People of the Swan

USA ▪ Canada ▪ UK ▪ Ireland

People

of the

Swan

Hubert Schuurman

Cover Design by Sue Westby

Note for Librarians: A cataloguing record for this book is available from Library and Archives
Canada at www.collectionscanada.ca/amicus/index-e.html
ISBN 1-4120-7962-4

*Printed in Victoria, BC, Canada. Printed on paper with minimum 30% recycled fibre.
Trafford's print shop runs on "green energy" from solar, wind and other environmentally-friendly
power sources.*

TRAFFORD
PUBLISHING™

Offices in Canada, USA, Ireland and UK

Book sales for North America and international:
· Trafford Publishing, 6E–2333 Government St.,
Victoria, BC V8T 4P4 CANADA
phone 250 383 6864 (toll-free 1 888 232 4444)
fax 250 383 6804; email to orders@trafford.com
Book sales in Europe:
Trafford Publishing (UK) Limited, 9 Park End Street, 2nd Floor
Oxford, UK OX1 1HH UNITED KINGDOM
phone +44 (0)1865 722 113 (local rate 0845 230 9601)
facsimile +44 (0)1865 722 868; info.uk@trafford.com
Order online at:
trafford.com/05-2860

10 9 8 7 6 5 4 3 2

To my wife Suzanne with love and gratitude
To my son Tristan for the joy he brought

I am especially grateful to Don Mclean for his encouragement and literary advice, to Trina Adams for her careful reading of the manuscript and corrections, to Barney Morrison for her thoughtful comments and all the friends who took time out to read the manuscript.
A special tribute to Ann Woodyer.

PROLOGUE

People of the Swan

The only sound in the castle tower was that of a shuttle flying across a large loom. At dusk it would weave intricate patterns of yellow and orange reflecting the colours of the desert landscape, which surrounded the ancient Alcazar. Princess Yaconda's slender hands sent the shuttle flying with great skill and Dominique her faithful maid watched in silence. Weaving was the only outlet that Yaconda had in her imprisonment, and Dominique knew that it kept the Princess from losing her sanity.

Dominique got up and peered through one of the tower's small windows. Below was a variety of cacti, whose flowers displayed an array of brilliant colours. Dominique raised her eyes to the dunes and beyond to the breakers of the distant ocean rolling onto the beach.

Across that ocean she and the Princess had sailed aboard Lord Imbrun's yacht. In good faith had they accepted his invitation. A trusted servant of King Arcturus for many years, no one at court had ever doubted Lord Imbrun's loyalty and devotion to the throne and his offer of an ocean cruise to help restore Yaconda's health, after a serious illness, had been accepted readily and with gratitude.

Yet, Dominique had had a foreboding that all was not well. Princess Yaconda had laughed, the kind of ringing laughter that sweeps away fear and suspicion, and is hard to resist. Dominique had felt the better for it and when she looked again at Lord Imbrun, she wondered how she could have had any misgivings at all. His handsome, noble features inspired such trust.

But she remembered well that day. On the dockside before they boarded, Lord Imbrun, gallantly, had offered his arm to Yaconda to board the vessel. Just as they came to the foot of the gangplank, the Dwarf Scimitar passed by, he halted, made a short bow to the ladies and then fixed his eyes on Lord Imbrun. Imbrun acknowledged the greeting, but his facial muscles twitched under the Dwarf's withering glance.

For nineteen years Yaconda's father, King Arcturus the Ninth, had ruled the Kingdom of the Seven Mountains. Yaconda's mother, Queen Miranda was the daughter of a High Elf Queen and a Prince of the Outlanders. Although the mixed marriage of her parents had raised many an eyebrow, it had helped to diminish long-standing prejudices, for the King and Queen had worked together to foster unity amongst the Kingdom's many different peoples.

When Princess Yaconda was barely ten, Queen Miranda died after a long illness. King Arcturus although heart broken, strengthened his resolve to achieve Miranda's hope of bringing about the unity of the Kingdom.

It took years of striving for King Arcturus to get Elves, Dwarves, Gnomes, Outlanders, Swannefolk and Mountain Fairies to agree upon a 'Common Book of Sacred Lore'. Wise counsel, patience and the great Unity Symposium held atop Mount Oneisis at full moon eventually realized the King's vision of unity amongst his people.

But not all subjects had attended the Unity Symposium. Most of the Elves had been keen to join the Kingdom and had followed their Queen Orchidae in taking an oath of loyalty to the King. A small group of disgruntled Elves decided to leave and seek their independence. It was the rebel, Cobalt, who led the discontented Elves across the river Sanctus to the remote forests of the northwest. They were last seen climbing the great plateau beyond the Sanctus followed by flocks of Merewings. These purple headed, black winged birds with a twelve foot wingspan were extraordinary gliders. Several had been spotted at the Unity Symposium on Mount Oneisis, circling at great height silhouetted by the light of the moon. Two of Queen Orchidae's Elves had been able to identify them because Elves have unbelievable eyesight and are able to recognize, at three miles distance, the face of friend or foe.

After the Unity Symposium on Mount Oneisis, King Arcturus died suddenly and thus his reign came to an abrupt end. His death astonished and shocked every living creature in the Kingdom.

The King's faithful servant, Septimus the Dwarf, had found him lifeless in his favourite chair, with the Common Book of Sacred Lore, open on his knees. There were no signs of violence.

The death of the King took place after Princess Yaconda had left the Kingdom on her sea voyage. With no legal heir to the throne present, great uncertainty had gripped the people of the Kingdom of the Seven Mountains.

The death of the King had been a terrible blow and left the nation from Outlanders to Fairies dumbfounded and dismayed. What had caused the King's death? Why had Princess Yaconda not returned from her cruise to the Western Ocean? Much speculation and gossip were afoot.

1

Cottage by the River

The sun cast its first warm rays on the little cottage on the shore of the Frivoli, that delightful stream, which meanders through the country of the Swannefolk. Between the cottage and the river stood rows of raspberry bushes. A few swans waddled among them, their long gracious necks occasionally shooting forwards, to pluck up a juicy snail. Old mother Annabelle appreciated the swans picking off the pests. She had grown rather rotund in her later years, in a jolly kind of way, and bending over did not come easily.

Annabelle's raspberry garden had been her sole source of livelihood, since her husband's death. One spring his gondola had been caught in a cataract and was swept over the falls. Annabelle had been left alone to raise her two children, Slim and Svanhild, in the little thatched roof cottage.

Slim had been only seven years old. A slight intense boy, with dark eyes and a questioning mind, he would sit often by the hearth, staring into the flames. One winter evening when Slim was in his seventh year Annabelle saw the light of the flames dancing in his eyes and asked, 'What thoughts are going through your mind Slim,'

'Mother, when I look into the flames I see father's face. His eyes are sparkling like the dancing of the flames and he whispers our names.'

Annabelle, tears in her eyes, put her hand on his shoulders.

'Slim, my dear Slim, the veil that shields you from the other world is but thin. Let it remain thus when you grow into manhood.'

Slim smiled. 'Mother what shall I do when I grow into manhood?'

'I think you know the answer Slim', replied Annabelle, who had seen Slim watch the swans for hours on end while they were being trained in water ballet, an art which had brought fame and prosperity to the Swannefolk.

'You will be a water ballet master, I think and train the swans in dance and pattern swimming, like your Uncle Svend. I will speak for you, that he may take you as an apprentice,' promised Annabelle. Thus it happened that young Slim began to work for his Uncle Svend. Slim had an eye for beauty, delighted in the graceful movements of the swans and he learned quickly. When he was only fourteen he choreographed his first ballet for swans!

Svanhild, a slender lively maiden, was three years younger than Slim. Her dreamy eyes had been the undoing of many a swain in the nearby village of Cascade. Svanhild's mind did not dwell on the common hopes and joys of the other village maidens. She dreamed of strange and wondrous places she had heard about in myths and legends. Perhaps her destiny would take her far beyond the borders of Swanneland, beyond the borders of the Kingdom!

Not that she was indifferent to the wooing and suing that came her way, but always there was a voice within.

'This is not the time, nor the place. Wait!'

Often Svanhild would follow the shore of the Frivoli until it vanished into the vast waters of the river Sanctus. Then she would walk along the bank of the Sanctus until she came to a row of willows. She would sit by the shore, her long fair tresses hidden by the branches of a great weeping willow.

While her brother Slim was training swans on the calm waters of the great river, she would watch these graceful birds respond to Slim's commands and sail lovely patterns on the black waters of the Sanctus. When Slim finished rehearsing she would watch him row upriver, with the swans trailing behind single file.

Once alone she let her eyes rest on the silent water. She knew that below the mirror surface of the river swift and powerful currents ran towards the western ocean. She wondered if below the quiet stream of village life, invisible currents surged that might one day seize her and carry her to unknown shores.

She would dream by the water's side until she could hear her mother's voice calling her back to the real world of warm earth, raspberry bushes, goats, wheelbarrows of manure, butter churning and other tasks that filled the lovely summer days. In the evenings leaning over her loom she would weave the cloth for the bright clothes the Swannefolk loved to wear. Swiftly flew the shuttle, and swiftly did the years fly by.

On her twenty seventh birthday Svanhild celebrated her flower festival, the traditional feast for young Swannegirls coming of age. Her fair hair had turned a lovely silver, a distinctive trait of the Swannefolk. At their coming of age their tresses turned a luminous silver.

Swannefolk's silver hair lasted until they reached their nineties Then it would turn a brilliant white. Svanhild's slight figure, dark green eyes and silver locks always charmed the Elves, Gnomes, Dwarves and others who came from different parts of the Kingdom to spend their holidays in Swanneland. She played the utelli, a stringed instrument which resembled a miniature harp. Often she would take the utelli on tour to play to the swans.

Svanhild was tall for a Swannemaiden, over four feet. Silver tresses framed a delicate face with deep green eyes, but within the frail looking maiden dwelt a feisty spirit.

Annabel was worried about her daughter's independent spirit. A year had past since the flower festival and she was still at home. Many a broken hearted suitor had walked out of the garden gate. No son-in-law or grandchildren on the horizon. It was strange and puzzling. The neighbours talked about it and Annabelle fretted. One evening quietly sitting in her rocking chair by the fire she made up her mind. She would invite Martha, the prophetess, to drop in for counsel.

It was an evening in spring when old Martha pushed open the wooden gate leading into the front garden of the little cottage. Trailing behind her on a leash was a bear.

Martha wore a brown homespun shift; white hair framed her blue eyes and gentle features. She tied the bear to the aspen tree in front of the cottage and walked in on Annabelle and Svanhild. Slim was out on the river, working with the swans.

'A sweet evening to you my dears,' greeted Martha in a soft whisper.

'Welcome to our home, ancient one,' responded Annabelle. 'The cider is heating on the hearth'

A smile appeared on Martha's face, there was a chill in the air and hot cider was her favourite drink.

'Ah yes, hot cider would be lovely and a raspberry square would make a good mate. No one makes them like you my love.'

Annabelle was proud of her baking and she warmed a sheet of squares in the oven of the cast iron stove. Martha looked at Svanhild leaning over the loom.

'Come hither my dear and sit with old Martha. We'll talk about husbands.'

Svanhild got up from the bench and sat down on a small maple stool opposite the ancient soothsayer.

'Dear Martha, it is so kind of you to drop in, but of husbands we must not speak. The time is not yet. Some of the youth have spoken to me but there is none that I take seriously. Besides mother needs me here and I am too young to tie myself for life.'

'Ah it is true my beauty there is yet time. You have only just celebrated the flower festival, but then the years fly quickly, and sometimes the right season comes and we know it not, and it vanishes beyond retrieval. Ah, I know it well, I have seen more than a hundred and fifty seven springs in this valley, and many a spring I failed to read its message. Give me your lovely hand, my winsome whelp.'

Svanhild laid her finely shaped fingers in the shriveled hand. The ancient seer brought the hand close to her faltering eyes, and uttered a muffled shriek.

'Ah you have spoken well my comely maid, the time is not yet. Now I must close my eyes and look at the inner world, for me it will be the only world. My eyes are quickly failing. Ah my sweetling, let me hold your hand a little longer. I see the river and dark is the sky. The clouds move swiftly. You are still alone, seated by the willow tree, and anxiously you scan the dark waters. Ah my lamb, I see a flash of light reflected from your hand. Is it a ray of moonlight on a silver ring, a gift of your betrothed? No a ring it is not. A silver dagger is clasped in that lovely hand.'

'Martha, Martha,' said Svanhild in a frightened voice, 'Is it the great darkness the legends speak of that your eyes behold?

Martha seemed far away, but then she put out her hand and stroked Svanhild's silver locks.

'I did not know it would be so soon. This is not the time for wooing. After the great darkness, my lamb, when the fire of suffering has swept the land, your love will find you. You were right the time is not yet. The silence was broken by Annabelle presenting a steaming tray of cider and raspberry squares.

'That will warm our hearts, my silver beauty,' sighed old Martha. Let us not dwell upon an old woman's vision, sometimes things turn out differently. Martha's gentle lilting laugh chased the gloom. Annabelle looked expectantly at the seer.

'The time is not yet, Annabelle. It is not a time for wooing. Be not distraught. Your daughter's destiny will lead her to lands beyond the Kingdom. She will play a part in great upheavals that are to wash over the land'

'No husband, no family,' whispered Annabelle.

'Ah I did not say that my beloved pumpkin. Other things must come to pass first, thereafter who can tell.

Slim had become an able assistant to his Uncle Svend. He had a natural eye for beauty and had just choreographed his second water ballet for swans. That eye for beauty did not fail to notice some of the young women in the county. Slim could only dream, for young men in Swanneland could not ask for a girl's hand until they turned thirty six.

One drizzly morning Slim sauntered down the narrow path by the rushing waters of the Frivoli. Trailing behind were seven cygnets, imprinted by Slim when they had been hatched. As part of their domestication program, the Swannemen would remove hatched swanlings from their parents.

Down below, the waters of the Frivoli rushed by to join the vast flow of the Sanctus. Slim stood still for a moment and let his eyes rest on the white and the green of the swift and restless water. Were not the years flowing by in the same remorseless fashion? He was close to manhood now and life had been kind to him. Uncle Svend had been like a father. For years they had worked together learning about swans, teaching them intricate swimming patterns and aerial ballet. Slim was much in demand in the county and beyond.

Life had brought success and even fame, but it rushed on like the waters of the river, year after year. Some days Slim wished that the predictable would become the unpredictable. At night he would read the legends of the Swannefolk and in his mind travel to strange and dangerous places.

The path meandered and dropped sharply, just before the wild watery horses of the Frivoli were caught in the silent waters of the Sanctus and joined the great migration to the sea. The seven swanlings followed Slim faithfully, chattering in a kind of trumpety way expressing joyous anticipation at their first class in the water arts.

Slim with his red jacket, white brimmed canvas hat and herder's staff, cut a dapper figure. Under that white hat and behind those blue eyes dwelt a keen mind. Little escaped him. Slim's eyes scanned the horizon, no change in sight from the cloud cover and the gentle rain. Yet there was a sense of foreboding and his internal barometer had fallen to storm levels. Maybe changes were afoot!

Today the training of the cygnets would begin. Slim was one of a handful of ballet masters in the land and traveled to exhibits and fairs throughout the Kingdom. The work suited him well, for at heart he was a showman, and on official occasions and sometimes on occasions not so official, Slim never missed a chance to dress up in the traditional attire of the Swannefolk. The men would wear their blue felt ranger hats, white shirts with blue sashes across the shoulder and red knickerbockers. The women wove their silver locks, which often reached to their waist, into a single braid and tied a green bow to the end. They embroidered their white blouses with bouquets of spring flowers and wore wide flowing green skirts. Both men and women wore black leather boots with toes turned up in a graceful spiral.

The water ballets directed by Slim and other Swannefolk had attracted visitors from many regions. In Cascade and other villages festivals were held from April till October. There were plenty of opportunities for Swannefolk to show off their traditional dress. A lot of complaining went on about having to dress up for all those foreigners, but ever performers at heart they secretly enjoyed it.

In earlier times Swannemen used to train swans for courier service, but now the Mountain Fairies had begun to teach the swifter pelicans to carry messages. The most gifted swans were trained in dance. Others learned to work in teams pulling the beautiful gondolas for which the Swannefolk craftsmen were so famous. From all over the Kingdom people traveled to Cascade to admire the Gondola's and watch the swan ballets.

Many wedding parties traveled on the Sanctus. One night Svanhild had counted nine teams of swans pulling gondolas on the river's moonlit waters. In the first gondola, caught in a beam of moonlight, were the bride and groom seated under an arch of roses. Behind them followed a gondola with musicians. Sailing in the remaining seven were family and friends. No wonder that more and more couples wished for a wedding in Swanneland! Dwarves, Outlanders, and even Gnomes and Elves traveled to Cascade to celebrate their nuptial feasts!

Tourism had become an important part of life in the county and at full moon many gondolas carrying young lovers, or sometimes lovers on a second honeymoon, could be seen silhouetted against the midnight blue, drawn by teams of seven, or sometimes nine swans. There were also the magnificent performances of swan ballets which attracted spectators from the Kingdom and beyond. Svanhild loved to help Slim with the swans and sometimes the two of them traveled together on the water ballet circuit. The swans were now firmly at the heart of local lore and tradition.

Slim whistled a gay morning tune that brought some brightness to the fog shrouded scene. Even the cygnets skipped a step or two, for they loved music. Slim turned around and walked backwards whistling and watching as the swanlings hopped happily to the music. Yes, this was a promising litter. Their mother Angelina had been a great dancer but alas no more. Over a week ago at dusk, she had been mortally wounded. Slim standing on the far shore had heard the death chant of his beloved swan winging over the waters of the Sanctus. When he reached the other shore he beheld his beloved swan lying in the bulrushes. The beautiful neck that always seemed to rise up to heaven had collapsed into the mud. Kneeling by her side, he caught the fading strains of her fleeing spirit.

Footprints in the mud left little doubt that a hound had rushed her. The pattern of the tracks showed that the dog had retreated walking on three legs. With her powerful wings Angelina must have broken the fourth.

Black dogs had been spotted in a neighbouring county. Slim learned at the local coffee house that a stranger had bought land on the other side of the Frivoli and was raising black dogs. It was likely that one of these had broken loose and killed his favourite swan, for Swannefolk seldom kept dogs.

At this time of year there were no tourists, but strangers had been seen passing through the valley, short stocky fellows. Most of the villagers did not like their looks but they had plenty of money and the businessmen in the community were keen to please them. Slim hoped that they would go away. He walked on towards the river and the joyful chattering of the swanlings wiped away the misgivings in his heart.

2

The Coffee House

Nestled in a horseshoe of ancient hills, where the Frivoli flows into the Sanctus, rose the village of Cascade. On the shore of the Sanctus stood an ancient inn, the Graceful Neck, a rambling old building, surrounded by stately poplar trees. A recent whitewash gave it a cheerful appearance and its lawns by the riverside were a popular rest stop, for visitors and locals alike.

The smell of bacon and coffee wafting from the inn's kitchen reached Slim on his way to the river. It was a damp and chilly morning and breakfast at home had been rather skimpy. It would be quite pleasant to sit down to a hot breakfast and shoot the breeze with some of his old friends. And there was another attraction, Rosemary. These weighty thoughts pulled him towards the front door of the old inn. But what about the cygnets? Slim ran down the lawn, all the swanlings running and tumbling after him and he parked the small birds in a tiny lagoon. There were a number of these, all closed in by fences made from willow branches.

He sauntered up to the inn and pushed open the creaky old door. Through a curtain of smoke Slim could see a number of Swannemen gathered around the long harvest tables. His favourite spot was still free. He walked over to the end of the bench next to the old cast iron wood stove. Being in a dampish profession Slim had a true appreciation of wood stoves. There was another attraction in the inn, a pair of pretty blue eyes under a mop of blonde hair, a white blouse and a wide red skirt. The mistress of these charming attributes caught Slims' wink. Moving towards him, Rosemary's black boots skipped easily across outstretched legs and other obstacles.

'The usual, Slim?' Slim smiled and nodded. When it came to talking to young ladies, especially when they were pretty, he was quite at a loss for words.

Waiting for a plate of pancakes and bacon Slim caught snatches of the conversation around him. Moose Martin sitting across from Slim leaned over.

'Slim, me boy, have you ever heard the like of it, after all these years of peace and quiet, our King dies a mysterious death.' Slim smiled.

'Come now Moose, Kings do die you know, and it may have been a heart attack'. Moose leaned closer.

'A heart attack? You are a dreamer, and always were. Have you not heard that he had a book on his knees when he died?'

'So he was reading the Book of Sacred Lore', countered Slim, 'what a way to go. Next best to passing on singing your favourite song'

'Would that it had been just that, my guileless friend. There was a pencil on the floor. The King had written a note, at the bottom of a page.' A hush fell over the harvest table and all eyes were on Moose Martin, 'Yes my friends, at the bottom of the page a message had been scribbled. The words were barely visible, but the Dwarf Septimus, the King's secretary, saw them right away. I heard it all first hand from the poultry farmer, who raises fowl for the royal table.'

By now a number of faces around the table were fixed on Moose Martin, keen to hear more.

'Out with it. Don't keep us on suspenders Moose,' and other shouts came from all sides. Moose cleared his throat and waited for the murmur to die down.

'The writing was faint, for the good King Arcturus was going out with the tide, as he wrote the words.' Even Slim was getting impatient with the old ferry Captain.

'Then speak the words Moose.' There was complete silence while Moose gravely repeated the King's last message.

"I am leaving these mortal shores. Trusted servants entangled in web of enemy. Princess Yaconda must be crowned and complete my mission."

'Those were the very words,' Moose Martin reflected in a solemn voice.

A somber mood prevailed among the men assembled at the harvest table. The words were all too clear. There had been trouble in the past. Perhaps this was the end of a century of tranquility and peace. Generations ago the Swannefolk had been able warriors, famous for inventing weapons and laying traps for their enemies. That was the past. Could it possibly happen again?

Slim took it all in. Certainly it was scary but on the other hand, there had been crises in the past and things generally had turned out all right. Perchance Princess Yaconda would return home and be crowned Queen. A coronation would call for a special swan ballet and in his mind swans were already skimming over the waters of the Sanctus in intricate patterns. These reassuring thoughts and the sight of a steaming breakfast sailing towards him, dispelled his misgivings.

Seated at the end of the harvest table, was Scimitar, a visiting Dwarf. He was barely visible for the smoke of many pipes had spread a blue cloud throughout the room.

Scimitar, Skimmy to his close friends had contributed generously to the cloud of blue, but now he took his pipe out of his mouth, cleared his throat, and stood up. The buzz of voices diminished and heads turned towards the venerable bearded head of the indomitable Dwarf. Before he raised his powerful voice, his penetrating eyes scanned the Swannefolk around the Table.

'Intrigue and mischief are once more afoot, and not wholly unexpectedly, my damp footed friends. We have enjoyed peace in this Kingdom, yet dwarf scouts on the alpine meadows have always kept lookouts along the outer borders. This tradition goes back to the time when the brotherhood of Witch Doctors was banished and our forefathers chased them over the mountain tops to the land of the red earth. Even then dwarf leaders knew that that would not be the end of it. The Witch Doctors were not their own masters and paid tribute to seven rulers in realms dark and distant. These Lords grew tired of the Witch Doctors' swindling and scheming, and began to recruit servants from among the local peasants, whom they have made into cold-blooded and calculating men.'

'Are these the Rovers that people living near the border talk about?' asked one of the Swanherders, sitting close to the Dwarf.

'Their masters in the land of the red earth call them Rovers. They are more dangerous than the Witch Doctors of yore and absolutely loyal to their Lords. When attacked on the Finnian range, behind Hammer Mountain, a party of our scouts killed two of them.'

'Actually knocked their blocks off?' gasped young Duckie in a tone of admiration. He was hushed up by some of the older men, but it was clear to the Swannefolk, that the Dwarves were a force to be reckoned with and there was general satisfaction that they were indeed on their side.

The jolly atmosphere around the harvest table subsided considerably and there were many frightened faces staring at the stern Dwarf's chiseled features. Slim piped up.

'Granny used to tell us tales that go back to my over-great-grandfather or great-over-grandfather. At one time she spoke about the Lords on the far side of the Finnian Range. She said that hearsay and scuttlebutt had it that they never aged. Power and wealth were theirs.'

'No doubt Slim, Grandma's words carried a grain of truth. The Seven have supernatural gifts. Perhaps the magic of an enchantress is behind it,' reflected Scimitar.

'Scimitar,' wondered Slim, 'if wealth and power are theirs why would they disturb our land, or hurt the King or Crown Princess?'

'There are no reasons Slim. All their secret desires are granted, but it never brings fulfillment. Fear is the shadow of desire, it spawns within, and that is where the evil rests and the threat to their undoing. But they see it elsewhere, in those around them, in neighbouring lands, in the Kingdom.' Some of the men looked flummoxed but most them, got the gist of it.

'This is pretty deep stuff Slim,' whispered Moose. Slim nodded and stood up.

'We certainly must be thankful that the Dwarves kept an eye on our enemies, but then Scimitar and his friends are excellent swordsmen, and flinch not in the face of death. Alas, we Swannemen do not have the skills to face an enemy in battle.' A slight chap with delicate features standing on the bench, piped up in a high-pitched voice.

'It is not just a matter of swordsmanship, Swannefolk are peaceful folk we do not have the nervous system for armed conflict. We haven't fought for generations and would all go to pieces!' An approving hubbub of voices confirmed the sentiment.

'Well, we can't all be heroes', sighed Scimitar. 'Yet, there dwells a warrior in all of us. The Path of the Warrior, a modest booklet penned by my brother Smithereen, may prove of interest to some of you.'

'Warmonger,' shouted a young chap sitting close to Slim. A few other nasty comments were mumbled here and there. Scimitar wisely ignored them.

'You spoke about rulers in distant lands, are there more than one?' asked Moose Martin.

'There are Seven', replied Scimitar in a solemn voice.

'Seven, whimpered one of the Swannemen aghast, 'Do we stand a chance against Seven?'

'We do, if the peoples of the realm work together. Now that the King is gone and Princes Yaconda, the heiress to the throne cannot be found, the Dwarves have asked each of the realm's founding races to send a delegate to Lambarina to form an interim Council, to guide the people of the Kingdom, until the rightful heir to the throne has been found.

People around the table could be heard shouting, 'Long live Princess Yaconda. May heaven protect her and guide her back to the land of her fathers!'

Princess Yaconda had vanished! The Swannemen around the table now showed genuine distress. Their beloved princess! How often had theirs been the honour of ferrying her in the finest gondolas pulled by teams of regal swans. Her words of gratitude and the light shining in her eyes had never failed to move them.

3

An Ocean Cruise

$\mathcal{P}$rincess Yaconda and her maidservant Dominique were standing on the deck of Lord Imbrun's yacht. The vessel was moored in Caplin Harbour a small fishing village west of Lambarina. The Princess waved to the festive crowd, gathered on the pier. Most of the cheering onlookers were women and children from the village come to bid her safe voyage, but some of her well wishers had traveled all the way from the capital.

Recovering from a long illness, Princess Yaconda had been pleased to accept Lord Imbrun's offer of an ocean cruise. The handsome nobleman was her father's trusted counselor and she had admired him since childhood.

King Arcturus himself had traveled to Caplin Harbor to wish his beloved daughter Godspeed. The royal coach drawn by four ponies had parked on the village square and the old King supported by his valet, managed to walk down the stairway to a small pavilion above the harbour. A fresh breeze blew his white locks and beard around his face and bracing himself on his long golden staff he raised his free hand in benediction to the travelers.

The Princess could see the purple of the royal robes far above the crowd. She recited a silent prayer for her father and for a moment the thought passed through her mind that she might never see him again.

Her joy at the coming journey had been darkened as she boarded the vessel on Lord Imbrun's arm. There had been that glum faced dwarf Scimitar. The scathing look in his eyes had sent shivers down her spine and for a moment even Imbrun had lost his cool. Had it been a bad omen? There was no point dwelling on it. Dwarves always were glum and dour, she told herself.

The cheering of her people drove the shadow from her mind and she waved enthusiastically to the jubilant crowd. As the vessel slipped its moorings the shouting and singing receded before the sound of lapping waves and sailors' voices.

A final hearty cheer from her well wishers carried over the water as the ship coursed from shore. The Princess and her maid were exhilarated by the spray and the salty breeze that filled the white sails and drove the vessel swiftly through the protected channel and into deep ocean swells.

Most of the crew were Outlanders, but Lord Imbrun had hired seven Mountain Fairies to work the sails. Moving across the deck in their dark blue toques, white shirts and blue tights, they looked like miniature dancers. The tiny creatures possessed an amazing agility and when ordered to trim the sails they flew about the rigging like squirrels in springtime.

Dominique looked down on a passing Fairy. The creature reached just to her hip. He stopped for a moment and jumped upon a coil of rope. She found herself looking into his eyes and sensed a note of warning. He was about to whisper in her ear. The Captain walked by, however, grabbed the creature by the back of his shirt and tossed him onto the forecastle.

'Begging your pardon ladies, we can't have those flying beetles bothering our passengers.'

Princess Yaconda just caught a glimpse of the Captain's face, before he moved on. A smile masked his harsh countenance. She shuddered and returned her glance to the calming movement of the ocean swells.

Once the coastline was out of sight, the vessel changed course and Princess Yaconda and Dominique watched the fairies race up the rigging and trim the sails. With grace and ease they danced back and forth on the spars. Once the sails were set they slid down the rigging, bowed to the Princess and withdrew to the forecastle.

Yaconda and Dominique sat down on a comfortable bench near the railing and looked over the play of waves and water.

Yaconca's misgivings about the journey receded into the background. Lord Imbrun had been most gracious and she chided herself for the mistrust that she had entertained for even a brief moment. The thrill of sailing! What a lovely change from the palace routine. Surely this trip would restore her health.

Lord Imbrun's valet walked over and offered to escort them to their cabin. They were expected to dine with his Lordship and the Captain later in the evening. Princess Yaconda wanted to have a rest before dinner, so she and her maid followed the charming Swanneyouth down below deck.

The Princess was delighted with the small cozy cabin. She could shed all the formalities of palace living and simply enjoy herself. After years of wearing sumptuous attire, morning, noon and night, being able to walk the deck dressed in skirt and sweater had been such a pleasure. She threw herself upon her bed and smiled at her companion.

Later in the evening the Swanneyouth arrived to accompany them to the dining room. Princess Yaconda had changed her sailor's outfit for a simple linen dress, with roses embroidered on the hem. Dominique, her fair tresses resting upon her shoulders, wore a dark green skirt and a white blouse,.

Lord Imbrun, attired in a dark brown gown with fur collar, introduced them to the Captain, a short square-chested chap with dark hair and a brusque manner.

Lord Imbrun appeared to be his old charming self, and yet there was the strain in his face that Princess Yaconda had noticed earlier. She had always admired the handsome lord, liegeman to her father King Arcturus, and in flights of fancy she had even pictured herself betrothed to him. 'The wild dream of a very young girl,' she mused. There was now something in his voice and manner that created in her a vague and indefinable unease. Trying to put it aside, she raised her glass in cheerful response to Imbrun's toast to a prosperous and happy journey.

The meal of fried fish and rice with fruits for desert was simple and tasty and an excellent wine loosened the stern looking Captain's tongue. He began telling stories of strange and distant shores and as the wine flowed, became loud and belligerent.

'The land of the red earth, a splendid place. Not like the stagnant back waters of these parts. People work from dawn until dusk and great works are rising, the Seven rule...' Imbrun shot the Captain a fierce glance and took the bottle away from him.

The Captain staggered out of the dining area and Imbrun tried to put a better face on things by talking lightly about the usual hard drinking, hard working sailors, driven to occasional indulgence by a harsh life at sea.

Back in their cabin Princess Yaconda could conceal no longer her unease. 'Dom is something not quite right?'

'I think not my Princess, the Captain is a queer duck but then we are not used to the company of sailors.

'Strange,' mused Princess Yaconda, 'strange men these sailors. It is quite an adventure this trip.'

For the next two days the weather was splendid and the yacht raced across the gentle swell of the western ocean. Lord Imbrun had been polite and attentive and the Captain had kept his distance.

Princess Yaconda and Dominique spent most of their time on deck. Leaning over the railing they rested their eyes on the ever-changing waves and talked to the dolphins swimming alongside. How leisurely these graceful creatures skipped the waves. A world of endless vistas and delight, no cloud on the horizon. It was at night resting on her gently swaying bed that anxiety returned. As a child she had loved the young Lord Imbrun, but now there was a veil between them. It was as if the young man she had known had vanished and a stranger taken his place.

On the third day out, while standing by the railing, Dominique cried out. 'Look astern Princess, look.'

Princess Yaconda turned around, raising a hand to shield her eyes from the sunlight. She descried a black speck in the distance and then another. The birds were flying at great speed and before long the Princess and Dominique discerned the outline of giant black wings, effortlessly propelling the creatures forward. Dominique put her hand on her mistress' arm.

'Princess, these are the merewings, granny told us about when we were young.' Yaconda could feel the hand on her arm tremble.'

Dominique looked up at the two large shapes circling overhead and shivered. Was it merely the memory of the old nightmare or rather the apprehension of new danger? Yaconda threw her arm around her shoulder and held her close.

The great birds landed on the bridge railing and Yaconda and Dominique watched the Captain take his pocket knife and cut a small container from the leg of one. Upon having spotted the birds, Lord Imbrun hastily joined the Captain on the bridge. There was a look of anticipation in his face, as if the birds' arrival had not been wholly unexpected.

Yaconda eyes were focused on the figures on the bridge. When the Captain handed Imbrun the small cylindrical container a glance of understanding passed between them.

Imbrun opened the little vessel and pulled out a scroll. Scanning it quickly he read a message to the Captain, who sadly shook his head and actually managed to shed a few tears. Imbrun feigned shock and dismay as he came down the stairs and walked up to the Princess and her maid.

Yaconda loved theater and she knew this to be one of the worst performances she had ever seen. For the squat little devil behind the helm to cry was as improbable as a crocodile shedding tears before breakfast.

As Imbrun's face came closer, she could see the mask of dismay, but his manner showed relief and a sense of power.

'My dear Princess,' began his lordship, 'your father the King.' He remained silent for a moment and looked at Yaconda. She returned his look with an icy stare not betraying any emotion.

'Go on my lord tell me my father has been murdered,' uttered the Princess without knowing what made her say it.

'Oh God... no, of course not,' muttered the nobleman thrown off guard. The beloved King murdered, that is quite impossible. No... he has suffered a heart attack, not entirely unexpected as the Princess well knows.'

A voice within sounded clear and convincing, 'Imbrun is a traitor.'

Suppressing her feelings her blue eyes looked through him.

'Then my Lord turn the ship around and return to Lambarina that I may bury my father and ascend the throne as legal heir and Crown Princess!'

The moment of truth had come, the mask came off.

'Alas Princess this is not possible, my new masters have other plans which will relieve you of the burden of royal responsibility.'

Dominique drew closer to her mistress, who wisely kept silent. From the bridge the Captain looked upon the drama below and burst into a fit of evil laughter frightening the crew and even the merewings feeding on a pile of fish, trembled at the sound.

'Where are you taking us Imbrun?' The steely edge in the Princess' voice cut him to the quick.

'Princess, rest assured, every courtesy will be extended to you. The Seven Lords in the land of the red earth will be your hosts. You and your maidservant will be met at the old Alcazar at the western cape by the Lords' personal representative.' Imbrun was feeling uncomfortable under Yaconda's searching gaze.

'My lady, it was but a matter of time before the Kingdom would have been taken over by the Seven Lords. There was no defense in place, no organization. Your father had been blind to the truth for years.'

She allowed him but one answer, 'traitor.' Anger flared in Imbrun's eyes, and he ordered one of the deckhands to take the Princess and her maid to their cabin. No sooner had the door closed behind them when they heard the key turn. They were locked in.

Lying on their bunks listening to the waves lapping against the side of the ship, the dreadful truth dawned. They were far from home, prisoners, and their fate was in the hands of rulers in a distant realm. Yaconda's grief for her father was laced with anger at the betrayal by one of his trusted friends.

Above the rushing of the water, a slight knocking sound arose. Looking at the porthole Yaconda espied a Mountain Fairy hanging upside down, pounding on the thick glass. A smile spread over her tear stained face at the droll sight. She opened the porthole and greeted the flushed fairy.

'What are you hanging on to my dear fairy?'

'My toes Princess, they are curled around the lower rung of the railing. We want you to know that we too, against our will, have been kept on this ship. We signed on for one journey and this is our sixth. It is easy for us to hide and we have overheard many a talk between the Captain and the Lord called Imbrun. The Captain, dear Princess is a servant of the Seven in the Land of Darkness. Lord Imbrun tempted by wealth and power has joined their ranks. Tonight we will arrive at the small harbour near the Alcazar, where you and your maid will disembark. Our best wishes to you and remember us when these evil days are past and your presence graces the throne of our beloved country.'

Yaconda blew a kiss to the loyal fairy, and his friends pulled him back to the deck. Heartened by the good wishes of the Fairies, the Princess and her maid began to pack all the warm clothes they could find.

An hour before sunset the yacht slipped into the small harbour on the western peninsula. Dominique and Yaconda standing on deck, looked upon the desert landscape lit by the warm orange light of the evening sun.

The yacht docked beside an old wooden ramp. The Captain looked down from the bridge and his twisted face broke into an evil laugh.

'Behold a guard of honour to greet you at your arrival in the land of the Seven Lordly Ones.' Imbrun was nowhere to be seen.

They stood at the railing and cast their eyes over the desolate sight before them. Near the dock stood a few ramshackle sheds and a great variety of cacti dotted the desert landscape. A rough track marked with rocks on one side led inland to the ruins of an old castle.

Dominique was the first to see a group of strange looking creatures walking among the shallow dunes. When they reached the trail they turned towards the harbour. A look of horror appeared in Dominique's face.

'Princess, these are Grolls!' They are going to leave us in the hands of a company of Grolls!' Yaconda kept silent, nothing could be done, and protest would simply amuse the Captain. A deckhand and a sailor picked up Yaconda and Dominique's luggage and carried it to the dock. They motioned Yaconda and Dominique to walk down the gangplank.

Standing hand in hand on the jetty they watched the Groll Officer and four of his regulars walking towards them. Upon reaching the dock, the Groll Captain raised his cap and made a bow. He looked at the Princess and her maid and a grin appeared on his scaly face.

'Captain Homarus, commander of fortress makes compliments to most pretty ladies. No fear, Captain and men very honourable. Make life very pleasant in castle.'

Grolls, creatures they had met in winter tales, told beside wood fires in the palace hall, tales that had sent shivers down their spine. Here they stood before them, these large, clumsy beings, covered with brown scales. Only their ankles and big flat feet had no scales and showed smooth brown skin.

Yaconda was speechless. Dominique, knowing they had to make the best of it, tried to mollify the fierce looking Captain.

'Thank you Captain,' said the practical maid, 'you may take us to our new quarters.'

'Soldiers carry luggage for gracious ladies. Very sorry to cause inconvenience. Poor Captain Homarus forced to carry out orders, how very unfortunate.' A lickerish smile twinkled in his eyes.

Before trudging on behind their escort in the hot sand, the Princess and her maidservant cast a wistful look at the quickly disappearing yacht.

Within a short while they could see the outline of a stone tower surrounded by a pile of bricks, the remains of the ancient Alcazar of the western Kings.

4

Scimitar's Warning

$\mathcal{T}$he black waters of the Sanctus were softened by a yellow sheen. The old willow trees on the bank of the river turned into canopies of golden leaves.

The warm rays of the spring sun put to flight the long damp winter and all along the river, Swannefolk could be seen tilling gardens, repairing boats and gondolas, training swans or simply hanging out in the sun.

Slim had begun to teach in earnest a new group of cygnets and life went on in its usual leisurely fashion. Yet there was an undercurrent of uneasiness. Princess Yaconda had not returned from her cruise and from the far reaches of the Kingdom no news of Lord Imbrun's yacht had been reported.

Anxious to hear scraps of news, Slim had made it a habit to drop in at the Graceful Neck. At midmorning he would park the cygnets in the small pond at the edge of the property, near the river and walk over to the old inn.

This morning as soon as he walked in, he could tell from the buzz of voices and the clouds of blue smoke rising from meerschaum pipes that something was afoot. Rosemary waltzed up to him and putting her rosy lips closer to his ear than necessary, whispered that Scimitar was staying at the inn.

Scimitar, traveling from his mountain stronghold, had spent the night at the inn. He was on his way to Lambarina for a meeting with delegates from the Gnomes, Mountain Fairies, Elves, Swannefolk and Outlanders to discuss the formation of a temporary Council to handle the affairs of the Kingdom, until the Princess returned to assume her rightful place on the throne.

Slim found a place opposite Moose Martin. When Rosemary placed coffee and pancakes in front of Slim, Moose raised his head and saw his friend sitting across the wooden table.

'Cheer up, Moose, I hear Scimitar is at the inn. He will steer us through these troubled times.' Moose was pleased to see him. He pulled a pipe from his pocket and filled it with tobacco.

'Good to see you Slim,' said the old sailor lighting up. It was then that Scimitar appeared at the bottom of the stairs and the hubbub died down to a few whispers.

The stalwart Dwarf leaned against the wall near the old woodstove and sent a thoughtful ring of smoke into the air. The buzz of voices had subsided, and Moose, feeling that someone should welcome Scimitar, stood up.

'Friends, we express our gratitude to Scimitar and his people. We owe them a debt. They had plans in case something should go wrong and something did go wrong. Something horrible has happened. We have had years of good health, no earthquakes, no floods, no swan bites[1], said I to myself, Moose Martin, this cannot be, some calamity is probably overdue. I should have known. Life has many pitfalls, and now this upheaval. Who knows what is going to happen next.' One of the businessmen rose.

'Let us not panic , I know the King has died under mysterious circumstances and that Princess Yaconda failed to return from a sea voyage on Lord Imbrun's yacht. But let us be reasonable, we need not suspect Lord Imbrun of foul play, the voyage may have run into trouble. Scimitar is helping to set up a Council to rule the Kingdom and things may go on much the same as they did before, until everything is straightened out.' There was a hum of approval from the business owners around the table.

'Well spoken Goldfinger. Don't let the Dwarf stir the brew,' and other shouts were plentiful. Scimitar pretended he had not heard and his eagle eyes scanned the throng facing him.

---

1   *Swanbites are extremely dangerous. They can lead to a coma, in which the patient often talks, revealing thoughts that he would rather have kept to himself. The condition can be treated with extract of boiled rattlesnake, however it takes a team of pelicans seven days to travel to the desert, capture a rattlesnake and return home with the remedy.*

'My friends, People of the Swan, I understand your reluctance to look at the danger ahead. Years of peace and prosperity have flown by like the waters of the great Sanctus. No armies are massed against us, yet the power of the Seven Lords from the land of the red earth is daily growing. New Rovers trained by the Seven, have been seen in the streets of Lambarina and other parts of the Kingdom.'

Snurfie, a Swanneman small in stature and known for his fine teams of swans and the beautiful gondolas that he had built, called out.

'I have seen them strangers in black leather jackets, hanging around my wharf. One had a black hound on a leash.' Goldfinger smiled.

'There are always fellows hanging around your wharf Snurf.'

'Black jackets Goldie, folks here in Swanneland don't wear black except at funerals,' retorted the gondolier. Mintpalm, the undertaker, cast a severe look at the small fellow.

'Small town prejudices .Working in the world of commerce we know about customs in other parts of the Kingdom and beyond. Those black-jackets have plenty of money. Everything is cash on the barrel, unlike some folks in this town, whose accounts are long overdue.' Scimitar blowing a cloud of blue smoke into the air rose again.

'Black dress is not unknown in some parts of the land, but the black dogs are trained by the Rovers. They are easily recognized by their great height and massive jaws.'

'Right you are, Scimitar, that was one of them I saw on the wharf. It gave me the creeps, the size of the beast.'

'Avoid the dogs, friends, even when they are on a leash. Accidents are bound to happen. A small bite can cause much suffering and bring death within weeks.'

'I wonder what a big bite would do,' wondered Duckie. A wave of fear and compassion passed over the Dwarf's face.

'We won't talk about that Duckie, but there would not be enough time to get the victim to the Convent of the Sisters of the Secret Crossing for the nettle treatment.'

At the mention of the black hounds a shudder had passed through the crowd. Death was bad enough, and the nettle treatment sounded frightening.

Moose stood up again.

'Fellow Swannemen, Scimitar is right. Unsavoury elements are moving into the county and something must be done to stop them!'

'The usual fear of foreigners,' muttered Goldfinger, 'these newcomers pay their bills.'

Scimitar wisely ignored the comments from the floor and shared his plans for future action.

'In Lambarina I will meet with Elves, Gnomes, Mountain Fairies and Outlanders. I hope that organized resistance will begin. If I do not return from my mission to Lambarina, be not dismayed. Work together to maintain the unity of our people. Oppose the evil that will fall upon us.'

With these words the grim faced Dwarf ended his speech and made his way towards the door. He turned once more to the throng around the harvest table and bade them farewell. Pushing open the creaky door he walked onto the porch, picked up his wooden staff and whistled for his faithful hound. Shouts of 'Godspeed, and fare thee well stout warrior,' could still be heard as the Dwarf strode across the porch of the old inn towards the river. Before stepping down from the porch Rosemary slipped up behind him and handed him a stone jug.

'Your evening meal Scimitar. Hold on to it, you are going to need it.'

Before he could say anything, she had disappeared through a side door into the inn.

The crowd was much subdued after Scimitar's departure and for a few moments Joris Goldfinger was stuck for words. When he rose to speak the eyes of the business community were fixed upon him.

'Companions in commerce, we know Scimitar, we know his brother Smithereen. Many Dwarves come to our festivals each year. They take themselves so seriously, they have to come to Swanneland to regain their wits. Do we blame them? Of course not. If we had to work underground in semi-darkness all year round, digging ore in mountain tunnels, we too would be sunk under buckets of gloom, dark forebodings would crowd the mind. Lack of daylight brings on melancholia, the Sisters at the Convent have told us about it.'

A sigh of relief could be heard from his companions, it all made very good sense. Molehills had been made into mountains. You had to toss it to Goldfinger, he knew his facts!

Through the windows of the coffee room, Moose and Slim watched the venerable Dwarf. Straight as an arrow he walked towards the river. With a powerful motion he launched his canoe and Patriot, his golden retriever jumped into the bow.

'There is a strength and single-mindedness in those Dwarves, Moose,' sighed Slim, 'Alas we Swannemen blithely wander about, taking life as it comes.'

'Never mind, me boy,' mused Moose smiling, 'Dwarves thrive on doom and gloom. Swannefolk don't take themselves that serious. They know how to enjoy life.'

'Nevertheless Moose Martin, without the Dwarves, we would be in trouble,' returned Slim.

Now that Scimitar had left, the whir of voices in the hall rose considerably. Some serious remarks could be heard, but most of the hubbub was the kind of small talk that Swannefolk love to carry on. It was just as well that Scimitar had left, for it was the kind of lightheaded twitter that drove dwarf visitors to distraction. To them it was just a dreadful waste of time.

At meetings in the land of the Dwarves, of which there were a great many, gibberish generally was called swannetalk. And yet those fierce warriors kept coming back to Swanneland. A good many had spent their honeymoon at the Graceful Neck!

When Slim had finished breakfast, Moose tapped him on the shoulder and motioned to follow him outside. When they stepped onto the porch, they could just see Scimitar, with powerful strokes, propelling his frail craft towards the capital, Lambarina. Patriot seated in the bow, scanned the horizon.

Slim and Moose wandered silently along the river. Slim had forgotten about the cygnets and Moose reminded him.

'You better give the cygnets a swim, Slim.' Slim ran over to the pond and unleashed the excited swanlings. They followed Moose and Slim to a quiet backwash of the river and glided gracefully into the water.

Moose sat down on a little hillock and listened to Slim talking to the swanlings. They began to play some of the games that Slim had taught them.

It was still a gray and misty morning but the golden sheen on the willow leaves and the cygnets floating in and out of the soft haze put them into a better frame of mind.

'The Witch Doctors are finished Slim, but Scimitar mentioned new servants, Rovers trained by the Seven in the land of the red earth. What about some of the strangers that have come through town in the last few years?'

Slim had to admit that some of the stocky fellows in their black coats gave him the creeps, yet they were courteous enough.

Moose hummed a little tune and watched the cygnets play.

'Ah, all is not well my friend, a life time on the ferryboats, gives you a sixth sense for heavy weather and I tell you, the glass is falling. Scimitar knows more than he lets on. The Seven in the Land of Darkness have designs on the Kingdom. And if you ask me, Princess Yaconda is not on a pleasure cruise. She has been kidnapped.'

Slim was shaken. Swannemen had an intense dislike of anything approaching trials and tribulations. They would put up with floods, terrible weather, long rainy winters, not without complaining of course, but without being rattled. But the trials that Scimitar had hinted at were the rattling kind, and jarred their finely tuned nerves. The very idea that strange and hostile forces might be present and threaten their quiet way of life was alarming.

'Well Slim I may be wrong, I have been wrong often enough.' Slim nodded.

'Perhaps Moose all this will drift over, Goldfinger could be right. We, Swannemen, panic at the first sign of trouble.' A voice from behind piped up.

'Nothing ever happens around here, I was hoping for a battle or two.' It was little Duckie who had wandered after them.

'Eavesdropping eh,' said Slim.

'Couldn't help it.' countered Duckie, 'I just have a good pair of ears'.

'One day you will understand why we, Swannemen, treasure our life style.'

'With respect Uncle Moose, my ma'am says you should say Swannefolk, for there are women too you know.' A grunt issued from Moose's throat. He knew when silence was the best policy when arguing with a precocious teenager.

Slim asked Duckie to collect the swanlings and herd them into a small fenced off area by the river. Moose and Slim watched him playing games with the cygnets. Using all his cunning, he succeeded in enticing them into the corral.

'Well done Duckie,' cheered Slim. 'Come and join us for a walk up the hill.'

'We could drop in at the Manor, Slim,' suggested Moose. 'The Marquis and Lady Erica may have more news about happenings in Lambarina and the Royal Palace.'

'Would I love to see the Manor,' exclaimed Duckie, sauntering behind.

The trio ambled up the hill at the edge of the village. Some of the pussy willows on both sides of the path were in leaf and birds were singing. In the distance loomed the outline of the old Manor belonging to one of Swanneland's noble families.

The Marquis, Ferdinand deCygne, was the only surviving male descendant in his family. Circumstances in the distant past under which the family had been elevated to the nobility, were murky. The Marquis claimed it was on account of bravery, but since bravery was equated with foolishness in the present cultural climate, Swannefolk did not pay him a lot of special respect. He liked to be called Marquis or Sir Ferdinand. The trades people in town soon found out that a little flattery goes a long way and it helped business along. Their bills were paid on time. Most of the village humoured the eccentric Marquis.

The Marquis was seated comfortably in his glassed in porch, enjoying a cup of coffee and a piece of scrumptious coffee cake, baked by his great aunt and housekeeper Lady Erica de Coscoroba.

'Keep the coffee warm Aunt Erica, I espy company coming up the path. It is that fine old gentleman, Moose Martin and some friends coming to pay their respects. The Marquis slipped out the sunroom into the hall, opened the front door, and bid his visitors welcome. Moose and Slim shook warmly the jovial nobleman's extended hand and followed him inside. Duckie didn't know whether he was invited, but he slipped in anyway.

'Welcome to the Manor of my forefathers, Lady Erica has kept the coffee warm.'

'Thank you Marquis, the smell is tempting,' responded Moose Martin.

'A new blend grown by the Gnomes on the south side of Mount Oneisis,' beamed the Marquis.

The Gnomes were well known for their coffee plantations, and Slim and Moose needed little convincing. It had not been an easy morning and they could do with a second perk.

Slim looked at portraits of forefathers hung in the great front hall, and the array of weapons on display. He had never paid much attention to the fierce swords and crossbows, but after this morning's news, he wondered if ever they would be used. It was reassuring to know that somebody in the village had a few weapons about. Perhaps the Marquis was not the useless figurehead some of the villagers made him out to be.

'That is all past glory Slim, the days when my ancestors fell in battle to save this land.' Slim shuddered involuntarily. The whole idea of falling in battle was upsetting, especially if you couldn't get back up afterwards.

'Have you heard anymore news, Your Lordship?' asked Moose.

'Very little after the death of the King. Yesterday Lady Erica gazed in the black pool in the courtyard, disturbing visions welled up from the deep.' Slim and Moose looked at each other. They knew that the waters in the black pool at the Manor often reflected events and people in space and time.

The Marquis took one of the swords from the wall, and inspected the edge. Pulling in his oversize tummy and taking a warrior like stance he stole a quick glance in the mirror hanging on the wall.

Pleased with himself, he stood at ease and related with some relish that the last member of the family to use the sword had been his grandfather Olivier deCygne.

'It was at the battle of the Crooked Tree. Most of the black priests had fled across the river, but a small group, accompanied by ferocious dogs turned back and attacked the Elven King and his bowmen. The King had been isolated and Olivier flew to his aid. Two large dogs in midair, ready to land on the king, were impaled on Olivier's outstretched sword, a perfect shish kebab. The Elven King's life had been saved, for even a small bite by the black hounds' long incisors is fatal. As a token of his gratitude, the King honoured Olivier with the Golden Rose.'

'Why a rose Sir,' Duckie wanted to know. The Marquis looked down to discover the youngster and laughed.

'An inquiring mind, I see. My young friend, to the Elves, the rose is the symbol of life. If a man risks his life to save another's, he is presented with a golden rose.' The Marquis raised his hand and all eyes traveled to the golden rose mounted on the wall near the window. Its delicately shaped gold leaves glittered in the early sun.

The Marquis lifted the sword back on the wall, and led Slim and Moose to the porch. Duckie, awestruck, touched some of the weapons with his hands. He was fascinated by the arms and stayed behind to study the many instruments of destruction.

Lady Erica invited the company to be seated at the dining table in the sunroom. Before long the conversation returned to events at the palace and Moose and Slim told the Marquis about Scimitar's speech at the Graceful Neck.

While pouring the coffee Lady Erica noticed Slim's vexed face.

'Where are your thoughts Slim?'

'It is the black dogs Lady Erica, the bites, are they always deadly?'

'It is true they are fatal, if not treated in time. There is a cure for the poison carried on the tainted fangs of the black hounds.'

'A cure for the tainted fang illness Lady Erica?' exclaimed Moose.

'Yes Moose, tainted fang is a terrible illness, but the Sisters at the Convent of the Secret Crossing, can heal its victims.' Alarm dwelling in their eyes, the company looked up. Lady Erica read their thoughts.

'Traditionally the Sisters of the Secret Crossing were known as spiritual midwives, who helped the souls of the dying to cross the mystic passage of time and space, into a new realm. And to this day they work with souls, who are about to leave the physical form. There is a small circle of healers in their order, who have preserved the healing knowledge left by the ancient Elven Kings. The victims of tainted fang must spend seven weeks at their Convent. There they are clothed in suits of nettle, woven by the Sisters. For seven weeks they burn with the sting of nettle, but then the illness abates and they recover.'

'Well I am glad to know there is a cure,' sighed Slim. He made a mental note to run for it, at the first sign of a black hound. Just being touched by a nettle leaf is painful enough, seven weeks in nettles! Lady Erica read his thoughts.

'The pilgrimage of life is a steep path Slim, strewn with pitfalls and broken glass.'

'Well, I can cope with the glass and the hidden pits, but savage beasts sinking their fangs into my flesh, it is just too horrible to contemplate.'

Lady Erica's face had an austere beauty and her intense green eyes shed a compassionate light upon Slim. The face softened into a smile. A smile hard to resist and one that cheered.

Metallic sounds from the hall, indicated that even the smell of coffee and cake had failed to draw Duckie away from checking out the shining armour in the great hall.

5

On The River

*T*he Sanctus flowed silently but its stillness was deceptive. Underneath the calm surface moved a swift current. Scimitar looked carefully around as he approached the bushes near the river. All was peace. The pussy willows hung perfectly still in the mist and the dew covered dogwood looked a brilliant red. Willows were in leaf and many gardens bordering the river displayed bright splashes of colour. Teams of swans drifted with the current or swam up stream near the far shore where the current was weaker.

Patriot, the golden retriever, seated himself in the bow of the canoe and Scimitar took his own place in the stern. The canoe was moored in a shallow lagoon. It took a few minutes of poling to push free, but once the frail craft floated on the water, the Dwarf swung his paddle, driving the canoe towards Lambarina. Turning around, he took a final look at the Graceful Neck framed by giant gently swaying poplars. Deep in his heart he had a great love for Swanneland.

The cedar canoe moved gracefully through the water, hugging the shore to avoid the strong headwinds in the middle of the river. He was driving the slender craft at high speed, for his presence in Lambarina was urgently needed. Only through unity and cooperation could they hope to oppose the infiltration of foreign agents into the Kingdom. The King had been a strong unifying force in the land and Scimitar knew his death and the imprisonment of Princess Yaconda, would give the enemy a chance to fan old prejudices and hatreds and drive a wedge between. Gnome and Dwarf, Mountain Fairy and Elf, Outlander and Swannefolk. Then the Seven Lords would make their move.

There was little doubt that there were those who would prefer Scimitar to arrive in Lambarina late or not at all.

The breaking of the water against the bow, the rhythmic splashing of the paddle and the soft misty beauty of the landscape conveyed a sense of wholeness and peace to the Dwarf's soul . For a moment he ceased to think about the overwhelming trials ahead and permitted himself a feeling of joy and gratitude. That interlude was but brief. Dwarves did not expect life to be happy or tranquil, they counted joy in moments that unexpectedly and sporadically cut across the thorny path of life. It was not long before Scimitar forced himself back to the here and now, focusing his eyes on the shore and carefully scanning the landscape.

Women poling barges upstream laden with milk and winter vegetables floated by. They would wave to the stern looking Dwarf driving his canoe at breakneck speed and wonder if the devil himself were at his heels. Scimitar returned their greetings with a mere nod, he simply did not want take his hand off the paddle.

Restlessly his eyes scanned the shore. Occasionally he could see the wagon trail that ran behind the farms. Then, he would slow his pace and watch the flow of morning travelers, farm labourers, hay wagons drawn by small horses, and women darting over to their neighbours for a quick visit and a cup of tea. Only once was his suspicion aroused. Perched atop a load of hay, behind the driver, were two farm labourers and a black dog. Scimitar knew Swannefolk rarely kept dogs. Patriot had caught a faint scent and the texture of his hair changed briefly. Scimitar dismissed the scene. There were at least a few old dogs left on the farms and likely this was one of them. The driver looked like an old farmer and the wagon moved slowly. In another hour he would be well ahead of the old cart.

The two figures on the farm cart had taken an unusual interest in the canoe, for the bow wave indicated the craft was moving at high speed. Swannefolk seldom hurried on principle. It would be wise to overtake the craft and check out this champion paddler. One of the fellows told the friendly farmer, who had given them a ride, to stop his wagon if he treasured his life. The jolly chap thought it was all in jest, but when he turned around, his eyes met the open jaws of a black dog and the icy stare of the strangers. He froze with fear.

'Come on you old coon, help us unload the hay.' The frightened farmer untied the lashings that held the load. The strangers pushed the bales over the side of the cart and climbed back on the box of the empty wagon. The whip flew over the old horse frightening the beast out of his wits. He took off in a wild trot.

Scimitar kept up the punishing tempo. He must reach Lambarina while the passage was relatively safe. Old farms and the odd windmill dotted his side of the river. This was still the land of the Swannefolk and Scimitar knew many of the families on the river homesteads. In the fall Scimitar and his brother Smithereen often traveled hither to pick fruit in the bountiful orchards that graced the water's edge. Working his way towards Lambarina, more farmhouses and orchards appeared and sometimes it was difficult to see the road.

Most of the orchards by the shore were owned by Swannefolk. Since the founding of the United Kingdom boundaries between Outlanders and Swannefolk were no longer clear-cut. Some Swannefolk had moved to Lambarina to try their hand at crafts, and Outlanders had bought farms in Swanneland. Two Outlanders had actually married Swannemaidens and planted orchards near the Sanctus. The weddings had raised a good many eyebrows and some of the older families had been indignant. Yet the flow of time like the flow of the Sanctus, had smoothed the waves of social outrage.

That morning Oliver Wendell walked to his orchard to do some spring pruning. How lovely the morning, beds of tulips and daffodils showed bright red and yellow, and buds were swelling, awaiting the kiss of spring to start their flowering.

As he was wont to do in the morning, Oliver sat down for a moment on the seat inside the small rose arbour between the orchard and the house and counted his blessings.

For generations the Wendells had lived by the Sanctus. It had been quite a shock to Oliver's father Mallard, when Sigurd, the Outlander, had bought the land next door. Sigurd had married a Swannemaid and old Mallard had been aghast. Soon afterwards old Mallard was taken to the Convent of the Sisters of the Secret Crossing and passed to the other side.

Oliver and his wife Magdalena developed a close friendship with their new neighbours and never thought of them as being different. Sigurd brought to the county many new ideas that proved useful.

The sun was burning off the morning fog and Oliver climbed up into one of his apple trees to prune the higher branches. Sitting on a sturdy branch to catch his breath, he overlooked the river. Sunlight spilling upon the still waters of the Sanctus unveiled barges and small craft laden with merchandise for the Lambarina markets. On the far shore windmills caught the first morning breeze. Entranced by the beauty of the moment Oliver forgot about pruning and rested his eyes on the soft pastel shades of the watery panorama. Life held many sorrows but moments like this made it all worthwhile. Touched by this, one of spring's mysterious moments, he sang softly,

when the fog is gently lifting
and the buds begin to swell
nature's secrets are unveiling
all is well, all is well , all is well

It was a reassuring kind of a song, and it was a good thing Oliver was singing it. As he repeated the last line a few times, changing a note here and there for the sake of musical fun, two figures walked into the orchard. Oliver noticed them as they passed the homestead. They looked like itinerant labourers, the kind that would come in autumn to help with the fruit picking. They were short sturdy fellows with tanned faces and angular features. These fellows did not look familiar. Behind them trotted a large black dog, with massive neck and jaw muscles. Oliver did not like the looks of them. From his perch in the tree he shouted, 'hi fellows, this is private property.'

They wore short leather coats instead of the casual wear of the run-of-the mill fruit picker. He came down from the tree, pruning shears in hand and leaned against the trunk. He tried to smile as the men came up to him. In a friendly tone of voice he explained that local bylaws forbade trespassing in orchards. The two men facing him were not impressed and the black dog seated by their side growled softly.

'Quiet Froth,' snapped the older of the two. Then he turned to Oliver.

'You listen carefully and nothing will happen to you.'

'Or your family,' leered his companion. Oliver realized suddenly that this was a situation unlike any other he had ever encountered. His fine weathered features turned a ghastly white. This was evil in the here and now, not the kind you read about in fairy tales or old legends. When Oliver looked properly intimidated, the elder fellow spoke.

'Just cooperate and we won't have to make an example of you. Tell us, did you see a Dwarf paddling down the river in a cedar canoe?'

'No, I have not gentlemen, no honestly, only women poling barges with winter vegetables. Oh yes, there were a couple of kids in a scow moving sheep. No Dwarves, absolutely no Dwarves. They only come in the fall to buy fruit.' The younger man frowned.

'You are lying, you filthy son of the soil.' He seized the pruning shears and poked Oliver in the stomach. Whether it was to protect himself or to hit his assailant was unclear, but Oliver raised his arms. The movement triggered a response in the black hound. It leaped at Oliver and locked its massive jaws on his left thigh, sinking the fangs deep into his flesh. Groaning with pain, Oliver sank to the ground. The older man hit the dog in anger and hissed, 'never attack until you are ordered to.' To his companion he sneered, 'we will not get any more information out of him and worse, the bite by Froth may be a clue to our identity.'

The two strangers walked off promptly lest they attract undue attention. At the river's edge they helped themselves to Oliver's skiff. Froth jumped in after them and they rowed quickly out of sight.

Oliver moaning softly, but conscious of what was happening, was still lying prostrate at the foot of the apple tree. The pain was terrible. He waited until he was certain that the villains were out of earshot, before crying out for help. Until they were gone, he did not want his wife and daughter on the scene.

Magdalena Wendell was putting the dinner plates back on the open shelves. The plates were a deep blue, swans sailing in the centre. Her daughter Helga, looking up from her spinning wheel, noticed that two of the plates were upside down.

'Ma'am, two plates on the left have the swans pointing their heads towards the bottom of the lake.' Magdalena smiled at her keen eyed daughter.

Some of the richer families had kitchen cupboards, but Helga loved the open shelves with the beautifully coloured plates, there for all to see!

Helga at seventeen was lovely, soft features, gray eyes and golden hair, reaching to her waist. There was about her an aura of mystery that was hard to define. It was as if her spirit lived in this world and the one beyond.

Scimitar on his annual fruit picking expedition last autumn had spent some time in the Wendell orchard. He was spellbound by Helga's beauty. For days he had been unable to get her out of his mind, a mind that was supposed to be dealing with grave issues. He had reprimanded himself for being fascinated by a maid. Dwarves are very severe with themselves in such matters, and easily smitten with guilt. After meeting Helga, Scimitar had retired to the woods and fasted for seven days. Alas, the image of Helga had but retreated into the deeper recesses of his mind.

Helga's mother finished the dishes and all the swans were right side up. It was silent in the kitchen, but for the whirring of the wheel. Sunlight filtered into the room. Helga stood up and walked to the window. She walked with a limp, yet it did not detract from her grace. She feasted her eyes on the mist unveiling the budding orchard, before returning to the wheel.

She had been disabled by a tragic accident. At the age of four she had been climbing trees in the orchard when a merewing had spotted her. Diving with the speed of lightning he clasped his talons around the braces of her playsuit. Then flapping his mighty wings, he had lifted Helga high above the orchard. Except for the swishing of air currents created by his huge wings there was silence. There were no cries and the child seemed to be mesmerized. Oliver had been standing by the shed smoking his pipe. Only when he raised his eyes to follow one of the blue rings of smoke gently spiraling into the sky did he see the heart rendering scene. He rushed into the shed, seized his long bow and sent an arrow flying. It pierced the marauder's right wing and forced him to release his prey. A cherry tree broke the child's fall and saved her life, but her right hip was crushed and had never healed properly. Perhaps it was this handicap that had set her apart from other children and given her the second sight.

Helga looked up from the spindle. The orchard and the river beyond were enveloped in soft sunlight. Larks were singing, but another sound rose faintly above the humming of the wheel and the singing of the birds. She lifted her foot from the treadle, the humming of the wheel faded and the magpies sang their final chord. The moaning was clearly audible and then a cry carried by the morning breeze reached her. It was her father, her father's voice.

She rushed out the door and walked as quickly as she could towards the shore. The cry for help was loud and clear and once she reached the last row of trees near the water, she saw her father lying in the grass.

When she came within sight, the moaning faded, but one glance convinced her that the situation was deadly serious. A trouser leg of his coveralls had been shredded. She bent over to comfort him and she took a small pair of pruning shears from a pocket in his coveralls and gently cut away the torn material around the wound. The injury was gruesome and the tissue around the teeth marks had turned black. Her intuition told her this was no ordinary bite. Soon her mother reached the scene and holding Oliver's hand, spoke words of hope and solace. After a few minutes he was able to tell them what had happened.

Helga walked quickly to the river hoping to hail a barge to move her father to a nearby hamlet where lived a woman who practiced the art of healing. Her eyes scanned the sunlit waters. No barges were in sight. Although teams of swans swam on the opposite shore, no vessels were near. She walked farther out where the willow branches no longer obscured her view and looked upstream. In the distance she espied the bow of a small vessel, probably a skiff or canoe rounding a curve in the river. The outline rapidly became clear. It was a canoe moving at great speed, in the bow stood a golden retriever. Whoever the master of the little craft might be, she decided to hail him.

She could now see the mariner. He was wearing a plumed hat, and with great power drew the paddle through the water. His determined stance told her he was traveling in great haste. Yet, she cried out for help. Scimitar, for it was the intrepid Dwarf, could barely hear the voice above the whirling water and the splashing of the paddle. Forcefully he continued to drive the craft ahead.

The golden retriever in the bow seemed restless. Patriot had picked up the scent he had smelled an hour ago, a smell that he had experienced only once before on a border patrol. All his protective instincts were aroused and he uttered a single piercing howl which sent shivers down even Scimitars iron spine. Scimitar looked up and saw the desperate maid waving her arms. He slowed the craft and steered for shore. He knew he was by the Wendell farm and that Helga was not one to raise a false alarm. He beached the canoe, jumped out and rushed up the bank. Within minutes he reached Helga. Scimitar saw the look of horror on her face as she led him through the orchard to the place where Oliver was lying.

Magdalena, who had just arrived at the scene, stepped back and Scimitar knelt over the victim. The warrior's sharp eyes examined the torn flesh and the black hue that was rapidly invading the surrounding tissue. A look of pity appeared on his face, then ire flamed in his eyes. Such fire Helga and Magdalena had never had seen.

Scimitar, instantly knew it was a case of 'tainted fang'. It was the first case in the Kingdom in many years. It meant the enemy had once more penetrated the borders. Only the massive black hounds of the servants of the Seven carried this venom. The local healers could not help Oliver, only the Sisters of the Secret Crossing in the Convent, had a cure for the deadly bites.

The scene of the two chaps on the hay wagon and the black dog flashed back into Scimitar's mind. Probably they had ditched the farmer and driven the horse at a fast gallop to be there waiting for him. The Rovers were well schooled by their Seven Masters. Careful in making plans and ruthless in carrying them out, they presented a much greater danger than did the old Witch Doctors. The Rovers and their horrid hounds had now arrived here in this quiet backwater of the Swannefolk and felled an innocent farmer, the father of the maid he had once fancied!

Scimitar bent over Oliver and told him that he must be taken, without delay, to the Convent of the Sisters of the Secret Crossing. Oliver looked panicky and whispered.

'Burning in suits of nettle for seven weeks, as it says in the legend.' Scimitar nodded silently. His severe features changed into a look of compassion, but only for a moment. The Dwarf was not one to be side tracked by his feelings not that he didn't have any as some of his relatives asserted. It was when he was alone in the wilderness that those feelings surfaced from the depth of his soul. In times of peril his mind was crystal clear.

Magdalena had rushed over to the neighbours to ask for help in transporting Oliver to the Convent in the hills north of Cascade. Oliver looked at Scimitar, pain in his eyes and said softly.

'They asked about you. They wanted to know if I had seen you on the river,' Scimitar realized no time was to be lost, it was clear the enemy wanted at all cost to prevent the convening of the interim Council in Lambarina, and Scimitar wondered if delegates might be waylaid on their journey to the Capital .

He laid his hand on Oliver's forehead speaking words of solace and gratitude. Well he knew that the attack on Oliver had given him fair warning and might have saved his own life.

Helga walked the Dwarf back to the canoe. From the back seat of the craft he smiled at her, dipping his paddle in the water.

He surprised himself that he could now smile at Helga without his heart strings quivering, or could he? Perhaps seven days of fasting had dispelled the illusion. No time must be lost. He pushed off quickly and picked up Patriot at a little tongue of land jutting into the river.

Dog and master now were keenly aware of the dangers around them. Patriot took his position at the bow again, analyzing all the scents that reached him from shore.

Helga walked back to her father. Oliver seemed to be recovering from shock. He looked at this daughter.

'Helga my sweetling, why has this happened to me? I could have thought of all kinds of terrible things, but not of this! Why me?' Helga took his hand and spoke gently.

'You ask why me? Sometimes we must ask, why not me? You may have saved the life of Scimitar. The black hound was the clue to the murderous intentions of the strangers, and without Scimitar, the Kingdom would be in greater peril. Remember father, when the merewing seized me, and my hip was crushed in the cherry tree? Yet in some strange way there was a gift hidden in that pain.' Oliver smiled at his daughter, her wisdom far beyond her years never failed to surprise him.

The sound of wheels snapping branches broke the silence and Helga could see the neighbour's horse and wagon approaching. Oliver was sitting up now and looked more relaxed. He tried to sound cheerful.

'Morning Sigurd. Thanks for coming swiftly.'

'Remember the old saying Oliver, better a neighbour near, than a friend afar. It says in the old legends that days of treachery and destruction will return to the Sanctus Valley. All will be well my friend,' soothed Sigurd taking Oliver's hand in his own. 'I will look after Magdalena and the orchard, while you recover.'

They made a primitive stretcher out of branches and twigs and gently lifted Oliver onto a bed of straw on top of the wagon.

'I will travel with him mother,' offered Helga. He needs nursing on the journey and I can help the Sisters of the Secret Crossing with the weaving of the nettle suits. We do not know what will happen. More folks may be attacked by the hounds, and the Sisters may need many hands.'

'Do come back dear. Do not join the order it would break my heart if you left us for ever.'

'No, mother, do not worry I will come back, but I cannot tell when that will be.' Sigurd helped Helga up onto the seat, climbed up himself, and spurred on the horse.

'Step on it my old friend, the climb will be steep and we are in great haste.' The horse seemed to get the gist of the message and broke into a swift trot. Sigurd's wife Anna, who had joined Magdalena, took her arm as they walked back to the Wendell homestead.

6

Lady Erica De Coscoroba

Lady Erica walked out on the balcony of her bedroom. The sun's first rays reflected in the windows of farm houses on the far shore of the Sanctus. The early sunlight cast the landscape in a rosy tint. Teams of swans, both black and white, rows of weeping willows, and the water itself emanated a soft beauty, only seen in early morning hours.

She came back to her room and sat down at her dresser. From its drawer she took an ebony comb and began to dress her silver hair. When finished she took a ribbon of blue silk and tied it into a pony tail. Unlike the Outlanders who turned gray in old age, the hair of Swannefolk turned silver at maturity, only grief or aging would turn it sheer white.

Her eye caught a portrait hung above the dresser. It was a pencil sketch of a young man dressed in the uniform of a border guard. It was over twenty years since she had seen Gustav. Along the Finnian range he had been in charge of a group of Outlanders who had assisted the Dwarves in guarding the borders of the Kingdom. On their journey to the mountains they had been quartered at the Manor.

He and she had met in the courtyard. Seated on the low stone wall which girded the pool in the center, she heard footsteps on the brick patio. Turning around she beheld the tall border scout. His fair locks were shoulder length, and strung over his right shoulder was a longbow. There had been a sparkle in the brown eyes that had touched her heart strings.

He greeted her courteously and she invited him to be seated. He told her of his adventures as a scout, of the danger that dwelt behind the Finnian Range and how few people took the threat seriously. Lady Erica too knew of the dangers. Visions in the black water of the pool had shown the shape of things to come. But she did not wish to dwell on them. She had been touched by the idealism of the young warrior and she wanted him to unwind and to speak of his home and family.

They had gone down to the river, taken a ride in one of the gondolas and watched a group of visiting Fairies dance on the lawn of the Graceful Neck. The lighthearted mood of a summer festival in Swanneland was contagious and the stern scout had let the world slip off his shoulders. Back at the Manor they had talked all night.

They shared tales about families and friends and about legends from strange and far off places. When dawn broke she had an odd feeling that truly they had entered each other's world. It was then that he knelt at her feet, took her hand and kissed it. She knew only too well that in the silent language of the Outlanders this gesture sealed for life a bond of friendship. Perhaps more than friendship, but that remained unspoken, for the fair scout with the fathomless eyes never returned from his mission on the frontier.

It was Scimitar's brother the formidable Smithereen who had been with Gustav, when the party was attacked by dozens of Gorghouls. Gorghouls have skin so tough that arrows do not even dent it.[2] Surrounded by dozens of Gorghouls the situation had been hopeless and surrender inevitable. The scouts were led away in irons to work the galleys of the Seven on the Wasa river. Only Smithereen had been able to escape. Swinging his terrible ball and chain the Dwarf by sheer force and speed was able to cut a swath through the Gorghouls.

The morning after the disaster, Smithereen walked over the scene of the battle and found a scrap of paper with a short poem addressed to 'My Erica'.

He had made his way to the Manor to tell Lady Erica the heartbreaking news and bring to her the note with Gustav's last thoughts before he was led away into captivity.

The tough Dwarf, by many considered a ruffian, could not suppress

---

2   *In the latter days the legend of gorghoul skin has inspired the creation of gortex, an unusually tough and water resistant material.*

his tears when he recalled the tragic scene of his friends walking off into slavery. When he spoke to Lady Erica about Gustav, his broad frame was bent with grief. With great love Lady Erica had looked upon the mighty warrior. He had put Gustav's poem in her hand and confided that he himself wrote poetry. Lady Erica had smiled, smiled at the great mysteries of nature that in the secret chambers of this rough hewn Dwarf, should dwell a poet.

The rays of the sun coming in through the window brought her back to the present. She took her eyes off Gustav's portrait, opened the top drawer of her dresser and took out the small aged piece of paper that Smithereen had given her, she sat down on the sofa and read the words penned more than twenty years ago.

To my Erica:
A bond of friendship
more than friendship meant
a bond of love, that cannot end
for you - my life, my love, my friend
G.H.

Although some of her silver tresses now showed streaks of white, an aura of beauty had never abandoned Erica. She moved with grace that was a pleasure to behold.

Clad in a purple gown, she walked down the spiral staircase. At the foot of the stairs a strong intuitive feeling moved her to go into the courtyard and gaze upon the black waters of the pool. The fruit trees in the sheltered square were in bud, the song of birds heralded spring, as she stepped into the sun filled air.

Two black swans at the far end of the courtyard flew up and settled beside her as she reached the low stone wall encircling the black waters. Her hands gently touched their feathers.

'Aske and Alma, I have come to look into the black waters of the pool.' She knelt down by the low wall and the swans by her side reverently bent their heads.

A ray from the rising sun shimmered upon the waters. For a short time the lady and her swans resembled a sculpture. The stillness was broken when Erica turned up her palms and intoned an incantation,

Oh sages now ascended
teachers of my soul
grant a vision
to those who dwell below

The swans by her side remained silent. Lady Erica looked into the black water, her eyes probing its depth. Perhaps it was because she had just looked at his portrait, but the first image that appeared was that of Gustav. By the shore of a great river, he was seated beneath a willow tree. White hair framed his features and his eyes were deep and clear. Suddenly she experienced a strong feeling that he was still in this world and had not yet ascended to the realms beyond. Next she beheld an image of a ship, a riverboat being rowed by many men. Was it possible that Gustav was working now as a galley slave for the Seven Lords?

The vision faded and total darkness returned. A new image floated to the surface. She could see the walled city of Lambarina and different people from the Kingdom trying to enter, but being repulsed by hostile forces. Then the vision faded. She knew immediately that Lambarina was in danger from within and that the meeting planned for delegates from the Dwarves, the Fairies, the Outlanders, the Swannefolk, the Elves and the Gnomes could never take place, in that city. But where could they gather and work out a strategy to deal with the crisis?

She looked into the pool again. She could now only see the courtyard of the Manor itself reflected in the dark water, no other images came up. Suddenly it dawned upon her. It was here in the Manor, that the meeting should take place. This backwater of the Kingdom in Swanneland, would never be suspect. If there were only a way to get a message to the Mountain Fairies, before it was too late, surely they would be able to pass the information on to Scimitar and other delegates.

The presence of many strangers had been reported in the capital, gypsies, birds of passage, backpackers, birdwatchers, hunters with dogs. Erica knew that the delegates must be prevented from entering the capital. If they walked into a trap, it would deprive the Kingdom of the men and women, who had the strength and wisdom to face the peril that lay ahead.

She must send word to the Mountain Fairies, asking them to forward messages by pelican to all delegates traveling to the capital and offering them hospitality at the Manor deCygne.

Carefully she inscribed the text on two pieces of peach wood and with blue ribbons fastened them around the necks of the swans. Then she added a personal note for Tuluga, Queen of the Mountain Fairies. This she put into a small silver container that she clipped onto a leg of the black male swan.

The black swans had been given to her as cygnets nine years ago. They were much attached to her and proud to accept this mission of trust.

'Fly only at night and the darkness will protect you, during the day you must hide deep in the marshes or in the woods, the enemy is afoot, and merewings have been sighted. If you encounter pelicans ask them to escort you to the land of the Fairies.'

The swans had to admit somewhat reluctantly, that the pelicans might be useful. Their extraordinary eye sight and speed were well known. Aske and Alma spread their wings and with a graceful motion created a current of air, carrying them aloft and into the rays of the early morning sun.

She whispered a blessing on the swans' mission and walked back to the house to dress and prepare breakfast for nephew Ferdinand, the eternal adolescent. He would be keen enough in this time of crisis to jump into the fray, and do something very rash. She smiled to herself. Yes, the Marquis even at mid-life, would dream of valour and go where angels feared to tread. And there was this silly business of the villagers calling him Marquis. Long since had she ceased use of her own title, Baroness de Coscoroba, and discouraged people from calling her lady. Ingrained habits died slowly among the villagers.

She entered the Manor by the backdoor and through the scullery walked into the large kitchen where Norma was kindling the massive brick stove.

'A sweet morning to you ma'am,' said the country lass who had just joined the household.

'Blessings to you,' returned Lady Erica in the proper traditional form.

'Ma'am, I was passing through the great hall and the Marquis was talking to young Duckie. He said something about Duckie becoming his page. What is a page ma'am?' A twinkle appeared in Erica's eye.

'In the last century my dear the tradition of chivalry was practiced. At that time we were still fighting for our freedom. Many a warrior had a page, a helper, to carry weapons, and learn the art of warfare.'

'Duckie wouldn't want to fight Ma'am, he is such a sweety,' flushed Norma.

'Duckie is a sweety my dear, but there's steel inside that soft core.'

Norma laughed and shook her head, Lady Erica had the strangest notions. Still, often she had predicted events that came true, although at the time villagers had snickered. Norma broke a couple of eggs on the edge of the cast iron frying pan when Duckie walked in for a chat.

As Erica left the kitchen she couldn't help smiling. The idea of Duckie becoming a page, was somewhat droll, but then it could have merit. Duckie was a canny boy, with both feet on the ground.

In the front hall Ferdinand was practicing a few sword thrusts in front of the mirror. Erica called out to him from the sun porch, 'Ferdinand, join me for morning coffee and breakfast.'

Ferdinand always enjoyed breakfast and the sight of steaming eggs, sunny side up, was dear to him. Comfortably seated in an oak armchair, overlooking his domain, he exuded a sense of contentment. Norma put a plate of eggs in front of him and he graced her with a benevolent smile.

Yes, a nobleman's life was a burden and a great responsibility but there were moments that made it all worth while. The only shadow on his sunny universe was the look that Aunt Erica cast upon him.

'My dear Aunt, you look concerned, I know you worry about me and you laugh when I try on the armour and check the weapons in the front hall. Do not forget we are living in dangerous times, you said so yourself, and I must be ready.'

'My dear boy, the enemy we are dealing with works under cover and with great cunning, you cannot go rushing off to slay a dragon or two. We need you here at the Manor. And at your age. Your hair is showing white and you are overweight.' Lady Erica's words sounded final, but Ferdinand made a last stand.

'Aunt Erica, I have trod this earth for over half a century, and what have I done. Dabbled in watercolour, written a poem or two, given a few speeches and presented the tenants with presents at the spring and harvest festivals. Out of boredom I have made floral arrangements and moved the furniture around.

I am a failure Aunt, my life is a tragedy, a tragedy of wasted time. To three girls I proposed, and each time was turned down.' Erica realized The Marquis was at a low ebb.

'It matters not my nephew dear. Did you not know that love cannot be solicited. It comes our way unexpectedly, at times and in places never imagined. My dear Ferdinand, you have always been a decent chap, and if three ladies turned you down, I am sure a fourth and better one is waiting for you somewhere. I trust you will help in the struggle that lies ahead, only remember Ferdinand you are not a young warrior, and the expeditions that are called for will not serve coffee and eggs sunny side up.'

Ferdinand began to feel a glimmer of hope. He might yet write his name in the annals of history.

'Thanks for putting things in perspective Aunt, but deep inside us lives a hero, an adventurer, waiting for a chance to break out. If he doesn't come out now, he could be walled in forever.'

Aunt Erica smiled. 'You better go and liberate that walled in warrior of yours and would you mind if I borrowed your page for a couple of hours?'

'Duckie' shouted Ferdinand, 'come here for a moment.' The youngster appeared instantly, a half eaten cinnamon bun in his hand.

'Duckie,' said Erica, 'Could you run down to the Graceful Neck, and see if you can find Moose Martin and Slim , and ask them to come up here. Then go to the village and leave this message for old Martha.'

'Martha, the blind prophetess?' asked Duckie, a little taken aback. 'I am scared to walk into her yard Lady Erica, it is the bear she has raised he is really big now'.

'The bear is all right Duckie his name is Grompuss, and very kind he is, when not provoked.'

'I won't provoke him Lady Erica,' shouted Duckie as he raced off the sun porch, message clutched in hand.

Ferdinand had put his feet up and now filled his pipe with Sweet Siren, a new tobacco mixture grown by the Gnomes. The suppressed adventurer deep within was temporarily put to sleep, and a rich fragrance filled the room.

Lady Erica enjoyed the smell of tobacco fortunately, and pouring herself a second cup of coffee cast her eyes over the sunlit hills beyond.

Against the dark rim of the distant spruce forest, a white fleck was moving uphill. She reached for the field glasses and looked again. Yes, it was a covered wagon pulled by one horse and riding towards the deserted mountain range beyond the Valley of Lost Hope. The only living creatures there were the Sisters of the Secret Crossing. Someone must be dying, and yet she had not heard lately of any serious illness.

The Marquis stared at Aunt Erica. He marveled at her serenity, a quality that had always eluded him. He was startled when a ripple of fear moved across the lovely face.

'Ferdinand, look up, on the north ridge, a horse and wagon are swiftly moving towards the Valley of Lost Hope.'

'Just a party traveling to the Convent of the Sisters of the Secret Crossing Aunt, one of the old men or women in the valley seeking solace in the Convent, before they leave this earthly plane.'

'Were it only so, my dear Ferdinand, I know of no illness amongst the people in the valley. A black aura surrounds the travelers. I can sense that evil has befallen the party traveling to the Convent. The enemy has penetrated farther down the valley, and the black hounds that travel with the Rovers may have attacked one of our people. I think that the wagon speeding towards the Convent is carrying a victim of tainted fang to the Sisters, for the nettle treatment!

Ferdinand shuddered and the hero inside did not stir.

7

Princess Yaconda

Princess Yaconda leaned out the narrow opening in the Alcazar tower. The sun rising behind the ancient walls cast its rays over the dunes and the ocean beyond. When she looked around the small circular room in the tower, the loom in the center and Dominique seated on the stone cot combing her long chestnut tresses, she wondered if it were all a nightmare? Perhaps she would wake soon and find herself back in the palace in Lambarina.

'Oh Dominique, what treachery has brought us here, and where will it all end? Imbrun, the traitor, told us that father had suffered a heart attack, but I know foul play caused his death.' Dominique continued silently braiding her hair. She looked at her mistress.

'Imbrun's words leave no doubt that he is in league with the Dark Masters. It is on their orders that we are kept in this desolate tower. The United Kingdom has been a thorn in their flesh for years. Once, it was divided into many enclaves and they could manipulate at will, Outlanders, Gnomes, Swannefolk and others. Now all the people in the Kingdom share The Common Book of Sacred Lore and pay homage to one throne. The Dark Lords have never forgiven your father for uniting the people in the Kingdom of the Seven Mountains.'

Princess Yaconda sighed. 'We know but little about the Dark Lords that brought about Imbrun's treachery. If they were able to win over Imbrun, their powers must be dark indeed.' Tears welled in her eyes. She had loved Lord Imbrun since childhood and his betrayal had been a sorrow to her.

One day, Dominique, I heard my father talk to the Elven Queen. He said that it was the enchantress Matista's magic that had bestowed upon the Seven Lords the gift of power and lasting youth.'

Dominique thought for a moment. 'Soon the Groll[3] will come to bring our daily rations, I will see if I can get him to talk.' Dominique got up and walked towards the narrow spiral staircase that led to the base of the tower.

Yaconda called after her. 'Caution Dominique, once they grab you there is no escape. They have claws like lobsters.' Dominique turned, smiled and went down the stairs.

The Grolls would always unlock the door, put the food inside and lock the door again, all without uttering a word. Listening, Dominique stood behind the door. Soon the sound of big leathery feet on sand alerted her. The door opened and she stared straight into the gruesome brown face of Captain Homarus. The Groll's first reaction was one of fear, for they had been forbidden to meet or even cast an eye on the prisoners and informers in the Seven Lords' realm were plentiful. He carefully looked behind and made sure that he was alone.

Grinning he spoke in a raspy voice, 'Beautiful lady has come to meet Groll, lady not satisfied with food?'

'No, no' said Dominique, 'I was just curious. When we met at the harbour we were too upset to have a good look at you or to have a chat. I have met Gorghouls, Goblins and Trolls before, but never had the honour of encountering Grolls and a pleasant surprise it is.'

The Groll quite taken by her praise, conceded that Goblins and Trolls were lower life forms. Dominique managed a smile, 'Oh greatly honored Groll you must have a high station with the Dark Lords, for they trust you with their prisoners.'

The Groll looked sheepish, as Grolls and wolves do at times. 'Crusty Homarus, Captain of the bodyguard at your command delicious lady.'

The word delicious caused Dominique some unease. Determined to find out more she went on asking questions, instead of slamming the door. Which she should have done.

----

3   *Grolls are large ugly creatures. They have scaly brown bodies and their hairy paws are capable of a viselike grip. They are the offspring of unions between Gorghouls and Trolls. They are generally dressed in a leather jerkin.*

'Great Captain Homarus, your Masters, the Dark Lords, what are they like?'

This question perplexed the Captain and he had to think for a minute, 'Seven masters have no fear, give no mercy, very hard on Grolls, cast net over all the land.'

'Have no fear,' exclaimed Dominique, amazed. 'Fear no dragons, no fear of giant wolves, or black hounds.'

The Groll made a rasping noise, faintly resembling the sound of laughter. 'Tame the dragons, tame black hounds.

'Oh Captain dragon tamer, you helped the Lords subdue these terrible monsters?' asked Dominique in a hushed voice.

Of all the flattery 'dragon tamer', greatly pleased the Groll, and he loosened up. 'Lords very great, fear no one, not one.' The Groll grimaced, carefully looked around him and then in a low voice confided, 'Fear no one, but one.'

'You speak in riddles, oh you clever Groll! How can one fear no one, but one?'

Captain Homarus was now really warming up and a mysterious gleam showed in his eyes. 'In council chamber, secret meeting, clever Groll hide in weapon chest and hear lords speak, fear no one, but one, the one, the elven child, they fear the elven child.'

The Groll fell into an evil laugh, as if the idea were somewhat preposterous, but the laugh ended abruptly. A strange feeling came over him, a kind of apprehension that all his actions were known to the Lords. Fear gripped him. Led on by this clever lady, he had been carried away, and had talked at his own peril. There were spies everywhere and the prisoners themselves might repeat his words. Then his doom would be sealed.

This sly lady had been the only one to hear his words. He knew he had lost his cool, but the error could easily be undone, and perhaps provide a juicy dinner in the bargain.

His arm shot out like lightning and gripped Dominique's wrist. The vise grip made her freeze with pain. And although she was a hefty maid, with little effort he swung her over his shoulder and carried her off into the desert. With her free fist she beat his back and her teeth tore at his left ear. This unexpected resistance made progress through the sand hills rather slow and painful.

Yaconda who had heard Dominique's cries, rushed down and opened the door only to see her faithful handmaid and the Groll disappear behind a cluster of cacti.

She left the door ajar and disconsolate returned to her tower, rested her arms on the window sill and let her tears flow freely. Through a veil of tears she beheld the huge breakers crashing on the beach, farther out the sunlight played upon the calm ocean swells. Then suddenly two tiny specks appeared. Gracefully they glided up and down the watery dales. She dried her tears and now could see clearly. In the hollow between the ocean waves stood two tiny figures. They were being carried ashore by the onrushing waves and stood perfectly still in their blue green ravine. The ocean trough moved swiftly toward shore, carrying the diminutive strangers in its hollow.

Princess Yaconda descried two wee creatures and they were riding surfboards. She looked again and saw the huge wave in front of them crashing on a sandbank. Yet they kept their balance and were carried towards shore on a quickly advancing wall of water. By their slight appearance she knew them to be Mountain Fairies. The fun loving creatures often took an ocean holiday, and the surf on this deserted coast was amazing.

'I must get a message to them, think of something to attract their attention,' she whispered to herself.

Fortunately for Princess Yaconda, Mountain Fairies are easily distracted. They are also incurable romantics. Edel and Weiss pulled their surfboards on shore and plunked down on the sand. They had grown up in the same village of the Kingdom and were inseparable. Often they had wandered in each other's company over the endless hills in the lake country, looking for wildflowers to decorate a fairy festival, of which there were a good many. One evening when they returned to the village their arms laden with edelweiss, a young girl had laughed at them and yelled, 'Look, here come Edel and Weiss.' There was a good deal of mirth about that and thenceforth the two were known as Edel and Weiss!

They knew very well they had disobeyed the Fairy Queen's command. Sternly they had been told to stay on the small strip of beach where the land of the Fairies touches the western ocean and not to cross the southern border.

But they loved surfing and for days on end had wandered down the coastline, camping by the shore at night and riding the surf during the day. Well they knew the best surf was at the end of the great desert peninsula, deep in the forbidden territory.

'Oh Edel, companion of my youth and friend in manhood, what fun, what excitement to ride the waves all day. We are free, free as a bird.'

Weiss got up and ran along the shore jumping over inlets of salt water.

Mountain Fairies can jump seven times their body length and Weiss moved with a grace and speed that was only rarely seen. Edel walked over to the little dune where they had left their clothes. He slipped on his leather shorts and white shirt and lay down in the sand to enjoy the heat of the sand and the sound of the surf. He picked up a large sea shell to shield his eyes from the sun and leaned against the incline of a dune. The sun warmed his slender, sinewy body and before long he found himself in a dream slaying dragons and snatching maidens from the jaws of Grolls and other acts of bravery, close to the heart of Mountain Fairies.

After a pleasant rest he rubbed the sleep out of his eyes, sat up and watched Weiss prancing in the water. Then he turned his eyes inland and saw the outline of the ancient castle tower amidst the ruin of the Alcazar. Weiss who had worn himself out was now standing beside him.

Edel looked up at him, 'Weiss, my light-hearted comrade, if this be the old Alcazar on the map, we must have come to the end of the peninsula and are miles and miles from home.'

Weiss took Edel's seashell and raised it over his eyes, the better to see into the light of the afternoon sun, 'The castle ruins make a perfect setting for romance. All it lacks is a Princess in distress.'

Edel smiled and looked Weiss in the eyes, 'Dream on my shining knight, dream on'. The look in Weiss' eyes intensified, his face expressed a sense of wonder, and his right hand pinched his cheek. He could only say 'Edel, dear Edel, am I hallucinating? I see a lady's face in the tower window, and her hand frantically waves a purple shawl.'

Edel saw precisely what Weiss was seeing. It was unlikely they would have the same delusions.

They had the presence of mind to hide their surfboards in a cactus patch, for they knew that this part of the land might be patrolled by Grolls. Then they leaped across the saltwater inlet to the next sandbank and into the desert. Sailing over cactus plants they reached the base of the tower within minutes. Looking up they beheld a maiden of great beauty leaning out the tower window, her wan face framed by golden locks.

Could this be the Crown Princess Yaconda, their beloved Princess imprisoned in this desolate ruin? Instinctively they knelt in a gesture of respect. While kneeling on the hot sand they could hear the plea from above to hasten to the north side of the castle and to enter the tower door, which was still standing open.

They ran around the castle jumping over crumbled walls and heaps of broken brick until they came to the front door that Captain Homarus had neglected to close when he carried off the unfortunate Dominique.

Up the stairs they flew, rushed into the turret chamber, and beheld the tearful Princess Yaconda sitting on the stone bench under the window. They jumped onto the bench, so that their eyes were level with the Princess'.

They bowed before her. 'Edel at your service Princess.'

'Weiss at your service Princess.'

Yaconda could not help but smile at the two ardent youths. 'Dear Edel and Weiss you bring to me the freshness and hope of the flower after which you were named and also memories of your dear Queen Tuluga. Edel and Weiss, I have been imprisoned here for months, kidnapped by the traitor, Lord Imbrun, and delivered to the domain of the Dark Lords. This morning my faithful maid Dominique was carried off by a Groll, oh how I fear for her life. Edel and Weiss please find her and bring her back to me, if it can be done.'

'If it can be done', echoed Edel. 'If it can be done,' sang Weiss. They looked at each other, clasped their hands together and danced around yodeling a fairy tune.

If it can be done
none will pooh pooh pooh it
If it can be done
we will do do do it.

They ended their little dance and kneeling on the stone bench shouted in chorus, 'It can be done!' Added Edel, 'When we return your maidservant, we can help you escape from this wretched tower.'

Here Princess Yaconda had to disappoint them. 'That cannot be my dear spirits from the mountain lakes. You can easily slip through the desert country without detection, but Dominique and I would be caught by the Grolls before the day is out. A worse fate would await us. But lose no time in finding Dominique's trail.'

'Your Highness,' reflected the cooler headed Weiss, 'we must return to our campsite first, to fetch our bows.'

Gratitude shone in Princess Yaconda's eyes, 'Would you fetch the weapons Edel, so Weiss can begin tracking the Groll. No time is to be lost.' Edel bowed and ran down the stairs, took a drink from the flask at his belt containing essence of orchid and leapt northward. His feet only touched the sand every four yards and his long saffron hair streamed in the wind. He had but one fear, that Weiss would perform some heroic deed before he returned. That fear proved to be unfounded.

Weiss left the tower moments afterwards. He looked at the open door and thought it wiser to close it. There might be other Grolls around. He pushed the door shut with all his might, and climbing on a few loose bricks he pulled down the raised iron bar. With a loud clang it fell into the metal groove on the side wall.

He looked about him, slipped on his fish skin shoes to protect his feet from the burning sand and began to follow the trail that the Groll's feet had traced in the desert.

Dominique was in a state of shock as farther inland she bumped and bounced on the Groll's shoulder. She realized that her beating and biting did not slow down the miserable fellow and she tried to collect her thoughts. Occasionally she could hear the Groll murmur to himself, 'Delicious lady, juicy, very juicy, rosemary and thyme, perhaps some garlic too, humm,' and there was a smacking of lips. It dawned on Dominique, with a sense of relief and horror, that the scoundrel's interest was entirely culinary.

The vegetation became richer and soon they came to a small oasis. Even her captor was exhausted. He dropped Dominique on the sand, dragged her over to a small palm tree and tied her to the trunk.

The oasis had often been used by Grolls and they were not creatures given to tidying up. Charred bones were spread around a barbecue pit and empty jars, some broken, littered the sand. Three vultures were perched quietly on a nearby shrub. A muddy creek could be heard trickling close by. Next to the fire pit was a stone cache. The Captain rolled away the head stone and reached in for a jar of fermented cactus juice, a potent brew. Captain Homarus took a couple of swigs and lay down to relax, his head resting on his hand. Yes. he had been careless, but that problem would be laid to rest very soon, in the form of an excellent dinner. He began to hum the groll drinking song.

Hey polly poll, pour gin into a Groll
he'll turn dazzling and droll
a Groll is not ghastly fellow,
gin makes him cute and mellow

Captain Homarus took another swig from the jug. The idea of a Groll turning cute and mellow was somewhat absurd and he grinned from ear to ear.

Immediately Weiss found the trail the Groll had left, and it was easy enough to follow. The footsteps were interspersed with places where the sand had been swept by Dominique's long skirt when she had slid off the Groll's shoulder. Soon small palms became visible and Weiss realized an oasis was nearby. He slowed his pace, positioned himself behind a cactus, and for a few minutes looked over the scene. A sound vibrated in his sharp ears, a faint voice crying for help. Approaching a hungry Groll without weapons was sheer folly, and it was Weiss' gallant heart that drove him to the scene of impending tragedy. Light footed and stealthy, he slid between the cacti and bougainvillea bushes until he came to the small dune in front of the barbecue pit. He tied this long golden hair into a ponytail and tucked it into his red shirt just in case.

Dominique's voice called out in despair. It was a last plea for mercy. The Groll thought this especially amusing, and it whetted his appetite. Weiss lifted his head above the ridge and saw the scoundrel approaching Dominique. He had a fiendish grin on his face as he hissed, 'Give no mercy, take no mercy, nasty does it. Silly Groll give secret away, now swallow it again.'

Pleased with his own sense of humour, he burst into a revolting laugh, and his vise like claws seized Dominique in a paralyzing grip.

A wave of pain came over her and as the life force ebbed, she slipped out of her body. First she rose to the top of the palm trees and then higher and higher. She could see her body, lifeless, but pretty in its green dress trembling in the lobster like grip of the Groll.

'It was just like a lecture she had heard on life after life, which the wise wood elf Seraphim had given at a meeting in Lambarina. There was her body down below, a little overweight, but sweet just the same, and that ghastly Groll squeezing the last ounce of life out of it. She shed a heavenly tear as she looked down on her earthly form yielding to overwhelming force.

Weiss took one look at the desperate scene and quick as lightning shot behind the little palm tree and climbed to the top. He picked a coconut and let it fly at the Groll's head. A resounding clash raised hopes that even the tough groll skull might now have a substantial dent in it. Captain Homarus yelled and staggered backwards into the fire that he had just lit. Now his fury really came into its own. He looked up and saw Weiss in the tree top. He forgot his lovely dinner tied to the tree and sprang to the palm and with terrible violence began to shake it. It was a good thing that Weiss was an expert surfer, for he was in for the ride of his life. The crown of the palm was like the center of a tornado.

Edel too had not wasted any time. With strides measuring up to fourteen feet he was practically flying over the sand. He attained the campsite within less than ten minutes, picked up the bow and silver arrows and retraced his steps along the beach.

When the Alcazar came back in sight he turned inland reaching the dunes and could be seen flying from dune top to dune top. A strange sight stopped him, in a clump of shrubs and small trees ahead of him, one tree was shaking violently, yet the afternoon was calm. Weiss stopped to listen and he picked up an invocation born on the wind, 'Farna varnada, helya ulyara,' It was the Fairies' call for help in this world and in the world beyond. It only was used in extreme peril.

Within seconds Edel stood on the dune ridge and watched the brute shaking the palm and dear Weiss hanging on for dear life. He drew his bowstring and a thin silver arrow winged its flight. It struck the Groll in the neck and for seconds he was stunned. Then he pulled the arrow out of his tough hide and let go of the tree. What was this new source of aggravation? The late sun shone on Edel's golden hair and when the Groll spotted the tiny archer, he sprang towards him, missing by mere inches.

Edel ran for it, and the Groll sped after him sending up clouds of dust as his angry feet stomped the sand. In a sprint Grolls did not stand a chance against the Fairies, but the endurance of the creatures was legendary. At first Edel was able to outdistance the heavy footed brute, but he could not keep up the flying tempo, and began to fall back.

Edel looked behind and saw the lumbering ruffian closing in fast. Then a shadow moved in front of him, the shadow of a large bird keeping pace. He knew it was a Pelican, but only when he looked up did he realize that it was Peli 1, a member of the Queen's Royal Guard. Queen Tuluga had sent her favourite Pelican, to look for them.

Peli 1 dipped his wings signaling Edel to follow him. Edel now turned south following in the flight path of his winged guide. The dunes diminished until he found himself running on a sandy plain and in the distance a strange steamy haze rose from the sand.

He could hear the pounding of groll feet coming closer. But when he reached the shimmering flats he felt under his feet a strange shifting of sand. Edel slowed down. Right behind him he could hear the Groll foaming and cursing, his big feet hitting the ground with a slapping noise. There was water on the sand. They had entered the great quicksand that separates the desert from the beach. Edel could now hardly move his feet. When he looked back the Groll was close to him, trying to pull his huge feet out of the wet sand. It was no use, Captain Homarus was sinking fast. He invoked the vengeance of his cohorts on the Mountain Fairies. His curses could be heard for miles around.

Peli 1 had dropped a piece of driftwood for Edel to stand on and regain his breath. The Groll's cursing was no longer audible, just bubbles rising from the sand, and then a strange silence prevailed. All that could be seen was he tips of the Groll's large pointed ears sticking out of the sand. Moments later, they too slipped away. Then against the luminous evening sky, rose a dark cloud from the shifting sand, at the very spot where the brute had vanished. Even Edel, who had never in his life been sad, looked solemn for a moment and pondered the mysteries of good and evil, and of the life beyond. Soon a smile returned to his mischievous face, as he thought of the delicious tales he could spin from this adventure at fairy firesides.

The Pelican had perched on a piece of palm tree stuck in the mud across from Edel.

'Peli 1, heaven be praised. You snatched me from the jaws of death!'

'A good thing the Queen sent me out here, to check on you, her Majesty had a suspicion you might have ignored her advise and wandered into foreign realms!

'It was awfully clever to lead the monster into that quicksand Peli 1.'

'Nothing to it, Edel, I was cruising at a comfortable altitude when I saw the Groll scampering after you I scanned the horizon and saw the haze of moist air rising from the quick sand. A perfect place to sink a Groll'

'Not worried about me getting stuck Peli 1?' asked Edel.

'Never for one moment, my young friend, Mountain Fairies have a lightness of being, which is quite puzzling,' said Peli 1 shaking his great beak.

Edel thanked Peli 1 and praised him for his quick thinking.

Edel began thinking of finding his way back to the oasis. Peli 1 sensing his dilemma began to hover over the quick sand, Edel grasped his legs and the great bird flapping his strong wings, dragged Edel across to a patch of firm ground. Edel walked across and then Peli 1 helped him traverse the next channel of shifting sand.

High above Dominique's spirit had watched the drama unfold. Her body lay motionless at the foot of the palm tree. She cast a loving glance at the sweet figure stretched out on the small dune at this moment of parting, as a rider bids farewell to a beloved horse. Suddenly caught by a noose of light she was pulled swiftly back to her earthly form. An instant later she regained her body.

She woke up with a start. The ropes still cut painfully across her middle and shoulders, and there was a stinging pain where the claws of the Groll had seized her arms.

The tree where she was tied was still swaying. A thud on her right told her Weiss had fallen out of the palm tree and she could feel him leaning against her. The sight of the Fairy on her side almost made her laugh. It was all like a terrible dream, but glory be, the dream had come to an end.

Weiss tried several times to stand up, but still found himself swaying. He recovered his balance, stood up and looked Dominique in the eyes, 'Lady Dominique, you are alive, thank heaven.'

Dominique sat up as far as she could and looked at the diminutive creature in front of her, 'So it was a Mountain Fairy I saw from on high, the Mountain Fairy who sent the coconut crashing on the skull of the Groll. A Mountain Fairy saved my life! Now if you can my dear Fairy, please cut these burning ropes!'

Weiss having regained his equilibrium pulled a knife from his belt and cut Dominique free. Just at that moment Peli 1 landed beside Weiss and bade him look south. There like a bouncing ball on the horizon Edel was hastening towards them.

Dominique watched as they fell into each others arms and did a kind of victory dance. 'You see Edel, now that we have saved the maidservant of a Princess and slain a Groll or at least sunk one, the Queen must forgive us for wandering beyond the borders of the land.'

Edel agreed wholeheartedly. Peli 1 had his doubts. Silently he shook his big beak. He knew why he had been sent out here, but this was not the time for reprimands.

They carefully set to cleaning up the area, removing all traces of the scuffle. Dominique took a drink of orchid extract to energize herself and they began the trek to the tower. For a short while Peli 1 hovered over them, and then sped homewards.

Soon the faint glow of a candle in the tower window became visible and Edel ran ahead to prepare Princess Yaconda for their return. Swiftly outdistancing Dominique and Weiss, he sped to the tower. Once he arrived he could not reach the heavy steel bar which locked the oaken door from the outside. He climbed onto a block of wood and reached for his bow. The bow touched the steel bar enabling him to lift it. But he quickly realized he would need the Princess' help to push from the inside. He ran around to the other side of the tower and threw a pebble through the narrow upper opening.

Yaconda seated by the loom, startled when a pebble hit the stone wall of her cell. She looked up for a moment and then a second pebble sailed through the narrow slit. Now she could hear Edel's voice. It made a remarkable sound for so small a creature and hope raised the curtain of gloom. She walked across the cell to the spiral stairway and as she walked down the narrow stone steps, Edel's impatient voice echoed in the tower.

'Push Princess, push the door when I raise the bar'.

Princess Yaconda's quickness of mind returned and when she heard the clanking of the steel bar she threw herself against the door. It was only Edel's quick reaction that prevented the Princess from falling on top of him as the door swung out. The fine sand outside the tower cushioned Yaconda's fall and she managed a smile when she saw the Mountain Fairy, by all of a foot, towering above her face! Looking into Edel's glowing eyes she knew that all was well.

Yaconda and Edel were standing at the tower door when Dominique walked out of the darkening desert night into her mistress' arms. Once back in the tower chamber, Edel and Weiss, seated in the window sills, took turns telling Princess Yaconda of the harrowing events that they had lived through and the demise of the Groll. Yaconda both laughed and cried throughout the tale.

'My dear Mountain Fairies, small in stature you may be but your gallantry and courage rank among the highest and are engraved within my heart. I shall write a note to my dear friend, the Queen of the Mountain Fairies, which I trust you will deliver safely.

Yaconda penned a short message for Edel and Weiss to carry to Queen Tuluga. Dominique and Yaconda walked down with them into the hall. Standing on the same level, the Mountain Fairies reached just above the Princess' knees. Yaconda knelt down and kissed the Fairies on the forehead and bade them Godspeed.

Edel and Weiss looked at her with gratitude and then slipped through the half open door. Working their bows together they were able to place the steel bar back in place. Then they were off, flying from dune top to dune top .

'We have been kissed by a Queen,' yelled Weiss at the top of his voice.

'Yes my noble friend, this is but the beginning of a life of adventure and what a beginning,' shouted Edel, resting for a moment on the last dune top before they reached the firm beach by the shoreline.

8

Dangerous Journey

Scimitar was driving the small canoe at great speed. He was well aware that the enemy had traced his movements and hoped to take him prisoner or worse. There was no sign of the skiff that had been stolen at Oliver's orchard. There were fewer swans on the river now, and orchards began to give way to dense woods. Occasionally there were fine stands of maple. The sugaring season was in full swing and columns of smoke could be seen rising from the huts where the sap was boiling. At other times Scimitar would have called at some of the outlander families who had homesteaded on this part of the river, and he would have been treated to hot maple syrup.

He permitted himself a few minutes rest to light his pipe and survey his surroundings. He spoke words of encouragement to Patriot, still on the look out in the bow of the canoe. Pipe clenched between his teeth, paddle firmly grasped in both hands, Scimitar's arms resumed the rhythmic motion, driving the canoe forward toward the capital. Many images floated through his mind, the agonized face of Oliver Wendell, the black tissue around the wound, and the solace in Helga's eyes. No doubt the attack on Oliver had saved him from an ambush. He could not help thinking of Lady Erica and regretted that he had not visited the Manor and asked her to gaze into the black pool. There had not been time.

He must keep his eyes on the river, and not let his mind wander, which even for a Dwarf can be difficult at times. The sun was setting and it was now time to look for a place to make camp. Visible a mile ahead was a small island covered with poplars and tall pines.

Skillfully he steered the canoe into an inlet and tied the painter to a poplar tree. Patriot happily jumped ashore and had a good run around the island.

Scimitar quickly built a lean-to between two trees and lit a fire. Then he remembered the jug of stew Rosemary had given him at the Graceful Neck. He went back to the canoe to fetch it, and put the jug next to the fire. He sat down on the soft sand resting against a fallen log and lit his pipe. His mind went over the events of the day, contemplating the first act of open violence in Swanneland. The news would spread like wildfire and people would wake up to the dangers that faced them. The death of the King and the disappearance of Princess Yaconda had shocked them already and now it would be more difficult for infiltrators to go undetected. The bubbling of the stew interrupted his trend of thought. It turned out to be a hearty meal and he couldn't help thinking how kind it had been of Rosemary to hand it to him on the porch of the Graceful Neck.

Before he fell asleep, the pained face of Oliver Wendell, his lovely daughter bending over him dwelt in his mind. He had tried to repress the image of the radiant maiden's face but now it surfaced again with renewed strength, it was totally un-dwarf like.

Patriot circled the island one last time before joining his master for a snooze. It was two or three in the morning when Scimitar awoke. The moon was a mere sickle but the sky was filled with glittering stars. When he sat up and looked over the black expanse of water, a feeling of great sadness came over him. He felt terribly alone.

He looked down on his unsheathed sword and saw the bare metal mirror a flicker of light. The light became more intense. When he looked up he was blinded by a white light. His eyes adjusted slowly and once they focused, he beheld the figure of a woman clad in a flowing turquoise dress. Her hands emitted a white light, and behind her golden tresses shone a bright halo. A smile appeared on Scimitars face.

She spoke softly, 'Oh my Dwarf, my noble Dwarf, how proud you are. How often have I said, Call on me in time of peril. Why forfeit the magic powers that could be yours?'

Scimitar lowered his eyes under the enchantress' questing gaze, 'Amaranth, my debt to you is great. How can I thank you.'

'My silly Dwarf, remember between us debts or ledgers cannot be. The same cause now claims us. Hide your pride and call on me, call when peril strikes or loneliness disheartens.'

'It is in a needful hour that you come to me Amaranth,' said Scimitar.

'Evil has fallen on this land. I see great suffering.'

Amaranth, a loving look in her eyes, spoke in a lilting voice, 'My stout and stalwart Dwarf, I have followed your adventures in these times of danger, and there is little I can do for you now. Yet a sword used in a righteous cause can be transformed by an ancient incantation! 'Oh takir inovit, oh takir sinika.'

Scimitar saw a flash of light issue from the fingers of her right hand, travel down his sword, turn blue in colour and then slowly fade.

'Oh Scimitar, my Dwarf, proud and intrepid you are. Yet remember you are mortal and do not disdain to call on me when evil overwhelms. Hear my counsel. Leave this island and paddle through the night until you reach the outskirts of Lambarina. Fare thee well my deep-souled friend.'

Scimitar saw the light fade and deep darkness returned. He recalled other times when Amaranth had come into his life. It had always been at a time of crisis and her advice he had not always heeded. She had called him my deep- souled friend. Scimitar pondered these words. People had called him brave, reckless, and even ruthless, but never deep-souled. Perhaps, perhaps, there was something about himself he had not yet discovered. The thought amused him, but this was not a moment for introspection. Amaranth had counseled him to leave the island and paddle into darkness.

He took down the lean-to and gathered his belongings. When he put his hand on the haft of the sword the blue sheen traveled along the edge.

He stood up, raised the weapon and let the edge fall on a maple branch. With but little pressure the sturdy branch was severed. Amaranth had given his sword a magic edge. Scimitar was grateful for this gift in time of peril.

He strode down to the shore. Standing by the water's edge, he stroked the fur on Patriot's back. It felt like a rough brush. The hair was standing up straight.

He peered into the darkness. Nothing could be seen, but Patriot pushed his head against his hand and he knew danger threatened. He bent down towards the water and listened carefully. A faint splashing could be heard, the splashing of paddles, many paddles pulling in unison.

Scimitar putting his hands on the gunwales of the frail craft pushed away from shore. He took his seat in the stern and Patriot jumped into the bow. The Dwarf's powerful muscles pushed the canoe forward at high speed and hugging the dark shore he steered west toward Lambarina.

Only after ten minutes of paddling did he look behind. In the faint moonlight appeared the outline of a large canoe. Dark shapes were propelling the craft forward, and on the bow a pair of green eyes glowed in the dark. Scimitar had seen black hounds at night, eyes burning bright green. No doubt Grolls were at the oars. He doubled his efforts and the canoe shot forward.

Whenever Scimitar stopped paddling for a few seconds, he could hear the plunging of many oars, reaching closer and closer.

Dawn was breaking and Scimitar could tell by the cattle in the meadows and the shape of the farmhouses that he was in an Outlander county and already close to Lambarina.

Farmers and milkmaids on shore could not believe their eyes when they saw a vessel commanded by two Rovers, and seated at the oars a large number of Grolls, in pursuit of the stout Dwarf. Many of them had met Scimitar and other Dwarves. Grolls and Rovers were known only from tales and legends. There was little doubt as to the intent of the fierce looking crowd in the large vessel in pursuit of the Dwarf. Such a threat of violence had never been seen in this century of peace, which had been their blessing.

Some brave farmers tried to slow the warriors by pushing small vessels and even barges in their path. The Rover at the helm was an able navigator and managed to avoid the barges. Some of the rowboats were crushed by the bow of the canoe. Yet it slowed them down and Scimitar was able to increase the distance between them.

The sun's first rays caught the Dwarf and the light glistened on his face, now drenched in perspiration. His plumed hat which had fallen overboard, the Grolls had picked up and wore it in turn. Mocking laughter echoed over the water.

Patriot barked suddenly. Scimitar turned and saw a black shadow moving over the water. He looked up to see a merewing sailing above. The bird dived and he pulled his paddle from the water to defend himself. The large wings flew straight at him. He raised his paddle and gave the bird a deadly blow. As the bird hit the water Scimitar's paddle flew out his hands, sailing into the water.

In the war canoe behind him there was a lot of cheering and laughing.

The Grolls were sure they had bagged their Dwarf and without any losses.

The bystanders on shore were horrified. One brave farmer jumped into his rowboat and pulled up to the large canoe. The Rover at the helm he managed to knock over the head with his oar, but paid for it with his own life. The boat swerved for a moment but another Rover took his place and steered it back on course.

The momentum of Scimitar's canoe took it to shore. He grasped his sword and jumped on land. Patriot was at his side. The noble hound uttered a fierce howl as the vessel carrying the Grolls drew closer, but Scimitar commanded him to stand back. He would not have a chance against the black hound.

Scimitar could see farmers running to his aid but he shouted to them to keep back, there was little they could do and already one life had been lost.

He could see the oarsmen clearly, they were Grolls dressed in brown jerkins. Seated in the stern, yelling orders was the Rover in a black leather jacket. His companion lay slumped over the side. The vessel was coming right at Scimitar.

'Forward Froth,' called a voice from the back of the canoe and the black hound bounded through the shallow water towards Scimitar. When he reached land Scimitar was ready for him. The sword raised high cast a soft blue sheen and when it came down the huge head of Froth dropped on the grass and rolled back into the water. The first of the Grolls to reach shore fell back at the sight, but prodded from behind they had no choice but to face Scimitar. In many a battle the Grolls' tough hide had protected them from serious injury, but there was something about the blue glow on Scimitar's sword that made them feel decidedly uneasy.

The first gruesome creature to reach Scimitar seized him by his left arm, but before he knew what happened he was filleted. The sad remains sank to the grass.

Half the Grolls had fallen in this inglorious manner, when two of them sneaked behind Scimitar and unfolded a large net of heavy twine. As the brave Dwarf was pressed back by the attacking throng, the net was pulled over him and a number of the brutes hurled themselves on top.

A huge Groll wrested the sword from the Dwarf, but as soon as it left Scimitar's hand the blue disappeared. The Groll looked at the sword which had decimated so many of his underlings, and just to check it out brought it down on the unhappy Groll standing by his side. It bounced harmlessly off his tough hide. Disgusted he chucked the sword aside amidst the reeds.

Scimitar entangled in the heavy twine called out to Patriot and ordered him not to come near. He knew very well that there was little Patriot could do in the face of such overwhelming force.

The one surviving Rover directed the Grolls to pack the immobilized Dwarf into a cage and to sail for the other side of the river. This the Grolls set about to do with great glee. Skrimp, the huge Groll who had tossed Scimitar's sword in the bulrushes, was a kind of strawboss, a fierce and frightful creature.

The light of the sun reflected in his foul eyes and an evil grin spread from his snout across his brown rippled face to his pointy ears. He mumbled to himself, 'Where did that snotty Dwarf find the sword?' It took a dozen Grolls to dull the blade. Skrimp ordered some of the other Grolls to go to their canoe and bring up the iron cage. They dragged the heavy cage ashore and rolled the entwined Scimitar down the meadow and into the open cage. Skrimp banged the door shut and secured it.

'Well done Skrimp,' said the Rover, the Lords have been looking for this one for a long time.'

'He is a nasty one Sir. It's good thing we had the netting.'

Patriot looked on from behind a clump of poplars while the cage was loaded into the large canoe. Soon many oars could be heard dipping in the waters of the Sanctus and the vessel swiftly moved upstream.

Once well on their way the Grolls cut most of the twine around Scimitar so that he could move freely in the cage. Now that Scimitar was more accessible Skrimp poked him a few times with his long knife. He smiled at his men. 'Dwarves are a pain, but this one is a real rotter, filleted some of our best men.'

The loss of their comrades had not dampened the spirits of the Grolls, for friendships run not very deep amongst these creatures. The rising sun and a decent breakfast put them in a jolly mood.

With Scimitar safely behind bars, their tongues quickly loosened. 'Hey there Fatty, you are going to pay for this. ... He looks juicy enough to fry in his own fat.' More choice comments followed as the Grolls kept poking Scimitar with their lances after each sentence, by dint of punctuation.

A discussion followed on whether Dwarves are best fried, poached or roasted. Throughout it all Scimitar sat scrunched in his cage. The fierce green eyes set deep in his stoic countenance expressed disdain.

One of the Rovers suggested they might want to smoke him.

'No boss,' said Skrimp, 'he is too big. We smoke Gnomes and we pickle Mountain Fairies, but Dwarves are too bulky.'

The Rover wouldn't begrudge his men a special treat, but he knew their Masters would want to question the Dwarf before disposing of him. After a short break and much levity, the Grolls began to swing their oars again and the heavy canoe started moving upriver.

Patriot had spotted his master's sword, clamped it between his teeth, ran across the meadows and farmyards to the main road and trotted off in the direction of Cascade.

The battle by the river and the capture of Scimitar had shocked the farming community. One of their own had fallen in a heroic effort to save the Dwarf. They well knew that the incident signaled the end of an era.

9

The Gathering

$\mathscr{L}$ady Erica de Coscoroba sat up in bed. She seldom woke in the middle of the night but this time it was as if an unseen hand had tapped her on the shoulder and she was wide awake. The weather had changed, clouds swiftly passing intercepted the rays of the full moon. Patches of light moving on the water of the Sanctus changed in rhythm with the fleeting clouds.

She was still seated on the edge of her bed with her eyes closed, when the image of Scimitar came to her mind, and a feeling of dread stole over her. Had something happened to the noble Dwarf? An intuitive fear gripped her. All had looked to Scimitar for leadership and skill in the art of defense.

Lady Erica put on her purple dressing gown, tied her hair into a pony tail and slid into her white rabbit skin slippers. She walked up to the window overlooking the Sanctus and rested her hands on the sill. How delightful was the river scene with its quickly changing patterns of light. For generations life in the valley had flowed like the river itself, with patterns of light and darkness, but it had flowed quietly and predictably and no upheavals had upset its gentle rhythm.

For most of the Swannefolk it was impossible to imagine that the flow of their traditional life was now seriously threatened. Some had had a foreboding of dark forces from realms beyond the outer boundaries. Martha the prophetess had spoken of it, but Goldfinger and other influential burghers in the county had ridiculed it as the musings of a senile mind.'

Some of the dark strangers traveling in the county had given quite a bit of work to the business community and paid handsomely in cash. Goldfinger and members of the Chamber of Commerce dismissed the suspicions that some Swannefolk felt about the strangers, as the prejudices of 'simpleminded farmers, lazy louts, shirkers and old biddies.'

Joris Goldfinger and his cousin John Mintpalm, were very much pleased with these new business opportunities and had begun to negotiate juicy contracts with the strangers. These men were much easier to deal with than the locals, who always argued about price, and thought nothing of letting six months slip by before payment and then only after many reminders and nasty notes! No, life was looking up in the county.

Lady Erica, too, had warned Goldfinger and his cousin, but they had laughed politely, and wished her a good morning. She recalled the incident now and smiled, 'There will always be collaborators,' she mused.

Fully awake now she scanned the moonlit riverscape.

Silhouetted against the moon, flocks of geese, eager to reach their nesting grounds in the northern desert, flew over the water. Her face caught the faint light of dawn. She leaned out the window and looked at the mist rising from the river. The intensifying light reflected the hazel in her eyes and a breeze from the waters of the Sanctus stirred her silver tresses .

A beam from the rising sun caught the vanishing geese in a line of light and for a moment Erica's mind flew back in time to Gustav. How they might have winged their flight and built a nest.

This had not been their destiny, but then they were not part of that world of nature which moves in quiet rhythms, predictable, harmonious, amoral. They lived in the world of nature, yet they were part of that greater world of consciousness that can create, invent, exalt and degrade. On this sea of consciousness there was no instinct to guide the patterns of life. Yet there were buoys that marked safe channels. How often these seemed hidden in dense mist and could be perceived only by those who knew about them and searched them out.

Her face, and tresses silver white, framed by the dormer window and illuminated by the orange sheen of the early sun, resembled a painting of pensive beauty. Erica tried to understand the web of destiny, the strands of good and evil woven into one cord. When meditating by the black pool in the courtyard, spirit guides had come to her. She knew the time was nigh, terrible trials would beset her people and the outcome was uncertain. She knew she could not run away, she was to play her part. A number of souls in Swanneland understood the danger that threatened their land, and they must be gathered here, at the Manor deCygne, to forge a ring of defense.

She hoped and prayed that the great black swans Aske and Alma had reached the land of the Mountain Fairies and delivered her message to the Queen. There would be then a chance that the delegates would not be waylaid on their journey into Lambarina and could be diverted to the Manor deCygne. Here in relative safety they would be able to consult and to find a way to defend the Kingdom and to maintain its unity.

The sound of Norma closing the cast iron door of the woodstove in the kitchen startled her. She rose, walked to her wardrobe, slid into a high collared black dress and clipped on a silver brooch. The emerald in the center caught a wayward sunbeam in a flash of brilliant green.

Ferdinand probably was in the sunroom waiting for breakfast. She could smell the sweet aroma of his pipe tobacco. Walking down the stairway she whispered a prayer that he would listen to her and not rush off like a knight errand on some outlandish adventure.

'Lovely morning, Aunt Erica.'

'A sweet morning to you my charming nephew'

'At least you see some charm Aunt', lamented Ferdinand, blowing carefully to the ceiling, a ringlet of blue smoke. 'The maidens in the village fail to see a trace of it. All they see is a dull , potbellied bachelor and they snicker at my lineage and title. By all the saints in heaven I will show them what a deCygne can do when the enemy is at the gate, and all tremble in dread of the black peril. Ah, it is true I may appear lethargic, but when danger strikes, we deCygnes come alive. Once aroused our wrath is fearful.'

By now he had worked himself into a fine lather and with knife and fork, mimed some fearful motions. Lady Erica couldn't help smiling.

'My Ferdinand, my Ferdinand', she soothed, 'your blood sugar is low, have some breakfast. These are trying times, but we must keep calm and not act hastily. Our actions must be planned by the Council that will gather here at the Manor deCygne.'

'Council and committees do not slay dragons or wrestle with black hounds!' exclaimed Ferdinand.

'There will be all kinds of opportunity for action nephew dear, but we must work together. There is a kind of energy in council, which is difficult to explain, but it weaves things together and gives them direction', reflected Erica. She slipped out of the room to hurry things up in the kitchen.

Ferdinand mumbled some more astringent comments, apropos of the new-fangled communal decision making and the superior nature of individual initiative. Norma approached carrying a large silver tray.

It is astonishing what the sight of eggs sunny side up, crispy bacon, sweet buns and steaming coffee did to the temper of this nobleman. A leisurely breakfast lightened the conversation. Towards the end of the meal Ferdinand conceded to Aunt Erica that given special circumstances, committees might have some use.

A hearty meal and a pipe of his favourite tobacco put him back on his philosophic perch. He moved to his easy chair and putting his feet on the coffee table looked rather thoughtful and contented.

As he surveyed the sunlit scene a smile showed on his face.

'Aunt Erica I see a dog down by the willow bushes, and I don't think it is one of my hounds. It looks like a golden retriever.' Erica moved closer to the window on the south side of the sunroom and looked at the low lying fields near the river.

'Look Ferdinand, the dog is carrying something. It looks like a large stick.'

A smile spread around the Marquis's chubby cheeks.

'Ah it takes the sharp eye of one trained in the art of warfare to see it is a sword that is clamped in the jaws of the beast.'

'I had a strange feeling when I awoke last night that something is amiss. Let us go down and see what the hound is carrying,' suggested Erica.

They slipped into the leather working boots, which Norma had just lined with hay from the marsh grasses that grow abundantly by the shore of the Sanctus and the Frivoli. The boots, watertight, made from the skin of wild boar roaming the northern forest, are well suited for work on the river.

Lady Erica and Ferdinand walked down the path to the Sanctus and could see the golden retriever lying in the lee of the willow bushes. He had dropped the sword, holding it securely under his front paws. When he first spotted them he let out a fierce bark. Then he stepped forward into the bright sunlight shaking the water out of his fur.

Erica recognized him. She put her hand on Ferdinand's arm and whispered, 'Patriot, it is Patriot, Scimitar's hound. What calamity has taken place that would separate Scimitar from his faithful companion?'

When the word 'Scimitar' reached Patriot's ears, he stopped barking and looked intently at Erica and her nephew.

Erica called softly, 'Patriot, Patriot come to us.' For a moment he stood still then he turned swiftly, picked up the sword, ran up to Erica and dropped it at her feet. Erica kneeled down and put her arms around the bedraggled looking hound. His eyes were full of self-reproach and she understood that look of contrition.

'Patriot, it is all right. We know you could not have saved Scimitar. The force must have been overwhelming and Scimitar ordered you to retreat. It is important that you came, now we know that your master was taken by the servants of the dark Lords. We will try to rescue Scimitar.'

A spark of life came back into Patriot's eyes and he made a faint effort to wag his tail. Erica remained kneeling, her right hand on Patriot's head. Ferdinand had just picked up the sword and thoughtfully regarded the blade.

'Extraordinary workmanship,' he murmured as he moved his left hand over the blade, only the gnome masters do work like this.'

Erica watched the hand of her nephew moving along the edge and a brilliant blue light emanated from the steel. She called out in astonishment,

'The blade has been tempered by the incantation of a wizard or enchantress of the highest sphere. If used in a righteous cause the spell will hold.'

'Splendid, splendid,' exclaimed the Marquis 'It could not have fallen into better hands. We, deCygnes, have long represented the arm of justice. Black imps beware, instant retribution awaits your foolery.'

'Remember the warrior who wielded this sword dear Ferdinand,' cautioned Erica, 'He was the greatest in the Kingdom. Alone we cannot hope to oppose this evil.'

A benevolent smile spread over the Marquis's face. He had to admit that there were times when Aunt Erica had come up with uncanny insights, but warfare had always been the specialty of the male line in the family, women simply did not know much about it.

He put his arm around his Aunt's shoulder and they walked slowly back to the manor, Patriot trotting ahead.

When they entered the front hall Duckie was checking out the crossbow that had belonged to Ferdinand's father and Norma was busy dusting the antique chests and chairs that graced the hall.

'My dear Ferdinand, I would like some time alone in the courtyard, so I will leave you with your page,' said Erica, giving Duckie a friendly tap on the head before walking through the hall which led into the courtyard. Patriot followed in her footsteps.

Ferdinand, ceremoniously, lifted the sword onto a small velvet lined shelf, mounted on the armoury's west wall.

'It looks like a mighty weapon Your Highness,' said Duckie with admiration.

'Mighty when swung by a mighty arm, and you need not say Your Highness, my fine fellow, Marquis or Sir will do,' the Marquis allowed.

'And how is that crossbow coming? Fine weapon the crossbow, my father, Albert the Great, was a perfect shot with the crossbow. Could pin a fox tail to a fence post with that weapon.'

'She will be ready in a jiffy and then we can go out for field trials,' chirped Duckie gaily.

"Practice, practice and then again practice," Papa used to say. Yes Ducky, we will do some target shooting when you are finished,' said the nobleman as he slid into the deep cushions of one of the comfortable lounge chairs and lit his pipe.

Duckie noticed a dreamy stare in his master's blue eyes, now veiled by a cloud of smoke and concluded that the Marquis was contemplating a battle strategy to oppose the coming danger. But such was not the case. The noble knight was dreaming already of the post- battle stage, of young women dressed in white throwing garlands of flowers over his head, while strains of the well known anthem 'In Praise of Heroes' wafted over the fields.

In the courtyard Lady Erica walked back and forth. It was a warm spring day and the cherry trees were blooming. Humming birds flew hither and thither among the flower beds and under the foliage of a lilac bush lay Patriot, sound asleep.

Her thoughts dwelt on Scimitar. How could they have a defense council without him? Was rescue possible? If only a few of the delegates could come at least they could make a start and talk about ways of freeing Scimitar.

Her train of thought was interrupted by the sound of wagon wheels crushing stones on the lane leading to the front door. Erica walked through the south wing of the Manor to the front door and onto the patio. An open wagon drawn by a mule was wheeling up to the porch. Erica recognized

Moose Martin and Slim on the box. Moose pulled in the reins and the farm wagon ground to a halt. On the wagon Martha, the prophetess, propped up by pillows was seated on a bed of straw.

Relief appeared on Erica's face. 'Welcome Moose Martin and Slim, and a welcome to you Martha.'

Once Moose helped Martha out of the wagon Erica embraced her.

'Lady Erica, it is an honour to be your guest, I am only an old biddy, and blind at that. I don't know if I can be of much use.'

'Oh Martha never say that. Your wisdom has saved many of us from peril.'

'Well my dear, we shall see, we shall see.'

Erica shook hands with Moose and then she turned to Slim and took his hand, 'Glad you were willing to come and leave your swans in Svanhild's care Slim.'

As she held his hand, Slim felt a current pass through his fingers and up his arm and suddenly resentment at being called away from the rehearsal for his upcoming swan ballet vanished. Erica let go of his hand and asked him to look down the road to see if Grompuss was coming.'

'The bear was a bit too heavy for the old farm cart and he shuffled behind until we passed some berry bushes,' added Martha.

Slim ran back towards the village until he saw Grompuss cruising from hedgerow to hedgerow, stuffing berries into his purple dyed snout.

Fortunately for Slim, Grompuss had filed his scent somewhere in the back of his bear brain and when he came up to him, the bear gave him a friendly push. Slim had often sent an intuitive message to his swans, and this too worked with Grompuss. The sense of urgency and danger was impressed upon the bear spirit and after one last foray into a bramble bush, branches entangled in his black fur coat, Grompuss trotted behind Slim to the Manor. When they walked onto the lawn, Martha whispered something in Grompuss' ear and the mighty bear plunked himself in the shade of a giant beech tree. Patriot trotted up to Grompuss and endeared himself by pulling the bramble branches out of his fur.

Ferdinand had joined the little group on the verandah and heartily welcomed Slim and Moose Martin.

'Delighted to have you here Moose and you Slim, I am not much of a committee man. Sitting around with old friends, drinking coffee and a thoughtful smoke is my style.'

'Yes sir I can relate to that, but I don't know if there is much I can do,

I have been a Ferry Captain all my life,' sighed Moose.

'That is just it Moose Martin. You have worked on the riverboats for over seventy years and know all the banks and inlets of the Sanctus. We need you.

Erica suggested that they move to the upstairs hall and have their consultation there. Ferdinand led them up the old spiral stairway leading to the second story of the Manor. Martha took a rest midway, leaning against the hand carved banister. Slim helped her up the last few steps and escorted her to an empty chair by the oval table.

The wall was covered with historic paintings. Some of the canvasses were battle scenes of the deCygne ancestors defending their homeland from forays by Gnome marauders and Outlander raiding parties. The large painting in the center portrayed the Unity Conference at Mount Oneisis. King Arcturus, his silver hair illumined by moonlight stands on a rock outcropping. Seated around him, in the moon shadow of pine trees, are Gnomes, Dwarves, Elves, Mountain Fairies, Swannefolk and Outlanders.

Slim was fascinated by the painting. Only when Moose Martin tapped him on the shoulder and startled him out of his reverie did he sit down. Soon all were seated around the ancient oak table. The backs of their chairs were crowned with carvings of flying swans.

The Swannefolk around the table looked more like guests at an afternoon tea than people gathered for a desperate effort to fend off a threat to their land and homesteads. The men wore casual dress, leather trousers, and blue woolen shirts, except for Ferdinand, who had slipped on his late father's mail vest. There was nothing extraordinary about the guests grouped around the table, yet these were the men and women that Erica had seen reflected in the depth of the black pool in the court yard. There was nothing to distinguish them from the many other capable upright citizens in the county, but following her vision she had brought Slim, Moose Martin and Martha here to the Manor for counsel.

Lady Erica took the lead and welcomed them. 'Dear Martha, friends, I am happy and relieved that you have come. We have sent messages to the Elves, Gnomes, Mountain Fairies and Outlanders inviting them to join us here, now that Lambarina is no longer safe.

'And in all these years I spent on the river,' commented Moose Martin, 'I nary saw any mischief. Now these black Lords send their servants skulking about and some of them dressed up as traveling workmen. It's a good thing we Swannefolk got silver hair. It is pretty hard to fake that. And then the merchants accepting money from these characters, but I have always had me doubts about some of these business folks!'

'This is the time that people will show their true colours Moose', reflected Erica, 'The task ahead is grim. The first sorrowful tiding I must share with you is the loss of Scimitar.'

'The loss of Scimitar,' exclaimed Moose Martin in disbelief, 'Scimitar has left us?'

'Scimitar was taken prisoner by the black louts,' interjected Ferdinand.

Martha spoke up in her soft brittle voice, 'Scimitar must be freed he was destined to lead us in a struggle that cannot be set aside or run away from. Goodness Gracious, this I had not foreseen!'

Moose Martin looked overwrought. He raised his tall frame from the chair and hands in his pockets, began walking back and forth. Then suddenly he stopped and repeated Martha's words, 'Struggle that cannot be set aside or run away from. Well we Swannefolk have always run away from thorny issues. If we can't sail around it or run away from it, by the Great Goose, we better get on with it!'

There was an expression on Moose's face they had not seen before, a kind of adamantine determination, focusing all inner resources on one goal.

Suddenly the large slightly stooped frame of the laid-back ferryman looked quite formidable.

Slim recalled Svanhild talking about the coming of the great darkness. This had been some years ago before the slight dark eyed water ballet master and his swans had gained fame in the land. What would happen to him, to Svanhild and their dancing swans if the towns they performed in, were overrun by bullies who served seven mysterious Masters?

Slim looked at the people around the table and his eyes rested on the face of Lady Erica. There was a sparkle in those soft hazel eyes. They emanated an energy tangible to all present. It was she, who understood the situation and would guide them through the tests and trials that lay ahead.

Duckie and Norma came in with a tray of sandwiches and a large earthenware pitcher of juice pressed from lomanas, the brilliant orange fruit which grew on wild shrubs and ripened in early summer.

The atmosphere relaxed, Erica took a sip from her beaker, smiled and began to talk.

'Thank you all for coming. There is a wisdom in consultation with trusted friends. Much knowledge is revealed in the waters of the black pool and visions gleaned from the dark waters have guided our people for generations. Yet many insights have been gained through the meeting of minds.'

'Well spoken my dear Lady,' interjected Martha, 'Wise words, wise words. I have lived alone for over a century and know well the pitfalls we dig for ourselves. We sit by the wheel spinning yarn and spinning thoughts, without a friend to call us down to earth. Some thoughts like ill knit garments, need unraveling at times.'

'Thank you Martha,' said Lady Erica, 'Together we must unravel the black web that surrounds us. We all know that after a century of peace and prosperity, the Seven Lords have risen again and threatened the quiet and safety of our people. They haven't massed armies this time but agents and small parties are wandering over the land. Lambarina is under their control and because we have no organized defense we are unable to resist.'

Moose Martin turned towards Erica, 'Yes it is true we have no defense, because this land has not known violence in all these years. It was the death of the King which finally woke us up, and afterwards the disappearance of Princess Yaconda. The Princess is beloved by all the people in the Kingdom. They would make great sacrifices to rescue her and restore her to the throne.' Lady Erica nodded.

'It is likely, Moose Martin, that Princess Yaconda has been kidnapped by the enemy. Without a ruler the people in the Kingdom are likely to drift back into their old prejudices and once more ancient squabbles will flare up between Gnomes and Elves or Dwarves and Outlanders. This is the hope of the Seven Lords, who live in the waste land of the red earth, beyond the ancient forests and the desolate marshes.

'Why, why,' threw in Slim, 'Why are there Seven Lords in some distant land seeking to extend their power to our Kingdom, and by means so foul!'

'They want to control us Slim, for deep within they fear that someone will find the means to challenge their power and put an end to their reign. There is much I do not understand, but some things have come to light and these I must now share with you.

'In the distant past, long before the Swannefolk had settled in the river valley of the Sanctus, King Norwalt reigned over the land. Prosperous was his reign, towns and settlements flourished. Wondrous tapestries were woven by the weavers at the court of King Norwalt and much of the music we hear at our high festivals, was composed at that time.'

Slim softly whistled a tune.

Lady Erica smiled. 'Yes Slim, the song 'The Rustling of the Sacred Leaves'

was written hundreds of years ago by King Norwalt's court composer. Most of us have seen the only sculpture that has survived from that era.'

'You are speaking of the marble image of Queen Netilda in the Lambarina museum.'

'Yes Moose, the Queen whose beauty was preserved in marble.'

'Such beauty has never been seen in mortal shape,' sighed Slim who remembered the day his mother had taken him to the museum in Lambarina.

'The Kingdom prospered,' continued Erica, 'Thousands of splendid gardens were seen throughout the country. At nightfall families would bring out the lyre, and music floated over hill and dale. The bliss and happiness of those days are still heard in poetry and music passed on by our forefathers. Each spring a great festival was celebrated on the terraces of the Royal Palace. Surrounded by flowering shrubs and fountains, musicians played and people sang. Nonetheless a shadow hovered over these fountains of joy. A shadow that goes back to the time when the King was still Prince Norwalt. His father the great King Stanislav ruled the land. Crown Prince Norwalt loved wandering through the hills and forests of the kingdom. One day hiking through the forests at the bottom of the Finnian range he met the dazzling sorceress Matista. The Prince was fascinated by the tall slim beauty. The touch of her slender fingers burned in his hand and her cobalt eyes electrified his soul. He pleaded with the King and Queen for permission to marry the comely enchantress. At first they were adamant in their refusal. When summer reached its height the Prince fell into a deep depression. His father and mother relented, they received Matista and were touched by the gracious manners of the bewitching beauty.

The King and Queen told the Prince to travel to the Kingdom's northern mountain ranges and live in the winter palace with his Godfather until a year had passed. Should he still wish to marry the bewitching Matista when spring returned he would have their blessing.

That winter, riding through a snow storm in an outlying fiefdom, he found shelter at Lord Kamenir's castle. He dismounted in the courtyard and upon entering the great hall he beheld the maiden Netilda, seated at a spinning wheel. The light of the flames in the great hearth cast a soft, warm light on her auburn tresses.

Prince Norwalt could not describe her features. Looking into her gray eyes he felt a peace he had never known before. Her eyes were deep like mountain lakes and the exultation in her face radiated joy.'

'The Prince was smitten,' laughed Martha.

'It seemed the image of the radiant figure behind the wheel unlocked a secret chamber in his soul, a chamber he had never known about,' reflected Lady Erica.

The Marquis lit his pipe and looked at Moose. 'Deep waters Captain Martin!'

'Deeper than any I have sailed,' whispered the retired ferryboat Captain, a baffled look in his eyes.

A smile played on Erica's face as she resumed her story. 'For weeks the Prince rode around the snow covered hills, trying to banish the image of the maiden from his mind. It was no use and he returned to the castle to ask Lord Kamenir for his daughter's hand.

The Queen and King were much relieved that Prince Norwalt had escaped the beguiling wiles of the enchantress, and joyfully bestowed their blessing on the union of the Prince and the lovely Netilda. Early in the new year they announced the wedding.'

Slim looked alarmed, 'Matista's fury must have been frightening Lady Erica.'

'Yes Slim. Terrible it was and so began a chain of events which shook the Kingdom. We have not seen the end of it yet.'

For a few moments silence prevailed. Martha drank her lomana juice and Moose Martin was doing a good job chewing up the mouthpiece of his soapstone pipe. Ferdinand blew rings of smoke muttering, 'Dazzling women are dangerous. One must be iron willed when temptation beckons.'

Lady Erica took a drink and went on, 'Even before Prince Norwalt returned home, Matista knew that he had fled her magic web. Scorned and banished from the court, Matista's wrath burned deep. She knew her time would come.

Joyful was the wedding feast of Norwalt and Netilda. Soon afterwards King Stanislav abdicated as reigning monarch and the newlyweds were crowned King and Queen.

The country prospered. Norwalt and Netilda traveled to every part of the Kingdom. They were loved and cherished by the people of the land. Of Matista there was no sign!

Years later, in King Norwalt's reign, signs of unrest appeared amongst the nobles. The chief elder of the Seven Counselors who advised the King, had long envied the sovereign's power and glory. It was then that Matista saw her opportunity. She invited Salan, Chief of the Council of Nobles to a secret meeting and planted the seeds of rebellion.

The Elven King, whose silent scouts had overheard Matista speaking to the rebels, giving them encouragement and advice, warned the King. The rebellion was squashed and the Counselors banished for life to a rocky island off the coast.

The flame of wrath that consumed Matista was only fanned by the adoration and love which the people of the Kingdom showered upon the royal couple. Matista decided to play her last card at the time of the spring festivities. She had discovered an ancient spell of great power. Well she knew that whoever spoke the fatal words would risk death, but life mattered not, revenge was sweeter. She traveled to the isolated rock where the seven rebels still clung to life and using her magic powers, restored to health, their haggard bodies.

She spoke to them in a sweet and beguiling voice. 'You will regain your rightful place in the Kingdom. Power will be yours and vengeance will be sweet! The game has now been played but one card I hold.'

'What trump is it that you hold in this deadly game, enchantress?' asked Salan.

'Noble Lord, do I hear a shade of doubt in your voice?'

'We have suffered on this wretched windswept rock for years Matista, if you had the power to change our fate, why did you not do so earlier?

'Salan, only now will the configuration of the heavenly bodies permit the casting of a spell. Patience my friend, the incantation I shall utter will subdue the Kingdom and its citizens and it will be yours to rule and to cherish.'

A spark of hope sprang into the eyes of the seven Nobles gathered around her. Long forgotten desires and ambitions returned.

'Our reign will be secure, enchantress?'

'No earthly powers can assail you! Wealth and power that you could not have dreamt in your fondest dreams will be yours. What you desire will be yours!' Then their leader Salan stood up and with a strange gleam in his eyes, kissed Matista's hand.

'Gratitude fills our heart. You have read our secret desires and your magic powers have hastened the hour of fulfillment. But great sorceress, tell us the terms of this bargain.'

'Oh Prime Minister', retorted Matista, 'The terms of this bargain offer all that life can offer. The spell gives everlasting youth and prime, delight and power. Death you will not suffer. But guard your realm well. Let no intruders enter for there is one spell that can undo the covenant that now protects you. Written on a golden tablet are words of light.' She did not finish the line and lowered her voice, 'This is all I know. It is of no concern for the tablet has been lost beyond times remembered.'

'Dear Matista your beauty we admire, and your grace we do implore, yet my soul is disquieted. If after many centuries death, by a fluke of fate, would find us, what would be our destiny?'

'Salan, wise one, waste not your time on idle speculation.'

The other six lost their patience, 'On these barren rocks swept by icy spray, we have suffered for seven years, no time shall be wasted, the hour is ours, power, beauty and reprisals await.'

Matista's black hair streamed in the icy wind and there was a smile on her finely drawn lips as she asked the Seven to seal the bargain for dominion, wealth and everlasting youth. Under the fatal lines the six eagerly printed their index finger dipped in blood. It was Salan who hesitated and again asked, 'If death does visit us, whence shall we repair?'

'I have always had a weak spot for you Salan. The questions you ask!

Salan, trust Matista. Nothing can befall you, greatness and enchantment will follow you through time!'

'Ah Matista whose beauty does bewitch, will you be there to bail us out if things go wrong,' whimpered Salan.

'Salan, Salan there is a streak of caution in your soul, and it will serve you well. Seize your dominions and guard them well against intruders and there will be no need to bail you out. Once the spell is cast I shall return to the caverns of darkness, whence I hail.'

There was a smile of victory and exultation on her countenance as she walked towards the sea. Standing on the beach, wavelets washing her bare feet, she raised her voice, 'Come hither servants of the deep.'

Out of the mist appeared a high prowed ship. Two of the sorceress' servants, clad in black robes, skillfully sailed the vessel through the surf to a narrow channel between two sandbanks. Matista waded through the water and climbed on board. 'Hasten, hasten to the Kingdom's shore, my faithful thralls.'

Matista's magic called forth a southern wind and the vessel raced across the water to the shores of the Kingdom.

She leaped onto the beach and commanded her thralls to return to the salt sprayed rock and to ferry the Seven to the Kingdom.

Following a narrow winding path she reached the festive grounds of the palace. Striding into the garden, her aubergine robes flowed in the breeze. Burning torches highlighted her milk white skin and the dazzling blue of her eyes.

King Norwalt and Queen Netilda were seated on the marble terrace, adjoining the palace. On each side of the terrace fine spray from the fountains caught the light from torches turning it into curtains of pearls. Servants and guests surrounded the royal couple.

Even before she reached the steps Queen Netilda spotted the solitary figure of Matista striding towards them. The crowd on the terrace instinctively drew aside.

Matista ascended the steps and fixed her gaze on the royal couple. A strange and threatening silence prevailed. Queen Netilda knew that her hour of trial had come. Yet, she looked calmly at Matista. She was conscious of the great and terrible beauty of the sorceress, as silently she stood on the marble terrace facing them. The enchantress raised her silver staff and spoke words that soared and seared through the happy throng, words that silenced the murmur of voices and fountains and would change joy and peace into strife and suffering.

'I have loved in vain, my presence has been scorned, my name reviled, my services forgotten. As you lived your smug and shallow lives, you banished from your minds the shadow of Matista. If life be but a game, the dealer threw to me one deadly card to play. The spell I now proclaim will end charades and the Seven will return to rule, to rule their slaves.'

She raised her silver staff and uttered the spell in a bell-clear voice,

" Sikinnik takor, isummi volti anorka."

Now Lady Erica ended her narrative and looked at the small band of friends around her. 'It was at this point in the book of legends that the written text ends. The ballads that our troubadours have sung throughout the ages tell us what happened after the spell was spoken.

A deep sleep overcame the dwellers of the Kingdom. Then the Seven Counselors rescued from their salt swept rocks landed in the Kingdom and became rulers of the land. The sleep, that Matista's spell had cast, lasted seven days. Upon waking the men and women of the Kingdom found themselves slaves of the cruel Overlords. The King was murdered and the Queen was exiled to the very rock were the Seven had been banished. Long afterwards fishermen from another land stumbled on her petrified body. The slender hands were fastened upon a crack in the rock. Miraculously the face had been preserved. The fishermen said it reflected an unearthly beauty. Lovingly they carried the body to their ship and brought it to the court of Arcturus II. There a death mask was cast and it was this mask which the great sculptor Deodatus used to create the marble likeness which Slim so admired in the museum in Lambarina.'

There was a moment of silence around the table and now that they knew the whole story, they felt a sense of relief.

'Old Martha spoke up, 'Of course we had heard some of the old legends, but to hear you tell it, brings it altogether. Those Seven sank into greater darkness as the centuries went by, and now no longer are content to stay within their own realm.'

'As their power grows, so does their fear,' added Lady Erica, 'that is what makes them so dangerous. Their reign is based on fear and terror. Thousands of slaves and prisoners labour in their realm. A secret dread that someone will penetrate their magic shield haunts them. Nothing threatens them from the outside. The fear dwells within.'

' What did Matista mean when she spoke about the golden tablet,' asked Slim.

'You know as much as I do Slim,' smiled Lady Erica. 'But news has come to us that some of the strangers traveling in the county have queried local farmers about golden tablets and offered a handsome reward if any one finds a golden plate.'

'Now you mention it,' Moose Martin observed, 'I have met a fellow or two in these last years on the ferry that showed a quaint interest in gold artifacts.'

'I wonder why Matista mentioned a gold tablet,' questioned Martha, 'It would have been easier and safer not to have said anything about it.'

'Ah ha, it might have been easier but she wanted to warn those Seven. There must be something to this business of a gold plate,' remarked Ferdinand.

'What happened to Matista? I sure hope she is not around anymore,' piped in a small voice. It was Duckie who had seated himself at the top of the stairway.'

'She has never been seen again young Duckie, at least not in my lifetime and that is saying a lot,' giggled Martha.

'I have an odd feeling that Matista in some shape or form may reappear,' mumbled Slim.

One must take the magic with a grain of salt,' mused Ferdinand, 'tales grow taller with the telling!'

Lady Erica was astonished, 'Nephew dear, jesting about the magic of a legendary sorceress is courting danger.'

'The only courting that I do without rebuff' said Ferdinand sheepishly. As if to reassure himself he added quickly, 'I am certain she is dead and gone to the darkness where she belongs.'

Moose Martin brought all of them back to the present, 'It is the Seven that threaten us. Scimitar must be freed and lead us in opposing this evil. Who will volunteer?'

'You are the one to lead the rescue attempt Moose Martin,' declared Erica, 'you know the river and all the streams that flow into it.'

'I know the river and the marshes well enough, but I am not a military man. I wouldn't know what to do if one of these dark fellows shows up, or a black hound charges.'

'I shall come along and bring Boudewine deCygne's crossbow, the weapon which skewered the Red Blighter to the old beach tree by the Inn.'

'Dear nephew, it is not the bow. It is the archer that sends the arrow true.'

'He is not doing too badly ma'am,' chirped Duckie, 'a couple of days ago, one of the arrows got stuck in the practice disk.'

'The crossbow might scare the black bandits, and how are they to know, the arrows don't always hit home,' said Slim. 'But prepared or not prepared,

we must do something.'

Ferdinand stood up and followed by Duckie, walked down the stairs and moments later a whizzing noise by the open window made clear that archery practice had begun.

'I remember Scimitar talking about his brother Smithereen', said Slim, Perhaps we could find him and ask him to come along on the rescue expedition.'

'Of course Slim,' Lady Erica agreed, 'Smithereen is the very person we must find. Who will go with Moose and travel to the alpine meadows in the Finnian Range and find the village of the Dwarves?

'I will go,' said Slim, 'but who will look after mother and Svanhild?'

'Your mother and Svanhild will be welcome here but have you ever thought about taking Svanhild with you?' As she posed the question, Lady Erica gauged the reaction of the group. She was pleased and surprised that there were no objections.

'When I took Svanhild's hand in mine,' muttered the blind prophetess, 'No love or fortune did I see, but a destiny to take her far beyond the borders of this land.'

'Svanhild has dreamed of adventure since she was a child,' smiled Slim. 'None can climb a tree or bring down a hare with a slingshot like Svanhild.'

The evening sun cast a soft orange light across the room. Most of the company tired of sitting began to move around. Moose Martin and Slim did some back stretches and then walked up to one of the large windows that looked upon the hills and forest to the northwest. The sun partly hidden by a dark cloud resolved into a spectrum of purple and red.

Moose was the first to catch sight of a solitary black swan skimming over the tree tops escorted by two pelicans. When Moose mentioned it, Lady Erica hastened to the other window to see the great black swan sailing over the berry bushes of the outer gardens. Aske flew close by the window and all could see the proud, erect and diminutive Tuluga, Queen of the Mountain Fairies astride the Swan's back, her golden hair aflame with the last rays of the sun. Erica hurried through the door leading to the terrace. The Queen dismounted by the stone wall and looked into Erica's eyes.

'I read the question in your eyes Lady Erica and though it pains me, I must tell you Alma's fate. When we were flying through the mountain pass of the Ancient Giants, a merewing appeared from behind a rock. He dived at lightning speed and mortally wounded your beloved swan, Alma. It all happened too quickly for the pelicans to intervene. Then the merewing returned and this time the pelicans attacked in formation and killed the dark fowl. We flew into the valley and landed near the knoll where Alma fell. While spreading her unseen wings for immortal flight, we could hear her sing. When we came close only her lifeless body remained. The pelicans formed a guard of honour, and I myself sang the death chant.

'Thank you Queen Tuluga,' whispered Lady Erica. She looked on the darkening landscape, Aske stood beside her, his neck resting on her shoulder. Queen Tuluga took a small vial from her satchel and offered it to Erica. It was a flower extract that brings tranquillity.

Queen Tuluga was a stern lady and she ruled her subjects with rather severe discipline. Fairies are lighthearted beings and without a strict Queen to keep them in line and limit the number of feasts and festivals to a manageable number, no doubt they would have ended up in a terrible mess. Queen Tuluga would broach no nonsense. Edel and Weiss had discovered that, to their chagrin.

Smaller in statue than any one there, she radiated a kind of authority and prowess that made people feel that nothing was impossible. Her presence was a welcome addition to the company.

Norma and Duckie were busy bringing up dishes for the evening meal. The sight of great pitchers of homemade wine and the smell of wild boar roasting in the kitchen fire brought cheer to the somber gathering.

Standing on her chair the Queen of the Mountain Fairies could look the company straight in the eye. She raised her glass and drank a toast to the Kingdom, the return of the Princess Yaconda and the rescue of Scimitar. Her boundless confidence was infectious and soon a merry band sat down to dinner. The wine flowed freely and tongues loosened. Marvelous tales were told that evening and Slim, lithe as a cat, danced one of the intricate dances in which hands and fingers speak. The Fairy Queen was in high spirits and her jesting and jollying turned the night into a merry ring of laughter. When Moose Martin played a gig on the ukase even Ferdinand loosened up and threw his legs into the air.

The next morning rain poured from a leaden sky and at breakfast in the sunroom, the mood was more subdued. Ferdinand was savouring his bacon and eggs, but the awful thought ran through his head that this was the day of departure and that in days to come, traveling on the river and through the marshes, breakfasts like this, were going to be rare,.

Svanhild and her mother had just arrived and they joined the breakfast party. Lady Erica took a seat next to Svanhild and poured her coffee. She recounted the happenings of the day before and explained to the Svannemaid the need for an expedition to rescue the Dwarf Scimitar.

'Of course he must be freed,' exclaimed Svanhild in an impassioned voice, 'Scimitar must lead the cause of freedom. Perhaps the great darkness that Martha prophesied is now approaching.'

'I am afraid my child that evil is overshadowing the land, and those of us that can resist, must resist.

'Resist we will Lady Erica.'

'Then will you join the rescue party Svanhild?'

'Deep within,' responded Svanhild, 'my spirit longs for adventure, I know my destiny was not to be behind loom and cradle!' Lady Erica put her arm around Svanhild's shoulder.

'Brave soul, may aid from the unseen guide you on this perilous mission.'

'I welcome it with all my heart Lady Erica, and after breakfast I shall be off to the kitchen to supervise preparations for the trip.'

Lady Erica whispered a prayer of gratitude that Svanhild had joined the company. She sensed that inside the dark-eyed slender maiden burned a fire that would spur the travelers on in the face of overwhelming adversity.

The Fairy Queen tiptoed into the dining room and holding a cup of mint tea in her hand, sat down on the windowsill. She abhorred bacon and eggs but had already drunk a beaker of honey and melon juice. In coffee she seldom indulged but there were times when she would take a little.

After most of the company had finished eating Tuluga Queen of the Fairies drank her last sip of mint tea, and standing up in the window sill, addressed the company seated at the table.

'Arcturus the Ninth brought Gnomes, Outlanders, Elves, Dwarves, Swannepeople and Mountain Fairies into one Kingdom. In that unity lies our strength. Neither the murder of our King nor the kidnapping of Princess Yaconda, can break our resolve to maintain the bonds that now bind and unite us.

We had a splendid party last night and I was loath to dampen your spirits with grave tidings. You all know that Princess Yaconda did not return from her cruise on Lord Imbrun's yacht. I suspected foul play. Alas, this has proven true.'

All faces around the table spoke dismay, and anxious eyes were fixed upon the tiny monarch.

'Two of my subjects, the scouts Edel and Weiss, have spoken to Princess Yaconda in the dreadful tower of the old Alcazar. There she and her maid Dominique are being held, by order of the Seven.

There were surprised shouts around the table, 'Where is the tower, has the Princess been mistreated? How did your scouts find her?'

'I shall answer the last question first,' smiled the Fairy Queen. 'The scouts Edel and Weiss were not supposed to find her at all. Flagrantly they disobeyed my commands, when they wandered onto the peninsula that juts into the western ocean. Of course they enjoyed surfing on the huge breakers near the old Alcazar. My special messenger Peli I found Edel in the Western Desert, a groll Captain on his heels. The brave pelican saved Edel's life in the nick of time.

On their return Edel and Weiss reported that they had spoken with the Princess and had saved her handmaiden Dominique from a fate so dreadful I will not mention it!'

A deep frown appeared on the Marquis' brow. He seemed to be rehearsing in his mind the various operations he would like to perform on groll Captains who terrorize innocent maidens! Lady Erica rested her hand on his shoulder and tried to subdue the deep rumble of indignation in the cavalier's soul.

'Could we rescue the Princess,' asked Slim anxiously.

'That is not possible Slim, Princess Yaconda and Dominique are guarded by the lifeguard of the Seven Lords. It is true the Captain of the regiment was waylaid by Peli I and Edel in the great quick sands and sank to his doom, but another and more fearsome Groll will take his place.'

'Quick witted chaps, these scouts,' mumbled Moose Martin to himself, but the Queen overheard him. 'Edel and Weiss are quick-witted, nimble and very cheeky. They have defied my authority and now they must do penance. Three months forced labour on the pelican ranch, wheelbarrowing fertilizer to the mountain gardens,' explained the Queen, a glint of glee in her eyes. 'Yet these incurable romantics love danger and after they have learned their lesson, could be of some use to our common cause.'

'Love danger,' whispered Ferdinand, 'unusual.'

'We are grateful to you Queen Tuluga,' said Lady Erica. 'Your indomitable spirit has cheered and heartened all. We wish the travelers Godspeed, as they set out upon their mission to free Scimitar.'

'Set out on their mission,' mused Ferdinand, casting a glance at the torrents of rain coming down. He lit a pipe filled with his finest tobacco. After all it might be his last one for days to come.

Duckie was rushing all over the place, packing last minute items. Svanhild improvised for Patriot a backpack, a canvas bag hanging down on each of the golden retriever's sides.

Moose Martin was bending over maps on the dining table trying to find the border settlement where the Dwarves lived. He succeeded in locating it on the Finnian range in the north eastern part of the Kingdom. It was there, they would be likely to find Smithereen.

A frown creased his forehead when he realized the distance that they would have to cover. Upriver for days and then through the marshlands covered by bulrushes and wild willows, according to legend the undisputed domain of the nymph Marsha.

Moose well knew that few Swannemen had traveled through the marshes and returned to tell the tale. Only Dwarves shielded by their iron moral code and indomitable will had succeeded in evading the beguiling charms of lovely Marsha, Queen of the marshes.

Strange and frightening dreams came to him that night, mud and maidens, steaming marshes, sirens singing, glasses ringing. Colourful gardens dissolved into muck and mire and he found himself sinking in deeper and deeper.

Grompuss might have been a useful companion on the expedition but the bear was simply too big for Slim's skiff. It was decided to leave the bear behind so that he could help guard the Manor. Queen Tuluga decided to stay for a few weeks to consult with Erica and Martha. They hoped that soon they would be joined by delegates from the Outlanders, Gnomes and Elves.

The Fairy Queen's pelicans were resting in a little pond in the north woods. The fishing was good and they were quite content to linger, for the flight home would be long and dangerous. This time the Queen would not ask Aske to carry her. To carry their sovereign home, four pelicans would carry one corner each, of a finely spun net.

10

Supper in Miranda

$\mathcal{M}$oose was still trying to free himself from a dreadful mire when he woke with a start. For a few minutes he sat on the edge of his bed recalling the horrid nightmare. Thank heaven, he woke up from that mess. His imagination had played tricks on him again. The Captain had been a navigator all his life, but navigating the inner waterways of his psyche did not come easy. He poured a pitcher of cold water over his head, dressed quickly and walked out into the fresh air. Feeling refreshed he joined the others at the dining table.

After breakfast, everybody got busy preparing for the journey. Svanhild, who had taken charge of the provisioning worked in the kitchen with Norma. Slim had gone down to the boat to make last minute repairs. Moose pored over maps, marking different routes they could take, and Duckie was packing weapons in the armoury. The Marquis was seated in his easy chair in the great hall smoking his pipe, meditating upon the enormity of the enterprise and indeed wondering whether it would not be better for him to stay behind and direct operations from a distance?

He arose, paced up and down the hall, casting an occasional glance at the portraits of his ancestors. 'No, by the teeth of the great dragon, I will throw myself into the fray,' muttered the nobleman.

Having made the decision, he ran up the stairs, two steps at a time. Pausing on the landing to catch his breath, he realized this trip was not going to be a picnic. Surely the outdoor exercise would put him back in shape! He began packing.

By noon the weather had turned and a steady rain was falling. Everyone was ready to go. Rain or no rain, there was no point in further delays. Without much fanfare the five companions left the Manor and walked towards the dock. Scimitar's retriever Patriot followed behind.

Lady Erica standing by the window in the sunroom caught a last glimpse of the travelers walking in a light drizzle towards the river. The plan was to row upstream on the Sanctus to the Tristana, the northern tributary that gathered the water of the marshes and the mountains beyond.

They had decided to use Slim's skiff. It was just large enough to hold five comfortably and Patriot could squeeze into the bow. Slim and Svanhild often had used the skiff when traveling with their dancing swans to the small northern settlements. The swans always swam behind.

Slim and Moose were sloshing through the soft mud by the side of the river when Slim got an idea.

'Moose we could take a team of Swans. They can swim behind the boat and anyone espying us from shore would conclude that we are on our way to perform a water ballet. It is best that only few know the purpose of our journey. I am sure that the agents of the Seven have eyes and ears amongst the local people.'

'I like that idea Slim,' reflected Moose. 'It would give us a good cover. Where are the swans now Slim?'

'Uncle Svend is minding them until we return. We can dock at his farm to collect the team. They can swim behind the skiff until we pass the last settlement, then I shall command them to fly home.'

Ferdinand, Duckie and Svanhild trailed some distance behind and Patriot made up the rear. Everyone was protected from the drenching rain by tightly woven capes. The men's were dyed dark blue, with light grey hoods. Svanhild wore the women's traditional dark green cape and the light green hood with silver trim. The capes were treated with resin to make them watertight. All wore a backpack and Patriot carried a heavy load in his saddle bags. Ferdinand had strapped Scimitar's sword around his middle, and was trying to adjust his gait to the swinging weapon. By the time they reached the skiff Ferdinand had taken a couple of tumbles in the mud and looked as well camouflaged as could be hoped for on a dark rainy day.

A small section of the boat near the bow was decked in and it was here, they stowed most of their gear. Lady Erica clad in a yellow cape emerged from the fog and walked onto the jetty for a last farewell.

Svanhild and Slim lifted the oars on the locks. Ferdinand wet, muddy and grumpy tried to alleviate his misery by lighting a pipe. The large hand carved briar bowl flared up for one hopeful moment and then was quenched by a torrent of rain. Patriot stood in the bow and Moose took the stern seat, resting his arm on the helm. Slim gently pushed the boat into the river. All looked up at the noble figure of Lady Erica, whispering a blessing on their mission. As the skiff turned north, rain and mist veiled her from view.

Five minutes of rowing brought them to Uncle Svend's place. Slim climbed out and walked to the farm house returning shortly with seven swans gliding down the narrow channel that connected the farm with the river. The great white birds with their black beaks kept up a lively chatter. They were delighted at the sight of Svanhild and eagerly followed the skiff as it headed upstream into the dense fog.

There was a strange stillness on the river, merely the sound of splashing oars and the bow cleaving the waters of the Sanctus. The seven swans swam single file, the great male Limonides leading. Svanhild was enchanted by the drama of the scene, but the rest of the company bedraggled and wet, failed to respond to her enthusiasm.

Every half hour they changed places at the oars, while Moose stayed at the back and skilfully steered the boat around floating logs and rocks. When the mist cleared for a few moments, they could see willows weeping by the shoreline and poplar leaves glistening with droplets. Farther up the river, cedar tops rose above the banks of fog and Moose knew that they must be nearing the lumber town of Miranda.

After five hours on the river Moose Martin spotted a fire burning on the southern shore. He pointed his hand and announced, 'Miranda, the last settlement of the Swannefolk, on our right, at the end of the inlet! Used to run in with cargo. Decent folks down there, keep a fire burning in foul weather for the shipping. A darn comfortable inn I recall.'

'Any reason why we should not spend the night in comfort,' asked Ferdinand.

'None that I can see Your Highness,' retorted Moose Martin, who glistening with rain and his teeth chattering, looked more like a walrus than a moose.

'Drop the Highness, Moose. When in the field on duty, only valour counts!'

'Quite right. Why spend a night on shore in pouring rain when the 'Golden Goose', is just within reach old boy,' quipped Moose taking the Marquis at his word.

'Forsooth, that would be an error Captain Martin, set course for the Golden Goose,' jollied Ferdinand. Drawing hard on the oars, soon they doubled their speed, passed the fire beacon and sailed up the inlet and into the harbour. Many lights were visible through the mist and they had no difficulty in finding a place to moor. They tied the skiff near the market square. The sign of the Golden Goose was clearly visible and Moose went ahead to talk to the landlady.

The Golden Goose, an ancient inn built with heavy timbers was owned and run by Hester Hollyhock. She was standing behind the bar serving drinks to some of the old timers when her ear caught the creaking of the oaken door and the dripping figure of Moose Martin appeared.

'Well well, if it is not the skipper himself. Sit down you old water rat,' greeted the friendly landlady. 'A hot toddy is on the hob. I thought you had retired and turned landlubber.'

' Aye Hester a pleasure to see you,' responded Moose rubbing the water from his eyes and casting a longing look at the roaring fire in the great open hearth. 'We would like to spend the night Hester, and there is a lady in the party.'

'A lady you say, an old widower like you traveling with a lady in this shocking weather. It's a shocking thing Captain.'

'Ah it is not like that Hester. I am traveling with the troupe that does the water ballet. Slim and Svanhild with a team of seven swans are at the harbour side.'

Hester smiled. Entertainers were always welcome at the inn.

'Of course you stay here. Where else would you spend the night? It has been pretty quiet of late, last week only a couple of strangers checked in.

'A frown furrowed Moose' brow, 'What are they like these strangers, Hester?'

'Burly dark fellows short and sturdily built but not used to the way of the Swannefolk. Yet they were clean, well dressed and friendly enough.'

'Why were they here, these strangers?'

Hester laughed, 'Ninety years I have run this inn, Captain, and I have learned not to ask people what they are here for. 'Not to worry Moose Martin these fellows left two days ago. Ah yes, they had a dog with them, a big friendly beast, black as night,' Hester added with a smile. Handsome tippers they were these fellows and paid their bills in cash!'

I can afford asking you why you are here, Moose Martin, for you have always been tight fisted and are unlikely to change!'

'Tut,tut, tut,' muttered Moose, trying to mollify the feisty landlady, 'I just came along with Slim and Svanhild to set up a swanneshow for the good men and women of the town.'

'A traveling show, now that is welcome news for folks in distant towns!'

Visits by artists were always prized and Hester who really was quite fond of the old ferry master, flushed in anticipation. When the glistening figures of Slim, Svanhild, Ferdinand and Duckie stepped out of the streaming rain and into the hall of the old inn, they received a hearty welcome.

Moose bent over and whispered in Slim's ear, 'Sorry Slim but I had to tell Hester that you will do a water ballet. Two burly fellows and a black dog passed through a few days ago. Luckily they have left. There are few other guests at present and there is plenty of room for all of us.'

'You did well to screen the purpose of our journey,' reflected Slim. 'When Scimitar spoke at the Graceful Neck, I had a feeling agents of the enemy had reached the outlying settlements. He said the peasants trained by the Seven are more treacherous than the Witch Doctors of yore.'

'They are likely the Rovers, Scimitar talked about but they left the inn a couple of days ago Slim. Probably they travelled down the Sanctus to Lambarina.'

Hester was flattered to have Svanhild and Slim stay at the inn. They were well known artists in the Kingdom, and their arrival in town was an event!

'But you Marquis deCygne,' turning towards Ferdinand, 'why are you with the troupe?

'Ah indeed I travel with the troupe. I have become lately a patron of the water arts and will foot the bill for our stay at your delightful inn.'

Hester looked flattered and reassured. She turned away from the Marquis, and slipped her arm through Svanhild's, 'You my love will share my apartment the others can bunk in one of the upstairs rooms.'

Duckie was probably considered a gopher attached to the show and he escaped Hester's special notice. Patriot tied up in the skiff had curled up under the back seat. Duckie got a couple of bones from the kitchen and took them to the patient hound. Walking back to the inn, he noticed the sky clearing and a stiff breeze blowing. A patch of moonlight passed across the harbour and he could see the Swans sailing in the breeze. From time to time, for a snack, they dipped their graceful necks below the surface. The weather augured well for the morrow.

Hester summoned her cook to prepare a solid dinner and a number of tables were set in front of the great hearth in the main hall. She sent her daughters around town to spread the news that Svanhild and Slim would be dining at the inn and that the Marquis deCygne, now a patron of the arts, would be giving, that night, a short talk about the water arts.

This was perhaps stretching it a little, but Hester was an excellent entrepreneur, and the news was sure to attract some of the wealthier folk in town for a dinner out.

Miranda was an isolated settlement and visiting artists or dignitaries were always a welcome diversion. The lumber trade had made the town prosperous and it had become a favourite with traveling performers.

Svanhild changed into one of Hester's daughters' dresses. She looked lovely, her silver tresses covered the upper part of the dark blue dress. A silver chain with a rosewood carving of a swan adorned her graceful neck.

She walked into the ancient dining hall framed by huge square hewn beams, from each of which was suspended an oil lamp. Casting a glance along the wood paneled walls, she saw a display of musical instruments. At the end of the room hung an ukase, a popular six stringed instrument. Next to it, hanging from a wooden peg, was an utelli. The utelli is a smaller version of the Outlander's harp. It was Svanhild's favoured instrument. Gently she took it down, seated herself at one of the tables and began tuning the strings.

As guests filed into the dining room, Svanhild touched the strings of the utelli and softly sang some of the traditional songs of her people. When playing the last chords of 'the Ballad of the Black Swan', a hunched shape halted by her chair. Svanhild was startled to see bending over her a face edged with age and surrounded by a bower of snow white hair.

'Aye my lovely songstress the melody and voice bring healing to my aching body. Sing on, sing on, my warbling thrush.'

Svanhild struck a new chord, but when she looked up, the ancient one was gone. She could see her shuffling towards a table in a corner of the hall.

There was something not quite right about the hunched figure that had stopped to talk to her. She ran her fingers lightly over the strings, reflecting on the stranger's appearance.

It was the voice, of course, that lovely voice that had addressed her in such endearing tones. It did not have the crackle one would expect from an old biddy. Voice and figure were like discordant notes! With a toss of her head she dismissed the mystery from her mind and played a lively jig.

Slim, Moose and Ferdinand, who had changed into dry outfits, picked a table close to the fire to drive the chill out of their bones. Hot toddies served by Hester's daughters, Fragrance and Fairlight, restored their dampened spirits. Hester brought Svanhild a glass of hot apple cider and sat down beside her. Duckie wandered about, talking to the guests.

The Mayor and his wife Annabelle entered the hall and as soon as they spotted the Marquis and Moose Martin, they walked over to their table. Annabelle was thrilled to meet Ferdinand deCygne in person and executed a curtsey. The Marquis was impressed.

The Mayor engaged them in an animated conversation about the role of arts in the community. He expressed his pleasure at the performance planned for the morrow by raising his glass and drinking to the success of the event.

Ferdinand succumbed to the charms of Annabelle. He was quite delighted to discover that there were still women with an appreciation for the nobility and for the finer points of life. Perhaps on his return he should spend some time in Miranda, where isolation had slowed the process of decay and real women could still be found.

Many of the people of Miranda had braved the pouring rain to dine at the inn. Smell of roast duck wafted into the great hall. All the guests were now seated and Fragrance, tall and stately, her dark hair hanging loose over her shoulders, carried the steaming dishes to the table. Slim could not help looking into the eyes of the lovely maiden. He had the soul of an artist and the image lingered in his mind. Fragrance was soon followed by her sister Fairlight, a slight blond maiden, whose light tread seemed to give her wings. She tiptoed among the tables filling glasses with wild bramble wine. A thrum of lively voices could be heard as food and wine were given full attention. After nibbling thoroughly clean his last drumstick, the Mayor turned to Ferdinand, 'My dear Marquis we are delighted to hear that you will give a short talk on the role of the arts'.

Without awaiting an answer from the astonished Marquis, the Mayor rose and spoke in the splendid baritone voice that had secured him his office in the last election.

'Fellow dwellers in the town of Miranda, we are honoured to have with us tonight the Marquis deCygne, patron of the water arts. We all remember his Lordship's efforts to preserve antiques in Swanneland and the fine display that he has mounted. It is not often that travelling troupes of performers brave a treacherous river and sheets of rain to reach Miranda. Miranda welcomes the Marquis, ballet master Slim, his lovely sister Svanhild and my old friend Moose who skippered them up the river.' Then the Mayor raised his voice and asked for a hand. There was a lot of hoopla and cheering, and when the excitement subsided, Ferdinand stood up, straightened his damp collar and spoke,

'Worthy citizens of Miranda, we are delighted to be here even if our trip was somewhat unexpected, and certain dangers attended the journey.' At this point Moose put enough pressure on the Marquis' toes with one of his big boots, to steer the speech into safer waters. 'By dangers,' continued the Marquis, 'I mean the natural elements, rather than the dangers posed by fellow creatures. Powerful waves and pelting rain did not deter us from pursuing our journey for the furtherance of the arts. I hope that tomorrow's performance will speak more eloquently than I can. Let us now go back to this splendid dinner Hester has prepared.'

This called for another hand, for if there is anything in a speech to which Swannepeople respond most heartily, it is brevity. Long and deep speeches were considered to be in bad taste.

Moose Martin, who had known the Mayor for many years, made it his business to ask about the strangers seated at the table next to Svanhild and Hester.

'Cornelius,' whispered Moose putting his hand on the Mayor's arm, 'the strangers, the two tall fellows, I don't remember seeing them in these parts.'

'The Mayor looked closely at his old friend, 'I see dismay in your eyes, Moose Martin, this is not like you. Is there is something I should know? But to answer your question first, the two tall men you asked about, are Ensten and Ulrik from Esteria. Solid gold those two. You need not be concerned. They are here to buy lumber from our northern forests. Master builders they are and woodcarvers. In Esteria, in winter, the snow reaches to the rooftops, it is then that they do their marvellous woodcarving. In spring and summer they travel to Miranda, to market the carvings and to help us with our building projects.'

Slim and Moose relaxed. Slim cast his eyes toward Svanhild and saw her smiling at the two brothers. Then as he scanned the lively scene he saw at the end of the hall another small table with a single guest.

There sat a woman, her slim frame bent with age and her snow white hair sweeping the surface of the table when she moved her head. The light of a single candle showed finely chiseled features and white skin laced with fissures like cracked pottery. Candlelight danced in her eyes and as her gaze turned upon him for an instant, Slim caught a flash of blue. He shuddered involuntarily and turned towards the Mayor.

'Mayor Cornelius, the lady, the ancient one, alone at yonder table.'

'No wonder Slim you noticed her, she is one of our local characters. It was twenty years ago that she arrived here tied to a raft and barely alive. Robbed, she had been shipped down the Sanctus. One of the families in Miranda nursed her back to life. We found her a small cabin in the marshes, and there she makes her living weaving willow baskets.'

'You forget my dear,' laughed Annabelle that many of the maidens wade through the marshes to her hideout, to have their future told.'

'Ah, you have to toss it to the old witch,' said Cornelius with the excellent wine getting the better of his faculties, 'She has an uncanny genius for reading people.'

'Cornelius,' Annabelle whispered in his ear, 'Never, never, speak like that again! Neva has a spooky way of divining what is said or even thought!'

'Neva,' mumbled Moose, 'not a name I have heard before.'

Slim decided to walk over to Svanhild's table to meet the builders from Esteria. Hester introduced him to Ulrik and Ensten and Slim soon was much taken by the warm jovial manner of the brothers. Wine flowed freely and Slim was captivated by their tales of the tiny country of Esteria in the snow clad mountains. A sudden desire to travel to these exotic places came over him. Many questions he asked and Ulrik was only too eager to answer them. Ensten, shy and studious by nature was quiet, yet little escaped his keen hazel eyes as they scanned the dining room.

The moon now shone through the large south window. It reminded Slim that tomorrow the sun would be shining and he would have to direct a performance of the swans in the morning. As he stood up and walked back to his table, he looked askance at the small table at the end of the hall. It stood empty, Neva the white haired fortune teller, quietly had slipped out.

Cornelius and Annabelle were just taking their leave, and Annabelle's parting curtsey quite convinced Ferdinand, that Miranda enjoyed cultural refinements, that sadly were lacking in his hometown.

'Remember Marquis,' were Annabelle's parting words, 'when you return for a visit, I would like you to meet some ladies from my circle, young ladies who take an interest in the arts.'

The Marquis bowed graciously and watched the Mayor and his wife depart. He sighed deeply and walked off towards the circular stairway, 'A remarkable woman, truly remarkable.'

Humming a melancholy tune, he walked upstairs to the dormitory. How delightful it would have been to stay in Miranda as Annabelle's guest, without this dreadful adventure hanging over him. If only they were now on their way back, the enemy pulverized, Scimitar liberated, and Annabelle's friends dancing around him, showering him with invitations to intimate dinner parties.'

Slim was standing by the open window looking upon the moonlit marshes. In his mind he went over the events of the evening. The image of Fragrance kept floating before his eyes. But he well knew Rosemary at the Graceful Neck would be waiting for him on his return. He had enough self-knowledge to know that he was easily touched by beauty, but he had only one heart to give and the image faded as his thoughts went back to the mission ahead.

Ulrik and Ensten had turned out to be delightful company and his suspicions had been unfounded. Yet he felt a lingering sense of danger. Just as he was ready to turn in there was a distant cry, a kind of muffled howl. Suddenly it stopped. Goose bumps crept up his arms and images of black hounds, nettle treatment and Sisters of the Secret Crossing, floated through his mind.

Slim lay down on his bunk fully dressed and smiled. His imagination was running away again, the cry was no doubt that of a hunter's dog in the marshes and totally harmless. As he began to drift off to sleep the image of the old fortune teller floated in his mind, snow-white was her hair and wrinkled her skin. Then the hair turned ebony black and the wrinkles vanished. Her skin now exuded a soft beauty and the face lit up. As he fell asleep he found himself sinking into the depth of her cobalt eyes.

11

Water Ballet

The morning sun caught Slim in a flash of light. He jumped out of bed and strode to the open window. The willows and poplars covered with a film of water from last night's rain, sparkled in the light. The blue leads into the marshes were mirror still and Slim's heart thrilled with excitement. The gloom of yesterday's journey forgotten, he was eager to explore the unknown.

There was much work to be done before the morning performance. He rushed downstairs, pushed open the heavy oak door and looked over the market square. A colourful scene greeted him. Farmers and their wives were putting up stalls for fruits and veggies. Wandering in the aisles were a few tinkers, packed high on their back were copper kettles, notions, bundles of wool, pots, fur trim and other household items. Roosters, chicks and ducks in wooden cages crowed and clucked.

Slim walked onto the square enjoying the sounds and splashes of colour. As he wound his way among the stalls to the waterfront, he could see the skiff swaying back and forth. Patriot rushed from bow to stern barking Slim a hearty welcome. Slim pulled the skiff to shore and Patriot jumped out. Together they walked along the harbour front.

When Limonides spotted Slim, his powerful webbed feet stirred the water and he glided to shore. Slim whistled twice and the swans responded by lining up single file. Limonides looked up as the ballet master outlined the water and aerial dance numbers for the morning's programme. The swans had performed the dances many times, and they chattered contentedly. This was not going to be one of those frazzling shows they performed in larger towns and there would be plenty of time for some quiet fishing before returning home.

Slim went back to the inn, feeling confident and peckish. Sensible it was that he made his way to the breakfast nook off the main hall. All the guests were there and the stack of pancakes and bacon was shrinking quickly. Fortunately Hester arrived with a large platter of dragon eye. Slim was very fond of dragon eye, and dug in with the others. Dragon eye is a traditional Swannefolk breakfast dish. A hole is cut in a slice of bread. Then the bread is put in a hot frying pan and an egg dropped into the hole.

Ferdinand gobbled down breakfast as if his salvation depended on it. He could not believe his good luck. Yesterday he had been quite convinced that he had eaten his last tasty meal for days to come. Now here he was again, having a splendid breakfast at a comfortable inn. He counted his blessings while they lasted.

Ensten, fiddling with his pipe, looked at Moose Martin seated across the table. He spoke in a soft deep voice, 'Moose Martin it was a pleasure to meet you. If your wanderings lead you to Esteria, a safe haven awaits you there. These are perilous times. Call on us or send a message. Trust the Grey Wolves, they will take a message for you to Esteria.' Leaning across the table he whispered, 'The black hounds fear the Great Grey!'

Moose smiled. He realized that Ensten had sensed that their mission would not end at Miranda. It was good to know that there was a safe outpost in the wild hinterland.

Moose moved closer to Ensten, 'First we will travel up the Tristana to the border country and try to find the Dwarf Smithereen.'

Ensten nodded, 'If the sky is clear you may spot the homestead of the Gnomes Oarflake and Ambrosia.

'Oarflake and Ambrosia,' repeated Moose pensively. Then it came to him. 'Yes, my father told us the story. Oarflake, the Gnome caught stealing gold dust and sentenced to perpetual banishment by the Sacred Chamber of Elders.'

'That's them. They live in the northern forest near the great marshes of the Tristana. It is true Oarflake broke one of the sacred gnome commands, and he and his wife were exiled to the forests near Esteria. We met them when first they arrived. The snow was so deep, it reached near their shoulders, and they could no longer move the sled loaded with all their worldly belongings. Ulrik and I got our large sleigh and packed the Gnomes and their belongings on top. A team of grey wolves pulled us all the way to the Lake of the Coloured Fishes and there we built for them a log cabin.

'No doubt you saved their lives,' exclaimed Moose

'I think we arrived in time,' said Ulrik who had joined his brother. 'The snow was too deep for them. Now we try to visit once or twice a year. They have built quite a wilderness retreat. Ambrosia is a great healer and the wounded and sick seek her help in their distress. She has the second sight, if your journey takes you to their homestead, seek her guidance.'

Moose sensed that Ensten and Ulrik knew more than they let on. He trusted the quiet lumbermen, and had a strong feeling that their path would cross again.

Slim and Svanhild already had left with all the props for the show. Moose and Ensten stood up and walked outside. All of Miranda seemed to have crowded into the market square. Hester had given Fragrance and Fairlight permission to watch the show and they joined the others at the harbour pier.

The Mayor himself, his charming Annabelle and the town's notables were seated by the water's edge. The sun shone brightly upon the merry scene and there was a bubbling mood.

Svanhild began to play the utelli and the swans lined up in a row and trumpeted the show's opening notes. All faces turned toward the water and the hubbub of the crowd abated.

Svanhild played an old dance tune on the utelli and Limonides sailed stately on the still water, then spread his great wings, gathered speed and once airborne skimmed over the blue surface. The others following in a straight line were mirrored flawlessly in the silent waters. As they rose above the water they changed into a V-formation, spiraling upwards to a great height. Suddenly Limonides dived and the others followed, shooting down toward the busy square. The increased speed released packages of ribbons tied to their feet and when they reached the crowd they were trailing purple and orange streamers. Skimming hats and fancy hairdos, they landed in a perfect V on the silent waters. All over the market square clapping and cheering resounded.

Svanhild and Slim went on to prepare the swans for pattern swimming. Around their necks they clipped golden rings from which hung tiny bells.

Limonides led the swans in a gentle spiral and swaying their necks, chimes rang across the water. The pattern changed now into a perfect circle, finally dissolving into a cloverleaf. Then they formed a tight circle, and moving quickly from the center, wing tips beating upon the water, created a star like pattern.

Ferdinand, enjoying his role as patron of the arts was holding forth to Annabelle on the fine points of the art of water ballet. Svanhild walked up to the Mayor and Annabelle, and invited them for a ride in a gondola. It was a tradition always to offer a gondola ride to the dignitaries in the towns that they visited.

Moose had found an older type gondola, moored in a small canal. Hester's daughters Fairlight and Fragrance were helping Moose with the decorations. Metal hoops were attached to the gunwales and the girls wove strands of wild flowers, which they wrapped around the metal frame. When Ensten walked by and saw the preparations, he went quickly back to the inn and returned with a large woodcarving of an elven child. He walked up to the gondola and placed it on the bow. Moose and the girls admired its laughing lightness. It was exactly what had been lacking. The little vessel looked transformed.Moose smiled and turned to Ensten, 'Is it one of yours?'

'It took me most of the winter,'said Ensten gravely,'For weeks I couldn't get the carving right. One night I awoke with a start and looked outside. All I could see was falling snow. Then the dark space in the window filled with a diffuse light and I saw the beauty that my hands had been trying to find in the wood I was carving. I beheld the face of an elven child her eyes sparkled and spoke of joy. She called me by name, 'Ensten, is it I you are looking for?' As she spoke, laughter played upon her face, I reached out to touch her but she receded into the snowy night, peals of laughter softly ringing. The lovely face wreathed in smiles, was still before me as I rushed downstairs, picked up my chisels and worked until I could see that laughing face in the woodcarving that I was holding between my hands.

Moose was not strong on the arts, but as he fastened his eyes on the lovely carving in the bow of the gondola, laughter rippled over the rough face of the old sailor and he realized that in the elven face, Ensten had caught something that could not be described in words, but spoke to the spirit within.

Slim was getting the swans ready for the traditional tour. He placed silver crowns on their heads, and Svanhild fitted the harnesses. She had woven the harnesses on her own loom, out of fine dark blue yarn. Then they walked over to the back of the harbour where the gondola was moored, the swans following behind.

Svanhild saw the gaily decorated vessel first and greeted Moose, Ensten and the girls. Then she descried the carving on the bow. Such gaiety was hard to resist and she burst out laughing. Slim's artistic spirit was captivated by the beauty of the face and for a few minutes his eyes rested on the delicate carving. He was touched by the expression of the elven child. For a moment it seemed that he could hear that laughter. The simple lumber trader from Esteria was a great artist. Svanhild, touching the carving, looked at him.

'You are a fine artist Ensten. Your work will bring delight and solace to many souls.'

Ensten did not speak but his face glowed. The compliment of the Svannemaid had touched a heart string. Ensten of course had to repeat the story of the carving, and the nocturnal appearance of the elven child.

When everything was ready, the Mayor and Annabelle boarded the gondola and Svanhild climbed on the stern seat, utelli on her lap. She signaled Limonides and gently the team pulled the little vessel through the small canal and into the harbour, along the market square. It was a splendid sight and the worthy burghers cheered heartily as the stately swans moved effortlessly on the blue water, the gondola gliding behind. Svanhild began to play a serenade on the strings and Annabelle waved kisses to the crowd.

A few of the men and women smiled at the sight of the mysterious wood carving on the bow, but not every one noticed it. Ferdinand, patron of the arts, failed to see it, but the ancient fortune teller Neva, sitting next to the Marquis on a rough bench , caught sight of it as the floating spectacle glided by. Ferdinand was just about to ask her if she would read his hand, when he saw her keen eyes follow the elven face. A momentary shadow marked her countenance. Ferdinand could hear her muse, 'Elven child, elven child, what is in an elven child?'

The thought slipped from her mind and a smile returned. She turned to Ferdinand and with her withered fingers grasped his hand. Long and silently she looked at it. 'Fine hand, powerful lines, reveals noble ancestors, born to great deeds,' she cast a questioning look at him. Ferdinand blurted out, 'Astonishing, simply astonishing, all so very true!'

The Marquis already buoyed by the very positive attitudes that he had encountered in Miranda, was impressed by the flattering words of the old soothsayer, who was still holding his hand.

'Ah you handsome rogue, love eluded your path, you misunderstood charmer, I see a woman who will cherish you and admire your hidden talents. Not in your home town, but far beyond the river and the marshes, the mountains and the desert, love may yet await you!'

The Marquis looked quite delighted. This old woman saw his hidden talents. It was crass to be called a rogue and a charmer, considering his lofty ancestry, but that could be overlooked from somebody too ancient to remember proper forms of address.

'You noble soul,' murmured Neva, patting his hand before letting go of it. The Marquis was visibly moved. The words of the ancient one had been a potent restorative for his ruffled ego. He hadn't felt so well in years. The women in Miranda were really quite remarkable! Suddenly the idea came to him that perhaps he should remain in Miranda. To be a patron of the arts was a pleasant role, suited more to the spirit of the times than the path of the warrior, and likely less troublesome! The party in that little skiff would be more comfortable without his bulky form! And perhaps Aunt Erica had been right, for a man his age to undertake these expeditions had been quite dewy-eyed. 'We, deCygnes, have the rare capacity to be honest with ourselves,' mused Ferdinand.

'You look deep in thought my handsome philosopher. Speak freely of your secrets, Neva will be silent as the tomb.'

'Wise and ancient soothsayer,' began Ferdinand, pleased to be able to talk to such a trusting soul about his inner conflicts. I come from a family of ancient warriors. On his deathbed my father whispered, 'Wield high the sword of honour. Alas the battlefield is not my element.'

'Indeed it is not my son. The vibrations are not those of a warrior. You are a child of the new age,' intoned the smooth fortuneteller.

'Well put Lady Neva. New ideas stir within, to be a patron of the arts, to live a peaceful and creative life.'

'Ah loosen the strings of your soul. It is a new era, the arts will triumph, warriors will be extinct.'

'We must move with the times,' responded Ferdinand feeling much relieved.

'Ah I see spiritual progress my noble friend,' confided Neva. 'You have caught the spirit! But tell me truthfully about this visit by your handsome artist friends. Is it just for a show in Miranda, or are there plans for travel inland, plans to rescue nasty Dwarves? The Dwarves have been always the troublemakers in the land.'

Ferdinand twiddled his thumbs a little. It was true the Dwarves could be troublemakers, and very snotty they could be. There could be no harm in confiding in this kind old soul, and explaining that Scimitar was a special kind of Dwarf. 'For even kind old ladies hold prejudices,' mused the Marquis.

While the Marquis was being gently reeled in by the ancient biddy, Ensten, standing a few feet away, overheard most of the conversation. The recluse from Esteria had an uncanny feeling that the Marquis would be caught soon in the scheming soothsayer's net. The Esterians in their secluded forest stronghold knew more about what was going on, than ordinary folks.

Ensten sidled up to Neva. His deep voice startled her.

'Greetings to you my merry diviner, a fine show today, and blessed by splendid sunshine.'

If Neva had been frustrated in satisfying her curiosity, she hid it admirably and greeted Ensten cheerfully.

'A fine day it is Ensten. Welcome to our market, may your business prosper.'

'Thank you Neva, if you will excuse us, I will ask Ferdinand to come with me. In his capacity as patron of the arts, I am sure he would like to see a display of our carvings, before we return to Esteria.'

Graciously he took him by the arm and led the baffled Marquis to a wooden table and benches where Moose, Slim, Svanhild and Duckie were enjoying an outdoor luncheon as guests of Mayor Cornelius and the lovely Annabelle. A fresh pot of coffee stood on the charcoal burner. The sight of Annabelle and the smell of fresh coffee mollified annoyance brewing in Ferdinand's breast, on being dragged away so rudely from that kind old soul. He hoped that her feelings had not been hurt.

While Annabelle smoothed the ruffled feathers of the Marquis, Ensten had a chance to tell Slim and Moose Martin about the conversation that he had overheard. The three realized that Neva's second sight had given her a glimpse of their mission, and that she had nearly beguiled the artless Marquis in confirming her hunch.

The luncheon on the lawn had now reached the coffee and dessert stage. Everybody was enjoying Annabelle's coffee cake. Ferdinand commented that it even excelled Aunt Erica's creations. He was rewarded by a warm smile.

A quartet of musicians, playing on their accordions traditional Swannefolk reels, walked into the market square. The gay rhythms set hands aclapping and feet atapping.

The festive atmosphere made it difficult to think of packing and traveling up the Sanctus to wild and uninhabited lands. Moose felt it was urgent that before any more information leaked out, they get on their way. Ferdinand was just finishing his coffee cake when he saw Moose get up and walk toward the Inn. This might be the right moment, thought Ferdinand, to approach him about his change of plans. He caught up with Moose at the entrance of the Inn.

'Moose, I have doubts about my going on this expedition. Although trained in the martial arts in the tradition of my forefathers, I have forgotten much and I am not as fleet of foot as you and the others. Well, you know that I am overweight and the boat is small. And then there are my new responsibilities as a patron of the arts. Perhaps it would be best if I stayed in Miranda.'

As he was wont to do when perplexed, Moose scratched his head. 'Look at it this way Marquis,' said Moose, putting his arm on Ferdinand's shoulder. 'If the intruders are not stopped, there may be no art to patronize.'

That was a powerful argument and Ferdinand lamented silently. He might be stuck with this group of adventurers.

'Marquis you might want to wiggle out,' added Moose, 'but once it is all over you may regret that you were not there.' This struck a sensitive chord in the Marquis. He had spent considerable time daydreaming about the cheer and glory that might befall him were he to survive this trip and return to a hero's welcome. If he fell in battle, they might well erect a statue or something, perhaps even get Ensten to carve it. He had a melancholy look in his eyes as he walked into the Inn to gather his belongings and to prepare for the journey into the wilderness.

Ensten and Ulrik came over to help with the luggage, and the party walked around the outside of the square. In the center the musicians and the dancers were in full swing, and few noticed the group walking toward the harbour.

Ensten standing by Svanhild's side stole a look at the young Swannemaiden. The lovely features, emerald eyes and silver tresses sang to his soul. And it was with a feeling of apprehension that he saw her step into the little skiff. He knew that perils awaited them.

Annabelle and Cornelius joined them at the dock, and Annabelle put into the Marquis' backpack a package with the remains of the coffee cake. Patriot already in the boat, wagged his tail at the return of his travel companions.

By now a number of Mirandans had noticed the travelers getting ready to board the skiff. They joined them at the quay to say farewell. Some asked Moose to take packages for delivery in Two Rivers. He accepted with a guilty conscience, for he knew well they wouldn't pass Two Rivers on this journey.

Cornelius put two gold pieces into Slim's hand, the customary reward for a performance. He then wished them Godspeed and invited them to return soon. At the last moment arrived Fragrance and Fairlight, carrying baskets of provisions which quickly were stowed under the stern seat. Annabelle, Hester and the other ladies waved kisses to the wayfarers. Ferdinand took an oar and pushed the skiff away from the dock and the swans lined up, swimming behind.

The crowd dispersed, only Fragrance could be seen, waving at the end of the jetty.

Patriot pleased to get away from the commotion and head for the wilderness had taken his place in the bow. He let out a happy bark as they rounded the corner and glided into the lead, which would take them from the harbour to the main channel of the Sanctus.

Moose and Ferdinand were at the oars, and the skiff cleaved the silent blue at a fair clip. The stately swans following behind were a lovely sight.

The narrow channel was flanked on both sides by marshes and the watery landscape was dotted by tall clumps of bulrushes, wild willows and clumps of cedar.

Once a fair distance from Miranda, Duckie piped up, 'Amidst those willow trees I can see the cabin of the fortuneteller. There in a poplar tree is one of the ravens she keeps. The chaps in Miranda told me about the ravens. They are her messengers!'

The rowers stopped for a moment and all eyes were on the small red roofed cabin in the marshes. Moose and Slim looked at each other, and Svanhild sensed their concern.

Slim spoke first, 'If the raven follows us and reports that we are turning north on the Sanctus, Neva will know that we are not a group of traveling artists. At present she may just be guessing.'

Ferdinand stood up for the soothsayer, and maintained, that for an old lady living alone, curiosity is quite natural.

The afternoon sun now low in the sky, shed a warm yellow light on the water and the bulrushes along the shore. The channel widened as they neared the Sanctus. Steering close to the north shore, they could see the dark expanse of the great river. Just then a black shadow flitted across the water and they saw a raven fly ahead of them.

Moose looked up, and as his eye caught the black fleck against the blue sky, realized that this was the end of what had been a pleasant river cruise. A grim look spread over his face and he asked Ferdinand to take out his crossbow and bring down the raven.

Ferdinand was not yet convinced that the lovely old lady who had held his hand and recognized his unique character could be in league with sinister powers.

Yet the Marquis had no love for ravens and he winched the crossbow tight and waited for the raven to return. The wily bird took his time before making a close pass on his return flight. With the sun behind him Ferdinand could clearly see the raven in flight. He released the string that set the arrow flying. It passed underneath the great black bird and dropped into the marshes. The next shot, even being farther off the mark, the Marquis concluded that some intense target practice would be called for at the next rest stop.

The raven returned, flying in a flouting way. Skimming over the water he boldly flew around the skiff, defiantly cawing at the crew. Ire mounted in the skiff yet they were powerless to silence the scoffer.

In a flash of anger Svanhild pulled her slingshot from her belt, armed the weapon and fitted a sharp stone into the leather patch. The raven glided again close overhead, casting a derisive look upon the commotion in the boat. Svanhild aimed and her right hand released the tension. Flawlessly flew the sharp stone and struck the raven on the side of the head. The mocking bird cawed no more, and dead, tumbled into the water.

The first shot in the drama engulfing them had been fired. The company in the boat sat silent, impressed by the precise aim of the fiery maid and the fearful realization that the picnic was over. At least they were free to move unobserved and darkness soon would cover their movements.

The rowers quickened their pace, and before long reached the wide waters of the Sanctus and made for a small island near the southern shore. Duckie and Svanhild built a fire and boiled water for tea. Ferdinand lit his pipe and wondered if he should have stayed in Miranda.

'Too late now old boy,' he mumbled to himself, 'the enemy has cast his eye upon us, death or glory.'

Slim called Limonides to the side of the boat and asked him to lead the team back to Uncle Svend's farm. Limonides although reluctant to leave Slim, obeyed and the seven lined up facing south.

Limonides with an undulating motion of his great wings rushed forward trailing water, then skimming the bulrushes, he rose into the darkening sky. High above the pine forests on the north shore, the seven white swans could be seen flying in the twilight.

It was dusk when they boarded their little vessel. Moose steered a north easterly course and before long they entered a part of the Sanctus that the Ferry Captain had navigated only twice before. They would have to journey at least three days before reaching the junction with the Tristana.

Closely hugging the shore they looked for a place to bivouac. Near the water were fine stands of poplars and aspen. Farther inland they could see a few pine, spruce and clumps of wild plum and apple trees.

Where small creeks and rivers joined the Sanctus, thin sand beaches had formed, suitable for campsites. Moose steered the boat into a little stream and landed the bow on a strip of white sand and pebbles. Everyone stumbled out, relieved to be able to stretch and move about.

The moon rose above the northern forest on the opposite shore, and cast an eerie light over the silent but swiftly moving waters of the Sanctus. Ferdinand and Duckie gathered firewood and Svanhild started to unpack the baskets of food that Hester and her daughters had provided.

Slim struck fire in the tinderbox and put some glowing moss under the pile of branches on the beach. Soon the fire chased away the chill of the cool summer night, and the company gathered around the blaze for an evening meal. Flames danced on their faces as they reflected on the events of the day.

'Welcome to our first cook out,' laughed Moose in a cheerful frame of mind. 'We covered a good distance and by the day after tomorrow should be close to the junction of the Tristana.'

'Must we cross the domain of the nymph Marsha?' quizzed Duckie who had picked up quite a lot of the old lore.

'Ah yes, Duckie, Marsha rules the bogs from the junction of the Tristana till the foothills of Donder mountain,' explained Moose.

'That impertinent hussy', Ferdinand exclaimed indignantly. 'Moral fortitude is the shield against the lures of marsh nymphs and such like.

'You don't say,' said Moose scratching his head and looking rather worried. 'The best thing would be to avoid her domain by taking the smaller leads on the southeast side of the marshes. Just in case.'

'Fret not for the morrow, we will take it one day at a time,' reproved Svanhild, 'Get your bowls and knives. Smoked meat of wild boar is sizzling in the fire.'

Coffee was set aboiling in an old copper pot and Ferdinand opened his backpack and pulled out Hester's candy cake. It was an excellent meal given the circumstances. They sat around the fire, enjoying the quiet evening. Moose, Ferdinand and Slim smoked their pipes, and Ducky tried his hand at carving one from a piece of oak.

Svanhild was already in her sleeping bag, and it was not long before the others followed. Slim built the fire for the night, and the glowing embers were a cheerful beacon for the friends. The night enveloped them. Patriot sat up wakeful and alert.

12

Svanhild's Disappearance

Slim was the first to rise. He got dressed, whispered to Patriot to stay with the others, who were still asleep, and walked along the bank of the little creek. Early rays of sunlight caught the silver fins of trout darting in the stream. Tall poplars and aspen flanked the shore on both sides of the beck and the early morning breeze caught the leaves, sending over the land a whisper of loveliness.

Slim loved the sound of quaking aspen and in a way it still felt as if they were on a camping trip. He was glad he had volunteered for this adventure. For years he had been wound up in water ballet and the care and training of the swans. It was his first love. Yet this expedition had brought to his mind many questions. Why are we here? Why has evil befallen the peaceful inhabitants of the Kingdom? How could a handful of Swannepeople help to stem the tide of oppression?

His mind went back to the events of the day before, how the raven had spied their movements and how Svanhild's flawless aim had killed the rascal. Deep within he knew his sister was the heroine in the party. She had more fighting spirit than ever he would have. Yet he had faith he would be able to play a part in the adventures that lay ahead. He knew that he had a good mind and a keen interest in strange lands and people. He always reacted to people with a kind of detachment that surprised him. Seldom was he intimidated or offended by the infinite variety of characters and personalities that crossed his path. Always they fascinated him. Perhaps that was why he had packed a small sketch book. At heart he was an artist. He couldn't imagine himself as a warrior. He didn't know how to fight and he never felt the inclination to do so, better gather firewood, and start cooking breakfast.

Returning to the campsite, he could see that the others were still asleep. He looked at the four figures in their sleeping bags, shaded by a large spruce tree and his heart sank. They looked forlorn in this wilderness and the whole journey suddenly looked like a wild goose chase. How were they going to stop dark Lords and fearsome creatures? How could this journey make any difference?

For a moment he sat down on a tree stump listening to the rustling of the leaves. Another sound mingled with the soft whispering of the aspen. At first it was like falling water, but then it rose above the leaves and he knew at once, the laughter of the elven child. It was the laughter that had resounded within him when he first saw Ensten's carving. He looked around, but there was nothing to be seen. Then a gentle voice sang out, 'Do not lose heart Slim, you are only few, yet you are a link in the creative chain that binds us all.'

To make sure he was wide awake, Slim stood up and rubbed his eyes. He could not see the elven child, but the laughter lingered. He felt cheered. They were a link, a small link in a chain of events that in the end would be for the good. There had been healing in the laughter. Thinking about the elven child, he wondered how her spirit traveled and visited people. Somehow he wanted to write it all down, but keeping a diary would not be practical on this trip, besides it could fall into the wrong hands. He would try to inscribe in his mind all the happenings and when they reached home, write it down.

His companions woke to a blazing fire. Coffee was ready and ample meat and bread was left from the food that Annabelle had provided. There were scraps for Patriot. Happy, the hound walked off with a bone and stretched out by the river's edge, enjoying the warmth of the sun's early rays.

They allowed themselves the luxury of sitting over a second cup of coffee. Even Ferdinand had to admit to himself that there was something thrilling about starting the day in the wilds of the hinterland after a fine breakfast. The weather held and by the time they launched the skiff the sun had burned off the early morning mist. Moose and the Marquis took the early shift at the oars, with Slim at the helm. Duckie, Svanhild and Patriot sat in the bow enjoying the view of the river.

Islands of reeds and willow shrubs appeared and Slim had to steer the skiff through the leads that wound among them. They could have gone farther out in the river, but the strong current was less troublesome near the shore. Moreover the small boat had little freeboard left and Moose did not want to take any chances in the turbulent waters of the main channel.

Some of the lagoons which they crossed were covered with water lilies in bloom. Slim loved the fields of white and delicate pink, and regretted that there was no time to paint the water lilies. Like his diary he would imprint the scene upon his mind and paint it at the journey's end.

When a small island came in sight they pulled to shore for a lunch break. After sandwiches most of the company caught a nap. Svanhild sat up watching islands of white clouds drifting on the deep blue sky. Then from behind one of the clouds two dark specks appeared. Svanhild saw wings approaching and soon they were soaring overhead. Moose was awake by now and he too looked up at the birds.

'I think that they are owls, Svanhild. If this is the land of the great forest owls or Wood Owls, we are not too far from the Tristana. I am sure that they flew over to check us out. By royal decree, they were granted hereditary rights to these woods in perpetuity, and the owls guard them jealously. Any strangers passing through would be suspect.'

'Would they give us trouble Moose?'

'I don't think Svanhild. Owls are wise, it doesn't take them long to find out what folks are up to!'

Svanhild, quite taken by the owls, kept looking for their return, but there was no sign.

When they launched the skiff, a headwind blew up and it took a lot of effort to keep moving upstream. There were fewer islets and they were more exposed. Moose, at the helm, kept the boat close to shore. They could have saved time by crossing some of the large bays that jutted inland, but Moose preferred to stay in the lee. That streak of caution in the old Ferry Captain served them well. Despite the wind, they took on little water and were still dry when they left the Sanctus and turned into a small lagoon to look for a site to overnight.

A narrow strip of sand at the end of the lagoon looked inviting. Large cedars, spruce and pine ringed the inlet and farther inland there were good stands of birch and beech.

Slim enjoyed gathering wood and lighting a fire. Since everybody else was happy to see him do it, Slim became the company's firemaker. He walked into the forest to gather kindling. When he came to a fine stand of birches, he stripped enough bark to start a fire. Before walking back to the site, he took time to look at stands of hardwood around him. Perched in one of the tall beeches, directly overhead he observed many owls watching him. He had heard about owls of course, but never had seen them in their habitat. He found himself staring into the fathomless depth of many owl eyes. A shiver ran down his spine, not a shiver of fear but of fascination at the many wonders of nature. The eyes looked like wells of wisdom, hiding secrets deep and dark. What interesting creatures! He wondered for a moment if they could be domesticated and perform in his show. No, they looked fiercely independent and would never submit to the commands of a ballet master. A pity though for he could think of some interesting scenarios. Looking up he knew that they could sense his thoughts, for a fiery gleam appeared in their eyes.

He packed up his birch bark and called out, 'My apologies for trespassing upon your forest, but we need some bark to start the fire.'

This seemed to mollify the birds and one of them said in a deep voice, 'You are welcome to the bark and the windfall, but drop any thoughts of dancing owls. We know about the swans, ballet master, very pretty and all that, but those birds have lost their freedom!'

These comments were followed by some grave hooting, and Slim thought it best to make his way back to camp. He bowed politely and took his leave.

On his way back he picked up more firewood. When he reached the campsite, Moose and the Marquis were finishing a lean-to and hanging from a cedar branch was a rabbit. He had never thought that his sister's skill with the slingshot would bring them so handsome a dinner. At home he had never understood Svanhild's love for hunting but on this journey it turned out to be a gift.

He kindled dry moss in the tinderbox and put it under the birch bark and a pile of branches. The sun was fading quickly and the flames brightened the deep shadows around the campsite. When Slim turned around he saw Svanhild coming out of the underbrush, another rabbit on her shoulder. Deftly she skinned it and hung it next to her first trophy.

Again a lovely supper was roasting over the fire and the Marquis felt very strongly that he had made the right decision to stick with it. The temptation had been great but perseverance too was a virtue and he felt pleased with himself.

The last of Annabelle's coffee cake topped off a fine dinner of roast rabbit. Duckie did the dishes and then joined the company around the fire. Sitting around the glowing embers, they talked about friends and relatives home in Cascade.

Moose and Slim missed their sessions with the boys at the Graceful Neck. And Slim thought with nostalgia of the pretty blue eyes and the mop of blonde hair that would skip to his side and slide a breakfast plate in front of him. When he saw her everyday he had always taken her for granted. He realized all of a sudden that Rosemary was important to him. She had a kind of springy cheerfulness that often startled him from his brooding moods and helped to bring the world back into focus. Thinking about inns, his mind went back to the Golden Goose in Miranda and suddenly the dark eyes of lovely Fragrance Hollyhock looked at him. The deep hooting of an owl startled him out of his reverie. He washed his face with cold lake water and reproached himself for day dreaming.

Moose and the Marquis smoked their pipes until the glowing embers darkened. To keep the fire smoldering through the night, Slim dragged a few big logs onto the fire. They unrolled their sleeping bags and the men took shelter under the lean-to. Svanhild preferred to sleep on the beach by the glow of the embers.

By the time the moon cast her gentle beams on the forest, they were fast asleep. Logs in the fire pit were still aglow and the soft babbling of a nearby beck blended with the hooting of the great forest owls.

Suddenly the hooting of the owls grew louder and Svanhild, sleeping at the far side of the fire, woke with a start.

She sat up and looked at the night scene. Moonlight played on the waters of the lagoon. The owl voices, like organ pipes, sounded deep and ominous. The men in the lean-to on the other side of the fire were sound asleep and even Patriot had dozed off.

Svanhild was enchanted by the nightscape and the sounds of the forest, but she failed to hear the note of alarm in the deep owl voices. She turned her gaze on the trees behind her. Faint glimmers of moonlight penetrated through the cedars. Clusters of pine were draped in blue-green light.

The hooting grew louder still, Svanhild strained her eyes but the great owls eluded her. Then she saw a shadow fleeting across patches of moonlight. It moved among the trees and came to a standstill at the edge of the beck.

Svanhild sitting up in her sleeping bag beheld the dark shape coming towards her. Mesmerized by the apparition, she watched silently as it drew closer. A ray of moonlight revealed a woman of striking beauty, arrayed in a black velvet gown. Patriot, awakened by a strange scent sat up, alert. Before he could utter a bark, the mysterious figure raised the wand in her right hand. The noble dog, unable to resist the magic, fell into a deep sleep.

Svanhild recovered her senses and looked at the regal beauty facing her. The comely face, ebony tresses and dark eyes, exuded an imperious air. From the dark velvet collar emerged a white swanlike neck. It was only when she spoke, that recognition dawned. The voice, Svanhild had heard that voice before, at the Golden Goose in Miranda.

'Svanhild, you must come with me,' she softly whispered, 'We are going on a trip together.' Svanhild felt as if a spell had been cast over her, and the will to resist ebbed away. She slipped out of her sleeping bag and walked towards the comely sorceress. Drawn by invisible threads, she sped onwards, following her bewitching captor deep into the forest. Only when she felt the cold night air in her face, did the spell begin to lose its power. She realized that she was moving against her will. She grasped the branch of a large cedar tree and hung on with all her might. The sorceress halted and addressed her in a melodious voice, 'It is too late my dear. If you resist this magic leash, my trusted helpmates will carry you onward. Gorghouls are obedient servants.'

The mention of Gorghouls frightened Svanhild. She closed her eyes and to her inner sight came the image of Seraphim the great elven teacher.

'The soul has many chambers. If one is crushed she weaves another, in worlds we know not of.' The words of the elven sage brought calm and her thoughts cleared.

The voice of the sorceress, yes, she had heard that voice before in Miranda. It was the voice of Neva, the ancient soothsayer. But how could this be, this youthful queenly figure standing in the moonlight before her?

They walked a short distance until they came to a clearing flooded with moonlight. The sorceress bade her be seated on a fallen log and then took a seat on a tree stump opposite. Svanhild looked intently at the apparition, trying to piece things together. The sorceress cut short her train of thought.

'I know the question in your mind and I will answer it. Behold Matista enchantress of the highest realm.'

To regain her serenity, Svanhild did some breathing exercises. Looking at Matista, she realized that she could be kept as a hostage or worse. Behind Matista, there stood among the trees, three miserable looking creatures. They must be Gorghouls. She remembered them from legends. With those ghastly ghouls around, escape would not be possible. This could be an opportunity to find out as much as possible. She asked innocently, 'Great enchantress, we know your fame from tales and legends, but why Neva by day and Matista by night? Why hide your beauty from admiring eyes?'

'An impertinent question young lady,' answered the sorceress, somewhat mollified by the compliment. 'It was a young wizard that cast the evil spell that transforms Matista's beauty into withered womanhood when dawn's light transforms all that lives and breathes into splendor and delight!'

'A young wizard?' Svanhild asked, feigning surprise, 'I was told that wizards are always old and wise.' It was clear from Matista's look that the mention of wizards had touched a raw nerve.

An expression of undiluted fury stole over her face. In a fiery voice she hissed, 'The black plague smite their elders and vengeance on their order, flames to their monastery, grasshoppers to their gardens, mites in their undergarments, rat poison in the soup, arsenic in the potatoes.'

The speech became garbled at this point, for the sorceress' blood pressure had risen to frightening heights. This was just as well. The appalling maledictions that spewed forth on the wizard and his brethren in the Monastery of the Luminous Horizon were rather awful.

When her wrath had subsided one of the Gorghouls offered Matista a beverage. It had a calming influence. Once the flaming red on Matista's cheeks subsided, Svanhild asked nonchalantly.

'The wizard who caused the trouble, is he still at the Monastery?'

'Your innocence is charming my fair maiden', said Matista, the flames of her anger smothered for the time being.

'Yes, he who caused the trouble is still there, Isumatak they call him, Isumatak the Wise. His black hair turned white centuries ago. It is he who is the Father of the Order. Long ago he came down from the snow covered barren lands in the far north.'

A melancholy look stole into her eyes. 'I first saw him coming down from the mountains clad in a deerskin parka, a tall and handsome boy with dark eyes and long coal black locks, a large whalebone bow strung over his shoulder. I asked what he hoped to find in these foreign parts and he simply said he wanted to find the truth. Hopelessly naive of course. Impervious to my charms he refused an invitation to linger for a day or two. Weeks later, wizards from the Monastery found him wandering in the forest, starving and exhausted. I should have clapped a spell on him before he learned their tricks.'

'It was centuries ago, I had just cast the great spell which sent an entire Kingdom into doom and perdition. It was a moment of triumph, the highlight of my career. The King and his flock became the slaves of my Seven Counselors. Queen Netilda, I banished to a rock forlorn in ocean waves. I had reason to be pleased and planned a well deserved vacation. There beside the vessel I was about to board for a pleasure cruise, illumined by the sun's flaming rays, stood Isumatak. Isumatak, the young upstart wizard. In a voice distant and imperious, he addressed me, the woman who had offered him shelter in years of yore.'

'Matista, enchantress of the seventh sphere, great indeed are your powers and great the mischief you achieved. I cannot undo the evil of your spell and restore happiness to the land of gloom. That must be left to other times and to other powers, but I will mar a beauty that beguiles and leads astray the innocent. He raised his bow and spoke in the northern tongue.'

'My powers cannot undo this evil spell,
Matista's fatal beauty, my words can quell
Never will the sun's fair rays grace
the comeliness of that face'

'He raised his cursed staff, and I felt myself shrinking into the hunched and withered hag Neva. How I hate her! Abhor her! I despise the light of day! It is when the red rays of the setting sun give way to dusk that I rejoice. Truly I am the enchantress of the night. For those precious hours of darkness, beauty and power are mine. But come that dreadful hour when dawn's rosy gleam appears, then vanishes, all that I hold dear. The shape of that old hag Neva enshrouds my spirit and I fling my curses on that wizard.' She stomped her feet in anger and then rested on the fallen log.

'And when night falls, you regain your ancient splendor?' asked Svanhild

'So it is my child. But there I have a choice. I can remain Neva the old biddy through the night if occasion calls for it. Sometimes it is easier that way, and it spares me the terrible pain that I suffer every dawn!'

One slender hand supported her head when the rays of the full moon caught her ravishing face in a wisp of light. Svanhild trembled with excitement and fear, when she beheld a beauty that had led a thousand lovers to the threshold of doom.

She whispered, 'It must be terrible for a woman of great beauty, never to be seen and admired in the sun's golden light.'

'Say no more my child. That wizard Isumatak went too far. His black locks have turned white, but forget the great grief that he has wrought, I cannot. The day of reckoning is nigh. Before the year is spent, the Seven Lords will ride.'

A shriek of frightful laughter followed. Even the Gorghouls shrank back and the hooting of the great owls came to a sudden stop. Svanhild had noticed the sudden silence in the forest, but Matista in her excitement paid no heed. Moments later Svanhild could hear the swishing of great wings and the rustling of branches.

Solomon, Chief of the great Wood Owls had called for a meeting in a clearing among the pines. A large number of birds soared over the moonlit meadow and perched in the trees. When the swishing and the crackling of branches diminished, Solomon hooted for order and the birds squinted at their Chief. Meetings are infrequent, for owls have a dislike of authority. Yet, there had been an unsettling note in Solomon's call and when danger threatened the wise old birds knew that they had better work together.

'My noble feathered friends, fellow owls,' began Solomon, looking solemn enough to get their full attention. 'Nasty business is going on in our forest. The sorceress Matista has captured a maiden from the Land of the Swans.'

This was received with muffled hooting. The owls were freedom loving to a fault and the capture of anyone, especially a fair maiden, made a deep impression.

'Furthermore, my brethren, there are Gorghouls in the party.' The capture of an innocent maiden was sufficient to raise the ire of the great birds, but the mention of Gorghouls sent them into a frenzy of anger. They remembered too many tales of owl stew and other atrocities. Confirming the need for united action, they bowed to their commander.

Matista had taken a liking to Svanhild. It was not often that the sorceress had an opportunity to unburden her heart. Witches too have feelings! Svanhild had played her part well and Matista let down her guard.

Turning to Svanhild with a wily smile she mused, 'You are in the winning camp my lovely one. Come and travel with Matista to worlds beyond your wildest imagination.'

For moments Svanhild was entranced by the proposal, but the sight of the Gorghouls behind the trees brought her to her senses. She realized that she must get away before falling further under the spell of the incomparable witch.

A faint light behind the tree tops signaled the coming of dawn. Soon Matista fell into the deep slumber from which she would awaken at sunrise as the hag Neva, bereft of her magic powers and bewitching beauty until eventide.

The Gorghouls had been instructed to take special care of the pretty prisoner during this time. Two of the gruesome creatures sat on each side of Svanhild. The third wandered around the campsite, but not for long. A fierce owl dived down from behind and snapped off his tail. This was a wise move, for a swishing gorghoul tail with its fierce green spines can be a formidable weapon. The gorghoul jumped up in pain and looked horrified at the severed tail, neatly coiled on the ground. This was imprudent for the owls wasted no time and sunk their terrible talons into the Gorghouls' faces. Blinded and terrified they ran for their lives, owls clinging to their head and neck. Svanhild saw her chance and rushed away towards the river.

Over forty owls aroused to righteous anger are a fearful sight. They drove the scamps out of the forest and into the marshes. Soon the Gorghouls were sinking in mud up to their thighs. Solomon raised his great wings motioning to the flock that the attack was over. He nodded in a snobby sort of way to a group of vultures seated on the branch of a dead poplar. Before long moon shadows of jagged wings and long beaks could be seen circling the Gorghouls, as they wrestled themselves deeper and deeper into the swamp.

Solomon led the triumphant birds back to the forest. The owls were quick to return to their personal perches in a stand of old oaks. The ancient trees stood in the forest to which King Arcturus had granted them hereditary rights. Only Solomon and his Deputy Kasper returned to the site of the assault. They found Neva sitting on a log, owl feathers and bits of gorghoul tail covering the ground at her feet. She looked up at Solomon and spoke in a melancholy voice, 'Silly birds, why deprive an old woman of her youthful companion, what good will it do?'

Owls have a reputation for wisdom. For these sagacious birds being called silly was painful. They sat silently across from Neva, their yellow eyes, like sunlit wells, were deep and motionless.

Although owls have terribly poor eyesight in the light of day, they had certainly noticed the transformation of the lovely sorceress into an old biddy.

Being polite they refrained from staring at her.

Neva rose, cast a withering look at the two birds, shook her head and flew off towards her cottage.

'That was not a friendly look, Chief.'

'Nearly scorched my tail feathers Deputy.'

'She looks a striking beauty in the depth of night Chief.'

'That is all that matters Deputy. It is in the depth of night that we owls do our looking. Remember only night reveals true beauty, daylight is for common birds.'

'Very true Chief,' mumbled Kasper, awed by the indisputable logic of his superior.

13

Lake Of The Coloured Fishes

Solomon and Kasper winked at each other as Neva vanished into the distance. The great birds breathed a sigh of relief. Well they knew that Neva's powers during the light of day were severely clipped, however, one could never be certain.

'Well, well,' hooted Solomon. 'The old witch is out of commission, at least until sunset. It's a good thing that the wizards keep an eye on her. But we better move, Deputy, and check on little Svanhild. I shudder to think what could have happened to her while alone with those Gorghouls.'

Kasper thought deeply and looked wise as only owls can. When the awful possibilities had been contemplated, his mighty wings shivered and he hooted a somber tune in a very minor key.

They spread their wings and became airborne, flying close to the ground until they came to the little inlet. There seated on a boulder was Svanhild. Bewildered by the events, she was trying to decide if it had all had been a dream. The owls landing in front of her resolved any doubt and she thanked the great birds for saving her from the Gorghouls. They responded politely by stressing that it had been entirely their privilege. The owls perched on an old log by the water and warmed themselves in the morning sun.

Svanhild stroked the rich brown feathers of the owls, and softly sang the 'Song of Thanks', an old tradition in the Land of the Swans.

thanks is just a word
dropped with ease
and often heard

with darkness all around you
when monsters fling
and dragons spring
thank the friend who found you

then thanks flow deep below
in silver vessels
and gratitude bestows
a wreath with golden tassels

The owls looked solemn and thought profoundly. Their stern faces did not give way to the surge of feelings within but there was a deep vibrato in Solomon's hoot as he thanked Svanhild. Kasper secretly wiped a tear with his wing tip.

When Solomon looked down the shore of the lagoon he saw Patriot trotting towards them. Slim and Moose Martin followed close behind. Patriot had picked up Svanhild's scent and was leading them on her trail.

This was the time for the owls to exit with dignity intact. Their great arched wings swished and they became airborne over the lagoon, and rapidly gained the crown of a nearby pine. From their lofty perch they observed the reunion of Svanhild with her brother and friends.

Kasper had a dreamy look in his eyes and hooted softly, 'A wreath with golden tassels would look splendid on you Chief, it would enhance your prestige.' Quite right Kasper,' quoth Solomon, 'An owl Chief must present a grave image and a ceremonial headdress would add stature, nothing personal, just the office one occupies.'

'Quite so,' echoed Kasper, 'and I could wear it when acting as Deputy.'

'That is another matter,' observed Solomon gravely, 'One that will require deep thought.'

'Of course, Chief. Deep thought is the owl's way, is it not?'

Slim was overjoyed to see Svanhild safe, and the party hurried back to the campsite. Duckie and Ferdinand had seen them coming at a distance and set about making a pot of coffee and pancakes. Breakfast revived Svanhild and leaning comfortably against a rock warmed by the early sun, she related the events of the night.

A dead silence fell over her fellow wayfarers. They realized the horrible dangers the Swannemaid had faced. At first Ferdinand could not believe that Neva, the lovely old lady who had sweet talked him in the marketplace in Miranda, was the dazzling sorceress Matista by night.

It suddenly dawned on Ferdinand that this trip was beset by hidden dangers, and that even behind the faces of sweet old ladies, fearful powers might be hidden. He uttered a deep sigh, emptied the coffeepot into his mug, and lighting his pipe, settled himself comfortably against the trunk of a huge pine. Disillusion had been his lot in life and it was clear that the world was a dangerous place. But the warm sun on his face and the softly swirling smoke of his pipe blending with the aroma of pine needles put him in a philosophic frame of mind. There was no graceful way out of this adventure. On the other hand, he had been bored at the Manor and had rushed at the chance for glory. Yes, he had been hasty, very hasty. How had his ancestors coped with all the terrible battles that they fought? With nerves of steel no doubt. Perhaps his nervous system was more refined and highly evolved; prepared no longer for the crude vibrations of Groll fighting and the wiles of wicked witches.

He closed his eyes and to his mind came an image of Seraphim. Seraphim had a reputation for uncanny wisdom. On several occasions Aunt Erica had dragged him out to the Graceful Neck to hear a talk by the aged white haired Elf.

'Discovering the Hero within', Yes, that had been the title of the last talk that he had dozed through. The details had escaped him. Perhaps somewhere deep within, a hero did dwell. But how to coach him to the surface?

If only Seraphim were here, he would have liked to ask a few questions, but Seraphim never took kindly to folks who dozed when he sowed his pearls of wisdom. Nonetheless the idea of a hero living inside was intriguing.

Unaware that he had put his hand on the sword by his side, a blue sheen caught his eye. For a moment, the mantle of fear that had rested on his shoulders lifted. Yes, Erica had spoken about it. The edge of the sword was endowed with magic when wielded by the hand of the just. He raised it by the haft and let it drop on a birch branch and without resisting the path of the steel, the wood parted.

Moose looked at him and read his mind. 'None of us was made for this sort of work Ferdinand. It was handed to us, so to speak, and we must make the best of it.'

'And why not?' piped Duckie, undaunted.

'A glorious adventure,' whispered Svanhild, who had regained her natural buoyancy.

'The immortality of youth,' mused the Marquis. A smile spread over his face as he inhaled the last breath of consoling smoke. He got up, knocked the ashes out of his pipe and began packing his belongings.

Duckie had washed the dishes in the lagoon and carried up some water to quench the fire. Moose was already in the boat stowing packs in their proper places and wiping dew off the seats. He pushed the boat from shore until she floated free, holding on by the rear painter. Svanhild waded quickly into the sparkling water and climbed aboard. She stretched out in the bow and as she looked up she saw the two great owls amidst the rustling leaves of a tall poplar. Solomon and Kasper dropped from their perch and soared overhead. Slim was startled by the shadows that crossed the water but Svanhild caught a winsome wink before the birds sailed across the lagoon and vanished into a clump of pines.

Ferdinand shouldered his pack and climbed aboard, he felt better for his meditation and enthusiastically placed himself behind one of the oars. Slim grabbed the other. Duckie, Svanhild and Patriot rested comfortably in the forward section. On the still waters of the lagoon, the skiff moved swiftly. Once they reached the Sanctus and turned north, the current slowed them down. They pulled harder at the oars, anxious to reach the junction with the Tristana. Moose scanned the wide expanse of river. In the distance, clouds drifted over the water. A change of weather was coming.

'Captain Martin,' asked Duckie, will we be coming soon to the marshes where the nymph Marsha lives?'

'Duckie, old tales speak of the nymph of the Tristana, but there have been no reports in recent times. We will sail up the narrower channels that cross the marshes on the south side.'

'Why avoid the Tristana if the nymph be only legend?' Duckie wanted to know.

'Just in case, just in case', muttered Moose.

'The prejudices that superstitious folks have broadcast about this lady of the marshes!' exclaimed the Marquis. It may be slander and prejudice that have ruined her reputation. Beauty always arouses suspicion. This lady of the marshes may turn out to be quite a decent type. I shall be pleased to meet with her and negotiate safe passage through her marshes.'

'And a handsome offer it is, Sir Ferdinand,' laughed Moose. 'I just hope it won't come to that.'

Moose Martin pulled his bosun hat farther down his forehead to keep the sun out of his eyes while scanning the river and both banks. If the weather changed it might take them another day or two before reaching the Tristana and there was much about which to be concerned. Matista could do little harm by day but at night her secret powers returned and she might have sent a message to the Dark Lords. Likely they would be watched.

Slim changed places with Duckie and sat beside Svanhild, who was still asleep. He pulled out his pocket knife and began working on a bow. As he sat carving the young yew tree that he had cut at the campsite, his thoughts wandered over the events of the last two days. No, he had no regrets, perilous as the journey would likely be. The Dark Lords had cast a wide web over the land and even in Swanneland, Rovers had won over some people in the community by handing out profitable contracts. Matista was a mystery, very dangerous, and yet he had a secret longing to see her by moonlight. They would soon reach the marshes and begin the long climb up the mountains to the stronghold of the Dwarves. Yet much could happen between here and the safety of the dwarf village.

A slip of his knife scraped his index finger and interrupted his stream of thought. He cast a quick glance over the water and along the shore. Just miles of cedar forest and occasional clumps of poplar, nothing untoward at first glance. The third time that Slim's keen eyes scanned the dense forest, he spotted a faint fleck of purple in one of the cedar trees. Hidden in the branches was a merewing. It was the purple beak that gave him away. Slim kept quiet until they were well beyond the cedar grove where the black bird with the amazingly wide wings had perched.

'Moose just half a mile back we passed a merewing in a cedar grove. I could tell by the purple beak.'

'A real merewing,' shouted Svanhild and Duckie, who only knew about the birds from legends. 'Sensible that you did not speak at the time,' said Moose Martin, 'He may think he went unseen.'

'I really wonder at times why the Dark Lords are so concerned about the five of us traveling up stream,' said Slim.

'It is fear my son, fear that makes them suspicious of anyone who has not fallen under their spell or who travels beyond the borders of the Kingdom.'

'Perhaps it is the fear that the golden plate, engraved with the ancient spell, will yet be found,' ventured Slim.

'Lost in the dim depths of time I fear,' mused Moose. A somber look fell over his face. 'And gone with it is the hope of an incantation to break the power of the Lords.'

'Do not lose heart, Captain,' said Svanhild in her lilting voice. 'Visualize victory as possible and all of us will hold that image in our mind's eye. How else could it possibly happen?'

Those words rang true. Her luminous eyes transfixed the old skipper and a cheery look returned. 'Heave to my hearties', his heavy bass sang out and as if their life depended on it, Duckie and the Marquis pulled at the oars. The bow wave waxed and the skiff shot forward.

Far, far off to the south, Slim caught the black silhouette of the merewing as it sailed towards the boundary of the Kingdom. He held his tongue, for there was enough to cope with for the moment. He bent over his new bow and notched the ends before stringing it.

Majestic pines lined the shore, casting a shade on the little vessel plying the channel. Beaver lodges abounded and deer moved silently among the pines. Slim was touched by the beauty passing before his eyes. When they reached a safe haven where he would be able work for a stretch of time, he would paint the scenes from memory. Perhaps they would overwinter in the mountain stronghold of the Dwarves. Then there would be time to write in his diary and paint the many images stored in his mind.

Ferdinand rowed with all his might. He had experienced some anxious moments and physical exercise relieved his fears. Recounting some events of the last few days, there had been much for which to be grateful. The meals had been better than one might have hoped for on an ordinary camping trip. The stay in Miranda had been absolutely delightful and there were still some provisions left in the basket, Annabelle's lovely daughters had stowed in the skiff. The Marquis knew fortune had smiled on him and he fervently hoped that it would continue to do so.

Moose, sitting at the helm, cast a concerned look at the sky. Clouds scudded across, turning the sun into a diffuse patch of light.

Larger and darker clouds rose from the horizon and a stiff breeze sprang up.

He steered closer to the shore. Now the oars were almost touching stands of bulrushes. The sky quickly darkened and rain began to fall. They stopped for a moment to put on their rain gear and fighting a strong current and headwind, carried on.

When a large island loomed ahead Moose steered the vessel into the right channel, hoping that indeed it was an island. The water became calmer and they found shelter from wind and rain. The channel turned inland and what they had hoped was an island appeared now to be a peninsula. They decided to follow the protected channel and look for a campsite.

Dense forest shielded them on both sides and Moose was grateful that they had left the exposed waters of the Sanctus. The channel seemed to peter out and they found themselves in a narrow passage, surrounded by reeds and willow bushes. Duckie and Ferdinand were now poling the craft through the dense vegetation. A few minutes later they were back in open water and after rounding a headland, a wide lake opened before them. Pine, spruce and cedar ringed the shore.

Dark clouds still drifted overhead but occasional shafts of sunlight touched the black waters. A strange magical feeling was in the air. For a few moments the rowers leaned on their oars and drifted with the wind. Leaning over the side Svanhild peered into the dark waters, now lit by rays of sunlight. Deep below, swimming through reflections of pine and hemlock, were schools of purple and orange fish.

Everyone was peering in the waters, fascinated by the moving spectacle of colours. Drops of rain woke them from their reverie. They sat up and looked around.

'This is the Lake of the Coloured Fishes that Ensten and Ulrik mentioned,' exclaimed Svanhild, 'The homestead of the Gnomes cannot be far.'

Moose was first to catch the scent, a whiff of wood smoke. He looked towards the far end of the lake and saw a fine column of white smoke rising into the air.

'There can be no doubt,' said the old Ferry Captain, 'The homestead of the banished Gnomes lies yonder.' The oars dropped back into the water and they made straight for the column of smoke. Before long an outline of buildings appeared on the horizon.

When they reached the end of the lake, they could see a barn and several sheds, surrounded by gardens and orchards. Nearby, to the right stood a little chapel built entirely of logs. Duckie and Ferdinand let the oars trail in the water and the skiff glided silently towards shore. Near the tiny chapel, a log cabin, half hidden by the forest came in sight.

Moose remembered Ensten telling the story of the Gnomes Oarflake and Ambrosia. 'The spirit forces have guided us to an oasis in this wild forlorn land,' he mused.

'Extraordinary!' Ferdinand called out, 'This may well be the only sign of human life between Miranda and the Tristana. Just as we finished the last of the sandwiches, we find this delightful looking homestead in the wilderness.'

Svanhild listened attentively. Strains of a hymn carried over the mirror surface of the lake. A voice was chanting in the little chapel.

To hear the music drift over the water, here in the middle of the wilderness was so astonishing. A spell fell over the travelers. The skiff drifted closer to shore and now the singing was loud and clear. The ancient hymn, praising the wonders of creation, was well known to all. The music filled the air with magic. The chanting seemed to reach up to another world and for a moment all fear and dread vanished.

Svanhild recalled, 'Old Martha spoke about Oarflake and the building of the chapel as an act of atonement.'

'It must have been hard for a Gnome to give up mining gold' whispered Slim, wiping a tear with his sleeve.

'Gnomes are deeply attached to the earth and its treasures,' reflected Moose, as skillfully he slid the bow of the skiff upon the sandy beach, 'Now he is mining another kind of treasure.'

Ferdinand was just about to make a profound statement about the melancholy nature of the earthly journey when Oarflake emerged from the chapel and strode towards the beach. This was certainly no melancholy Gnome striding cheerfully towards the shore and greeting them with a voice that rang with laughter.

'My friends welcome, welcome. No visitors have set foot on this shore since the ice left the lake this spring. Come to the house and be our guests. Tonight shall be a banquet to celebrate. Ambrosia, Ambrosia come hither.'

There was a sudden movement in the raspberry patch and they could see Ambrosia running between the bushes which formed a canopy above her.

A roly poly figure emerged from the rows of tall raspberries and rushed down the hill. A red pointed hat sat on the white wavy locks resting on the shoulders of her blue frock. She walked onto the beach and heartily welcomed the little band.

Patriot had jumped ashore and could be heard barking at the edge of the clearing. 'He has picked up the scent of the grey wolves,' laughed Oarflake, 'They will not harm him and he will soon befriend them. Come friends let us go to the house for rest and merriment.'

'Rest and merriment,' the Marquis whispered to himself. The very words worked like a powerful restorative on the nobleman, exhausted as he was from a long and vigorous row.

Oarflake led the way to the log house and held the door as they walked in. The house was spacious inside and had attractive log furniture. Along the walls were rough hewn benches and before long they were comfortably seated. Ambrosia lit the stone hearth and a cozy glow chased the late afternoon chill.

Oarflake and Ambrosia wanted to know everything about their journey and Moose related their adventures. Oarflake nodded gravely. Yes, he knew about the threat to the Kingdom. Ambrosia was not surprised to hear about the double life of Neva, the soothsayer in Miranda. The Esterians had had their suspicions.

In winter Ulrik and Ensten had traveled hither. The Great Grey had pulled their long sled swiftly across forest trails and frozen lakes. The journey had taken less than two days. What a joy it had been to see the kind Esterians arrive in the lonely winter hours. They had brought much news and had asked Oarflake and Ambrosia to report any sightings of merewings or servants of the Dark Lords.

Svanhild knew she could confide in their kind hosts and told them about the Golden Goose and the shriveled biddy Neva, whose bell toned voice had rung a note of dissonance. When she came to her encounter with Matista, Ambrosia put her arm around Svanhild's shoulder.

'My dear girl here you are safe,' comforted Ambrosia, 'The Great Grey watch over us.'

Moose continued the story, with Duckie piping in here and there. Slim described the Swan ballet in Miranda and the Marquis praised the reception they had received in the small lumber town.

'Thank you for sharing this with us,' said Oarflake, 'We must all oppose the evil that threatens the Kingdom. No doubt you heard the story of our banishment. There is little that we can do here in the wilderness. Alas, our banishment is for life and I cannot join my fellow Gnomes in the fight for freedom. Here we can only keep watch and report to the freemen of Esteria our observations. The Great Grey carry messages back and forth to Esteria.

The Esterians have tracked enemy scouts for years. They keep close watch on events.'

Duckie cast a glance at the weapons hanging on the wall. They looked frightfully fierce and he knew the Gnome meant business.

As he spoke again, a veil of sorrow fell over Oarflake's features.

'Now you know the story of my crime and banishment and I welcome the opportunity to atone. The fire of remorse has burnt to ashes and I have found peace. The cosmic spirit has touched my soul and daily I offer thanks in the chapel. It is a terrible thing for a Gnome to steal gold dust, but I was young at the time.

'That is enough Oarflake, don't live through it again,' soothed Ambrosia.

Dusk settled over the homestead. Slim looked outside and caught sight of Patriot flanked by two grey wolves. He was wagging his tail and seemed pleased with his new found friends.

'The Great Grey are always close,' Ambrosia reassured them. She looked at her guests comfortably seated, their faces lit by the fire. As they dozed off one by one, she smiled. This was the time to cook a hearty meal, and the larder of the Gnomes was well supplied. Ambrosia opened a trapdoor in the floor and went into the root cellar to fetch provisions and a couple of bottles of Oarflake's dandelion wine.

14

Journey Through The Marshes

Darkness descended upon the homestead of Oarflake and Ambrosia. A pale moon illumined the sturdy log cabin set against a background of pine and cedars. The wolves and Patriot were draped on the front lawn fast asleep. Ambrosia smiled at the sight. She knew that at any unusual sound or scent they would spring into action.

In the kitchen, the slumbering figures on the benches began to stir.

Ferdinand's eye caught the outline of a bumbleberry pie being pushed into the brick oven behind the hearth. Stuffing his pipe with some of the tobacco that Oarflake had put out on the table, he went to the fireplace for a light.

Leaning comfortably against the rough hewn logs he blew rings of blue smoke. The philosopher within began to speak. Indeed these Gnomes were fine people. He had never realized that these small creatures could be so hospitable and prepare scrumptious meals. Were he to return from this journey in one piece and with his nervous system intact, he should use his influence to put in a good word with the Gnome Sacred Council of Elders. Perhaps this decree of perpetual banishment could be rescinded. It was a noble thought, worthy of a Marquis of the Blood.

Svanhild was helping Ambrosia and querying her about life in the wilderness. Ambrosia told Svanhild of Oarflake's conviction, thirty-three years ago, by the Sacred Council. The pain and humiliation Oarflake had suffered and the shock when the sentence of perpetual banishment was pronounced. Then came the dreadful journey in the middle of winter to the forests at the bottom of the Finnian Range. Had it not been for the Esterians and the Great Grey, they would have perished in the deep snow. Swinging their double edged axes, Ensten and Ulrik quickly had built a cozy log cabin.

'They saved our lives my dear. In the little chapel, Oarflake and I pray daily for our friends from Esteria. These times are filled with danger and Esteria is close to the land of the red earth where the Seven rule.'

Svanhild felt that she could open her heart to Ambrosia. She told her all about her encounter with the enchantress Matista and her rescue by the owls.

Ambrosia cast her a caring glance, 'That was a narrow squeak my peach. It is true the owls are brave, very brave when their sensibilities are offended.' Ambrosia picked up a wooden ladle and stirred the gravy.

'Ensten knew about the old biddy Neva. A sleeper she is, living quietly in Miranda for more than twenty years. A few years ago, trouble started on the border. It was then that she began to stir and we learned about her nocturnal powers. Ensten and Ulrik told us about her. They had learned of her secret powers from the Monks and Wizards at the Monastery in Esteria. There is also a Convent in Esteria, the House of the Sisters of the Third Woe. Never get a word out of them, silent as the tomb. Imagine, they are not allowed to talk!' Ambrosia shook her head and stirred the bubbling stew. Svanhild could hear her muttering, 'Not allowed to talk. What has the good Lord given us a voice for?'

'Our voice can get us into trouble,' reflected Svanhild, 'Things can blurt out so quickly, often we regret what we have said and feel foolish afterwards.'

'If we didn't make a fool of our selves betimes, we would never know how foolish we are. That is how we learn my maid'

'Ambrosia,' said Svanhild, 'Your friends Ensten and Ulrik have helped you out so often. Have they ever talked to you about Isumatak, the Abbot of the Monastery in the deep forests of Esteria?'

'They have not my love but I do know Isumatak has been there since time out of mind. Some of the Monks are also Wizards and learn magic spells and all, but seldom do they intervene in worldly matters. Very holy they are, the Monks of the Luminous Horizon. That is the name of their order you know.'

'Yet Isumatak, their Abbot', reflected Svanhild, 'Clipped a spell on the enchantress.'

'Indeed he did my lassie. It was the fire of youth. He was young and inexperienced and not yet fully steeped in the discipline of monastic life.'

'It must have slipped out,' said Svanhild thoughtfully.

'It did, it did so buttercup,' mumbled Ambrosia with a telling wink at the silver haired beauty by her side.

Oarflake raised a large terracotta vessel and poured wine into silver beakers. Then he lit the tall candles in the wrought iron candelabra on the harvest table.

Oarflake invited all to stand and hold hands while he spoke words of praise and gratitude to the Cosmic Spirit for bringing the company to his table. They took their seats on the benches and helped themselves to the wonderful spread.

Revived by rest and warmed by the gnome couple's hospitality, good cheer returned to the company. Oarflake sat at the end of the table flanked by Moose and Ferdinand. Wine beakers were filled again and again and tongues loosened. Duckie got up to bring Patriot and his newfound friends a large bowl of bones that Ambrosia had saved.

Once the mirth had subsided, Oarflake turned to Moose and asked about the journey ahead. Moose told him about their plans to trek up the Finnian Range in order to find the Dwarf, Smithereen. A frown appeared on Oarflake's forehead. 'Captain you spent most of your life on the river, surely stories of the nymph Marsha must have reached you.'

'Many a tall tale of that fair lady was told by travelers from afar,' laughed Moose raising his beaker of wine. 'But even if there were a grain of truth in the myth, we will turn south before we reach the Tristana and sail up one of the smaller channels to give the domain of the Queen of the marshes a wide berth.'

'Perhaps, perhaps,' muttered Oarflake,

'Oarflake,' remarked Slim suddenly, 'Moose told the story of the Dark Lords and their fear of a golden plate. Legend tells us of an incantation encrypted on its rim. If intoned by an elven child it will undo the power of the Seven. Is it true that Gnomes have a sixth sense for the presence of gold?'

Oarflake nodded gravely. 'Yes, my friend and master of the dancing swans, it is true. A strange and irresistible force draws us to the noble metal but of the golden tablet and the incantation I have not heard before. It is true that long ago secret spells were often encrypted in gold. Many of these have been lost for centuries and it is unlikely they will be found. Throughout the ages, mud slides, lava streams, spring tides and other natural disasters have wiped out villages and outposts. Gnomes like to dig for artifacts but if gold tablets had been found we would have heard about it. Nevertheless, other Gnomes must be alerted about a possible gold tablet. I will send a message to Ulrik and Ensten and ask them to send the news on to the Elders. I, myself, will seek for clues.'

'We will seek for clues, my long bearded partner,' interjected Ambrosia, smiling at the guests, 'I too get goose bumps all over whenever I am within miles of nuggets, rich in shiny gold.'

'Quite right my love, I meant the two of us.' A grin spread across the Gnome's face. 'In winter the Great Grey pull our sled through the deep forest snow and once on the frozen marshes, they move like lightning and we have to hold on for dear life,' he laughed. 'Often we cross the border into the forbidden land of the Seven. Ambrosia makes notes of all that we see and hear and the wolves carry the news to Esteria. If ill befall you in the marshes and you end up in the domain of the nymph Marsha, send a message Captain Martin. Once the marshes freeze, we can travel thither by wolf sled.'

'When winter comes, we will be far beyond the marshes, in the high country of the Dwarves,' said Moose with a smile.'

'The nymph Marsha does not concern us,' said Ferdinand, blowing a ring of smoke, 'The unfortunate lady may have been abused in childhood and now vents her anger on unsuspecting travelers. A role model of a kind and an upright male might do wonders.'

'Fiddlesticks,' sputtered Ambrosia, 'Spiders will spin webs and witches fair, set their snares. Watch your step, Sir Ferdinand. If, heaven forbid, you should meet the enchantress of the marshes, do not waste words. While you can, make your escape!'

The Marquis listened politely to the warning but he seemed not convinced. These Gnomes had been isolated from the mainstream of society and probably were not familiar with new thoughts on the consequences of child abuse. Kindness and understanding might work wonders with the maligned lady.

The Marquis drew on his pipe and watched rings of smoke rise in the candle light. His mind wandered off and he saw himself seated by the side of the fair nymph of the marshes, offering spiritual counsel.

The laughter and banter around the table called Ferdinand back to the here and now. Lifting his wineglass he proposed a toast. 'To Ambrosia and Oarflake, to the home that has been a refuge to the weary traveler, a beacon of light in this dark forest.'

As the company clinked their beakers, the Marquis looked Ambrosia and Oarflake in the eye. Laughter and gentle banter went on until a veil of drowsiness fell over the company.

Oarflake, seeing his guests nodding and dozing at the table, spread rugs on the floor. One by one, they got up and stretched their weary limbs on the padding that he had provided.

Slim watched the light of the flames dancing on the ceiling, dissolving into dancing swans and maidens singing. And then a single voice, wistful, wondrous, melancholy with foreboding, soared high above the maidens' chant.

The morning sun caught Slim's face. He woke with a start and for a moment, fear lingered in his breast. He rubbed the sleep out of his eyes, rose to see dawn cast a golden sheen over lake and forest and smiled when he recalled his dream. The tricks we play on ourselves.

Ambrosia already had lit the hearth and was stirring a steaming pot of porridge. 'The dancing master is the first to catch dawn's light. Would you like a coffee, my dear?'

'With pleasure Ambrosia. A cup of coffee will clear my mind from last night's dream.'

'Dream? master Slim. You wouldn't care to tell mother Ambrosia your dream. The gift of soothsaying came to me when I was but a mite.'

'Dear Ambrosia, strange and wonderful voices sang to me, maidens blonde and beautiful danced a circle round and round. Then a single voice soared and chanted, enthralling, threatening.'

'Master Slim,' said Ambrosia firmly, 'it was the voices from the marshes singing in your dream. Avoid the Tristana. Danger hides in the wetlands. Many have vanished there without a trace. The nymph Marsha and her handmaidens rule the marshes. I know the young folks do not believe the lore of yore. If you hear voices chanting Slim, take heed, take heed.'

Moose, the Marquis and Svanhild, sat down at the table and soon were filling up on hot gruel. Duckie, who had taken Patriot for a romp in the garden joined the others. Oarflake poured the coffee but there was no lingering over second cups. Moose was anxious to push off and reach the marshes before nightfall.

As they were packing up, Ambrosia's blue eyes shot Slim a glance. Slim knew that she wanted him to mind her words. When she caught him smiling, Ambrosia looked relieved.

Oarflake and Ambrosia walked down onto the dock to wave farewell. Tears flowed down their cheeks. Visitors were precious and they knew that the wayfarers' mission was perilous. High above, Svanhild descried two great birds circling. They were too distant for recognition but in her heart she knew that Kasper and Solomon were near.

It was indeed the Chief of the owls and his Deputy. They had been so taken by Svanhild that in order to check on their protege, they had diverged from their usual flight path.

The mornings were becoming cooler and a curtain of mist covered the water. Moose skillfully guided the skiff across the lake into the channel through the marshes, and then found the narrows leading to the Sanctus.

White clouds sailed across the blue sky, portending a change of weather.

Flocks of geese flew southward and a few stands of birch and poplar showed glints of golden yellow. A stiff headwind slowed the vessel's speed. Ferdinand and Slim were at the oars, straining against the cutting wind. Only Patriot enjoyed the wet spray splashing over the gunwales.

Towards evening the sky turned slate grey and a fine rain began to fall. They had covered but half the distance to the Tristana and exhausted from battling wind and water, they looked for a campsite.

Ferdinand knew that his luck had run out and that life was dropping quickly below the comfort zone. Slim sat in the bow grim faced, scouting for a spot to land. The trees along the shore were shorter now and glistened with a film of water. A profusion of bulrushes lined the shore. The Sanctus became narrower at this point and even through the mist they could see trees on the opposite shore.

When a small island came into view they lost no time making a landfall. Wet and tired they clambered ashore. To build a fire, Slim set about gathering birch bark and wood. Within a short while they were drying their damp gear by a warm blaze.

They found some deer meat that Ambrosia had put under the front seat of the skiff. Slim skewered the meat over the flames and Svanhild scooped spoonfuls of coffee grains into a pot of cold water and hung it from a tripod over the fire. Ferdinand, slumped against a tree trunk, opened his eyes and mumbled something about the rocky road to heroism. The leaping flames and the smell of coffee brought some consolation. After supper they built a lean-to and covered it with cedar branches. Before going to sleep Slim piled heavy logs on the fire to make it last the night.

At midnight Moose woke. He heard a soft moaning coming from the marshes. He got up and gazed over the fenland. A soft moonlight shone through the rising mist, but he could not make out anything unusual. After a while the moaning subsided and Moose crawled back into his sleeping bag. 'Strange,' he mused, 'the lament of the marshes, what deep secret dwells in those endless fens?' He made up his mind to rise early and lead the company well beyond the wetlands by sunset.

Morning revealed a grey rainscape, yet the embers were still glowing. Slim quickly brought the fire back to life and put on the coffee. Breakfast was a skimpy affair. After washing the dishes in the Sanctus, they pushed off for the Tristana.

The wind had slackened, but a fine rain kept them damp and clammy. The forest on the shore was thin and stunted, and the fenlands stretched for miles.

By afternoon they could see water meadows filled with rushes and patches of blue and white flowers. Narrow channels snaked through the reeds. Moose was at the helm scanning the shore for the junction with the Little Tristana, the small tributary that emptied into the Sanctus several miles before the Tristana itself. For some time a small flock of wild swans, staying just ahead of them, had been following the shore line. Slim kept an eye on them. Suddenly they vanished into a stand of reeds and bulrushes. Moose steered for shore and they all looked closely for an opening in the dense stands of reeds. They could hear now the trumpeting of the swans farther inland and knew that there must be a narrow lead.

'This could be the beginning of the Little Tristana,' said Moose, 'It has not been used for navigation for years and the delta may have filled up with reeds.'

Svanhild was the first to see the wild swans again, emerging from a mass of rushes. Moose pointed the bow toward the place that Svanhild indicated. Duckie and Ferdinand stood up and began poling the craft through the dense marsh-plants. It was hard going for awhile, but soon the channel widened and they could row again.

'The Little Tristana no doubt,' cheered Duckie.

'I don't like it,' said Moose, 'The weeds and rushes have almost blocked the channel and to get through to the boundary country we may have to divert to the Tristana proper.'

They rowed for awhile, until the channel funneled to a mere trickle and once more they used the oars to pole the craft forward. After half an hour of poling and pulling oars out of the mud, a sound of rushing water could be heard, babbling and splashing. A new channel veering to the north east came into sight. Moose moved the helm and the lively water catching the boat whisked her into a new direction.

It was a narrow passage, no more than seven feet across, but a surging deep current moved the little craft swiftly forward.

There was no turning back. As the little vessel plowed through the marshes, huge stands of bulrushes flashed by and startled water fowl rose from their nesting grounds. Svanhild, standing in the bow, was exhilarated by the sense of speed and the fleeting water meadows daubed with blue and purple lilies.

'Uncanny current,' muttered Moose, a deep frown tracing his forehead. We have no longer any say where this boat is going. She has a mind of her own.'

They were drawn deeper and deeper into the marshes and the sinking sun cast a deep orange over fens and water meadows.

A few clumps of poplar were silhouetted against a dark sky. The current abated, the channel widened and soon they found themselves drifting on a lake. Just as Ferdinand was about to settle the oars back into the locks, a scent wafted over the waters, Svanhild picked it up first, an exotic, fragrant perfume that enveloped the lake. A smile spread over Ferdinand's face.

'A delightful place to shelter,' mused the Marquis. The deep frown on Moose's face vanished and he seemed pleased.

The vessel drifted towards a strip of soft sand, still warm from the summer sun. Slim jumped out and pulled the vessel up. He too was enthralled by the enticing scent but in his mind's eye he saw Ambrosia and the warning in her eyes. He whispered to Svanhild, 'We must take heed, this perfume bodes ill.'

By the time that all were seated on the sandy beach, still warm from the day's sunshine, the sky had turned deep purple and the moon had risen over the marshland. The men in the company felt exhilarated and the beguiling fragrance endowed all their senses with a wondrous appreciation of the beauty of the wetlands. Yet Svanhild's mood was not affected and Patriot was driven frantic by the scent, burrowing his muzzle into the sand.

In the stillness of the night, voices drifted over the wetlands. Moose, Ferdinand and Ducky stood up and peered over the moonlit marshes. They espied a narrow trail winding among the water gardens. As if drawn by an invisible force they wandered down the path. Exquisite flowers glistened in the moonlight.

Slim rose and caught up with them. How lovely was the view and how bewitching the scent! Surging within him was a deep longing to follow his friends. Before he could take another step forward, Svanhild seized his hand and called out, 'For God's sake Slim, come back, peril dwells within these marshes!'

Reluctantly Slim remained by her side. Svanhild could still see Moose, Ferdinand and Duckie silhouetted in the moonlight slowly moving farther into the wetlands. She shouted to them at the top of her voice. For a moment they hesitated and looked back. Then a distant sound drifted over the shimmering marshes. The voices of maidens singing could be heard and soaring high above was a queenly voice, setting reeds atrembling and hearts aflutter. Enthralled the trio moved deeper into the marshes.

Svanhild hanging on to Slim, watched with growing despair as her friends wandered farther into the gardens. Even Slim with Ambrosia's warning bells ringing in his ears was enchanted. It was only Svanhild's firm grasp that held him back. Svanhild called out again to Moose and the others, but no answer came. She stood up still holding onto Slim and scanning the darkness. There was no trace of them. The marshes had swallowed them up.

Moose Martin felt scales falling from his eyes. Scenes from his youth came back and feelings of long forgotten delight rushed through his veins. The Marquis was thrilled by the perfume and the beauty of the water gardens they were passing through. The enchantment had escaped young Duckie, but spurred on by a sense of loyalty and adventure, he followed his master.

A girl's voice sweet, soft and enchanting could be heard nearby. It drew the three yet farther away from the beach. Then appeared a white figure silhouetted against a purple sky. The scent had put them in a dreamlike state and they walked towards the graceful white maiden beckoning. They came closer and she motioned them to follow. Treading in her light and graceful footsteps, they wandered deeper and deeper into the night.

Strange and wonderful fragrances drifted across their path and the moon shed a soft light on exquisite flowers beds. Raised paths crossed these gardens and arched wooden bridges spanned the many small leads and canals. Bewitched by the beauty of the gardens and the charm of their guide, they walked on. Domes appeared among the gardens and high fountains reached up catching moon rays in a fine spray. At the base of a large dome, the guide raised her hand and a heavy carved door opened silently. They entered the palace of the Queen of the Marshes.

Svanhild, still holding on to Slim's hand stood on the moonlit beach. The singing had faded and only a faint scent remained. The spell was broken and Slim looked at Svanhild with fear in his eyes.

'The nymph of the marshes, no myth is she,' breathed Svanhild.

'There is no sign of Moose, Ferdinand or Duckie,' sighed Slim peering into the distant fens. Then his ear caught the sound of a distant lingering voice, sweet and sorrowful and a sense of deep regret came over him and a longing to experience the enchantment and to see the beautiful Queen of the Marshes. In a strange way he felt left out. Svanhild seemed to read his thoughts.

'You might never return Slim,' whispered Svanhild, pressing his hand.

The singing stopped and the scent was gone. Slim gathered some dry reeds and made a small fire to boil water for tea. Svanhild spread reeds on the sand and with a pot of tea between them, they sat side by side, 'Your determination and Ambrosia's warning saved me from the spell,' Slim sighed.

'You seemed reluctant to be saved,' smiled Svanhild.

For a moment they remained silent. The only sound was the rustling of the reeds in the cold night air. Patriot was asleep. Slim raised his head and turned into the wind. A somber fugue-like sound seemed to be rising from the marshes. Svanhild stood up and looked towards the water gardens, where the whimpering voices seemed to originate. A green sheen was visible in the distance and here and there patches of green popped up at water level.

The deep moaning drew closer and yellow spots could be seen in the green patches. The yellow spots appeared in pairs and Slim realized that they were eyes, yellow bulbous eyes glowing in the water meadows. The moaning sounded like the base pipes of an organ. It was the green creatures with the yellow eyes that voiced the haunting notes. The bodies of the strange froglike beings were buried in mud. The upper part of their faces showed above the swampy surface. A sense of horror seized Svanhild. The yellow eyes turned towards them but the creatures could not articulate speech. Yet, trying to draw attention, they filled the night with their melancholy humming.

'Who are these mudsprites,' wondered Slim, 'Their moaning breaks my heart.'

Svanhild knelt down close to one pair of yellow eyes and listened carefully. The sprite, looking at her with his luminous golden eyes, raised himself on a sunken stump. Half seated on this platform his froggy legs still under water, he managed to speak.

'My name is Theophilus. Before I was trapped by the nymph of the marshes I was a prosperous trader in Lambarina. Now I am a frog-like creature, prisoner seventy nine. For seven years we have been enslaved in the marshes, building dykes and water gardens for the Queen.

We, too, were travelers through the marshes, unaware of hidden dangers when the voices of the maidens drew us to the underwater palace. We were overcome by the perfume, enthralled by the beauty of the gardens and went down the garden path. The underwater palace is magnificent. Black marble paths lined with flowering bushes wind among fountains and birds of brilliant colour fly freely through the passageways. It was in the great dining hall that first we sighted the Queen, a small graceful figure with brilliant sharp features, her long black hair with a tinge of white falling over her shoulders and blending with her dark velvet dress. The bewitching creature wore no shoes and her bare feet were white as virgin snow. With grace and lightness she tiptoed over the marble, gravity itself seemed defeated. She seated herself on a carved pedestal and bade us welcome.'

"You have come to a place of rest my weary travelers, rest from the harsh marshes and the weary ways of the world. Here, you will escape the toil and boredom of your humdrum lives."

'For nineteen days we were her guests of honour. Music, wine, singing and dancing maidens were all around. The gardens displayed flowers in every colour of the rainbow and the fountains spouted jets of water. What beauty! What delights! At night we danced in the light of the full moon. The thrill of youth had returned to our hearts! Alas, alas, the illusion did not last.

The Queen's honey-tongued words stroked our vanity. For her, we would do anything. The snow white feet dancing on the marble-black entranced us.'

The mudsprite wiped a tear of remorse from his round yellow eyes. Slim winced and Svanhild wept, wept for the fate of their friends and the mudsprites.

The green slimy thing slid back into the water and with great effort continued his tale. 'Somewhere deep within I knew the spirit of independence had died. Slowly we were reeled in.

It was new moon, the nineteenth day of our stay and we were seated amongst the maidens in the banquet hall enjoying all the sweets that life could bestow. Suddenly she entered, adorned in a sweeping gown black as a moonless night, her green eyes shooting fire and the lovely white feet gliding across the marble. Her raised right hand clutched a golden wand.

A shiver ran across my spine. What had caused the terrible change in our lovely hostess. That voice ever gentle and crystal clear, spoke now in hoarse and hissing sounds, scattering the very birds that floated on the pool before her. All the birds but one flew away to hide in the shrubs. A brave pelican, intent to see and hear what happened, remained. This bird stayed calm when the Queen's eyes caught fire and she addressed me and my travel companions.

"You have expressed your devotion and gratitude to the Queen of the marshes. Now you shall prove it. You have admired my gardens and fountains. Now you will build and maintain them. Terraces and bridges you will build and you will beautify the gardens, to please me and my Seven Masters."

When she mentioned those Seven, a wave of fear engulfed us. Next she sang the incantation that would end our life as we knew it.

"Anista trima, vulcano bestami," sang out the triumphant voice of the evil sorceress. "Till the end of your days, you will serve the Queen of the Marshes."

Her magic overcame us and changed us into mudsprites. Our days of endless labour are spent beautifying the gardens or working in the palace dungeons. If only there were hope of escape.' Svanhild looked Theophilus in the eye and spoke softly,

'Hope sparkles in the depth of night, hope puts fear to flight. Everything is possible Theophilus. Things are always changing in this world. The web in which you have been caught could one day dissolve and the spell be lifted.'

Was it the look in Svanhild's eye or the words she spoke? The veil of fear dropped from the green creature's face and a light shone in his yellow eyes.

'The Seven Lords, Queen Marsha's Masters, do they visit the palace and the gardens?' asked Svanhild.

'It happens once a year, my friends from Swanneland. The Queen gets in a frenzy of preparation and all is polished to perfection. The Seven Lords from the Land of Darkness stay for a few days of rest and recreation in this underwater paradise. Sometimes we catch a glimpse of the Seven, highlighted by the light of the moon and surrounded by the Queen and her maidservants, who sing and dance to please those frightful men. Take heed, take heed and flee when voices soar on the evening breeze and scents divine suffuse the air of night.'

As he ended his story, a look of hopelessness returned to the green face of the poor sprite.

A soft moaning came from many parts of the marshes as numerous mudsprites watched their spokesman slide back into the swampy pool. Svanhild reached out her hand and before he sank out of sight, touched his head. A small green hand broke the surface of the pool and waved a gesture of gratitude.

Svanhild walked back to the sandy beach and began to gather dry reeds to light a fire. Slim filled the kettle but neither of them spoke. Only when both were seated on a rock, sipping a mug of steaming tea, was the silence broken.

'It is at new moon, the Queen changes her guests into froglike creatures. We have two weeks left to rescue our friends.'

Svanhild nodded, but said nothing. At last she smiled.

'Look at Patriot,' she mused, 'His muzzle is still buried in the reeds, poor dog. At least he and I did not fall for the scent.'

'You remember when the mudsprite spoke of the pelican amongst the exotic birds in the Queens palace. The Queen of the Mountain Fairies may have planted one of her pelicans in the palace as an observer. We must try and get in touch with that bird.'

'You make a sleuth of the first water, Slim,' laughed Svanhild sipping her tea. But how do we contact that pelican bird?'

Slim got up and wandered close to the algae covered surface of the nearest pool and sang in a low voice,

mudsprites of the mire
invoke the sacred fire
hope succeeds despair
frogs turn into princes fair

Ripples broke the green moonlit surface of the pond, pointed ears poked up and the mudsprite reappeared.

'Well-meaning friend,' mused the sprite, shaking his dripping head. 'The sprites listened to your words of hope, but words are only words and words don't always work.'

'Sprite, words spoken in the right spirit to the right sprite must go hand in hand with action.'

The green face broke into a smile. 'Let us hope,' he whispered, 'I am the right sprite.'

'You are the right sprite, Theophilus, and you must help us. In time perhaps we will be able to overcome the Dark Lords who hold the nymph of the marshes in their power.'

When he saw Slim's determined face a gleam of hope returned to Theophilus's eyes.

'Theophilus, it is important that we talk to the pelican in the palace.'

'My dear friend,' muttered the sprite. 'We are slaves and lowly froglike creatures and do not enjoy freedom of movement in the palace, but each Sunday morning the Queen and her maidens issue forth from the palace doors, to walk and play in the gardens. Many birds accompany the party and often we peek from our pools to see the sunlight play on their gorgeous coloured wings. Yes, I remember the pelican, always near the Queen and her maidens. He seldom seems to play or flutter. A serious bird, one could say.'

'Listen Theophilus, on Sunday morning, two days from now when the flock of merry birds follow the troupe into the gardens, try to attract the attention of the pelican.'

'My friend from the land of the swans, the pelican is always close to the Queen. If I showed myself in the gardens that would be the end of Theophilus as you know him. Being a froglike sprite is bad enough, can you imagine being changed by the Queen's fury, into a crayfish or a clam?' Slim stopped to think. At least frogs can turn into princes, but as a clam Theophilus, fate might be grim indeed.

'Theophilus, do you remember the national anthem of the Mountain Fairies?'

'Of course, of course,' nodded the green sprite glowing in the moonlight, 'and a lovely melody it is.'

'Hum it when you see the Queen and her entourage. If the distance proves too great, get your fellow sprites to join in unison. There are only few wild pelicans left. All the others have been domesticated by the Mountain Fairies. This bird may be one of the pelicans in Queen Tuluga's Royal Guard.'

In the eyes of the sprite, a light appeared.

'I understand that solemn bird may be a plant in the palace. We shall gather the mudsprites together for a secret choir practice. If the big bird twigs to the anthem, we shall know that he can be trusted.'

'He must come quickly to the shore of the lake. Tell him that the dancing master from Swanneland and his sister are camped on the beach and are in desperate need of help. The Queen and pelicans of the Royal Guard have seen us perform on the Sanctus, in front of The Graceful Neck. If the pelican was one of them he will remember us.'

The sprite too recognized Slim and there was a twinkle in the yellow eyes.

'Dancing master, this very night I will swim to the scattered pools, wake the sprites and gather them for choir practice. In my youth, I spent two years with the Lambarina Choir Boys, Hallelujah,' the green creature sang out.

Cheered by the prospect of action, Theophilus climbed on the stump, leapt into the air and with a graceful dive, vanished underwater.

Slim laughed silently as he sauntered back to the campsite to tell Svanhild.

That night Slim and Svanhild woke thrice and heard a faint humming from the marshes. The melody of the anthem of the Mountain Fairies drifted on the mist, at first halting and unsure but by the time the sun gained the horizon the sprites sang well and harmoniously.

15

Peli 1

A dense morning mist hung over the marshes and Slim felt cold and damp as he crept out of his sleeping bag. He tried to light a fire but the wet reed stalks would not catch. Sitting on the damp sand, shivering with cold, he wondered if this trip had just been a mad dash into the unknown. How could the rescue of Scimitar stem the wave of evil that was rolling over the land? But then perhaps their journey was a part of a greater plan, the end of which could not be fathomed. He recalled the words of encouragement and laughter of the elven child and he felt better.

A swishing sound high above drew him out of his reverie. As he looked up, two dark shapes hovering in the mist, descended in graceful spirals. Slim woke Svanhild who raised herself while rubbing sleep out of her eyes. As the birds drew closer the outline of the wings could be seen. Svanhild recognized Solomon and Kasper sailing through the haze. Patriot began to bark until Svanhild folded her hands together, the 'all quiet sign' that she had seen Scimitar use at the Graceful Neck.

The great owls had kept the party under surveillance. They suspected that the Gorghouls would not lightly forget their humiliation at beak and claw by the united owl force. Even the Grolls, offspring of the unions of Gorghouls and Trolls, might have heard about it and although very selfish, they had a certain regard for their notorious ancestors. And then there was the Queen of the marshes. In their deep owl minds they knew that the wiles of the Queen would not work on the fair Svanhild. Only the male members of the party were vulnerable. Evil rumours about Marsha of the marshes had been passed on by birds that had escaped from the palace. The owls suspected that the wayfarers might have run into trouble in the marshes. If truth be told, the proud birds had been enchanted by the Swannemaiden and had a secret desire to look once more into those deep emerald eyes.

'Kasper, Solomon,' cried Svanhild, 'What a wonderful surprise! This visit must have taken you miles away from your hereditary forest.'

'The marshlands are a pleasant change of scenery. Is that not so, Kasper?'

'Indeed Chief, but what a joy to get back to the forest,' sighed the obliging Deputy.

'My dear feathered friends meet my brother Slim, the dancing master.'

Solomon made a deep bow and Slim, still shivering with cold stammered, 'My gratitude to you for the rescue of my sister, Chairbird of the Wood Owls.'

'Chairbird', Kasper repeated to himself shaking his head, 'Democratic humbug. Chief sounds a lot better.'

'Times are changing!' prompted Solomon

Kasper couldn't help himself. He blurted out, 'And if times are changing why are the swans kept in captivity and made to dance to the Swannefolks' piping?'

'Watch your p's and q's Deputy,' whispered Solomon, 'You know very well that the swans choose to work in Swanneland of their own free will and enjoy working with the Swannepeople.'

Slim smiled at Kasper, 'I understand your feelings Deputy. Owls are freedom loving birds and strong on wisdom. Swans are devoted to the arts, and we work together.'

Kasper felt that he had let his feelings get the better of him and that to live up to the owlish reputation of wisdom, this had to be corrected. Freebooter at heart, it was beyond him, this business of swans making a career in dance.

'To each his own, dancingmaster. Deputy Chief at your service.'

Kasper made a polite bow and cast Slim a conciliatory glance.

Svanhild walked up to Kasper and rested her right hand on his feathery head. The fierce look mollified and there appeared a shade of contrition in those deep wise eyes.

'Kasper,' called out the Chief, 'Slim and Svanhild are chilled to their wingtips so to speak. Is there anything that we can do to get that smoldering mess of reeds burning?'

'There is Chief, there is,' hooted Kasper, 'A short flight away there is a birch wood.' With that Kasper lifted off. High up in the air he was still reprimanding himself for flying off the handle. Having regained his equilibrium, he swooped into the little birch wood and by flying around and around the trunks of the trees, peeled off large sheets of birch bark.

The birch bark burned high and fired up the bedraggled reeds. In minutes the coffee was on the boil. Revived by the heat, Slim and Svanhild told Solomon and Kasper about the dire fate that awaited their companions.

The owls did a lot of head shaking. Their deep yellow eyes grew larger as if to say that only earthbound creatures could be so foolish as to be taken in by the guiles of the nymph Marsha. Svanhild told the owls about the appearance of the mudsprites and the terrible fate that they suffered.

'Abysmal ,' muttered Kasper, shaking his feathers, 'life without wings must be a test. We understand the slippery slopes of life below, being led down the garden path, chasing the illusion of love. Perhaps it is a frustrated desire to have wings and fly. Is that not so Chief?'

Solomon cleared his throat, straightened his feathers and then recited in a deep voice,

earthbound beings without wings
do silly things
chase phantoms in the sky
for by and by
they really want to fly

'A ditty that my grandfather taught me when he was hereditary Chief.'

'And a great Chief he was,' echoed Kasper politely, 'One might say a legendary bird.'

Quite pleased by this response, Solomon winked at Kasper and proceeded to address the issue at hand.

'Action is called for, owlish action, instant and decisive. Once the spell is cast and your friends are metamorphosed the game is up.' sighed Solomon.

The horror of the situation dawned anew upon Slim and Svanhild. Svanhild looked at Solomon. 'Noble chief once you saved me and I implore you now to save my companions.'

Svanhild's emerald eyes sent the heartstrings of the owls into a deep vibrato. Svanhild knew that she could count on the assistance of the owls. No task would be too great.

'My dear friends of noble feather, fly across the marshes to the Sanctus and follow the great river to the shores of Swanneland. On a hilltop on the north side of the river you will spot the Manor deCygne. From the air it looks like a long box with a courtyard in the middle. It is the ancestral home of the Marquis deCygne, who has fallen under the spell of Queen Marsha. His Aunt Erika and friends are assembled there and you must tell them of our fate. I pray that they will come to the rescue before our friends join the green army of mudsprites.

The birds began moving their great wings and Svanhild knew they would oblige her.

'Watch for merewings,' prompted Slim.

'For all their size, their eyesight is but poor,' retorted Solomon

'All wings and no brains,' added Kasper.

Svandhild stood between the two birds, her hands resting on their plumage.

'Fare thee well my gallant flyers, Godspeed.'

The owls rose swiftly into the morning haze and Slim and Svanhild waving on the beach below, soon lost sight of the Chief and his Deputy.

Slim and Patriot explored the shores of their little peninsula. When they found a thick patch of reeds, they dragged the skiff along the beach and pushed it well out of sight, into the rushes.

Svanhild, left alone on the beach, meditated on the palace of Queen Marsha. In her mind's eye she visualized Moose, Ferdinand and Duckie making their escape from the palace. It had all happened so quickly. That the Marquis might have been mesmerized by the scents and singing, she could understand, the Captain however, always as solid as a rock, she couldn't imagine wandering off the straight and narrow. Sadness filled her eyes as she recalled the events of the last few days. She looked at the still surface of the lake and a sparkle came into her eyes. There reflected in the water was the image of the wood carving that had been mounted on the prow of the Gondola in Miranda. She couldn't help laughing when she watched the elven face wreathed in smiles. Then, she thought of Ensten, the woodcarver and her sense of hopelessness vanished.

She went up to the lake, washed her face and hands and tried to focus on the problems at hand. Yes, of course they must find another campsite less exposed. She wandered along the beach and found a sheltered spot surrounded by willow bushes.

Slim and Patriot found her at the new site and Slim helped move their gear. By afternoon the sun had warmed the sand. They stretched out on the beach and slept until the sun turned the marshes a fiery red.

A festive atmosphere pervaded the underground palace. The Marquis, seated on a low marble wall encircling a fountain, had lit his pipe. Rings of smoke drifted into the fine spray rising from the water. At his feet were three of the Queen's favourite handmaidens embroidering roses on a linen table cloth.

'Queen Marsha is pleased to have a nobleman as her guest', said one of the maidens.

'Tell the Queen that the pleasure is entirely mine, we deCygnes, thrive in this kind of setting, for an appreciation of luxury and refinement is entirely natural to us. Days of travel and hardship will be soon forgotten'

'Sir Ferdinand,' laughed one the sirens innocently, 'what took you from your ancestral castle to these remote marshes?'

His mind still sparkling with the excellent wine served at lunch, Ferdinand leaned over to the trio and whispered, 'I speak to you in confidence my lovely companions. A rescue expedition took us through the marshes on our way to the Land of Darkness, the rescue of the Dwarf Scimitar.'

'Our lips are sealed,' responded the tallest of the three with a look of admiration on her face. 'Such work must be terribly dangerous, Count.'

'Marquis, my lovely mistress,' laughed Ferdinand, 'Counts are two steps down so to speak. As for danger, it has been the daily fare of the males in the family. There was uncle Henry who skewered the Red Blighter and Thomas deCygne who barbecued...'

The tall girl butted in. 'Marquis, you speak of the males in the family. What about the women? They bore children, withstood terrible sieges when the men were gone and poured boiling lead on enemies scaling castle walls. If the Queen heard you speak like that, she would be upset.'

Ferdinand was flummoxed. The thought that heroism extended to the fair sex was quite sobering. His sparkle subsided and suddenly it occurred to him that he might have said too much.

He sucked on his pipe and consoled himself with the thought that things said could not be unsaid, and that the girls had promised not to talk. Could it be that the lovely damsels at his feet were not trustworthy? Such beauty not trustworthy? A contradiction in terms, philosophized the nobleman, sending a ring of blue smoke aloft and suppressing the wavelet of fear that stirred in his psyche.

Moose and Duckie, wandering through the splendid halls and gardens, admired the profusion of fountains and statues. Painted on the walls were murals portraying bare arid landscapes covered with red earth and cacti. Rivers wound among the low dunes and blue mist obscured the horizon.

Some of the Queen's handmaidens were seated in small groups working at their looms while others knitted or practiced their string instruments. Wherever they went a charming smile greeted them. Duckie approached one of the girls to ask about the murals.

'The paintings on the walls, my lady fair,' said Duckie with a polite bow. 'They give me a somber feeling, landscapes even the Captain has never seen.'

The smile on the face of the blonde maiden died quickly. She took Duckie's hand and pressed it gently.

'Dear boy the paintings were gifts of the great Lords, our Queen's Seven Masters. Once a year they spend a vacation in these halls. Look at the statue in yonder fountain. It is a likeness of Salan, the greatest of the Seven. Statues of the other six stand in the smaller fountains along the garden paths. It was the Queen who had their images carved in stone.

Duckie cast a glance at the statue in the fountain. Suddenly he felt anxious. 'Have we made a mistake coming to this palace, Captain Martin?' reflected Duckie.

Moose Martin responded with a stream of laughter cascading through the halls. The Captain was entranced by the sight, scent and sounds around him.

'Duckie my boy, for a few days we will live in the kind of splendour dreams are made of and then we will worry about crossing the marshes.'

Perhaps it had something to do with extreme youth and lack of hormones but young Duckie had never been fully captivated by the scents and sights of the palace and the Queen's honey tongued speeches. Looking at the grim statue in the fountain had cleared his head very quickly. There was something fishy going on. Captain Martin, always an incarnation of common sense, appeared slightly off his rocker. Maidens were all right, pretty and all that but nothing to lose your head over. Captain Martin was certainly making a bit of a fool of himself. It was all very well to talk about leaving within a few days but how in the name of the Great Goose were they going to find their way out of this underground palace, with its endless halls and pavilions? Moreover they would have to persuade the Marquis to come along. The Marquis, thanks to liberal libations of the Queen's wine, walked on air!

Ferdinand deCygne glowed, years of boredom and rejection were behind him and now all his secret dreams were unfolding. The maidens sat with him at table, massaged his weary limbs and listened patiently to his tales of glory past. These girls understood his unique identity and capacity for heroism.

He lit his pipe and wandered through the halls, blowing circlets of smoke into the air. As he drew away from the fountains and the music, some exotic birds perched on his shoulders. When he entered a small pavilion, the sound of a spinning wheel caught his ear. A girl, tall and stately, moved the treadle of the wheel and the fine down, gliding through her fingers, spun into silver wool.

Standing beside the comely maiden, his eye caught sight of a pelican. It was not unusual that he should find a pelican among the many colourful birds in the palace. The penetrating gaze of the bird however, unsettled the Marquis' ebullient mood. It was as if a look of reproach dwelt in those eyes.

The Marquis chuckled to himself and muttered, 'Quite astounding how our imagination works. A bird, an ordinary bird of the pelican variety, and I see disparagement in his face, my guilty conscience.' He laughed at his own acumen. The wine had done its work.

Ferdinand deCygne sat down on a marble toadstool opposite the charming spinster. She raised her eyes and a melodious voice said, 'You are a member of the trio that arrived at the palace last week.'

'Yes my lady fair, Marquis deCygne at your service.'

She responded with a smile only. Ferdinand sensed a solemnity in this little pavilion and it brought some calm to the surging waters of his mind.

'Your name fair spinster?' asked the Marquis bowing deeply.

'Dorothea, my name is Dorothea,' sounded the lilting voice.

'A noble name and no doubt the daughter of a noble family,' said the Marquis, wiping perspiration from his forehead.

'My family were commoners from Esteria, Marquis. My father, worked in the woods. Alas, he died of grief when I was kidnapped as a toddler.'

'Kidnapped?' echoed the alarmed nobleman.

'Yes Marquis, playing in the woods, listening to the singing of my father's saw, I did not hear the swish of diving wings. Taken by a merewing, I was brought here to be raised as handmaiden to Queen Marsha.'

The tragic story moved the Marquis and a degree of sobriety returned to him. Great God, strange things were going on in this palace. Perhaps all was not wine and roses.

'Marquis,' the sylph maiden intoned with a frown on her lovely countenance. 'Marquis, be on guard when you speak to the Queen!'

'Gracious lady,' mused the nobleman, his hand touching Dorothea's bare shoulder, 'It is true that rumour has painted that splendid lady with a dark and cruel brush. Yet an understanding ear and the sympathy of a fellow aristocrat is all that are required to bring forth the nobility that dwells in those lovely eyes!'

'Marquis, I speak in earnest.'

'Ferdinand to you my dear friend, Ferdinand please'

'Ferdinand, you are a kind and charming man but terribly naive,' continued the undaunted girl.

She looked at the portly figure, his blue eyes full of zeal and lofty sentiments and smiled. Somewhere deep within she wanted to shield this hopeless romantic from the fate that awaited him. She was surprised at her own feelings. She sensed a warmth of heart in this man that touched her. Innocent and vain no doubt, yet a man without guile.

'Ferdinand for your own good, stay away...' She stopped in mid sentence. Across the hall, softened by the fountain's fine spray, appeared the small striking figure of Queen Marsha. Before taking her leave, Dorothea rose and bowed.

Slowly, majestically but menacingly the Queen approached along the semicircular wall of the fountain and placed herself next to the Marquis. Her eyes like mountain lakes revealed a black depth.

'Delighted to meet you, Marsha of the marshes,' beamed the Marquis with the usual confidence of a member of the upper classes. He was taken aback when the Queen retorted haughtily,

'Majesty, to you Ferdinand deCygne.'

'Pardon me Queen, majesty, the pleasure is all mine,' flustered the nobleman.

'My maidens tell me Marquis that a special mission took you to my marshes. I have met the Captain and the cute little boy but were there others with you on this foolish journey?'

Ferdinand's confidence ebbed away. Those beautiful eyes were very unsettling.

'Others, Queen? No others, Queen. It was just a fishing trip. The old Captain knows the waters.' His face flushed crimson.

'Telling fibs, Ferdinand deCygne, telling fibs in front of a Queen, whose eyes can read the truth.'

The Marquis knew that the game was up. The maidens had tattled. Beauty and trustworthiness did not always go hand in hand after all. Wiser to tell the truth since the Queen knew it anyway.

'Queen we are to rescue the Dwarf Scimitar and do a little fishing on the side.'

Queen Marsha burst into laughter. 'The old Captain, the cutie-pie youth and Ferdinand deCygne are going to the mines at the Black Peak and rescue the stuck-up Dwarf and do some fishing on the side.' The Queen doubled over in laughter. Looking at the perplexed nobleman she admonished, 'Stick to fishing Ferdinand deCygne. Armies could not rescue the rogue Scimitar.'

The thought of Scimitar subdued her mirth. 'Scimitar the troublemaker, the warmonger will meet his doom in the dark mines.' Fire swept over the black lakes when she recalled the Dwarf. Many times, impervious to scent and singing, the Dwarf had crossed the marshes. The very thought was maddening!

The Marquis and his friends, soon would be turned into mudsprites. It was but twelve days to new moon, when the spells could be cast. A smile played upon her lips. The Marquis would make an interesting creature no doubt, a kind of noble frog on the tubby side. Too many frogs had been kissed into princes, the time had come to change the tradition and turn a few princes into frogs. How amusing.

'You Ferdinand deCygne,' scorned the Queen, 'will have the privilege of serving Queen Marsha, your fellow aristocrat!'

Ferdinand realized the Queen had eavesdropped on his conversation with Dorothea. Deplorable behaviour and what was this about serving her? A

deep frown appeared on his face. It began to dawn on him that all was not well and a wave of fear engulfed him. He must flee this palace and all its splendour.

'Dorothea dear, accompany the Marquis to the dining hall,' said the Queen as she dismissed Ferdinand with a brusque gesture.

It was a very sober nobleman Dorothea lead by the hand. Yet there was a smile on his face. This humiliating interview might have its uses. The Queen had mentioned that Scimitar was imprisoned in a mine near a black peak, this could be a landmark that would help find the captive Dwarf. Intelligence gathering is part of the hero's path. It was not exactly what had led him to the palace but then... A smile played upon his lips. Yes he must get out of here but what about the maiden at his side? Dorothea was unlike anyone he had ever met.

Pain dwelt in Dorothea's eyes. Twelve days to new moon, when her knightly companion would join the chorus of green nocturnal moaners. Was there some way to warn this charming dreamer?

The dining hall came into sight and a joyous sight it was. Wine flowed freely and musicians, strumming their instruments, wandered among the banquet tables. Seated between lovely maidens, Moose helped himself liberally to the Queen's wine, and burst into one of his old sailor songs.

Dorothea had quietly walked up to the Marquis and whispered in his ear, 'Ferdinand, the wine contains a magic potion. Take heed. When he looked into her eyes he read danger and a sense of dread came over him. What was it that the Queen had said about serving her? This was not what he had in mind. The wave of anxiety that flowed over the Marquis had a decidedly sobering effect.

The concern of the maiden by his side touched his heart. She could be trusted and perhaps help them to escape?

How were they to get out of here? Moose Martin was several sheets to the wind, the mind of the old sailor had slipped its anchor. Only Duckie was pert and sober, always asking for hot chocolate when offered wine, much to the amusement of the maidservants who had a weak spot for the charming youngster.

The food was excellent and Ferdinand regained his composure. Without thinking he picked up a glass of wine but before putting it to his lips his eye caught sight of the pelican solemnly shaking his large beak. The Marquis turned deftly around to admire the fountain and then emptied his glass in the swirling water.

16

Conference At The Manor

Sunbeams dancing on the water touched the faces of the forlorn figures sleeping in the willow copse. Slim dreamt of distant voices singing, coming closer, closer. When he woke and rubbed the sleep out of his eyes, he could still hear singing, it was no dream. It was a chorus of mudsprites, humming the Mountain Fairies' national anthem. He washed his face in the waters of the lake and woke Svanhild. Both of them listened to the rising chorus. If the Pelican worked for the Mountain Fairies he could not fail to recognize it and he would slip away from the garden party to listen to the mudsprites' plea.

Suddenly the singing stopped. Slim looked at Svanhild.

'The pelican must have left the party and landed amongst the mudsprites Slim.'

'It is good sign, Svanhild. The sprites will send him out here I trust.'

They lit a fire and drank their morning tea while anxiously scanning the marshes. It was Svanhild who first caught sight of the Pelican. To escape detection, it was flying low, its great beak touching the bulrushes. The strong wings angled and the pelican reduced speed until it touched the water and swam ashore.

Svanhild, her silver hair on fire in the early sunlight, knelt by the water's edge and touched his wingtip. 'Thanks so very much for responding to our call, pelican. Now we know you serve Queen Tuluga of the Mountain Fairies.'

'When I heard the singing of my people's anthem I knew my presence was required, my lady.'

'My dear pelican we are grateful you have come.

'Peli 1 at your service swannemaid,' spoke the bird in a courtly manner.

Slim too moved closer to the water and thanked Peli 1 for his prompt response. 'You may have guessed the reason for our plea for help Peli.'

Peli nodded gravely before opening his beak, 'I have been a sleeper in the palace for months and have seen many a traveler lured to his doom.'

Peli 1 was a bird of few words and had a rather brusque manner but as a member of the Fairy Queen's Royal Guard, he was used to keeping things to himself.

'Tell us about the Marquis, Moose Martin and Duckie,' urged Svanhild.'

The large beak opened as he cleared his throat, 'The boy Duckie has escaped the spell and the Marquis is showing signs of common sense. It is the skipper that has gone off the deep end, reeled in by the Queen and her nymphs, hook, line and sinker. The great beak covered a wide arc as the solemn fowl shook his head.

'The Captain,' cried Svanhild in dismay, 'There is not a mean bone in his body. He stands for all that is good and noble.'

A smile played in the pelican's stern eyes. 'Daughter of innocence, many great men have a chink in their armour, and few travelers in the marshes do not succumb to the scent and the singing. Only the Dwarves escape the Queen's magic. They can be seen at full moon driving their canoes at great speed through the narrow channels. No wiles beguile them.

'Dear pelican, what can we do to break the Queen's spell,' sighed Svanhild. The great bird shook his head, 'The spell cannot be broken until the fall of her Seven Masters.'

'Our friends Peli, what can we do to avert this terrible fate befalling our friends?'

'They are safe, child of the Swannepeople. They are safe till the sickle of the new moon appears in the sky then the Queen will voice the incantation that will change them into frog-like creatures.

Slim put his arm around Svanhild, 'Peli, we have sent a message, with the Chief of the Wood Owls and his Deputy, to our friends in Swanneland and help will be forthcoming. Your Queen Tuluga is likely to be at the deCygne Manor, attending a conference of delegates from different regions of the Kingdom.

At the mention of his Royal Mistress the pelican made a slight bow.

'I must return to the palace, my friends. Prolonged absence would raise suspicions. I shall await a message when help arrives.'

The bird turned quickly and swam away from shore. With a powerful stroke of his pinions he rose above the waters, banked steeply and set course for the garden party. Gaining height, Peli 1 saw the Queen and her retinue walking back to the palace. He flew a semicircle far behind the long line of singing and dancing retainers and descending in a steep dive, caught up with the rearguard of the revelers.

The de Cygne Manor was veiled in a dense mist. Inside the guests were seated at breakfast. The gnome, Quicksilver, after a harrowing journey, had reached the manor only days ago. One of the swarthy strangers had spotted him outside Lambarina and sent a black hound after him. Gnomes are smaller than Dwarves, but they can move quickly and their mail vests, finely woven from secret alloys, are impenetrable.

Quicksilver running as if the devil himself was chasing him, jumped on a wood stack behind a farmhouse. Tossing chunks of firewood at the black fury, he held him at bay until the woodpile shrank in size. Then the hound seized Quicksilver by the sleeve of his mailvest. His fangs fastened upon the fine mesh of metal, wildly shaking the poor gnome. The black brute failed to see the farmer, carrying a well honed ax, coming out of the woodshed. The kind fruit farmers on the shore of the Sanctus would not hurt a fly. The news of the attack on Oliver Wendell had traveled quickly however and at the sight of the black hound the gentle farmer's eyes turned into burning coals.

The Gnome was being pounded against the woodpile, his head spinning, when suddenly the vortex stopped and he fell to the ground. The black jaws of the hound were still clamped to his right arm, but a well aimed blow from the farmer's ax had felled the beast.

The farmer tapped the fangs caught in the mail and lifting the dazed Gnome from the ground, carried him into the house.

The farmer's wife treated Quicksilver's bruises with comfrey extract.

'Heaven be praised. The skin is not broken,' exclaimed the kind woman.

Relief showed in the Gnome's face for he well knew the deadly effect of the tainted fangs.

'It was a close call, my dear woman,' whispered the Gnome. 'The magic vest held until your brave husband dealt the monster a mortal blow.'

A couple of hours rest and a bowl of oatmeal restored the bruised Gnome. Anxious to resume his journey, he thanked his hosts with a deep bow and moved swiftly onward.

The company at the Manor heartily welcomed Quicksilver. Now only delegates from the Outlanders and the Elves were missing. Erica guided the exhausted Quicksilver to a comfortable window sill where promptly he fell asleep.

After breakfast Erica and Queen Tuluga stepped into the sunroom. The mist was clearing and the waters of the Sanctus reflected the sunlight. Soon the last fog banks burned off and they had a clear view of the river and the red roof tops among stands of tall poplars. The little town of Cascade, at the confluence of the Frivoli and the Sanctus, looked quaint and peaceful. Yet tales and rumours from the village were disquieting. Local business was booming and dark strangers were handing out profitable contracts. To welcome the new investors, Joris Goldfinger had given a speech at a Chamber of Commerce dinner. Heads were nodding and tongues wagging. Things were not so bad. It was true, the newcomers demanded prompt service but money was flowing freely. There was a reckless atmosphere in town. Prices were spiraling upwards and speculators were buying properties. With many strangers coming to town there was a shortage of accommodation and bed and breakfast signs were sprouting up on every street. More men arrived every day and moved in with the locals. Business at the Graceful Neck was brisk.

Some of these stocky men in their leather coats had been seen lingering around the Manor. After Grumpuss tossed a couple into a patch of bramble bushes, they kept their distance.

Standing on the coffee table, Queen Tuluga reached Erica's shoulder. Playfully she drew her fingers through her white and silver tresses and whispered in her ear, 'Gustav is alive my dear. My pelicans spotted him in one of the Dark Lords' galleys, do not lose hope.'

Tears came into Erica's eyes as she reached for the diminutive hand of the Queen of the Mountain Fairies.

Tuluga scanned the horizon on the far side of the Frivoli. She uttered a startled cry when she saw two dark dots moving towards them. She put her hand on Erica's shoulders. 'They are not pelicans, but what could they be? Wood owls perhaps?'

Indeed it was Solomon and Kasper who were approaching the Manor.

Chatting amicably, the Chief and his Deputy soared over the Sanctus. High above the owls a dark shape appeared. Queen Tuluga spotted it first. Its shadow skimmed the waters. Then the black wings folded and Tuluga let out a cry, 'The merewing, the merewing diving for the owls!' Thrice she whistled a long shrill signal. The Queen's pelicans were enjoying a breakfast of fresh trout on the north pond, when the high pitched sound reached them. 'Red alert,' yelled Roderick, the Queen's Soarmaster. Instantly the pelicans spit out the fishes they had stored in their beaks and lined up for take off. The pelicans, rising swift and true, flashed over the Manor.

The end of their mission in sight, the owls had been somewhat complacent and were also involved in a tricky discussion on rights, privileges and perks, owing to Chiefs and Deputies. So it was that the merewing caught them unawares. Screeching overhead, he grabbed both of them, Solomon in the right talon and Kasper in his left.

'Two in one sweep,' he sang to himself, a grin appearing on the airborne pirate's purple face.

The owls stared in dismay at each other. 'Chief,' stuttered Kasper as they rose rapidly upwards. 'Are we goners?'

'Situation grave Deputy, our terrestrial journey may be nearing its destination.'

'Those eyes, those emerald eyes of the Swannemaid, Chief, they float before me.'

'A bad sign Deputy. Visions of that nature forebode serious trouble,' reflected Solomon, a touch of envy in his voice.

'How do you keep your cool Chief?' gasped Kasper.

'A Chief keeps his cool Deputy. That's why I am Chief.'

The logic was airtight and the terrified Deputy never again questioned the station of his superior.

Solomon was the first to see the rays of the sun intercepted by a triangle flashing past. Suddenly light began to shine through holes in their captor's wingspan. More and more holes appeared in the wings hovering above the owls. Nose-diving, the pelicans bored their long fierce beaks through the merewing. Losing height quickly, he was forced to drop his prey. There was little wing left when the purple head tilted downwards and the evil bird spiraled to his doom.

Solomon and Kasper, flying under their own power, breathed a sigh of relief and expressed their gratitude to the pelicans.

At the Manor, all had congregated on the terrace to witness the aerial battle. Loud was the cheering when the black fowl went into a dive and splattered on the rocky shore of the Sanctus. The pelicans politely dipping their wings as they passed their Queen, landed on the north pond. After smoothing their feathers they settled down to the business of finishing their breakfast of fresh trout.

Kasper and Solomon touched down upon the stone wall encircling the terrace and were greeted by Queen Tuluga. Solomon bowed and thanked the Queen for dispatching the pelicans. Erica asked in an anxious voice, 'Have you tidings, tidings from the wayfarers?'

'I have, my lady. Fear not, all are alive and well. But the Marquis, the Captain and the boy Duckie are guests at the palace of the Queen of the marshes.'

A shadow fell over Erica's face. She decided to wait for details of the story because she knew the owls had been through an ordeal and they badly needed rest and comfort.

'Come inside dear birds. Rest and refresh yourselves and I will sooth your ruffled feathers.'

Kasper and Solomon hopped into the sunroom, perching on the back of two chairs. Erica, standing between them, smoothed their feathers, mussed up by the merewing's talons. Erica gently stroked their pinions. A blissful gleam appeared in their wise brown eyes.

When the birds had regained their poise, Erica offered them some of the blue cheese left on the dining table.

'Quite excellent food,' commented Kasper.

'Indeed Deputy,' confirmed Solomon, 'it's got a bite to it and a hint of moldy mouse.'

The prophetess Martha and Grumpuss bear had repaired to the rose garden to escape the commotion on the porch. Suddenly Grumpuss rose on his hind legs and in a kind of dance step started swaying back and forth. Martha turned to her companion and shook her head but then she, too, could hear a gay tune floating through the air. Before long the happy whistler, a tall lanky figure, appeared from behind the bramble hedge and walked across the lawn to shake hands with Martha. Grumpuss shuffled up first and hugged the stranger with a kind of bear hug that one never forgets. Grumpuss had a great love of music and those who make it! Once freed from the well meaning bear, the happy whistler's collapsed chest filled with air, and he shook hands with Martha. 'Volker, the name is Volker.'

'Ah Volker the Lark, 'laughed Martha, 'If I remember well, the musical secretary of the Outlander's Council.'

Volker had a habit of whistling songs and melodies at the oddest time. It just happened. His tunes had frozen speakers in mid-sentence and once had put to sleep, the entire Council. Stories about Volker the Lark had cheered many a winter evening gathering.

Blushing somewhat, while trying to brush his blond locks from his eyes, Volker explained that the Chairman of the Council was ill and that he himself had been chosen as delegate to attend the meeting at the Manor.

The lovable double-jointed Outlander was known by most of those gathered at the Manor. Whistling the traditional battle hymn of the Swannefolk of old, two steps at a time, he climbed the stairway and joined the gathering in the upstairs hall.

Kasper and Solomon were once more in fine feather, their self-respect restored. It was true that they should have been more alert, however, it had all happened at the end of a long tiring flight. 'Owls are wise but not infallible,' affirmed Solomon.

'A lesson in humility, Chief,' intoned Kasper. The owls were perched at the end of the long oval table. All eyes were upon them, anxiously awaiting news of the wayfarers.

No Chairperson had been elected. It was by an unconscious process that Lady Erica had become the leader of the little band. She gave Solomon an encouraging nod and he took the floor.

Solomon's grave eyes and sonorous voice sent a tremor through the room and all eyes turned to the wise bird's commanding face, even those that had been napping perked up.

'The Wood Owls send their greetings to the delegates of the Kingdom of the Seven Mountains gathered here at the Manor of the deCygne family . We honour your late King Arcturus who granted the owls hereditary rights to the forests on the southern shore of the Sanctus. A noble soul who took flight prematurely. May he rest in peace.'

Moments of silence followed the Chief's opening words.

'Slim and Svanhild, well out of reach of the Queen of the Marshes, are camped on a beach. Yesterday we touched down at their campsite and they asked us to fly to the Manor deCygne and report their news. Alas, the Marquis, Captain Martin and the boy Duckie were enticed into the palace of Queen Marsha and are in great danger,' concluded Solomon. The news that all the travelers were alive was greeted with a sigh of great relief, but the enchantment of the Captain, the Marquis and Duckie put a damper on the spirits around the table. It was clear from the owls' expression that they considered the misfortune of those three the result of foolishness.

'Slim and Svanhild asked us to tell you that help is needed to free the captives from the clutches of the Queen of the Marshes.'

'Dear Svanhild stranded on a beach in the wilderness. I knew that her destiny would take her to strange and perilous places,' sighed old Martha the prophetess. 'Is she well my little pumpkin?'

Solomon fixed his gaze upon Martha. 'She has recovered, my dear lady from a frightful adventure. The Wood Owls played a modest part in her recovery.'

'Recovery?' queried Lady Erica.

'She had been kidnapped, my Lady. The enchantress Matista enticed the Swannemaid deep into the forest.'

At the mention of Matista, eyes around the table stared in disbelief at the somber owl.

Lady Erica was the first to speak. 'Matista has returned after all these years?

'She has lived for some time in the remote town of Miranda. There she was known as the old soothsayer Neva, my lady. My Deputy and I had the privilege of playing a minor part in rescuing Svanhild from the clutches of the enchantress,' the owl reported with proper humility.

'Our pleasure, entirely,' echoed Kasper, his eyes downcast.

As Solomon's story unfolded, it became clear that the owls' role was not so minor after all. Grateful and admiring eyes looked at the stern birds as Solomon told the story of the owl attack on the Gorghouls.

Queen Tuluga expressed gratitude to the owls for their valour in the rescue of the Swannemaiden and undertaking the journey to the Manor at great peril. Then she took out of her satchel two golden bands, stepped onto the table and clipped them around the necks of both owls. The Golden Collar was the second highest decoration in the land of the Mountain Fairies. It was worn on festive occasions and entitled the bearer to be addressed as honourable. The owls radiated satisfaction.

Honourable has a fine ring to it Chief,' whispered Kasper. Solomon gleefully imagined the faces of the other owls on hearing the news. It would be hard to take for some of the young upstarts. Solomon tried to feign a somber stare, a kind of disdain of worldly honours look, quite becoming in one with a reputation of higher wisdom. Queen Tuluga moved across the table towards Lady Erica.

'Friends,' exclaimed the Queen, 'There are eleven days to new moon. Once the crescent of the new moon appears, it is too late. We must rescue the trio from the palace. Of course, they should have their heads examined, falling as they did for the lowly nymph's charms.' She shook her head and paused.

'Any suggestions Queen Tuluga?' smiled Quicksilver.

'Yes, my dear Gnome, we must get them out. Help must be sent. I talked earlier about the scouts, Edel and Weiss, assigned to odious duties at the Pelican Farm. They might welcome a change.'

'Brilliant Queen Tuluga,' burst out Lady Erica, 'Cheeky and disobedient they are but also bold and ingenious. I think that somehow they would find their way into the palace.'

'But, but, but,' spluttered Volker, 'the singing and the scent and the handmaidens, are Mountain Fairies quite impervious to that sort of thing?'

'My dear and innocent Outlander,' laughed the Queen, 'For Mountain Fairies, love exists on a higher plane.'

'But new Mountain Fairies keep appearing,' blurted the blushing Secretary.

'Secretary Volker, you want to know how we perpetuate the race? Have you not heard how lovers in our land rise at dawn and wander hand in hand where water lilies grow? Gently they step on giant floating leaves and walk to a flower, brilliant white. Over the bright white petals, their breaths intermingle touching the dew drops gathered deep within. When the sun sinks in the west the petals fold for the night. The next day the lovers open the flower and find within a tiny Fairy.'

In utter astonishment the nonplused secretary looked around the table.

All eyes that met his stare said clearly, 'Of course quite natural and beautiful. We have known it all along.'

'We all trust,' said Erica with a twinkle in her eye, 'that the Mountain Fairies are immune to the traps that led astray members from our company. We welcome the services of Edel and Weiss.'

Nodding of heads around the table made clear that all were in agreement. Out of habit, Volker pulled a notebook from of his pocket and wrote down the decision, including a footnote about the propagation of Mountain Fairies.

Queen Tuluga jumped from the table to the windowsill, leaned out the open window and whistled. Roderick perched on a branch near the window, made a slight bow. 'Roderick hasten home and tell the elders to release the young whippersnappers, Edel and Weiss, and command them to hurry hither. Take only two other pelicans for an escort and order the remainder of your wing to rest on the north pond.'

Roderick wasted no time and moments later three pelicans flew past the south window and vanished into a cloudless sky.

When Solomon saw the pelicans flying off it reminded him that he and Kasper had better get back to home base.

'It has been days, Kasper since we left the flock in the woodlands. We better return and assert our leadership, just in case.'

'Very wise chief, some of the younger birds may have forgotten your station as hereditary Chief.'

'Never mind Deputy. I'll put them in their place.' Solomon hooted, with the kind of new sternness that success and decorations tend to evoke.

Erica saw that the owls were eager to get going. She expressed the Council's gratitude and asked them to tell Svanhild and Slim about the arrival of the Mountain Fairies.

'At your service,' said Kasper with a wink, 'We will just touch down in the woodlands to remind some of the young owls of who's who, my lady, and carry right on to the marshes.'

Soon Kasper and Solomon were airborne and with great precision they plotted a course for their native forest.

17.

Edel and Weiss

The air was filled with the happy chatter of Pelicans. They had just returned from their daily fishing expedition to supply the palace kitchens of the Queen of the Mountain Fairies. Leisurely floating on the pond, they enjoyed the sight of Edel and Weiss working like a pair of pack horses.

'They had it coming Rosy,' snapped a female in full plumage, 'Disobeyed the Queen!'

'You don't say Flighty,' countered Rosy with a serious nod. 'Troublemakers those two. I have a long memory. Pulling tail feathers and worse.'

'Let them sweat. It may burn off their karma,' mumbled Flighty.

The birds sailed majestically past the two delinquents. They returned the Mountain Fairies' greeting with a haughty nod.

'Stuck up birds,' grumbled Weiss, wiping sweat from his forehead. 'Work seven days a week, rain or shine and entertain the pelicans.'

'It is not the work Weiss. It's the smell. That is what will be the end of me,' sighed Edel, shovelling another scoop of manure into the wheelbarrow. Weiss lifted the wheel barrow and guiding its front wheel over a series of wobbly boards to a large pit, dumped the load over the edge.

'Time for a break,' shouted Edel, climbing to the top of a little hillock overlooking the ranch. Weiss leaped from island to island in the sea of muck and joined Edel.

Both stretched out on the tall grass, the wind singing them to sleep.

They dreamt of rescuing princesses and gaining eternal glory until footsteps woke them to the reality of muck shoveling. They rose to see coming towards them three elderly Fairies. The overseer accompanied by two white haired elders walked up the hill. Edel felt a wave of panic, what had they done?

The senior elder barely reached above the tall grasses. His white locks streamed in the wind and his blue eyes looked kindly at the youths.

'It is not what you have done Edel,' he laughed, 'It is what you are going to do that brings me here.' A gleam of hope appeared in Edel's eyes.

'I cannot tell you much but the Queen needs two dauntless, nimble fellows for a rescue expedition and your names were mentioned in a message carried by Roderick.

The Fairies jumped for joy. 'A thousand thanks ancient one,' cried Weiss, 'we are ready to leave this very instant.' 'Or sooner,' added Edel, looking askance at the grim faced overseer.

'No, my friends, you must hasten back to the town of Windekind and there present yourselves to the Chief Archer, for new outfits and instructions.'

Edel and Weiss looked at each other. The words of the ancient one bespoke hope and glory of which there had been precious little at the muck ranch.

The elders thought of their own youth almost two centuries ago and their smiling eyes followed the two racing for town, their feet but skimming the ground.

The chief archer was inspecting a troop of new recruits when the muck covered Fairies rushed onto the field.

'Master Bull's Eye, shouted Edel, 'We have come by Royal Order.' 'Never mind the Royal. To the bathhouse you two river rats. Scrub yourselves clean and get new jumpsuits before you talk to me,' grumbled the unruffled bow master. Spic and span was the great archer's password. Under ordinary circumstances their appearance would have spelled trouble but master Bull's Eye knew that Edel and Weiss could send an arrow far and true if they weren't daydreaming. With the old marksman, that counted for a lot.

Edel and Weiss looked splendid in their new suits and even Master Bull's Eye cracked a smile when they walked out of the armoury. He accompanied them to the store clerk who issued two fine yew bows and plenty of arrows. Backpacks with survival gear completed their outfit and before the sun had dipped below the horizon, the two Fairies were climbing the high ridge that would take them around Lambarina and to the Manor deCygne. Master Bull's Eye caught them in his field glasses as they emerged from the trees close to the summit. Once they gained the bare ridge, moving at great speed, they vanished into the gathering dusk.

On the morning of the second day they spotted the pelican flock fluttering over the north pond by the Manor. They began their climb down.

Grumpuss bear picked up the scent but never saw them. The Mountain Fairies in their green jumpsuits and deer skin jackets were well camouflaged. Fleet of foot, they moved lightly through the orchards and gardens and before anyone had seen them, walked into the Manor.

Queen Tuluga had just returned to the Council meeting when Edel and Weiss jumped on the edge of the table and greeted her with a bow.

'Welcome Edel and Weiss,' smiled the Queen. 'You have traveled at great speed and arrived earlier than we expected. You were anxious to leave the pelican ranch?'

'Most anxious indeed, Majesty,' returned Weiss, 'we are grateful for your clemency.'

'I am not sure that this is clemency my scouts,' laughed Tuluga, 'Your next job is arduous and dangerous. The Marquis deCygne, Captain Moose Martin and the boy Duckie have been lured into the palace of Queen Marsha of the marshes and they must be rescued before it is too late!'

'A wicked Queen,' exulted Edel, who sensed an opportunity for glory 'We will slide and slither through those marshes and weasel our way into the palace!'

'Wait, my boys . Easy it will not be, the palace is protected by a bodyguard of Grolls.'

'We sank a Groll in the quicksand on the western shore, Majesty.'

'I remember my brave scouts but there will be many Grolls in the palace. Slim and his sister Svanhild are camped on a beach nearby. First consult with
them. Do nothing rash.'

Tuluga explained about the presence of Peli 1 in the palace, the suffering of the green moaners and at new moon, the dire fate awaiting Duckie, the Captain and the Marquis.

'Find Slim and Svanhild and together make plans to free the captives. Leave tonight and under cover of darkness, travel as far as you can. Once you reach the marshes watch for the Wood Owls. They will guide you to

Slim and Svanhild's camp. One of my pelicans will take a message to the owls.'

The Mountain Fairies could hardly wait. The prospect was dangerous but spine tingling and after three months on the pelican ranch, very welcome.

'No my scouts not yet. First you will dine with the company and Lady Erica will provision you before leaving.'

Norma brought from the kitchen a splendid dinner. Wineglasses rang and twinkled in the candlelight as the company saluted the Fairies and wished them Godspeed.

Later in the evening, with half the company dozing around the table, Edel and Weiss slipped out the front door and onto the terrace. Before they vanished into darkness, Lady Erica hastened outside and handed them a small box.

'Norma sends these oatcakes, they contain spores of black mushroom and will speed you on. Heed the black hounds but do not fear the Great Grey. Fare ye well Edel and Weiss!'

They followed a well trodden path along the north shore of the Sanctus. On their right were stands of bulrushes and beyond, the waters of the Sanctus reflecting the moon's rays.

'A splendid night for traveling Weiss,' sighed Edel, 'Pure air at last, after months at the Pelican Ranch.'

'And rushing into the night to outfox a wicked queen,' rejoiced Weiss.

'Glory be,' exulted Edel speeding through the bulrushes.

It was not long before the lights of the Graceful Neck came into sight and Edel and Weiss stopped for moment to catch their breath.

'Quaint old inn Edel,' whispered Weiss.

'The Swan Festivals we danced at, Weiss. I well remember the gondolas lit with torches and pulled by teams of swans.'

For a moment, curiosity getting the better of them, they moved closer to the inn. Most of the windows were lit up and Edel and Weiss tripped quickly up the front porch. They climbed the ivy growing by the dining hall windows and peered inside. A group of businessmen smoking and drinking ale were seated around a trestle table. Rovers in black jackets sat at a table nearby. Between the groups, there was a lively exchange. They appeared on the best of terms. At one of the Rover's feet dozed a black hound. The sight of its massive jaws intimidated even the indomitable ones. They quickly slid down the ivy, rushed back to the river and resumed their trek eastwards.

Soon they reached the junction of the Sanctus and the Frivoli. Here they decided to cross to the south shore of the Sanctus. They started building a raft by weaving logs together with willow twigs. The moon provided ample light and absorbed in their work, they were startled by the sound of oars dipping in the river.

A ray of moonlight revealed a small rowboat coming towards them. Edel and Weiss moved into the shrubbery and watched. The little vessel glided onto a bank near the shore. A figure cloaked in grey was seated on the middle seat. The hands resting on the oars were delicate and white in colour.

'The hands of a lady, Edel,' whispered Weiss, 'I think we need not fear!'

The mysterious figure freed one hand and pulled back the hood that shaded head and shoulders. The lunar light cast a halo behind the mysterious rower and this they thought to be a good omen. Oars were resting on the gunwales and the vessel gently rocked on a ridge of sand, six feet from shore. Edel and Weiss jumped easily from shore to the sandbank.

'A couple of jumping jacks,' sang out a melodious voice, 'and fairies at that, Mountain Fairies, we don't see much of you folks in these parts since the troubles began. I remember Mountain Fairies staying at The Graceful Neck yonder to perform at the great swan festivals. Wonderful dancers they were!'

'Alas those days are gone,' lamented Weis. 'A shadow has fallen over the land of the swans.'

'A shadow has fallen over the Kingdom my light-footed friends,' intoned the mysterious rower.

Edel returned to the task of weaving willow branches around the logs. The nocturnal visitor watched the Fairy wrestling with the unruly twigs.

'It will take hours to make a decent raft my Fairies dear and chances are that the current will take you half way to Lambarina before you reach the other shore. Jump into my boat and I will row you to the south shore.'

Edel and Weiss looked at each other and each knew what the other was thinking. The halo had been a good omen, there was nothing to fear.

The Fairies leaped into the boat and trusted their fate to the cloaked figure with the golden tresses. Silently dipping oars into the water, she swiftly moved the little vessel to the main channel of the moon swept river.

'What might your name be wise one,' queried Weiss, 'and whence your knowledge that we are heading for the other shore?'

The moon illumined an ageless face of great beauty. Her uncovered hair was rimmed by a golden glow and her blue eyes sparkled. Letting the oars trail in the water, the current carried the little vessel along.

'One thing at a time my dapper fairy. My names are many and they change from age to age. Amaranth you may call me.'

Weiss, who knew the book of ancient lore from cover to cover, squeezed Edel's hand. 'It is the enchantress Amaranth, Edel.'

'Seldom would I take this risk to expose myself and well you could have built your own little raft, but it would have taken precious time. Your mission cannot wait. Lady Erica called upon me in the black waters of the pool.'

Taking up the oars she swiftly rowed towards the far shore and landed the craft at a promontory surrounded by reeds.

'Hark ye well, brave boys.' The Fairies' eyes lit up in astonishment. As she spoke a haze of light enveloped her and before them stood the great enchantress. Stars sparkled on her sea blue gown and a crown of light adorned her brow.

Even the irrepressibles were subdued and made a deep bow. Amaranth smiled and said in bell-clear tones, 'Hurry, hurry, hurry, there is nothing else that I can do. My presence is required elsewhere. I have always had a weak spot for the Dwarf Scimitar. The rescue expedition must succeed, much depends upon the intrepid warrior, now a prisoner of the Seven.'

'Remember the grey wolves. The Great Grey can be called upon for help. Ulrik and Ensten from Esteria have spoken to Leonardo, leader of the pack. There is little time left. Make haste for only nine days remain before the new moon rises.'

They picked up their packs from the bottom of the boat and sprang ashore. Amaranth pushed off and turned the little craft down stream.

A grey mist enshrouded the enchantress and a trace of light on the dark waters was the last that Edel and Weiss saw of her.

They sat down on a tree stump. 'Amazing Weiss, I am overwhelmed to have seen the enchantress. I won't be able to sleep a wink tonight.' Edel's eyes sparkled with excitement.

'That is just as well,' retorted his Weiss, 'There is no time for sleep, only nine days to new moon.'

'No fiddling, no games, no meandering,' laughed Edel, 'We must travel night and day.'

Once they put their mind to something Edel and Weiss wasted no time. They shouldered their packs and in giant leaps traveled eastwards. They traveled at a speed that would leave Gnomes and Dwarves far behind. But Gnomes and Dwarves have great endurance. After a day of travel Mountain Fairies are forced to rest, whereas Dwarves and Gnomes keep slugging along.

Edel and Weiss were still flying swiftly when dawn broke over the river. Covering great tracts of land, they had crossed two tributaries to the Sanctus. By noon the going became heavy for the riverbanks were covered with dense shrubbery. They stopped to pick berries and drank the crystal water of the Sanctus. Refreshed, they sat down by the trunk of a willow tree and dozed off. The sun was nearing the surface of the water when a cool breeze called them back to the banks of the Sanctus and to the need for haste! They jumped up and grabbed their packs. This time they didn't last long, running along the shore they were soon overcome by a wave of fatigue, and slowed down. They had been traveling at great speed for over eighteen hours and their reserves were spent.

The shrubbery had begun to give way to evergreens, tall and stately, their branches swaying in the evening breeze. It was easier to walk under the pines for there was little undergrowth and they were able to pick up speed. A canopy of needles overshadowed the tiny figures moving over the forest floor. By dusk they had to stop and Edel suggested that they should bivouac soon.

'It is true Edel we must replenish our strength,' sighed Weiss, 'I will climb a tree and look for landmarks.

Weiss slowly worked his way to the gently swaying treetop and rested his eyes on a dark sea of needle woods reaching to the horizon.

In the faint light of the waning moon he spotted a single column of white smoke rising high above the jagged tops of a ridge of giant spruce.

Edel had fallen asleep on the soft needles. Weiss climbed down quickly and shook him by the shoulders. 'Edel there is a cabin in the woods, perhaps three miles from here. We must try our luck and find shelter if we can.'

Edel pulled himself up and painfully they began their march inland. Sometimes crossing a clearing they would catch a glimpse of smoke in the distance. As they walked on they nibbled on Erica's oatcakes. Edel was dizzy with fatigue and leaned on Weiss to keep his balance. The darkness was now complete and the towering pines became low vaulted catacombs. They felt the great trees were weighing upon them and exhausted, they sat down and leaned against the foot of a giant pine.

As the darkness deepened, a sense of dread flowed over the Fairies, a sense of dread they had never felt before. The saucy, cheeky, very much taken with themselves Mountain Fairies collapsed on the mossy forest floor. Life had been a lark, a happy dance and the two daredevils had thought themselves immortal. Now they experienced a fear they had never known before.

They lay still, unable to move. A sense of foreboding crept closer and closer. 'Edel.' spoke Weiss, grasping his hand, 'Edel, death exists even for us. Let us be grateful there is death, for death is surely more welcome than this paralyzing fear. It is as if all the evil spirits of the forest gathered in this darkness and are holding us in their clutches.'

'I hear footsteps Weiss,' said Edel trying to sit up. Weiss, still trembling, managed to stand up and leaned against the rough bark of a pine.

'Lights,' Edel, 'hundreds of little lights are moving towards us.'

They could see the flaming torches coming closer but the torchbearers themselves could not be seen. As the flames drew ever closer, Edel and Weiss broke out in a cold sweat.

'Weiss, they are Elves, clad in black.'

'The Black Elves Edel, the elf wing that defied the Elven Queen when she brought the Elves into the Kingdom of the Seven Mountains. They broke away and crossed the border.'

Weiss had picked up a lot of mountain lore. It had been whispered that the very Elves who had walked away from the unity conference at Mount Oneisis in order to gain independence from the Kingdom had allied themselves with the Seven Dark Masters. They had abandoned their traditional colourful clothing and had adopted the black standard of the Lords. Carrying torches in the dark forest, only a shadowy outline of the dark column could be seen.

A physical pain crept over the Fairies. They slid to the bottom of the pine tree, too tired and miserable to attempt escape. They put their bows and backpacks behind the tree and lay flat on the moss. Perhaps the Elves would ignore them. Vain hope! A merewing strutting alongside the marching troop had just brought instructions to report all suspicious activities. Cobalt, Captain of the Black Elves had little use for Mountain Fairies. Their Queen had a sharp tongue and there had been some humiliating incidents in the past.

When he spotted the prone Fairies by the trunk of the tree he did not entertain seriously the idea that they might be involved in some nefarious activity. After all Mountain Fairies were playboys, useless pranksters, incapable of any project that was worthwhile.

Perhaps he could give them a good scare or turn them over to the Grolls who would serve them as appetizers, preferably pickled in wine sauce. The very thought was quite hilarious and Cobalt was in a jovial frame of mind. He bent down and prodded Edel and Weiss with the end of his silver halberd.

Edel and Weiss knew that they were beaten and slowly they got up.

'Mountain Fairies, eh?' snarled the Captain. 'Your names please.' 'Edel and Weiss,' responded Weiss for the two of them.'

'Edelweiss,' snickered the Captain. 'A lovely flower, a delicate flower,' mused the grinning Elf, 'Quick to bloom and quick to wither.' Of course Cobalt had heard of Edel and Weiss, tales of the fairy mischief makers had spread far and wide. And Cobalt knew these practical jokers, these good-for-nothings, were dispensable, his masters couldn't possibly be interested in them.

His command to march was accompanied by a couple of kicks and the exhausted Edel and Weiss dragged themselves along.

'Cobalt the traitor,' whispered Weiss a little too loud, and another swift kick followed. Not all the Elves had laughed at the crude behaviour of their leader and some were pained by the violent kicks that Cobalt dealt so generously. Some recalled how Cobalt's fiery speeches had swayed them to choose separation and independence. Now marching through the dark forest in their drab outfits many longed for the past. They remembered with nostalgia the dancing, the brilliant colours, the festivals and the fellowship that they had shared with Gnomes, Dwarfs, Outlanders and Mountain Fairies. And the wonderful feasts in the land of the Swannepeople. Cobalt's promises of independence and great powers had come to naught. Quite a few of the Black Elves marching in the column dreamed of escape and of returning to the Kingdom, if only an amnesty could be arranged. The promise of freedom had turned out to be a straitjacket.

They had not marched far before they came to a clearing. Here the Black Elves stopped to spend the night. Five of the Elves grabbed Edel and Weiss and stuffed them into a burlap bag. Tying one end of the rope to the bag they flung the other end over the branch of a large pine. With a good deal of merriment they pulled the free end of the rope and Edel and Weiss rose high above the forest floor. Escape would be impossible.

They could easily look through the rough burlap mesh and down below they saw the Elves lighting bonfires, one for each of the four companies of the troop.

The Elves lay on the pine needles, feet towards the fire. Peeking through the burlap, to Weiss it looked like four cartwheels with fiery centers.

Mountain Fairies are rather double-jointed and although mortified, they were not terribly uncomfortable in their burlap prison.

Down below Cobalt was talking to Lightfoot, his second in command. They made sure every word could be heard by the prisoners.

'I think they prefer to pickle them Cobalt. For all their rough manners, Grolls are dedicated to fine dining,' offered Lightfoot.

'It certainly would put us in their good graces Lightfoot.'

'I say Captain, we will turn them over when we reach the border. The Grolls can do the stuffing and the curing.'

'Indeed Lightfoot let them do the dirty work,' laughed the Captain.

'Useful work, Captain, who needs them? Bums, vagrants, hobos, a pair of lackadaisical lotus-eaters.'

'This is no way to go, Edel,' murmured Weiss. 'If we are to check out from this terrestrial plane, we must go in a blaze of glory. Our reputation is at stake.'

Weiss was peering at their captors through the mesh when in the light of the flickering flames a huge figure loomed. Weiss could see shuffling gently towards the center of the clearing, feet the size of a small boat.

The Elf Captain turned to Lightfoot, 'I think our Landlord has just arrived.'

A look of discomfort spread over Lightfoot's face and he whispered.

'Poor timing Cobalt. We may have some explaining to do.' It was indeed the Landlord of the Elves. After years of wandering the breakaway Elves had found shelter in the woods of the ancient forest troll Heronymus. Heronymus had lived for more than half a millennium in the ancient pine forest.

Trolls keep growing like ancient trees until they reach half the height of the pines. Heronymus looked impressive. The huge Trolls are quite harmless and they treasure their privacy. Old and lonely in his latter days, in return for small favours, he had given the Elves a home. The jaunty black creatures amused him.

One thing pained the giant Troll. Many young male Trolls, distantly related, had married Gorghoul maidens and the offspring had turned out badly.

Young Grolls had roamed the land and had robbed and terrorized the old and defenseless.

Although Grolls were smaller than their ancestors, they were fearsome warriors and some had even harassed their troll forefathers. Many had drifted to the domain of darkness. Blood lines are important in troll life and when the Grolls swore allegiance to the Seven Masters it had pained the ancient Trolls.

It was not that the giant Trolls had a highly developed conscience. They had rather a nebulous kind of feeling about good and evil. They would listen to that inner voice sometimes, especially if it did not upset their comfortable lifestyle.

They tried to forget about being related to the Grolls, but when horror stories surfaced, it grated just the same. The whole situation reflected poorly on the image of the giant Trolls and whenever Grolls were mentioned, Heronymus blew his stack.

He had overheard the talk between the Captain and Lightfoot and their plans to present the Fairies as a good will gift to the Grolls. Any illusions he might have had about the offspring of the young Trolls and the Gorghouls had long since been shattered and well he knew the fate that awaited the Fairies. The whole thing would reflect badly on his reputation and his fury was in full spate.

Lucky for the Black Elves, Cobalt and Lightfoot had shouted a warning as the Troll strode towards the sleeping Elves. The giant feet would have done honour to a steamroller. The Elves however, always nimble and quick, sprang out of harm's way.

The sight of a troop of terrified Elves vanishing into the underbrush rather amused the Troll and his anger soon abated. He sat down close to the very spot from where Cobalt and Lightfoot had scrambled into the bushes.

'Out with you Cobalt,' shouted Heronymus, 'If you do not appear this instant, I will waltz you and your elf troop into the ground.'

Cobalt knew Heronymus to be as good as his word and his big feet could flatten a lot of Elves in a very short time. The Captain made an appearance, quite confident that he could handle his volatile landlord. He climbed the tree against which Heronymus was leaning and perched himself on a branch that was level with the Troll's head.

'What is this nonsense you were talking about, elfie? Do I hear you have a present for the Grolls?'

'A jest Your Highness,' said Cobalt trying to placate the Troll, 'We just wanted to scare a couple of good for nothing Mountain Fairies. They are hanging up there in the burlap bag.'

Heronymus had a feeling that the Black Elves were engaged in a foxy scheme. He decided that he would look into the matter. He got up with a huff and a puff that blew Cobalt off his perch and without paying any further attention to the elf leader sprawling on the forest floor, went up to the burlap bag swinging on the large pine, picked it up, and swung it over his shoulders.

Soon Edel and Weiss were bouncing on the back of the striding Troll.

Heronymus lived in an old log house on a height overlooking the forest and the Fairies could hear him puffing as he climbed up the steep path.

It was pitch dark when he went in through the front door. He put the burlap bag on the dining table and lit the candles in the wrought iron chandelier.

Heronymus was exhausted after all the excitement and decided that he would deal with the contents of the bag after a good night's sleep. He tied the bag to the chandelier, snuffed out the candles and climbed into his huge bed at the far end of the living room.

Dawn's first light was breaking when Heronymus woke. Streaks of deep red drew across the purple sky and he rose slowly with a feeling of foreboding. After dressing he opened the front door and walked into the garden. He was clad in lederhosen and a bright red shirt. Long white hair framed a gnarled face on which time had carved the story of centuries. He picked a bouquet of roses and wandered over to the grave of Trollanka, through many years, his faithful companion. He shook the roses until the petals covered the grave and seated himself on an old tree stump. Tears were running down his face, wetting the collar of his shirt.

'Ah Trollanka,' wept the ancient one, 'Two centuries have flown by and trouble nothing but trouble. Our great grand children, the Grolls, work for the Dark Lords and my only source of amusement, the Elves, have turned black and cruel. Your cooking and your singing no longer cheer my spirit. What am I to do? Life is turning into a tragedy.'

Trolls tend to become melancholy when they grow old and Heronymus was feeling weary and sorry for himself. He rested his great head between his hands and hummed a haunting tune.

Edel and Weiss had finally fallen asleep in their burlap hammock. They wakened at first light and set out energetically to fight themselves out of the burlap bag. This did not prove easy. The burlap was tough and it took a lot of chewing to make a hole in it.

'By the Great Pelican, Weiss, I have never been so frightened in my life,' confessed Edel.

'That ancient giant saved our skin Edel,' cheerfully piped Weiss.

Once the hole was large enough, they had their mouths full of burlap fibre. With an artful jump they landed on the dining table.

'Where has he gone Weiss,' asked Edel, looking around the room.

The pair took a flying tour of the large house but there was no sign of the Troll. The door stood ajar and they walked onto the porch. There was the Troll, seated on the tree stump in the garden, rivulets of tears running from his eyes.

'Edel,' whispered Weiss touching his hand, 'This journey is unlike any other. Fear and grief are our fellow travelers.'

For the first time in their lives the two pranksters touched a depth that they had not known before. Both knew that they must try and comfort the disconsolate figure in the garden who only hours ago, had snatched them from the jaws of death.

Edel was about to rush down the garden but Weiss caught him by the arm. 'Edel look, look up.'

Against the red and purple sky of the early dawn moved the outline of a woman veiled in light. The apparition drew closer, moved across the grave, came to a halt behind the slumping Troll, and rested her right hand upon his head.

'Faithful companion of my youth, you too must leave this puckered, wizened body. Our ancestors await your coming.'

The Troll, electrified for a moment, reached out to Trollanka.

Edel and Weiss stood motionless, tears welling in their eyes.

A hand of light touched the gnarled hand of her ancient companion and he looked up at her spirit. 'You have come to fetch me and I will leave these mortal shores. But the Mountain Fairies hanging from the chandelier, what will become of them? I was going to take them down and serve them breakfast.'

'It is all right,' shouted Edel and Weiss, rushing into the garden, 'We chewed our way out of the burlap bag and we are here at your service'

A smile played upon the Trolls' face when he looked down on the young eager faces.

'A last request by an ailing Troll,' said Heronymus.

'We will do anything you could wish,' shouted Weiss, 'you saved us from a horrible fate.'

'The Grolls, they were going to feed you to the Grolls. The Black Elves betrayed my trust. My sons will come and set things aright. Black smoke is the sign that we agreed upon, burn wet branches in the fire place. Tell the boys to banish Cobalt and his Elves beyond the eastern border and into the realm of darkness.'

Edel and Weiss looked attentively at the Troll. His lips were still but there was a light in his eyes. Suddenly his spirit seemed to leave his ancient body and he slumped forward onto the layer of rose petals covering Trollanka's grave. As they rose above the grave, their hands touched. Two flecks of light speeding through the purple sky.

The Fairies stood in silence. There was nothing they could do now except rush up to the house and light the fire. Edel started the fire with dry kindling and onto the pyre, Weiss piled dew covered fir branches. Soon the sky was darkened by a black column of smoke. The Mountain Fairies looked at each other.

'My God Edel, how much we have lived through in the last day and a half. We must stop and have a bite to eat. Let us climb the dining table.'

First they jumped on Heronymus' huge chair and from there it was an easy hop to the surface of the table. At the far end they found a stack of waffles and a large bowl of cranberry sauce. To Edel and Wise the waffles looked the size of wagon wheels. They soon cut themselves some manageable pieces and had a decent breakfast.

'Now we must climb onto the roof Weiss,' shouted a revitalized Edel, 'and look out for Heronymus and Trollanka's sons.'

This was easier said than done, for by fairy standards, the troll house was more than seven stories high. At the corner where the logs interlocked they found good purchase and clambered to the ridge. Black smoke was rising straight up into the brilliant blue and Edel and Weiss, comfortably seated on the ridge of the thatched roof, awaited the arrival of the next generation of Trolls. The view was glorious and the love of life, always hidden in their hearts, rose quickly to the fore.

Edel and Weiss saw the pines undulating and heard the earth tremble as the giants forced their way to their father's house. When the six large Trolls emerged from the trees, they loped across the meadows and moments later arrived at their father's house. Snort, the eldest, walked up to the grave yard and saw his father's lifeless form lying by his mother's grave. Standing still he began to chant. The other five joined him at the graveside and raised their voices. They sang in unison, setting the forest aquiver.

When the chanting stopped, the six figures by the graveside straightened up and looked around them. Weiss waving his arms, shouted, 'Son of Heronymus, we have a message for you.'

Snort turned quickly and looked up at Edel and Weiss, still balanced on the ridge. When he saw the diminutive creatures on the roof, he couldn't help laughing.

'Come down my pretties,' thundered the giant. He stretched out both hands and Edel and Weiss jumped neatly into his palms.

Weiss filled Snort in on what had happened, stressing his father's last request about banishing the Black Elves.

Snort knelt down gently and deposited the Fairies on the porch.

'Stay for the funeral and the wake, my pretties.'

'Alas, great Troll,' sighed Weiss, 'Our mission is urgent and we must leave soon. We owe a great debt to your father. He saved us from the Black Elves.

Captain Cobalt intended to give us to the Grolls to be served as appetizers.'

Snort chuckled inwardly, not that he wished the fairies ill, he simply had a perverted sense of humour.

'Fare thee well, my dainties.' Edel and Weiss went through the open gate and hand in hand walked for a few paces. Then they turned around and called a last farewell to the six brothers who had lined up by the old wood fence.

No time was to be lost. Following an old cart track the Fairies flew forward at high speed.

Some miles away Cobalt and the Black Elves heard the sound waves echoing against the rocks. It made them decidedly uncomfortable. It had been a snap to befuddle old Heronymus but Snort was another matter. He had a short fuse and pulling the wool over his eyes had proven to be an unprofitable exercise. Snort had been known to sneak up on the Elves with a huge broom and sweep half the troop into a dustbin. Some of the Elves had been traumatized by the experience. Then Heronymus had been there to save the day.

No, it was time to move before Snort and his brother ruffians did something that could not be undone! The chanting had a decidedly quickening effect on the Elves and within a very short time they were on the move.

'That devilish sound of those six organ pipes gives one the creeps, Chief,' moaned Lightfoot working his way up a narrow path by the side of a beck.

'With those six pile drivers in charge, our time in the great forest has come to an end Lightfoot,' retorted Cobalt, 'to the land of the Seven Lords we must go. Onwards friends!'

Cobalt and his troop of seventy seven Elves hurried along the shore of the Mork. Only when they had put a safe distance between themselves and the Trolls did they stop for a meal and rest.

After a short break they carried on along the Mork's shore. The going was rough with lots of shrubs and bramble bushes along the water's edge. When they came to a clearing Cobalt called a halt and told the troop of his plan to lead them to the Seven Lords in the Land of Darkness.

'Those of you, who have the courage, follow me to the new land. We will build a raft and the Mork's swift current will carry us to the border country and then onto the Lake of Shadows, where flocks of Merewings are raised and trained by servants of the Seven. There we will be under the protection of our new Masters and depend no longer upon the whims and whisks of ancient Trolls.'

Many of the Elves cheered Captain Cobalt and set about building a raft. But there was a small group that stood watching silently. At a sign from a small Elf standing in the center of the group, they took off their black jackets and threw them into the Mork.

'Disgruntled, I see,' laughed Cobalt. 'Pulling out just as we are about to reach the land of promise.'

'Many years we have been reaching that land of promise, Cobalt,' said Starlight speaking for the seventeen Elves that wanted to return to the Kingdom. 'Freedom, fie and folderol, we have learned our lesson. Whenever we moved we left but one dependence for a greater one. Freedom, fibs and fiddles. Nowhere did we have the freedom and felicity that our brethren enjoy in the Kingdom of the Seven Mountains. We will return and beseech Queen Orchidea to grant us amnesty.'

'Away with you, Starlight, you never did have the pluck to persevere. The Kingdom you are returning to may surprise you. Our new Liege Lords will control the Kingdom before long and if there be an amnesty it will be short-lived,' scoffed Cobalt.

'The future is not ours to see, Cobalt. We will follow our guidance come what may. Be it our last righteous act.' The dapper Elf walked away from the jeering of Cobalt's crowd and joined his fellows at the far end of the clearing.

They packed their few belonging and began the long trek home. Within minutes the seventeen had vanished into the shrubs. The faint strains of the Kingdom's National Anthem could be heard and it grated much on Cobalt's cross-grained soul.

In their scrape with the Elves, Edel and Weiss had lost bows and backpacks. Unencumbered, they were now moving like a pair of gazelles and many of the traditional forest dwellers were amazed to see the two fly by.

A couple of badgers, comfortably meditating at the foot of a large birch, looked up at the speeding Fairies and shook their heads.

'Lack of planning Berend,' muttered the elder.

'A common failure amongst bipeds, Ludwig.'

'I say, they may know where they are going, Berend, but the why has escaped them.'

'Mountain Fairies, Ludwig, the most volatile species in the Kingdom.'

'That may be so Berend but it is no excuse just the same.'

'Very true Ludwig, very true,' mumbled Berend, 'all fluff and no depth.'

Edel and Weiss' mad dash came to an end at the shore of a lake. They caught their breath and sat down at the water's edge. After a short rest Edel stretched out on his stomach and bringing his face down to the water quenched his thirst. Resting his head upon his hands, he stared down into the water.

'Weiss, the colours in the lake are magic. Fishes, purple, black, red and yellow. All the colours of the rainbow swimming around.'

Weiss joined Edel and together they watched a kaleidoscope of colours moving in the lake's crystal waters. Fascinated by the sight, they did not notice a tiny craft moving along the shore until a deep voice echoed over the water.

'Hail Mountain Fairies, hail. Far from your native land you have wandered. Welcome to the Lake of the Coloured Fishes.'

'Edel and Weiss sat up, startled. They saw a tiny boat glide into view and a small figure at the oars steered the craft towards them.

Whatever misgivings they might have harboured dissolved when Oarflake's singsong voice welcomed them.

'Strangers have visited us in our exile but no Fairies from the land of Queen Tuluga have come to the Lake of the Coloured Fishes. A warm welcome to you my Fairies. Come to our humble home and be our guests at the evening board.'

Edel and Weiss bowed, thanked the Gnome and in the wake of his little boat, followed the shoreline. Weiss, who knew the story of the exiles filled Edel in. Edel was thrilled to visit the famous Gnome couple in their perpetual banishment.

'What adventures Weiss, what stories to tell when we return.'

'If we return Edel. Queen Tuluga spoke about a dangerous and arduous journey,' cautioned Weiss, trying to get Edel's feet back on the ground.

Soon they came to a clearing and could see a column of smoke rising at the edge of the forest. Ambrosia met them near the dock, took their hands and led them through the gardens. They could see a quaint log cabin flanked by fine stands of spruce.

Coming closer, Edel gave a start and grasped Weiss' arm.

'Look Weiss, by the well in front of the house.' They stopped in their tracks. A huge grey wolf rose from his haunches and sauntered towards the anxious Fairies. He stopped just short of the two, a puzzled look on his face.

'Fear not my friends,' boomed Oarflake's voice near the house, 'Come hither, come hither, Leonardo will not hurt a fly unless I tell him to.'

The wolf had an amused look in his blue eyes. He gave the two guests a friendly lick, walked back to the well and spread himself out on the sunny lawn.

Weiss had told Edel the story of the banishment of Oarflake and Ambrosia, and they felt delighted to meet the couple that tales had already shrouded in mystery. Oarflake told them about the visit of the travelers from Swanneland and then Edel and Weiss told Oarflake and Ambrosia how the Marquis, Ducky and Captain Martin had been lured into the palace of the Queen of the marshes. A frown appeared on Ambrosia's face.

'Alas my dear friends none of those lured into the Palace has returned to tell the tale.'

'Fear not mother Ambrosia,' burst out Edel, 'We will find a way into the palace and before the new moon appears, snatch our friends from the clutches of the Queen.'

Ambrosia, with a wooden ladle, stirring a large pot of stew, smiled at the enthusiasm of the ephemeral creatures by her side.

While listening to the Fairies' tale, Oarflake got the table ready.

Seated around the table supping hot stew, the story became more animated. When the Fairies told of their capture by the Black Elves, Oarflake and Ambrosia were so excited, they forgot to eat.

'A close shave I'd say, nearly turned over to the Grolls,' murmured Oarflake with horror in his eyes.

But when Weiss told them how Snort had banished the Black Elves, Ambrosia and Oarflake seemed relieved.

'It will take at least three days for Edel and Weiss to reach Svanhild and Slim,' reflected Ambrosia. 'It might be too late. Tomorrow they must ride Leonardo to the domain of the nymph and gain Svanhild and Slim's campsite by sundown.'

'Well spoken Ambrosia,' intoned Oarflake. 'I will make new backpacks for our guests.'

After the evening meal Edel and Weiss walked out on the lawn and with some trepidation, approached the well where Leonardo was dozing. Edel stretched out his hand and stroked the wolf's fur. With a kind of trumpet sound Leonardo turned on his back and Edel and Weiss gave him a tummy rub that put the gentle brute in a state of bliss.

I believe that we have established a relationship,' said Weiss, 'which is just as well before riding into the wilds on the back of this giant wolf.'

'I say we have, 'grumbled Edel, trying to brush myriad wolf hairs from his trousers.'

Edel and Weiss had a sound sleep that night and after a breakfast of hot porridge and sunflower seed, they felt full of bounce. Ambrosia came out of the house with two backpacks filled with sandwiches and nuts, and Oarflake presented the Fairies with camp knives. There was no time to be lost. They must leave at once.

'Fare ye well my fairy friends, Leonardo will carry you swiftly to your goal.'

'Can you believe it, Weiss,' cried Edel, 'we will be wolf riders, I never dreamt of such a thing.'

Ambrosia smiled at the two Fairies, caught up as they were in the excitement of adventure, without a thought about the dangers that surely must lie ahead.

Leonardo although not endowed with powers of speech understood quite a lot. He began doing leg stretches, for he had the distinct feeling that a lot of running was in the offing. 'Those two Fairies, I'll give them the ride of their lives!' There was a mischievous twinkle in Leonardo's blue eyes.

'Come hither Wolfie,' called Oarflake, there is some cargo to be packed before the riders climb on your back'

Leonardo stood quietly while Oarflake hung the two rucksacks over the wolf's broad back. Edel and Wise climbed aboard.

Ambrosia threw them a kiss, Oarflake waved and Leonardo moved off at a gentle trot.

18

Palace In The Marshes

$\mathcal{W}$olf riders, we'll be known as wolf riders Weiss,' shouted Edel.

Keep your mind on the path ahead, Edel. Never mind what we'll be called. First we have to get there.'

Those words came none too soon. To vault a stream, the wolf who had been ambling along broke into a full gallop. Edel, seated behind Weiss was still in the middle of a daydream. In the great reception hall of the royal palace, Queen Tuluga pinned a Golden Wolf on his jacket and the soaring voices of a choir of fairy maidens, raising the national anthem, thrilled his soul. When Leonardo leapt across the water, Edel slid off the wolf rump and splashed into the rushing stream. He was already under water when the lovely music in his mind dissolved into the sound of swirling water.

Leonardo halted on the other side and Weiss rushed down the hill to see his dripping friend hanging by a willow branch. The current was swift at this point and could not easily be forded. Then a deep howl reached his ears. Leonardo had sounded the alarm. Weiss looked upstream where a raft was shooting the rapids. Small black figures were busy steering the craft through the racing waters of the Mork.

The sight of the wolf by the shore sent a wave of fear through the company of Black Elves but it also alerted them and Captain Cobalt spotted the Fairy hanging by the willow branch and many ready hands plucked Edel from his precarious hold and tied him to the timbers of the raft.

Rescue was impossible. The raft traveled swiftly down the Mork and the shore was lined with jagged rocks and wild brambles. Cobalt, his sixty remaining Elves and their fairy captive were well on their way to the border country.

Weiss was horrified and helpless. Leonardo, seething with anger, was unable to jump the fast moving raft. This was not the first time the Black Elves had worsted him and he had a deep yearning to sink his fangs into them.

Weiss knew that he must go on. The mission was vital and in the end, even Edel's lot might depend on it. Edel, always dreaming about tales now was caught in a tale he might never tell. Weiss shivered as he climbed onto Leonardo's back.

The great wolf followed a winding forest trail, his anger spurring him into a flying gallop. On the undulating wolfback, Weiss bounced like a rubber ball. His surfing experience stood him in good stead and he kept his balance. The trees became fewer and fewer and soon they entered the marshlands.

The sun was high in the heavens and when they crossed a warm sandy beach, Leonardo slowed down to have a rest. Weiss lay down next to the great beast hoping to catch a quick nap, but Leonardo's wet snout kept poking him. At last, Weiss got the message, the wolf wanted his tummy scratched. He got down on his knees and rubbed Leonardo's tum until his charger fell asleep. Weiss spent some time brushing wolf hair from his suit and reluctantly accepted that the price of wolf riding is having long sticky wolf hair all over your outfit.

Leonardo, possessing an inner sense of duty, woke up as soon as his splendid physique was ready to go back into action. He ate Edel's lunch with relish, did a few leg stretches and they were off on a mad dash through the marshes. Weiss was heartbroken but he held back the grief flooding his soul. He must stay on the bounding wolf back. Leonardo was moving with giant strides across the wide expanse of swamp country.

The white waters of the Mork washed over Edel as the raft traveled down stream. Cobalt steered the craft skillfully as it shot down the last set of rapids before it left the Kingdom of the Seven Mountains and entered the black and silent waters of the Lake of Shadows. Dusk had fallen and the rocks at the end of the lake were set afire by rays of the setting sun.

Edel now could breathe more easily. Water no longer washed over his face and he could see stars sparkling in the dark blue sky above. He shivered with cold and fear, and a sense of guilt stole over him. His daydreaming had done him in. When Leonardo jumped the stream, he should have paid attention.

Before long his mirth loving spirit returned. Was it not possible that he would learn important facts about the enemy, escape, and bring the intelligence to the Council at the Manor deCygne? Out of this disaster some good might yet come, reflected the ever optimistic Mountain Fairy.

The Black Elves paddled the raft to a wooden dock where a company of Grolls met them. A groll Sergeant jumped onto the raft and on behalf of the Rover Captain at the outpost, welcomed the Elves. After the first greetings Cobalt pointed to the Fairy tied down to the logs. 'We brought you an appetizer Sergeant.'

'A welcome change after weeks of fish and potatoes,' said the Groll smacking his lips.

Edel was cut loose, still dazed from his ordeal. The Groll picked him up, tucked him under his arm, and carried him to the field kitchen in one of the barracks. The brute dropped him onto a wooden surface. Edel, fully conscious, realized that he was lying on a kitchen counter. An ill omen indeed. He rolled over hoping to drop off the edge but a quick witted cook caught him in time and pinned him down with a fork.

'Smells like a Mountain Fairy. Get me one of the glass jars from the storage room Gaffer,' the cook ordered the Groll, who had dropped Edel on the counter. 'And while you are at it bring some brine and a cabbage leaf.'

High above, Solomon and Kasper were circling the marshes. They had successfully removed any doubts among the woodland owls concerning legitimate leadership and the troop of Wood owls left behind in the pine forest looked subdued and miffed.

'Splendid chief,' said an admiring Kasper, 'Your speech took the wind out of the old boilers and some of the young turkeys tumbled off their perch.'

'No point flapping around the bush Deputy. Choosing leaders by a show of wings, it is against nature.'

'Entirely unheard of Chief, I say horse feathers, poppycock and flapdoodle.'

'Well put Deputy, quite literary. It puts the whole thing in perspective.'

Solomon and Kasper serenely soared over the wetlands, looking for Slim and Svanhild, when they caught a grey shape streaking through the marshes. Banking into a steep glide, they soon espied Leonardo with Weiss bouncing on his back.

'It looks to me as if there is only one Mountain Fairy on the back of the wolf,' observed Kasper.

'Creatures without wings are in for a bumpy ride Deputy, especially on wolf back. One must have bounced off. We better show wolfie a short cut to the beach. The Great Grey have a good sense of direction but it does not hold a candle to celestial navigation.'

'Of course not Chief, that art is unique to higher fowl.'

The owls skimmed the marshes. When Weiss spotted them he shouted at the top of his voice, 'Leonardo, Leonardo, the owls will guide us. Follow the owls!'

Leonardo changed course and sprang forward in the gathering dusk. High above the marshes the rays of the setting sun still caught the owls in flight and the great wolf followed them.

Slim and Svanhild, a sleeping bag wrapped around their shoulders, were seated by a small fire when they saw Solomon and Kasper glide overhead. Moments later, Leonardo broke through the willow shrubbery. The wolf by himself would have frightened them, but the dapper Mountain Fairy seated on his back, dispelled their fear. When the wolf came closer to the fire, Svanhild recognized Leonardo and knew that he could be trusted.

Patriot, who had made his peace with the grey wolves at the log cabin of Oarflake and Ambrosia, cheerfully wagged his tail.

Weiss dismounted and told Slim and Svanhild that the Council at the Manor deCygne had sent him to offer what help he could.

Slim and Svanhild extended a warm welcome and thanked him for coming to their aid. Slim pulled up a log and Weiss, still dazed, from the loss of Edel and the grueling trip, seated himself by the fire.

Leonardo worn to a frazzle sat on his haunches puffing and panting. Svanhild offered him a bowl of water and stroked the massive wolf head until his breathing calmed down. Solomon and Kasper, perched on a willow branch, with deep and wondering eyes, gazed at the little group.

Slim hung a tea kettle over the fire and Svanhild who had been watching Weiss walked over and put her hand on his shoulder. 'Weiss, we remember you from the festival in Swanneland. You and your friend Edel danced in front of the Graceful Neck.

'Fair Swannemaid,' spoke Weiss with tears running down his face, 'Edel traveled with me on this mission and should have been sitting next to me on this very log by your lovely fire listening to the singing of the kettle.'

'Edel traveled with you on wolfback? Tell us my fairy fair, what befell your lively companion.'

'He fell in the Mork and was captured by Black Elves rafting downstream. They tied him to their raft and carried him to the land where the Seven rule.'

Svanhild put her arm around Weiss and tried to comfort him.

Solomon reflected, 'the raft will have crossed the border by now. Rescue is even beyond the wisdom of owls but we will fly over the border area and keep an eye on all that moves down below.'

Weiss thanked the owls and tried to pull himself together.

'Do not lose hope Weiss,' consoled Slim, 'All of us are in danger and we will do what we can.'

'Before new moon we must whisk Moose, Ferdinand and Duckie out of the clutches of the Queen of the Marshes,' Svanhild warned.

'Two days grace before they turn into green moaners,' added Solomon gravely.

'Could you sneak into the palace Solomon?' asked Svanhild.

'Alas, my Lassie of the Swans,' retorted the Chief, 'Queen Marsha invites exotic birds into her palace. Birds of wisdom are not welcome.'

'That says a lot about the lady of the mudflats, Chief,' snapped Kasper.

'It says it all Deputy,' Solomon responded with a deep hoot. A moment of silence followed the Chief of the Owls' definitive statement.

'The last news from Peli 1, came yesterday. Duckie and the Marquis had regained their senses but the Captain was still three sheets to the wind,' reported Slim.

'Strange,' mused Svanhild, a puzzled look in her eyes, 'that retired ferry Captain solid as the rock of ages, now a philanderer and libertine, reeled in by the maidens of the Queen. How can that be Solomon? Can the Owls' Book of Wisdom shed light on so strange a transformation?'

Solomon stretched his wings, blinked his eyes and in solemn tones, hooted,

the quiet landscape of the soul
hides strangers down below
who secrets keep
in caverns deep

when the sentinels of mind ,
are lulled by scent and wine,
then, they rise to havoc wreak
they feast and dance and run
into the web the Queen has spun

After a few minutes of silence, Svanhild remarked, 'How terrible, Solomon, that below the surface of our consciousness do strangers live.' Solomon fixed his gaze upon the Swannemaiden.

'Svanhild, we must turn within. Face the creatures in the underworld, listen to their secret wishes and guide them to the light of day. Ignore them and they will haunt us.'

'Unto thine own self be true,' concluded the Chief of the owls, quoting the inscription on the title page of the Owls' Book of Wisdom.

'Care to add anything Kasper?' asked Solomon turning to his Deputy.

'Quite awesome Chief, I should study that ancient volume daily, self discipline, self discipline,' muttered Kasper to himself.

'Indeed Deputy,' whispered Solomon, 'Especially if there is to be any hope of you being Chief one day.'

This last line from the Chief made an impression on Kasper and he appeared lost in meditation.

Leonardo looked baffled, the words of the owls' speech escaped him but he got the gist. 'Pretty deep stuff,' he muttered to himself.

'What can we do Solomon, to bring the Captain back to reason?' asked Svanhild.

'In silent meditation the powers of the soul will rise again and oust the intruders. The Captain must be led to a remote chamber of the palace and spend time away from dance and song and maidens.'

'I must sneak into the palace and scout the secret rooms and dungeons,' piped up Weiss, 'And find a way to lock the Captain out of harm's way.'

'Connect with Peli 1, Weiss,' said Slim, 'He knows our plans and will do all he can.'

'We better get some rest,' suggested Svanhild, 'Weiss is exhausted from the long journey and needs a good night's sleep before venturing into the palace.'

Slim got up and put some more logs on the fire and the friends curled up around the rising flames. Weiss rested his head on Leonardo's neck and quickly fell asleep. Only Svanhild stayed up to talk for a while to Kasper and Solomon. She put her hands on the heads of the two owls and thanked them for guiding Leonardo and Weiss to their campsite and sharing secrets from the Owls' Book of Wisdom. The Chief and his Deputy had a dreamy stare in their eyes, for Svanhild's lilting voice always had a peculiar effect on them and that ancient volume offered no satisfactory explanation of this phenomena.

Solomon and Kasper rose up in faint moonlight and winged their way back to the pine grove in the woodlands. Strange things happen to woodland owls when a vacuum in leadership occurs and Solomon knew his presence would be required for a long period of time.

Brilliant sunshine woke the party on the beach and even Weiss felt refreshed and strengthened. Saddened by the loss of his bosom friend, he was all the more determined to aid the party in recovering their friends at the Queen's palace.

Svanhild unpacked the bag of provisions which Leonardo had brought from the homestead of the Gnomes. Slim got a fire going and Svanhild cooked hot cakes and coffee over the blaze.

Leonardo had caught himself a fish in the shallow waters near the beach and lay down on the sand licking clean the bones. The great wolf, his mission completed, prepared to depart and return to his pack in the forests of Esteria. The party waved farewell as Leonardo bounded into the marshes.

Breakfast and hot coffee raised the spirits of the three figures around the fire. Just as Weiss prepared to leave in order to scout the palace grounds, a moaning sound was heard. Slim rose up and walked to the nearest pond, there in the middle stood the mudsprite Theophilus. Weiss and Svanhild joined Slim on the edge of the pond and Slim introduced the Mountain Fairy to the sprite.

'I must be brief, I am in great danger, exposed as I am in clear sunlight. We overheard your conversation and know that Weiss wants to rescue the Queen's victims. Some time ago, on orders of the Queen, we dug a secret tunnel into the palace. Months of back breaking labour. Perhaps we can try to smuggle Weiss into the palace. Meet me here at sundown Mountain

Fairy.' With these concise instructions Theophilus vanished underwater.

For a second cup of coffee, the party returned to the fire. Of course it would be far more sensible for Weiss to go with one of the trusted sprites who knew the marshes inside out.

'Synchronicity Weiss,' exclaimed Svanhild, 'it was meant to be this way, but you need a day of rest before setting out on another adventure.'

While sipping her coffee Svanhild told Weiss about the tragic fate of the mudsprites. Weiss realized that the kidnapping of Edel was but one of many terrible events that had happened since the rising power of the Seven Lords.

He got up and walked to the shore. By the water's edge he sat down, leaning against a log. Weiss' eyes rested on the waving reeds and the ripples on the lake. He never knew whether it was the beauty of the view, the warm rays of the sun or a magical spell that sent him into a deep sleep. In his dream the enchantress Amaranth walked on the water, waves running over her bare feet, her dress a brilliant red, golden hair streaming in the wind.

She leaned over him and whispered, 'Once you enter the palace, you must attempt to prevent the Captain from drinking the Queen's wine. The wine contains a secret potion that befuddles the Captain's common sense. Then idle fancies and secret longings overwhelm him. Once the Captain escapes from the Queen's clutches, this elixir from the fire flower will put him to sleep. It will aid him to recover and regain his sanity.'

Weiss woke with a start. The lovely vision was gone but on the log stood a small transparent flask filled with an elixir that scattered the sunlight into a spectrum of brilliant colours.

He jumped up, stepped into the water and splashed his face. Now wide awake, he looked upon the lake. Over the dark surface of the water, far from shore, moved a figure. The rays from the rising sun caught a fleck of red and gold vanishing over the horizon. Amaranth had stood amongst them and all had slept through her visitation. Weiss woke Slim and Svanhild. Quickly they washed in the lake and sat down to hear Weiss's dream. When he finished he took from his pocket the crystal flask. Slim's eyes sparkled with delight.

'Heaven be praised,' exclaimed Svanhild, 'We are not alone. Help has come our way. How I wish I could have seen the enchantress.'

'I think you will meet her one day,' Weiss smiled.

The sun had set and it was time for Weiss to leave for his rendez-vous with Theophilus. He embraced Slim and Svanhild and walked swiftly into the marshes. At the edge of the pond he found Theophilus and his friend Greenpiece sitting on a submerged stump.

'Welcome Mountain Fairy,' said Theophilus, 'we, the wretched mudsprites of the marshes, wish you well on your mission. May your work help to unseat our evil mistress and her masters and change us back into the Swannefolk and Outlanders that once we were. It will take time I know. Let me introduce you to Greenpiece. He was a locksmith in Lambarina before his fall, a master at breaking and entry. If anybody can get you into the palace, Greenpiece will.

Theophilus dove under water and vanished. Greenpiece motioned Weiss to follow him. As they made their way to the palace, the Mountain Fairy and the mudsprite were hidden by the bulrushes. Greenpiece told Weiss about his family back home and his hopes that one day the Queen's curse would be lifted.

Tears ran down Weiss' cheeks as he learned about the terrible things that were happening, tears for the fate of the mudsprites, tears for Edel, tears for the imprisoned Princess and tears for the loss of his own innocence. He could never again be the carefree spirit that roamed the world, creating mischief and playing pranks. Dark forces were at work and he, like the others, must put his shoulder to the wheel.

'Grieve not for us Mountain Fairy. Our fate is our own doing. We should never have fallen into temptation,' Greenpiece lamented in a fit of self-reproach. Weiss put his arm on the sprite's clammy shoulder to bring some solace to the remorse stricken creature. He recalled the words his mother sang at bedtime.

in the darkest night
a star will twinkle bright
to guide an erring being
to life, to light, to seeing

'A lovely thought, were it only true,' groaned Greenpiece.

Weiss had never really thought about it but his hand slipped into his pocket and there was the lovely oval bottle with the elixir from the fire flower. Amaranth had come to them from the unseen worlds to help their mission.

'It must be true Greenpiece. Things happen at times and places for reasons that we cannot see. You must believe it. Believing is seeing!' Greenpiece felt moved by his companion's enthusiasm and through him flowed a surge of energy.

The two trudged along a narrow path until they came to a pavilion. A small fountain in the middle was surrounded by flowerbeds. Wooden garden chairs, beautifully crafted stood around the perimeter of the little garden. Light of the waning moon was reflected in the lustrous red slate covering the area.

'Yes, she has exquisite taste, the Queen of the Marshes,' observed Greenpiece, sliding into one of the comfortable chairs. Weiss climbed onto the wide armrest and looking at the sprite asked, 'How is it Greenpiece that a lady who adores beauty can be so wicked?'

'That is a knotty one, Mountain Fairy. In some strange way she believes that what she is doing is useful, admirable. She wants to please her Masters. Perhaps deep inside that blistering beauty, lie hidden seeds of virtue. We, the green sprites, were upright fellows before our fall. Did we carry seeds of self-ruin within?' mused the green creature in a doleful voice.

Mountain Fairies, unlike Dwarves and Outlanders, are not given to wandering in the deeper valleys of self reproach but Weiss' quick mind followed the trail of Greenpiece's journey within. Putting his hand on Greenpiece's shoulder he asked, 'Are we not like the wooden dolls that the Gnomes carve in winter by the fireside? You open one and you find another inside. You open that one and another one shows up.'

'You are learning quickly,' rejoined Greenpiece pressing Weiss' hand. 'On the journey within, strangers keep appearing.'

'That is how the Chief of the owls explained it,' said Weiss.

'Owls are wise, they have got it together,' mused Greenpiece.

'I think, Greenpiece, that even the best of us sometimes have a little doll inside that we really don't care to know about and the worst amongst us may have a glimmer of light hidden within.

'The Queen a glimmer of light? Well, I will not gainsay it Weiss. It is just hard to fathom.' They lingered a few minutes longer and listened carefully for any signs of life. Weiss' sharp ears could still pick up the distant sound of footsteps in the palace.

'We must wait until all is quiet, Weiss. Keep listening and tell me when the coast is clear.'

It took another half hour before Weiss signaled to Greenpiece that all was silent. They scanned the bushes and gardens around them to make sure that no spies or guards were anywhere near. Then Greenpiece lifted some of the pieces of slate that concealed a trapdoor to the tunnel. Since Greenpiece himself had installed the lock on the door, it didn't take him long to pick it. Weiss entered the tunnel and Greenpiece followed, pulling the door down behind them. They walked in total darkness. The froggy locksmith knew every foot of the secret passage and taking Weiss by the hand moved swiftly forward. They had to be careful not to trip for any sudden sound would alert the palace guards.

They arrived at a heavy wooden door with wrought iron strapping, secured from the inside by a heavy metal bar. Greenpiece knocked seven times and again, three times. Weiss heard a scraping sound as many hands raised the iron bar and the door gave way. Five mudsprites stood inside the dungeon as they entered. Greenpiece explained that the sprites, who had raised the bar, were trusted friends assigned to palace duty. Greenpiece took his leave and worked his way back through the tunnel, locked the trapdoor and rearranged exactly as they had found it, the red slate in the pavilion.

The five sprites took Weiss all around the dungeons and the underground passages. They had worked in this part of the palace for years and knew every nook and cranny. At the end of the tour, they took him to their sleeping quarters. The clammy underground cellar was lit by candles and the only furniture was a rough wooden table and benches.

There was little to do at this time of night but get some rest. Weiss stretched out on the table and covered himself with a blanket the sprites had provided. He could not fall asleep, for the dank underground cavern was a horror to this child of light and flowers. He thought about Edel, the terrible fate of the green moaners and the strange and perilous mission that he had undertaken. For a Fairy known for his lightness of being, he had landed in deep and murky waters. Only when the vision of Amaranth returned to his mind was he able to unwind and fall asleep.

Jeremiah, the eldest of the sprites woke him in late morning and served a meagre breakfast of watered down oats. Afterwards the green creatures sat down with him and showed him a rough sketch of the palace.

After looking at the sketches, he felt he had a good idea of the layout of the palace grounds. The sprites suggested he wait before venturing upstairs until late afternoon when there would be more activity in the palace and much less likelihood of discovery.

He spent time talking to the sprites and the Fairy's blithe spirit revived their hopes for deliverance. By late afternoon they could hear a din of activity upstairs, footsteps, laughter, conversation and musicians tuning their instruments.

The sprites guided him through an underground passage to a narrow stone staircase leading to a gallery near the palace gardens.

On parting, all five were eager to shake hands and Weiss took time to speak words of hope and cheer to the sad looking creatures. Quietly he tiptoed up the stairs and reached a small hallway lit by torches. Weiss thought it best to find his way first to the indoor gardens. There he would be likely to find Peli 1.

There was no visible sign of life but distant voices and music could be heard interspersed with peals of laughter. The clinking of glasses and the clatter of dishes told him that dinner was in full swing. He moved lightly and carefully along the walls. Flaming torches mounted on the wall threw islands of light on the marble floor and after he had moved several hundred feet, he saw the shadow of a tall figure holding a spear in his right hand. Pressing against the wall he slid closer and saw the rough scales on his legs. He was fascinated, this was the legendary Groll skin which no arrows could penetrate. Lower down, around the feet and ankles the skin was smooth. He was tempted to touch the legs, but good sense got the better of him. His mind went back to Princess Yaconda in the Alcazar and the rescue of Dominique from the hands of the groll Captain, the same smooth flat feet. Yes, it was a Groll all right. Weiss was frightened and excited at the same time. It was fortunate he measured less than two feet without his hat on, and the piercing green groll eyes, scanning the hall missed him by a couple of inches. Weiss pressed even closer to the wall and slid noiselessly forward, turning at the next passageway which took him to a brightly lit gallery.

Oil paintings graced the wall on his right. A large canvas in the center of the wall arrested him. It depicted a beautiful young woman kneeling before a lady in aubergine robes with ebony tresses and deep blue eyes. Weiss drew closer to read the caption, 'Queen Marsha greets the Sorceress Matista.'

The din from the dining hall grew louder. He slipped silently to the end of the gallery and peeked around the corner. A great banquet table ran the length of the hall. At the far end of the table presided a lady dressed in black satin with guests seated in rows on each side. Birds of brilliant plumage were perched on the back of chairs, on picture frames hanging from the wall and on the three magnificent chandeliers suspended over the table.

On the far side two maidens played the harp. Close to them stood the figure of a stately pelican, seemingly absorbed in the music. Weiss pulled back for a moment. Thank Heaven, Peli 1 was here. The black lady at the head of the table must be Queen Marsha and the loud male voice coming from that part of the table likely was the Captain's. Weiss peeked again, on the other side, next to a maiden of great beauty, sat a portly figure, the Marquis no doubt.

Dorothea watched Ferdinand closely and pressed his hand. 'Ferdinand, watch the Captain's eyes. He has wandered far into the Queen's web. Alas the touch of those lovely lips turns princes into toads.'

There was a lull in the music. Weiss picked up the voice of the Captain, now on his feet, raising his glass in a toast to the Queen.

'Hail to the Lily of the Marshes. Gone are the dull days of a retired Ferry Captain. The energy of youth pulsates through my veins and I have awakened from a long and dreadful sleep.' He looked deep into the Queen's eyes and deep he drained his goblet of red wine. The Captain did not hear the words that the Queen whispered in response to his toast but he imagined that a telling smile played on her lips.

Weiss watched the Captain closely and knew that no time was to be lost. Duckie was easily spotted for he was close to where Weiss was standing, seated between two girls who broke out into peals of laughter whenever Duckie spoke.

He waited until the laughter subsided and then whistled. Duckie turned just in time to see the tiny Fairy disappear through the archway. He slipped away from the dining table and walked through the entry portal. Weiss grabbed him by the sleeve and in a few words explained his mission and the desperate urgency for speedy escape. Duckie was horrified when Weiss told him about the green moaners and the danger that awaited them at the next new moon.

'Duckie, Peli 1 is standing behind the musicians. Wander over and ask him to meet me in the pavilion with the tall fountains and the rose bushes, but return to your table first and pretend that all is well.'

Duckie rejoined his pretty companions and suggested they walk over to the end of the hall and greet the musicians. 'You go by yourself, sweetie,' laughed the girls, 'The harpists will be pleased to see you.'

He got up and leisurely walked over to the little orchestra. Everybody in the palace knew him and the musicians welcomed him with a warm smile. There was a kind of innocence about Duckie that amused the Queen's maidens. The girls playing the harp winked at one another and motioned him to stand behind them, while they continued their performance.

Perched on the mantelpiece was Peli 1. That solemn bird loved music. It was one of the few pleasures that made bearable his stay in the palace. He flapped gently his great wings to the beat of the music and from a distance it looked as if the pelican was conducting the musicians. He had spotted Duckie but he did not let on. Duckie turned, looked up and said softly, 'In the pavilion behind the archway. No time to lose.' Peli did not stop the flapping of his wings, but blinked his eyes. Duckie knew the crafty bird had understood the message. A little later when the music stopped, he saw Peli sailing through the archway.

Weiss anxiously was waiting in the rosebushes when Peli touched down. 'Relieved to see you Peli, the Queen sends her greetings and hopes to see you back soon.'

The Pelican remembered Weiss from their adventure at the old Alcazar and the rescue of Princess's Yaconda's handmaiden.

'The sooner we are out of here, the better,' Peli whispered, 'the vibes are poor and the constant chitter chatter of airhead birds gets me down.'

'We must get the wayfarers out of here Peli.'

'I know all the nooks and crannies in this palace of moral lassitude. If we find a way of taking the guzzling Captain in tow, we will be gone in a flash.'

A shrewd look showed in the dark eyes of the big beaked bird.

'Ah my fairy fair, we must prevent the Captain from drinking the wine that the Queen so liberally serves him. It contains a magic powder. The handmaiden of the Queen, Dorothea, has a tender spot in her heart for the Marquis and his fellow travelers. Perchance she knows about the secret potion mixed into the Captains wine. Write her a note and I will take it to her.'

Weiss penned to Dorothea, a note about the planned escape, asking if there was a way of hiding the magic powder which the Queen's maidens had been slipping in the Captain's wine. Peli took wing and soaring amongst the coloured birds in the great hall, landed behind Dorothea. His beak nudged her hand, she felt the piece of paper and quickly hid it up her sleeve.

Excusing herself, she went to her room in the royal apartments to read the message. 'At last,' she murmured, 'they may yet escape before the lunar sickle rises in the sky.'

With the abandon of a maiden in love and oblivious of the dreadful consequences were she to be discovered, she slid into the royal suite and approached the Queen's boudoir. She took from it a porcelain vase decorated with roses and resolutely walked it into the kitchen and flushed down the drain, the contents of white powder. Quickly she located a jar of icing sugar, filled the vase and deftly replaced it on the boudoir.

While walking back towards the great hall she met Peli 1 in a small pavilion. Peli bowed and looked at her. She came close to his great beak and whispered, 'It is done my pelican, in four and twenty hours the Captain's soul should once again be in command.'

'Then you must flee with us maiden, before the Queen finds out that you meddled with the powder.'

'It is not possible my dear bird, I have given my word to serve the Queen and I would be a hindrance to the travelers and there are others that I hope to save before it is too late.'

'The Marquis will not leave without you Dorothea,' insisted the shrewd bird.

'The Marquis must leave without me. He will not see me before he leaves and you must tell him, it is my wish. If heaven wills, we shall meet again in this world of being, if not, in the realms beyond.'

Peli's wingtip wiped a tear from his eye and with a bow of his mighty beak, he left. In the gallery he met Weiss who was just on his way to the dungeon, to spend the night with the mudsprites. Weiss told Peli 1 that he had spoken with Duckie and the Marquis and that they had decided to meet the next afternoon, hoping that a window of sanity would appear in the Captain's mind.

The sprites, grateful for Weiss' safe return, served him a light snack, and wrapped him in blankets to keep him from shivering in the damp underground chamber. For several hours they questioned him about the outside world and were surprised to learn about all the changes happening. Before Weiss dozed off they discussed plans for the escape. They promised to talk with Greenpiece and to arrange for him to meet Weiss and his companions, at midnight the next day.

When Weiss awoke, already the green sprites had prepared breakfast and he was pleasantly surprised to see coffee and bannock on the table. Some of the older sprites on kitchen duty had spirited away some flour and coffee.

That morning Peli found the Marquis still seated in the small pavilion, Peli 1 conveyed Dorothea's warning that danger threatened and he must attempt escape that very day. The Pelican assured him that Dorothea trusted that they would meet again at another time. If he tried to get in touch with her, it would be at her peril, and his own. Peli 1 did not tell the Marquis that Dorothea had disposed of the Queen's magic potions. No point in getting him upset.

Next Peli 1 decided to shadow the Captain and see if there was any change. The old sailor came first into view around lunch time and headed for the usual buffet. He helped himself to a generous dish of smoked fish and marsh rice and filled his goblet from a crystal carafe of red wine. A smile spread over his face and Peli heard him murmur, 'The wine, so red, is even sweeter at this hour when love awaits me. The Lily of the Marshes, does she love me, yes or no?' He counted the golden buttons on his new navy jacket, sewn by the royal tailor. But, on the tenth and last button, it was no. The Queen loved him not.

Peli soared overhead, perched on the chandelier and watched the lovesick sailor. This was the time, to get his attention, so Peli picked a candle from the chandelier and dropped it on his plate. Some fish sauce splattered onto the table and the Captain looked up, amused to see a pelican sitting on the chandelier. With a jovial gesture, he invited him down for a bite of fish. Peli sailed down and took his place by the Captain's feet, well out of sight of the other guests.

The Captain had a weak spot for pelicans. His mind went back to the time when he stood at the helm of his ferryboat cruising down river, flocks of pelicans passing overhead. Images of the past welled up. A gondola ride with his betrothed, the beautiful Marinda, laid to rest in the convent garden of the Sisters of the Secret Crossing. A scent of orange blossom enveloped him and he felt Marinda standing by his side, her hand touching his shoulder. Moose Martin felt a current passing through his body, beginning at his feet and rushing upwards.Peli realized the Queen's magic potion had lost its power. He said softly, 'Captain follow me, I have urgent news.' Without waiting for a response, he soared out of the banquet hall. Moose walked out of the hall and into the gallery, where he heard the soft clicking of Peli 1's beak. He turned and saw Peli beckoning. He had to walk briskly to keep up with the hopping bird. Only after they had descended into the underground passages of the palace did Peli stop to tell the Captain that he was taking him to meet a messenger from the Manor.

Soon they were deep in the labyrinth of underground pathways and even Peli wasn't sure where they were going. Jeremiah, accompanied by small sprite appeared and led them quickly to their quarters. When Peli led Moose into the room, Weiss and the mudsprites breathed a sigh of relief.

Moose sat down at one of the tables. Weiss jumped in front of him and made a polite bow. Moose was exhausted and disoriented but the sight of the Fairy evoked a faint smile.

'Welcome Captain, My name is Weiss, servant of Queen Tuluga. Drink to our friendship. Weiss handed him the crystal vessel of elixir from the Fire Flower which Amaranth had left on the beach. Captain Martin drained it to the last drop. Before Weiss had a chance to speak, the Captain's head rolled onto the table and he fell into a deep sleep.

'Well done Weiss and Peli,' praised Jeremiah. 'You snatched him from the Queen's power on the very eve of the new moon. May his release hasten our redemption.'

'Every small victory will bring that hour closer,' reflected Peli in a solemn voice. The Captain will regain his sanity but as long as he remains within the walls of this sordid castle, he is in danger'

Weiss asked one of the mudsprites to take him back upstairs into the palace to find Duckie and the Marquis. They spotted Duckie in one of the fountains fooling around with his playmates and Weiss had no choice but to expose himself. Fortunately no Grolls were nearby. Weiss slid into the fountain, waded through the water and grabbed Duckie's hand.

Duckie was astonished to see Weiss darting through the spray. The maidens were quite delighted at the sight of a Mountain Fairy and both wanted to take turns holding him. To be treated like a cuddly toy was irksome and Weiss playfully jumped atop the statue in the center. The girls danced around him but Weiss was able to whisper to Duckie, 'Find the Marquis and bring him to the picture gallery as soon as you can.

Duckie disentangled himself from the girls and Weiss took a flying leap and landed behind the fountain wall and was out of sight in a jiffy. He made his way to the picture gallery, hid behind a curtain and waited for Duckie to return with the Marquis. Actually finding the Marquis however was another matter. Duckie searched the palace, but there was no sign of him.

That morning, after coffee Ferdinand deCygne had walked over to the little pavilion behind the small waterfall. It was there, in a small bower of rhododendrons that every morning Dorothea faithfully had waited for him. As he came nearer, he could hear the splashing of the little waterfall. Approaching Dorothea, his heart began to sing. Love had cast its net over the middle aged bachelor.

He crossed the little wooden bridge and entered into the pavilion. There she stood, a white dove perched on her shoulder.

But why did she not come forward to welcome him? There was no greeting, neither did a smile play upon her lips. The dove on her shoulder didn't stir as the Marquis drew closer and an eerie silence pervaded the bower.

He halted and thought for a moment. Had there been a change of heart? The icy stare in Dorothea's eyes frightened him. Rejected once more? What had he done this time to spoil his chances? A wave of self doubt washed over him. In her hearts of hearts, Dorothea had accepted him, he knew it. Surely it must be a slight indisposition that had brought about that icy look.

He took a few steps and reached for her delicate hand. He held it in his own. It was like grasping cold marble and an icy current ran through his fingers and up his arms. The truth began to dawn. He had not been rejected, rather his beloved Dorothea was powerless to respond. He touched her face, her hair and even the dove on her shoulder. All was stone cold marble. He wasn't imagining things. This was real. His Dorothea had been turned into a marble statue. A statue of transcendent beauty but the spirit of life had flown.

He sat down on the little bench by the waterfall, his head touching the marble hand which had always brought him solace. Tears welled in his eyes. He was brought to his senses by strains of laughter cascading through the palace. When he raised his head, he saw the Queen of the Marshes looking down upon them. At last the truth dawned. It was the Queen who had petrified his Dorothea. Her evil spell had turned his beloved Dorothea into marble.

He wandered about, a soul forlorn, sank down onto a rock and buried his face in his hands.

Duckie, trying to locate the Marquis, remembered the Marquis and Dorothea's trysting place and timidly approached the pavilion. He espied the marble statue and saw the wonderful resemblance to the comely Dorothea but where was the lovely maiden? He stepped farther into the pavilion and saw the Marquis lost in grief. Panic seized the young page.

Far away he could hear the Queen's laughter and Duckie knew something horrible had happened. Whatever had happened, he knew he must get his Master away from the scene and he took him by the hand and guided him to the picture gallery.

Hidden behind a curtain, Weiss had been impatiently waiting in the gallery. Grolls had been moving about and Weiss sensed that security was tight. When Duckie and the Marquis appeared he poked out his head and whispered, 'Here behind the curtain.'

Duckie guided the stricken nobleman into the hiding place and explained to Weiss what had happened. Weiss tried to console the grieving Marquis but even the light touch of the Fairy could not reach into that well of despair. Only time could heal that wound.

Weiss explained to the Marquis that it was Dorothea's last wish that they might escape in time, before they would be turned into green sprites. Indicating that he understood, the Marquis nodded.

The footsteps of a group of Grolls brought the Marquis back to reality. When the sound passed, Weiss cautioned them. 'Wait, I will check whether the coast is clear.' Slipping from behind the curtain, he surveyed the passage leading to the stone stairway. He returned in a few minutes and whispered, 'Take off your shoes and follow me.' Carrying their shoes they followed Weiss, moving silently across the gallery and down the narrow stairs leading to the dungeon.

Peli met them at the foot of the stairs and guided them to the sprites' sleeping quarters. The sprites, caught up in the excitement of the escape, were jubilant when they appeared but when they learned that Queen Marsha's wrath had turned on her handmaiden Dorothea, their joy turned into sorrow.

Weiss told them how Dorothea had gone to Queen's chambers, emptied the vase with magic powder and filled it with icing sugar. The fate of Dorothea was a terrible blow to the mudsprites. It was clear to all that the Queen upon finding the icing sugar in the vase, had burst into a fit of fury and cast the fatal spell that changed into cold marble, the lovely maiden and the dove on her shoulder.

Moose Martin was still in a deep sleep and the Marquis overcome with grief, so Weiss and Peli 1 planned the escape. They decided that once they were out of the palace, it would be best to strike west first. If the Grolls tried to track them they would not lead them to the beach where Slim and Svanhild were camped. After the Grolls gave up the search they could find their way to their friends' campsite. When dusk fell over the land, Weiss and the sprites picked up the sound of feet running through the underground passages.

'The Grolls are on the rampage,' shouted the chief sprite, 'the Queen has discovered the disappearance of her guests, and has ordered the Grolls to search the palace.'

Soon the racket grew louder as the brutes rushed through the underground passages and tunnels. Many got lost in the underground labyrinth and kept crashing into one another.

'It will take time for the Grolls to find this hideout, the way they are carrying on,' smiled Theophilus.

A small sprite near the door looked worried, 'They are coming closer, I think we should call for help.'

'Why don't you whistle Tiny and invite master Ratticus for a chat,' said Theophilus. 'The Master and his freebooters do owe us a favour.'

Tiny blew a silver whistle sending its thrill tones echoing through the underground passages. Presently there appeared a large rat dressed in green trousers, white shirt and a tall pointed red hat. He planted himself on the table facing Theophilus, lifted his hat and made a gracious bow.

'Greetings Theophilus,' piped the jaunty rodent.

'Welcome Master Ratticus, the Grolls are downstairs raising cane and looking for our guests. Perhaps you and the troopers could discourage them!

Duckie fascinated by the large elegant rat butted in, 'Master rat, is it not true that Groll skin is pikeproof?'

'Pikeproof it is, but only from the ankles up! Besides what is a pike when held up to a rat's front cutters! Lookie here young fellow,' Ratticus lifted his upper lip and Duckie bent over the table to admire two razor edged fangs.'

The Captain, who was now awake, took a look at the rat's formidable snaggles and chuckled, 'The Grolls will be counting their toes tonight.' Everybody laughed, realizing the Captain was quickly becoming his old solid self again.

The hurly burly got louder and to rally his troopers, Ratticus dived through a hole in the wall. Pandemonium broke out. Dashing and bashing through the maze of tunnels had pushed the Grolls beyond their frustration threshold and once Ratticus raised the battle cry and his troopers charged, the Grolls went berserk. Yelling with pain and anger they began to run for the two narrow stairways leading to the palace.

Some Grolls had three or four rats hanging onto to their feet. Others managed to shake them off, toes and all. As they jostled up the stairways, Grolls were bruised and beaten by their brethren.

Once the din had subsided Theophilus advised the party to leave before other evils might overtake them.

The Marquis' grief had turned into a feeling of uncontrollable fury. It took Weiss and Duckie to calm him down and to make him understand that rushing upstairs in a fit of anger would endanger all, besides the Grolls would make short shrift of him.

Duckie, the Captain and the Marquis still wore their splendid outfits, made by the Queen's tailor. They looked an unlikely threesome as they followed Tiny into the tangle of passages that led to the outside door, Peli 1 making up the rearguard.

When they came to the door, Tiny knocked three times and waited until a bang was heard from the outside. Then with the Captain's help, he removed the heavy iron bar. Greenpiece welcomed them and swiftly led them to the tunnel entrance in the pavilion. Here Tiny waved good-bye and silently they followed Greenpiece, who, just in case they were being followed, led them on a winding course through the marshes. From time to time they halted and listened for any signs of groll feet slapping the mud. No sounds could be heard for the Grolls were still in the palace nursing their torn feet.

Greenpiece and Weiss decided that they could head for the beach. Peli 1 breathed a sigh of relief, stretched his strong pinions and rose into the cool night air. 'Free at last' he whispered and joyously flapping his mighty wings, soared in the faint moonlight until he spotted the campfire on the beach. Skimming the lake, he made a perfect landing. 'How lovely to trail one's feet in the waters of a real lake after months of palace watching,' muttered Peli 1, as he paddled the last few feet to the beach.

Slim and Svanhild were seated on the sand by the faint light of glowing embers. When the swishing on the water caught their ear, they rushed to the water's edge and descried the silhouette of the pelican in the faint moonlight.

'Welcome Peli,' whispered Svanhild. 'Are our friends safe?'

'The mission went according to plan Svanhild,' the bird reported with a polite nod, 'Greenpiece will guide them to the beach.'

An hour later, with a triumphant smile, Greenpiece jumped on the beach. Patriot barked joyfully but Slim quickly motioned him to be quiet.

Duckie appeared first and Svanhild and Slim gave him a warm hug. The Captain and the Marquis looked heavy-hearted as they stepped out of the reeds at the edge of the sand. Slim and Svanhild' enthusiasm at their reunion assured them that all was forgiven.

Greenpiece watched with a flicker of hope in his eyes. It was a small victory but perhaps in time the spell might be broken. Hope, faint hope, is better than no hope and it was enough to keep him going! He turned quickly and hastened back to the marshes.

Svanhild, seeing him vanish, called farewell. Greenpiece just caught a trace of her voice before he dived into a pond and joined the other sprites building new dykes for the Queen.

Svanhild sat herself by Peli's side, stroked his feathers and thanked him for his help. She knew he was anxious to return to the land of the Mountain Fairies and to report to his Queen. Before leaving, Slim asked Peli to make a small detour and bring news of their escape to the Manor deCygne.

Peli made a solemn bow, his beak touching the sand. Remembering the excellent fishing in the trout pond north of the Manor, he said he would be delighted to make a short stop to report to Lady Erica and her friends.

The Captain still had a sheepish look but his common sense had returned. After a cup of hot tea he suggested that they leave for the Dwarf strongholds in the high mountains, far from the spells of the Queen and the wrath of her groll guards.

Soon the skiff moved down the dark lake carrying the band of adventurers far from the domain of the Queen of the marshes.

19

Land of Darkness

Under the specter of snowclad peaks, amidst the alpine meadows rises a cluster of log cabins. It is the village of Turania, home of the Dwarves. Turania is close to the summit of the Finnian Range and on the other side of the range is the realm of darkness, where rule the Seven Lords. Bitter experience has made the Dwarves security conscious and a stone wall encircles their settlement. Summers are short but glorious. The meadows burst into myriad colours, and flowers and berries appear everywhere. The women herd goats, grow hay and garden. Many of the men tunnel for ore, some silver, but mainly iron for the blast furnaces in which they create tools and weapons. Their artists use the silver to create lovely brooches, necklaces, spoons, goblets and ornaments. The silver craft was much sought after in the Kingdom.

Most of the homes are built from logs that they fell in the forests below and haul up the mountain. Winters are severe and heavy snow falls keep the Dwarves shoveling for several days a week. Toward the end of winter only rooftops can be seen, with columns of smoke rising from the chimneys. Banks of snow as high as seven feet rise on both sides of the street and tunnels lead you to the front door of their houses.

Inside, all is snug and cozy. A roaring fire in the cast iron cookstove keeps the family comfy, and cooking and eating are favoured pastimes. Between meals the men clear snow, split firewood or work on their tools and weapons. In the evenings, they sit in their rocking chairs by the fire and smoke wooden pipes carved from birch bowls. The women spin, weave, and knit colourful sweaters which, in better times, they would take to the festivals in Swanneland and put up for sale on the lawn of the Graceful Neck.

In spring, the snow tunnels melt and the whole village becomes a pool of soft mud. Dwarf wives are great gardeners and once the sun dries the ground, the women are out in their gardens. They grow flowers, vegetables and all kinds of small fruits. They are fond of berries and their gardens are hedged by black current bushes. The men mix currant leaves into their pipe tobacco, which accounts for the sweet aroma and the deep blue colour of the smoke. This blue smoke is favoured by the judges at the annual pipe smoker's ring blowing contest.

In early summer, the men march down the mountain, cross-cut saws slung across their shoulder, axes tied to their belts and their voices echoing against the cliff sides.

with a hey and a ho
and a dide-o.
for winterwood we go
saws will sing and axes ring
and a mighty swing
brings down the timber

Once the winter firewood is secured, the men return to the mines and tunnel for ore. They also work on their fortifications. In their mountain vastnesses they have created an elaborate defense system and the Dark Lords on the other side of the range wisely decided to leave them be. Their agents, when traveling to the Kingdom of the Seven Mountains, use mountain passes farther south to reach Lambarina.

The Dwarves have always been a vexation to the Seven Lords. They had considered occupying the mountain stronghold but felt the cost would be too high. The capture of Scimitar, their military leader, had been a stroke of luck. With the warmonger out of the way, there was no reason to be concerned about the sloppy bunch of miners and tunnelers on the other side of the range.

From the top of the Finnian range, looking east towards the domain of the Seven Lords, a rocky slope runs half way down the mountain to meet the first rows of spruce trees. The great spruce cut the horizon like a set of jagged teeth. At lower elevations, the forest slowly gives way to red rocky desert ground that occupies most of the land between the Finnian range and the sea.

Numerous brooks run among the trees, mingling and merging into larger streams which rush into the plains, surging in concert to become the Wasa, the great water way, that winds through the rocky desert and empties into the Eastern Ocean.

Beyond the plains and east of the Wasa lies a desert region with high plateaus of red rock. On the first plateau stands the giant castle of the Seven Lords. In clear weather their lookouts can see the plains to the west where prisoners labour in the fertile fields. The Wasa runs through the realm of the Seven and gives them easy access to the Eastern Ocean. Galleys rowed by prisoners constantly travel the great waterway.

In their palace on the great plateau, the Lords were seated at a long table in the great hall. Salan, once prime minister in the ancient Kingdom, before the rebellion, is still their acknowledged leader. He sits on a red velvet cushion in a high backed oaken chair, his arms resting on the hand-carved supports. A smile plays on his lips for he has reason to be content. Their power has been consolidated. Although they did not occupy the Kingdom of the Seven Mountains, the Rovers have infiltrated Lambarina and are in effective control of the city. Salan is pleased. Time has erased his fears. His agents have combed surrounding lands but no gold tablets have turned up. Matista's incantation has given them power and lasting youth. It has never been challenged. The Dwarves were still a problem but they could be isolated in their mountain strongholds. Scimitar, the warrior soothsayer, had traveled around fermenting fear and warmongering, but he was tucked away in the black mine, spending his days cutting marble blocks for seven new villas to be built, complete with gardens, ponds and fountains.

The Seven Lords spent time talking about the small enclave of Esteria, west of the Dwarves' stronghold in the great mountain forests. It was the home of a handful of lumber traders. Some of their agents had bought lumber in Esteria to build mine shafts for the large mining developments below the Black Peak. Esteria is but a small region outside the Kingdom and, for the time being, could be ignored.

Today the atmosphere was relaxed. The hostesses wore skimpy dresses cut from the finest silk and their shoes were crafted from splendid crocodile hides. The crocodiles were raised in deep pools under the palace. They were a useful resource, for they made wonderful leather and played their part in disciplining wayward Grolls and punishing runaway galley slaves, providing at the same time, light entertainment.

The high-heeled shoes of the servant girls tapped a gay rhythm on the white marble floor and soon silver trays with cups of cappuccino and apple fritters arrived at the conference table. Salan actually smiled at the coffee maiden by his side, an exceptional gesture for a Lord so stern.

The talk today centered on the building of the villas and the pools. The maidservants, to work in the seven villas were in training at the palace of the Queen of the Marshes. Queen Marsha always picked the pretty ones and life in the new villas, with their lovely gardens and private pools, looked promising.

There had been some tensions amongst the Seven living in the palace and Salan felt that the villas would give each member of the Council an opportunity to indulge in some of their favoured pastimes without arousing jealousy or nasty comments from the others.

After some light banter they got down to serious business. Some of the Groll regiments had to be disciplined for neglect of duty. More agents were required in Swanneland, whence came rumours of the formation of resistance groups. Routine stuff but it had to be attended to.

Towards the end of the meeting, some of the army chiefs came to report on fortifications and just before they broke up, a groll commander rushed in to report the escape of three men from Queen Marsha's palace in the marshes. Salan gave orders to intercept them and dismissed the Groll. Turning to his colleagues he smiled.

'If we capture them we will make them sing and Queen Marsha can turn them into green slaves at the next new moon.'

'What if they find their way to the Dwarf Village?' one of the Lords asked.

'Not to worry' spoke a voice at the end of the table, 'If they reach the mountain stronghold of the Dwarves, they will never get out again. Without Scimitar, the Dwarves will soon learn to toe the line.'

Grunts of approval met this remark. The Dwarves had always been a thorn in their side. Counselor Kuluk, a short squat figure with cunning green eyes spoke next.

'Of course we can capture the escaped prisoners. Yet this should not have happened. Security at the palace of the Queen of the marshes has always been lax. Can the Queen be trusted? Are her magic powers more potent than she lets on? We must keep a watch on her as we do on all our allies. What if she turned us into green moaners?' Waves of laughter resounded through the hall.

'You can't be too careful,' mumbled Kuluk, a sheepish smile upon his face.

'Your words were spoken in the right spirit, Counselor,' soothed Salan. We must place a spy in the palace in the marshes.'

Next Counselor Torzak, Vice Chairman of the Council spoke about the heir to the throne of the Kingdom of the Seven Mountains. 'Why keep the Princess and her handmaid in the old tower by the sea. While she lives, there is hope of restoration. Tell the Captain of the guard to snuff the maids.' A steamy smile spread over Salan's face.

'Fie, fie Torzak , why snuff a pretty Princess when all that loveliness could be mine, I'll wed the pining beauty, enhance our prestige and chop the line of succession.'

The Council was quite taken by Salan's creative approach. You had to toss it to him.

'Let us drink to the wedding,' shouted Counselor Mortimer. Servants ran in with decanters and glasses resounded, amongst shouts of 'Hail to the Master and his bride.'

Below the red cliffs of the plateau where the palace stood, stretched a rocky desert until one came to the wide waters of the Wasa. At the shore of the great river, docks ran out into the water to meet the galleys from the Eastern Ocean. Unloading freight, slaves and prisoners laboured in the hot sun. Arms for the groll regiments, building materials for fortifications, cattle to stock the farms on the upper plains and delicacies for the tables at the palace, arrived daily. Sometimes crates were carried ashore containing jewelry, fine linen and silks to stock the wardrobes of the hostesses at the palace.

The galleys were skippered by short stocky men in leather vests, members of a mountain tribe in the remote reaches of the domain of the Dark Lords. They had proved to be faithful servants over the centuries and were well rewarded. Wide brimmed hats made from black leather protected them from the sun. They were experts in handling forty foot whips, cut from crocodile leather. Standing on the stern of their vessel, their whips would leap out to the prow of the ship and catch any slave that might be resting on his oar. They were so proud of their expertise that every spring, they organized a whip wielding contest.

A large galley had just docked and the slaves were busy loading crates onto the mule-drawn wagons by the dockside. Craving a cold beer the skipper had vanished into one of the small wooden buildings. The crew knew that he would be safely tucked away in the small tavern for hours yet and when they finished transferring the cargo, the galley slaves sought shelter under a weeping willow by the water's edge. Here they often found a brief respite from their life of unending hardship.

Two of the older galley slaves walked out on a small strip of land jutting into the river. Long white hair resting on sun burnt shoulders told of age and suffering. When they came to the end of the promontory they rested on the shore, dangling their feet in the waters of the Wasa. Gustav and Thorwald, border guards from Swanneland, had been captured by the Grolls two decades past.

'The miracle is that we are still here. Many of our friends perished in the Wasa.'

'The lucky ones,' retorted Thorwald with a quick glance at the distant palace.'

'My mind dwells on worlds beyond, beyond the prison of the lords, beyond the prison of the body.'

'Then throw yourself into the Wasa.'

Gustav gently put his hand on Thorwald's wrist and said dreamily, 'Companion of my youth and fellow wayfarer on this sea of adversity, is it not the way of providence? We must endure these ills, not leave this stage till our part is played. Soon enough the time will come when Sisters of the Secret Crossing will row our souls on the opal sea to distant shores. To the wonder in their fathomless eyes, we will reply, yes we endured. We endured until, from mystic strands, trumpet calls signaled our release.'

The friends stared silently at the waters of the Wasa and found strength in each other's company. Gustav tossed a pebble into the smooth dark waters sending rings rippling outwards. Softened by the rippling of the rings, the image of Erica appeared, seated by the black pool. Gustav saw streaks of white among her silver tresses, a delicate hand rested on the neck of a black swan. He could hear her sing song voice travel over the river.

endure my love forlorn
endure till a new day is born
endure this play entire
endure the cleansing fire

The Wasa surged forwards and the image faded. The voice lingered. 'There is no separation, together we weave a pattern on a timeless loom.' A spark of hope burned in Gustav's eye and Thorwald caught the spark. Together they walked back to the galley and began cleaning the vessel. Soon the skipper would return and before his whip began to do the talking, it would be better to have things in order.

20

Elves Arrive At The Manor

$\mathcal{P}$eli 1 caught the first rays of the sun long before it rose on the world of men, gnomes, fairies and other earth bound beings. High he soared following the Sanctus. By the time that the sun illumined the water and the meadows along the shore, Peli had reached the Frivoli. Soon he espied the Manor on the hilltop and went into a steep glide.

He flew a wide arc over the trout pond, eyes boring deep into the water, yes, things looked promising but he found himself humming the little ditty his father had taught him.

> *lofty is the plight*
> *of Pelicans in flight*
> *just one measure*
> *duty before pleasure*

By an act of will he left the pond behind, heading directly for the Manor and touching down gently on the terrace wall. Lady Erica was helping Norma set the breakfast table when she descried the Pelican. She rushed out to welcome him, anxious for news. Peli assumed a serious stance.

'The news is positive my Lady, the profligates have been brought to their senses and reunited with the party.'

'Wonderful Peli 1, wonderful,' responded Erica overlooking any aspersions cast on the Marquis's character. Erica knew Pelicans had a severe sense of moral rectitude, typical of higher fowl. For those bound by gravity, it was hard to live up to.

'Join us for breakfast Peli, and tell us about your adventures.'

Peli hopped into the sunroom. Most of the friends had gathered around the table and Erica rushed out to find a stool, placed it at the end of the table, and invited Peli to perch.

Also seated on high stools were the Gnomes, Gneiss and Grit, representing the Sacred Council of Gnome Elders. Quicksilver had returned to his family and they had taken his place. Annabelle and Martha the prophetess were there and so was Volker, the Outlander, his little notebook at the ready. Lady Erica introduced Peli 1 to the Council members, praising his courage and cleverness in rescuing their friends.

All were spellbound as Peli 1 narrated the adventures at the palace. Smiles and chuckles greeted the news that the Marquis had fallen in love with a handmaiden of Queen Marsha. But the glee quickly froze when Peli related Dorothea's sacrifice and the dreadful penalty exacted by Queen Marsha.

'A great sacrifice,' mused Martha.

'Forsooth, a noble deed,' exclaimed the Gnome Gneiss. 'Once Princess Yaconda is freed and takes her place as Queen of the Kingdom, Dorothea's name will be carved in the stone wall of the palace hall, along with the names of other heroes and heroines who fought for our freedom.

The fate of the selfless maiden and mention of the future Queen and her captivity cast a veil of sadness over the party.

'There is more ill news, I fear,' added the Pelican. The fairy scout Edel was captured by the Black Elves. Queen Tuluga will be distraught.' Peli's stormy look betrayed some mixed emotions. He remembered all too well the practical jokes Edel had played on the Pelicans, in fact he had been a pest. But Black Elves, no he would not wish Black Elves on anybody. 'Be magnanimous Peli, remember altitude,' he mused to himself, 'Altitude of soul, the motto of higher fowl.'

Norma served breakfast and the plates of hot food and coffee lifted the prevailing gloom. Peli had an aversion to eggs and Norma rushed back to the kitchen for fried fish and potatoes. The potatoes were a treat but Peli could never understand why Swannefolk spoiled trout by frying it. Anyway, he would have a brief stop at the trout pond on his way home!

Lady Erica thanked Peli and asked him to convey her warmest greetings to Queen Tuluga and also an invitation to return to the Manor as soon as it was safe to travel again. The appearance of numerous merewings had made air travel dangerous.

Peli wasted no time, he made a deep bow to the assembled guests and hopped through the doorway onto the terrace. Norma timidly tip toed out of the kitchen and knelt down beside him.

'Peli tell me, is young Duckie safe?' Peli's eyes lit up and he smiled.

'Sensible young man that Duckie. He drank hot chocolate instead of sparkling wine, no enchantress could draw that youth into her web and the Queen's maidens failed to charm him.'

Peli cast her an encouraging look and took wing. A well deserved stop at the trout pond was short but delicious and he stored some lunch in the bottom of his large beak. He rose high above the mountain range and turned west, following the range and taking advantage of the updrafts during the heat of the day.

Norma walked slowly back to the kitchen door, a thoughtful look on her face. Duckie was safe, what a relief. But immune to the charms of the maidens. That was both reassuring and worrisome. But then he was young and as her late mother used to say hormones take their time coming and going.

After a meal break the Council repaired upstairs to the hall, used now as a Council chamber. The news Peli 1 had brought led to lively discussion and the possibility of Scimitar's rescue kindled a ray of hope. Were Scimitar to return to the mountain stronghold of the Dwarves he would be able to lead the resistance against the agents of the Seven and prepare the defenses on the Finnian Range. Only the Dwarves had kept up a tradition of martial arts and military skills. Other peoples in the Kingdom, Swannefolk included, long since had abandoned warlike traditions.

Then the talk shifted to Princess Yaconda. Was there a way to rescue the beloved Princess? Even if rescue were possible, where could they find a safehouse? In the high mountain ranges of the Dwarves, perhaps? Certainly not in Lambarina or Swanneland. Rovers had infiltrated many towns by now. In Cascade most of the business community had been won over. The Rovers paid handsomely and Joris Goldfinger and Dennis Mintpalm had built splendid mansions and like proud peacocks, strutted around their fine gardens.

Volker's secretarial skills stood the company in good stead. He was always making notes and brought some order to their discussion and future historians no doubt will be grateful. He was still in the habit of whistling tunes at the most inappropriate times and seemed entirely oblivious of it himself. The company around the table gladly put up with the eccentric Outlander. Volker raised the topic of the Elves.

'Why had not the Queen of the Elves sent delegates? Lady Erica knew internal squabbles had plagued the realm of Orchidea. Now that the Black Elves were gone, harmony should have been restored. Could evil have befallen the delegates on their travel to the Manor?

Security at the Manor was discussed. There was a lot of animosity in the town. Immediately the Gnomes volunteered to patrol the property. They were small but exceedingly tough and they could always call on Grumpuss who took great delight in tossing shady characters in the huge bramble bush behind the hedge of the estate. Then he would find a comfortable spot from which to watch his victims scramble from the bramble. Those standing close by could hear a deep belly laugh, especially if the poor devils had to slip out of their clothes to escape the fierce thorns. This was not an admirable trait and Martha had attempted to speak to Grumpuss, but to no avail. He simply enjoyed himself too much. He really was a very gentle bear, except when provoked or when Martha was threatened. Then he would turn into a ball of fury, fearful to behold.

The Gnomes lost no time in starting their guard duty. Martha introduced them to Grumpuss. Gneiss and Grit each carried a small pickax and a horn on their belt. The horn was only sounded when evil threatened. Gneiss blew a short haunting note for the benefit of the bear. When the Gnomes raised the alarm, Martha told Grumpuss to come instantly. Grumpuss understood. Though he did not have the gift of speech, his intuitive understanding was profound.

Erica was seated on the stonewall in the courtyard. A transparent muslin veil covered her silver white tresses, which met her wine coloured silk dress just below the shoulders. In the stillness of dusk she was gathering her thoughts. Gratitude welled within for the escape of Ferdinand and his fellow travelers. The sacrifice of Dorothea and the tragedy of her petrification had deeply touched her. She could feel the bond between the maiden and her nephew Was there anything that could be done? She leaned over the black water of the pool and gazed into its depths.

It was as if her mind spoke to the dark waters. Images appeared deep below the surface, black images with silver writing and titles in a florid style adorned the top of these tablets. Erica's eyes scanned the headings as they flitted by, levitation, healing, wizardry, broomsticks, prophecy. It was as if enlightenment on many topics could be hers. A tablet entitled, Spells, Casting and Undoing, caught her eye. As she focused on the illuminated script, she could read the headings and scanned the spells that could be cast. Unbidden, the tablet scrolled down and soon Undoing spells appeared. Involuntarily her eyes were drawn to one of the last passages on petrification.

The motion slowed and she was able to fix the words in her mind.

'Petrification. Evil the witch who casts this spell. Seldom undone by mortal man or woman.[4] The images faded into darkness. Erica remained seated on the wall of the pool, and thought about Ferdinand and Dorothea. Ferdinand had found his love. His love had been requited and then snatched away from him, but true love will survive. Seldom undone by mortal man or woman, she reflected. It did not say never and hope returned.

Lady Erica walked back to the terrace and looked over the sunlit gardens. Two slight white figures walked between the rose beds. The Elves had arrived. Grumpuss had looked somewhat nonplussed when he saw the elven maidens walk across the green lawn. The bear knew innocence when he saw it and returned quietly to some berry picking. Lady Erica rushed out to welcome them.

'Greetings Lady Erica,' sang the voices of the Elves. 'Queen Orchidea sends kindest wishes to you and to the delegates gathered at the Manor.'

'Welcome, welcome, I am so pleased to see you. We are glad that you arrived safely and can join the Council. The taller of the two bowed.

'We are honoured to join the Council and hope that we may be of some use.'

'Pray, tell me your names dear Elves.'

'I am Silfida and with me is my sister Sidonia. Queen Orchidea suggested that she accompany me. Sidonia has the gift of vision and can recognize a face two miles away. Twice on our journey hither she spotted merewings and Rovers at a great distance and we were able to hide in time.'

---

4   *Reading tablets of the cosmic mind was well known practice in ancient times .Many necromancers and lay witches derived formulas and spells that way. In the latter days when the inner light failed, external techniques for retrieving information were devised. Computers and other devices are but a reflection of ancient inner information highways.*

'Truly a great gift,' exclaimed Lady Erica, 'one that we will need at the Manor. The enemy is all around and the ring is closing.'

Lady Erica took the Elves by the hand and led them towards the Manor.

Secretary Volker, upon seeing the delicate white beings crossing the garden, burst into a spontaneous whistle medley. Only when Lady Erica entered the porch and presented the Elves to the other delegates, did he cease his welcome concert. The Gnomes Gritt and Gneiss, who had met the elven sisters in Lambarina, walked over to greet them and then returned quickly to their duty of patrolling the grounds.

Lady Erica, led the Elves upstairs, where they took a seat at the table. She felt a sense of assurance now that the Elves were here. Only a delegate from the Dwarves was missing. Alas, Scimitar's chair was empty.

She knew that the Elves, though slight of body, had unusual psychic powers. They could tell whether people were well or ill by the colour of their auras. There were times when they had visions of happenings far beyond the borders of the Kingdom.

Lady Erica told the Elves about the Council's concerns. They already knew about the capture of Scimitar and the rescue expedition. Queen Orchidae had warned them that the powers of the sorceress Matista could once more bring disarray and chaos in the peaceful life they had enjoyed for the last century.

When Lady Erica told of Svanhild's disappearance and the rescue by the owls, they understood that Queen Orchidae's warning had been in earnest.

Sidonia and Silfida were shocked to hear of Edel's capture by the Black Elves. They both knew Cobalt and feared the worst. Rumours had reached Queen Orchidae about a group dissenters that had left Cobalt and his troop and were returning to elven land, to seek an amnesty.

'Have you received word that Captain Martin and the other wayfarers arrived safely in the land of the Dwarves?' inquired Silfida.

'Not as yet. Peli 1 flew in a few days ago and brought the good news that the Marquis, Captain Martin and Duckie had made a successful escape from the palace of Queen Marsha and were last seen rowing across the long lake that stretches to the foothills of the Finnian Range. I know of no dangers that would stand between them and the Dwarf stronghold. They should have reached the land of the Dwarves by this time.

Silfida looked around the room, taking in the shapes and colour of a setting that was entirely new to her. For a moment she rested her eyes on a painting of the Marquis. Erica descried consternation in her face.

'A black veil covers the portrait of your nephew, Lady Erica. The Marquis is in mortal danger. I feel the will to live is ebbing quickly.'

All looked at Silfida with astonishment, to them the painting appeared perfectly clear. Silfida looked at her sister. Sidonia too had seen the veil. 'Alas friends,' a black shroud covers the image, a portend of great peril.'

Erica knew Elven lore and doubted not the elven sisters had perceived a sign from the unseen. Silence prevailed for a few minutes. Then Lady Erica spoke.

'I fear that unexpected danger may yet befall the company before they reach the dwarf village of Turania.'

Secretary Volker whistled in a minor key and his thoughts appeared to be far away. Lady Erica suggested that they deal with the issues at hand and not let the vision weigh them down. 'Of course danger surrounds the travelers on their rescue mission but even here at the village of Cascade unrest and hostility are present. Most of the business community and many of the villagers have been won over by the Rovers, agents of the Dark Lords. Ill feeling and resentment have been incited against the Manor and even against the Royal House.'

Sidonia recalled, 'Silfida and I walked through Cascade on our way to the Manor. The cheer and warmth of years of yore seem gone. People walk with their eyes averted to the ground. Few returned our greetings and smiles were rare. Gone were the bright white auras that enfolded folks on the street. Many an aura appeared deep purple and even black.'

'The people in Cascade are drawn slowly into the web of the black Masters,' sighed Lady Erica, 'Hatreds buried long ago surface once again.'

Volker's whistling had started again, deep and somber tones floated on the air while he pulled out his notebook and filled a page with his observations.

Martha pulled herself up in her chair. 'The great darkness of my dreams is now approaching. Swannefolk and other peoples of the Kingdom have become entangled in the black web of greed and power. Tempted by promises of gain and fame, they have been cut loose from their peaceful moorings. Shades of night are falling.'

'Deep within the people of the Kingdom are kind and generous,' said Silfida, 'We must counter the darkness and illumine their souls.'

'What can be done Silfida, what can we do here at the Manor?' Lady Erica wanted to know.

'The Elves have practiced creative visualization for centuries, we must use it here to send a ray of life to the Marquis and to change the hearts of the people in Cascade.

Sidonia will you lead us into meditation?'

Sidonia stood up while the others remained seated. She was dressed in white and her golden hair caught in a ray of sunshine.

'We will all stand, hold hands and form a circle. With our inner sight we will behold a light descending. With the mirror of our minds, we will reflect that light to the centre of the circle.'

Sidonia's singsong voice led the company into an inner world.

'The light is now descending. Let it flood your mind and bend the rays toward the Marquis. I see him standing amongst us enveloped in light.'

For a few minutes all stood in silence, while the image of the Marquis remained with them. Then it faded into black.

'Now the men and women of Cascade enter our circle. We see them struggling with all the fears and desires that overwhelm them. It is the seesaw of fear and desire that robs us of our inner peace. Cast your light on the people of Cascade. Visualize them as spiritual beings rising above the troubles that have beset them. See the waves of darkness receding from the village and the light returning.'

Silence prevailed for some time before Lady Erica spoke, 'Our gratitude to you Sidonia for taking us through this meditation. Please continue to lead us in this practice until spring returns to the meadows of their hearts.'

The Gnomes Gneiss and Grit had quietly slipped into the room and had watched the last part of the meditation. Their faces looked rather grim. Erica heard Gneiss murmuring to himself, 'New fangled spirituality. A clout on the snout works very well with those rogues out there.'

'We must defend ourselves Gneiss, of course, there are souls that cannot be reached but most of the men and women in Cascade are good at heart,' said Lady Erica

'You ironfisted warriors.' laughed Sidonia. 'There are other ways of reaching people than by knocking them over the head.'

'Your work must be done Gneiss, if you and Grit didn't guard the Manor we would be in trouble,' soothed Lady Erica.

'That is the truth ma'am,' blurted Grit, 'the Rovers themselves seldom show up but they have recruited ruffians to do their dirty work. I tell you without that bear we would have been in trouble. He has perfected his aim and few thugs land far from the center of the bramble bush.' A grin appeared on the little warrior's face.

'We must do both Grit, defend the Manor and try to change the hearts of the people in the village.'

The jaunty warriors returned to their duty on the grounds. Erica standing by the window could see the tough little fellows walking out onto the lawn, with hands on the pickaxes tied to their belts. It occurred to her that if all the dwellers of the Kingdom were just into spirituality, things would have been a lot worse!

21

The Mountain Trek

*T*he skiff moved swiftly down the lake. Weiss was sleeping with his head resting on Patriot's back. Slim and Svanhild, fresh and rested, were at the oars. Slumped in the back were Moose and the Marquis, the Marquis lamenting the calamity that had befallen his Dorothea and Moose wringing his hands and agonizing over his foolish infatuation with Queen Marsha. His self respect had been shattered.

Duckie was the only one who had escaped from the palace with a clear mind. He kept eyes and ears open for any unusual sights or sounds. Only the singing of thousands of frogs could be heard and he could see a faint outline of bulrushes by the shore and patches of white water lilies floating on the water, their blossoms piously folded for the night. Their course at the moment was simple, to put as much distance as possible between themselves and the palace of Queen Marsha.

Duckie joined Weiss and Patriot in front. Patriot was delighted at the return of his playmate and joyfully licked his face. Weiss now fully awake climbed onto the bow and directed the rowers. For the next hour they moved swiftly over the mirror surface of the lake. Before long they would be beyond the reach of the Grolls. But now the lake narrowed and patches of reed slowed their progress. Mist began to rise from the water and even Weiss could no longer make out any landmarks. They were lost in the marshes and in the dense fog there was little they could do. The skiff stopped moving. Slim and Svanhild dozed over their oars and an eerie silence enveloped them. Only Weiss was alert. His keen eyes scanned the darkness and through the haze he spotted a faint outline of the new moon. Dark shapes flitted across that sickle of light, merewings soaring through the night. There was no point in waking his fellow travelers. There would be little danger till first light, for merewings see but poorly in the dark.

The Marquis, the Captain and Duckie had escaped in the nick of time. Queen Marsha's fury would know no bounds. Weiss shuddered as he thought of the mudsprites. She would certainly vent her wrath on the poor green creatures.

If her Grolls overtook them they too would join the froggy dyke builders.

His agile mind tried to visualize ways of escaping from the mass of tangled reeds and lilies. There was little time. At first light surely, they would be spotted by the wretched purple beaked birds.

His mind ran around in circles but no answers came. In a final gesture of despair he folded his hands and prayed to the spirit world. Mountain Fairies are very action oriented and turn to prayer only if all else fails.

Weiss remained silent for a while and then whispered,

I searched the realms of my mind
and can no answers find.
Send a guiding ray
to a fairy in dismay.

He remained in silent meditation for a few moments, for Fairies find it hard to keep still for very long. A noise alerted him, Svanhild climbed by his side and together they stared out over the dark expanse of water and reeds. The silence was broken only by the swish of merewings sailing overhead. The giant birds' poor sight saved them from detection but dawn was only hours away.

Svanhild rested her hand on Weiss' shoulder. Suddenly she felt the tiny body tense up. He was peering ahead, touched Svanhild's hand and pointed up. Far above the horizon Svanhild could see a spot of light moving upward into the sky. At first it appeared to be a sparkling star, but soon moving across the heavens, a train of light appeared. 'A celestial procession!' Weiss exclaimed, enchanted by the sight.

'Oh, Svanhild, I pray Edel could be here to see these wonders of the universe.'

They looked at each other in utter amazement. The train of dizzying light came closer and closer, tracing through the bulrushes a furrow of light and halting at the bow of the skiff. Looking at the head of the procession, Svanhild saw a small sparkling creature. Hundreds of luminous beings were lined up behind her. She gazed at the parade of lights and remembered the Wolly Wobs. She recalled her mother telling stories about Wolly Wobs.

'Weiss, it is a visitation by the Wolly Wobs,' exclaimed Svanhild. Weiss' eyes lit up with delight.

The sparkling apparition responded with a smile. 'It is true my children. We are the Wolly Wobs. Yes, we are in the fairytales that your mother told you and alas, the stories are all too true. We live on the rim of the seventh circle of the celestial realm, where the foolish virgins and mischievous spirits are sent, after they leave this earth and travel the secret crossing to the world of immortality.'

> *wearied of our froward way*
> *we pray*
> *a day will dawn*
> *when we cease to mourn*
> *days when we made hay*
> *no more do we delight*
> *in dancing and in singing*
> *and pray*
> *to find a way*
> *of true joy ringing*

'How we wish, my children, to leave the rim of the seventh circle and to gain entrance into the deeper world of the spirit. Now we seek to help those in need and earn our release from the chains that we forged in merry making. We know your plight and will be your guide through the morasses of the wicked Queen.'

Weiss and Svanhild were touched and fascinated by the Wolly Wobs. Svanhild couldn't help asking. 'Wolly Wob, tell me please, how did you spend your days on earth?' The Wolly Wob drew closer and the sparkling light shone upon Svanhild.

'I can see, my dear girl, that you are a Swannemaiden. Then you know the Graceful Neck? I was a nightclub singer in Lambarina, but once every year we played in that quaint inn on the shore of the Sanctus. I must admit that I was famous at the time. Often I performed at the Ecstasy Café in Lambarina. The applause, the showers of flowers and the men at my feet, those wonderful days of yore.' A wave of nostalgia swept over the Wolly Wob. Her companion touched her with her short wing of light and whispered, 'Violetta, remembering the past will not set us free. We must serve and help these mortals to find their way.'

Svanhild saw tears of light flowing from Violetta's eyes. Quickly she pulled herself together and said in a resolute voice, 'Sisters let us mark a trail to lead our friends through these evil marshes.'

A great throng of Wolly Wobs, resembling a sphere of light, had gathered around the skiff. Like wool unwinding, they traced a line of light across the marshes. Svanhild woke the others and as they rubbed the sleep out of their eyes, they beheld a stream of light winding through the marshes.

'Wolly Wobs,' laughed Svanhild, 'The Wolly Wobs have come and are marking for us a channel through the morasses.'

Even Moose and the Marquis were now fully awake. They beheld a sparkling trail vanishing into the night. Every one in the Kingdom had read in the Sacred Book of Common Lore, the parable of the Wolly Wobs. Yet to see them here responding to the needs of those that dwell below, was a marvelous sight. Duckie was enchanted to see the trail of lights traveling through the reeds and lilies.

Moose was overcome with a feeling of gratitude and humility. Once again help had come when peril seemed to be overwhelming. His mind traveled back to that dreadful fall into darkness at the palace in the marshes, that deeper morass, the spiritual abyss, into which he had well nigh vanished. Yet, there too, he had been rescued. He took his place at the helm and fixed his eyes on the winding lights.

The Marquis and Slim grasped the oars. First they backed out of the blind lead and then turned to the markers of light. The bow of the little boat cut a fair wave and glided alongside the thread of sparkles. Before they knew it they were sailing in a wider channel and found themselves floating on a large lake, free from the marshes.

Slim and the Marquis let go the oars and all looked back. The thread of light rolling into a bright ball of sparkles rose up into the heavens whence it had come.

Weiss' acute hearing caught a distant squishy sound, no doubt groll feet splashing in the mud. They pulled on the oars with all their might, creating a fine bow wave and the skiff shot across the mirror surface.

Only when the first rays of the sun illuminated the expanse of blue water, did they let the oars rest in their locks. Floating on the lake that bordered the foothills, they had a meager breakfast and drank lake water.

Being on a large body of water cleared the Captain's head and he told the company that a day's sailing would take them to the foothills of the mountain range.

'At long last' sighed the Marquis 'There will be hope of a decent breakfast in the village of the Dwarves.'

'It is only the second breakfast that you have missed since we left home, your Grace,' said Duckie who had become a lot bolder since the palace incident.

'The coffee, my boy, lake water is all well and good but when one reaches my age and station in life, a breakfast in style and the sound of coffee perking, bring to the inner man, a special kind of solace,' mumbled the Marquis. He had moved to the bow of the boat, dreamily staring over the water. Slim and Duckie took to the oars and Moose turned the helm, pointing the bow toward the distant mountains. Svanhild tied a fishhook to a silk thread and trailed it over the gunwale, and it was not long before several lake trout leapt into the boat.

The Marquis was depressed. The love that had flown into his life had turned into cold marble. The sacrifice of his one and only love had purchased their freedom. Nonetheless, the prospect of frying trout over an open fire returned signs of animation to the nobleman's face.

They rowed and rowed but the mountains did not seem to come any closer. In the early afternoon, a breeze sprang up and Moose rigged a sail. Running with the wind, the skiff picked up speed and by sunset the mountains loomed ahead. The setting sun cast an orange tint on the slopes above the tree line. Svanhild gazed at the mountain range. The snow-covered peaks towered high above and the trek up through the forest and the bare rocks above, looked forbidding.

When the bottom of their vessel slid onto the gravel beach, the sun was on the horizon and only the top of the range was caught in an orange blaze. Exhausted, but wide awake and grateful for a safe crossing, the party drew the boat farther ashore and unloaded the few supplies they had left.

Slim began to gather driftwood on the beach, the others cut poles for a make shift tent. They tied all the poles at the top and spread the bottom ends in a wide circle. An old tarp completed their tepee. Slim brought inside, a pile of driftwood, dug a shallow fire pit and lit a bit of moss with his tinderbox. Birch bark and bits of driftwood caught fire and the smoke drifted through the opening at the top.

A blazing fire, the smell of frying trout and a few oatcakes raised hopes for a decent meal. Even the Marquis admitted that given the circumstances, it was a fine dinner. Patriot was happy to be on land again, joyfully prancing around and chasing ravens uphill.

A touch of fall was in the air and they arranged themselves in a close ring around the fire. Ferdinand carefully laid Scimitar's sword by his side and soon fell asleep. Slim went out to find more driftwood and walking by the shore he rested on a log. The light of the new moon illumined the mist rising from the water and the scene conveyed to the young ballet master a feeling of peace. It was true that he had left all that was dear to him and yet he felt that he was following his destiny. He was not a warrior, but had a clear mind, even in the midst of danger. It had surprised him, but he knew it could serve them well in times to come.

He looked back at the silhouette of the tent by the water's edge, smoke rising in the faint moonlight, and tried to engrave the image upon his mind, thinking always of sketches and paintings, he would make on his return.

It was Svanhild's voice from the tent that ended his reverie. He got up, picked up a large chunk of driftwood and dragged it back to the fire pit. The fire banked for the night, they crawled into their sleeping bags and watched the glowing embers until they fell asleep.

At first light of dawn, Svanhild got up. She had slept well, yet she felt weary. The stress of the journey was beginning to take its toll. She looked at her travel companions, fast asleep. She dressed and to wash her face and hands, walked to the lake. A fine mist rose from the silent expanse of water. She turned around and lifted her eyes to the mountain peaks backlit by the rising sun. The aspen and maple on the lower slopes had turned red and gold. Higher up the dark green of spruce reached up to bare rock and snow covered peaks. She sauntered by the shore reflecting upon the events of the past few weeks. Her life in the quiet back waters of Cascade had taken a sudden turn and she felt as if a whirlwind of events had carried her onward.

She looked back at the little party overshadowed by the vastness of the mountain scenery. Her eyes fixed on the mirror surface of the lake, mist was still rising from the water. Thinking back upon the events of their journey, a shadow crossed her mind. The quest seemed hopeless and no doubt more dangers awaited them. If she were to die young, she would accept it. She remembered the words of the wandering sage who used to give talks at the Graceful Neck. 'On life's canvas a miniature of beauty will delight the angels. Strive not for a large and melancholy design.'

Suddenly she felt a hand touch her elbow and heard a singing voice, 'I read your thoughts, my daughter. Indeed the loveliest scent comes from the crushed flower, but think not of death. The living must work together to resist the evil that is upon us.' Svanhild turned and beheld the face of Amaranth, dressed in white, her hair flowing loosely to a waistband beset with gems.

From the hand under her elbow, Svanhild felt a vibration flow through her body. She felt as if she had drunk from the cup of life. The forests and the mountains, the lake with birds askimming and the presence at her side, assumed a supernatural beauty. She knew that she was in the presence of an enchantress, who hailed from the highest realms.

'You are greatly favoured my child, the path that you have chosen out of your own free will, is a blessed path even if the outcome is unknown. I have come to lift your spirits and to give warning. The merewings have carried to the Seven Lords, the news of your escape. Their agents, those stocky fellows in black leather jackets, I think they call them Rovers, have crossed the mountain range. Always at their side, the black hounds, who carry the tainted fang illness, which only the Sisters of the Secret Crossing can cure.'

'There is so little that I can do. Hasten back and tell your friends to pack their belongings. Quench the fire and leave the open beach. Trek up into the aspen and maple woods, where there is at least some protection from the eyes of the merewings. Be cautious my daughter and do not seek the company of any dwellers in the forest, accept no hospitality from anybody, until you reach the land of the Dwarves. Godspeed my daughter.'

Before Svanhild could bid the fair enchantress farewell she had vanished. Only a trace of light lingered in the mist, moved across the water and disappeared. Svanhild turned around and saw Weiss standing nearby.

'Weiss, I too have seen Amaranth. She gave warning of Rovers and Grolls on this side of the mountain. Please rush back to camp and wake the others!'

'Rovers and Grolls,' Weiss queried, 'No doubt they will have the black hounds at their side.'

'Yes, Weiss, I fear Amaranth mentioned the black brutes that carry the dreaded illness. Hurry Weiss there is no time to lose.'

Slim had just lit a fire. The others were comfortably seated around the blaze, waiting for the kettle to boil, when Weiss flew into the tent and told them of the forewarning that the enchantress had conveyed to Svanhild.

Amaranth's words and the mention of Rovers and dogs spurred them into action. When Svanhild arrived, she quenched the fire and removed all traces of their overnight stay. Their belongings were few, and packing was done quickly. Moose pushed the skiff back into the water, hoping that it would drift to some remote part of the lake where discovery was unlikely.

Sitting on a fallen log, they had a drink of lake water from the leather pouch that Slim had filled, and ate the sad remains of fried fish from last night's dinner. The meager repast took only a few minutes. They shouldered their packs and walked across the beach to the first stand of trees.

Patriot trotted ahead and made the going easier by leading them to a deer trail. The path took them through an aspen grove. The leaves trembled in the early sunlight. Svanhild halted for a moment to enjoy the magic of the rustling leaves.

The Marquis, panic-stricken by the thought that they might encounter the Rovers and their hounds, quickened his pace and even forgot to complain about a wretched breakfast.

The deer track petered out but there was little undergrowth and they were able to head straight up the slope. Slim cut himself a hiking stick and led the party through the aspen wood and into stands of maple. The climb was steep and after a while the party had to rest to catch its breath.

Weiss sat on a patch of moss, leaning his head on Patriot. Moose was trying to figure out how long it would take them to reach the alpine meadows and the settlement of the Dwarves. 'Two days of climbing will take us there, if we don't meet up with the Rovers,' figured the Captain who was quite his old self again.

A shiver ran down Ferdinand's spine, 'May heaven protect us from black hounds,' mumbled the Marquis.

'Let me go ahead Captain to find the Dwarves and warn them of your approach,' volunteered Weiss. Moose knew that the Mountain Fairy could swiftly run up the slope and that in the present climate of suspicion it would be wise to alert the Dwarves of strangers approaching.

'It is a good idea Weiss. You could make it by tonight and tell the Dwarves we will arrive in a day or two.'

'I'll fly up that mountain Captain and find Smithereen. If I don't see you safe and sound in the Dwarf village in a couple of days, I am sure the Dwarves will send out a search party.'

The others gathered around Weiss and wished him a safe journey. Svanhild bent over and kissed him on the forehead. 'Godspeed, my fleet-footed friend. Your blithe spirit and angel wings will delight those dour Dwarves.'

They were all grateful that Weiss would forewarn the Dwarves. If ill befell them on the mountain, it was reassuring that those sturdy warriors would know about it. Weiss strapped on a small pack, bade farewell to his friends and like an arrow released from a tight string, sped up the mountain.

As their lighthearted friend disappeared into the trees, they felt a sense of foreboding. Svanhild was the first to start moving, and Slim and Duckie quickly followed her up the steep path. The Captain and the Marquis, still weary and depressed from their experiences in the palace of Queen Marsha, had difficulty in keeping up with Slim, Svanhild and Duckie, and often they stopped to rest. By the time the evening sun lengthened shadows, they were exhausted. Darkness was rapidly falling and when the little stream they were following widened, revealing a narrow strip of fine gravel, they halted and set up camp. They didn't bother building a lean-to. Slim set to his accustomed task as firemaker. There were fine stands of birch and he collected sheets of silver bark. The birch bark flared up and threw on the dreary scene more light than Slim had intended. The bright glow brought solace to the weary wayfarers. They just hoped that no merewings were overhead.

'Risky but pleasantly warm,' laughed Svanhild. She stood by the fire, holding her hands up to the flames, when a sharp tapping sound blended with the crackling of the wood. Alarmed, she turned around only to see a red woodpecker swinging on a birch branch. 'I thought I'd knock before appearing, fair maiden,' spoke the bird in the staccato voice so typical of the species.

'We keep an eye on the black gliders with the purple beaks. When one of the ugly buzzards is spotted, we hammer out a message that fellow birds repeat from tree to tree. None has been sighted, enjoy your fire,' chirped the bird, hammering a piece of hardwood with his beak, at the end of each sentence by way of punctuation.

'We thank you noble bird,' responded Svanhild.

'No thanks required. Pick up a basket and I will lead you to a patch of chanterelles.'

Svanhild took a small canvas bag and followed the black and red feathers darting through the trees, to a patch of mushrooms.

The chanterelles, a bit of left over fish and huckleberries that they had picked on the way, was more than they could have hoped for. They enjoyed their meal by the bright blaze. Before crawling in their sleeping bags they piled heavy timbers on the fire. The distant tapping of the woodpeckers provided a sense of security and they fell into a sound sleep. Their feathered friends were on guard.

The Marquis was the first to get up, which was unusual, but several times nightmares had disrupted his sleep. Black hounds had chased him over the mountain top and straight into a band of fierce Grolls. It was better to get up and shake off those images. There was only one thing on his mind, to reach the safety of the Dwarves' mountain stronghold.

'Facing a fierce foe in the field is one thing,' he said to himself whilst stroking the edge of his sword. 'My forefathers reduced many a foe to rubble, but villains and venomous hounds hiding in the woods, sneaking up on victims from behind. Great God, it defies the laws of nature.'

Moose put a hand on his shoulder. 'There is much that defies nature today Ferdinand. Heaven willing, we will live to see a better future.'

They decided to dispense with breakfast, quickly packed up their few belongings and doused the fire. Svanhild took the party along a narrow lead by the side of the stream, singing softly lines that came to mind,

of the land of swans I sing
of sunlit meadows
of great white wings
on silver water skimming
of the land of swans I sing
of the cottage by the river
where joy and laughter ring

How keen she had been for this adventure and yet, there was that twinge that pulled her back to the humdrum life she had left behind. Humdrum, but from here it looked so lovely. The early morning sun scattered light among the trees. They climbed at a good pace and only when the slope steepened, did they slow down. Spruce trees began to appear among the birch and maple casting shadows on the forest floor. Svanhild halted and suggested that they stop for a snack. They found a fallen log in a patch of sunlight and finished the leftovers. As soon as they got up and strapped on their packs, the sound of the woodpeckers became louder. They began tapping a tattoo, hundreds of beaks hammering in perfect harmony. Svanhild recognized the rhythms. We are leaving their habitat,' she explained, 'It is their way of signing farewell.'

They were still following the stream. It narrowed again, the ground along the shore was muddy and water began sloshing in their boots. Only the odd beam of sunlight reached the floor of the dense spruce forest and a chill was in the air. They kept plodding up the slope. Sometimes they halted for a drink from the little brook. By late afternoon no sunlight penetrated the needle canopy and they worked their way through the dense web of spruce branches. Large mushrooms grew on the mossy carpet, some a deep purple with white dots, others a fierce red or a phosphorescent green. The spruce branches and stands of giant ferns slowed their pace. A light rain began falling and an eerie and gloomy atmosphere settled over the spruce forest.

'It is true,' mused the Marquis. 'No Rovers or hounds would likely enter the inner darkness of this spruce cathedral. But what of hobgoblins and ancient Trolls?' Now the philosopher within took over. Was there not always something to fear, if not one thing then another. Yes, the world indeed was a dangerous place. He recalled a talk by Seraphim at the Graceful Neck, 'The fear that dwells within.' It was the fear of death, the shedding off this mortal coil. That is what the old greybeard had stressed. We must die, learn to die and accept our death, then fear itself would die, while yet we lived. The soul of his beloved Dorothea had left her marble body and winged its way to other realms. He must grieve no longer. Thoughts of such profundity called for a pipe of tobacco. Alas his pipe and tobacco had been left at the palace. The Marquis sighed and trod on, the party behind following in silence. Darkness descended quickly and Moose called the party to a halt.

For Svanhild the dark greens of the spruce forest, the reds and purples of the mushrooms, the rushing of the stream, conveyed a feeling of magic. Moose, Ducky and Slim felt exhausted and miserable. The rain was still falling and it would be difficult to make a fire. Yet they might have to spend the night here.

The Marquis, who had seated himself on a tree stump by the stream, looked far away. Moose savoured the sweet smell of moss and ferns, he inhaled deeply. Then another scent caught his attention, a trace of smoke. Somewhere in this remote forest a wood fire was burning. With the evening breeze blue smoke drifted down the slope. The others caught it too. Duckie jumped up and looked at Moose.

'Captain, the fire seems close. Let me scout the source. We may find food and warmth.' chirped Duckie quite prepared to rush forth.

Moose nodded approval. Following the trail of smoke, Duckie moved prudently through the tall ferns. Before long he heard a voice softly chanting, a woman's voice. He halted for a moment and listened. It sounded like an ancient hymn. Mystified, he wondered whether he was hearing voices from above. As he came closer, the sound became louder. Clearly it came from a terrestrial source.

It occurred to him that he might have come upon a hermit's hideaway. He knew that to commune with the spirits, men and women retired at times to a retreat. They would don the hermit's garb and live alone in the woods. He stepped out of the ferns and saw in front of him a small log cabin. On the porch sat an old woman, her foot moving the treadle of a spinning wheel to the time of her song. The voice was clear with a slight tremor. She was clothed in a simple nun's habit. A black cape covered her shoulders. She stopped her singing but the treadle kept moving. Dark laughing eyes, welcomed Duckie.

Good eve, reverend mother,' Duckie called out with a slight bow. 'We had not thought to meet living creatures in this distant forest.'

'Ah my little man,' replied the hermit, 'it is not too distant and not too dark for the Sisters of the Third Woe.

Duckie's curiosity was kindled. 'Sisters of the Third Woe. What is the Third Woe ancient one?'

A smile spread over the wrinkled face. 'My innocent whelp, as yet untouched by the woes of the world. Sisters of the First Woe have forsworn the allures of the flesh. To attain unto the Second Woe pride must be overcome. The Third Woe is the greatest burden that holds back our progress on the path of the spirit: the mischief of the tongue. Malicious whispers, become raging storms destroying ties of kin and friendship, toppling kingdoms. Thus we are a silent order and permitted only to speak when addressing an outsider. Why don't you go and bring your friends, for you do have friends nearby? I am sure they are anxious for a good meal and the glow of a bright blaze.'

'Many thanks mother, gladly will we partake of your hospitality.'

Duckie rushed back to the stream, to share the good news. After Duckie reported his meeting with the holy sister, Svanhild reacted. 'Never heard of the Sisters of the Third Woe.'

'They live in a convent in Esteria, Svanhild,' Moose put in, 'the brothers Ensten and Ulrik mentioned them to me. They spoke highly of the charitable work of the sisters. Sisters of the Third Woe are revered in Esteria for their healing powers. Esteria is not that far from here and for the holy sisters to do penance, it is quite possible that the Convent maintains cabins in the woods.'

Svanhild remembered Amaranth's warning. They were almost in the land of the Dwarves and surely the holy sisters could be trusted. She shivered in the evening chill and looked forward to the comfort of a cabin and a hot dinner.

'A wonderful offer of hospitality,' reflected the Marquis, 'An answer to our prayers.'

They followed Duckie as he made his way under the dark arches of the evergreens. The ferns were wet and the spruce branches shed water as they were moved back to gain passage.

Svanhild made up the rear. Her hood protected her from some of the water falling and she failed to hear the hammering of the single woodpecker that had followed the party. For a moment she stood still and imagined she heard a faint knocking. Water falling from the branches? She could now see the welcoming light of the cabin, the promise of warmth and shelter. Quickening her pace, she caught up with the others.

Soon the bedraggled travelers found themselves seated by the fire, sipping hot soup. Duckie had explained about the oath of silence taken by the

Sisters of the Third Woe and that they communicated only when necessary. Thus none of the company was surprised that the bent figure shuffling between the wood stove and the table, said precious little.

After serving soup, their hostess returned to her spinning wheel, humming a wistful melody. A black cat curled by her side. Svanhild's eyes scanned the cabin, it was austere indeed. It was, what was not there that struck her. Nowhere did she see the Common Book of Sacred Lore or the Silver Mandalas that were so prominent in all the holy houses. She had a vague notion that she knew that voice singing behind the spinning wheel and a feeling of unease settled over her. Everything had gone so well. They had found this charming refuge in the dark forbidding woods, offering warmth, hospitality and a generous evening spread, and yet ...

The soup and the fire relaxed the worn out travelers. The Sister got up from her spinning wheel and walked over to the stove. A pot of barley malt was simmering. She poured the drinks and put in front of her guests the steaming mugs. No words were spoken and she returned to the spinning wheel.

'It was good fortune indeed, to stumble across this humble abode of a holy woman,' spoke the Marquis in a soft voice. 'I have always admired the pious practices of monks and sisters. At one time, I contemplated taking holy orders, myself. My grand Uncle Amadeus was an abbot in the House of Mystic Seekers.'

'Warriors and holy men in the family tree,' admired Duckie.

'Alas I have always wavered between the two,' sighed the Marquis, keenly aware of the identity crisis that these conflicting tendencies had caused him.

'Perchance, if we return from this journey, my young friend, I will bid you all farewell and seek spiritual solace in one of the stricter houses of spiritual discipline,' the nobleman concluded wistfully. His Dorothea was lost and what was to be done? If only he had a pipe and a pouch of fragrant tobacco to help him traverse the psychological abyss that had opened before him.

The travelers had enjoyed the meal and the hot drinks, all but Svanhild, who felt on edge and barely touched the food. The barley drink she poured deftly into a flower pot behind the bench.

Patriot hiding behind a spruce tree peered at the cabin. His inner dog sense had told him that there was dipsy doodle in the works. The reverend Sister of the Third Woe was spinning silently on the front porch humming an old hymn and the company inside slid softly into a deep sleep. Only Svanhild was alert. Her intuition had told her to refrain from food and drink. It was clear as the light of day that the soup or the barley drink contained a sleeping potion.

Although wide awake, Svanhild closed her eyes and like the others rested her head on the table. What could be done? And who was the old woman pretending to be a Sister of the Third Woe? Svanhild's ears caught the words of the hymn she was singing.

sleep sweetly children dear
the journey's end is near
sleep my doting friends
sleep in innocence

A raspy laugh, barely audible drifted into the cabin and blended with the loud purring of the black cat now stretched out in the center of the dining table. A shiver ran down Svanhild spine. 'Sister of the Third Woe, flimflam, hokum,' she whispered to herself. Despite her anger, she still pretended to be asleep. She could hear the sister getting up and walking into the cabin. Those footsteps were not the sound of old feet shuffling. Then a lovely voice rang out, a voice of such beauty that it would make divas weep with envy.

'Svanhild daughter dear, I know you are not asleep. It was clever of you to pour your drink into the flowerpot. Asleep you are not, for I can hear the vibrations of your mind.'

Svanhild remembered that voice all too well, it was no use pretending, and she raised her head. The Holy Sister of the Third Woe, in her pious habit had vanished. The pretense was gone and before her stood the comely Matista. She couldn't help herself. She was fascinated by the majestic figure dressed in a gown of heavenly blue that flowed upward in a collar around her swanlike neck. Ebony tresses flanked a face beyond compare. Fascinated as she was, yet Svanhild felt anger.

'Sacrilege, sacrilege, Matista, to play the part of a holy sister and for mischief use their sacred retreat.' For a moment Svanhild was stuck for words but then she blurted out. 'You are a fake and I despise your wiles.'

For a moment even Matista, veiled in her aura of power and mastery was unnerved. The deep fire burning in those innocent eyes unsettled the great witch but she recovered her poise quickly. After all, few could match her powers. Why be concerned about the fire in Svanhild's eyes? The swannemaid's anger was rather amusing and made her reluctant to turn her over to the Grolls.

'We have met before Svanhild. At that time your friends the owls repaid my hospitality by attacking my bodyguard of Gorghouls. Alas, Gorghouls make poor guards. It is fortunate that we are close to the Land of Darkness, for a Rover and a troop of Grolls will soon be here to collect those sleepy heads on the table. Grolls make better guards my dear. Not pretty mind you, but few escape their lobster claws. The union of Trolls and Gorghouls was a fortunate event. Their offspring has proved useful. Grolls have no scruples and they make excellent guards. They may not act politely when they come to collect you.

Svanhild tried to think. Her friends were fast asleep and she doubted not that Matista's sleeping potion would keep them under until a Rover arrived with a troop of Grolls. It was pitch dark outside and the candles that Matista had placed on the mantelpiece cast a flickering light on the sleepy heads resting on the table. A cold draft blew through the cabin, Svanhild shivered. Matista looked at the slight maiden and walked to the fireplace. She threw some dry spruce branches on the dying embers and pointed her delicate fingers at the wood. Sparks leaped from her finger tips and instantly a bright blaze sprang up in the hearth. Light and heat radiated into the cabin.

Matista stood gazing at the blaze her magic had lit. She was well pleased with herself. Listening to the crackling of the burning wood, she did not hear the sound of paws on wood as Patriot leapt across the porch. He pushed open the door and sprang forward landing on the witch's back. She lost her balance and fell face first into the fire. Svanhild's first impulse was to rush to her aid, but Matista succeeded in raising herself and with her hair aflame, like a human torch, she rushed over to the water barrel and dipped her head in. Svanhild took the opportunity to rush out the open door. She ran into the forest followed by Patriot.

Matista quickly recovered her wit and fixed her gaze on the small mirror on the wall. Her face was burned and all her hair gone. She invoked an incantation: 'Aelis nastrum sicimous.' A sphere of deep red light glowed around her face, and the burns on her face and scalp began to heal immediately. She knew that her hair would grow back but it would take time, magic could not restore it. She covered her head with a white linen scarf. Again she looked into the mirror, and was pleased to see her lovely skin almost completely restored, except for a spot in the center of her forehead where she had hit the red hot gridiron. Magic could not erase it, the burn was too deep. It would mar her face. Cosmetics would hide the blemish, but the wound to her pride was grave. She strode out onto the porch. No sign of Svanhild, but there on a patch of moss, stood Patriot determined to block the witch's path in pursuit of Svanhild. Matista had no plans to run after Svanhild. She was sure, that the Swannemaid would not get far in the dark forest and surely the Rover and his Grolls would find her. The sight of the dog that had pushed her into the fire, sent her blood pressure soaring. Overwhelmed by rage, she let out a dreadful shriek which seemed to have a calming effect. A few moments of silence followed and she regained her poise. Then an incantation fell from her lips. Patriot froze in the defiant pose that he had assumed. The light brown fur turned slowly into the dark grey of rock. The noble hound had been turned into stone by the enchantress' evil spell. Had he only had the good sense to keep running, but then he would not have become that symbol of courage embodied by the grey stone statue, which for centuries has graced the old forest.[5]

A smile played on Matista's face as she looked at the handsome statue, a tribute to her powers. She was not to be trifled with. Let no one forget it, man or beast. The sweetness of revenge pleased her and she turned around and walked back into the cabin.

She looked at the wooden table and smiled. The Svannemaid's fellow travelers were sound asleep and Svanhild would not go far by herself. It was still dark and the path was steep and narrow. At first light the Rover and his Grolls would enter the forest.

Another quick glance at the mirror confirmed her fear. The burn on her forehead was still there. It had burned into her inner shape. 'Fie, fie, fie,' exclaimed the sorceress . 'A price must be paid for this grievous insult. These wretched travelers who caused this havoc will end up in the stone quarries of the Seven Lords. It will be a learning experience.' The very thought made her giggle.

'The girl, that girl, I will take her with me on my travels and break that rebellious spirit. She will serve and obey me, I will teach her magic.'

Matista leaned back and smiled. Even in the life of a great enchantress there comes a secret longing for a companion, a sorceress' apprentice to share the magic and the power. What a lovely thought. An almost maternal feeling came over Matista. A smile played upon her lips. She recalled a talk by an old wizened Elf, she couldn't think of his name now, but she recalled the talk had been about the stages in one's life.

Yes, she had reached a new stage and she was ready for a new relationship. She would teach the Svannemaid the art of magic and she would share with her, both the power and the glory. So taken was she by this idea that

---

5   In the latter days, the forest has become a National Park and the stone image of the handsome retriever stands now in the center of a memorial pavilion. Now after a millennium of peace, tourists and kennel clubs, come from all over the Kingdom, to pay tribute to the noble hound.

she failed to hear the voice of caution that welled within the depth of her psyche.

She repaired to the porch and took her place by the spinning wheel and with her right foot pushed the treadle. A ray of moonlight reached down among the trees and illumined the clearing around the cabin. The humming of the wheel calmed her frayed nerves. It is generally believed that great witches are never beset by anxiety, this is not true. They experience chasms of fear, and strive for ever greater powers to counter the threats that they perceive.

The secret magic used in the gardens of Queen Netilda had given everlasting youth to the Seven Lords in the Land of Darkness. They were beholden, therefore, to the enchantress who had rescued them from the forlorn isle in the western ocean. The quiet humming of the wheel led her mind back to that hour of victory amongst the fountains and the lighted pavilions of King Norwalt and Queen Netilda. From the deep wells of her memory rose the story of the lost tablet of purest gold. The tablet that contained a secret spell that could undo the magic that had given the Seven power without end. Although agents of the Lords had combed the land, no sign of a golden tablet had ever been found.

'It is good to indulge in self analysis at times,' mused Matista. 'It is true that the possible discovery of such a tablet has been the cause of much anxiety, however, most fears spring from the demons of the mind and have no relation to reality.'

She breathed a sigh of relief. There had been reason for concern but now it was evident that the tablets were but a myth, a myth spread by the enslaved men and women in the land of the Seven. She recalled another fairy tale, a story about an elven child chanting the words encrypted on a golden tablet. 'Quite absurd, fiddle faddle, folderol,' she laughed to herself. How foolish to give credence to these folk tales.

She took her foot off the treadle and the wheel came to a stop. The spinning had calmed her nerves. She looked out upon the forest. A partially cleared sky allowed moonlight to dance on the raindrops covering the spruce branches. No sign of Svanhild, but she could not have wandered far into that tangle of wet spruce branches. Matista waited quietly until dawn clad the great trees in a mist of somber light. Not long after Matista heard heavy footsteps crushing through the underbrush and a Rover followed by a troop of Grolls appeared. She could see Svanhild flanked by two Grolls holding her wrists in a lobster like grip. Two black hounds made up the rear of the procession.

Matista stepped down from the porch to welcome the Rover and to thank him for capturing the fair Svanhild. 'Tell your men to be gentle with her,' She could see the pain in the girl's eyes. 'I will deal with her after the men have been taken care of.' Several Grolls stepped up to the porch and entered the cabin.

Matista approached the hounds sitting on their haunches. They knew the power of the enchantress for they allowed her to pet them. Or was it the stone statue of Patriot that intimidated them?

'Welcome puppies,' she whispered resting her hands on the huge heads. 'In the cabin there is a treat for you.' Matista walked back up the steps and through the door.

Duckie, Slim, the Marquis and the Captain, their heads resting on the table were still asleep. The Grolls were standing about, not knowing how to rouse them. Matista broke out laughing at the sight.

'We have attempted to wake them your ladyship,' said a tall Groll.

'Try knocking their heads on the table,' suggested the great witch.

This simple method worked well and Duckie, Slim and the Captain were startled into wakefulness.

Yes, the travelers would soon be taken care of. Matista's laugh rattled the mugs and bowls on the table. Before they knew it Grolls were tying their hands to their back and being none too delicate about it.

The Marquis, still half asleep opened his eyes, to find a black hound staring at him. 'A dream,' he whispered, 'A nightmare of the first water. It must be the unfamiliar food.' He distinctly remembered having read that indigestion could produce such hellish visions, but the prod by a Groll standing behind him felt uncommonly real. 'Sweet mercy,' he muttered, 'If it only were a dream, I should be able to wake right out of it.'

After his terror subsided, a frightful rage overtook him. He called down upon Grolls and hounds, the wrath of his ancestors. Unfortunately, it was ineffective. Matista laughed at his ranting. 'Indeed Marquis, you come from a long line of distinguished warriors and you may well be the last one, very few, my dear nobleman, survive the quarries by the Black Peak. My Grolls must tie your hands and resistance will be useless. The black hounds would enjoy a little romp.'

The Marquis was terrified. The hound facing him, froth covering his jaws, eyed him constantly. It would be best to resign himself to his lot, but even if he survived the Grolls and the hounds, life in the quarries would be unbearable.

The Marquis recoiled at the thought of slave labour. It was entirely against his philosophy and totally beneath his dignity. A large Groll holding a rope seized his left hand. The claw bit into his flesh. It was then, totally unexpectedly that the hero, hidden deep within, arose. It burst forth like a volcano. His free hand reached down and gripped the sword lying under the bench and up in the air it soared, the blue sheen glowed brightly and seconds later the Groll trying to bind him, now neatly divided in two parts, hit the ground. Shouting the old family motto, 'Glory unto Death,' in a towering rage, swinging his deadly weapon, the Marquis tore across the cabin. The sword's blue sheen gave the blade a magic edge and Grolls were falling all over the floor. Matista climbed onto the table and looked upon the scene in utter astonishment. Some hidden aspect in his psyche she most certainly had overlooked.

It was an uneven contest and new Grolls replaced their fallen comrades. When the Rover entered the cabin he tripped the whirling Marquis. The fierce hound that had been watching the Marquis, seized his chance. He jumped the fallen nobleman, sinking his fangs into his shoulder. The brave warrior was immobilized by pain.

The Marquis was writhing on the cabin floor. With a mixture of admiration and pity Duckie stared at his master. What a splendid fight, it would go down in the annals of the deCygnes, and live in folklore for centuries to come.

Matista shook her head. What foolishness and all for nothing. She knew that the tainted fang illness soon would take care of the Marquis. She told the Rover to let the Marquis go. He would die in the forest. Ferdinand got up after a few minutes, staggered out of the cabin and wandered off into the trees. There was nothing that the Captain, Slim or Duckie could do. The eyes of the huge hounds were fixed steadily on them, watching for any movement.

Now that the hubbub had subsided, Matista stepped onto the porch. The Grolls were still holding Svanhild. She told them in a stern voice to release their grip on the Swannemaid. In a haze of pain Svanhild fell forward. The enchantress caught her in her arms, placed her on a chair, and put her hands on the torn flesh of her wrists and forearms, the burning pain eased. Svanhild felt a warm soothing feeling flow through hands and arms. She looked into the eyes of the sorceress, and for a moment Svanhild' eyes penetrated those deep dark lakes. She could see the scars of centuries: struggle, humiliation, hurts and triumphs, the love for the Prince, the fall of Queen Netilda, the ascendancy of the Seven Lords. All appeared in a flash of insight and a mixture of pity and contempt filled Svanhild's heart. Although freed from the Groll's lobster claws, now she felt bound to the enchantress by invisible cords. Matista's touch had dissolved her will to escape.

Matista told the Rover to lead his Grolls and the captives to the land of his Seven Masters. The Rover bowed and asked if he could take the girl. 'Never mind the girl Captain, she shall come with me.'

'The fat fellow that got bitten by the hounds, should we finish him off, ma'am?' asked the conscientious chap.

'Let him be, nature will take its course, within days, death will overtake the nobleman. March the prisoners to the camp under the shadow of the Black Peak in the land of the Seven. Working in the stone quarries will be a wholesome experience.'

The Captain and Slim were overcome with grief by this new turn of events. Almost within reach of the safety and comfort of the Dwarves' alpine village, evil had befallen them. Only Duckie was mad enough to give his guard a kick in the ankles, where the Grolls are supersensitive. His captor yelled and the claws dug deep into Duckie's arms. They could hear in the distance Ferdinand's faint moaning and realized there was little chance their friend would survive his ordeal.

The captives and their guards disappeared into the spruce forest and Matista set about cleaning the cabin of the Sisters of the Third Woe. The next Sister on retreat would not find a trace of the deception and violence that had taken place in their holy hideout, but the vibes might tell.

Svanhild had fallen into a trance in which Matista appeared to her through a blue haze. 'Svanhild dear, the time has come to return home. We will travel to my Chateau in the foothills of the Northern Range. There we will rest and meditate and I will teach you the uses of enchantment.' Svanhild's will to resist had ebbed. Matista gripped her hand and pulled her along. It was as if a mysterious force propelled the great witch. Her feet barely touched the ground and Svanhild felt almost weightless, as if a magic band pulled her along. They came to rest on the shore of a great lake.

Matista and Svanhild sat down by the shore. Svanhild's mind was in turmoil. A terrible attraction to the enchantress collided with an urge to escape, to tear herself loose from the magic that enchained her. Deep inside she knew that it was too late to turn back.

The first red haze of dawn appeared on the horizon. Svanhild looked at the enchantress beside her. She had just put on a grey cape. Its hood fell over most of her face and sunglasses covered her eyes. Svanhild realized that it would not be long before the sun's first rays would rise over the water and the bewitching Matista would change back into the old woman, Neva, her beauty masked and her powers curtailed until daylight faded into the dusk. The sun's rays illumined the hills across the lake and Svanhild cast a furtive glance at her companion. The ravishing face was wrinkled and the raven tresses were pure white.

'Confound the light of day and that Wizard Isumatak who stole my beauty.' whispered the old hag by her side. 'At least the night is mine and perhaps the evil can be undone. Once we reach the Chateau at the far shore of Fireweed Lake, I will have time to think.'

Svanhild looked up at the sun filled waters and descried that the lake was wreathed with a profusion of fireweed. A sail on the horizon caught the early light and swiftly it drew near the shore. The single helmsman lowered the sail and let the bow of the boat slide gently onto the beach. The Rover that skippered the vessel jumped onto the beach and bowed to Matista. He was clad in a colourful shirt and shorts, his hair reached to his shoulders and his face did not have the usual cruel lines of Rovers. Unlike the squat bodies of the other servants of the Seven, he was small and slender. His manners were pleasing and he helped Svanhild into the boat.

'Welcome home my lady and a welcome to your guest. I trust that all went well?'

'All turned out well in the end Finch. But there were trials and I have been grievously hurt. Outrages have been committed. I am generous, but there are limits.' Unconsciously, she moved her hand to the spot burnt into her forehead.

'I have returned Finch, for rest and recreation. I must soothe my shattered nerves. Svanhild will be my guest and we will study the art of magic.'

Svanhild thought it wise to change the subject. 'Why did you call him Finch, Matista?'

Matista stretched out her hand and rested it on the shoulder of the young man.

'He is different from the other Rovers, Svanhild. Considered useless as a warrior, he was about to be sent to the mines. I was at the palace in the land of the Seven at the time and asked if I could have him for a servant. They were pleased to let him go and my Finch was delighted to get away from his rough comrades. His love of bright clothes and music and his disdain of violence had already made him a laughing stock among his fellow Rovers. He has a lovely voice and sings like a Finch. Most Rovers are cold and calculating, their obedience springs from fear. Finch has feelings, his loyalty springs from the heart.'

Svanhild looked at Finch sitting at the back of the boat and realized how slight and youthful he looked. His black locks came almost down to the seat. He gave Svanhild a warm smile as he stepped forward to hoist the sail. Svanhild's mind began to clear and she realized that Finch was trusted by the enchantress. Unlike the regular Rovers, he was not likely to inform on his mistress to the Seven. Matista cherished her privacy.

The morning breeze caught the sail and drove the boat to the middle of the lake. Svanhild could now see clearly two dark towers silhouetted against the sunlit mountains.

'The Chateau my daughter,' whispered Matista. 'Home sweet home, my pet. There we will perch and rest our weary limbs. I will work in my hall to perfect my arts and teach you the secrets of power, my little hummingbird.' The great witch cast a maternal glance at Svanhild and dreamily looked out over the lake. Svanhild was wide awake now and alarmed. She knew she must remain alert before she became entangled in the hypnotic web that her hostess was busy spinning.

The boat moored at a small inlet. The young Rover jumped ashore, tied up the vessel and then helped Matista and Svanhild onto the dock.

'Come, my daughter. Welcome to the Chateau'

There were few trees and Svanhild saw the great edifice rise before her. The walls were built of natural rock, deep red in colour and towers flanked the building on both sides.

They walked along on a path of crushed shells. Beds of lovely pink roses lined the sides. Looking up, Svanhild saw two merewings perched on the roof's ridge. By the entrance, a Groll stood guard. The heavy oaken doors swung on their iron hinges and both enchantress and apprentice walked through. In the lobby, they were welcomed by an older woman with a handsome face and charming manners.

'Welcome back mistress,' greeted the lady in a soft voice.

'Thank you Meadow,' returned Matista. We are glad to be back. Kindly bring some refreshments to the hall.'

They walked from the lobby into a large hall with windows overlooking the snowcapped mountains to the north. Bookshelves lined the walls and on the window sills stood bottles filled with coloured liquids.

Svanhild was too tired to take it in. She had been chilled by the early morning crossing of the lake and she was relieved to see a fire in the open hearth. Matista led her to an easy chair, close to the fire. She sat down and held her hands up to the flames. By the time that Meadow arrived with a tray of tea and open sandwiches, she had sunk into the cushions of her chair and fallen into a deep sleep.

22

At The Home Of Smithereen

$\mathcal{W}$eiss sped along. By dawn he had traversed the spruce forest and entered the alpine meadows. Sunlight turned millions of dewdrops into diamonds and edelweiss blended with the reds and blues of berry bushes. He sat down on a rock and for a quick breakfast, took a bite of dried fish out of his satchel. Two eagles soared above and made a threatening pass. It occurred to him, that weighing a mere twelve pounds, he could be a candidate for an aerial journey. He moved down on the wet grass and pressed himself against the rock. There was no reason for anxiety. The two birds landed on a hillock and the larger of the two, greeted Weiss politely.

'Fear not little fellow, we are members of the Celestial Covey, an elite group of birds in search of spiritual truth. We have forsworn the consumption of higher life forms.

'Just eggs and fish,' added the other bird with a sour look on his face.'

'Don't begrudge it Nightglider, we have embraced wholeheartedly the rules of the Covey,' said Servatius with a reprimanding nod towards his companion.

'I am delighted to hear about the Celestial Covey,' Weiss exclaimed with a look of relief. 'I have always admired eagles.'

'Well there are eagles and then there are eagles, my little fellow,' said the great bird, Thank your lucky stars that you did not meet up with a flock of Dauntless Divers. Rough customers they are. Know them by a blood red comb. Good hearted deep down, diamonds in the rough but no refinement or discrimination,' sighed the great bird, with a patronizing look.

Weiss had certainly heard speak of them and told the eagle that he was greatly honoured and relieved to meet with a bird of spiritual stature. This pleased the eagle, who made a deep bow, 'Servatius at your service.'

'I am very anxious to reach the stronghold of the Dwarves.'

'If my eagle eyes do not deceive me, little fellow, you are a Mountain Fairy. Why is a Mountain Fairy traveling to the dwarf stronghold?'

'Noble birds this is a long story, but my friends are still back in the forest struggling up the mountain side. It has been rumoured that a Rover and a troop of Grolls have crossed the range. They could be in danger.'

The great bird nodded, 'Grolls are not to be trifled with, rather revolting creatures. What might your name be my fairy friend?' Asked Servatius.

'I am sorry Servatius, I am Weiss.'

'Weiss,' repeated Servatius to himself, 'Short and to the point.'

'Well Weiss, the Mountain Fairy, you had better climb onto my back and throw your arms around my neck. You can tell me the rest of the story later. Now we shall show you a view of the mountains, terrestrials seldom see,' said Servatius.

Wolf rider, eagle flyer! How wondrous to be small and under twelve pounds, thought Weiss. 'Edel wish you were here,' whispered the Fairy.

'And who is Edel, asked Servatius, who had just begun to stretch his pinions, 'I like that name. Where did it come from?'

The story of how together they had picked Edelweiss for the flower festival and how they got their nicknames, amused the eagles.

'Edel and Weiss, I like the ring of it,' mused Servatius. 'Where is Edel now?'

Tears ran from Weiss' eyes while he told the eagles of Edel's abduction by the Black Elves. Servatius and Nightglider were moved and promised Weiss they would bring the matter before the High Council of the Celestial Covey.

No more time was to be lost and Servatius walking to the edge of a precipice lifted off. The graceful motion of his great wings easily propelled the eagle and his passenger high up into the mountain air. Close behind, followed Nightglider.

Weiss was enthralled, the view was awe inspiring. Down below, glaciers, patches of newly fallen snow and alpine meadows emerald green, flashed by.

He held on for dear life. The icy mountain air streamed around his face, yet, it was exhilarating. What a gift to be able to experience all these wonders of creation. Now, they were following the snow covered ridge of the Finnian Range. On the left, evergreens ran down the mountainside and beyond, Weiss could see a red haze hanging over the land of the Seven Lords. It was the very first time that he had looked upon the dark realm. He trembled and dug his hands deeper into the eagle feathers.

He looked to the right and espied columns of smoke rising from a small settlement surrounded by alpine meadows, the dwarf village of Turania at last. Servatius banked to the right and began a long glide down. They made a perfect landing in front of the guardhouse of the dwarf stronghold. The fort was made of logs and surrounded by a circular rock wall.

On the down slope side of the village were piles of heavy rocks that could be set off by a slight shove and crush any intruders approaching from the forest below. At the gatepost stood two grim looking Dwarves, dressed in mail vests and sporting wicked looking swords. They had shiny helmets with visors to keep the sun out of their eyes.

'Top of the morning to you master eagle,' spoke the tallest of the two guards, 'I see you bring a passenger to our gates.'

'Greetings Sergeant Crusher. At your post as usual, I am glad to see it. These are dangerous times.'

'They are, they are, my feathered friend, rumours of marauding Grolls on our side of the mountain.'

By this time, Weiss had slid down and walked up to Sergeant Crusher. The stern looking guard cracked a smile at the dapper diminutive figure facing him. 'Well by the great dragon himself, what do we have here. I'll be skewered if it isn't a Mountain Fairy. And what can we do for you my light weight?'

Weiss climbed on a rock and looked Sergeant Crusher in the eye.

'My name is Weiss, Sergeant and my mission a matter of life and death. I traveled with a party from Swanneland. It was in Swanneland that your leader, Scimitar, was ambushed by the Grolls and transported to the mines under the Black Peak, in the land of the Seven.'

The mention of Scimitar startled the guards. They knew about his disappearance, but no details had reached their remote settlement.

'Who is in charge while Scimitar is gone,' asked Weiss, 'I must see your deputy Chief at once, take me to him, if you please?'

'It is a her, my plucky pixie. Scimitar's older brother Smithereen would have taken over, but for the illness which befell him. Sunflower, his wife of many years is at the helm. I will take you to her presently.'

The eagles knew that it was time to go. Servatius nodded to Nightglider, there was a rush of air, wing shadows passed over the guards and the eagles gained altitude.

'Take over Tuffkote, and I will take this featherweight to the lady,' hollered the Sergeant to his companion. Sergeant Crusher was astonished how effortlessly Weiss danced from rock to rock. The Sergeant, taking long strides, had trouble keeping up. Soon they came to an alpine meadow with tall grasses, and here it was Weiss who fell behind. Flowers tickled his nose, pollen made him sneeze and angry bees buzzed around his head. At the end of the meadow they passed through a wooden gate and into a garden. A lovely log cabin surrounded by scrub birch and huckleberry bushes met Weiss' eyes. Seated in a rocking chair on the porch was the figure of a huge Dwarf, dressed in a green smock and leather vest. His grizzled head leaned against the high back chair. He did not look up when Weiss and Sergeant Crusher approached.

'It is Smithereen, my tiny friend. Once the sight of him would set friend and foe ashivering in their boots, now he just sits there rocking back and forth and whispering to himself.'

'He is ill then?' whispered Weiss.

'They says it is an illness all right. I see nothing wrong with him, strong as an ox.' The burly guard looked flummoxed. 'Depression they calls it. Fudge and folderol, never heard anything like it before. Folks should pull themselves up by their bootstraps.'

The screen door opened and a dwarf lady stepped onto the porch. She wore a bright flowery apron, and below a mop of curly white hair sparkled a pair of light blue eyes. 'I bring you a Mountain Fairy ma'am. His name is Weiss. He says that he comes from Swanneland and has news about Scimitar.'

'Welcome stranger, welcome. Thank you, Sergeant Crusher, for escorting my guest hither. You may return to your post.'

'Yes ma'am,' The Sergeant saluted and turned around.

'Thank you Sergeant Crusher,' said Weiss.

'Fare thee well, Tiny.' In a low voice and with a broad smile, Crusher added, 'Watch the lady my fairy fair, a lovely lady, a lovely smile and a steely streak under that apron with the pretty flowers.' Sergeant Crusher was on his way. Weiss sprang onto a small lawn table and bowed before Smithereen's wife.

'A Mountain Fairy has come to the stronghold of the Dwarves, a first in our history, but then the world is shrinking.' A hearty laugh followed. 'Smithereen and I were honoured to meet your Queen Tuluga. It was at the Unity Conference in Lambarina, before tragedy overtook our King and Country. You may wonder why I still laugh, now that Scimitar is gone and my husband has sunk into a deep depression. Laughter wells up from within, it is my nature. As long as there is life, there is laughter and where there is laughter there is hope. Besides, dwarf husbands are picky, pious and pure, which makes for very dull fare. If we dwarf women didn't have a plentiful store of giggle and glee, the whole village would clot into a gooey lump. Dough without yeast, you know!' Cascading laughter filled the garden. 'Laughter is a great healer, my Mountain Fairy, but come down and meet Smithereen.'

Effortlessly, Weiss jumped from the table and walked to the bent figure in the rocking chair.

'A Mountain Fairy has come to visit us, Smitty.'

'From the land of Queen Tuluga? I can't believe it!' whimpered the dark figure in the rocking chair.

'Then open your big eyes and see for yourself.'

Smithereen raised his head and looked at the wee figure now seated on the porch railing. For a moment a ripple of mirth showed on the dark face. 'A Mountain Fairy here in the land of the Dwarves and all alone.'

'Alas, all alone, Sir. Edel, companion of my youth and closest friend, was snatched by the Black Elves and rafted down to the domain of the Seven in the land of Darkness.'

'Nasty lot those Black Elves,' muttered Smithereen, 'Rumours of their dealings with the Seven have drifted up into the mountain regions. Sad business. My brother Scimitar disappeared seven months ago, no trace.

'Smithereen, Sir, there is a trace. The Marquis learned from Queen Marsha in the wetlands that Scimitar is a slave in the quarries under the Black Peak, in the land of the Seven.'

Astonished, Sunflower and Smithereen looked at each other. 'Scimitar is alive. Cheer up Smitty,' said his sunny wife, but it was not enough to dispel the black cloud that had enveloped Smithereen.

'Labouring in the quarries, a slave in the land of the Seven, perhaps worse than death,' lamented the Dwarf. Weiss knew that Smithereen was in no state of mind to deal with an urgent mission and he took Sunflower aside and told her quickly that his companions, still in the spruce forest below, hoped to reach the dwarf village the next day. For a moment a cloud moved over that sunny countenance.

'Danger dwells amongst the dark spruce trees. Grolls have been spotted on the mountain passes and the forest badgers told us that an old woman has moved into the hut that the holy sisters use for their retreat.'

Sunflower lost no time. She seized a ram's horn hanging on the side of the cabin, filled her ample chest with air and sent a haunting note echoing off the mountain side. Quickly there could be heard the stomping of heavy feet, silver helmets glistened in the sun and warriors gathered in front of the garden gate.

Leaning on their swords the troop listened to Sunflower as she told them about the other wayfarers still working their way up through the black spruce.

'We had better go down to the forest, Lady Sunflower,' said a short, barrel-chested Dwarf, Grolls on the loose you say, I doubt not that they have along a few doggies. If you expect company, we had better go and give them a hand, just in case. A strange sister in the hermit's hut? The holy sisters weren't due till next week. Could be a mummer I'd say.'

'There is also a girl amongst our friends in the forest, Bullneck. I thought I better let you know!'

A murmur of indignation moved through the ranks. 'A girl traveling with three men? Unheard of, entirely improper.'

'What is the world coming to Sunflower? Have these outsiders lost all sense of propriety,' exclaimed a gaunt little Dwarf with a pained expression on his face.

'Scrub your mind Prissy and you won't see evil, where it is not. Different customs must live side by side in the United Kingdom, we may as well get used to it!'

Snickers were heard round and about and whispered comments were plentiful. 'A straight shooter that one. You've got to toss it to her. Put Prissy in his place. Don't tangle with Sunflower.'

Bullneck made a slight bow, 'We must make haste. We will march to the spruce forest and find the strangers.'

'Godspeed my men,' Sunflower shouted as the warriors descended the mountainside towards the forest. Weiss and Sunflower stood on the porch, watching until the last of the warriors had disappeared.

'Come on in Mountain Fairy. We will leave Smithereen alone for a while,' Sunflower held open the screen door for Weiss to pop in. A cheerful cabin it was. A lovely soapstone hearth warmed the kitchen where most of the living took place. Benches and a sturdy table made from rough boards stood across from the stove. In the living area on the other side of the cabin stood a loom, a wide blanket in the making stretched across its frame.

Weiss jumped upon the edge of the loom and looked at the blanket's design; dolphins diving in a deep blue sea.

'Ms. Smithereen, it is so lovely,' exclaimed Weiss, have you traveled to the ocean?'

'On our honeymoon, sprightly one. We sailed down the Sanctus to the western coast and camped by the old Alcazar. I would sit on a dune top and gaze at the breakers at my feet and when I lifted my eyes I saw the dolphins dance.'

'Oh, lady Sunflower, you saw the old Alcazar where the Princess lies imprisoned?'

'Our beloved Princess Yaconda shut in the Alcazar? Tell me the whole story, news seldom reaches here.' Sunflower seated herself in a small rocking chair and took up her knitting.

Weiss leaned comfortably against the loom's frame, put his feet on the warp and told Sunflower of the surfing holiday that had brought him and Edel to the old Alcazar where the Princess and her handmaid lingered in prison. Sunflower's knitting needles had stopped in midair. Her eyes sparkled and within her surged a deep longing for travel and adventure. When Weiss told of their homecoming he paused for a moment.

'Tell me everything Weiss, what did Queen Tuluga say?'

'We were disciplined, Lady Sunflower, shoveling manure on the Pelican Ranch.'

Sunflower burst out laughing, 'Yet, your Queen knew your worth Weiss, otherwise she would not have asked you to undertake this mission.'

Then Weiss told her about their travels and the episode in the palace of the Queen of the Marshes. When he came to Edel's capture by the Black Elves, Sunflower wept and walked over to the stove to make a drink. They both sat silently sipping hot goat milk, mixed with a bit of malt and honey.

'Weiss, did the eagles tell you that they would bring Edel's fate before the Celestial Covey?'

'They did so Sunflower lady.'

'Be of good cheer, my fairy friend. The Celestial Covey are all upper echelon birds, a bit snobbish to be sure, but they have the power. If they are moved by Edel's fate, things may happen.'

A gleam of hope sprang in Weiss' eyes. He looked outside towards the mountain peak and whispered a silent prayer. His eyes caught the outline of Smithereen in his rocking chair on the porch and he looked at Sunflower.

'Will Smithereen recover, he seems so sad, is there anyone who can help him?'

'The moping illness is a terrible thing, Weiss. Quite a few of the men in the village have suffered from it. Perhaps they take themselves too seriously. Merriment chases gloom and the herbs gathered by the goat lady have often cheered their spirits.

'The goat lady?' queried Weiss.

'High above the village on the upper meadows the ancient one lives. Her real name is Angelica. She has lived there as long as any one can remember. She lives alone with her goats and spends much time in meditation. Her hair is white, her figure bent and her grey eyes sparkle in a face that knows no age. She talks with the eagles and gathers herbs on the mountainside. Her hands have healing power and she has saved many a life, the ancient one. I dare say she's got the second sight.'

'What herbs does she gather Sunflower?' asked Weiss who always had had an interest in plants and flowers.

'She gathers borage and comfrey and other herbs. She talks to the ill and tries to uncover the demons that dwell deep inside and beset their soul. Dwarf husbands are a solemn lot, too solemn, and I say it is a pleasure to have a lightweight, like a Mountain Fairy, visit here.'

Weiss, pleased that his presence was so welcome, did all he could to put on his best lightweight appearance. He helped Sunflower around the house and the next few days passed quickly. He nimbly climbed the roof and cleaned the chimney, he dusted all parts of the house which where difficult to reach and weeded the strawberry patch. In the afternoons they went off together, huckleberry picking high above the village. From there on a height of land they would anxiously scan the meadows at the edge of the forest for any signs of the dwarf warriors and the company emerging from among the trees.

In the high mountains of the Finnian Range, far above the dwarf village and in the shadow of a giant peak was a small plateau. Around Grand Master Grimmbeak, thirty eagles had gathered in a semi-circle. Servatius and his companion Nightglider had just told the meeting of the Celestial Covey about their adventure with the Mountain Fairy Weiss and the sad story about Weiss' bosom friend Edel. They wondered if rescue might be possible.

Grand Master Grimmbeak seemed doubtful. 'It would be unwise for the Covey to become involved with the squabbles of earthlings. We will never see the end of it,' spoke the mighty one, shaking his head and flapping his pinions. 'Sad business, Black Elves. Bad karma. No doubt, they handed the tiny mite over to the Rover overseers at the mine under the shadow of the Black Peak.'

At the end of the half circle stood a young eagle, eyes veiled with tears, 'A Mountain Fairy will never survive chain gangs in the quarries, Grand Master,' spoke the noble youngster. Most of the older birds were not impressed, but Servatius felt that he must support the idealism of the younger birds.

'Master Grimmbeak, remember the black smoke from the smelter near the mine? Trees on the far side of the mountain are dying. The environment will suffer and sooner or later we may have to choose sides.'

Dying trees had a powerful effect upon the Grand Master's world view and deep inside he had a weak spot for Fairies. 'Thoughtless whimsical windflowers they are, yet there is a lightness in their being that makes me think of tinkling bells and angel wings,' mused that old bird. A sort of inward laugh tickled his ribs. Stern eyes did not betray his inner mirth.

'Get off your perch young Theodorus and check out the quarry. If Edel is not in the quarry, survey the bordering desert country in case he has escaped,' snapped Grimmbeak casting a piercing look at the young bird.

Theodorus lost no time, he rose rapidly to the ridge and soared quickly out of sight. Grimmbeak called for a recess and the eagles flew off to a nearby mountain lake to do some fishing.

By the time Theodorus returned, the birds of the Covey had reassembled. The young bird took his place at the end of the half circle, wiped away some tears and with a quivering voice painted a picture of the prisoners' wretched condition.

'My feathered friends, the men are chained together and driven mercilessly by a Rover. There was no sign of the Fairy. The smelter behind the mine billows out plumes of black smoke, the air smells foul and sometimes it was difficult to get a clear view. I made a number of passes.'

Even Grimmbeak looked grimmer than usual. 'The Fairy may have escaped on the way to the mine. Lithe and whippy creatures they are. If he got away, he will be trying to make his way to the Dwarves.'

He lost no time in issuing commands. 'Nightglider and Servatius will undertake surveillance flights and look for the Mountain Fairy.'

Weiss and Sunflower had spent the afternoon picking huckleberries. An orange glow was shining on the peaks when they shouldered their packs, heavy with berries, and began the descent back to the village. They had crossed the last meadow before entering the gate when Weiss saw two dark shapes silhouetted against the glowing peaks. One of the birds appeared to have a ring around his neck. In the quickly fading light, wide wings circled the meadow and flew directly overhead. Weiss espied a small shape mounted on eagle back, arms fastened around the great bird's neck.

Then, he heard a sound, the yodel of a Mountain Fairy, its high notes bouncing off the mountain range. Heavens above, it was Edel! The eagles had been as good as their word. Servatius and Nightglider landed at the end of the meadow. Weiss rushed towards Edel and in a wild dance of joy, spun him around. The eagles perched on a rock and Sunflower, standing nearby, watched the reunion of the friends.

'You have added a note of joy to this world of ours,' said Sunflower.

'It was so little.' returned Servatius, in the idiom used by birds in the northern regions. 'It was a welcome adventure. We swept high above the last ridge and spotted two merewings standing by a pile of rocks that blocked the entrance to a small cave. They were madly pecking away trying to pry something out of the cracks. We knew that something fishy was going on. With the sun behind us we dived down and the black buzzards didn't see us until it was too late.'

'We knocked the stuffing out them,' Nightglider explained, with ill concealed glee. Servatius cast a stern glance at his younger companion.

'Was I ever relieved when the long purple beaks stopped pecking at me,' exclaimed Edel.

'But it took some time to convince our Fairy that he could climb safely out of his stone tomb,' added Servatius with a modest bow.

'We will fly him to your cabin Sunflower. The poor mite got chilled in the upper air currents and should be sitting by a hot stove.'

Edel had recovered sufficiently to climb on Nightglider's back. He lay forwards, put his arms around the eagle neck and minutes later stepped onto the porch of the log cabin.

Sunflower and Weiss rushed down the mountain. When they reached home, Edel and the eagles were already inside. The eagles perched on top of the loom and Edel cuddled up to the hearth. When Sunflower and Weiss entered, Edel sprang up to give them a hug. His energy was quickly returning.

Smithereen was still seated in his rocking chair in a corner, a gloomy veil over his eyes. Once or twice however, the sight of the exuberant Fairies brought a smile to his face. Sunflower's neighbour Pristina and her hubby Bullneck dropped in to find out what all the commotion was about. Sunflower had begun to cut vegetables for a lamb stew and Pristina joined her at the counter. While they were preparing the evening meal, she filled Pristina in on the events of the day.

The pot of lamb stew filled the small cottage with a lovely aroma. A few more neighbours dropped in and soon a merry crowd was seated at the evening board. The eagles preferred their perch, so Sunflower put a plank across the loom and served them a generous portion of lamb stew.

'Lamb stew, Servatius, not quite kosher, is it?'

'Servatius thought deeply. The stronger the smell of lamb, the more deeply he thought.

'One has to be sensitive to the people around us Nightglider. The sunny lady has gone out of her way to give us a treat and it would be impolite to reject it.'

'That is true, very true,' mumbled his companion, a piece of lamb in his beak.

'This lamb is cooked Nightglider.'

'That alone Servatius puts the matter in a different light,' Nightglider rejoined solemnly.

'Creative consultation can solve knotty problems Nightglider.' Servatius was much pleased with himself and the dinner turned out to be immensely satisfying.

'Nightglider, you recall my grandfather?' asked Servatius

'I do indeed, a twelvefooter.'

'Mighty wingspan could lift a lamb as if it were gossamer!'

'The Covey has changed our life style, my friend.'

'Spiritual progress Servatius,' said the young bird casting a woebegone look at his companion.

'When we get home Nightglider, the Covey will be anxious to hear of our adventures. When it comes to this splendid lamb stew, we must be delicate.'

'Most delicate. Only few birds in the Covey understand about the spirit of the law.'

'You are perceptive Nightglider.'

After the main meal a bowl of dandelion wine was passed around and the eagles drank a generous portion. Weiss drank a toast to the eagles and thanked them for their rescue of Edel. Sunflower concerned about Edel's weakened state had refrained from asking him to tell his story. She need not have worried. The stew, huckleberry crumble and the dandelion wine had done wonders.

Edel stood upon the bench and thanked the eagles for saving his life. He looked a little shaky. Sunflower reached for a wooden bowl, turned it over on the table and put Edel on it. Seated center stage, surrounded by a circle of eager listeners, it was hard for the Mountain Fairy to resist telling his tale. He took a sip of dandelion wine before speaking.

'Thanks to the spirits above, thanks to Servatius and Nightglider I am here to tell my story. Weiss has told you about our trip on wolfback, how I slid off Leonardo's back and into the river Mork. Addle-headed daydreamer that I am, the icy waters of the Mork swirling about my ears brought me back to the real world. I could see Leonardo and Weiss standing on the opposite shore, but there was nothing that they could do. I was hanging from a willow branch and could see the raft with the Black Elves bearing down. It was they who plucked me from the waters and tied me to the raft's beams. Most of the journey to the Land of the Seven was made underwater. Only God in heaven knows how I survived.'

Even Smithereen seemed caught up in the tale. When Edel looked at the slumped figure at the end of the table, he could see a light in his eyes.

'Through the Lake of Shadows, we entered the land of the Seven, and when we docked Cobalt presented me as a gift to the Grolls. When Grolls catch Fairies, they like to pickle them and I knew that I was a goner.'

Sunflower wiped a tear and filled Edel's glass. Smithereen pulled himself up in his chair.

'The Groll Captain tucked me under his arm and walked me over to the field kitchen. I was dumped onto the counter and they had begun covering me with cabbage leaves, when a Rover, asking for the prisoner, walked in.

"The prisoner is under a cabbage leaf about to be rolled up and dumped in a pot of brine Chief."

"Not this time," explained the Rover, "There are new regulations from the palace, all prisoners must be transported to the Black Peak, for questioning and for quarry duty."

The Groll laughed, "You say quarry duty? This pint sized piddler carry stone?"

The Rover ignored the Groll's protest and before I knew it I was whisked from under my cabbage leaf and dumped into a cart outside. A couple of Grolls tied me up and hitched a mule to the cart. The Rover jumped onto the box and the cart started bouncing down the rough trail to the Black Peak. The Rover knew little about Mountain Fairies. Wriggling out of those ropes was no harder than sliding out of my pants,' laughed the willowy Fairy.

'Thirty seconds later I found myself standing in a cloud of red dust, and saw the mule and wagon vanishing over the hill. Where to go? Grolls could show up at any time. There was no food or water anywhere and the only hiding places were rocks scattered over the landscape. I knew it would not take the Rover long to discover that his prisoner was gone. I ran away from the cart trail and towards the Lake of Shadows. Soon a few shrubs appeared and I could see larger trees behind them. It was a ray of hope, if only I could make it to the shore. But then, my ears caught a stomping sound, Groll feet were on my trail. One of the black hounds must have caught my scent. I could hear him scurrying through the bushes. I ran faster, it was no use. The black peril was leisurely loping in my tracks. Hiding behind a rock, I peeked around the corner. The monster had come to a stop and I could see him licking white froth from his chops. I froze. In a foolish way I wondered if he would swallow me whole?'

'Oh my God,' exclaimed Pristina, 'it is too horrible to fancy.'

The party around the table sat in stunned silence. Weiss rubbed his eyes to convince himself that Edel was really sitting there on his upturned bowl, alive and well.

'The ghastly beast simply stood there, smacking his jaws and enjoying my terror.'

It was then that I heard a voice. It appeared to come from the ground below my feet. At first I didn't dare look. Then the voice spoke louder. "Down here pixie!" A large Mole was standing by the entrance to a tunnel. Immediately I dived down and the Mole scurried after me.

'In the nick of time Tiny,' gasped Sunflower. Even Smithereen opened his mouth. 'Moles are good fellows, lucky you fitted in that hole.'

'I couldn't stand up,' Edel went on, 'I crawled farther down and found soon that the tunnel widened and I could move comfortably. For a while I could hear the yelling and the cursing of the Grolls, but as I went even farther down the tunnel, all was silent. Deeper down, the tunnels gave way to dome roofed chambers, carved from earth and red gravel. Walls were decorated with colourful pictures and illumined by candlelight. I sat down on a small chair and had an opportunity to look at my guide who was standing in front of me. He wore a brown cloak over a yellow vest. On his head he wore a yellow cap. He pulled spectacles out of his vest pocket and balanced them on his long snout. He took a long look, shook his head and said, "What foolishness to be wandering around in Groll country. It was a near thing you know. Those hounds have a healthy appetite."

I thanked the Mole for saving me from the hounds and their masters and told him how I had escaped. The Mole lifted his cap, made a slight bow and told me he was Ben the Mole. I introduced myself as Edel the Mountain Fairy. Then he told me to follow him, explaining that for questioning, all unexpected visitors had to be presented to the Board of Judges.

My host took the lead and easily walking upright I followed. The deeper tunnels were much higher. We entered a sizable hall with a table in the center, at each end of which was seated a Mole. My guide took a seat in the center and motioned me to sit across from him. Anchored in the red rock above was an elaborate chandelier shedding an eerie light.

My guide who turned out to be the third judge, told my story. The other judges' grave look made me feel uneasy. The older one on my left explained that I was now in the presence of the Three Judges of the Mole Confederacy and I had better tell the truth. Giving me a penetrating look through his specs, he asked, "Do we have here an unsavoury element? Has a criminal mind invaded these sacred premises? Does a putrid smell emanate from the suspect?" All moved their long snouts towards me and inhaled deeply.

"The smell is tolerable," muttered the judge on my right.

"The suspect is a Mountain Fairy," explained my guide, who was also the Chief Justice of the Confederacy.

"Ah so my worthy collegue," responded the figure on my left, this puts a new light on the case, a better light. Queen Tuluga, she has a good reputation. We only hope that this Mountain Fairy wasn't exiled for mischief."

I told them my name was Edel and that while on a special mission for the Queen, I had been kidnapped by the Black Elves. This seemed to satisfy them.

The Chief Justice explained that all strangers were suspect until proven sound and upright. It is the way that their system works. They conferred for a few moments, their heads huddled together and I could hear them mumbling, "Not a criminal mind, no jarring vibrations. The smell of wildflowers and mountain air, not the invigorating scent of damp earth, wet peat and dripping rock. Acceptable just the same."

I knew I had been cleared. My guide invited me to follow him home until they decided what could be done for me. Well my friends,' smiled Edel looking at the astonished eyes around the table. 'A whole new world opened up before me. We wound our way through comfortable tunnels, where heavy wooden doors on both sides opened into cozy apartments. Some moles, seated in little rocking chairs by their front door, asked us to come in and have a peek. The furniture was lovely, in the modern style, with light woods and colourful designs. Chandeliers cast a gay pattern of light.'

'Never heard anything like it. Didn't know the moles had it in them.' exclaimed Sunflower.

'If we didn't have the beauties of nature around us Sunflower, we too would do something about the inside of our houses,' laughed Pristina

Edel sipped some wine and took a moment to catch his breath.

'How are the women dressed?' Pristina wanted to know.

'Well,' began Edel, hesitating for a moment, 'mole ladies are not built like mountain fairy maidens.'

'We know that, you little twit,' Pristina burst out, a twinkle in her eyes. 'Dwarf wives aren't either you know.' There was quite a bit of snickering around the table. Edel quickly added, 'The mole ladies wear long woolen skirts, embroidered blouses and lace caps with small golden plaits suspended from the sides. They look very beautiful.' Sunflower and Pristina were thrilled, but the men could be heard muttering, 'Hoity toity, stuckuppiness, frills and frazzles, sinful pride.'

Edel wiped his forehead and took another drink. 'My friends, that underground world was full of charm and grace. My host's apartment was at the end of a tunnel. The heavy wooden doors are never locked and I just walked in after Ben. Ben's wife, Rochelle, standing in the kitchen, couldn't believe her eyes. "What in mercy's name have you got in tow now, Ben the Mole?"

"A Mountain Fairy, my honeycomb, already cleared by the High Court."

"Vindicated for crimes that never took place," Rochelle laughed. "A mildewed practice, run by moss-backed male moles."

Ben laughed and introduced me to his feisty wife. Rochelle liked the sound of Edel and kept singing the name to herself. Lovely name she concluded and when I told her how I had come by it, she was thrilled. Ben and Rochelle knew that I was anxious to join Weiss in the land of the Dwarves and Ben promised to consult the other Judges.

Their home, like the others that I had seen, was beautifully furnished. I sat down on a comfortable sofa, and Rochelle served snacks and tea. Roasted roots were a new experience but quite tasty. As soon as I had finished eating I collapsed on the sofa and slept right through the night. It was strange to wake up in the morning without the sun shining through the windows but the dining room was brightly lit with candles. Ben the Mole pulled a gold watch out of his vest pocket and informed us that it was nine o'clock. Over a breakfast of roots, nuts and dandelion coffee, I learned some surprising news. Three elven sisters live in the Mole Confederacy. During the great upheaval when the Black Elves revolted, these girls had been abandoned in the forest, north of the Sanctus. When the moles found them, they were starving. They took them in and have cared for them ever since.' Sighs and whispers could be heard around the table.

'Noble moles, well done, never heard the like of it. Elven children in the dark tunnels, poor mites.'

'Oh no,' exclaimed Edel, 'The tunnels are well lit there are playgrounds, fountains and evening entertainment. The moles are good musicians. Although they have poor vision, they have a good ear.'

'Have you seen the elven children, Edel,' asked Sunflower.

'I met them that same morning. They had just come back from a music lesson and were sitting at the edge of a fountain. They were very pleased to meet me and wanted to know all about the outside world. We had a long chat. It was the youngest of the trio that I remember most vividly. Small in stature, rosy cheeks, a face wreathed in laughter. I can never forget it.'

'I wonder, I wonder,' mused Sunflower, 'why those children were abandoned and raised by the moles?'

'Tiny just told you,' said Smithereen.

'But Smitty, things happen for a reason. There are no accidents, my love.'

It took Smithereen a while to digest that pill. While Edel carried on, he sent a few rings of smoke gently drifting to the ceiling.

'It was the innocence of the youngest elven child that touched my heart, her laughter was like falling water, her eyes like morning dew.'

Weiss looked up at Edel and wondered if it was the wine that made him misty eyed. No, not the wine just Edel. He had made a speedy recovery and his romantic genius was in full flower.'

'Praise be,' intoned Angelica, who had slipped in after dinner, 'The elven children were saved and cared for by the good moles. The moles have saved many a soul. A large stock of healing roots they have and often they help me out.'

'It is true,' said Edel, 'they do have a large selection of herbs and ground roots, and Rochelle served me a special drink to make me recover my strength.

After two days with Ben and Rochelle, I felt well again and on the third day I was summoned to appear before the Judges. They told me that since I had been cleared of suspicions, I was welcome to stay as long as I wished. I replied that I was anxious to reach the land of the Dwarves. They huddled for a minute and then offered to take me to the end of the western tunnel. This was the tunnel that surfaced near the last ridge of the land of the red earth, and only a day's journey from the alpine meadows.'

The last evening of my stay with Ben and Rochelle, they took me out to dinner. We went to a little restaurant on the edge of the great central plaza. Three mole girls played the violin and delighted to have a Fairy amongst the guests, played some of my favourite tunes. They danced around me as they played and touched me with their bows, to make sure I was real. What marvels one discovers underground.

Early in the morning I bade farewell to my hosts. Rochelle's long wet snout planted a kiss on my forehead and she strapped a small pack of provisions on my back. Ben gave me a hug. When two guides appeared at the door, he explained that they would take me through the labyrinth of tunnels leading to the edge of the Alpine meadows. We worked our way through many tunnels and whenever we met a group of moles they would wave and wish me well.

When we reached the western exit, my guides were not content to let me go off on my own. They stuck their hunting knives in their belts, and put on slitted wooden goggles and ranger hats, for protection from the fierce sun.

We passed through some caverns and then I could see daylight through the cracks. My guides and I squeezed through a narrow opening to find ourselves in the red desert. After all that time underground my spirit was cheered by the light of the sun. The moles, well protected as they were, grumbled and I could hear them say that they simply could not understand why anyone would choose to live above ground.

We plodded through rough terrain until we came to a trail running up the slope. Here, they saluted, turned around and hurried back to their tunnels. I thanked them several times, but I am not sure that they heard me.

The sun was high in the sky and I began running towards a distant ridge. Once across it, I would be in the land of the Dwarves. Several hours later I sat down on a rock, overlooking the realm of the Seven Lords. I scanned the mountains and in the distance I saw the black smoke from the blast furnaces near the quarries under the Black Peak. I pulled a root from my pack and began chewing. When I felt revived I stood up to look at the ridge above. My heart skipped a beat. Perched on a rock above me, there were two black specks.'

' Merewings,' breathed Pristina. A tremor passed through the company around the table.

'I think they had been watching me for some time. Once they knew that I had seen them, they spread their wide wings and soared towards me. A hundred yards off, on my right, some large boulders were piled together in front of a small cavern. I made a dash for it and wiggled through the opening between two boulders. The merewings couldn't enter, but they poked their long beaks through every crack that they could find. I danced around in my dark chamber, dodging the sharp bills coming at me. Suddenly I heard two thuds and the frantic stabbing ceased.'

Edel paused for a moment and looked at Nightglider and Servatius, still perched on the loom. Nightglider cleared his throat and picked up the tale.

'We had spotted the merewings miles away. But it was the violent pecking at a clump of rocks that intrigued us. We circled overhead, dived with the sun behind and knocked them out. When you meet them in the air they can be a handful, but catch them on the ground and they simply crumble. That's what happens when your wings are too big for your pinions. It took a few minutes of explaining to convince our Fairy that we were indeed the good birds!'

Edel laughed, 'You can't be too careful. But once they mentioned Weiss, I knew that all was well. I climbed out of my prison and jumped on Servatius' back. And here I am sitting amongst friends in a cozy cabin. Heaven be praised.' Sunflower patted him on the head and raised her glass.

'To the eagles and the Celestial Covey,' her voice sang out and the ringing of glasses echoed through the cabin.

'A splendid evening,' mused Smithereen. 'It will live in history.'

Late that night Servatius and Nightglider rose from the porch and over the moonlit peaks, winged their flight home.

23

Smithereen Rises

When Bullneck led his men down the mountain, they appeared to be a loosely organized troop, but their casual appearance was deceiving. They had been on many expeditions together and they knew well how to work as a team.

Long swords glittered in the sunlight, Bullneck and some of the older Dwarves had balls and chains draped over their shoulders. A few of the men carried spears. Dwarves are excellent spear throwers and had won many a Gold Beaker at the national games in Lambarina.

As they walked down the mountain trails, banks of fog floated over the slopes and their favourite martial songs echoed from the cliffs. It was only when Bullneck spotted the black shape of a merewing gliding through the mist that he motioned his men to stop the singing. They were walking single file through a narrow gorge when a rather rotund Dwarf stopped in his tracks and pointed his nose towards the cliffs on the left side of the ravine.

'What's up Sniffer,' sounded several voices. 'Grolls galore on top of the embankment, the smell is foul, and I think there are black hounds in the party.'

A ripple of fear spread through the troop and they reached for their swords. The Dwarves abhorred the hounds. Several of their brethren had died a painful death from the tainted-fang illness.

'They have traveled farther than I thought,' said Bullneck, 'Likely captured the strangers and are on their way back to the land of the Seven. The Merewings must have spotted us and informed the Rover and his Grolls.'

The Dwarves, sword in hand, took defensive positions behind rocks. When the sun's rays dispelled the mist, they could see the enemy high above lined up along the edge of the cliff. Their weapons were useless and the Grolls roared with laughter when they saw the Dwarves running for shelter. The face of the Rover standing behind them looked cold and cruel. By his side stood five dogs anxious to get into the fray. The Grolls had a good stock of rocks piled up and leisurely they began pelting the Dwarves in the gorge.

'We walked into a trap,' muttered Tuffkote, narrowly missing a projectile by springing under an overhang. 'We have got to get a message to the village, or we'll all be knocked cold.'

He looked around and spotted a crevice in the face of the cliff. Crawling on the ground, shielded from sight by bramble bushes, he was able to reach the opening and crawl inside. He could see the blue sky high above and he realized that he was inside a chimney. He dropped his weapons and pushing his back against the narrow passage he was able to wiggle his way to the top. When he pulled his head over the edge, he could see the Grolls on the opposite side of the gorge, tossing stones on his friends below. Behind the Grolls sat the prisoners, tied to a rock, helplessly watching the uneven contest.

Tuffkote pulled himself up and ran towards the village. One of the black hounds standing near the Rover caught a whiff of Tuffkote's scent and let out a menacing growl. The Rover scanned the rough grounds on the other side of the ravine, but Tuffkote already had disappeared behind the shrubs and bushes. To make sure that none of the Dwarves got away to raise the alarm, the Rover ordered the hound to go after the quarry. The black brute licked the foam from his lips and in an almost playful manner and certain of his prey, bounded after Tuffkote.

Bullneck managed to light a fire and its smoke partially hid the Dwarves and drifted up into the Groll's eyes, slowing down the shower of stones raining down upon them. Two young warriors had been killed and the Dwarves were hard pressed. Some were sorely hurt. Bullneck had seen Tuffkote vanish on the cliff face and knew that he had found a way out. He prayed that help would come in time. Tuffkote, running as if his life depended upon it, paused for a moment on a shallow bluff and looked back. It was then that he saw the black shape winding between rock and bushes. In the distance he could see the wall ringing the village and he rushed forward. Fear gave him wings. Like a mountain goat, he loped across the fields.

Seated on a hillock, outside the village gate, sat the great Smithereen, contemplating the meaning of life. The solitary figure in the alpine meadow presented a lonely and forlorn aspect. The once great warrior had lost his self respect. Battle was all for which he was famous. People had described him as a great brute. Nobody praised his intelligence and sensitivity. He wrote poetry in secret and twice the Lambarina Gadfly had published one of his poems under his nom de plume, 'Buttercup'. Dwarves by and by had little use for poetry and even less for poets. Shirkers, sissies, slackers, libertines given to the ways of the flesh, were some of the epithets that his stern brethren had used. And yet some of the poetry that these shirkers had written had moved Smithereen's soul. Life was perplexing.

Smithereen admired the lilies growing by his side. The beauty of the lilies was like a poem, greater than a poem. At least there is beauty in the world, a beauty that transcends the squabbles and paradoxes of life around him. No, he must abandon his martial career and develop his creativity, his deeper talents. Wasn't that what the old Elf Seraphim had talked about when he spoke at the Graceful Neck in Cascade?

Smithereen looked upon the sunny landscape and for a moment, the black cloud hanging over him dissolved. The alpine meadows in their autumn colours were glorious to behold. Wings of butterflies caught the rays of the sun and a gentle breeze sent waves traveling over the tall alpine grasses. Smithereen's interlude of serenity was short lived. In the lovely alpine meadows he saw a figure cutting a swath through the undulating grass. Behind the sprinter bounded a black shape. Poetry and beauty were forgotten. The inner sentry awoke and all the martial instinct, dormant for many months, resurfaced.

The figure darting through the fields was a Dwarf, probably Tuffkote. One could tell by the way he moved. Smithereen's energy returned. His huge frame trembled as if an engine had started up inside. The shape of the fleeing Dwarf flashed by Smithereen, right behind, fangs bared, the black hound took a flying leap and was only inches away from Tuffkote's thigh. Swift as lightning Smithereen grabbed the rear leg of the airborne hound and held it in his iron grip. Slowly he began to spin the beast around, faster and faster. He reached a dizzying speed and then let fly. The body of the brute hit the town wall and breathed his last. Smithereen marched over to the guardhouse where the exhausted Tuffkote stood panting against the wall. Tuffkote looked up.

'It was you, Smithereen who smashed the venomous beast and saved my life,' exclaimed the warrior.

'What is the situation Tuffkote?'

'The Rover and the Grolls caught us in a trap. Your nephew and another soldier have been killed and the others are in great danger.'

Deep fury smoldered within Smithereen as he walked into the guardhouse and returned with ball and chain. Tuffkote followed him down the meadow.

'They are in the gorge Smitty,' shouted Tuffkote, trying to keep up.

'Have a rest before you join the fray,' returned Smithereen, now moving at a punishing pace.

The smoke that had been bothering the Grolls on the height above the gorge diminished. They returned with zeal to their task, tossing rocks down on the defenseless Dwarves. The Rover nodded approvingly. The Dwarves had always been a nuisance and this was an excellent opportunity to clean them up for good. Looking over the sunlit alpine meadows with the village in the background, a smile played upon his lips, a rare occurrence. In a short time, these pleasant meadows and the village would become part of their domain.

His train of thought was interrupted by a strange phenomenon. A black disc floating above the meadows moved toward his troopers at an astonishing clip. In the center of the flying circle was a burly shape. The Rover was fascinated. The apparition approached the first row of Grolls who were busy rolling stones over the edge. But now an amazing sight greeted him and the smile celebrating new domains vanished. Grolls began flying over the edge and became a greater hazard for the ducking Dwarves, than did the falling stones.

The Rover uttered a command that sent the hounds rushing at the mysterious figure, who appeared to be whirling a black object. None broke through the circle traced by Smithereen's gyrating ball. The infuriated Dwarf was spinning his weapon at phenomenal speed. Within seconds, the remains of the poisonous hounds were scattered at the bottom of the ravine.

The Officer and a few remaining Grolls ran for their lives. The dizzying ball came to rest on the ground and Smithereen walked up the edge to look down. Bullneck who had come out of hiding, spotted the face of their old leader. He stuck two fingers in his mouth and whistled the 'all safe'. Dwarves crept from behind rocks and emerged from overhangs and crevices. Bullneck raised his right hand and all the men cheered Smithereen.

They loaded their fallen comrades and the wounded on stretchers and began the retreat from the gorge. In a short while they reached the end of the ravine and then they made a steep turn and started climbing up to the plateau. There Smithereen was standing, still huffing like a steam engine from the immense expenditure of energy. They crowded around him and in the din of voices could be heard gratitude for their deliverance and mourning for their fallen comrades. They had almost forgotten, in the excitement of the drama, the prisoners tied to a rock nearby.

Slim , Moose and Duckie, with great anxiety, had watched the battle from a distance. When Smithereen appeared they knew the tide had turned and their freedom was in sight. Yet Slim kept a watchful eye, for some Grolls or their hounds might be still be hiding down below in the trees. Scanning the edge of the forest, he spotted, camouflaged by shrubs, the massive head of a black hound. A Groll voiced a command and the hound rushed forth from the bushes, heading for the huddle of Dwarves. Slim yelled at the top of his voice, 'The hound, mind the hound!'

Rick the Reamer, son of a long line of spearmen caught the warning and turned around. As the black hound shot forward, his flight was intersected by an iron spearhead. With a dull thud, the body hit the ground. Bullneck sprang forward and severed the monstrous head. The Dwarves took their battle stations and two archers caught sight of the fleeing Groll. Knowing that their arrows would not penetrate the scale covered skin they aimed for the lower legs. The Groll lost his footing and fell head first on a sharp rock. There was no sign of life when the Dwarves approached and they tossed him down the ravine to join his brethren.

The battle was over and it was Slim's powers of observation that had saved them from the Groll and his hound. Bullneck walked up to the prisoners, still roped to the rock, cut them free and gave them a warm hug.

'Only three men from Swanneland. Where is the girl that the Fairy told us about?' wondered Bullneck.

'There were supposed to be four men Chief, as well as the girl,' said Sniffer. Bullneck looked at Slim.

'Tell me what befell the Swannemaiden?'

Tears welled in Slim's eyes. 'When my sister rushed out of the cabin she was caught by the Grolls. I fear that the sorceress Matista cast a spell and kidnapped her.'

The Dwarves shook their heads. This indeed was grim news.

'And the fourth man in the party?' asked Sniffer.

'Ferdinand deCygne was felled by the fangs of a black hound,' lamented Moose, 'he staggered into the forest and is at death's door.'

'The Marquis from Swanneland, brother to Lady Erica,' exclaimed Smithereen.'

'Alas, it is he sir,' answered Duckie in a distraught voice, 'I was his page and failed to protect him.'

'There is nothing you could have done,' reassured Slim, putting his arm around the youngster's shoulder. He then explained to the Dwarves the ruse that Matista had played on them. 'She appeared in the guise of one of the holy Sisters that use the retreat. The drinks she served contained a sleeping potion. We fell in a deep slumber and woke only when the Grolls banged our heads upon the table. Startled, we opened our eyes and beheld the enchantress standing before us in all her worldly splendour. Even her laugh had an exotic charm. She was flanked by a Rover and two dogs and behind each one of us stood a repulsive Groll. It was then that the Marquis astonished us all. He seized his sword, endowed with a magic edge and mowed down Grolls and dogs all around him.'

Dwarves could be heard muttering. 'Splendid. Jolly good fellow. Groll slicer. Three cheers for the Marquis.'

A small Dwarf piped up, 'Where is the Marquis now Slim?'

'He is close to the Sisters' retreat. A Rover tripped the Marquis from behind and a black hound jumped him, sinking his fangs into his shoulder muscles. The Grolls let him wander off, to die in the forest.' A wave of horror rippled through the troop.

'Left in the forest to die a warrior's death,' sighed Bullneck, a trace of envy in his voice.

'We could not help him,' explained the Captain, 'Our hands were tied behind our backs. We were taken outside and roped together.'

Sergeant Crusher who had been listening quietly, sprang onto the rock beside Bullneck and looked at the Captain, 'Nothing could have been done by you or your friends to aid the Marquis, but where there is life, there is hope. I will lead a party down the slope and bring the Marquis to the village. We should, within the hour, be able to reach the hut of the Sisters of the Third Woe. Raise your hands, those who are willing to come with me.'

To a man the Dwarves raised their hands. Crusher picked four swift runners and within minutes the Sergeant had led the party down the slope. Sword in hand they raced down the forest path, their steps echoing against the mountainside.

Forest badgers, awakened by the pounding of dwarf feet on the moss, came out of their holes and shook their heads. The Dwarves were sensible beings. This stomping of feet augured ill. A major calamity must be afoot. The badgers withdrew deep into their holes and just in case, started to take stock of their larders.

The Dwarves knew that every minute counted. At breakneck speed, they ran over rocks and tree roots and crashed through the underbrush. Farther down, the heavy spruce canopy admitted little light and a raised root caught Tuffkote's foot. He went catballing down the steep path and came to a halt at the foot of a tall spruce. When the others caught up with him he was already standing up, none the worse for wear. Sniffer took time to take a deep breath. 'We are close, I smell traces from a battle scene.'

They spread out and before long Sergeant Crusher could hear the faint moaning of the fallen nobleman. Parting a clump of shrubs, Crusher looked down at the Marquis, whose face was white as an angel's wing. A stare of resignation dwelt in his eyes.

'The Dwarves,' he whispered, 'You have come at last, and I will not die in solitude.' Crusher could see that the will to live was diminishing quickly. He took the Marquis' numb hand and spoke to him in a firm voice.

'Not yet Ferdinand deCygne, the time is not yet. We will take you back to the village of the Dwarves.' The Marquis held on to the Sergeant's hand as if he were holding on to life itself.

The Dwarves unleashed their axes and cut small spruce trees to build a stretcher. It took only minutes to lash together the stretcher and strap the Marquis on top. They raised the Marquis easily, resting the stretcher on four shoulders. The sturdy dwarf legs pushed uphill at a steady pace.

Stillness pervaded the forest. Only the footsteps of the stretcher bearers could be heard. When the forest dwellers caught a fleeting glance of the Dwarves carrying the Marquis, his face a ghostly white, they knew that the shadow of death was passing. Woodpeckers stopped their hammering and chipmunks froze on branches. Badgers looked out of their portholes and concluded that things were bad indeed and returned to their stockrooms.

It was late in the afternoon when the procession reached the tree line and minutes later joined the main party. Slim, Moose and Duckie rushed up to the Marquis to speak to him words of solace. Ferdinand visibly moved by the words of his old comrades in arms whispered, 'Fare thee well my friends I will be leaving these mortal shores and sailing for distant strands. Pray may your mission succeed.'

'Do not leave us Master,' Duckie implored, 'Hold on tight to the thread of life. You are needed here.'

'Ferdinand,' said Moose taking his hand, 'The Dwarves will take you to the Convent and the Sisters of the Secret Crossing will cure you.'

'The nettle treatment,' exclaimed the stricken figure on the stretcher, 'It is too late, I am prepared to check out and leave this place of grief and sorrow.'

All realized that it was best to let the Marquis rest for the time being. Bullneck took one look at the Marquis's face and knew that not a moment was to be lost. The stretcher bearers were relieved by other Dwarves and the party moved swiftly forward to the village. The Marquis was in great pain. The sound of his whimpering touched the hearts of the warriors and they raised their voices in song, hoping to bring comfort to the patient. Trailing behind were other stretcher bearers carrying the bodies of fallen comrades.

Weiss and Sunflower were picking huckleberries near the south gate when suddenly Sunflower stood up and turned her head to the wind. 'I hear them Weiss, I can hear their voices on the wind.' Sunflower and Weiss walked down the path several hundred feet and listened. Weiss, too, could hear the voices, a faint melody wafting over the alpine meadows. Sunflower touched Weiss' shoulder, 'My fairy fair these are no joyous sounds that announce their coming, ill has befallen them.' The mountainside echoed the sound of deep base voices, drawing closer.

'The Song of Solace,' said Sunflower with tears in her eyes. 'Tragedy must have struck, death and suffering are their companions. Rush up the mountain Weiss and fetch Angelica, the goat lady. Bring her to my home. For healing hands will now be needed.'

Sunflower saw the Mountain Fairy leap from rock to rock. Being herself somewhat on the heavy side, she could not help but smile as she watched the Fairy dance across the alpine meadows with the lightness of an angel, that seemed to defy gravity itself. Oh, to be able to dance through life barely touching the ground. Perhaps when she shed this mortal coil and ascended to the realm of light, she too would dance like angels. 'Vain thoughts, deal with the here and now,' sternly she told herself. The men were approaching and a crisis had to be dealt with. She listened to the words of the chorus whose clear sounds were mirrored by the mountains.

gentle wings of light
soften dark shades of night
name our comrade's name
heal the searing pain

Grief dwelt in her eyes as she beheld the somber procession drawing closer. And yet in that grievous sight she perceived a spark of joy. There was her husband, marching at the head of the troop. He had spent months in his rocking chair suffering from the moping illness, but once again his great heart had risen to save his friends in peril. Pride shone in her tearful eyes.

The Dwarves were close now, and as they approached the gate, their voices dropped to a whisper. Sunflower climbed onto a stone wall near the gate and watched the troop file by. Smithereen had stepped aside and let the others pass. He put his arm around Sunflower and together they followed the last stretcher bearers.

The dead were taken to a stone cavern reserved for warriors who had fallen on the field of battle. The Marquis was carried to Smithereen and Sunflower's cottage and gently lifted onto a straw mattress next to the loom.

Sunflower and Smithereen knelt by his side. The white countenance of the Marquis spoke for itself. Her eyes met Smithereen's. 'Mangled by the tainted fangs?' His silent nod confirmed her worst fears. 'The Mountain Fairy has gone to fetch Angelica. She will be here soon.'

Weiss was still running up the mountain, dodging the goats who seemed to be everywhere. It was higher up than he had expected, but soon he saw the small hut where the goat lady lived. It was just below the snow line. He burst through the door and found Angelica stirring a wooden spoon in a large cast iron pot bubbling on a wood fire.

'Angelica,' shouted Weiss, who had climbed onto a chair in order to be on the same level as she, 'Angelica you must come now to the house of Sunflower and Smithereen. Ill has befallen the party returning from the woods.'

'Ah, a Mountain Fairy, I have had feeling in my bones that there was a Mountain Fairy in the neighbourhood. Light feet bounding over meadows, a nice change from those heavy dwarf feet stomping the mountainside.' All the wrinkles on her face danced together as her face broke into a smile. Weiss would very much have liked to have had a chat with this interesting lady, but he knew no time could be lost.

'Lady Angelica, great haste is called for. One of the men may be dying.'

'I know, I know, my wisp,' mused the ancient one patting Weiss on the head. 'Never be hasty, my good mother used to say. One thing at a time and that is what I am doing, one thing.'

'Then what is the one thing that you are doing mother,' asked Weiss full of wonder.'

'I am stirring a brew Mountain Fairy with a wooden spoon.'

'I can see that goat lady, but that will not help the wounded warrior.

'And how do you know that?' laughed the ancient one. 'How do you know the brew I am stirring will not help the wounded one?'

Weiss looked mystified. 'You don't know what wound or illness has afflicted him.'

'But I do know fairy dear, I saw it happen. Sitting by the fire gazing at the flames I saw the black hound attack the Marquis. My brew will not heal him, but for ten days it will give him a window on life, time to reach the Convent of the Sisters of the Secret Crossing, the only place where healing can take place. A few more minutes and this fusion of Devil's Claw and Deadly Shade of Night will have steamed long enough. Only a small portion is required, too much is dangerous.' Angelica wobbled over to the counter and took a small wooden cup with a neatly carved lid, she went to the pot, spooned some of the hot potion into the cup and covered it.

'Now fleet foot, run this over to the cabin where the patient lies and tell Sunflower to pour it his into his mouth. I will follow after, as quickly as my feet can carry me.

Weiss lost no time. Jumping from rock to rock, sometimes landing on goat backs, he sped on to the village, the small wooden container tucked safely under his jacket. When he walked through the door, Sunflower was still on her knees by the side of the Marquis. Weiss handed her the wooden container, repeated Angelica's prescription and Sunflower quickly drained the contents into the Marquis' mouth.

Moose Martin, Slim and Duckie, partly hidden by the loom, were seated on the benches in the living room. Exhausted and saddened by events they were delighted to see, sitting on the loom, two Fairies instead of one. The Fairy seated next to Weiss could be none other than Edel, rescued from the Black Elves.

'Edel and Weiss, it has a nice ring to it,' laughed the Captain, 'we welcome you to our company. Comfortably leaning against the frame of the loom, Edel told them all about the cruelty of the Black Elves, the wonders of the Mole Confederacy and the rescue by the eagles.

The door opened again and Angelica arrived with the rest of the brew that she had prepared. Sunflower, bending over the Marquis, gave him another drink of the concoction.

'Dreadful taste,' muttered the stricken nobleman, the first words that he had uttered since his arrival at the cottage.

Sunflower looked at Angelica and smiled. 'The life-forces are returning , Angelica.'

'They are, they are, Sunny. My medicine will suppress the symptoms of the poison, but not for long.'

The Marquis who had heard her words, tried to sit up. Sunflower reached for a large pillow and propped it behind his back. He looked at Sunflower and said, 'It should not end like this, felled by a foul hound while a prisoner of the miserable Grolls. My noble forefathers fell on the field of battle, their chests cloven or their heads chopped off, in honourable fashion but, I Ferdinand, meet my end at the maw of a wretched dog. My life has been wasted, no fame has come my way and now I depart these mortal shores in a state of disgrace.'

The Marquis had gone into a tailspin and Sunflower put her arm around him and her blue eyes smiled.

'Ferdinand, if I may call you Ferdinand.'

'Call me anything you fancy,' whispered the forlorn figure.

'Then Ferdinand it is,' affirmed the indomitable Sunflower, with a smile so sparkling that the Marquis was heartened by it.

'You have earned our honour and admiration. To have chosen to go on this long and dangerous journey was an act of courage. Whether a Rover's sword cut you in half, or the foaming jaws of a black hound tore into your shoulder, it matters not and furthermore you misunderstood the ancient one. Angelica meant that the medicine will, for a short period of time, suspend the poison. A dwarf team now is preparing to carry you down the mountain and across the river to the Convent of the Sisters of the Secret Crossing, where healing will take place.

A spark of hope sprang into the eyes of the Marquis. He lowered himself down again. He twisted uncomfortably on the floor. Angelica kneeled beside him and moved her hands back and forth over the savage wound. Slowly the pain receded and the body of the nobleman relaxed.

'The ancient one has healing hands,' explained Sunflower.

'I hope she can help Smithereen too,' said Weiss, looking through the window at Smithereen slumped in his rocking chair. The battle scene had galvanized Smithereen and he had saved the day, but the outburst of energy soon subsided and the mighty warrior once more sat on the porch brooding about the meaning of life and death.

Small groups of Dwarves had gathered in front of the house, talking about the foray against the Grolls and their dreaded hounds. Sunflower walked out on the porch. Standing behind Smithereen, she placed her hands on his shoulders and spoke to the small crowd that was lingering in front of the cabin. 'Angelica's medicine has revived the Marquis. He must now travel to the convent of the Sisters of the Secret Crossing. No time is to be lost.'

There was a sigh of relief from the men and women that had gathered around Sunflower.

'Anything we can do to help?' wondered one of the women.

'We need provisions for the team that will carry Ferdinand deCygne to the Convent of the Sisters.' The crowd dispersed to their root cellars, to find dried fruits and smoked boar meat.

Sergeant Crusher arrived to report that he had recruited a fresh team of stretcher bearers to carry the Marquis to the Convent.

'How long a journey is it, Sergeant Crusher?'

'At least eight days Sunflower, if we have no trouble crossing the Sanctus. The Esterian lumbermen at the north end of the Sanctus might send us a raft, if there were a way of sending a message.'

'We must ask Master Grimmbeak for help.'

Seeing Richard the Reamer leaning against a rock, Sunflower asked him to raise the distress signal on the flagpole in the center of the village square. The tall spearsman directly rushed to the community centre to find the ensign to be raised to attract the eagles' attention.

By a stroke of fortune Master Grimmbeak himself, accompanied by young Theodorus, was airborne. He had decided that he needed to spend some time with the overly sensitive bird and harden him up a bit. They were soaring high above the peaks when the Grand Master sighted the blue banner down below.

'The Dwarves are in trouble. Most unusual Junior, when the Dwarves raise that banner there is real trouble. Not that we want to be involved. Remember we are here to judge, not to meddle.' Fortunately Grimmbeak was better than his word. Deep inside that hard boiled bird, there was a soft spot.

Sunflower saw the great wings sailing towards the cabin and the eagles land on the porch railing. She thanked them for paying heed to the signal and opened the door. They hopped in and perched on the loom.

Grimmbeak looked down upon Angelica and the stricken Marquis. 'Death is near, I feel it in my feathers. What can be done lady Sunflower?'

'Bitten by a black hound, Master Grimmbeak, the tainted fang illness. A team of runners are now preparing a stretcher to carry the Marquis to the Convent on the other side of the Sanctus.'

'A Marquis, no doubt from a noble family,' observed Grimmbeak, rather impressed, 'What a tragedy, we are at your service.'

'If they can reach the Convent within ten days, he may yet recover. They must cross the ice filled river where the men from Esteria are rafting logs. Please dispatch one of your eagles to the logging camps to speak to Ulrik or Ensten and ask if a raft could be built to ferry the party across the waters.'

The mysterious eyes of the Grand Master of the Covey stared for a moment at Sunflower and then he nodded solemnly. 'Theodorus, an opportunity to save a life, a noble life. Follow the Sanctus to the logging camps and stay in the area until the party has safely crossed the river. Report to the stretcher-bearers, the presence of any merewings or other furtive creatures. Once the Marquis has safely reached the Convent of the Sisters, you may return to our mountain home.'

Grimmbeak and Theodorus bid farewell to the company and amid shouts of thanks and good wishes, they hopped out of the door and rose quickly into the alpine air. After they had been airborne for a short while, Grimmbeak's wing touched the tip of Theodorus' and motioned him to begin his long glide down to the river.

It was dusk when four sturdy runners carrying a stretcher arrived at Sunflower and Smithereen's log cabin. No time was wasted in loading the Marquis on the stretcher. Sunflower and Angelica covered him with woolen blankets and goatskins and bid him Godspeed. The four Dwarves shouldered their rucksacks, lifted the patient on the thick layer of straw that covered the stretcher and in the gathering darkness began their journey towards the spruce forest.

Sunflower walked back into the cabin and looked at her downcast guests. Slim was heartbroken by the disappearance of his sister, the Captain was wearied and unable to forgive himself for succumbing to the wiles of the Queen of the Marshes. Only Duckie had recovered. He went onto the porch to talk to Smithereen. The formidable warrior was amused by Duckie's cheerful prattle, but soon he sunk back into a slough of despondency.

Angelica and Sunflower stood by the woodstove whispering to each other, trying to find a way of dispelling the doleful atmosphere and uplifting their guests' spirits.

'A dinner party Sunflower. A pot of boar stew, bumbleberry pie with goat cheese and a few bottles of dandelion and huckle wine.'

'Angelica, it is a grand idea. Weiss would you pop over to Bullneck and Pristina and ask them to join us for dinner? Tell Bullneck bring his ukase, we need music to cheer the spirits of this bedraggled lot.'

Weiss was reluctant to leave Edel who was still recovering from his adventures, but Edel motioned him to go. Sunflower spun into a whirl of activity and Angelica set the kitchen table. Festive candles were lit and before long a tempting smell filled the cabin. Sunflower asked Smithereen to leave the now dark porch and to take his place at the table. The Dwarf got up from his rocking chair and joined them at the kitchen table. His heart was not in it, but he did it to please his vivacious wife and the company.

Weiss returned with Bullneck and Pristina. All took their seats around the dining table. A couple of pillows on the weaving bench brought the Fairies above the table top by a comfortable margin.

Being seated in the cosy kitchen with a splendid spread on the table restored a sense of well being and hope for the future. Moose Martin pulled himself together and raised his glass of huckle wine, 'Gratitude fills our heart when we think of all that the Dwarves have done for us, Sergeant Crusher and his men saved our lives from a fate worse than death. Smithereen and Sunflower have opened their home to us. Angelica's herbs and her healing hands have brought a window of hope to the Marquis.'

Glasses rang. Edel and Weiss stood upon the bench and joined in the toast. Slim raised his glass and with tears in his eyes spoke of Svanhild.

'My beloved sister's brave and loving spirit has sustained us on this journey fraught with danger. Casting a secret spell, the sorceress Matista tied her with an invisible cord and carried her off into the forest.' Slim seemed heart broken, Angelica put her arm around his shoulder and tried to comfort him.

Even Smithereen was moved and could be heard muttering, 'Where are my ball and chain. Things have gone too far.'

'Higher powers than ball and chain are required to right this violation of the spirit my dear Smitty, but your heart is in the right place. Your sentiment is right.'

'I say my sentiment is right,' bellowed Smithereen with a defiant smile. For a moment all around the table could see a fire burning in the eyes of the warrior. Alas, it did not last and he slumped back into his chair.

'I am afraid our journey has yielded but little fruit,' remarked the Captain. 'Our beloved Princess Yaconda, heir to the throne, is still imprisoned, Svanhild is in the hands of the sorceress and the Marquis is at death's door.'

'Not so my dear Captain,' retorted Angelica. 'What really mattered is that you undertook this journey. Your enterprise, my dear navigator, has awakened a spirit, that in time, will bear fruit.'

Sunflower stood up. 'You must stay the winter, dear friends and recover from your travels and trials. Your presence here will help Smithereen to recover. If Providence favours us, the Marquis and your lovely sister Svanhild will join us once again when next the blue bells bloom on the alpine meadows.'

24

At The Chateau

*T*wo merewings skimmed above the ice of Fireweed Lake and on reaching shore, rose sharply to perch upon the roof of the Chateau, the enchantress Matista's remote residence. The birds had just completed their daily patrol and were enjoying a brief rest in the morning sunlight. It was the duty of the merewings to report intruders in the sorceress' domain and to raise an alarm when anyone was seen leaving the Chateau, especially if it was apparent that more than an innocent walk was intended. It was a cushy job for the birds with the large black wings and purple beaks. There was plenty of game to keep them happy and often they could be seen diving for rabbits or marmots.

In the main hall of the Chateau, a fire burned brightly. Reflections of the flames danced in the glass bottles that lined the shelves and tables. They contained the powders and potions Matista used for her magic arts. At the far wall ancient volumes stood on sagging shelves. There she would sit for hours scanning musty pages until she found a spell or incantation, needed for her wily schemes.

Often Matista would leave the Chateau to travel in disguise to different parts of the Kingdom. A few days ago she had left to visit the Seven Lords in the red desert. During her absence, the Rover Finch, had been left in charge and in the event of unexpected visitors, a couple of Grolls wandered around the grounds. Two elderly ladies, widows from the Land of Darkness, ran the household. At least they considered themselves to be widows, for their husbands had vanished years ago. Many farmers who lived in the realm of the Seven Lords had disappeared. Some had been trained as Rovers, the ruthless overseers and agents who worked for the Seven, others had been sent to work camps. Most had never been heard of again.

Gertrude and Maria had been dispatched to the Chateau, as a present from the Seven to the enchantress Matista. The only other servant at the domain of the sorceress was her old friend and companion, Meadow, who assisted with research in witchcraft and experiments in magic.

Meadow came from a large family in Lambarina. She had been always a shy retiring girl with an interest in the occult. One evening, feeling lonely and forlorn in the busy town square, she saw emerge from the milling crowd, a woman of uncommon beauty. In her wake she left untold admirers. Great was Meadow's surprise when the determined clicking of high heels on the cobble stones overtook her and she found herself looking up into a pair of ravishing blue eyes. A delicate white hand touched her cheek and her loneliness vanished. She was captivated.

It was the first time in Meadow's life that she had felt wanted. The enchantress exuded a charm and warmth that made her glow and when Matista offered her a position at the Chateau, she jumped at it. When Svanhild arrived, Meadow already had been at the Chateau for years and she was glad to have a new companion in that remote wilderness retreat.

Svanhild had not been brought to the Chateau by brute force. In the cabin of the Sisters of the Third Woe, Matista had cast a spell that linked Svanhild to the enchantress by an invisible cord. In a trance had she traveled in the footsteps of her fair abductress, unable to resist. The two traversed the forest until they arrived at Fireweed Lake. The forest badgers, Berend and Ludwig, had seen them flying along the trail. They could tell that the innocent maiden was being pulled along against her will but there was nothing they could have done about it. They had shaken their heads and crawled back into their comfortable home, to discuss the situation.

'Caught in the sorceress web, Berend.'

'I say Ludwig, this bodes ill indeed, the abduction of innocent maidens.' The end of common decency as we know it, Berend.'

On this conclusive remark the badgers retired into their rocking chairs by the fire to enjoy their hot chocolate and contemplate the signs of the time.

It was more than a month since Svanhild had arrived at the Chateau at the far end of Fireweed Lake. The enchantress hoped to break her defiant spirit and to initiate her into the mysteries of witchcraft. For years Matista had dreamt of an apprentice, an adopted daughter to share her magic and her power. The fire burning in the emerald eyes of the Swannemaid fascinated the enchantress. Yes, Svanhild would be tempted by the wonders of witchcraft and the thrill of magic. Well she knew that supernatural powers beguile the innocent and she would draw the maiden into her secret world and weave a magic web for the Swannemaid. Once caught in it, there would be no escape.

Meadow had been a faithful servant and companion but she lacked the ambition to become an enchantress of the highest sphere. When traveling through the blue spruce forest, a passing beam of moonlight had revealed the comely features and the fire in Svanhild's green eyes, Matista knew that it was she who would make a worthy daughter and companion in her secret world.

Svanhild, a book on witch craft on her knees, was seated in the great hall. She closed the cover and looked at the flames dancing in the hearth. Her thoughts went back to her travel companions and how Matista had lured them into the retreat of the Sisters of the Third Woe. There, they had been attacked by a Rover and a troop of Grolls. Slim, Captain Martin, and Duckie had been captured and the Marquis deCygne attacked savagely by a black hound. She doubted that he was still alive. Now for the first time since her arrival at the sorceress' chateau, she found herself alone. Matista had left for a few days and Svanhild had a chance to take stock and to think about the future. She was conscious of a strange attraction to the enchantress. This perhaps was the greatest danger of all. She must escape before becoming entangled in the magic web of sorcery.

During the night, it was hard to resist Matista's fatal attraction, but at first light, the ravishing sorceress changed into the hag Neva and all that loveliness shrank into the body of an old woman. This was the curse that the Wizard Isumatak had cast upon her. But even then, during daylight hours, there was a strength in the voice and eyes that were hard to resist. Once the sun's rays sank below the waters of the lake, she would assume her nocturnal beauty.

Attraction and repulsion had paralyzed Svanhild's mind and at first made it difficult to decide on a plan for escape, if escape were possible.

Now, alone at last, she knew that she must flee, although it might take time before an opportunity for flight would present itself. During her forced stay at the Chateau she would learn some of the magic lore that would shield her from spells and incantations in future encounters.

The voice of Meadow startled Svanhild from her reverie. 'Lunch is served, Svanhild'

'I'll be there in a moment, Meadow.' Svanhild got up and put back on the shelf the volume on spells and incantations.

They lunched together in the solarium at the back of the Chateau. Meadow and Svanhild were seated at a round cast iron table covered by a slab of black marble. They were surrounded by an abundance of planters filled with herbs, flowers, and small shrubs, which Matista used to create potions for her craft.

Svanhild asked Meadow where the enchantress had gone.

'My dear she travels hither and thither, arranging affairs here and there. She disciplines troublemakers and suppresses revolts. She is the trusted friend and confidante of the Seven Lords yonder, in the sands of the red desert. Alas the folks in the Kingdom and Esteria have not yet learned that opposition to the Seven Masters will bring nothing but loss and grief.' sighed Meadow. Svanhild knew that Meadow worshipped Matista and that she had never seen the dark side of the enchantress.

'Tell me about the wizard Isumatak, Meadow.'

'Isumatak, the upstart wizard whose curse clipped my mistress' powers and hides her beauty in daylight hours.'

'Why did he do it?' asked Svanhild, keen to find out more about the enchantress.

'Spite and envy, my dear, spite and envy. Matista was then at the peak of her career. She had just toppled the reign of King Norvalt, the King who had banished his Seven Counsellors for conspiring against him.'

'Was it the incantation Matista uttered that subdued the Kingdom?'

'It was indeed my dear. It was an extraordinary achievement in the science of witchcraft. All the dwellers of the Kingdom fell into a deep sleep. Matista brought the Seven Counsellors back to the land and restored their powers. At least, that is how I understand it Svanhild. It all happened centuries ago and much of the story is lost in time.'

'And those Seven Counsellors are the Seven Lords who reign in the Land of Darkness?'

'I see, that you have caught some snatches of the ancient lore. Yes

Matista's arts restored their health and gave them the gift of lasting youth and power.'

'No spell can break that gift, Meadow?'

'I think not. There have been rumours about ancient incantations carved in golden plates and the like. But the servants of the Seven have combed the land and no tablets can be found. Hearsay and scuttlebutt, you know.'

Svanhild knew that there was little point in telling Meadow about the things that were happening in the Land of the Seven, the slavery, the terror spread by the Rovers and their companies of Grolls, the black hounds, the kidnapping of Princess Yaconda. Meadow adored Matista and would only believe what the enchantress told her.

'Will she be gone for long, Meadow?'

'A week perhaps. She always returns to the Chateau to rest. She watches what happens in the world and when something displeases her, she rushes out to set it aright.'

'How can she learn what happens in the rest of world when she lives here at her Chateau on the outer rim of nowhere, hundreds of miles from other living creatures?'

'My child, Matista is no common witch, indeed she is insulted when she hears that word. She is an enchantress who hails from the highest spheres. Her power extends into this world and to worlds beyond. Her knowledge goes back in time and reaches into the future.'

They sat in silence overlooking the snow clad forest on the slope behind the Chateau. The trees rose gradually, thinning out near the top of the range.

Finch, carrying a tray with coffee and cakes, entered the sunroom. He always had a pleasant smile and Svanhild could not help liking the young Rover. He was so unlike any of the others whom she had met.

They took their coffee, sank into a couple of easy chairs on the sun filled porch and soon the elderly Meadow drifted into a gentle sleep. Svanhild enjoyed the silence and rested her eyes on the large cedars at the edge of the garden. She was startled when a soft shadow stole over the snow covered branches. A dark shape perched near the top of the tree and another swooped down beside it. Then she knew. The birds on the cedar branch were Solomon, Chief of the woodland owls and Kasper his deputy. There was no way to talk to them, but at least they had spotted her and could report to her friends, her whereabouts.

The Owls knew that they were being watched by the merewings, and there was no time to lose. They winked their yellow saucer eyes, by way of greeting. There was an audible swish of great wings and they lifted off. The cedar branch swung upwards, scattering a veil of fine powdery snow. Svanhild felt a sense of relief. At least the Dwarves would know where she was detained and might attempt a rescue. She was sure that Solomon and Kasper would continue to survey the area. If she were able to make a getaway they might help her to find her way back to the Kingdom.

The owls quickly gained altitude and circled around the end of the lake before setting course for the great forests where they had lived for generations and enjoyed hereditary rights in perpetuity.

'At last, we found the Swannemaiden Chief,' said Kasper in a wistful voice.

'I suspected that the enchantress had absconded with her,' muttered Solomon, 'Last spring we freed her from the clutches of the witch's Gorghouls. It seems that Matista had her eye on the fair maid and bided her time.'

'The sorceress will try to mesmerize her Chief, and entangle Svanhild in her web of witchcraft.'

'The danger is great Deputy, but there is a spirit of defiance in the Swannemaiden. She may surprise us.'

Meadow, just waking up, smiled at Svanhild. 'I am sorry dropping off on you like that my dear.'

'Drink your coffee. It'll help you to come to. With Matista away, we can relax.' Svanhild ventured gingerly, 'Meadow you said that Matista travels hither and thither. How does she know where trouble brews or where her magic powers are required?'

'You will learn all that. You are fortunate Svanhild that Matista has chosen you as her apprentice. Soon you will know more than I have picked up in all these years.'

Svanhild was just about to confide to her elder companion that she had no intention of becoming the sorceress's apprentice, but she thought the better of it.

'I guess some of the news that Mastista gets is carried by the Merewings?'

'That is so my fair maid.' Leaning over to Svanhild, in a low voice, Meadow continued, 'Matista can see any place on earth. It is the broken mirror.'

'A broken mirror Meadow? What good is a broken mirror?'

'If you but knew. There is magic in the glass. Several times I have been permitted to look at the glass fragments. I have seen far off places. It is no ordinary mirror.'

'Tell me more Meadow.'

'Ah, my deary, the tale takes us back in time,' mused Meadow taking a sip of coffee and leaning into her wingback chair. 'I may as well tell you now, for soon you would learn it anyway.'

'In the dim recesses of time, an Elven Queen ruled in a far off land. Her beauty was beyond compare and many an admirer traveled months, even years, for an opportunity to behold her lovely countenance. Yes, even the prude Dwarves traveled to that distant land to catch a glimpse of her radiance. As you know, Dwarves set little stock by feminine beauty, at least so they say,' laughed Meadow, a merry twinkle in her eye.

'I know it well Meadow,' chuckled Svanhild, 'It hasn't changed to this day, I fear. How often have I tried to crack a smile on those stern faces.'

'One wonders how the dwarf population grows,' mused Meadow.

Svanhild, looking at the mop of white hair and the innocent smiling eyes, laughed heartily.

'It is a riddle my precious,' Meadow went on, 'but I must not lose the thread of my story. Yes Dwarves too, traveled far and wide to steal a glance at that lovely countenance. It was a Dwarf that brought the Queen the gift of a mirror, mounted in a silver frame of rare beauty. She was astonished and delighted with the mirror. Truly, it was a work of art. The Queen raised the mirror and saw her comeliness framed in gloriously crafted silver. Overcome by her own beauty, she could not let go of the vision.' Meadow raised her head and in her eyes, Svanhild caught a melancholy look.

'To possess such beauty must be a test, Meadow.'

'Alas, vanity has tripped many of us. And you, a sorceress' apprentice, must guard against it.'

'I will watch my step Meadow,' smiled Svanhild. 'But tell me what happened next?'

'Every day The Elven Queen would raise the silver mirror and always, startled at her own beauty, would pray for the appearance of a handsome prince, deserving of her loveliness. Many suitors paid her court. Alas, none could measure up to her high standards. Alone and lonely did she spend her years.'

'Did age not show on her Meadow?'

'Elves can live for several hundred years, without any visible changes. In time they do age, but they don't wrinkle and turn white as we do. Their features fade in the mist of time. It is as if a dense veil hides their faces and we can see but a dim outline of their former beauty.'

'This is what happened to the Elven Queen?' asked Svanhild.

'It did Svanhild. The beauty that had obsessed her began to fade. The shock must have been terrible. When she raised that precious mirror the lines that once sketched all that loveliness receded into white mist.

She looked at the beautiful silver that framed the faint image in the glass and then cursed the mirror that had enclosed her in the prison of self, for so many of these years. "Vanity," she cried in a fit of remorse, "Never, never, again must this mirror imprison a maiden in its frame!" She then intoned an incantation,

within this silver frame
let no one face solace find
the glass must show
the face of all mankind

'Ah it was deep my daughter, a cry from the heart. It rent the souls of all who had gathered around her.'

Svanhild wiped a tear from her eye. 'How very sad Meadow, to see only one's folly when the end of life comes within sight'

'Yet, my dear, her remorse released a magic power. Although she didn't know it then, the invocation she had voiced was fulfilled. With the last strength of her fading body she seized the mirror and flung it through the window. High it flew over the flowerbeds, the silverwork capturing the red flames of the setting sun. It soared to the edge of the cliff and then down, down, it went into the deep ravine beside the castle. The glass shattered into a thousand fragments, although still held together by the silver frame.'

'Amazing that the frame held together Meadow.'

'It is so, my sweet companion. The ancient silversmiths in the land of the Dwarves had skills that none can equal.'

'What happened to the mirror?' queried Svanhild, keen to hear the end of the tale.'

'It was an Esterian who found it. He was felling lumber in the gorge when a ray of sunlight caught the glass and almost blinded him.

He picked up the silver frame and wiped it clean. Although the glass was broken into countless pieces, he knew it to be a valuable find. He took it home to his log cabin, and after supper, by the light of the fire he raised the silver frame and looked at the shattered surface. The leaping flames danced in the tiny fragments of glass. At first he saw, playing in the broken glass, but a reflection of the flames. When he brought the mirror closer and peered at each tiny sliver, he began to see places and people in different parts of the land.

Some he recognized and others seemed to be far off places that he had never seen before. Each wee piece of glass showed people the world over. The curse or the blessing spoken by the Queen in her torment had come true, it was the face of all mankind that the old woodsman beheld in the broken glass.'

'What a wonderful story Meadow.'

'Quite amazing, but that was not the end of it. The old man in Esteria did much good with his precious find. When the mirror showed people in distress he would travel thither and render aid. After a few years his wife protested that he was spending all his time gazing at the silver mirror. The wood was not cut, there was no food in the cellar, and at night his wife found herself alone in their bedstead, while he sat glued to the magic mirror, looking at strange faces and sights around the world.'[6]

'Oh, oh,' mumbled Svanhild, 'the beginning of matrimonial trouble.'

'You are wise for your years,' chuckled Meadow, 'No, that situation could not last.'

'I guess it didn't Meadow?'

'No my pet. At the next yard sale his wife put the mirror, along with a lot of other knick-knacks, on a wooden table in front of the house. A traveling witch doctor working for the Seven, picked up the mirror for a song and presented it to Salan, the leader of the Seven.'

'I guess he wanted to curry favour with his masters,' commented Svanhild.

'He did indeed my dear. Salan appreciated the marvellous silver frame, but I think he never realized its power. He presented it to Matista. Perhaps he thought that the precious silver work would please the enchantress.'

'Did it, Meadow?'

---

6   *All this happened in times not remembered. In the latter days the rediscovery of the magic of the broken mirror led to new technologies. The internet and the worldwide web appeared and today too men are known to sit looking at the 'glass' deep into the night captivated by sights and sounds around the world.*

'It pleased her immensely, she could sense the potent vibrations of the gift bestowed upon her. When first she brought it home, she spent days looking at it and soon realized the powers that would be hers.'

'Could we see the mirror, Meadow?'

'I would not dare touch it Svanhild, but I think there is no harm in just looking at it. After all you are her apprentice.'

'Where does she keep the mirror? It is certainly not in the hall.'

'In her boudoir, my dove, where all the deep secrets are kept. But I know where she hides the key,' chuckled Meadow. She stood up and beckoned Svanhild to follow. They left the sunroom and walked up the curved stairway to the second storey. Meadow stopped before a heavy wooden door and kneeled. With her long finger nails, deftly she flipped up the key hidden in a crack between two floorboards.

'I hope no trouble comes of this,' breathed Meadow, as silently she turned the key to the enchantress' inner sanctum.

'I think not Meadow,' Svanhild reassured, 'Matista would not object to us taking a peak at the mirror.'

Meadow had her doubts, but Svanhild pushed open the heavy door and they walked in. There by the side of a large window, resting on a simple wooden easel and illumined by the light of the late winter sun, stood the silver mirror.

Svanhild was delighted by the beauty of its frame, exquisitely shaped by the artist. She came closer, seated herself on the chair in front of the mirror and gazed at the glittering surface of broken fragments. Meadow walked up and resting her hand on Svanhild's shoulder, looked down.

'This is the mirror of a thousand fragments. Look closely and you will find yourself traveling in strange and wonderful places.'

Svanhild began to scan the tiny pieces of glass and soon found that once she had spotted a scene that interested her and she focused her attention, the image would become magnified and she was able to see details. She could see Dwarves stacking wood, Gnomes tunneling for ore and then Lambarina, the Capital of the Kingdom of the Seven Mountains, appeared. It was a gloomy sight. People hurried through the street, a frightened look on their faces and everywhere there were servants of the Dark Masters about.

'Heavens above, they have taken control of the city,' she whispered to herself. Meadow peeked over her shoulder. Living in the Chateau in a remote wilderness, the sights and sound of other places and faces were a welcome change.

Meadow turned and looked out the window. A reddish tint lay on the snow covered branches. She knew that the sun would soon be setting and perhaps they better hurry downstairs. The other servants might be looking for them or, heaven forbid, Matista might return unexpectedly.

She tapped Svanhild on the shoulder and pointed to the door.

'You go ahead Meadow, I'll be only a minute,' said Svanhild who had just discovered an ocean scene that looked intriguing. Gnomes were walking on a beach by the Eastern Ocean. She could see them boarding small vessels and stowing gear. They would row a few hundred yards from shore and then letting their oars glide, climb onto the gunwales and dive into the ocean. She waited for more details to appear. As the image expanded, she could see them swim down, down, to the bottom of the sea. What were they searching for?

Svanhild pushed back her chair and cast at the mirror, a last glance. A golden shimmer caught her eye. They were salvaging treasures. No doubt many ships had been wrecked on the shoals and rocks of that remote coast. Sea Gnomes? She had never heard of them before. But it made sense, Gnomes had a remarkable affinity to gold and could, miles away, sense its presence. They must be distant relatives of the mountain Gnomes and their search for gold had led them to the bottom of the ocean, prospecting for hidden treasures.

She must talk to Oarflake and Ambrosia about the mirror of a thousand fragments and ask them if they knew legends about Gnomes migrating to the shores of the eastern ocean. They might be able to confirm her vision. Did the fragments of the mirror reflect reality or merely magnify her imagination? It seemed that each tiny piece of glass showing people and places interacted with the mind of the viewer and revealed different facets of each place. How she longed to be on the shore of the Lake of the Coloured Fishes to visit the dear Gnome couple.

'Svanhild hurry,' called out Meadow from the doorway.

'I am coming Meadow,' replied Svanhild looking around the room. A sudden thought struck her. What if Matista looked at the mirror and saw the Sea Gnomes diving for gold. No, that must not be. The Dark Lords had combed the land for gold tablets and it would be best if they remained in ignorance of the Sea Gnomes on the Eastern Ocean.

She reached over to a sewing basket on the table under the window and picked up a needle. With great skill and patience she pried loose the tiny fragment of the mirror that showed the Sea Gnomes at work, wrapped it in her handkerchief and tucked it into her dress. She hurried out of the room, and found Meadow waiting for her in the hall.

'Quick Svanhild,' whispered Meadow, dropping the key back into the crack, 'Matista is expected at any time.'

As they were about to run downstairs, the front door banged shut. They hid behind a wardrobe and just in time. They heard Finch welcome his mistress, but the enchantress ignored the greetings of her favoured servant and stormed up the stairs.

'Dear me,' whispered Meadow, 'her ire is up, something must have happened to annoy her. Oh my, I fear her blood pressure is rising, she is prone to it.'

Matista had picked up the key and vanished into her boudoir. Meadow slipped from behind the wardrobe and tiptoed downstairs. Svanhild hoping to find some clue to her anger, walked up to the door, and kneeling down, peeked through the keyhole. Matista was seated by her mirror. Her breathing was back to normal, but deep was her wrath.

She could hear Matista muttering. 'The Dark Lords were not pleased. The prisoners didn't arrive. The Nobleman, no doubt died in the forest. No one ever survives a bite by tainted fangs. But the others? The Grolls had orders to march them across the Finnian Range to the quarries, under the shadow of the Black Peak.'

When the enchantress stamped her feet in anger Svanhild jumped, but quickly she brought her eye back to the key hole and saw an evil smile spread on Matista's face.

'Working in the mines would have been a wholesome experience for the Captain. Never mind the boy Duckie, he was kind of cute.' she mused.

'The Ballet Master, an arrogant chap. Hauling stone under the shadow of the Black Peak would have made a man of him. Eating humble pie builds character. Never worked in his life, just stands by the shore and watches his swans prance around.' Alas, for all her magic powers, the great witch had no appreciation of the arts.

Svanhild now putting her ear to the keyhole, could hear her whisper. 'The Master of the Dancing Swans thinks himself safe in the dwarf stronghold. His sister is my guest and if worst comes to worst, a pretty hostage she will make.'

Evil laughter cascaded through the door and set a crystal vase vibrating in a minor key. Svanhild had heard enough. Thank heaven that her brother, the Captain and Duckie were safe. The Dwarves must have rescued them.

But if she were used as a hostage, Slim and his companions could be manipulated to yield up their freedom. It was another reason to hasten her departure from this gloomy castle.

She slipped down the stairway, walked into the great hall, took one of the books from the library and sat down by the open hearth. The book resting on her knees, she peered at the flames and tried to gather her thoughts. Any illusion that Matista had her interest at heart had been dispelled. She was but a pawn in the enchantress' game and, if the need arose, she would be wiped off stage.

She must make her getaway. Before long Matista might discover that a tiny fragment in the mirror was missing and her fury would know no end. The attraction and repulsion that she felt for Matista had often left her in turmoil. Now her mind was made up. There was no time to lose.

She opened the volume on her knees and leafed through the yellowed pages. A heading caught her eye: Shielding Against Evil Spells. She read quickly the entire chapter and found no secret formula to ward off spells and curses. It spoke only of an attitude of mind. 'Visualize a shield surrounding you and hold the vision till the danger passes.' It also stressed frequent practise. 'When an incantation of evil intent is spoken, the shield must be recalled instantly.'

Hearing a noise upstairs, she got up and put the book back on the shelf. She determined to practise visualizing the shield until it became an instant and effective response.

When the enchantress calmed down, she returned to the hall, greeting Svanhild and Meadow with a reassuring smile. She sat down across from Svanhild and warmed her hands by the fire. Svanhild looked at the enchantress' wrinkled face enveloped in a bower of white hair. The amber rays of the sun were sinking fast and a blue mist shrouded her countenance, then it lifted like a curtain and old Neva was no more. Seated across in her nocturnal splendour was Matista. The deep blue eyes seemed to read her very thoughts. Even after weeks in her presence, Svanhild felt a thrill at each eventide when the enchantress metamorphosed into a loveliness beyond compare. Night was Matista's season. All who came close to her were captivated by her comeliness and electrified by her radiant energy.

'Tonight my dear companions we will dine in style.' She arose and walked to the dining room. Svanhild and Meadow followed in her footsteps. Silver candelabras illuminated the table and Gertrude and Maria served a wonderful dinner. Wine from the palace cellars of the Black Lords, was poured by Finch and for a location so remote, the scene reflected a rare elegance.

After dinner Matista invited Svanhild and Meadow to accompany her for a soak in the hot tub. The large wooden tub stood on the balcony overlooking the lake. Her two Grolls were detailed to fetch buckets of water from the lake and to pour them into cast iron pots hung over a blazing fire. Once heated, the pots were hauled upstairs to the balcony. The Grolls growled and grumbled over the odious task but dared not complain. A soak under the star studded sky was an indulgence the enchantress cherished. She could relax only when Svanhild and Meadow joined her in the tub. For all her powers, she had a strange dependence on those who were close to her.

Meadow and Svanhild shed their clothes and slid into the steaming pool. The blue ice on the lake reflected the soft light of the moon and caught the outline of the enchantress as she slid out of her dressing-gown. Matista's body exuded an unearthly allure.

Svanhild held her breath. Such comeliness. Such wickedness. Moving with infinite grace, the enchantress stepped into the pool. Svanhild couldn't help wondering about the men in Matista's life. There had been, centuries ago, her love for Prince Norvalt. Had the bitter resentment of his rejection hardened her heart forever? Svanhild knew very well that one does not pry into the love life of a witch, and wisely she kept quiet.

The enchantress moved around the pool with the lithe movements of a ballerina. It was a joy to behold. Meadow's eyes sparkled, for to her the perfections of her mistress were a source of pride. The exuberance of the enchantress was infectious and Svanhild enjoyed herself, but this time her resolution to escape did not waver. She rested her eyes on the plane of blue ice ringed by spruce forest. Memories of her childhood came to the fore. The frozen lakes in Cascade! Her first skates. How Slim had taught her to race on the long metal irons, wrought in the smithies of the gnomes. When they returned to the great hall, they grouped around the open hearth and Marie and Gertrude served spiced tea and muffins.

The morning sun lit up the solarium where Svanhild and Meadow breakfasted. Matista worked through the night and preferred to sleep during daylight hours.

'Our mistress is in need of rest, Svanhild. She told me this morning before retiring, that she would like to have her spinning wheel and the small loom brought down from the attic. She looks forward to spending a few days working on her crafts. It relaxes her. 'Could you climb up the narrow stairs into the attic Svanhild and see if you can find them? It hurts my back to climb to the top storey.'

'I shall be pleased to do so Meadow,' said Svanhild who always had wondered what was hidden behind the little wooden door. After they had finished their morning coffee, Svanhild changed into an old jacket and Meadow gave her the key to the attic door. She climbed the spiral stairway, turned the key and pushed open the little door. Sunlight streaming through a skylight caught the many cobwebs strung across furniture and artifacts, stored under the rafters.

Sitting down in an old rocking chair, Svanhild looked over the variety of articles before her. An old sled, candelabras, and a number of lovely dresses strung over an old chair. The spinning wheel and the handloom near the door she dusted off best she could. She was about to leave when she bethought herself. Now might be her only chance to take a good peek at this collection of odd items. She made her way among old birdcages, flower pots and paintings. She tripped over a piece of metal, leaned over and picked it up. It was a skate, much to her surprise, mounted in a block of wood, with leather straps attached. She rummaged around until she found its mate. Then she put the skates with the other items to be taken downstairs.

She made her way to the gable at the end of the attic and looked through the small window which rendered a view over the frozen lake. The skates, the blue ice on the lake, this would be her chance.

Matista was seated in the solarium when Svanhild brought to her the spinning wheel and loom.

'Put it here by my side. Thank you my dear, spinning is a laudable pastime for an old woman.'

It always struck Svanhild as odd that at break of day, when Matista metamorphosed into an old biddy, her voice retained its lovely youthfulness. If you closed your eyes you could never tell. She was going to ask Matista if she could try out the skates, but she thought the better of it. She would wait until after sunset. Arrayed in her nocturnal glory, the enchantress would be more generous. At dusk, moonlight flooded the frozen lake.

Svanhild walked up to Matista who was mixing powders on the large table in the hall. 'I found a pair of skates in the attic Matista. I would like to try them out on the lake.'

'Of course my love. Don't break a leg. Skating is dangerous, and don't forget that dinner is an hour from now.'

Svanhild dressed up for the brisk winter weather and walked down the garden path to the lake. Matista stepped over to the window and watched her, skates slung over her shoulder, stroll towards the lake. A shadow of suspicion crossed her mind. The Swannemaid had been unusually pleasant in the last few weeks, but one never knew what really dwelt behind those deep emerald eyes.

Matista could see her two Grolls walking towards the ice. They had spotted Svanhild, putting on her skates by the lakeshore and following Matista's instructions they were keeping an eye on her. Matista was pleased that duty in this remote part of the wilderness hadn't dulled their wit. There were other Grolls of course, patrolling the lake shore. No, it would not be easy either to leave or to enter the Chateau without being noticed. Matista was enjoying the winter scene, when Meadow walked in and asked permission to go down to the ice, to keep Svanhild company.

'By all means. It is a lovely winter evening, enjoy yourself.'

Svanhild had her skates on by now and tried to stand upright, but before long she tumbled down. Only when Meadow walked onto the ice and gave her a hand was she able to keep her balance. She tried a few times to move on her own but each time she sprawled onto the ice.

The Grolls found the scene amusing and their raucous laughter could be heard in the Chateau. Matista smiled at the sight of the friends frolicking on the frozen lake. The next day Meadow found herself an old pair of skates and whenever the weather was fair, the two would gambol on the frozen lake. The Grolls didn't bother watching anymore. Only Matista would sometimes look out the window and smile at the twosome tumbling on the ice.

One morning Marie and Gertrude went out to fetch firewood for the kitchen range. After they had finished piling wood on a small sled, they paused to watch Svanhild clowning on the ice.

'You and I used to skate Marie,' wistfully sighed Gertrude.

'I remember it well Marie. It was before darkness fell over the land and they shipped us off to serve the witch.'

'Watch her skate, Marie,' laughed Gertrude, 'She clowns in a very skilful way.'

'That girl knows her art well,' exclaimed Marie putting her hand on Gertrude's arm.

For a moment, they looked at each other.

'We must help her,' said Marie, a whisp of excitement in her voice. We will never know freedom again, dear companion of my youth, but let us pray that the Swannemaid will fly free from this sombre spot.'

'Let it be so Marie, but what can we do?'

'We must talk to her. First of all, she may not know about the Grolls that patrol the far shore. If she makes a getaway it should be at full moon, when the Grolls go slightly luny.'

'At night Marie? The enchantress will be at the height of her powers.'

'Even in daylight, in her old shrivelled body, she can do a lot of harm.'There was no denying that. The two friends returned to the kitchen and pouring a drink, they sat down at the round table.

'It it will be full moon five days from now!' whispered Gertrude, 'If she waits another month, the ice might melt or be covered with snow.'

'We must take care of the merewings, they might trip her on the ice.'

'They could certainly be a right out nuisance, Marie. I will put some lake trout out in the old chicken coop, and lock them in.'

'What will happen when the witch finds out?'

'We are old women,' Gertrude shrugged, 'We will know the joy of seeing the young maid flee this wicked place.'

Later that day Marie slipped Svanhild a note and when the coast was clear Svanhild quietly walked into the kitchen.

'Sit down, deary,' said Marie, putting on the stove some water for tea. 'Like you Svanhild we were brought here against our will. That was many years ago and we reckon we will be here for the remainder of our days. You, who have your life before you, must flee this unholy house.'

'Then you know,' whispered Svanhild.

'We saw you skate my dear. It takes a good deal of skill to flounder on the ice like that.' Svanhild looked anxious.

'Not to worry my love. Gertrude and I grew up on skates, we could tell. Nobody else had an inkling, I am sure. You must leave at the next full moon, four days hence. At full moon the Grolls go balmy and you will have a better chance. We will fix the merewings.'

'If Matista finds out what will happen to you?' Svanhild asked, a concerned look in her eyes.

'The enchantress needs us here my dear, I think we will survive.' Marie replied wryly. Tears in her eyes, Svanhild hugged Marie and Gertrude and made her way to the main hall.

The next few days passed quickly. Matista, still recovering from her trip spent much of the time in her boudoir. Sometimes when she passed through the upstairs hall, Svanhild would pause, peek through the keyhole and see the enchantress seated before the magic mirror. One day she heard her mutter, 'The Rovers gained control in Lambarina. My Seven Lords will rule the land before long. The King is in his grave. Princess Yaconda, heir to the throne of the Kingdom, is tucked away in prison, but not for long.'

Svanhild held her breath, the beloved princess Yaconda, what was to befall her? For a minute all she could hear was an evil giggle. She put her ear to the door and Matista spoke again. 'Salan found the answer. He will marry her. Ah I suspected there was a lusty streak in his dark soul. Splendid, Splendid, a stroke of genius.'

The witch's laughter burned in Svanhild's ears. She had heard enough. The princess would be transported from her prison to the palace of the Dark Lords and be forced to marry Salan, the leader of the Dark Council. She must warn the friends gathered at the Manor DeCygne in Cascade.

During the next few days Svanhild and Meadow often went for walks in the snow covered garden and when the weather was fair they would skate at night by the light of the moon.

Svanhild knew that she would not be able to take with her any provisions and that skating away in the winter wilderness, even if she managed to elude the enchantress and the Grolls, would be a foolhardy undertaking. The next day would be full moon and she must take her chances. To stay at the Chateau for even another month would be perilous. It was Matista in the radiance of her nocturnal glory that Svanhild feared. The terrible wondrous beauty of the witch electrified her. Flee, she must, before the powers of the enchantress proved irresistible.

25

Like A Whirlwind

*L*ight was waning quickly and the full moon was diffused by a curtain of snow. Svanhild was sitting at the kitchen table when Marie walked in the door. 'All set my love. The black buzzards are in the chicken coop, gorging themselves on fish and the door is locked. Make haste, before the snow gets worse.'

Svanhild embraced Marie and Gertrude and before closing the kitchen door she turned around.

'You will be always in my thoughts, always!'

'And you, my love are our link with life and freedom.'

Svanhild wiped her eyes before walking back to the hall. Approaching the enchantress, she was struck again by her beauty, illumined by the blazing logs in the hearth. But her determination did not waver.

'Matista, this may be our last chance to skate on the lake. The snow will put a stop to it. Meadow and I would like to play on the ice for half an hour.'

'Be back before dinner, my daughter, in time for a soak in the hot tub.' mumbled the enchantress absent-mindedly, preoccupied with a new experiment in her laboratory.

Svanhild and Meadow strolled down to the lake and tied their skates.

The Grolls seated on a couple of tree stumps, watched Meadow and Svanhild frolic in the soft moonlight. They were rather lively tonight and their whistling and singing carried across the ice. Svanhild's mind was on her coming flight but Meadow overheard some bawdy lines. Full moon always sent the Grolls into a frenzy. Suddenly, they leaped onto the ice and started a kind of savage dance. It came to a sudden stop when they fell through the ice where earlier in the day Marie and Gertrude had done their trout fishing. The icy water had a sobering effect. The shouting and yelling of the Grolls attracted the attention of Matista, who was soaking in the hot tub. She stood up, flung a dressing gown around her shoulders and looked over the lake. At the sight of the dripping Grolls crawling onto shore, she smiled, but her smile did not last.

When the Grolls fell through the ice Svanhild knew that her time had come. She let go of Meadow's hand, slid gently backwards on the ice and came to a stop.

Matista looking at the moonlit scene with a few snowflakes falling, wondered why Svanhild was now leaning forward, with one hand behind her back. The girl stood perfectly balanced. This was not the usual tottering and clowning on the ice at which, so often, Matista had laughed.

Svanhild pushed back her right leg and moved forward on her left skate. Then her right skate slid forward and she gathered speed with a powerful stroke of her left leg. Startled, Meadow's eyes followed her, as she swiftly moved over the ice. The Grolls, still moon struck, figured it was some kind of innocent trick.

Svanhild turned and caught sight of the enchantress wrapped in a cloud of steam. There was a fleeting twinge of guilt and then she leaned into the wind and skated rapidly away from shore.

Matista was astonished by the grace and speed with which her apprentice moved on the ice. Then the truth dawned. She had been deceived, betrayed by the Swannemaiden, who flew over the ice with the skill of an accomplished skater.

She dressed quickly and peering into the winter night, all she could see was a tiny figure gliding rapidly toward the horizon. Standing by the steaming water, she rose to her full height, and intoned a dreadful incantation. A beam of fire shot into the night chasing the fleeing maiden, but it petered out a short distance from shore.

The enchantress' fury was awesome to behold. Well she knew that incantations do not work unless each letter, each syllable, each comma and space is properly observed. A minor slip nullifies the effect. She would have to calm down before she could hope to intone her curses properly.

Meadow stood on the ice, utterly amazed at the ease and speed with which Svanhild was gliding towards the far shore. Never had she seen anything like it. Svanhild had deceived her too. Yet she felt a strange warmth for her young friend and prayed that she would survive her foray into the winter wilderness.

Meadow returned to the Chateau to find the enchantress dressed and seated by the fire in the great hall. Matista had regained her composure and now realized that the merewings had failed to respond to the crisis. She got up and walked into the kitchen. Marie and Gertrude stood by the stove. Matista could tell by their faces, that they had trapped the big birds.

'Where are my merewings,' snapped the enchantress.

'Well my lady, we had some fish left over.'

Matista ignored them and marched out the back door. She could hear the miserable buzzards cawing and screeching. Their great black wings flapping and their purple beaks poking through the mesh of the chicken coop, they presented a nasty sight. Matista freed her feathered friends but it was too late to send them on a mission. Their night vision was but poor. She just hoped that the Grolls patrolling the other end of the lake would sight the fleeing maiden.

The gall and the cheek of those kitchen women in aiding the brazen girl to fly free. The deception and treachery was shocking. She stormed back to the kitchen. Marie and Gertrude were standing by the counter, tears in their eyes, tears of joy that Svanhild had managed to escape the sorceress' tyranny. Matista approached them, raised her hands and uttered a fearful curse. A flash of fire singed their eyes, blinding them. Matista stalked out of the kitchen, leaving Marie and Gertrude in a state of shock.

Meadow who had now returned from the lake, saw Matista rushing up the stairs, no doubt to consult her magic mirror. She walked into the kitchen to find Marie and Gertrude seated by the round table, their hands covering their eyes.

'She blinded us Meadow. We trapped the merewings in the chicken coop to give Svanhild a chance.' There was a note of triumph in Marie's voice.

'How horrible Marie.' For the first time in her life, Meadow felt a loathing for her mistress. She went to the sink, made cold compresses and placed them on their eyes. It soothed the pain. Later when Marie removed the wet towel for a moment, she called out, 'Gertrude, I can see light, it is the candle, the candle's flame.'

'The tears in our eyes protected us. Heaven be praised. We may yet regain our sight.'

Svanhild had reached the middle of the lake. With smooth and graceful strokes she flew across the ice. The snow had let up and the moon shining brightly, revealed jagged spruce on the far shore.

That night the badgers Ludwig and Berend, out for their evening stroll by the lake, seated themselves on an old log that they had dragged to shore.

'A peaceful spot, Ludwig.'

'That's why we moved here Berend, no kafuffles. Far from the madding crowd. Peace and quiet are precious these days. A moonlit sheet of ice without a creature stirring, the sight smoothes the wrinkles in one's soul. And then a pleasant fire, hot chocolate and bran muffins.'

They had an enjoyable sit on their favourite log, resting their eyes on the moonlight reflected in the ice. Suddenly, Berend stirred.

'A fleck in the middle of the lake, Ludwig and it is moving fast.'

'High speed is an ill omen in this rustic neck of the woods, Berend. We must prepare.'

The badgers retreated behind a hollow tree and unearthed a couple of sturdy oak sticks just in case unsavoury elements would intrude on their quiet life. Inside the hollow tree was a trapdoor that gave way to their cozy home.

Each standing on one side of the tree, they looked over the lake. It was clear that a creature was gliding swiftly over the ice. They waited quietly, watching the unusual spectacle. A sound of heavy feet slapping on the snow startled them. 'It is the Groll, Berend, patrolling the shoreline.' Then the sound came to an abrupt halt and silence returned.

'The brute is hiding in a clump of cedars, Ludwig.'

It was the Groll, and Ludwig and Berend could see his head sticking out above the cedar trees. He too, had seen the figure moving on the ice and seemed to be waiting for it to reach shore.

Berend climbed up the hollow tree, in order to get a better look. 'It is the Swannemaid Ludwig, skating like a whirlwind and heading straight for the open arms of the ghastly Groll!'

'The Swannemaiden, Berend?'

'The very same Ludwig, the one who was kidnapped by the sorceress last fall.

'And the blinking Groll is waiting for her. This augers ill Berend.'

Svanhild breathed a sigh of relief when she realized that she was not being pursued. She had visualized a shield surrounding her to deflect the inevitable curses that would follow her. Sometimes she felt buffeted by force-fields that seemed to pursue her, but these diminished as she drew swiftly away from the Chateau. She was skimming over the ice and could see the far shore looming in the moonlight.

Only when she approached close to the evergreens covered with a sprinkling of snow did she slow down and glided deftly onto the snow bank at the end of the lake. Right into the arms of the grubby ruffian.

'Great God Berend, the Groll, he's got her in his vice grip. Should we do something?'

'If we meddle with the Grolls, Ludwig, it'll be the end of serenity as we know it.'

'If we don't meddle Berend we will suffer guilt till doomsday. Imagine hot chocolate and bran muffins by the open hearth, with a Swannemaiden buried in a shallow grave by the hollow tree. Guilt burrows, Berend and we know what that is like. Fear hovers, but we can cope with that,' said Ludwig reaching inside the hollow tree and pulling out an old bugle from his militia days. A ghastly note from the rusty instrument shrilled through the night air.

It startled the Groll and he looked behind him into the dark forest. Svanhild was dangling from his right claw. Her skates were still on her feet and with all her might she drove the iron on her right foot into the Groll's knee.

He uttered a yell of pain and looked down at her, wondering how to put her out of her misery. The badgers trembling with righteous indignation quietly crept on a knoll behind him. Blows from their oak clubs rained upon the ruffian's head and all he could see was a myriad dazzling stars. He dropped Svanhild and rushed away in a daze, sliding onto the ice. His large leathery feet could be heard slapping the ice as he staggered away from shore.

The badgers helped Svanhild onto their log. Her right wrist was badly bruised and she was shivering with shock and cold.

'We will take you to our home, Swannemaid. A bright fire will thaw you out and we will look after your bruises. They untied her skates and Berend slung them over his shoulder. Supporting Svanhild on both sides, Ludwig and Berend walked her to the hollow tree. Berend opened the trapdoor and went down first. The entrance was tight but once down, Svanhild found herself in a comfortable living room that was connected by tunnels to other chambers. Ludwig found an extra chair and flanked by the two badgers, Svanhild sat down in front of the fire.

'Dear badgers how can I thank you. You risked your lives attacking that fierce Groll' said Svanhild who had begun to thaw.

'Don't mention it my dear girl, we were just lucky there was only one of them. A nasty lot those Grolls,' chuckled Berend.

Svanhild looked around and she was surprised to find such a comfortable home underground. There were paintings on the wall, pots and pans on the table and a cheery hearth. At last it dawned on her that she was safe in this place. Thank heaven.

'We presume that you hail from Swanneland, dear lady?' queried Ludwig.

'I am sorry Mr. Badger, I should have introduced myself. My name is Svanhild. My brother is Slim, the ballet master.'

'Of course. Slim and his flying swans. We have heard about your brother. Water ballet is quite an acceptable art form. Badgers have always supported the arts. Berend and I do a bit of painting in our spare time, of which we seem to have a good deal. Ludwig turned his head towards one of the walls displaying their work. I am Ludwig.'

'Ludwig and Berend. They sound like Badger names.'

'Indeed, they are Badger names, my dear girl,' smiled Berend. 'Before you tell us your story, we must have a mug of hot chocolate and bran muffins, Svanhild. It is a tradition in this home, every night it is hot chocolate and bran muffins by a cozy fire. Something to look forward to, you know.'

'I shall be delighted to drink hot chocolate and eat bran muffins,' exclaimed Svanhild, who was starving.

At breakfast next morning the badgers served porridge and tea, while Svanhild told them of the many adventurers that had befallen her. The badgers were amazed at everything that was happening in the outside world and hoped that their small outpost in the wilderness would be spared the commotion. After breakfast Svanhild sat by the fire and thought about the journey ahead. She must try to reach the Lake of the Coloured Fishes and consult the Gnomes Oarflake and Ambrosia.

When she told Ludwig and Berend about her plans they offered to make her snowshoes so that she could travel through the deep snows of the spruce forest. That very same day the kind badgers set about weaving a set of snowshoes and provided her with proper winter clothing for the long trek. In the evening they sat by a cozy blaze and drank their hot chocolate and nibbled on bran muffins.

Svanhild woke early next morning and peeked out the trapdoor. Hoarfrost covered the trees and sunshine sparkled on the snow. The badgers cooked her a hearty meal and stuffed her backpack with provisions. They knew of the Lake of the Coloured Fishes and on a piece of bark, Ludwig sketched a rough map. She gave them both a warm hug, tied on her new snowshoes, shouldered her pack and walked down the trail leading into the spruce forest.

She knew that the trek ahead would be both arduous and dangerous, but she was free from the powers of the enchantress. Matista's magic web had drawn her closer and closer to its centre and her flight had been in the nick of time.

Walking among the snow covered evergreens, her spirit lifted. She felt free at last, and anxious to see the Gnomes and then to return home to Cascade. The snowshoes felt strange at first, but soon she learned to walk briskly on the deep snow and made good progress.

Ludwig and Berend saw her vanish behind a rise in the forest and felt sad at heart. They returned to their home for an extended breakfast. The blithe spirit of the Swannemaiden had cheered the badgers and for a fleeting moment, they doubted if being far away from the madding crowd was all that it was cracked up to be.

Ludwig got his mind off the problem by working on one his paintings. Berend snuck out through the trapdoor and looked inside the hollow tree.

There, hanging from a broken branch were the skates the Swannemaid had left behind. Speed was taboo in badger society, but the sight of Svanhild flying over the ice, effortless, serene, and swift, had touched a chord in Berend's heart. He must try on these strange looking iron shoes.

He walked to the lakeshore and tied them on. Badgers have a good sense of balance and before long he was confidently gliding on the ice. After several days of practice, he attained a phenomenal speed and Ludwig, watching from the shore, shook his head in reproach. Thereafter Berend did his skating when Ludwig wasn't around.

Badger society still frowns on speed, however the skill of skating was passed on by Berend's nephews and nieces and in each generation you can always find a few badgers that covertly enjoy skating on remote wilderness lakes.[7]

Svanhild kept up a brisk pace. The trail wound through a forest of snow covered evergreens. Sunlight filtered through in patches and the beauty of the winter forest sang in her heart. At midday she came to the edge of a frozen lake, and rested on a log. The badgers had packed her a hearty lunch including a generous helping of bran muffins.

Svanhild took her time over lunch. Afterwards she picked some spruce branches, piled them on the snow and stretched out, leaning against the log. She could feel the warmth of the sun on her face and before long she fell asleep.

When darkness fell, a cold breeze swept the ice and touched Svanhild's face. Sitting up she took a handful of snow and rubbed it on her cheeks.

Gone was the brilliant winter scene that had greeted her arrival at the lake. Spectral moon shadows rose now before her eyes. She got up and walked to the edge of the ice. She was free, free at last and she longed to reach the homestead of her old friends, the Gnomes Oarflake and Ambrosia.

It would be a long trek through these remote northern forests. Rovers, Grolls and other creatures might well be travelling through these parts. A shiver ran down her spine. She had escaped from the Chateau, but was she really free from Matista? Her powers were not limited by space and time. Foreboding enveloped her, she could almost feel the presence of the sorceress. She raised her head and looked out at the ice. At the far end of the lake a dark mist obscured the moonlight. Slowly it crept over the ice, and in its centre a black wraith appeared.

A shiver rippled through her body and she did a few breathing exercises to control the fear which was about to paralyze her. She could now see that the centre of the black throng pulled forward and it took the shape of a phalanx. As it drew closer, Svanhild descried distinct shapes. The figure at the centre could be none other than Matista and in her wings moved countless dark creatures. Svanhild knew who they were, spirit servants from the underworld. She had read about them in one of the enchantress' books

---

7   *In the latter days sightings of badgers on skates have been rare. Wilderness Societies have waged bitter battles to ban Eco Tourism from lakes where the phenomenon has been observed. Birdwatchers using cameras with high shutter speeds have snapped a few shots of skating badgers, but even these look streaky.*

on witchcraft. It was clear that she had marshalled them to overwhelm her. A feeling of resignation beset her. The dark cloud drew closer and now she could see the splendid figure of Matista flanked by streams of dark beings. They were dancing forwards, their upper bodies moving in tortuous patterns, writhing and wringing. Svanhild knew that if they reached her side of the lake, they would surround her and carry her off.

All was finished, all had been in vain. When she looked up to meet her fate, the black procession had come to a halt. The wild frantic dance of Matista's companions had changed into slow grave movements. Heads were turned up, arms and hands were raised, as if to ward off some terrible pain.

Svanhild discerned a haze of light hovering over the ice, blocking the path of the black demons and shielding her from their approach. The light intensified and revealed the outline of a stately figure. She beheld the noble features of the ancient Wizard Isumatak. Within her heart she knew that it was he. For a moment his eyes met hers, and then he turned around and raised his arms. A wall of light spread across the lake and his luminous voice called out, 'Return, daughters of mischief, to your wretched abode on the outer rim of darkness. Abandon the service of Matista and you may yet escape your bitter lot!'

The dark army shrank back. Only Matista stood still for a minute and faced the Wizard. Her anger at the sight of Isumatak was terrible. She tried to hurl a curse the Wizard's way, but she was incoherent and could not even get through a simple incantation. Uttering a terrible shriek, she turned around and flew across the lake in the footsteps of her dark handmaidens.

Isumatak lowered his arms with an abrupt gesture, and approached Svanhild.

'Fear not my child. The Queen of the Night will not return. The monks at the Monastery of the Luminous Horizon have prayed for you Svanhild.'

'When I saw the dark wraith appear, my spirit wavered Isumatak. Your presence saved me.'

'Twice you have been captured by the great witch, Svanhild, and twice you have withstood the temptations that she set before you. You were shown the secrets of the occult and the power of sorcery, but you rejected the spider's invitation and escaped the magic web. You have passed these grievous tests and the enchantress will not attempt to capture you again.'

Svanhild raised her head and her eyes met the loving gaze of the ancient sage.

'Isumatak, is my brother safe?' A smile appeared on the Wizard's face.

'Yes, Svanhild. Slim, master of the dancing swans is safe with the Dwarves on the Finnian Range. We pray continually for the handful of brave souls in the Kingdom of the Seven Mountains, who oppose the tyranny of the Rovers and their Grolls. In time the Dark Lords will try to occupy the Kingdom. So far they have been content to let their minions control events.

At the Monastery, we can only pray, the brethren are not permitted to carry arms or intervene.'

'Once you did intervene, Isumatak!' Svanhild knew she should have held her tongue, but the words slipped out!

A smile spread over the timeless features of the Wizard. 'It is true my daughter, I was young and inexperienced and anger overwhelmed me.'

'Take heed Isumatak, the sun has never risen again on that radiant countenance and the enchantress has never forgiven you.'

Svanhild felt secure in the presence of Isumatak, Wizard and Abbot of the Monastery of the Luminous Horizon. He radiated a sense of reassurance and she felt that the efforts they had made, however small, were not in vain.

She took a small parcel from her pack and unwrapped it. The light of the moon shone in the fragment of glass that she had lifted from the Matista's magic mirror.

'It is a bit of glass Isumatak, taken from the Mirror of a Thousand Fragments. It is the mirror crafted by the Dwarves of old, the glass in which Matista sees the face of all mankind.'

'This explains much Svanhild, often we have wondered how Matista knew about events in the Kingdom and Esteria.'

'The whispered wish of an Elven Queen in times not remembered Isumatak, gave magic powers to the glass. It was the desperate plea from a dying Queen who loved her own image, but failed to love mankind. Her dying wish penetrated the heart of the universe and the glass became enchanted.'

'The mirror that could have benefited humankind fell into the wrong hands. You have seen the magic glass my daughter?'

'I have Isumatak. Exquisite silver work holds the glass that shattered into a thousand pieces when the unhappy Queen tossed it out the castle window.

'And you took a tiny piece,' laughed Isumatak, 'for a keepsake.'

'No Isumatak, I wouldn't have risked it for a keepsake. It was the fragment that showed Sea Gnomes diving in the Eastern Ocean. I thought it best perhaps, if Matista did not know about it.'

Isumatak smiled. 'If Gnomes are diving, treasures must abound. You know about the golden tablet Svanhild.'

'I do Isumatak, I know the chances are slim, but the discovery of the Sea Gnomes raises new hopes.'

Isumatak placed the tiny piece of glass between his fingers. 'Please take it Isumatak,' urged Svanhild, 'I'd rather not carry it,'

'You must keep it Svanhild, and carry it back to the land of the swans. When this present darkness passes, the museum in Lambarina will be delighted to add it to their collection.'

After several moments of silence, the Wizard said quietly, 'My time is up Svanhild I must return to the Monastery in Esteria and assume my worldly shape. Go and talk to Oarflake and Ambrosia, my daughter. They will be able to tell you about the Sea Gnomes if indeed there are such creatures. Fare ye well, my child, and hasten to the homestead of the Gnomes.'

There was a lightness and youthfulness about the ancient sage that surprised Svanhild and it filled her with a sense of peace. She looked at the Wizard's mysterious countenance, now wrapped in an aura of light. The light intensified and the outline of his figure softened. Soon only a haze of light remained. Yet the strength in the Wizard's eyes, etched in her mind, gave her new hope.

Dark clouds moved swiftly past the moon and patches of light danced upon the ice. With a light heart Svanhild tied on her snowshoes and shouldered her pack. She would cross the lake tonight.

The expanse of ice seemed endless. At last the faint green line of jagged spruce came closer and she could see the outline of separate trees. She reached the far shore and stepped onto the beach, where she gathered birch bark and dead branches and soon had a cheery blaze going. She dragged some bigger logs on the fire and dozed by the glowing embers until dawn's first light.

Soaring high above Fireweed Lake and the Chateau, Chief Solomon and Deputy Kasper caught sight of the sun long before its rays reached the forest dwellers below. During the past few days, they had made several passes over the Chateau, but there was no sign of Svanhild.

'The maiden may have flown the coop, Deputy.'

'I wouldn't put it past her, Chief.' rejoined Kasper.

'How could she have made her way across the lake in midwinter Deputy?'

'We had better fly a grid across the lake and the forests beyond and look for clues, Chief.'

The owls flew up and down the lake and by the shoreline. There was no sign of Svanhild. They ventured farther into the woods.

Soaring on an updraft above the treetops Kasper spotted a black animal with white stripes moving on a lake below.

'Could be a badger, Chief.'

'Moving at that speed, Deputy? Badgers are, on principle, opposed to speed.'

The owls landed on a log on the hillside overlooking the scene. There they saw Berend flying across the ice, sliding up a snow bank, and coming to a stop, close to their perch.

'I see Badgers have discovered speed,' hooted Solomon.

'Badgers,' exulted Berend, 'have discovered change. We have stood still for centuries, but now we are on the move.' He turned around in a flash and raced to the end of the lake and back.

Solomon shook his head. He had read in the Owls Book of Wisdom about desires and aspirations dormant for ages, pushing to the surface.

'My noble badger,' said Solomon.

'Berend is the name,'

'Berend Badger, we would like to know whether a Swannemaiden has been spotted in these parts?'

'These very skates are hers, my feathered friends. Ludwig and I snatched her from the vice grip of a Groll. We sheltered her for a few nights and provided her with snowshoes, winter clothing and a bag of bran muffins. Now she is on her way to the Lake of the Coloured Fishes.'

'Not a moment to lose, Deputy.'

'Indeed not, Chief,' said Kasper, flapping his pinions.

'Haste ye thither forest owls, fly fast, speed is everything.' triumphantly exclaimed the badger, gliding on one skate over the smooth black ice. High above Solomon and Kasper watched the tiny dot speeding across the lake.

'Berend Badger challenging time honoured traditions Deputy. It is the tip of the iceberg.'

'Berend Badger has discovered the new age Chief, portentous.'

'Portentous, I like the sound of that word Deputy. You do have remarkable literary talent. Portentous.'

Svanhild ate a branmuffin for breakfast. The sun was up but the end of the lake was still in the shade. Feeling chilled she lost no time strapping her snowshoes. She looked at the map that the badgers had given her and realized it would take another two days to reach the homestead of the Gnomes. Into the dark spruce forest she walked. She descried deer tracks and followed in their imprints. The trail was narrow and struggling with overhanging branches and numerous snow drifts, she covered nine miles. It was going to be a long journey.

The owls had tried to spot Svanhild. By the time that they reached the lake where she spent the night, she had vanished under the forest's dark canopy.

'We have lost her, Chief,' ventured Kasper

'We will head for the homestead of the Gnomes, Deputy, and tell Oarflake and Ambrosia, Svanhild is on her way.'

The owls touched down at the dock near the log cabin where the Gnomes Oarflake and Ambrosia lived. After their banishment they had homesteaded in this remote wilderness, where their orchards and gardens flourished.

Like many other forest dwellers, the owls opposed cultivation of the wilderness, but they had to admit the Gnome couple had built a prosperous farm on the shore of the Lake of the Coloured Fishes. Well they knew that many wounded or sick birds had been nursed back to health by the kindly couple. Oarflake standing on a snow bank had spotted the Chief of the Wood Owls and his Deputy, well before they landed on the peaked cap that covered the well in front of their cabin. Ambrosia who had been inside, stirring a stew, heard their friendly hoot. Anxious for news, she opened the door and invited them inside. The owls, catching the scent of a good meal brewing on the stove, flew into the house and perched on the drying rack by the stove. They felt more comfortable in the dim light of the log house, for the bright sparkling snow irritated their eyes.

'The Chief and his Deputy, very welcome you are,' joyfully exclaimed Ambrosia. 'We haven't had visitors since last summer. Share our dinner and tell us about happenings in the outside world.'

Solomon spoke in a solemn voice, 'Major changes are afoot Lady Ambrosia.'

'Apocalyptic!' voiced the Deputy

'It sounds worse than we had expected,' exclaimed Oarflake, an expression of utter dismay upon his face.

'The Deputy has a literary touch,' explained Solomon casting a glance at Kasper. 'It may not be quite as bad as all that.'

'I should hope not,' sighed Ambrosia, 'that word gives me the shivers.'

'Limit your literary impulses Deputy. It tends to overpower. Modesty and simplicity in speech is a capital virtue. Memorize the ancient Book of Wisdom.'

The Deputy Chief looking a little miffed, muttered, 'three hefty volumes, I can hardly lift them. To memorize the Book is the privilege of a chief.'

Solomon kept quiet and fixed his gaze on the little meatballs bobbing up and down in the stew. Ambrosia stretched out her hand and smoothed his ruffled feathers.

'But tell us what happened,' urged Oarflake. 'Last summer travellers from Swanneland spent time with us. Slim and Svanhild, the Captain, the Marquis and little Duckie. Are they safe and sound?'

'And the Mountain Fairy Weiss and his friend Edel,' added Ambrosia.

'The eagles reported that they had rescued the Mountain Fairy, Edel.

Edel and Weiss are safe with the Dwarves in the alpine meadows. Alas, the Marquis was bitten by a black hound and we don't know his fate. The remainder of the company were captured by the Grolls. In a fierce battle on top of the Finnian Range, the Dwarves crushed the Rover Captain and his Grolls and liberated the prisoners. The Mountain Fairies, Moose Martin, Slim and Duckie will be spending the winter with Smithereen and Sunflower and other dwarf families.'

'Oh, my stars!' exclaimed Ambrosia, 'Who would have thought.'

'Is there anything we can do?' asked Oarflake.

'That is why we are here my dear Gnome friends,' communicated Solomon. 'Svanhild was kidnapped by the witch Matista and abducted to the Chateau at the far end of Fireweed Lake. She made her escape a few days ago. The badgers, Berend and Ludwig, saved her from the Grolls and told us that she is travelling to your homestead. We have tried to find her but now she is in the spruce forest and cannot be spotted from the air.'

'The spruce forest,' Ambrosia echoed with dismay, 'A dreadful place in winter.'

'I will travel thither by wolf sled,' Oarflake concluded in a determined voice. 'She may run into heavy weather at this time of year.'

'Before we do anything Oarflake, we must sit down and have dinner.' The owls had been eyeing for some time, the meatballs floating in the stew. They perched on the bench and lost no time digging in.

'There is something about Ambrosia's stew,' said Kasper picking out a meatball, 'That one seldom finds in the wild.'

'Homesteading and cultivation have their merits Deputy. One could easily get used to a cozy cabin and Ambrosia's cooking.'

After a very satisfying dinner the owls thanked their hosts and then took flight for their hereditary patch in the forest. Oarflake and Ambrosia, standing in front of the cabin, waved farewell. Solomon and Kasper tipped their wings and soaring over the little log house vanished into darkening clouds.

Ambrosia went back into the house but Oarflake stayed outside and looked over the lake. Shadows moved over the vast expanse of white and a few snowflakes floated in the air. The wind began to gather force and dark clouds rolled over the lake. Oarflake made his way back into the cabin, sat down in his rocking chair by the fire and filled his pipe. The crackling fire and the clicking of Ambrosia's knitting needles were the only sounds that could be heard. Years of exile had accustomed him to the loneliness of long northern winters and the visit from the owls had been a welcome change.

The only other visitors had been lumbermen from Esteria who dropped in on their way down to the Sanctus. There they spent the autumn felling timber and floating it down to Miranda and other mill towns. Since their banishment, no Gnomes had ever visited. Not even their relatives!

The brothers Ensten and Ulrik from Esteria were their closest friends. Whenever they travelled to the upper reaches of the Sanctus they would stay for a day or two with the Gnome couple. Ambrosia, her knitting needles resting on her knees, looked at a small carving that Ensten had brought her as a gift. The woodcarving showed a Mountain Fairy, one leg already in the air, leaping from a rock. The sight of it cheered her. The fire in the hearth flared up and Ambrosia looked at Oarflake.

'Yes, my dear the wind is gaining.'

Oarflake walked to the window and listened to the howling wind. It was dark outside and heavy snow was falling. A frown traced his brow when he returned to his seat.

'I fear for Svanhild my dear, no wolf team can be gathered until the weather clears.'

26

Wily Weasel

The rising sun had turned the snow covered forest into a vista of dazzling white. Cheered by the sight, Svanhild tied on her snowshoes and leaving the lakeshore behind, she followed a narrow trail into stands of giant spruce. Branches curved by a burden of snow formed an arch and sunlight highlighted the trees' upper reaches. She found herself walking into a cathedral of light and for a brief moment shed the fears and worries that weighed upon her.

This lightness of being lasted through the morning but after lunch fatigue and weariness returned and she felt forlorn in the wilderness. Yet her determination never faltered and through the deep snow she trudged onward. The sun had disappeared. A cold breeze swept through the tall trees, swaying branches and shedding snow below. When Svanhild looked up she saw dark clouds sailing across the sky. Snowflakes fell among the trees. She struggled for a few more miles until she reached a clearing. It was snowing hard now and drifts were beginning to form. The wind whistled across the open space and blowing snow made it difficult to see. She paused and watched the swirling snow. A blizzard was blowing up and she knew that for shelter it would be best to tunnel into the snow. She took off her snowshoes, sank on her knees and dug a hole in the snow. Shivering and weary she crawled inside and curled up.

The howling wind and a sense of isolation led her mind back to family and fellow wayfarers. She wondered how her brother Slim had spent the winter in the Dwarf Village on the Finnian Range. She knew that he would be writing in his diary and making sketches of all the wondrous sights that they had seen. He was an artist at heart and had a marvellous memory.

In her mind's eye she relived the battle in the cabin of the Sisters of the Third Woe, and the terrible fate of the Marquis. She could still hear the doleful moaning of the stricken nobleman. How had she been able to live with the sorceress who had been the cause of all this misery? Yet she had been fascinated by Matista's beauty and the depth in those blue eyes. Svanhild's fingers traced the icy walls of her snowy prison and for a moment she quivered. Her secret attraction to the great enchantress had frightened her more than the dangers of the forest.

In the darkness and isolation her mind travelled back to the town of Miranda. It was in Miranda that she had met Ensten and the thought of the handsome woodcarver chased her gloom.

She recalled the tall Esterian holding up his carving of the elven child. Had the laughing elf really appeared to Ensten, or had it been a figment of his imagination? The carving was so lifelike and irresistible. When sleep stole over her she dreamed of Ensten and his carving.

It was ringing laughter that woke her. She opened her eyes to see an elven child leaning over her and feel elven lips touch her forehead. A sweet voice sang out, 'I am Elmira, a figment of the imagination, I am not. From the hands of the enchantress, Amaranth, I received the gift of spirit travel. Fare thee well Svanhild. Our prayers go with you.'

The elven child, wearing a gown of light receded into a white mist. Distant laughter lingered in Svanhild's ears long after darkness had returned. The experience had been so genuine, she felt convinced that the visitation had been real. She recalled the myth about an elven child who would intone the mystic writ engraved on a golden plate that could break the power of the Dark Lords.

A gleam of sunlight filtering through the opening of her refuge told Svanhild that the storm had passed. Out of her snowy prison she crawled into bright sunlight. Spurred by the thought of reaching Oarflake and Ambrosia's homestead, she stepped into her snowshoes, tied the strings and hurried forward. In the newly fallen snow her snowshoes left an oval print.

The great spruce forest covered a large area between the outer frontiers of the Kingdom and the Finnian Range. It had always been uninhabited and only in recent years had rover scouts patrolled the area.

Captain Zorf of the Dark Masters' Life Guard, accompanied by his Groll servant and a black dog, was returning from a reconnaissance trip when he spotted snow shoe tracks.

'Remarkable Scaly,' said the Rover in an amused tone of voice, 'This is not one of ours.'

The Rover and his Groll, striding on short wide skis began to follow the tracks. He was convinced the intruder was a Dwarf. No other dweller in the Kingdom would have had the audacity to enter the Great Spruce Forest now claimed by his Masters. They slid smoothly over Svanhild's trail and had it not been for the lumbering black dog, who kept sinking into the fresh snow, they would have overtaken her. The Rover and his Groll were forced to wait for the panting brute to catch up.

When Svanhild stopped to rest, the sun was casting long shadows. A soft following breeze had sprung up and only when she came to a halt did she catch a waft of the foul scent borne on the wind. Immediately her mind went back to the attack by the Grolls in the cabin of the Holy Sisters. The dreadful smell of foam and saliva had been etched upon her memory. A black hound was near.

She walked on for several hundred feet until her eyes lighted on a giant spruce split by lightning. There was a hole in the trunk, eight or nine feet above ground. She untied her snowshoes, climbed a neighbouring birch and leaning forward was able to grasp the lower edge of the hole. She pulled herself in and landed on a soft mossy floor. Perhaps the danger would pass. She would wait quietly and visualize a safe arrival at the Lake of the Coloured Fishes.

After awhile she put her ear against the burnt side of the hollow tree and listened carefully. In the winter stillness no sounds could be heard. She closed her eyes, breathed deeply and tried to relax. She knew that Rovers and Grolls would occasionally patrol the forest, but was it possible that they had passed earlier and that their scent had lingered? She must anticipate the best.

A faint rustling caught her ear. Svanhild looked up and in the dim light of the hollow tree appeared an elegant white shape. The natty creature made a polite bow and raised a pointed red hat. 'Greetings fair lady and welcome to my winter quarters. Wily Weasel at your service.'

There was an impish gleam in his green eyes and the name was a little unsettling, but the creature's deportment spoke in his favour. After all, what is in a name? Svanhild had known enough folks with fancy names who had turned out to be rats.

'My apologies Master Weasel for invading your winter quarters. For a moment, while travelling, the air reeked foul and it reminded me of the black dogs that accompany the servants of the Dark Lords. I thought to hide until the danger passes. I am travelling to the homestead of the Gnomes, Oarflake and Ambrosia.'

'Friends of the Gnomes my dear, are friends of mine. Their banishment has been our gain and they have been a blessing to the forest dwellers. Many a wounded weasel has recovered at their cottage.'

Svanhild felt she could trust Wily, despite his name and told him in a few words about the importance of reaching the Gnome homestead as quickly as possible. The green shining eyes turned serious. He hopped on the edge of the hole and sniffed the air.

'There is no doubt Lady of the Swans,' said the weasel who was familiar with the Swannepeople, 'The hound and his master are not far off.

Foul reeks the air and I can hear a dog panting.' Svanhild sighed, so close to safety and now another threat to face. She looked at the sleek weasel.

'How long would it take to reach Oarflake and Ambrosia's homestead Wily?'

'It can be done in less than two hours, Lady Svanhild.'

'Hasten thither my noble weasel and tell them about my fate.'

To be called noble lifted the spirit of the gallant weasel. He had a penchant for trouble and his relatives had called him by many a name, alas, noble was not one of them. Wily took an immediate liking to Svanhild.

He made a polite bow, shot out of the hole and before rushing off had a quick word with members of his family.

Svanhild pulled herself up to the edge of the hole to see his lithe white body move along the spruce branches. Avoiding the trail and taking a different direction, he headed in a straight line for the Lake of Coloured Fishes.

She caught a glimpse of the weasel flying between treetops before her fingers grew stiff and she slipped back to the soft floor at the bottom of the hollow tree. Moments later she could hear the sound of voices and the dog's panting and scratching the bark of the tree. The Rover and his Groll were standing close by.

'There is somebody inside Captain,' growled the Groll, 'Foamy wouldn't make a racket for nothing.'

'The tracks stopped by the tree and there is a pair of snowshoes lying on the ground. We may conclude that the owner has found refuge inside the hollow trunk.' A sheepish grin showed on the Groll's face.

'I'll take a look, Captain.' Locking his vice like claws on the edge of the hole he pulled himself up.

'It is a girl, Captain, curled up inside.' That was all that the brute was able to say for Wily's extended family had gathered around the hollow tree and at a sign by Wily's great grandfather, rushed at the Groll. Grandpa, who had dealt with Grolls before, stood on a hillock giving orders. 'Go for his ankles fellows, no scales below the knee.' A good many weasel fangs sank into his feet and ankles. Dreadful curses fell from his lips as he crashed to the ground.

'Get the vermin Foamy,' shouted the Rover. The black dog lashed out at the weasels, now flying in all directions, up and down, backwards and forwards. They looked like terrestrial humming birds. The dog's fury ended in frustration and exhausted, he sank down in a pile of snow.

Leaning against a tree opposite the hollow trunk, the Rover took stock.

'Let us take it easy Scaly time will do the job for us.'

'Why bother captain? It is only a maid.'

'Never mind Scaly, we get a bounty for any able body we bring back. All the men have been called up for army duty and our Masters need slaves to work the farms and the armouries.'

'The big push Captain?'

'First we will deal with the wretched Dwarves and then the rest of the Kingdom, Scaly. No more dilly dallying and trying to buy the cooperation of the folks down below. Opposition is growing in Lambarina and Cascade, and an underground movement is afoot that could spell trouble. Some of our men and their servants have been attacked in the dark. The Lords want to occupy the Kingdom.'

Svanhild could hear every word and she realized that the Captain was a high placed officer in the enemy camp. What she heard was vital information that must reach Lady Erica and the Council in Cascade.

'You can bring in the prisoner Scaly and keep the cash,' said the Rover in an unusual fit of generosity.

'I have to get her out of the trunk first,' snickered the Groll.

'Simple as cake Scaly.' Peel some birch bark with those lobster claws and pile dead wood on top.'

Grolls are dense when it comes to innovation but understanding began to dawn and a grin spread from ear to ear.

'Smoke Captain, smoke and she'll come out of that hole as meek as a mouse.'

The Captain was well pleased with the intelligence displayed by his Groll. He seated himself comfortably to watch his companion snapping branches with his powerful claws and starting a blaze at the foot of the hollow tree.

Svanhild could smell the acrid smoke and crawled into the lowest part of the trunk, where the smoke was least likely to penetrate. She uttered a silent prayer and waited silently. The heat inside the tree slowly rose and the smell of smoke made her cough. To make things worse she could hear the chortling of the Rover and his Groll, who considered the whole affair quite entertaining.

'Splendid barbeque Scaly,' muttered the Rover munching his supper.

Svanhild recalled the time that she had been seized in the vice grip of a Groll's claws . Death would be preferable to the pain and slavery that she would experience if captured. She dug deeper under the roots of the spruce, where the earth was still cool. The smoke began to irritate her throat and her frequent coughing spells were a source of merriment to the Captain and his servant.

At the Lake of the Coloured Fishes drifting snow swooshed around the log cabin of the Gnome couple. Oarflake sat in his rocker by the fire. Smoke curling up from his long stemmed meerschaum pipe was drawn up the chimney by a strong draft.

Ambrosia's knitting needles lay still on her knees and her eyes looked into the flames. Oarflake knew that stare in Ambrosia's eyes, she was in a trance. She had the second sight and he wondered what secret vision glowed in those dancing flames. Ambrosia turned from the flames and looked at her hubby.

'Trouble Amby?'

'Rovers are patrolling the spruce forest, my noble Gnome.'

Oarflake sensed an emergency. 'Is it Svanhild my love?'

'Flaky, I hear her spirit calling. You must find the wolves and harness the team. No time is to be lost.'

Oarflake rose from his comfortable rocker and Ambrosia fetched his deerskin parka and helped him into it. He slipped into his mukluks, packed emergency provisions in his rucksack and from a peg on the wall Ambrosia fetched his ivory horn, the gift of a unicorn. Years ago the unicorn had been wounded by a Rover's arrow. Oarflake and Ambrosia had heard her cries in the autumn night and helped her to reach the cottage. Before she expired the unicorn had expressed her gratitude to Ambrosia and Oarflake and asked Oarflake to take her horn upon her death. Ambrosia had sensed the horn's secret powers and Oarflake discovered that if he blew through the spiralled ivory instrument, deep vibrations would travel through the air and awaken the creatures in the forest.

He stepped outside and put the smooth ivory to his lips. The grave tones of the magic horn sped through the trees echoing from hills and mountains. It woke squirrels from hibernation and startled badgers fast asleep in their cozy underground homes. Some badgers stuck their heads out their entry halls, but the doleful sound convinced them that trouble was afoot and quickly they retreated, double locking their front doors.

Leonardo was in the middle of a pleasant dream. It was springtime and he and his lady friend Andante were trotting along by the side of a babbling brook. The sound of the horn abruptly ended his nocturnal escapade with the charming she-wolf. His thick silver fur aquiver, he sprang up, shook the heavy snow from his coat and woke his team mates. Leonardo was a magnificent specimen. Even among the Great Grey, he stood out for his size and strength. Badgers avoid trouble at all cost, but not the Great Grey. Leonardo was totally action oriented and the penetrating oscillations of the unicorn horn had galvanized him.

For a few minutes he listened as the deep sounds rebounded through the forest. He knew that the call was urgent. Leonardo's verbal skills were limited but he had a sixth sense and realized that here was a chance for him to prove his valour. He signalled to his team mates and they lined up single file. Moving swiftly through the heavy snow they reached the cabin of the Gnomes in record time. Oarflake and Ambrosia, waiting on the porch, bid them a hearty welcome.

Ambrosia explained to Leonardo how she had heard Svanhild's spirit calling and he grasped the situation instantly. Svanhild had made a deep impression upon him. The fact that the dark eyed Swannemaiden was in trouble and that black hounds might be involved, stirred a chord in the noble wolf's soul. The Great Grey had a deep loathing for the black dogs and fortunately they had acquired immunity to the poisonous fangs.

Oarflake's sled was loaded with provisions, including his yew bow and a set of iron tipped arrows. The wolves were hitched in a jiffy and off they were, racing over the frozen surface of the Lake. Oarflake standing on the back of the runners held on to an upright handle and shouted encouragement to the team.

They sped across the Lake of the Coloured Fishes. The snow had stopped falling and stars sparkled in the midnight sky. After an hour's run, Oarflake called a halt for a few minutes to give the wolves a chance to catch their breath. They sat on their haunches, tongues hanging out and steam rising from their deep fur.

When Oarflake looked up clouds were moving swiftly and patches of moonlight fell on the forest clearing. He wondered how they could travel faster, for even the Great Grey would not be able to keep up that punishing tempo in the deep soft snow.

Resting against a tree he caught a white flash. It seemed to move from tree to tree and before he knew it, a weasel appeared on a branch. He made a polite bow and raised his red hat.

'Master Oarflake, it is me Wily Weasel. Oarflake didn't recognize the gleaming white creature immediately, for weasels do look very much alike. After a few moments he identified him by his jaunty manner. He and Ambrosia had treated many a sick weasel at their homestead and he was pleased to see Wily. Wily did not waste any time.

'Svanhild is in danger Master Oarflake. She hid in the hollow tree that happens to be our winter home. A Rover and a ghastly looking Groll have laid siege to it and a drooling black hound sits by their side. I fear that they will set the tree on fire.'

'How far from here Wily?'

'The way you are travelling two or three hours. But there is another way higher up where the weather is colder. On the barrens there is a string of lakes where the ice is frozen solid. Follow me and in half the time we will attain my winter quarters.'

Wily led the party swiftly up the mountain. Once the wolves reached the height of land, they loped across the frozen lakes and the barren lands at a tremendous pace. Wily couldn't keep up and jumped on the sled. Standing in front of Oarflake, his red hat in hand lest it blow off, he directed Leonardo and his team with great skill and verve to he hillside above the hollow tree. Leonardo was trembling with impatience to rush to Svanhild's aid. Oarflake lost no time unhitching the team.

Captain Zorf and his Groll had spent the night by a cozy fire that slowly burned into the hollow tree, home of the weasel family and Svanhild's refuge. The heat inside was intense but the Swannemaid had no intention of giving herself up to Captain Zorf and his charming companion.

Dawn was near and the bottle of liquor that had kept the Captain in good humour was nearly finished.

'Get more wood Scaly,' yelled Zorf. 'We have to get her out of here in a hurry.' He could hear moaning sounds from inside the tree and a look of satisfaction appeared on his scarred features. The Captain's joy would be short lived. The first sign of trouble was the dog's growling.

'Quiet Foamy,' snapped the Rover who enjoyed listening to Svanhild's cries. But Foamy could no longer contain himself and jumping up, stared at the path leading to the plateau. Grey shapes came rushing down and a strong wolf scent caused him considerable anxiety. He turned his drooling head and took a look at the glade down below and rushed off. It was too late. Leonardo, heading the wolf pack, flashed past the Rover and the Groll. Moments later his great teeth gripped the hound by the scruff of his neck and shook him so violently that the huge black head lolled over to one side and the brute sank into the snow.

One of Oarflake's arrows had pierced the Groll in the neck. His large body falling right across the flames subdued the fire.

Captain Zorf was bewildered by the speed with which things were happening. He too, ran to the glade below. But the Great Grey ringed the Rover. He drew his sword, slashing at the wolves but it was no use. The wolves slowly tightened the circle around him.

Oarflake had taken his small axe and was chopping a hole in the already weakened tree and within minutes pulled Svanhild into the fresh air.

Wily Weasel and his family had moved spruce branches to the foot of a nearby tree and Oarflake lowered the semiconscious Swannemaid onto a bed of green needles. Her face and clothing were black with soot, but no serious burns showed on her skin.

With snow he gently washed Svanhild's face and brushed off her clothing. The fresh air brought Svanhild around and she sat up against the tree trunk. Her eyes adapted slowly to the snow scene and it took a few minutes before she could see clearly. A smile played on her lips when she discovered that a family of weasels had gathered about her.

'We thank our ancestor, the Great Weasel, for your delivery Lady of the Swans,' said Wily with a polite bow.

Thank you Wily,' said Svanhild with a sigh of relief, 'when you flew off like an arrow, I knew help would arrive in time.'

'Wily saved the day Svanhild,' added Oarflake, a happy smile on his face, 'he took us up to the frozen lakes, saving hours of travel through heavy snow.'

The entire weasel family seemed pleased to hear Wily praised. Svanhild had an inkling that Wily's mischievous spirit had often been a source of grief to the family. To see the young weasel cast in the role of a hero was a good omen and no doubt a turning point in his life.

'Wily reached your home in the nick of time, Oarflake. I am so grateful'

'Wily never reached our home, Svanhild. He met us halfway and guided us hither. In the middle of the storm Ambrosia heard your spirit calling and we knew that not a moment was to be lost. I blew the unicorn horn and Leonardo and his mates rushed to our homestead.'

For a moment Oarflake had forgotten about the Rover Zorf. He looked down the glade and saw the nine wolves in a tight circle with Captain Zorf in the centre. Zorf, evil to the core, was no coward. Oarflake and Svanhild watched the Rover's tragic end. He thrust valiantly at the wolves but they were too quick for him. Whenever he swung his sword at one of the Great Grey, the wolf behind him would leap up, sinking his fangs either into his back or neck.

Svanhild turned her head away in horror, but Oarflake watched the circle draw tighter and tighter.

'Let the punishment fit the crime,' he mumbled. The weasel clan was delighted at the spectacle and clapped heartily every time one of the wolves lunged forwards. As the circle closed, Leonardo, filled with righteous fury, flew at the Captain, knocked him down and quickly put an end to his misery. The scoundrel sank in the snow. The Captain of the evil Lords was no more. Only a whiff of black mist could be seen spiralling into the blue sky.

The weasels watched the black column rising. 'Wonder where he is going?' mused one of the elders of the clan. 'Plenty warm, a lot hotter than the hollow tree he baked the Swannemaid in. Cooked his own Goose.' Other comments abounded.

The wolves walked back up the glade, but Leonardo went straight up to Svanhild who put her arm around his neck and thanked him heartily.

Svanhild put on a brave performance, but the Gnome knew she was exhausted and he prepared a seat for her on the sled. The wolves lined up behind Leonardo and Oarflake hitched them up.

The weasel clan waved goodbye and Wily accompanied the team for the first little while. Only when they reached the lakes stretching across the barrens did he halt and waved his red hat to the party speeding by.

Svanhild, wrapped in a blanket, sat up and Oarflake stood behind, his feet planted firmly on the runners. It was a magnificent sight, the great wolves dashing across the sun drenched barrens, Svanhild's silver hair streaming in the sunlight and the Gnome singing words of praise for their deliverance. A strange procession indeed. Two hares standing by a dwarf birch did a double take when the train flew by.

'Unparalleled Phillip,' said the taller of the two.

'I say Alexander, they are practically moving at hare-speed and if I am not mistaken, the silvery flash was a pretty maid.'

'No mistake Phillip,' said his cousin, who like most hares, had the ability to freeze a moving image in his visual memory and recall it with perfect clarity.

'The maid was lovely, luminous silver tresses, fine bone structure and all that. But as to travelling at hare-speed, rest assured my young friend they were nowhere near it.'

Ambrosia was standing on the porch when the sled pulled onto the shore of the Lake. Within minutes Svanhild found herself in Ambrosia's arms. What a relief to be back at the home of her dear Gnome friends. Ambrosia took her inside and sat her down in a chair by the hearth.

'Be back in a minute my dear, I must feed my wolfies, they have worked hard.' Ambrosia took a pot of porcupine stew off the stove and carried it outside. The wolves made short shrift of it. When Ambrosia returned to the hearth, she put some goat milk on the stove for hot malt drinks.

Before leaving for their lair deep in the forest, Leonardo stole into the homestead and pressed his wet snout against Svanhild's cheek. Svanhild rubbed his head and thanked him for rescuing her.

Oarflake and Ambrosia went onto the porch to wave farewell to Leonardo and his team mates and watched them vanish into the dense forest.

The moment Oarflake relaxed in his rocking chair, a deep weariness stole over him and after a hot drink he dozed off, but Svanhild and Ambrosia talked deep into the night.

27

Oarflake and Ambrosia

*S*unshine and the smell of fresh coffee woke Svanhild early in the morning. It took a few moments before she realized where she was. Ambrosia's smiling face reassured her, she was among friends.

'Have a cup of coffee my dear. Take a bath before breakfast and scrub off that soot. Oarflake is heating the water. I washed your clothes last night and they are drying by the woodstove.'

After months of danger and imprisonment Svanhild found herself once more in the home of the dear Gnomes. Tears welled in her eyes and Ambrosia put her arm around her shoulders and wiped her face.

'Will these trials ever end, Ambrosia?'

'Trials never end my love. They are part of life, and without them we don't grow. But triumphs too will come to us and we will live to see them. Now, away with you and into the bath!'

When Svanhild joined the Gnomes at breakfast, she felt refreshed. Hot porridge, sausage, cheese and coffee stood on the table. Ambrosia knew many a recipe from Swanneland and on the hob nearby simmered dragon eyes. Eggs, dropped in a hole in the centre of a slice of bread, and fried to perfection.

Svanhild was delighted at the spread before her. It brought back memories of the little cottage by the Frivoli where, for many years, life had flowed so quietly. Was it only last summer that the first rumbling of approaching peril had reached Cascade and stirred its people into action?

Safe and secure in the loving care of the Gnome couple, Svanhild began to unwind. In the evening seated around a blazing fire, she told them about the battle in the cabin of the Sisters of the Third Woe and the terrible fate of the Marquis, her escape on skates from the Chateau and how the badgers had saved her from the Groll. Oarflake was impressed to hear how Ludwig and Berend had stuck their necks out to save the Swannemaid and his opinion of badgers shot up a couple of notches.

The Gnomes were thrilled when Svanhild told of the light surrounding Isumatak and how the great Wizard had prevented Matista from recapturing her. But it was the image of the Sea Gnomes in the Mirror of a Thousand Fragments that caused a flurry excitement.

'Flaky,' burst out Ambrosia. 'Some Gnome families may have wandered to the Eastern Ocean and learned to dive for treasures on the bottom of the sea.'

'If there is gold on the bottom of the sea, Gnomes will find it,' laughed Oarflake.

'The Dark Lords have combed the earth for a mythical golden tablet for years and that tablet could be resting on the ocean sands.' exclaimed Svanhild.

'We must travel thither Ambrosia and befriend the Sea Gnomes. They are our distant kin and I doubt not but that they will help us in our search.'

'Once they realize we have no ambition to dive for gold or treasures they will welcome us,' chuckled Ambrosia. 'In summer Oarflake must travel to the seashore and find our distant relatives. I am afraid the journey would be too much for me, the joint-ill has laid me low.'

'How I wish I could go,' sighed Svanhild.

Svanhild closed her eyes and the image of Sea Gnomes came back to her. 'Strange,' she thought, 'this remarkable attraction to gold and the uncanny knack of finding it had lead Oarflake into trouble long ago, but now it might uncover a crucial secret.'

Oarflake lit his meerschaum, but sleep was catching up with him and he was gently snoring when Ambrosia removed the pipe from his hands. She took up her knitting, settled down in her chair by the fire and stared at the flames. Her mind dwelt on all the strange events that had happened, and how they all were linked in some mysterious way.

Next morning at breakfast Ambrosia took Svanhild's hand. 'My love you must stay until the ice breaks up in the Sanctus, we will be glad of your company and travel would be safer and easier in early spring.'

'Alas, Ambrosia I must hasten back to Cascade and speak to the Council at the Manor DeCygne and talk to Lady Erica. Imprisoned in my hollow tree, I overheard Captain Zorf talk about plans to crush the Dwarves and occupy the Kingdom.'

'So far the Seven have been content to send their agents into Cascade and Lambarina, Svanhild. Why would they risk open warfare?' questioned Oarflake.

'The Rovers have bribed the business community Oarflake, but their rough and ruthless manners have created resentment amongst the people in the Kingdom. The men and women of the Sanctus Valley, who have not seen conflict for more than a century, at last are organizing a resistance movement. Rovers, Grolls and even black dogs have disappeared without a trace.'

Oarflake smiled, 'It is true Svanhild that long ago folks in the Kingdom were cunning fighters. The spirit of the warrior once buried deep, has risen again.'

'The Dark Lords will not broach opposition,' cautioned Ambrosia, a frown crossing her brow. 'If they break through the passes on the Finnian Range their armies will sweep Esteria and the Kingdom.'

'The Dwarves are formidable warriors,' reflected Oarflake, 'Yet, unaided they cannot withstand the armies being mobilized by the Dark Masters.'

'Who would come to their aid Flaky?' queried Ambrosia.

'Master Grimmbeak and the Celestial Covey might support the Dwarves. Once Grimmbeak sees the damage that the Dark Lords wreak on the environment, he'll take sides.'

'I did not tell you Svanhild,' said Oarflake, 'Young Theodorus, one wing paralyzed by an arrow wound, was carried hither in late fall. He had been shot by a Groll archer. Master Grimmbeak will not let that one pass lightly. Then there are the men of Esteria, and they would bring the Great Grey along.'

'When the Kingdom is occupied, the Woodland Owls would lose their hereditary rights to their patch of forest. Then the owls would certainly join the battle for freedom!' exclaimed Svanhild.

'We will have to see what happens Svanhild,' said Oarflake, 'but it is important that you reach Cascade and bring tidings to your friends gathered at the Manor.'

Svanhild felt a sense of urgency to reach Cascade but she needed a few days to recover. In the mornings and evenings she joined the Gnome couple for prayers in the little chapel. At night Oarflake went to the chapel to chant and his deep bass resounded through the winter night. When Svanhild heard his voice, she would don a winter coat and go out on the porch to listen.

One night he sang prayers from the Common Book of Sacred Lore, the sacred scriptures compiled by King Arcturus. 'How marvellous,' mused Svanhild, 'that all the peoples in the Kingdom have been able to accept the book.'

The next day a fearful snowstorm swirled around the little log cabin and the three of them were forced to stay inside. After years of isolation it was a joy for Oarflake and Ambrosia to have Svanhild with them for a short while yet. In the evenings they talked of times past and of times to come. Ambrosia loved to hear Svanhild describe the great Swan Festivals at Cascade. She told of the dancing Swans and the splendid feasts on the lawns of the Graceful Neck. When she described the procession of newlyweds in gondolas pulled by teams of Swans, Ambrosia whisked a tear from her eye.

'Perhaps one day Oarflake and I will see that splendid sight.'

'Of course you will see it. When peace returns and Queen Yaconda ascends the throne, your banishment will be rescinded. You will be my guest in Cascade and sail you will in our finest gondola. Limonides will lead the team of Swans that will propel you on the Sanctus at full moon and I will serenade you on the utelli,' laughed Svanhild. Ambrosia's eyes sparkled and she took Oarflake's hand. 'Sometimes we must dream Flaky.' A flicker of hope sprang in the Gnome couple's eyes and that night they dreamed of gondolas and moonlight.

The snow turned to rain and the trails leading down to the Sanctus remained impassable. At full moon the weather turned and Svanhild knew that soon she must be leaving. That night Svanhild stood by the lake side and watched the light of the moon reflected in the water covering the ice.

At the sound of footsteps she turned and saw Oarflake step into the chapel and moments later, borne on the evening breeze, the sound of his deep voice reached her. The words were not familiar and she realized he was singing a lamentation that he himself had written.

oh fleeting years
of exile and distress
years that endless seem
awaiting a message to redeem
a trespass from the past
Oh spirit of the ages
that breathes in all living things
cleanse the blemish off the pages
that man's folly brings

Svanhild could not help but smile and she mused silently. 'This wonderful man has nurtured and loved all the creatures in this great forest around the Lake of the Coloured Fishes and still he is tormented by a shadow of his youth. How dearly he paid for that handful of gold dust.'

The last echoes of Oarflake's words vanished into the night. Svanhild was about to turn around and walk back to the cottage, when she saw two moon shadows fleeting across the ice. Solomon and Kasper circled overhead and perched upon the branches of a pine.

'Dear Solomon, dear Kasper, how good of you to come and visit.'

'The pleasure is entirely ours, Swannemaid,' responded the Chief of the Owls.

'The privilege Chief, it is more telling.'

'Ah, the privilege Svanhild, in literary matters I bow to my Deputy, a well read bird!'

'Oh, Solomon,' burst out Svanhild, did you hear Oarflake singing? Why does the folly of his youth torment him to this very day? Why hasn't the Gnome Sacred Council forgiven him?'

Solomon's yellow eyes glinted in the moonlight. 'It is a deep question, daughter of the Swans. Yet, it is not that the Council has not forgiven Oarflake. They know about his noble life by the Lake of the Coloured Fishes. They simply haven't rescinded his banishment.'

'In the land of the Gnomes a law cannot be bent or broken,' added Kasper.

'Of course. That is why it is a law,' concluded Solomon, with the kind of finality that Kasper had learned to respect in his Chief.

'No Svanhild, it is not a message from the Sacred Chamber of Elders that

will lift Oarflake's burden. The last Volume of the Book of Wisdom speaks of judges. The sternest judge dwells within our psyche. It is this judge's message that Oarflake is waiting for.' Tears sprang in Svanhild's eyes, as she listened to the learned owl.

'Knows the Book by heart,' sighed Kasper, 'All three tomes. It makes me sick.'

Svanhild had great respect for Solomon's wisdom, yet recognition for all that Oarflake and Ambrosia had done would not be amiss. The next morning the owls joined Oarflake, Ambrosia and Svanhild for breakfast. A gleam appeared in their eyes when they spotted a bowl of meatballs on the table.

'Have you flown over the upper Sanctus in the last few days?' queried Oarflake.

'Some of the younger birds passed by. The ice is breaking up and it will be clear in a few days,' replied Kasper.

'Speaking of younger birds,' groaned Solomon, 'we must get back to the Woodlands. Some of the young turkeys are under discipline.'

'Sprang out of line again,' added Kasper, winking at the Gnomes. 'Talking of legitimate leadership and other impertinent questions. The Chief took them down to size with a few choice quotations.'

'Knowing the text has its uses Deputy,' snapped Solomon slyly.

'After you settle things back in the woodlands Solomon, could you fly a message to my brother?'

'It will not take long to settle things in the woodlands Svanhild. We will be delighted to fly to the Finnian Range and convey your greetings.'

'Tell him Solomon that I escaped from Matista's clutches and will soon be travelling home. Warn the Dwarves that the Dark Masters are massing armies to storm the passes and that they will attempt to seize the Kingdom.'

A dark shadow appeared around the large yellow eyes. Kasper turned to Solomon. 'If the armies seize the Kingdom, it is the end of freedom and hereditary rights.'

'Quite so Deputy, our duties are clear. I will call a meeting of chiefs.'

The owls bowed to Svanhild and the Gnomes, hopped onto the railing of the porch and rose quickly into the morning sunlight.

Soon after the owls had left, Svanhild packed her belongings and got ready to depart. She embraced the Gnomes and promised that she would return in the summer and join Oarflake for an expedition to the Sea Gnomes.

Halfway down the lakeshore, she turned around and waved a last farewell to Oarflake and Ambrosia who were standing on the porch of the log house.

Walking briskly, she tried to cover as many miles as possible while the snow was crisp. By midday she hoped to reach the glade leading down to the Sanctus Valley. The evergreens were covered with hoarfrost and rays from the rising sun transformed the towering spruce into a crystal canopy. The ground was firm and Svanhild skipped along merrily. The silence was broken only by woodpeckers hammering away. The appearance of birches and a maple here and there, told her she was approaching the great river.

The canopy of evergreens shielding her from the sky had disappeared and Svanhild was afraid that merewings might spot her. It was as if someone had read her thoughts, for suddenly a woodpecker appeared on a maple branch.

She knew by the brilliant red feathers that it was the very same bird that they had met on their trek to the Finnian Range.

He pecked a little tattoo by way of greeting and spoke in his usual rattattat voice.

'Daughter of the Swans, rest assured the skies are clear. Last night a passing moon shadow caught our eye and we saw overhead a formation of black buzzards returning to the Land of the Red Earth.'

'I am so very pleased that we meet again, Roland Hammerfast,' sang out Svanhild, 'and thank you for tracking the movements of the merewings.'

'I am afraid they have not vanished for good, Swannemaid. Messages have been hammered out and relayed to us by fellow birds from the other side of the mountains. The nasty buzzards are training for some evil event. Yet, for now, the path to the river is clear. The men from Esteria are driving their logs down the river and we can hear their voices sing. A hearty welcome awaits you Svanhild.' The dapper bird beat a gay pitter patter and was gone.

After walking another mile down the valley, Svanhild found a sunny spot sheltered from the wind and sat down to enjoy the lunch that Ambrosia had slipped in her pack. After a short rest she walked down to the river, wondering if Ensten would be amongst the loggers on the upper Sanctus. A light twinkled in her eyes and her pace quickened!

Her thoughts went back to the Golden Goose in Miranda where first she had met the handsome woodcarver. Then, the company had still been together. Most of her travel companions were safe in the village of the

Dwarves, but no one knew if the Marquis had survived. Once across the Sanctus, she would travel along the great mountain ridge to the Valley of Lost Hope, and call on the Sisters of the Secret Crossing to learn the fate of the Marquis. It was back in the autumn, that the party had been attacked and she remembered the moaning of the Marquis in the forest. She wondered if the Dwarves in Turania had been able to reach the nobleman in time, and carry him to the Convent.

28

Run For Life

The Marquis' stretcher rested on four rocks. Angelica, the goat lady knelt over the nobleman to administer a sedative draught. The Marquis dazed with pain, perceived the gesture as the ministration of the last rites. Surprise shone in his eyes and he seemed far away, as if listening to a distant voice. Angelica saw his lips moving and she leaned over attempting to make out what he was saying.

> *it is Dorothea calling*
> *her voice like water falling*
> *farewell my friends*
> *I sail for distant strands*
> *cut loose the moorings*

'Marquis, please,' urged Angelica. 'It's not the end. This cup contains but a sedative to comfort you on a healing journey. Dorothea's voice is calling upon you to endure and attain victory. You must not let go. If the right incantation can be found, Dorothea's spirit will return and her marble body transformed, once more, into living cells.'

In a gesture of gratitude, the Marquis grasped the hand of the wise old woman and leaned back on the stretcher. Angelica waved farewell as four stout Dwarves lifted the stretcher and walked through the gate to begin the long trek to the Convent of the Sisters of the Secret Crossing.

Sergeant Crusher marched at the head of the team and in his backpack carried the medicinal drink that he was to administer, twice a day, to the Marquis.

'Dreadful concoction,' muttered the Sergeant, 'Devil's Claw and Deadly Shade of Night, strange to imagine how that could save a life, but the goat lady knows her stuff by golly and her art has saved many a man.'

Sergeant Crusher knew that the mixture of Devil's Claw and Deadly Shade of Night would, for only ten days, protect the Marquis. There were nine days left to reach the Sisters of the Secret Crossing. Only they knew the art of weaving the nettle suits that could save victims of tainted fang. It was the fluid secreted by the nettle leaves that would kill the fatal virus that had entered the Marquis' bloodstream. Sergeant Crusher shuddered at the thought of anyone spending seven weeks in a suit of fire.

Soon after their departure, darkness enveloped the landscape. Although a gibbous moon shed a faint light on the path winding down the mountainside, they were forced to slow down. Many boulders were strewn on the ground and carrying the stretcher, they could not risk a tumble.

After several hours, the dark jagged edge of the spruce forest drew near. There was a well worn trail through the forest but moonlight barely penetrated the spruce canopy, and it took over an hour to cover a few miles.

Just as Sergeant Crusher was about to call a halt, he caught the scent of wood smoke. He knew they were close to the retreat of the Sisters of the Third Woe, the very log house where Matista had caught the travellers from Swanneland in her snares. Sergeant Crusher suspected that the Nuns had heard about the deception and had hurried hither to exorcise any evil vibes that might still be lingering in that holy place.

After motioning the bearers to slow down, he walked ahead towards the hut and stopped for a moment by the stone statue of Patriot, the Golden Retriever who had attacked Matista and earned her wrath. Her evil magic had turned him into stone.

At a few yards distance from the log house, he hollered in a deep voice. 'Sisters of the Third Woe fear not, it is Sergeant Crusher from Turania in the Finnian Range, we are on a mission of mercy. The Marquis deCygne is mortally wounded.'

No sooner had he called out then a Sister in black habit appeared on the porch, a veil covering her face. 'Sergeant Crusher you speak in the tongue of Dwarves. We bid you welcome. Bring the dying man into the house. You and your warriors may sleep on the porch.'

The Marquis, still semi conscious, was carried gently into the hut and lifted onto the sofa.

'Dreadful what happened here, Sister, treachery and deception in this holy place! The Marquis and his fellow travellers were lured here by the sorceress Matista disguised as a Sister of the Third Woe. The Marquis was bitten by one of the Rover's black dogs.

The Sister shed tears as she looked at the lifeless form of the Marquis. 'What of his travel companions Sergeant Crusher? Were they transported to the labour camps under the shadow of the Black Peak?' A grin spread over the Sergeant's face.

'No Sister, the Dwarves trounced the Rover and his Grolls. Smithereen, ill with the moping sickness, shed the torpor that had weighed him down and he rushed to battle. His dreadful ball and chain demolished them, it was frightful to behold. The bottom of the ravine was covered with Grolls.'

Although very much committed to the path of peace, Sister Matilda and her two companions couldn't help chuckling.

'We do hope, Sergeant, the great Smithereen has recovered from the moping illness.'

'Alas, Sister, when the crisis passed Smithereen fell back into depression.'

'We will pray for him, Sergeant, please tell him so.'

'Thank you Sister. I am glad that you decided to retain the retreat.'

'That this holy place was used for evil came as a great shock to us. We contemplated taking it down. The vibes were loathsome and we scrubbed the walls with prayer,' laughed Sister Matilda. 'We have decided to keep the retreat. Sister Sofia reminded us that it had also been a place of heroic battle.'

'So it was ma'am, the Marquis rose up against overwhelming odds. The stone statue of the noble hound Patriot, in front of the cabin will be a memorial and a place of pilgrimage for dog lovers in generations to come.'

'I am afraid Sergeant when that time comes we will have to find a retreat in more remote regions.'

Sergeant Crusher handed the bottle of medicine to Sister Matilda to be given to the Marquis at night. Walking out of the cabin he cast a look at the snow white face on the sofa. Two younger sisters kneeling beside the motionless figure intoned a healing chant and remained with him through the night.

It was still dark when the three Sisters served the men a hearty breakfast on the porch. The Marquis was barely conscious when he was lifted onto the stretcher and carried down the path leading towards the Sanctus. Sergeant Crusher stayed behind to thank the Sisters. He expressed his joy that they had decided to keep the retreat. Not that he was a man of prayer, he had other methods of dealing with the world, nonetheless, he considered it a good omen. He knew the Sisters would soon change the evil stigma that had attached to the cabin in the forest.

As he stepped off the porch and walked into the forest a ray of sunlight broke through the clouds. His eye caught a gleam of metal amongst the leaves, bending over, he removed some leaves and needles, and there in front of him glittered the metal of a handsome sword. The sword of the Marquis. Moose Martin had told them how the Marquis had arisen in a fit of fury and dispatched a dozen Grolls. He could only guess that after the black dog had mortally wounded him, the nobleman had stumbled out of the cabin into the forest and dropped his sword. Sergeant Crusher picked up the weapon and walked down the path into the forest. He could see in the dim light under the spruce branches, a blue sheen glowing on the weapon's edge. A light appeared in the warrior's eyes. No wonder the Marquis had created havoc among the Grolls. He lowered his arm and the edge sliced through a sturdy branch. He looked closer and saw carved on the haft, an inscription. It was Scimitar's signature. Sergeant Crusher wondered at the marvellous edge on the steel that had lit up when he grasped the haft. Perchance the enchantress Amaranth had cast a spell on the weapon. Sergeant Crusher had always suspected that the enchantress had a weak spot for Scimitar.

How Scimitar's sword had fallen into the hands of the Marquis was a puzzle to the Sergeant. He would take it to Smithereen on his return. Certainly carrying it along on this dangerous journey would not be amiss.

Breaking into a trot, he caught up with the stretcher bearers. The sun had disappeared and a fine drizzle spread over the forest. The spruce branches glistened with water and a thin film of mud covered the path. They slowed down to prevent sliding and the stretcher flying off.

By dusk they were exhausted. Coming to a clearing, they halted and let down the stretcher. They woke the Marquis and managed to pour into his mouth, a portion of the horrible drink the goat lady had concocted.

A huge fire dried their clothing and kept the Marquis warm and for supper they enjoyed smoked boar meat and huckleberries. Although the team was dead tired, they needed to unwind, and a pot of coffee perked over the embers as they lit their pipes.

Talk centred around the sword. It was Tuffkote who suggested that Patriot, Scimitar's faithful hound, might have carried it away when Scimitar was ambushed by the Grolls. It seemed likely enough, and Sergeant Crusher figured that the golden retriever had taken the weapon to the Marquis.

The rain stopped and a ghostly moon rose in the sky. The men lay down on skins around the glowing logs. Looking up, the Sergeant spotted a black shape soaring overhead. One of his men got up and reached for his bow, but he put a restraining hand on his shoulder.

'Wait Valkirk, I think it is an eagle. It could be young Theodorus, Master Grimmbeak of the Celestial Covey sent him to the upper Sanctus to ask the river drivers to meet us with a raft on the southern shore.'

Theodorus had seen the fire and made a graceful landing in the meadow, where he was welcomed by the Dwarves. Perching on a tree stump, he folded his wings. His magnificently curved beak and piercing eyes, illumined by the dancing flames, gave him a fierce look. Yet he was a softie at heart and often had his entreaties mollified Master Grimmbeak's harsh judgement. Theodorus remained silent for a moment before raising his voice.

'I am relieved to have found you Sergeant. The fire was visible for many miles and we may only hope that merewings have not spotted it.

'It is the Marquis, Theodorus, we have to keep him warm.'

'I understand,' said the young eagle, casting an anxious look at the prone nobleman.

'The men of Esteria are building a raft and will be waiting to ferry you across the river.'

'This is good news,' exclaimed Sergeant Crusher.

'Take heed my friend,' warned the eagle, 'I have sighted a Rover and a troop of Grolls on the shore.'

'Black Hounds?' asked Valkirk.

'Only one black dog.'

A shiver ran through the men. The dogs were unpredictable and often it was difficult to dispatch them, without receiving a scratch or bite from the deadly fangs.

'We better get some rest men,' said the Sergeant, bedding down by the fire, 'Tomorrow could be tough going.'

Theodorus felt it was his duty to stay around until the Marquis was ferried safely across. He had orders to aid the Dwarves with aerial surveillance, but not become involved in actual battle. Master Grimmbeak's philosophy was simple: the task of the eagles in the Celestial Covey is not to meddle or to take sides, the task of eagles is to judge.

Sergeant Crusher knew Theodorus would do all that he could to change the Covey philosophy. Master Grimmbeak might yet alter his stand. Smelters under the shadow of the Black Peak were working day and night making armaments for the Dark Lords. Ghastly black smoke rose from their chimneys and trees had been smothered by the poisons spewing into the air and Grolls had burned large tracts of forest to improve defences. Master Grimmbeak retained a dignified aloofness about the world below. But trees dying! That was another matter.

Perched on a little birch tree the young eagle looked upon the moonlit clearing. The dying fire cast an orange sheen over the five warriors and the stricken Marquis. Theodorus's keen mind reflected on the scene before him.

'It is all very well for Master Grimmbeak and the old boilers to stand on their mountain peak while the world below is dissolving into chaos. The Master and the older birds may have to do a paradigm shift, and forget this notion of neutrality,' mused the young eagle.

By dawn the stretcher bearers were on their way. Sergeant Crusher, sword in hand, marched well ahead of the team. Theodorus had left the campsite in the dark and now was nowhere to be seen.

It was a warm sunny day and the sombre mood of the night before had lifted. Birches and maples in gold and red attire appeared among the spruce. The Dwarves sang their favourite songs as they marched down the path. To watch the strange procession, woodpeckers stopped their hammering, and badgers put their eye to the little peek holes in their doors.

Close to noon they reached the top of a hill and there before them spread the waters of the Sanctus. Sergeant Crusher silently scanned the river's shimmering surface. There were no signs of other creatures. Theodorus had reported Grolls but they might have moved on. It was strangely quiet and there was no sign of the young eagle. He told the bearers to find a sheltered spot in the bushes and to wait for him. Carefully, he crept down to the shore. The stout warrior had a great love of water, and the sight of the Sanctus never failed to move him. He sat down on a small dock and watched the play of light on the wavelets. A few minutes later Tuffkote appeared by his side.

'Sergeant Crusher,' whispered Tuffkote,'I hear a moaning sound yonder by the bulrushes.'

'Cover me with your bow,' retorted the Sergeant, 'I will check it out.'

The old warrior slipped down the bank. Standing by the water, he could hear a high pitched whine. Crusher had a gut feeling that it was the young eagle crying. He waded through the water, parted the dense reeds, and there lying on one side, was young Theodorus. An arrow had penetrated his right wing. The arrow head had lodged in the muck and the slightest movement caused terrible pain. The warrior lifted the magic sword. Effortlessly he sliced the arrow on each side of the wing and pulled out the remaining piece of wood. Immediately the pain lessened and the young eagle made an effort to perch. Looking at the shaft, Sergeant Crusher recognized the traditional Groll arrow with its heavy iron point.

'A bad wound Theodorus,' said the Sergeant bending over the eagle. On our return we will carry you to the home of the Gnomes by the Lake of the Coloured Fishes. Their healing hands will speed your recovery.'

Theodorus felt an enormous sense of relief. He could move and bend down to drink water. No longer was he a sitting duck!

'It is fortunate, indeed, Sergeant Crusher that you have not been detected by the enemy,' said the young eagle in an apologetic tone of voice.

'I was pinned down by the Groll's arrow and unable to warn you. The raft sailing across the river to meet you, was attacked by a party of Grolls as it passed close to a strip of land, jutting into the bay. When Grolls and a black hound sprang on board, the men ferrying the raft were terrified. They jumped overboard and swimming downstream found refuge on a small island.'

'Nasty blighters those Grolls,' mumbled Tuffkote, 'attacking unarmed lumbermen.'

'Where is the raft with the Grolls now Theodorus?' asked Crusher

'They ran aground on a rock in the shallow part of the bay. They had planned to ambush you near the dock. I suspect that they are not skilled rafts men but they could come around the point at any time,' cautioned the young eagle.

The Sergeant didn't lose a moment. He picked up Theodorus, put him on his shoulder and walked up to the clearing where the other Dwarves and the Marquis were hiding. He gently placed the eagle upon the forest floor and asked him to tell the men what had happened. Turning to Tuffkote, he motioned him to come along. Seizing his bow, Tuffkote rushed after the Sergeant.

When they returned to the river, they hid amongst a stand of poplars and shrubbery near the water. It was a comfortable spot and shielded them from view.

'The Grolls must be pleased,' muttered Tuffkote, 'Tossing innocent river drivers into the icy current is the kind of thing that turns them on.'

'Quite so Tuffkote. Here they come.'

The raft drifted into sight. On the front stood a hatchet faced Rover in a black leather jacket, his right hand resting on the massive head of a black hound. Grolls were scattered all over the raft. They seemed to be enjoying the September sunshine. Some sat at the back trailing their large flat feet in the cool water of the Sanctus. The raft moved randomly with the current. In the scuffle most of the pike poles had fallen overboard. One huge Groll had salvaged a pole and running from front to back, pushed the raft towards the dock.

'I gathered from Theodorus that they had planned a surprise party for us at the dock. By the great dragon, it is fortunate that we arrived early,' whispered the Sergeant.

'Shall I pick off scarface standing up front?' queried Tuffkote.

'No Tuffy, knock off the black dog first. He is likely to catch our scent.'

Tuffkote pulled an arrow from his quiver and positioned it on the string. The muscles on his arm swelled as he drew back a ninety pound weight. The arrow flew true and seconds later the huge head of the hound hit the water.

The relaxed atmosphere on the raft changed in an instant. The Rover shouted commands and Grolls scrambling over the raft tried to form a defensive position. Unfortunately they had precious little cover. The arrows Tuffkote sent travelled at high velocity and hit true. Four Grolls rolled overboard. Groll archers fired a number of arrows into the dense stand of poplars without doing any damage. Any efforts to steer the raft had ceased and it drifted aimlessly down the river. After the arrows stopped coming, Sergeant Crusher parted the shrubs to take a look. It was clear that the raft was drifting away on the icy waters.

Crusher knew that they must cross the river that very day. The Marquis had only six days left and the trek to the Convent on the other side of the river could take up to five days. He scratched his head and looked at Tuffkote who was staring into the distance.

'Over on the other shore, Sergeant, I see men moving about on a sea of logs.' Sergeant Crusher raised his eyes and looked. Men were racing across a log boom and at the end they loosened a number of logs and began riding them across the river. Skilfully they handled the long pike poles and riding their slippery twirly logs moved swiftly across the water.

A grin spread over the face of the old warrior, 'The river drivers from Esteria.' he sang out. 'They are coming hither.'

The raft carrying the Grolls was well out of bow shot, and the Sergeant and Tuffkote left their hiding place and walked to the water's edge. Dozens of Esterians riding logs converged on the raft. Nimbly they moved their feet to maintain an upright posture, deftly balancing the long pike poles. One tall Esterian, ducking Grolls' arrows approached close to the raft, swung his pole and knocked the archer into the water. The next Groll to raise a bow was knocked out by one of the Esterians, who came along the other side. With the archers gone, the Grolls had to rely on their spears and swords. They didn't stand a chance against the dozen river drivers who had circled the raft. The long pike poles were clad with iron points and the Esterians put them to good use. On all sides Grolls were tumbling into the icy waters. Some tried to seize the logs or even to climb up. The river drivers only laughed and twirled the logs with their feet and sent them swimming.

From shore, Sergeant Crusher and Tuffkote watched the spectacle and cheered the loggers on. The last to go was the Rover. Two pike poles hit him at the same time and he went flying head first.

The Grolls and their commanding officer were carried down the icy current and it was not long before the last of their bobbing heads sank below the surface of the Sanctus.

Two of the river drivers steered their logs ashore. Sergeant Crusher gave them a hearty cheer and told them that the Marquis was lying on a stretcher a few hundred yards back. Other Esterians boarded the now empty raft and poled it quickly to the dock.

Tuffkote had gone back to tell the others what had happened and the Dwarves raised the stretcher onto their shoulders and carried the Marquis down to the river. Before boarding the raft, Sergeant Crusher consulted the river men about young Theodorus. A tall youth stepped forward and volunteered to run the eagle up to the Lake of the Coloured Fishes.

'Very well,' said their foreman, 'Nimbus is a fine runner and one of the other men can cover for him on the river.'

Valkirk offered his backpack of provisions and Sergeant Crusher rushed back into the forest to bring out Theodorus. Carefully he lifted the young eagle onto the runner's shoulder and thanked the wounded bird for all that he had done.

Nimbus was delighted with the challenge. He had always been a first rate runner and here was a chance to put his training to the test and distinguish himself. The Sergeant put some stuffing under the shoulders of his jacket to provide protection from the talons. The Dwarves smiled at the young runner racing up the path. Theodorus was bobbing on his shoulder, his talons anchored firmly to the athlete's jacket.

The Dwarves gently placed the Marquis on the raft and the men pushed off. The Sergeant cast a last look inland as the runner and his feathered charge disappeared over a hill top.

'One of our best runners,' said the foreman, 'he'll be at the homestead of the Gnomes by early morning.'

The raft, now in the hands of skilful river drivers, moved swiftly across the river. Midstream they moored at the small island where the men, dumped by the Grolls, had found refuge. All were helped aboard. On the north shore Ensten and Ulrik heartily welcomed them and Ensten urged Sergeant Crusher and his men to rest and spend the night at their camp.

The Dwarves joined the river men for dinner in the field kitchen. The cook served a roast and Ensten, holding a silver pitcher, went around pouring huckleberry wine. The drama of the long day was the talk of the meal. Wine flowed freely, tongues loosened, and stern Dwarf faces mellowed. Some actually could be heard laughing.

After his men had turned in at the bunk house, Sergeant Crusher stayed up. He sat by the kitchen hearth looking at the dying embers. His face was brooding and he regretted the time that had been lost by leisurely dining and drinking. It was not dwarf like, but then the tension had been high throughout the day and perhaps the men needed to let their hair down. He tried to square off with himself. Alas, Dwarves have this perpetual sense of guilt. That, perhaps makes them the intrepid warriors that they are.

When he went to check on his patient, he could hear the Marquis moaning. He sat down by his bunk and listened. The Marquis had a high fever and was muttering incoherently.

'Dorothea's hands, cold as marble.... I am turning into a toad. Flowers bloom and voices sing.... scents divine drench the senses. Queen Marsha beckons, such beauty cannot broach deception.'

The Sergeant was flummoxed by the feverish blabber of the Marquis. It didn't make much sense. Dwarves knew that pretty faces always meant deception, and Dwarves' senses were never drenched by scents divine, even their women said so. 'Folly and folderol!' muttered the Sergeant.

Ensten woke the Sergeant and his men before dawn. The cook had made pancakes and bacon and the Dwarves joined the lumbermen at the long table in the dining hall. Sergeant Crusher had to tell all that had happened in the last few weeks. When he mentioned Svanhild's kidnapping, a shadow passed over Ensten's face.

It was still dark when Ulrik and Ensten waved farewell to Sergeant Crusher and the stretcher bearers as they began their long climb to the mountain ridge, which they would follow for the next two days, before descending into the Valley of Lost Hope.

The woods north of the Sanctus were a mixture of birch, maple and evergreens, and a smooth path made the going easy. Yet it took four days before Sergeant Crusher spotted the sandstone walls of the great Convent. Relief flooded his heart. They would make it in time with half a day to spare.

The light coloured sandstone of the Convent stood out against the evergreens and the flaming maples. A spacious inner court contained lovely gardens and fruit trees. The corners of the massive structure supported graceful towers.

The north-west tower had a sewing room on the top storey. Since there had been an influx of men bitten by the black dogs, the room was being used for weaving nettle suits. It had been many years since a victim of the tainted fang illness had been brought to the Convent and the Sisters had been shocked, when last spring Oliver Wendell, his left thigh lacerated by the dreaded fangs, arrived at the Convent. His daughter Helga who had accompanied him on the journey, stayed to join the Sisterhood as a lay worker.

Sister Esmeralda, seated in the tower, a nettle suit on her lap, remembered it well. The Convent had been in a flap, for none of the Sisters remembered the cure.

Thank God, the knowledge of the nettle cure for the fateful virus had been preserved in ancient manuscripts. There were no instructions for the weaving of the nettle suits, but Esmeralda and some of the older sisters quickly taught themselves. They weaved the stalks together with the leaves intact and with fine silk thread, fastened the sleeves to the vest. There were plenty of nettles around the Convent. Fortunately, detailed in the ancient text, were all the root extracts and herbal infusions needed for the treatment.

Helga had quickly learned to weave the suits and Esmeralda had grown fond of the Swannemaiden. 'That must be her now,' mused Sister Esmeralda, for the feet treading the stone steps sounded an uneven rhythm. In childhood Helga had suffered a hip injury that had left her with a limp.

Helga's father had made a good recovery, and four months after the attack, he was able to return home. Esmeralda was grateful that Helga had decided to stay behind. She had not yet celebrated her flower festival, but the selfless maiden with the golden tresses had a wisdom far beyond her years. She radiated a quiet joy that cheered patients and Sisters alike. Esmeralda secretly hoped that she would stay and enter the novitiate.

They worked quietly together, sometimes resting their eyes on the red and gold foliage rising to the top of the ridge.

'Something moves among the trees,' burst out Helga, 'it is not a horse and wagon. It appears to be bobbing up and down.'

Sister Esmeralda's sight was poor, but after awhile she too, could see it. 'It is a stretcher, Helga, carried by four short men, Dwarves. They must be Dwarves my love!'

Through a gap in the trees, they could see four stout Dwarves balancing a stretcher on their shoulders trotting down the wide trail as if their lives depended on it. Sister Esmeralda seized the bell rope hanging from the spire. The tolling of the great brass bell announced the arrival of a sick or wounded party. Sisters rushed out to the gate and the great door swung open, just minutes before Sergeant Crusher ran into the courtyard. Panting for air he shouted, 'The Marquis deCygne, felled by a black hound!'

Moments later the stretcher bearers stormed through the gate. Mother Hyacinth, Abbess of the Convent beckoned the Dwarves to follow her. She led them through a long hall to a room at the south end. The Dwarves lowered the stretcher and gently the Sisters moved the Marquis onto a comfortable bed.

Snow white was his face and his eyes were closed. Only after one of the Sisters gave him a powerful restorative did his eyelids move.

Mother Hyacinth invited the Dwarves to the common room. There they found Sergeant Crusher resting by the fireplace. All sat down in the comfortable chairs, arranged in a half circle by the hearth and rested their weary legs on logs standing on end. The Sisters served them bread with cheese and hot malt drinks. After the refreshments, even before they had a chance to light their beloved pipes, the Dwarves dozed off. Only Sergeant Crusher remained awake and told the Sisters of the attack by the hound that had felled the Marquis.

Later in the evening, the Sisters had to help the Dwarves to get up. They could hardly move their leg muscles. They took them to a bedroom, where they tumbled upon the bunks and fell into a deep sleep.

Next morning, it took a lot of stretching before the Dwarves made it to the breakfast table. Mother Hyacinth shared the meal with them and expressed her admiration and gratitude for their gallant efforts to reach the Convent in time. 'An hour later,' she added, 'and the Marquis would have slipped through our hands.'

Other Sisters joined them at the table and after they had finished breakfast, which took a long time, the Dwarves lit their pipes and told the Sisters about their trip. Little news from the outside world found its way to the Convent and the adventures of Sergeant Crusher and the stretcher bearers caused a great flurry of excitement. Esmeralda was worried about Theodorus's wing, but when Sergeant Crusher told the Sisters that the young eagle had been carried to the home of Oarflake and Ambrosia, they were reassured. They already knew of many creatures that had been healed at the little house on the shore of the Lake of the Coloured Fishes.

The Sisters gave the Dwarves a festive send off. Their backpacks were well provisioned and they would stock up again at the logging camp of the Esterians.

Sister Esmeralda and Helga walked into the Marquis's room. He was still in a deep sleep. They took his measurements and decided to finish his nettle suit that evening. The Marquis was the ninth victim of tainted fang and the Sisters knew he should rest before undergoing the shock of donning the fiery nettle suit.

Sister Esmeralda could see that Helga was exhausted and she suggested that they walk to the gardens in the inner court to rest. There would be plenty of time after supper to finish the nettle suit. Arm in arm they sauntered among the shrubs and flower beds and found a seat in a pavilion surrounded by roses. The autumn sun was still warm and Helga dozed off. When she came to a number of girls had gathered around Sister Esmeralda, eager to hear more about the lives of the Sisters of the Secret Crossing.

Eight Swannemaidens had come to the Convent to help in the crisis. Some intended to stay and join the Sisterhood, others, when they could be spared would return to Cascade and the surrounding farms. Yet, all were anxious to know more about the work of the Sisters with the men and women who had come to the Convent to spend their last days before making the transition to the world beyond.

The girls formed a circle around Sister Esmeralda. Helga looked at Kyria sitting beside her. Kyria came from the farm next door. They had been friends since childhood. She knew that Kyria would be entering the novitiate and was keen to learn more about life in the Convent.

'Sister Esmeralda, we have nursed, for months, the victims of tainted fang. When will we learn to work with the dying?'

'Of course Kyria,' laughed Sister Esmeralda, 'that is the true mission of our order. Nursing the victims of tainted fang is a task we have taken on, for no other House of Healing in the Kingdom knows how to the treat the illness. Although we never thought we would be faced with a case of tainted fang again, our Sisterhood kept a record of ancient healing traditions. This scourge will not last my children, I trust peace and prosperity will return to the land.'

'How do you assist souls to cross the great divide Sister Esmeralda?' asked Helga.

'Look around you girls. The men and women resting on the lawn will not be with us long. Our love supports them in these days of transition. Soon they
will bid farewell to their bodies, bodies that served them well on this earthly journey.'

'How they must grieve to part from these faithful companions,' mused Helga.

'It is true Helga, for some it is painful, for others it is a relief to shed a shell that is worn and diseased. When that moment comes, we prepare for our task as spiritual midwives.'

'Sister Esmeralda, what happens when the souls leave their shell? Is it like a rider bidding farewell to a faithful horse?'

'Yes, Kyria. The soul bestows a blessing upon the horse and takes its leave. Whither it goes, the horse cannot follow.'

'But Sister Esmeralda, what happens once the souls fly free? Where do they go and how can you accompany them if they are invisible?'

'Why do you think it takes nine years Kyria to become a Sister of the Secret Crossing? We, too, leave our bodies and in that state we see the souls as clear as crystal. We travel side by side, fingers touching and then enter the secret passage that leads to the other side. We travel with them to the midway point.'

A hush fell over the girls seated at Sister Esmeralda's feet.

'You look puzzled Kyria,' laughed Esmeralda.

'You don't abandon them halfway down the tunnel Sister?'

'It is at midway, my love, that we meet the guides from the other side. There they take over and accompany the souls to the new light.'

'Have you ever travelled beyond the midway point?'

'I have Kyria.'

'One time the Sisters from the other side invited us to travel with them through the remainder of the tunnel. When we came out at the other end, we passed through a portal of light and entered upon the shore of the opal sea. We watched as the souls that we had loved and cared for, were guided aboard a crystal vessel. Swiftly did she course from shore. I remember the faces, once fraught with pain, now radiant and wreathed in laughter.'

A hush fell over the girls gathered around Esmeralda.

'When I become discouraged girls, I recall that vision and find the strength to carry on. Those of you, who intend to join the Sisterhood, will be initiated in the true mission of the Sisters of the Secret Crossing.'

Helga was fascinated by Sister Esmeralda's words. She looked at Kyria, Sophia and the other novices with a touch of envy. They would be entering the novitiate, but she had half promised her mother she would return home. Of course she knew that was not the reason. In the secret chambers of her heart lived the image of Scimitar. She was certain the handsome Dwarf had once loved her and yet he had disappeared without a word. She believed the Dwarf's love for her had not died and that one day he would return. She would stay with the Sisters as long as she was needed for the laborious and painful work of weaving the nettle suits.

Tonight she would be up late, finishing the sleeves for the Marquis' suit. They hoped that by morning he would be well enough to withstand the shock of the burning nettles. Kyria offered to help and after supper they climbed the spiral stairway to the workshop. Sitting side by side, patiently they wove the nettle stalks together. The girls had been given gloves to protect their hands, but often they would drop the gloves and work the fierce plants with bare hands. It was quicker and easier. When they finished their hands were afire and they walked downstairs to the courtyard, to cool them in the pool.

The Marquis deCygne had passed a quiet night. The potions that the Sisters had administered upon his arrival had revived him and he was breathing normally. Sunlight filled his room and he blinked his eyes.

'Marquis deCygne!' exclaimed Sister Ophelia who had spent the night in a rocking chair, by his bedside.

The Marquis opened his eyes and beheld the elderly Sister. His eyes fixed upon her simple head cloth, a white scarf fastened at the back of her head. It covered part of her forehead and showed a golden pin depicting a swan in flight, the emblem of the Sisters who had been initiated into the order of the Secret Crossing. The Marquis, still hazy and confused, recognized the golden pin on Sister Ophelia's headdress and knew that his time was up.

'Have I left this wretched body yet, poisoned by the dreaded fangs?'

'Poisoned, Marquis, but not beyond recovery.'

'The nettle suit,' sighed the nobleman.

'It is almost finished my dear fellow, do not despair.'

'I do despair dear Sister, what good is all this suffering?'

'It purifies the soul, Marquis.'

'It is undignified. There must be better ways to purify the soul, dear Sister. If I do recover I shall enter holy orders and meditate on the matter,' sighed the Marquis.

He sank back upon his pillows and lost consciousness. Two hours later Esmeralda entered the sick room followed by Helga carrying the nettle suit. The window stood open and a warm autumn breeze rustled the nettle leaves.

At the touch of Helga's hand, the Marquis awoke. Opening his eyes he beheld the rustling leaves. 'By the teeth of the Great Dragon,' shouted the nobleman, 'that it should come to this!'

Helga deftly removed the covers and slipped on the nettle trousers. Esmeralda pulled the vest over his head and the sleeves up his arms and Helga fastened them to the vest. At first fatigue and shock protected him from the burning of the leaves, but it was not long before he woke to the pain.

Slowly the Marquis' face turned red as the fiery nettles secreted the sap under his skin and a vibration running through his limbs restored him to full consciousness. The sensation of burning was overwhelming, yet at the same time hope sprang up within. When he sat up in bed, Helga turned around, picked up the nettle headdress and pressed it halfway down his forehead. The whole operation was so smooth that within minutes the astounded nobleman had been transformed into a huge green bird in full plumage.

'My apologies Marquis,' said the Swannemaid, 'this completes your outfit and will speed your recovery.'

The Marquis cast a strange look at the women standing around him, and with a sigh of resignation, leaned back upon his pillow. Helga watched him closely and was astonished to see a broad smile spread over his countenance.

The Marquis tormented by the burning nettles and the indignities heaped upon his person, hit bottom. Once more, wholly unexpectedly, the hero hidden in the depth of his psyche rose to the fore and The Marquis laughed out loud.

'Helga,' said the nobleman who remembered the Swannemaiden from earlier times, 'fetch me a mirror.'

Helga slipped away and returned with a mirror. She set it up at the end of the bed. When the Marquis raised himself and saw his face red as a tomato in a wreath of green nettle leaves, laughter cascaded through the room. The Sisters standing around couldn't help themselves and joined in. For a moment mirth prevailed.

The head piece had provided the finishing touch. Seeing the nettle leaves aquiver from head to toe, he heaved with laughter. Sister Ophelia knew that the upsurge of spirit would ebb again, but she rejoiced that the Marquis had gained the first victory in his long and uphill battle.

For two days he managed to cope with the pain, but as he gained strength, he became restless. On the seventh day they brought him a new nettle suit to maintain a steady flow of secretions into his blood stream. For the first few hours he put on a cheerful front and seemed to have reached a kind of equilibrium. The Sisters withdrew quietly but Helga stayed, she wanted to be there when his spirits ebbed and the fire of the nettles overwhelmed him.

It was afternoon when the Marquis awoke from a restless sleep. The calming draft of valerian which Sister Ophelia had given him subdued no longer, the waves of fire that leaped around him. Helga looked at his purple face and knew that a crisis was brewing.

Suddenly he jumped out of bed shouting, 'The end is at hand. A deCygne does not die in bed. Out into the field my friends. Death or Glory!'

He rushed down the hall, seized a poker in passing and burst into the courtyard. With superhuman strength he opened the heavy gate and ran into the fields behind the Convent.

The old badger Olaf was sunning himself before his front door when the green apparition flew by declaiming, 'The end is near, Glory be.' There was only one thing to do. He jumped inside shouting, 'Ragnar open the door to the secret tunnel, it is all over. The ancient prophecies of doom have come true. The green fiends have taken over!'

The Marquis ran onwards down the fields, towards the ravine behind the building. The Sisters watching from the window were horrified as they saw him rushing down the slope.

The hares Philip and Alexander had wandered down to the Valley of Lost Hope for a track meet. The sight of the Convent's veggie garden had proved too much of a temptation. They were enjoying a lunch break of fresh carrots, lifted quietly from the garden, when the Marquis flew by with his green plumage streaming in the wind.

'Heaven help us,' cried Alexander, 'a monster.'

'Prehistoric,' rejoined his cousin Philip, who had read some natural history. 'We could trip it and donate it to the museum in Lambarina.'

The hares shot forward at phenomenal speed, overtook the Marquis and blocked his path. He tumbled and came to a stop at the edge of the ravine. His headdress had fallen off and parts of his nettle suit were in tatters.

The hares shook their heads when they saw the creature lying in the tall grass. What was the world coming to?

Soon they heard the shuffling of many feet and when they saw curtain of white skirts moving through the tall grass they panicked and Alexander prepared for take off, but Philip raised his paw and held him back.

'It is not about carrots, Alexander. It is the green phenomenon that they are after.'

The Marquis, half dazed, was sitting up when the Sisters arrived. The foray into the meadow had depleted his energy and when the Sisters gently coached him back to his room, he did not object. They administered a sedative and before long he fell into a deep sleep. The Sisters repaired his nettle suit and prayed that he would accept his cure.

Sister Esmeralda stayed behind and to the startled hares explained the strange appearance. She thanked them for their presence of mind in stopping the Marquis before he dived into the ravine. Well she knew who had stolen the carrots from the convent garden, but this was not the time to bring up the matter. 'Even veggie stealers can play a part in the plan of the creative force,' she mused, as she walked back to the convent.

29

Return To Cascade

Spring had come to the Sanctus. The sinking sun highlighted birch and maple buds near the shore and Svanhild's reflection in the water was veiled in a reddish hue. The calm surface of the black water was deceptive, for swift currents flowed deep below.

Svanhild had begun her descent to the great river, skipping light-heartedly over the frozen ground but by late morning the crisp path had turned into a muddy soup. When swift brooks blocked her path she was forced to follow the shore until an easy fording could be made. Thank goodness, no merewings or Grolls were anywhere in sight. Reassured by the cheery woodpecker's message, Svanhild had been happy to contend only with the trials of nature.

It was near dusk when she reached the waters of the Sanctus. If it had been daylight, the river drivers would have spotted her. At night they retired to the bunkhouses on the north shore.

An occasional ray of moonlight showed the camp's outline and the glow of fires was reflected in the windows. Svanhild ate the last of the smoked meat that Ambrosia had dropped in her backpack and filled her cup with water from the Sanctus.

Ensten and Ulrik, who supervised the logging operation, had their own cabin. Ulrik, exhausted from the day's work, already was asleep. Flames from the fireplace and a couple of candles lit the small table where Ensten was patiently chipping away at a block of wood, slowly revealing a swan in flight. He couldn't help thinking about Svanhild's captivity.

While his mind went back to Svanhild, his eyes wandered around the cabin and came to rest on the carving of the laughing elven child. To the sombre face of the lonely woodsman, it brought a smile.

He picked up his fine chisel and the chips began to fly. As he worked away he recalled the words of the Dwarves. Their scouts had reported the mobilization of armies on the other side of the Finnian Range and they feared an attack in the spring.

Last fall, Sergeant Crusher and his men, carrying the Marquis to the Convent, had spent the night at the camp. The Sergeant had recounted Edel's tale about the Mole Confederacy. Ensten had been fascinated to hear of splendid tunnels lit by torches, the well furnished apartments and the moles' love of music. When Sergeant Crusher came to the elven children living with the moles, Ensten had looked at the carving of the laughing elven child, standing on the mantel piece and wondered. The candles began flickering and he put away his chisels.

Leaning back in his chair, he looked at the fleeting moonlight on the river. A peal of laughter stirred him from his reverie. He swung around and in front of the glowing embers stood the elven child, her face wreathed in smiles.

'Ensten,' sounded a gentle voice.

It was the first time that the elven child had called him by name. He was startled. 'You have the gift of speech, child.'

'Spirits speak, like all beings endowed with intelligence,' explained the elven child as she turned around and looked at the carving on the mantelpiece.

'I am flattered Ensten.' she laughed. 'You are an artist.'

'Thank you, elven child. Tell me your name.'

'I am Elmira the youngest of three sisters.'

'It is you who live in the tunnels of the Mole Confederacy?'

'My sisters and I were raised by the moles, Ensten. They are our godparents. They found us in the forest at the time of the rebellion and raised us in their splendid underground dwellings.'

'Yet your spirit travels beyond the underworld,' ventured Ensten, a look of wonder in his eyes.

'It was a gift from the enchantress Amaranth. We were seated by the fountain looking up at the stream of water rising to the centre of the great dome and falling in silver droplets; then I saw her. She floated gently down in front of us, and speaking in a sweet voice, told us how pleased she was to find us safe and thriving in the Federation of the Moles. She said that we must be grateful for the protection of the Moles. Elven children had been kidnapped by the servants of the Seven, for the Dark Lords took serious the myth that words voiced by an elven child could threaten their reign.'

'An elven child,' mused Ensten, 'innocence and laughter would multiply the force of an incantation.'

He marvelled at her story. Reading his thoughts Elmira continued.

'The enchantress made each of us a gift before she left. My older sister Annabelle received the gift of music, my middle sister Galatea, beauty; and then she turned to me and said, "You, Elmira will have the gift of spirit travel so that you may see the world above. Your laughter will cheer the sorrowful and bring to those who dwell in darkness, a sparkle of joy." Elmira exuded glee but the fine outline of her face began to soften and diminish. Before Ensten realized it, Elmira had vanished from sight, but her laughter lingered. Then her voice rang true and clear, 'Do not get lost in your carving Ensten. Cast a look across the river.'

For a few moments he remained seated, his gaze fixed upon the place where the elven child had stood. Then her parting words sank in, and striding over to the window, he scanned the dark waters of the Sanctus. On the distant shore he spotted the faint glow of dying embers. It was dangerous to step into the darkness, yet he believed Elmira must have had a reason for mentioning the far shore.

Dressing warmly, he ventured out to the water's edge, jumped into his small skiff and poled the frail vessel through the bulrushes. Once in deep water, he lowered the oars on the locks and under his powerful strokes, the skiff shot ahead. He moored at a small dock a few hundred feet from the glowing logs and drawing closer saw the silhouette of a slender figure seated by the fire. A passing ray of moonlight caught the traveller's silver tresses. A tremor swept the woodcarver's body. The visitor was a maiden from the Land of the Swans. Ensten knew in his heart that the mysterious stranger was the Swannemaid who he had fancied in Miranda. Svanhild must have escaped Matista's magic web.

So as not to frighten her, he whispered softly, 'Svanhild, it is Ensten calling. Welcome to the river camp.' Svanhild, waking with a start, saw the tall woodcarver standing by a birch tree.

'It is you Ensten. Bless my heart. I prayed that my fire would be seen.' Ensten took her hand and bade her welcome. Hand in hand they walked to the shore and boarded the skiff. Svanhild watched Ensten as he propelled the craft across the water and rejoiced that their paths had crossed once more.

Ensten poled the vessel through a narrow channel where Ulrik was waiting for them. Surprised and delighted to see Ensten in the company of Svanhild, he stepped into the cold water and lifted her to safety. Ulrik had rekindled the fire and the cabin was filled with light and warmth. He brought out smoked meat and spice tea and they talked long into the night. Ensten and Ulrik were not surprised to hear that an assault by the armies of the Dark Lords was being planned. They had noticed that fewer Rovers and Grolls were about, and that merewings were seldom to be seen.

The brothers looked at each other. They knew that they must return to Esteria to help prepare the defence of their town. Once the dark armies crossed the Finnian Range, Esteria would not be spared. Svanhild looked worried.

'Will the armies of the Lords lay siege to Esteria before turning to the Kingdom, Ensten?'

'I doubt not that they will, Esteria is a strategic town on the way to the Kingdom. They wouldn't risk bypassing it.'

'Will you call on Leonardo and ask for the support of the Great Grey?'

'It is not a question of asking Leonardo to stand by, Svanhild. Leonardo is all too keen. It is matter of restraining the great wolf and his team mates, until they can be of the most use. Leonardo is always anxious to jump into the fray,' laughed Ensten.

'I am on my way back to Cascade to warn the Council gathered at the Manor deCygne. It is urgent that they learn of all the recent events. No time is to be lost. I shall leave early in the morning,' decided Svanhild.

'I will travel with you as far as the ridge of the mountain range that will take you to the Valley of Lost Hope.' Svanhild cast Ensten a grateful glance.

It was long after midnight when she dropped upon her bunk. A wayward beam of moonlight caught her face and for the first time in many months the stern lines around her eyes relaxed and a smile played on her lips. Strange, she thought, Ensten and I haven't spoken much to each other, but it is being with him that brings me a sense of peace.

The next morning they took their time over breakfast. When sunlight had flooded the riverbank, Svanhild and Ensten shouldered their packs and bid Ulrik farewell.

The ground was firm and setting a good pace, they hiked up the mountain path. Sometimes on a steep incline of rocky ground, Ensten would take Svanhild's hand and guide her up. She felt a bond with Ensten. Destiny had linked them in some mysterious way. Deep in her heart, she knew that if they both survived these times of trials, their friendship might catch fire. This was not the time to dream. Turmoil and danger lay ahead. Any links forged now might later be severed by the sword. Neither of them spoke about their feelings. First they must traverse the dangerous ledge that loomed ahead. At the top of the ridge, it was a formal handshake that parted Ensten and Svanhild. Only their eyes spoke a different tale.

There was a song in Svanhild's heart as she skipped merrily along the ridge and in the steps of the woodcarver there was a spring as he loped down the mountain towards the waters of the Sanctus.

Dusk lingered in the Valley of Lost Hope and the Sisters of the Secret Crossing had settled their patients for the night. Sister Esmeralda and Helga sat in the dining hall of the Convent, their feet stretched towards the fireplace. Esmeralda had insisted that she take the evening off for Helga's hands were badly swollen from nettle stings.

Two more men had been brought in with tainted fang disease. Helga had worked long hours in the tower room, weaving nettle suits.One of the victims was Joris Goldfinger, the very leader of Cascade's business community, who had advocated collaboration with the enemy. Joris Goldfinger had prospered and built a splendid mansion. The locals had never seen anything like it, the shingles were slate from the land of the Gnomes, exotic fruits grew in a solarium and black swans sailed gracefully on a pond surrounded by flower gardens.

Grudgingly, the villagers had admitted that old Joris did have an eye for beauty. That impression was strengthened when comely ladies were seen travelling down the river to visit the Goldfinger mansion. Often Rovers would join the party and the people of Cascade were convinced that the Goldfinger residence, for all its charm, had turned into a den of iniquity. Voices muttered that such evil would not go unpunished.

The Rovers, who had been courteous at first, became more and more demanding. They requisitioned part of the new mansion to quarter their

Grolls and simply ignored Joris's protests. Black hounds ran amok in the gardens and killed the Swans. Joris made the mistake of tossing a rock at one of the brutes. The animal stopped in his track and gave him a cold stare. He bent down to pick up another rock, but before he could throw it, huge jaws seized his arm and fangs sank deep into his flesh. The pain was fierce, but worse was the laughter of the Rovers, the very men with whom he had collaborated. When the good people of Cascade loaded Joris onto a covered wagon, that was to take him to the Convent of the Sisters in the Valley of Lost Hope, pain and guilt had overwhelmed him.

To soothe the burning of the nettles Helga dipped her hands into a bowl of aloevera juice. She wondered about Joris Goldfinger. Even if he did survive, after everything that had happened, it would be difficult for him to return to Cascade.

Throughout the long winter Helga had spent many hours at the Marquis deCygne's bed side. Often she would sing to him to sooth the pain of the burning nettles or tell stories to distract his mind. When the burning became intolerable she would administer a sleeping potion. The nobleman had made a good recovery. He had been out of his nettle suit for several months now and soon would be able return to the Manor deCygne.

The Marquis rejoiced at the first signs of spring and was anxious to go home. He joined Sister Esmeralda and Helga in the hall. Since he had shed his nettle suit, the stay at the convent had been quite pleasant. The Sisters were good listeners and the Marquis was more than willing, to relate his adventures, all of which gained a good deal in the telling. The story of Dorothea's petrification had made the rounds in the Convent and for his tragic loss, Ferdinand deCygne had received a great deal of sympathy from the Sisters. It had softened the edges of his grief.

'I think there is still hope Marquis,' said Sister Esmeralda, 'I have talked to the Sisters who work on the other side, Dorothea has not been seen on the shore of the opal sea, her spirit may yet linger in the palace of Queen Marsha.'

The Marquis frowned and his mind travelled back to the palace of the Queen of the Marshes. That place of worldly delights had been almost his undoing. Had it not been for Dorothea, he would have been turned into a green toad, along with Duckie and Moose Martin.

In his mind's eye he could see Dorothea sitting by the spinning wheel, her delicate foot pushing the treadle, and golden tresses reaching to her waist.

'Golden no more,' he whispered to himself, 'White ice-cold marble.'

Helga's sharp ear caught the whisper and she knew that his mind was back at the palace. While still in his nettle suit and shivering with fever, often he had talked of the tragedy that had befallen his Dorothea.

'You must forgive and forget Ferdinand deCygne,' soothed Helga.

'Forgive myself,' retorted the Marquis a deep frown shading his face. 'It was I who fell for the regal beauty of the Queen of the Marshes, such beauty I believed could only be capable of good. In my innocence I believed that beauty and truth walked hand in hand.'

'It is not so Ferdinand deCygne,' smiled Helga and sang an old rhyme from Swanneland.

> *when beauty's eye caught*
> *pride's golden sheen*
> *she threw a parting kiss*
> *where truth had been*

The Marquis could not help but smile at Helga's wisdom, so far beyond her years. Looking into his eyes, Helga laid a hand on the Marquis's arm.

'Ferdinand deCygne, do not despair. You have regained your health, and soon you will travel home. In my heart I know that your Dorothea is not lost for ever.'

'Lost to me in this world,' sighed the nobleman. It would have been better had I left this mortal coil and followed the Sisters on their crossing to the other side.' A melodramatic look spread across his face as he rested his head in his hands and stared into the flames.

'You must never say that Marquis.' Helga spoke now in a stern voice. 'It was meant that you recover your health and follow your destiny. Is it not possible that the frightful curse of the Queen of the Marshes will be lifted? May not an incantation be found to undo the evil? In a few days you will be back at the Manor deCygne. I think Lady Erica will be able to help for she is learned in mystic lore.' The Marquis rejoiced at the thought of being reunited with his aunt, the Lady Erica de Coscoroba.

He walked to the mirror at the far end of the hall and took a good look at himself. Few at the manor would recognize his emaciated features. He was pleased. Gone was the pudgy nobleman and standing now in the glass was a heroic figure, a true knight, purified through the fire of suffering. Henceforth he would walk the path of self-denial. He might even enter holy orders in one of the Monasteries. The new persona of the tragic hero suited him and his arrival at the Manor would stir pity and admiration. With a contented look on his face, the Marquis returned to his chair and dozed off.

Helga went back to the workshop in the tower. Before settling down to weaving yet another nettle suit, she scanned the path leading to the mountain ridge. She espied a slight figure hurrying to the Convent. Moonlight caught the stranger's silver tresses and Helga knew it was a Swannemaiden who had celebrated her flower festival.[8]

The Marquis, when he was in bouts of delirium, had often talked about his fellow travellers. Surely this lone maiden must be Svanhild, sister to Slim, the ballet master. She had met them both at festivals in Cascade. She rushed down the stairs as quickly as her damaged hip would allow, walked through the courtyard and using all her strength, pushed open the gate. Svanhild ran through the archway, straight into Helga's arms.

'Welcome Svanhild,' burst out Helga, 'The Dwarves told us about your captivity. What a relief to see you safe and sound.'

'Helga Wendell, you have joined the Sisters of the Secret Crossing.' exclaimed Svanhild in surprise.

'Not yet, Svanhild, I am working as a lay sister, weaving nettle suits for victims of the black hounds.'

Svanhild cast her a questioning look. Helga understood. 'The Marquis, he is alive and well. The good Dwarves brought him here in time for the treatment. I will take you to him.'

Holding Svanhild's hand, Helga led her to the great hall. Svanhild barely recognized the haggard figure asleep in an easy chair near the hearth. When she drew close, the Marquis awoke, and at the sight of the Swannemaid, rose up.

'Svanhild, what a joy to see you safe and sound.'

'Thank heaven, Ferdinand deCygne, you reached the Convent in time and recovered from that dreadful attack.'

'Thanks to the Dwarves and the Sisters here.'

Several of the Sisters gathered around to welcome Svanhild. Many questions were on their lips, but they could see that Svanhild's eyelids were heavy with weariness. Helga took her to a guest room. Svanhild lay down upon one of the beds and before she had a chance to undress, fell asleep.

---

8   *After Swannemaids celebrated their flower festival at the age of twenty seven, their hair turned silver and their hand could be sought in marriage.*

Next morning, in the dining hall, Helga joined her for breakfast.

'I must leave this morning Helga, it is urgent that I reach Cascade.'

'In three days time the wagon train will arrive with supplies and the Marquis will be travelling back on it. Wait until then. You would not arrive any sooner, if you were to leave on foot this morning.'

Svanhild volunteered to help in the Convent, but the Sisters would not hear of it. At night they gathered around her and Svanhild's tales took them far away from their daily chores and the world of the Convent. They met the old biddy Neva at the Golden Goose in Miranda and watched Slim directing the dancing Swans in the harbour.

Through her tales they travelled with Svanhild up the Sanctus to the splendid water gardens of the Queen of the Marshes and learned how Dorothea's sacrifice had saved the Marquis and his friends from turning into toads. Svanhild told of her capture by the Grolls near the cabin of the Sisters of the Third Woe. A sigh of horror could be heard, for the Sisters had seen the deep scars on her wrists and realized the terrible force of the Grolls' lobster claws.

You could hear a pin drop when she took the Sisters to the Chateau of the great enchantress and told of the Mirror of a Thousand Fragments. When she skated to freedom across Fireweed Lake, there was a sigh of relief and many lips whispered a prayer of praise and thanksgiving.

'Wonderful that you learned to skate on the lakes above Cascade,' sighed Sister Esmeralda, 'How often do innocent pastimes in childhood serve us in later life?'

'That was not the end of it Sister,' Svanhild explained in a halting voice, 'It was Isumatak who forestalled my capture on the way to the Lake of the Coloured Fishes. If it had not been for the help of the Abbot of the Monastery in Esteria my escape would have been foiled. When Matista and her handmaidens crossed the frozen lake I thought all was lost. Then Isumatak summoned the hosts of light.

The Sisters were thrilled. What strange and astonishing events were afoot. The slender figure in the centre of their group was not a dwarf warrior or a male knight relating his forays into danger. It was a woman like themselves, some one who had lived through these perils and returned to tell the tale. The heroine sitting in the centre of the circle was a maiden from the Land of the Swans.

A ripple of excitement spread through the group. 'A harbinger of the new age,' exulted Esmeralda. Many were the questions the Sisters asked and it was well after midnight when they escorted Svanhild to her room.

Svanhild's story had given the Sisters a new vision. With new hope and joy, they returned to their work.

'It is true,' said Sister Esmeralda to Helga and Kyria, 'we are far removed from the world in this Convent, in the Valley of Lost Hope, yet we are part of it. We are here to shepherd the heroes and heroines that complete that frightful, joyous journey across the stage of life. We are here for them at the end of that journey and to help them make a gracious exit and enter that other world of the spirit.'

Before Svanhild realized it, she had been at the Convent for two days. Early on the third day, she saw the covered wagon with supplies pull into the courtyard. It was a lovely spring morning and leaves were sprouting from the birch trees on the hillside. She felt rested and refreshed.

When Svanhild and the Marquis climbed onto the box, the Sisters and the lay workers gathered in the courtyard to bid them farewell. The driver was eager to get going and the horses strained their hind legs to move the wagon up the steep trail leading to the mountain ridge.

Another day and they would be home, reunited with friends and family at the Manor deCygne. Joy sang in Svanhild's heart. The days at the Convent had restored her energy and her natural cheer. The Marquis and Svanhild turned around and caught a last glimpse of the Sisters waving, just before the wagon entered a hairpin curve and vanished from sight.

The hares Philip and Alexander were seated on a tree trunk nibbling fiddleheads when the wagon passed.

'My word Alexander, the chap on the wagon, it is the face of the dragon we tripped last fall just before he fell into the ravine,' shouted Phillip.

'Lost his green scales poor fellow. Summer is coming and he is moulting already,' reflected his cousin philosophically.

30

Swannemen Arise

$\mathcal{T}$he morning sun cast a golden veil over the thatched roofs of the cottages in Cascade. Svanhild nudged the Marquis and startled him out of his nap. He looked dazed but his eyes brightened when he saw, nestled between the waters of the Sanctus and the Frivoli, the ancestral Manor of the deCygnes. The houses, painted in all the colours of the rainbow, always delighted travelers approaching town.

Svanhild's heart skipped a beat at the sight of her beloved home town. The driver, casting a sideways glance at his passengers, shook his head. 'Cascade is not what it used to be, my friends.' Svanhild turned to him with a query in her eyes. 'Ah, my lass,' mumbled the old reinsman, 'you have been away for a year. Things have changed and not for the better.'

Sunlight played gaily on the Beechway, the town's main artery. The smell of freshly baked loaves drifted from the bakery and Svanhild recalled the many times she had spent at the bake shop meeting friends over coffee and croissants. But the moment that she looked at people's faces, her joy was dimmed. Few bothered to look up when they passed.

'Sad business ma'am,' muttered the carter, 'used to be a lively town. Now folks are divided into different camps.'

They passed a Rover walking his black pet in the company of Dennis Mintpalm. Svanhild knew that some folks in the town had thrown in their lot with the agents of the Seven. No doubt they must have been bribed or intimidated. Fear and suspicion veiled now the faces of the once easy going and openhearted burghers.

It was likely a few Swannefolk had accepted as inevitable the Lordship of the Seven. Perhaps they had abandoned hope of successful opposition. Svanhild's heart sank.

She looked at the canopy of beech branches that formed an arch over the street. Sunlight dancing on the trembling dome of leaves evoked scenes from her childhood and she recalled dancing and singing with her playmates on the Beechway. At the end of the Beechway they turned up Hazelnut Lane. Wild roses, splashing dabs of red on the green foliage had sprung up among the hazelnuts. Roses, birds in song, how strange and wonderful it felt after a year of hardship in the northern forests to be back in this gentle valley, lush and verdant.

The mist had lifted on the hills and the Manor deCygne stood out against the blue sky. The Marquis beheld the sight and his face lit up. He returned home, battle scarred, a warrior who had reduced to shards, a dozen Grolls. No longer would the Knights of yore in their golden frames chuckle when he walked in.

Martha, the blind prophetess, and Svanhild's mother Annabelle were seated on the terrace. Annabelle was knitting a sweater for Slim, when Martha laid her hand on her arm and the needles came to rest.

'Annabelle,' whispered the ancient one, 'Svanhild is near. Her aura shines in the darkness that surrounds me.'

Annabelle seized Martha's hand and looked at the garden gate. Nothing could be seen. However in the lower garden Martha's bear, Grumpuss, had become restless. He raised himself on his hind legs, sniffed the air and catching an unfamiliar scent, lumbered to the garden gate. Martha picked up a faint creaking of wagon wheels. She took Annabelle by the hand. 'Come, my love we'll walk to the rose garden.'

The wagon was just passing through the gate when Annabelle and Martha reached the pavilion. The horses stopped short of the rose beds. Svanhild, seeing her mother and Martha amidst the flowers, jumped off the wagon and in a flash found herself in her mother's arms.

Grumpuss bear poked his head inside the covered wagon and looked for possible intruders. A look at his mistress convinced the mighty bear that none of the black-souled rascals were on board. Disappointed, he waddled down the garden. Tossing the Rovers into the dense bramble patches had been one of his joys, but there were few left now and they avoided the Manor.

Lady Erica, attracted by the voices on the lawn, stepped outside. When she beheld Ferdinand talking to the carter, she felt a wave of relief. The moment he became aware of her, he took leave of the good reinsman and strode across the lawn. She caught him in her outstretched arms. After the first greetings, she stepped back and looked at him. The pudgy, middle-aged bachelor of yore was gone. Was this really her nephew Ferdinand standing before her? There was barely enough flesh on him to keep his bones from rattling. A deep melancholy dwelt in his eyes. It was clear that the loss of his beloved Dorothea and the attack by the tainted fangs had exacted a frightful toll.

The Elves Silfida and Sidonia attracted by the jubilant voices, hastened outside. Svanhild was sitting with her mother in the pavilion when she descried the Elves lightly skipping across the garden. Silfida walked up to Svanhild and gently took her hand. At her touch, Svanhild felt an immediate flow of energy. She looked at the sea blue elven eyes and felt a bond with this stranger whom she had never met before. A bond stronger than with friends of yore. Sidonia brought a gift of silverwork and presented it on behalf of Queen Orchidae. It was a pendant, a swan carved in black soap stone and mounted in silver. When Sidonia slipped the silver chain over her head, Svanhild flushed with pleasure.

A merry tune floated on the air and the whistling Secretary of the Outlanders arrived. While carrying on his musical serenade, he made a polite bow. Svanhild accepted it all in good grace.

The Gnomes Gritt and Gneis, too, joined the welcoming party in the rose garden. Svanhild surrounded by friends and family, drank in the beauty of the gardens. It all seemed so overwhelming. Why ever had she left? But she knew that there was that other part of her, that longing for adventure and the unknown, tugging her away from all that she loved so well.

Lady Erica took Svanhild's hand and together they walked to the terrace, below the sun porch. She sensed that Svanhild had urgent tidings and cast at her an enquiring look.

'You must have heard, Lady Erica that nearly all the Rovers and their Grolls have left. It is not that the Seven have given up their designs, they are massing their armies to overrun the Kingdom.'

'I had suspected as much Svanhild. Gazing at the waters of the black pool I beheld armies storming the Finnian Range. Let us wait until after lunch and then tell the Council all that happened.'

She suggested to Svanhild and Ferdinand that they rest first before joining the others for a light meal in the sunroom. They wouldn't hear of it.

Seated among friends, on a comfortable chair, the Marquis began to unwind. His eyes wandered from the splendid paintings of swans to a rack displaying a number of his finest pipes. Heavens above, he hadn't tasted tobacco in months. After the meal, he would light up.

Most of the members of the Council had joined them at board. Only the Gnome Gritt was missing for it was his turn to do guard duty in the lower garden. Volker was still whistling and only when food appeared, did he halt his musical serenade. Fortunately the Marquis had heard about the eccentric musical secretary and appreciated the unusual tribute on his return.

Lady Erica told Svanhild and Ferdinand that Queen Tuluga of the Mountain Fairies had spent a few days at the Manor to consult with the Council.

'We are grateful to Queen Tuluga for sending her scouts Edel and Weiss to our aid,' said Svanhild. The Fairies are wonderfully swift and quick-witted and without Weiss, the rescue of Captain Martin, Ferdinand and Duckie would not have been possible.'

It was just as well that the Marquis was out of earshot. The episode at the palace was a painful reminder of human foibles and the loss of his beloved Dorothea. He had just lit his favourite pipe and as he sank into an easy chair, a look of bliss appeared on his stern countenance. Gneiss and Volker pulled their pipes out and filled them with the excellent tobacco that the Gnomes had grown in their gardens. A soft and fragrant aroma filled the sun porch.

After luncheon the members of the Council seated themselves at the round table in the hall at the head of the stairs. Silfida welcomed Svanhild and the Marquis into their midst and gave thanks for their safe return.

When Svanhild told of the conversation between the Rover Captain and his servant Scaly, it dawned on the company that events had taken a dramatic turn. The trouble they had seen paled before the appalling fate awaiting them. The Kingdom might be flooded by murdering Grolls from the realm of the Seven.

'The danger is greater than we thought,' sighed Lady Erica. Secretary Volker took his pen out of his mouth and whistled a mournful tune. After a moment of silence Lady Erica spoke.

'The Seven attempted to control the Kingdom by murdering the King and kidnapping his daughter, Yaconda, our beloved Princess and heiress to the throne. They sent Rovers to buy the cooperation of our people, and yet all they accomplished was to bring division and chaos into the land. Resistance groups are forming in Lambarina and the villages along the river. Rovers and their dogs have been attacked in some towns. The Seven Lords have learned that they cannot gain control by stealth and now they plan to march their armies through the passes in the Finnian Range and occupy the Kingdom.'

The Elves, Sidonia and Silfida, were terribly upset. They had always resorted to prayer and meditation to settle conflict and hoped that prayer could now forestall this wave of violence approaching the Kingdom. For Elves, a call to arms represented a desperate gesture.

Lady Erica cast the Elves a loving look. She admired the elven maidens and their abhorrence of violence. If prayer and creative visualization could not forestall the suffering and violence looming on the horizon, at least it would shorten it.

Lady Erica motioned to Silfida to take them through the spiritual exercises the Elves practised so faithfully. Silfida closed her eyes and asked the friends to join hands and to send thoughts of peace towards the Land of Darkness, beyond the Finnian Range. Silfida chanted, 'Oh Spirit of the Ages carry a message of peace on waves of light. Let it penetrate the heart of darkness and heal the lesions that divide.'

They closed their eyes and remained quiet. After a few minutes Lady Erica looked at Silfida, whose face had turned a deadly white.

Sidonia spoke first, 'Alas, a field of energy surrounds the minds of the Seven. The messages that we sent, bounced back. Our thoughts cannot penetrate their shield.'

All had hoped that all out war would never happen. Now it seemed that nothing could stop a massive attack on the Kingdom. The prospect was frightening.

'The armies will try to defeat the Dwarves in the passes on the Finnian Range,' reflected Lady Erica, 'If they break through, they will take Esteria and then sweep down upon the Kingdom. It would be difficult to send men into the high mountains but we must ask for volunteers to aid in the defence of Esteria.'

'The Esterians are preparing their town for an attack' said Svanhild, 'They could quarter and train Gnomes, Elves, Outlanders, Mountain

Fairies and Swannefolk who can find their way up to their enclave.'

'Then we must send a message to Queen Tuluga of the Mountain Fairies. Her pelicans will take the news to other parts of the Kingdom.' suggested Lady Erica.Members of the Council nodded in agreement. Silfida and Sidonia looked grief-stricken. Yet they knew that now the evil confronting them could only be met by force.

'How can we send a message to Queen Tuluga?' asked Secretary Volker.

'I will fetch Slim's lead swan, Limonides,' replied Svanhild. He will gladly undertake the mission. Limonides and the dancing swans have been boarded at Uncle Svend's farm. I will go across the river and speak to him.

'I think it would be best my dear,' encouraged Annabelle, 'with Slim away in the mountains, I doubt Limonides would listen to anybody else.'

Volker stood up and volunteered to row her across the Sanctus. Svanhild did not know whether Volker had much boating skill, but the eccentric secretary certainly would be good company.

After Svanhild and Volker took their leave, Lady Erica wrote a message to warn of the approaching danger and ended with a request to send volunteers to Esteria. Queen Tuluga's pelicans would relay the messages to the Elves, Gnomes, and Outlanders.

The Marquis had said little thus far. Sending a fine ring of smoke on its way to the ceiling, he reflected, 'It would be wise for the warriors to trek to Esteria. In the village of the Dwarves, there is no space for them, and to wage war on the alpine meadows and the mountain passes takes the kind of skill and endurance that only Dwarves possess. Esteria can offer accommodation and a training base. It will take the enemy time to prepare their armies. Nobody knows when they will strike. If there is time the Dwarves will attempt to rescue their commander Scimitar, imprisoned in the mines below the Black Peak.'

The company had retired to the sun porch when Limonides made a graceful landing on the lawn. Lady Erica went into the garden to welcome him. Shortly afterwards, Svanhild and Volker returned and Lady Erica handed Svanhild a small container to fasten around Limonides' neck. Stroking his feathers, she whispered words of encouragement.

The great wings moved, a rush of air fluttered Svanhild's tresses, Limonides was airborne. Gracefully he soared towards the dark green ribbon of spruce, north of the Manor. As they watched the white wings rise on an updraft, Lady Erica put her arm around Svanhild's shoulder. They soon lost sight of the swan, but the Elves watched him speed for miles above the ridge and in the ancient elven tongue, whispered a prayer for his safe arrival.

After supper, all gathered by the open hearth in the great entry hall. The atmosphere was more relaxed there and Svanhild shared some of her adventures. Throughout the year, bits of news had reached the Manor, but for the friends seated around the fire it was a special thrill to follow Svanhild on her fearful, wondrous journey.

The Lady Erica was astonished to hear of the Mirror of a Thousand Fragments in the Chateau of Matista and the glass sliver showing the presence of Sea Gnomes on the Eastern Ocean. Was there a remote chance that the long lost golden tablet was resting on the ocean floor?

When Svanhild finished, the Marquis paid tribute to Dorothea and her sacrifice in the Palace of the Queen of the Marshes that had bought their freedom at such a terrible price.

'You suffered a tragic loss when the enchantress petrified your love. When Queen Orchidae returns she and I will scan the black pool together to search for keys that might undo this evil spell,' consoled Erica.

Hope shone in the Marquis' eyes. He had met the Elven Queen and knew her spiritual powers. Once when he had been deeply depressed, she touched his fingertips. A flow of energy had pulsated through his arms and spread throughout his entire body. A soft light had radiated from the diminutive figure of Queen Orchidae and he had been enveloped by a sense of healing and well being. The thought of the Elven Queen brought to him hope and solace.

Lady Erica now turned to Silfida.

'In your next message to the Queen, please urge her to return, for her presence is precious to us all. There is much written in the black pool that I cannot decipher. Queen Orchidae is skilled in reading the tablets of the Cosmic Mind, hidden in the black waters.'

Volker was busy writing down everything that had happened. Some Council members had their eyes closed and it was difficult to say whether they were trying to concentrate or actually were asleep, but when Norma came from the kitchen with hot drinks and apple strudel, everybody perked up and indulged in light-hearted banter.

Next morning they gathered in the council chamber and talked about finding volunteers in Cascade, to send to Esteria. Swannemen loved their comfort and the very thought of an exhausting trek up the mountains to Esteria would appal them. Fighting a ruthless enemy who could easily chop your head off or commit some other irreversible act would be hard for the average Swanneman to contemplate. Swannemen didn't mind hardships of the reversible kind, falling in icy waters and being fished out afterwards and that sort of thing, but loosing one's head as a volunteer in battle was a bitter pill to swallow. In the not too distant past, nonetheless, their forefathers had been shrewd and cunning warriors.

'Every morning the men gather at the Graceful Neck to drink coffee and talk about events. The Marquis could go down and speak to them,' suggested secretary Volker.

Ferdinand had been dozing in his chair, but the words of the secretary roused him. He thought for a minute and blew a few rings of smoke. The truth of the matter was that he had never deigned to mix with commoners. All his life he had lived in Cascade and never once had he or any other deCygne, for that matter, entered the coffee room at the Graceful Neck. His ancestors had led burghers into battle, they had given speeches on festive occasions on the lawn of the old inn, but never had there been any hobnobbing with the men who gathered there for coffee in the morning. Lady Erica read his thoughts. 'Times are changing Ferdinand. It is a new age and we are facing a crisis. Going down there would be a first step to opening the minds of the men to the fate that awaits them.'

The Marquis, who had great respect for his aunt, mulled it over. He was delighted to have once more a pipe of tobacco at his side. The philosopher within arose. Social relations were changing and if this was the coming of a new age, he certainly ought to be at the cutting edge. It was only proper a nobleman should take the lead. He would speak to the men. Perhaps he could persuade them, and even lead them to Esteria. He looked up at the painting of Sir Oliver deCygne and thought that for a moment, he could see the ancient warrior blink.

The next morning the Marquis had the kind of breakfast that he had not had since his stay at the inn in Miranda. He was amazed how easily he adapted to all the little luxuries of life at the Manor. He had to watch this. He rather cherished his lean ascetic image and if truth be told he spent some time in front of the mirror, trying different postures. In the Lambarina museum, he had admired paintings of Saints and travelling monks and he was startled to see how they resembled the figure he was looking at in the glass. Of course he had often contemplated taking holy orders but this was not the time. Pensively, he sent a ringlet of smoke into the air. What if Dorothea were revived? An oath of holy orders would not do, it would not do at all!

A fine mist hung over the valley as he left the Manor and turned down the laneway leading to the Graceful Neck. As usual most of the men in the village had gathered this morning in the common room. A fire in the woodstove had chased the damp away and Rosemary was bustling around serving breakfast.

When the Marquis walked in, the buzz of voices came to a dead stop. Every face turned towards the tall nobleman. It was as if the appearance in the doorway had risen from the dead, for scuttlebutt and hearsay had the Marquis as dead as a doornail.

It was Ferdinand deCygne all right, standing there, alive as a flying squirrel. And yet it was not the old Ferdinand deCygne. The jolly podgy Marquis was gone and standing before them now was a figure, emaciated, hollow eyed and wraithlike. A mixture of shock and awe swept across the crowd and the men removed their caps.

The collective memory of the men in the room went back to the old legends, to a time when their forefathers had been warriors. Some of the tradesmen who had worked at the Manor recalled the paintings of fierce warriors leading Swannemen to battle. That was long ago and belonged to the past. The new generation had evolved beyond that kind of thing. It had no use for the glory of battle, let alone the misery. Now a sixth sense told them something was going to be asked of them, something that they might not like.

Kirk, shipwright and Gondola builder moved over and asked the Marquis to take a seat. In centuries past the titled members of the deCygne family had been looked up to. Their forefathers had fought under the command of Sir Oliver to ensure the freedom and independence of the Swannefolk. Those days were over, however, and titles now meant little. Before he left Cascade few of the men had taken the Marquis seriously and he had been the butt of a good many jokes.

The men didn't quite know what was coming, but they greeted him politely. Never before had a deCygne come down to the Graceful Neck to sit at coffee with the common folk in town.

Looking at the changed figure of the nobleman they were not inclined to laugh anymore. Deep lines were etched on his countenance, lines of pain and suffering. All was not well. The Marquis had come to the Inn to warn of danger, and in their hearts the men knew that they would have to take a stand. Joris Goldfinger had encouraged them to work with the Rovers, yet in the end, he had been cheated and attacked by the black hounds. It was Kirk who broke the silence.

'I think, I speak for all of us, Marquis, when I say that we are mighty glad to see you well and alive. Rumours had it that you were a goner. Pleased to have you back Sir.'

'I am grateful to be alive, Kirk.' The Marquis said gravely. He had decided wisely, before calling for volunteers to fight in Esteria, to give the men a firsthand account of his experiences. Rosemary brought him a coffee and he took a few sips before speaking.

'Men of Swanneland, Swannebrothers. I will share with you my adventures so that you may know what is afoot beyond the borders of our Kingdom.

'Calls us Swannebrothers,' muttered Jimmy Pikepole, one of the old Gondoliers. 'Quite flattering, I say, to call us common ducks, Swannebrothers. We will pay for it.'

Some of the old gaffers blew thoughtful rings of smoke into the air.

'Quiet please,' shouted Kirk, 'Give the Marquis a chance to tell his tale.'

Ferdinand de Cygne began to talk and it was not long before the men were listening with rapt attention, as they learned how the company had been enticed by the beautiful Queen of the Marshes and the tragic lot of the Outlanders, metamorphosed into toads, the treachery at the retreat of the Sisters of the Third Woe and the capture of Slim, Moose Martin and Duckie by the Grolls.It touched the hearts of the men. Deep and ancient chords were stirred in their collective unconscious. As he looked around Jimmy Pikepole felt on edge. The men had always been an easy going lot. Now the faces bore a grim expression.

'Ah well,' he muttered, 'we have been sucked in and we have got to make the best of it.'

The year before when Scimitar had spoken at the inn, few had taken him seriously. All remembered the stern flinty-eyed Dwarf, who had warned them of dangers brooding behind the Finnian Range. Now the mood was different. Sombre faces sat in silence chewing their pipes or sipping coffee. Then unexpectedly, Kirk sprang up and raising his right hand piped up.

'Your Grace.'

'Drop the title,' interrupted the Marquis, 'Those times are gone. Shoulder to shoulder will we stand to oppose this evil now menacing our land and our loved ones!'

'Ferdinand deCygne,' responded Kirk with a broad smile, 'in the weeks before your return, most of the Rovers left. We hoped that the tide had turned and that they had left for good.'

'Were it only so,' sighed the Marquis. 'No, the Seven realized that their policy of infiltration didn't work. Resentment and resistance grew throughout the Kingdom and it became more difficult for their agents to buy favours. Now the Seven will launch their armies and occupy our land.'

Gasps of horror could be heard. Life as they knew it might well come to an end. The Marquis put his coffee down and stood up. The man standing now before them had seen battle, had been wounded savagely and returned to tell the tale. Whatever they had thought of him in the past now was set aside. They knew the evil that Scimitar had warned them about was real. Something must be done and Ferdinand deCygne was going to ask them to do it. Swannemen, loath to change their lifestyle, would resist every inch of the way, but when danger threatened their lives and freedom, they would rise to the challenge. They were ready to listen to the Marquis.

'A year ago the traitor, Lord Imbrun kidnapped our gracious Princess Yaconda and a few days later King Arcturus was murdered. Outlanders, Mountain Fairies, Elves and Gnomes have gathered at the Manor to consult and they will counsel and guide our people until the Princess Yaconda is rescued and assumes her rightful place as Queen.'

'Is the Princess imprisoned in the palace of the Seven?' one of the gondoliers wanted to know.

'Queen Tuluga of the Mountain Fairies, told Lady Erica that the Princess is imprisoned in the old Alcazar, situated in the dunes of the peninsula where the western and eastern oceans meet. Lady Erica has gazed into the waters of the black pool and the images in its depth foreshadow mortal peril for both the Princess and her maid.' A wave of anger swept through the crowd.

'How can we save Princess Yaconda from the Seven?' asked Svanhild's Uncle Svend.

'The rule of the Seven must come to an end,' the Marquis replied in a tremulous voice. Svend sensed his hesitation.

'Ferdinand deCygne, even if the Seven were driven back at the passes of the Finnian Range, it would not be the end of their rule or Yaconda's imprisonment. We could never cross the mountains and invade the land of the Seven and break their power.'

The Marquis looked distraught. 'I have no answer, Svend, we take it one step at a time. First we must prevent the occupation of the Kingdom.'

Many of the men nodded silently. Jimmy Pikepole's imagination had conjured up the most dreadful thing that could be asked of them. Since the real thing could not be worse, he challenged the Marquis.

'Ferdinand deCygne you have come to ask something of us. Out with it!'

'Friends,' responded the Marquis, 'Lady Erica and the Council have sent messages to the peoples of the Kingdom asking volunteers to go to Esteria to oppose the enemy. Esteria must be held at all cost.'

The prospect of occupation by a ruthless force and the threat to the life of their beloved Princess had roused the men to action.

Kirk jumped onto the table and raised his right fist.

'To Esteria men!'

'To Esteria!' thundered a chorus. The dull resentful faces that had greeted the Marquis were transformed and the old wooden floor of the coffee room resounded with stomping feet. Shouts flew through the air.

'Down with the Seven. Long Live the Princess!'

The old warrior spirit, buried by layers of peaceful generations, resurfaced.

The men had been touched when the Marquis told them to drop his title. Yet in a strange way their mind went back to times of old, when Oliver deCygne had led the fight for freedom. Martin Mudpole climbed on the table.

'Three cheers for the Marquis,' shouted the old gaffer. The men cheered and spontaneously raised the old deCygne anthem.

Lord of the Manor
praise and Glory be
we march for thee
wave high the banner!

'To the Marquis,' ran the toast and for want of something better they clanked, with vigour, their coffee cups and Rosemary picked up the shards.

The Marquis was not wholly insensitive to their tribute. A warm glow flowed over him. His self-esteem climbed quickly, perhaps too quickly for cool and reasoned judgement. For years nobody had taken him seriously and being cherished was an agreeable sensation.

The change amongst the Swannemen was astounding. Once they decided to go, they put their hearts into it. Old Martin Mudpole suggested that they leave within two weeks time. By then the spring run off would be at an end and the current in the river would begin to abate. When Ferdinand deCygne departed the old inn, he left behind an enthusiastic throng.

Back at the Manor, merriment danced in Lady Erica's eyes as her nephew told of the meeting at the Graceful Neck. The Council members were pleased that the Swannemen would be joining the volunteer corps in Esteria.

'I will lead the men in person,' added the Marquis.

'You have two weeks to rest up Ferdinand.' said his aunt, 'and prepare for the long trek up the mountain.'

It was the news about the Sea Gnomes that had surprised the Council. Every one knew of the Gnomes' affinity to gold.

'We know not if the lore of the golden plate holds true. Nevertheless, no stone must remain unturned. Perchance force will stem the tide, but turn it? I think not! I will travel with Svanhild to the Lake of the Coloured Fishes and then on to the shores of the Eastern Ocean and the Sea Gnomes,' volunteered Sidonia.

Silfida turned pale at the prospect of her elven sister leaving. She knew that she herself had neither the strength nor the temperament to deal with hardship and danger. Yet, she admired Sidonia's noble offer and took her hand.

'I will pray,' she whispered, 'my thoughts will encircle you. If ill befalls you, call on me.'

The Council members had been worried by the idea of Svanhild setting out alone and were relieved at Sidonia's offer to be her travel companion. Sidonia's spiritual insight and astounding eyesight were a wonderful gift.

Lady Erica knew that few people in the Kingdom set much store by the myth of the golden tablet, but the Dark Lords had not ignored the old legend. It had been a source of fear and their scouts carefully had combed the land for signs of gold. For all their power, luxuries and lasting youth, a germ of fear gnawed at their felicity. The dangers they perceived had been spun in the caverns of their souls. Their thirst for power and control was driven not by greed, but fear. She had shared her thoughts with the Council and they knew that there was little time left.

'We may be grasping at straws,' sighed Lady Erica, 'but a sign came to Svanhild when she caught a glimpse of Sea Gnomes in the Mirror of a Thousand Fragments.'

'Sidonia and Svanhild must lose no time exploring the beaches on the eastern shore,' suggested Silfida with a note of sadness in her voice.

Svanhild and Sidonia left the table and went to their rooms to pack. Annabelle got up and putting an arm around her daughter's shoulder, followed her downstairs.

'I know now, my love,' she whispered, 'why there was no wedding after you celebrated your flower festival. Martha read it in your hand when she prophesied the great darkness. Times of suffering and tribulation are at hand and you were meant to play a part in it.' They sat down on the sofa in the hall, Svanhild holding her mother's hands.

'I could never have been a bystander Mother. I must play my part in the drama that now is unfolding before our eyes.'

'All this will pass my love,' soothed Annabelle, 'then you will return home and many a swain will seek your hand.'

Svanhild blushed. Annabelle breathed a sigh of relief. To her the blush was a sign that her daughter was still connected to that world of small joys that Annabelle loved so well, family, children, animals, the veggie garden and the berry bushes, life on the even keel, Swannefolk held so dear.

Svanhild did not have the heart to mention to her mother the meeting with Ensten. The very thought of her friendship with a stranger from Esteria would have been a terrible shock to Annabelle. Neither did she wish to dwell on it, for present dangers could foil future dreams.

Sunlight streamed through Erica's window and a wayward ray caught the pencil sketch of Gustav. It was over twenty-five years ago, that he had been taken prisoner and sent to the galleys on the Wasa river. Every morning upon rising she would look at the sketch and say a silent prayer. She knew deep in her heart that he was still alive.

Thank heaven that the Swannemaid had removed that tiny sliver from the Mirror of a Thousand Fragments. Lady Erica hoped and prayed that it had been enough to prevent Matista from seeing the image of the Sea

Gnomes. If the Seven learned of it, the shores of the eastern ocean would be swarming with Rovers and Grolls.

She finished dressing and sat down upon the bed. Her mind had been busy sorting all the feelings and thoughts of the last few days and she did some breathing exercises to calm herself and to gain perspective. After a short meditation she walked down the stairway.

She was surprised to see Sidonia and Svanhild all packed and ready to leave. The weather was fine and it would be best to have an early start.

She embraced them both and joining hands, they walked down to the dock. Svanhild carried a bow and a quiver of arrows and from her belt hung her faithful sling shot. When they reached the water, Silfida, carrying last minute provisions for the journey, caught up. Uncle Svend's skiff was waiting.

Svanhild felt refreshed. The visit at the Manor and the days at the Convent of the Sisters of the Secret Crossing had been an inspiration. Sunlight glistened on the water, poplar leaves whispered words of comfort and cheer.

Uncle Svend welcomed them and stowed their packs in the sturdy boat. To take advantage of a fair breeze blowing from the south, a mast had been stepped in the bow, with a small sail attached. Lady Erica and Silfida kissed the travellers and they boarded. 'Where will you take them Svend?' asked Lady Erica.

'Up to Mary's Landing, ma'am. From there a path leads to Miranda.'

'We will spend the night at the Golden Goose,' decided Svanhild.

Svend hoisted the sail, lowered the sideboards and swiftly the small craft coursed from shore.

Lady Erica and Silfida waved until the boat was a mere speck on the great expanse of water. Silfida lingered, she could still see clearly, both Sidonia and Svanhild's faces and visualized their safe arrival at the Lake of the Coloured Fishes. Running up the hill, she caught up with Lady Erica on the lawn of the Graceful Neck.

31

Rescue Scimitar

*F*lying high above the northern forests, Solomon, Chief of the Wood Owls, spotted black clouds glowering over the Finnian Range. When they left the Lake of the Coloured Fishes to courier Svanhild's message to the Dwarves, sunlight sparkled on the snowy forest below. Now flying in the foothills, high winds slowed them down. Suddenly they found themselves in the midst of a snow squall and Solomon motioned Kasper to follow him down into the trees. They perched in the top of a giant spruce and shook the snow off their wings.

'Better wait it out, Chief. The weather may clear in a day or so.'

Kasper turned his head and saw the dark glint in the deep yellow eyes of his superior.

'Did we make a commitment to the Swannemaiden, to carry urgent tidings to the Dwarves?' Kasper knew what was coming but kept quiet.

'A Chief of the Wood Owls honours a commitment to a Swannemaiden. The tidings are urgent, Deputy. We'll fly through this storm, be it our last flight.'

The idea of being on his last flight was a difficult notion for the Deputy to get his mind around. He hoped it wouldn't be his last flight. It was in moments like this that it came to him, why Solomon was Chief. Solomon's stern face turned to Kasper.

'The freedom of the Kingdom hangs in the balance, Deputy. If the

Kingdom falls, what will happen to our hereditary rights?'

'It would not auger well, Chief,' conceded Kasper.

'We complain about the way things are run in the Kingdom, Deputy. If the Seven from the Land of Darkness seize the country, will there be owls left to complain? Owl stew is an ignoble way to end your flying days.'

There was but one answer to this latest dressing down. In a defiant gesture Kasper flapped his wings and flying straight up into the swirling snow, headed for the peaks of the Finnian Range.

Solomon, with a powerful stroke of his pinions, rose from the spruce tree and flew into the wild night. Snow packed into their wings and ice pellets stung their eyes, but the intrepid birds flew on. The trees below vanished and high above the alpine meadows, they found themselves in a sea of white. Battered by gusts of wind, they struggled on. Turbulence dropped them into deep troughs, lifted them up again and left them gasping for air. Yet their celestial imaging never failed and they knew precisely where they were.

Once over the dwarf village they descended swiftly. At first all they could see was swirling white but closer to earth a glimmer of light showed. Sergeant Crusher had stoked a blaze in an iron barrel and standing in the lee of his guard post, held his hands to the flames. When the old warrior looked up he saw two dark shapes drifting towards him. He dismissed the notion that merewings were approaching. Their oversized wings would never have survived the storm.

When the bedraggled shapes of the Wood Owls materialized in front of the Sergeant, the warrior's features broke into a grin.

'Owls, Wood Owls, if my frozen eyes do not deceive me. You are way off course my feathered friends,' bellowed the Sergeant trying to shout above the howling wind. 'To the village of the Dwarves you have strayed.'

'We are precisely where we planned to be Sergeant,' answered Kasper a little miffed.

'What might your names be?' asked Sergeant Crusher in a conciliatory tone.

'Solomon, Chief of the Wood Owls and my Deputy, Kasper.' The owls bowed politely.

'Sergeant Crusher at your service. Tell me my good birds what made you fly through this dreadful soup to reach our outpost in the mountains?'

'We carry tidings for the Dwarves from the maiden, Svanhild.' Sergeant Crusher looked dumbfounded.

'The sister of the ballet master, living with Lady Sunflower and Smithereen?'

'The very same Sergeant. We met the fair maiden at the homestead of the Gnomes Oarflake and Ambrosia. She asked us to carry tidings to Lady Sunflower and Smithereen.'

'Svanhild, alive and well, at the homestead of the Gnomes. Escaped from the enchantress' magic web.' chuckled the warrior. I'll strike the mother lode if that isn't news. Perch on me shoulders.' The birds couldn't move, their wings had iced up. Sergeant Crusher planted an owl on each shoulder and struggling through a maze of snow banks, the sturdy warrior reached the home of Sunflower and Smithereen.

Smithereen was sitting in his rocking chair, wrapped in deep thought, when the snow covered Sergeant appeared in the doorway, a white figure standing on each shoulder. The great warrior looked flummoxed.

'My stars, Sergeant, what are those frozen statues on your shoulder?'

'Wood Owls, Smithereen, up from the Lake of the Coloured Fishes. Chief Solomon and his Deputy.'

I'll be crushed if I ever saw the like of it,' muttered Smithereen.

Sunflower turned around from her loom. The sight of the Sergeant and the frozen birds sent her into a fit of merry laughter.

Solomon and Kasper began to thaw out a bit and managed to hop from the Sergeant's shoulder onto the backs of two chairs. Crusher, anxious to get back to the gate, slipped out the front door.

Sunflower bade the owls a warm welcome. She lit the kitchen lamp and took a close look at her guests. The large birds were shivering from cold and exhaustion, so this was not the time to query them about their mission. She took a towel from the line and gently dried their feathers. The woodstove flared up and a pleasant smell of stewed lamb wafted through the air. Perched close to the stove and with a generous dish of lamb in front of them, the owls revived.

Edel and Weiss tiptoed quietly into the parlour and climbed onto Sunflower's loom. Solomon and Kasper, deep into the lamb stew, didn't notice them.

'Edel, my love, run next door and ask Moose and Duckie to come over,' suggested Sunflower, 'once the owls thaw out a bit, they will tell us what is happening in the outside world.'

Mountain Fairies do not take well to the cold, so Sunflower had sewn the two Fairies tiny parkas embroidered with alpine flowers. Edel threw his parka around his shoulders and flew to the neighbours. The Mountain Fairies and Slim had spent the winter at Sunflower and Smithereen's. Moose Martin and Duckie lodged with Pristina and Bullneck, who lived next door. Slim joined the guests at the kitchen table and a few moments afterwards, Edel returned with Moose and Duckie.

Smithereen's spirits were still dampened but he took an interest in the owls and wondered aloud why the birds had braved so savage a storm.

Solomon, recovered after a second helping of Sunflower's stew, had heard Smithereen muttering.

'Haste was called for Smithereen. We carry news from the Lake of the Coloured Fishes.'

Kasper couldn't hold his tongue and blurted out.

'Svanhild is free. She escaped from Matista's Chateau.'

Solomon cast his Deputy a severe look. He had planned to make the announcement in a dignified manner.

In whatever way it was made, the effect was electrifying. Slim's eyes filled with tears. Sunflower, who had grown fond of Slim, rejoiced with him. Even Smithereen, still down with the moping illness, looked pleased. Edel and Weiss, thrilled at the news, began a dreamy joyful dance on the top beam of Sunflower's loom. The half-finished throw on the warp made a perfect trampoline and the light footed pair flew all around. Pirouetting atop the beam they barely cleared the ceiling. The tense muscles on Smithereen's face relaxed and the gloomy warrior broke into laughter.

Solomon and Kasper frowned. Rebuke shone in their yellow eyes, they were not amused by Edel and Weiss's antics. In the circle of birds, committed to higher wisdom, the reputation of Mountain Fairies stood low. Incurable romantics they were. Owls, wise as they are, have no feeling for the arts. Life is grave and lightness of being is frowned upon. Solomon, living up to his reputation, held his cool. He had enough dismal news left to bring them to their senses. To get the company's attention, once the mirth had subsided, he sounded three hoots in a minor key. Sunflower saw dismay in the owl's eyes.

'We rejoice at the escape of the Swannemaiden, friends. Svanhild, on her flight from Matista' domain was forced to hide in a hollow tree. It was there she overheard a Rover talking to his Groll. The Dark Lords are massing armies on the planes of the Wasa River. They plan to storm the passes on the Finnian Range, mop up the Dwarves and overwhelm the Kingdom.'

These ominous words had a sobering effect upon everybody. Only Smithereen came alive. The prospect of a major calamity raised the old warrior from the slough of despondency.

Disbelief spoke in the eyes of the group seated around the kitchen stove. Bullneck and Pristina had joined the company earlier and now Bullneck raised his voice.

'There has been talk of activity along the shore of the Wasa, plumes of black smoke pouring from the smelters and the armouries by the black peak.'

Sunflower knew that the question of organizing the defence would come up. She looked at Smithereen. He had phenomenal strength, but alas his straight-laced soul did not have the cunning required for military leadership. Smithereen knew it only too well. He raised his huge frame from the rocking chair and looked around the room. 'The hour for Scimitar is now,' boomed his mighty voice. 'He must be freed and command our forces before it is too late.'

Bullneck looked sombre and shook his head. 'A desperate undertaking. No one has escaped from the slave labour camps in the quarries under the Black Peak. Guards are posted every hundred feet. No one can leave or enter unseen.'

'We can, we can.' came voices from the loom. 'Mountain Fairies can.'

'They can do it,' said Slim in a matter of fact voice. 'Captain Martin, Duckie and I will travel with them to the barrier that surrounds the quarries.'

'Count me in,' shouted Bullneck.

'A noble mission, into the eye of the storm,' rejoiced Edel.

'Into the heart of darkness, glory be,' responded Weiss.

After a snowbound winter, Edel and Weiss had a bad case of cabin fever. They were itching for action and dreaming of glory.

Solomon and Kasper were half asleep on their perch and did not hear the Mountain Fairies' outburst. They abhorred impulsive action. The Book of Wisdom advocated sober, clear and systematic planning.

By nine o'clock, food, wine and the heat from the woodstove had had its effect and there was a lot of yawning. The hubbub died down and heads were nodding. Sunflower suggested they retire for the night and wait for morning to begin preparations in earnest.

There were patches of blue in the morning sky and Sunflower, standing by the window, could see that a rim of light lined the mountain peaks. In winter they blocked sunlight from reaching the village. Now each day the light grew stronger and soon the sun would be chasing the shadows from the alpine meadows.

The owls were wide awake, anxious to make the best of the change in weather and to head for home. Sunflower served them smoked meat of wild boar.

'Excellent food, Chief,' Kasper mumbled between bites. 'Smoke enhances the flavour, we don't find that kind of thing in the wild.'

'True Deputy, terrestrials may not be able to fly, but they have got other things going for them.'

After a satisfying breakfast, the birds hopped out onto the balcony, perching on the railing. Sunflower stroked their feathers and thanked them again for bringing news to their wintry outpost.

Soaring high above the mountain range, Solomon turned to Kasper.

'The touch of the Sunny Lady's hands was a pleasant sensation, Deputy.'

'Indeed Chief, vibrations rippling through the feathers, moving the Chi and energizing the pinions'.

'That was deep, Deputy, well phrased.'

At the home of Sunflower and Smithereen members of the rescue party talked around the breakfast table. Coffee and a pot of oats boiled in goat milk, bubbled on the woodstove. Bullneck spouted orders for the preparation of the expedition. They would leave to set up a base camp in a grotto, close to the Black Peak and the quarries that fell under its shade.

I wonder if the eagles are willing to come over to our side?' pondered Slim.

'Not likely,' Smithereen commented from his rocking chair. 'Blinking fence sitters, too high and mighty for their own good.'

'Don't speak too soon, hubby, the Grandmaster may change his mind,' soothed Sunflower. 'Black smoke has been pouring out of the chimneys at the Black Peak. Many birds in the Covey are upset.'

The party planned to leave within two days. Travelling by night they could move swiftly on the frozen snow. They would travel on skis except for Edel and Weiss, who were light enough to skip on top of the snow's thin crust.

The Dwarves had taught Moose, Slim and Duckie to ski and a good part of the winter had been spent out of doors exploring the mountains. Dwarves are expert skiers. The tradition goes back thousands of years and it is believed that Dwarves invented the ski.

The prospect of action had an electrifying effect. No sooner was the breakfast table cleared when packing began. Bullneck had made a list of all the provisions required and he assigned the tasks. Sunflower and Pristina prepared the food for the expedition.

Angelica, the goat lady, called that morning with a basket of healing herbs. Slim looked at the basket and recognized a mixture of devil's claw and deadly shade of night. He shivered and tried not to think about it, but always there was the danger of being bitten by a black dog. The potent mixture gave a two-week window on life, hopefully long enough to reach the Convent of the Sisters.

In the evening, a meeting was called in the community hall. The news of the Seven Lords massing armies on the other side of the Finnian Range had travelled through the village like wild fire, gaining momentum as it went along. That night, families from the village and even some from outlying farms filled, to overflowing, the spacious log building.

Smithereen, still feeling low, stayed home. Since coming down with the moping illness he suffered panic attacks when in crowds. Sunflower knew a sensitive soul lived in that formidable body of her hubby and she had taken it upon herself to chair the meeting.

She welcomed the audience. Since Sunflower was chairing the meeting, most of the Dwarves had taken their wives along. All the benches in the hall were filled with Dwarves anxious to hear what was happening. Sunflower shared all the news the owls had brought. There was a sigh of relief, for flying rumours already had the enemy overrunning the outlying farms, murdering the men and shipping the women and children off to the realm of the Seven. Sunflower reassured them that in fact no soldiers from the enemy armies had crossed the range.

'They are mobilizing their forces on the plains of the Wasa.'

'How much time do we have to prepare our defences, Sunny?' Sergeant Crusher wanted to know.

'Three or four months, Sergeant. I think that by late summer scouts will cross the range to test our defences. Help may be coming our way from Esteria.'

A ripple of excitement moved through the crowd. The Esterians were famous for their archery. Once iron tipped arrows were released from their tall yew-bows, they seldom failed to hit their mark.

Men, women and children volunteered for service. Sunflower's joyous bubbly nature had a flint of steel in it. She lost no time organizing a women's brigade to build fortifications and to pile rocks on the heights, flanking the pass the enemy was likely to storm.

Sergeant Crusher took charge organizing the warriors and provisioning the armouries. The ball and chain was still a favourite weapon and many new ones had to be forged. It was the only weapon that would put a substantial dent in a Groll skull. The Dwarves were also excellent spear throwers and a large stock of spears had to be produced.

The formal part of the meeting did not last very long. Men and women were standing around in small groups talking about the hundred and one things that had to be done. Before stepping down from the stage, Sunflower announced that an expedition to rescue Scimitar would leave the next day. The crowd cheered. Grimfaced Scimitar, the handsome bachelor with the fine chiselled features and long pointed beard, had never failed to fluster the village women. The thought of Scimitar returning was a cause of anxiety for some of the girls. Other commitments had been made and could not now be broken.

Sunflower observing the flushed looks had a fair idea of the goings on. Good luck to the maid who would take on Scimitar, if ever he did return. Dwarves made poor husbands. Moral to a fault, they carried a burden of guilt in their gunney sacks. Compulsive workers and formidable warriors, it would take many drops of dew from a very lovely rose to soften the hardened clay of that warrior's soul. Sunflower smiled when the blushing maidens walked on stage to volunteer.

The atmosphere inside the log building was charged with energy. Warriors walked on stage to share stories of battles from the distant past. Men, women and children were ready to give their all for the defence of the mountain gorge that guarded their lives and liberty.

Home alone, sitting in his rocking chair by the stove, Smithereen contemplated the universe. The great warrior had no use for community meetings. There was no room in his soul for the hype and slogans of mass rallies. Many a battle had he fought. He had seen the carnage of the battlefield and worn the laurels of victory, but how empty its rewards.

For months, the village had been in semi-darkness and the long winter night had taken its toll. It had been a blessing for Smithereen to have the

Mountain Fairies living with them. Edel and Weiss' frolics and eternal optimism had lifted his spirits. Smithereen had gone back to writing poetry, composing verse in secret in a little sanctuary at the back of the house. Once Edel and Weiss had sneaked in and peeked over his shoulder. The cheering and clapping of the Fairies had taken Smithereen by surprise. Yet, Edel and Weiss' enthusiasm gave a lift to his soul. Perhaps one day he would travel to Cascade and share his poetry with Lady Erica. Then he would go on to the artist colony in Lambarina to meet kindred souls. They might even ask him to give a public reading? The thought brought solace.

He looked at the flames dancing in the hearth, picked up his pen and began to write.

spring brings in
a scent divine
of hyacinth,
receding snow revealing
a thousand blue bells pealing
laughing waters streaming
in meadows of my inner being
there my soul will dance
amidst a myriad hues
and clap its hands
in morning dew

Smithereen read the poem to himself and hummed a tune that would suit the words. He knew it still needed work but it was a beginning and a smile spread over the gnarled face.

For years he had been a soldier and had even penned a military tract, The Path of the Warrior. He was revered only for his brute strength, the formidable ruffian! Yes, he had been going through an identity crisis and suffered from the moping illness. One day he would find his true calling.

Among his fellow Dwarves there was no recognition of his literary efforts. He would learn to accept that. The stout fellows would listen to a battle ballad, but poetry no. Even when they looked at the vivid, graceful designs on their wives' looms, they would shake their heads and mumble, 'frills, foppery and finery.' They were puritans, austere, severe, stuffed shirts, intrepid just the same. Smithereen sighed. If only he were known as deep instead of macho.

He looked at the glow of dying embers and thought of his brother Scimitar, a born leader and cunning warrior. Were Scimitar here the Dwarves would stand a chance against the armies from the Land of Darkness.

When Sunflower returned from the meeting, she found Smithereen dozing in his rocking chair. Quill and writing board lay on a small table by his side. She moved closer to look at his face and there saw a ripple of mirth. He was gaining the upper hand in an inner struggle that for years had paralyzed him. Her heart felt lighter.

A few minutes later, the Mountain Fairies burst through the front door and landed on the armrests of his rocking chair. Smithereen woke with a start.

'Well, my dainties, was the meeting a success?'

'A splendid affair sir, Sunflower has a magic touch for organizing.'

'I know it well my boys,' laughed Smithereen.

All pulled their chairs up around the hearth and before retiring enjoyed a mug of hot apple cider. Tomorrow they would rise early and complete preparations for the expedition to the grottos near the Black Peak.

Many miles to the east of the village of the Dwarves, the moon shed its mysterious light over the high mountains. Black shadows could be seen moving over ice covered plateaus. Eagles, flying in from all directions, converged upon the traditional meeting place. Covey meetings did not always have full attendance, but this time Master Grimmbeak had called a special session and urgent messages had been flown to all full-fledged members of the Covey. Hundreds of eagles had taken to the air and the traditional meeting place was filling up quickly.

The occasion was young Theodorus' return to the Covey. Wounded in his right wing by a Groll's arrow, he had been forced to spend the winter at the homestead of the Gnomes, where Oarflake and Ambrosia had nursed him back to health. One sunny day in late winter he had taken flight and winged his way back to the Covey. Master Grimmbeak had been delighted to see his protege safely back home and he had asked Theodorus to address a plenary session of the Covey.

Grimmbeak standing on a large rock looked down with satisfaction at the sea of feathers before him and bid a hearty welcome. He knew that some thorny issues would have to be tackled, but it would be better to hold back his carefully prepared speech until Theodorus had finished his story.

Theodorus had the birds practically hanging on his beak, as he told of his near fatal flight. How he had evaded several volleys of Groll arrows before an arrow pierced his right wing, his crash landing into the bulrushes, the rescue by Sergeant Crusher and the harrowing trip on the shoulder of the Esterian runner into the healing hands of Oarflake and Ambrosia. When the young bird finished, anger flared in the eagles' eyes. Their long cherished neutrality had been violated.

While Servatius and Nightglider were serving light refreshments, a buzz of indignant voices rose from the assembled birds. For centuries they had been above squabbling terrestrials. They listened, watched and judged as eagles are supposed to do. Never had their impartiality been questioned and for the first time within living memory, a member of the Celestial Covey had been attacked. Black smoke and dying trees are aggravating, but an unprovoked attack is quite another matter. The Grandmaster's yellow beak gleamed with anger as he took his stand on the rock.

'Friends, birds of noble feather, companions of the Celestial Covey, a wanton attack on one of our brethren marks a new day in our history. A day of infamy! Henceforth, a state of war exists between the Covey and the emissaries of darkness.'

A current of excitement swept through the waves of dark feathers crowded around Grimmbeak. 'We will take a stand and wage war. With all our strength we will attack the evil forces gathering in the plains of the Wasa. If merewings are sighted, pursue and destroy!'

A century ago the eagles had been engaged in a police action, but deep in their feathers they knew that this was going to be different. They would be opposing the Lords of Darkness and their massed armies.

The Grandmaster asked for a show of wings. Support was overwhelming.

'Master, will the Dauntless Divers join us?'

'No doubt, Servatius. They are always spoiling for a fight. They may lack refinement but savage fighters they are. Their precision diving would be an asset in any battle.'

Grimmbeak sent Nightglider and Servatius to parley with the Dauntless Divers. He took it upon himself to visit the Dwarves and to tell Sunflower and Smithereen of the Covey's resolve.

The expedition to free Scimitar had left in the evening and Smithereen spent the night in his rocking chair pondering the chances of success. He feared for the safety of his friends. The Mountain Fairies might get into troubles. The foolish daredevils in their quest for glory and romance would go out on a limb or a twig for all that. He already missed Edel and Weiss riding on the armrests of his rocking chair. Their boundless merriment had lightened the dark winter months.

When the sun's rays rose above the Finnian Range he walked out of the house and followed the trail winding up the mountain. Halfway between the village and Angelica's cabin, overlooking the village, he rested on a rock. The red roofs glistening in the sun, stood out against the brilliant white. Snow was melting everywhere and water was streaming down. In the heart of the great warrior, a rill of joy trickled to the surface.

He raised his eyes to the peaks above and the deep blue sky. Suddenly he realized that he had reached a turning point. His mind must travel beyond the bonds of the warrior culture into which he had been born, and search for new horizons. He knew that darkness would return but this moment of light would give him heart to pursue his journey.

When he returned home, he found Sunflower leaning on the porch railing. She could tell by the way he walked that there was a change in Smithereen. In her heart she was grateful to the Mountain Fairies. Their exuberance and fantastic flights of fancy had brought mirth and laugher into the house and healing to Smithereen.

She put a hand on his shoulder and together they looked at the patches of green in the alpine meadows. Spring flowers were blooming in myriad hues. When Sunflower raised her eyes she was startled to see Grimmbeak descending in a graceful spiral. The Grandmaster perched on the railing and made a polite bow.

'Master Grimmbeak,' exclaimed Smithereen, 'an unexpected pleasure.'

Grimmbeak's penetrating look took in the scene before him and he realized that Smithereen was coming out of his slump. The great bird was not one to waste words.

'The pleasure is mine, Smithereen and Sunflower. I have come to tell you of a landmark decision made at last night's Covey gathering. The eagles' neutrality has been violated. We will side with the Kingdom, opposing the gathering forces of darkness.'

'Master Grimmbeak we will be grateful for your help in the struggle ahead,' exclaimed Sunflower. The Grandmaster heaved a deep sigh.

'Alas, my friends, no longer will we be able to judge the world for we will be players in it. Centuries of tradition have been wiped out overnight.'

Grimmbeak was visibly upset, Sunflower put her hand on his windblown feathers. Her smile and touch worked their magic and Grimmbeak relaxed.

'Change,' mused the great bird, 'seems to be the new law of life, we stand at the threshold of a new era.'

Sunflower went into the house humming a cheerful ditty. The support of the eagles was heartening. She found some fresh fish and brought it out to Grimmbeak. A bowl of trout restored his equilibrium and he was ready to return home.

Sunflower and Smithereen thanked him again and told him of the expedition to free Scimitar. Grimmbeak listened carefully. He was interested to hear that Edel and Weiss were involved and made a note in the back of his head to have Nightglider and Servatius check on the two Fairies.

The Grandmaster rose majestically from the porch railing and Smithereen sat down in the spring sun to enjoy a pipe of tobacco. Sunflower went next door where Pristina had organized a prayer meeting for the rescue of Scimitar.

32

Svanhild And Sidonia

Leaning over the bow, Svanhild watched the skiff slice the waters of the Sanctus. A powerful west wind was driving the craft upstream towards Miranda. Uncle Svend, sitting at the helm, held onto the small sail.

Sidonia's phenomenal vision caught the frail figure of Silfida standing between two willows on the lawn of the Graceful Neck. She could feel the mind of her elven sister visualizing a safe arrival at the Lake of the Coloured Fishes. Only when Silfida turned and walked among the poplars towards the old inn, did Sidonia lose sight of her.

Before she turned her eyes to the bow, Sidonia descried a line of white flecks floating on the water. Swans! A team of swans was following them. Sidonia, delighted by the lovely sight, called out to Svanhild.

'The swans are swimming in our wake.'

Svanhild sat up and looked back. All that she could see was a patch of white, but she trusted Sidonia's sight and feared Limonides and his team mates might have taken it into their head to follow them.

For years she had worked alongside Slim, training the swans in water ballet and Limonides was much attached to her. Svanhild and Slim had been away for more than a year and Limonides and the swans had spent that time at Uncle Svend's farm. During her short stay at the Manor deCygne, Svanhild had talked to the swans and explained the reason for their long absence. Now she sensed their impatience and feared that Limonides might try to follow her.

When the skiff sailed by the farm, Limonides had been floating on the waters of the deep pond behind Uncle Svend's barn. A tremor had flowed up his long neck and he raised his great wings. The image of the Swannemaiden flashed into his mind and he felt her presence. The other six swans alerted by Limonides' reaction, formed up single file behind the great swan. They swam through the narrow canal that linked the pond to the Sanctus and spotted the little boat sailing up river. Limonides decided to keep his distance. He realized that if detected too soon, they would be sent back but he didn't know about elven eyes.

'Oh Sidonia what are we to do, it would break my heart to part with them again.'

Sidonia remained silent, her eyes resting on the reflection of the tall poplars in the waters near the shore.

'Let them travel with us until we come to the landing where the trail begins, then you can talk to Limonides and ask him to follow Uncle Svend back to the farm.'

Svandhild looked at the procession approaching in the distance. Uncle Svend had learned in the last year that Limonides had a mind of his own. The swans moved with silent majesty. When they caught up, Limonides swam up to the stern and Svanhild's arm reached out to him, her hand touching the tall, graceful neck. Limonides uttering a deep haunting cry, rested his beak on Svanhild's arm.

Uncle Svend wiped a tear from his cheek and Sidonia cast Svanhild an imploring look.

'You may come as far as the landing stage, Limonides. Then you must return with Uncle Svend. We will not be long this time. Slim and I hope to return before the first snow. Svanhild looked at the six swans circling around Limonides. She had known them as cygnets and now she called each by name, Flicka, Saskia, Pavlova, Tristan, Lancelot and Prince.' They were delighted to hear the voice of the maiden who had sung to them as cygnets and had played the utelli when they danced.

There was not much time to linger and Uncle Svend set the skiff back on course. When they approached the bulrushes on the other side of the bay, he steered the boat through a narrow lead to an old rickety dock. Svanhild and Sidonia clambered onto the jetty and Uncle Svend handed them their packs.

'This is the old cart trail to Miranda. It is an early spring and you should be able to keep your feet dry. It swings south passing below Miranda harbour, and then turns back to the settlement.'

'It was good of you Uncle Svend, to bring us here,' said Svanhild throwing her arm around the old swannemaster's shoulder.

'It was so little. I just hope and pray that by nightfall you find yourselves at the Golden Goose. Remember me to Hester Hollyhock. Godspeed girls.'

Uncle Svend took his time turning the boat around and Svanhild knelt on the dock to talk to Limonides.

'Follow Uncle Svend, Limonides. Slim is on a mission high up in the alps, I trust that he will return soon.'

Limonides would not gainsay Svanhild and he followed the skiff back to the Sanctus. Uncle Svend was making good time rowing downstream and the distance between the swans and the old ballet master increased steadily.

When the skiff disappeared behind a small island, Limonides slowed down and the others swans huddled around him.

He remained in deep thought as a whirling current floated the swans into a circle. Swans do not think in a linear fashion, but their intuition is acute. A strong feeling came to Limonides that Svanhild was travelling to Miranda and that they must meet her there. They had performed in Miranda the year before and he knew that the distance was not great. The other swans sensed his purpose and their long necks swayed in unison. The great wings created a powerful air current. A rush of air rippled the water and the swans leapt forward. Once airborne, they turned around and headed for Miranda.

Walking down the jetty, Svanhild and Sidonia found themselves in a stand of poplars. They shouldered their packs and began the trek to Miranda. The poplars gave way to cedar. Large puddles appeared on the old trail and it was not long before their feet were wet. Close to Miranda the ground rose and cedar gave way to spruce. Only a few rays of sunlight reached the forest floor and a cold ground mist chilled them through and through. After an hour's hike they could see Miranda across the lake and occasionally they caught glimpses of red and blue gables.

Resting on a log at the next clearing, they gained an unobstructed view of the town. The sky had cleared and a sinking sun shed a warm light on the brightly painted houses surrounding the market square. What a surprise to see seven white swans, regally floating past the town docks.

Limonides sensed that Svanhild was close by, but he pretended not to see her. It would be better to give her time to get used to their being there. They swam out of sight. Svanhild couldn't help laughing. The swans always did have a novel way of interpreting her commands.

Half an hour later, they walked into the market square. Hester Hollyhock was watering geraniums in the flower boxes by the Golden Goose. At the sound of sloshing wet feet, she looked up and dropped her watering can.

'Svanhild, what a joy to see you well and at liberty. News of your escape from the evil witch reached us months ago. And you returned in the company of an elven maid. Welcome my dear,' greeted Hester, resting a hand on Sidonia's white tresses. Hester was delighted to see Svanhild but she was not surprised. When the swans swam into the harbour her hopes had been raised that the ballet master or his sister might follow.

At the sound of their voices, Hester's daughters, Fairlight and Fragrance skipped into view and embraced them. They rejoiced to see Svanhild and to meet Sidonia. Elven visits to Miranda were rare.

Limonides had been watching the scene out of the corner of his eye. The joyful sounds of the meeting with Hester and her daughters echoed over the lake and the great swan considered it a good omen. He trusted there would not be any serious reproach about their unexpected arrival.

Hester's practical turn of mind brought the reunion back to earth.

'Look at your feet girls. You are soaked right through. Fragrance, take them upstairs and pour a warm footbath. They shall have clean socks and shoes, for surely you will stay overnight. By morning your boots and socks will be dry. Fairlight, run over to Cornelius and Annabelle and tell the news.'

Hester never lost her business sense in the midst of excitement. She knew that the presence of Svanhild and her elven friend meant a full house at the inn for the evening meal. Hester prepared for the girls, an upstairs guest room to rest until supper hour. Before guests started arriving, Fragrance walked in with an armful of dresses. For Sidonia there was a lovely blue satin that Fragrance had outgrown. When Sidonia walked into the dining room, voices fell to a whisper, people were astonished at the grace and comeliness of the elven maid. Svanhild followed in black silk, silver swans embroidered on the hem.

Hester seated them at the Mayor's table. Cornelius and Annabelle embraced the girls and bade them be seated. There were a thousand questions and Svanhild did her best to satisfy their curiosity.

Annabelle, who had taken a special interest in the Marquis, was thrilled to hear of the desperate rescue by the Dwarves and the trip to the Convent. To Cornelius, Svanhild mentioned the need for volunteers to travel to Esteria.

Brief snatches of news had reached the people of Miranda but when Cornelius stood up and told the tale of the Marquis and Dorothea, there was a wave of emotion. Within living memory nothing like it had been heard in this quiet lumber town. The Mayor raised his glass and proposed a toast to the Marquis. The ringing of crystal echoed through the hall and Cornelius knew this to be the right moment to break the news about the request for volunteers to follow the Marquis to Esteria. The response was overwhelming and a good many of the men signed up.

After the last course was served, the guests asked Svanhild to play the utelli. Svanhild looked over the musical instruments displayed on the wall and picked the utelli that she had played before. She took the finely crafted instrument and began tuning the strings. The silver ring on her finger felt tight. She took it off and laid it aside.

She whispered to Sidonia standing beside her and when Svanhild had played a few chords, Sidonia broke into song,

in the face of lilies I see love
in rustling leaves a voice above
sings of elven dreams
of worlds where no weapons flash
nor foes do clash
a world without war
darkness will be no more

elven eyes brightly shine
elven ears do hear
a bell from distant years
it tolls on time's horizon
it sings of light descending
peace and joy extending
a world without war
darkness will be no more!

Sidonia's vision of the future lifted the sombre mood that had settled over the guests. Cornelius was fascinated by the fragile elven maid, with the sparkling turquoise eyes and crystalline voice. When the evening came to a close, Cornelius thanked Svanhild and Sidonia and assured them that the men in Miranda would be joining the Marquis on the march to Esteria.

Fragrance and Fairlight joined Svanhild and Sidonia for breakfast. The pretty sisters deluged them with questions. Was it a ray of the rosy morning light or a blush on Fragrance's cheek when Svanhild spoke of Slim?

Svanhild hadn't failed to notice and wondered about Rosemary, Slim's first flame. Hearsay in town had the pretty waitress at the Graceful Neck seeing a rich burgher in Cascade. On the long trek up the mountain Slim had spoken of Fragrance. She had paid little heed at the time, but now she wondered. Slim's heart was hard to fathom. Perhaps he didn't fathom it himself. How often we fail to hear the murmur of the deeper currents that flow within us.

The stomping of heavy boots interrupted her reverie. An old logger walked into the dining room. It was Fiddlehead. He had walked the trail to the Lake of the Coloured Fishes in his younger days and Hester had asked him to talk to Svanhild and Sidonia. The hunched old fellow had a long beard and snow white locks touching his belt. His comments were not encouraging.

'The Lake of the Coloured Fishes, folks go there no more. The trail, she is a nasty one, all grown in, dark as a Dwarf's tunnel. Nasty the creatures that dwell in that stinking mess of rotten wood and wet moss, may as well move into a root cellar. But if your heart is set on it, cross the lake and find the giant yew, there you'll find her, if your eyes be sharp.'

Shaking his head and softly snickering, he shuffled to the kitchen for a cinnamon bun and a chat with old Sarah. Walking through the doorway he muttered in his beard.

'Them doodle-brained girls wants to hike the old trail, she is haunted I say.'

'If those youngsters wants to find out for themselves, it is none of your beeswax, ye old rascal.' laughed Sarah. 'Youngsters these days don't hold with the old tales we learned when we was young. Let them find out if they must.'

'Ah so be it, Sarah. Give me that mug of coffee and a bun, and by and by I'll row them to the other shore.'

Before shouldering her pack, Svanhild walked into the sunlight and knelt at the water's edge. Limonides swimming around the harbour sailed gracefully up to his mistress.

'This time, Limonides, please return to the farm. If you do not come back, Uncle Svend will wonder if ill befell you.'

Limonides lowered his tall neck and his beak touched Svanhild's face. Svanhild understood his ambivalence and lovingly stroked his feathers. When she turned around, Fiddlehead was walking towards his punt. It was now time for leave taking.

Hester and Sidonia had just lowered their packs into the punt when Svanhild arrived, followed by Fragrance and Fairlight. When Svanhild and Sidonia took their seats, Fiddlehead was still sputtering comments. 'Foolish featherheads, must learn the hard way.'

Voices of well wishers on shore drowned his homily and once he started pulling the oars, he had no breath left for snarly comments.

Heavy hearted, Hester returned to the inn. Never before had she met a maiden like Svanhild. For courage, talent or endurance, even amongst the men, there were few who could equal her.

Walking through the dining room, a flash of light caught her eye. A sunbeam glittered on a silver ring that had been left on one of the tables. Raising it to the light she saw that it was the ring presented to Svanhild upon the celebration of her flower festival. Set in the finely crafted silver was a small oval stone. Engraved in the stone was a rose surrounded by four flames. The rose, for the beauty of womanhood and the flames for the fire of suffering that must be traversed to obtain the gift of the spirit.

'Beloved Svanhild,' whispered Hester placing the ring on the high shelf of a glassed-in cabinet.

Fiddlehead was still shaking his head when the shallow bottomed punt slid on the sandy shore. Svanhild and Sidonia jumped on land near a clump of poplars and thanked the gloomy boatman. Fiddlehead pumped one of the oars by way of farewell and leisurely steered the boat back to harbour.

Fragrance and Fairlight, seated in the sunshine by the water's edge watched Svanhild and Sidonia until they disappeared under the branches of the giant yew. The swans sailed around the harbour and Fragrance and Fairlight wondered what they were up to.

Limonides had been dismayed at seeing the two maidens entering the spruce forest. Deep in the swans' collective unconscious dwelt memories of dark forests and lakes. A dim awareness of danger came to Limonides. He remembered from the distant past, birds that once had been closely related to swans, birds that saw naught but evil and who black mouthed all who crossed their path. Deep in time, the swans had broken away from the dark-feathered beings that had cast a shadow over them. They had fled the gloom of the spruce forest to find light and liberty on the plains of the Sanctus. Freed from the dark past, they developed the grace and beauty that they manifest to this very day.

A faint imprint of these memories passed through Limonides' mind. He tried to give shape to his feelings but could not. Pavlova sensed Limonides' reluctance to leave Svanhild and her elven friend in the dark regions that their forefathers once called home.

'An ill wind whispers through the spruce branches Limonides. Let us wait until Svanhild and Sidonia arrive at the Lake of the Coloured Fishes, before flying back to Cascade.'

Limonides thought for a moment. They had been told to return, but a day or two later would serve just as well. Pavlova's sixth sense had never failed her. Danger dwelt under the deep green canopy that had swallowed Svanhild and Sidonia.

'It is well Pavlova. We remain in the harbour until we know that they are safe.'

The men and women of Miranda were surprised to see the seven swans remain near shore. At dusk couples ambled onto the board walk delighted at the sight of the great white birds, so full of grace. Limonides leading, they swam around the lake that provided the town with a natural harbour. Having worked in show business all their lives the swans thrived on the admiration of the audience on shore. Excited by the attention, Limonides lead the swans into a simple water ballet exercise. Pavlova did airborne caprices, complementing the movements of the swans below.

By now most of the town's people were seated at the water's edge, enchanted by the dancing swans. Cornelius and his wife Annabelle were amongst the onlookers and concluded that Svanhild had asked the swans to stay and treat the town to a show before returning to Cascade.

Crawling under the overhanging branches of the yew tree, Svanhild and Sidonia confronted a jungle of small shrubs and nettle plants. Fortunately they were prepared for roughing it in the bush. Annabelle had provided them with travelling outfits, blue slacks and white pullover jackets made out of canvas. Cut from the same cloth were wide rimmed hats. It was a strange sight to see the girls in the same dress, but Annabelle's practical mind had foreseen the hardships of travel and ignored tradition.

They pushed their way through the thick undergrowth to a large rock. Sidonia climbed on top and overlooking the shrubbery, spotted a faint indentation in the greenery, where the path might have been. She fixed her sight on a tall poplar, some distance away and they struck out for the landmark.

They reached the old trail but the dank air made breathing difficult. Suddenly, Sidonia reached for Svanhild's hand.

'Hark, my dear!' Svanhild turned her head and picked up a faint tapping.

'Sidonia, it is the signature of Roland Hammerfast, the red woodpecker that guided us last year on the mountain trek.'

The woodpeckers had watched the girls for quite some time and their telegraph system had relayed their presence from tree to tree, until it reached Roland Hammerfast. Announcing himself with a polite knock, the red bird emerged from behind a tree. He bowed and voiced a greeting. Sidonia had difficulty in understanding the staccato speech of the rakish looking bird, but Svanhild was used to it.

'Greetings to you and your feathered brethren, Roland Hammerfast. We gratefully remember your help on the mountain slopes when the leaves were gold and yellow.'

'It was so little, Svanhild. This is a different part of the forest and for four or five miles the going will not be easy, then the path will rise and the ground will be firmer. We wish you good luck. Our scouts have spotted the faithful swans floating in Miranda harbour, awaiting your return.'

Svanhild flushed with anger. This was twice that Limonides had disobeyed her. There was nothing that she could do. Turning back was not possible.

'Thank you Roland Hammerfast, we remember your kindness.'

'It is nothing my dear swannemaiden, also very pleased to meet the elven lady.' added the dapper bird. 'Farther up the mountain one of our far flyers spotted small creatures encamped in a forest glade. Elves perchance?'

Sidonia's eyes spoke disbelief.

'Forsooth, fair maid, that is what our bird saw and I do not think his eyes betrayed him.'

'We will find out when we reach thither Sidonia, but now let us resume our trek. At least we know that the walk through these chillsome corridors will soon end.'

As they shouldered their packs and set out they could hear Roland Hammerfast calling after them.

'Halt not for a night's rest till you clear the height of land and begin your descent to the Lake. Heed not the call of creatures furred or feathered. Tales of mischief in the dark of the forest abound.'

They thanked the jaunty bird and with new courage attacked the spongy forest floor. Behind them they heard Roland tapping a short tattoo by way of farewell.

Heeding the woodpecker's warning they trudged for hours until they came to a slight rise and the going became lighter. Upon reaching the ridge of the small hillock, rays of sunlight reached down through the black canopy. Sidonia suddenly halted and raised her hand. Svanhild could hear only the soft singing of the evergreens, but Sidonia seemed fascinated.

'Svanhild, Svanhild, elven voices carried on the wind. The woodpeckers were not deceived.'

The sound of elven tongues seemed to have a magic effect upon her travel companion and Svanhild had difficulty keeping up with her.

'How can it be Sidonia, elven tongues in the wilderness, far from the domain of Queen Orchidae.'

'The sound is fading Svanhild and all I pick up now is a faint knocking. Perhaps it is Roland Hammerfast's suggestion and my wishful thinking,' laughed Sidonia slowing her pace. At the top of the next knoll they looked at each other. A clear chopping sound came from the valley below. The trail turned right and once they had rounded the corner, a sun filled glade reached up to the horizon. At the lower end of the glade, small trees were falling. Sidonia squeezed Svanhild's hand.

'Elves. They are Elves cutting firewood, I can see a lodge farther up the glade. Elves have set up camp in this lovely meadow. How can this be?'

They were not left wondering very long. The woodcutters at the lower end of the glade, had spotted Svanhild and Sidonia and they came running downhill at lightning speed. Whether Sidonia actually recognized one of the runners or if it were extra sensory perception, Svanhild never knew, but Sidonia burst out at the top of her voice, 'Starlight, angels above. It is Starlight.' And indeed it was Starlight. Starlight, who as an elven youth had joined the rebel Cobalt and his troop of Black Elves.

Starlight had been standing in the glade watching the strange twosome wandering down the trail. They were a fair distance off, but even in her strange outfit, he recognized Sidonia's face. They had grown up together. He rushed down followed by his companion and came to a stand-still at a short distance from Svanhild and Sidonia. He cast an apprehensive glance at Sidonia, not knowing whether to extend his hand. She might refuse to touch the hand of a rebel. He underestimated the elven maid's great heart, for she threw her arms around the tall Elf standing before her. He looked into her eyes and answered the unspoken question.

'There are seventeen of us who left the Black Elves and broke with Cobalt and his rebels. We are on our way home and will plead for an amnesty at Queen Orchidae's court.'

Relief and joy welled up within Sidonia's heart. She introduced Starlight and his companion, Timmy Tightstring, to Svanhild. 'Stringy for short,' laughed the small Elf. Starlight invited them to come to the lodge and meet his companions. The large-cone shaped structure was held up by poles meeting at the centre. The spaces between the poles were filled with cedar branches and moss. Once inside the lodge they beheld the whole company seated around a fire. Sidonia knew most of the Elves and she and Svanhild went around shaking hands with every one of them.

Rosehip tea was boiling and mugs were passed around. Starlight was keen to redeem himself in Sidonia's sight and related their adventures.

'After Queen Orchidae led our nation into the United Kingdom, Cobalt persuaded seventy seven of us that we were in danger of losing our freedom and culture. We set out to fulfil our dream of independence, only to find that life with Cobalt and his clique became a straightjacket. Black uniforms and discipline replaced our gay habits and carefree life. I knew we had made a terrible error and seventeen of us broke away.'

'What happened to Cobalt and the other Elves, Starlight?'

'I fear Sidonia they rafted down the river Mork and swore fealty to the Lords of Darkness.

'The power of the Seven Lords must be very great if they can draw Elves into their web of deceit,' sighed the elven maiden. Sidonia was shaken. She knew all the Black Elves and feared that in the end, their choice would lead to disaster. 'Oh, Starlight, providence enabled you and your companions to free yourselves while you could. Tarry no longer. Return to our people. With open arms Queen Orchidae will welcome you back. All will be forgiven. Why not return forthwith, companion of my youth? What is to be gained by dawdling?'

'We are afraid that our plea will be rejected Sidonia, hence we lingered through the winter at the home of Snort, the eldest son of the late Trolls Hyronymus and Trollanka. In early spring we set out for the homeland.

Yet, we fear the wrath of the Queen and her councillors and we have been unable to decide who amongst us should travel ahead and request an amnesty.'

'Oh, Starlight,' burst out Sidonia, 'wrath never did dwell in the Queen's heart. Only grief dwelt there. When our nation joined the Kingdom and Cobalt led his followers beyond the borders, the Queen's lament was deep. Had Cobalt repented, how great would have been her joy.'

The anxious faces of the seventeen Elves around the fire broke into smiles. The doubts that had plagued their minds and delayed their return vanished and it was quickly decided that they would all travel together and plead for mercy. Caught in a wave of excitement, they talked of nothing else but memories of Elvenland.

At the home of Snort they had discarded their black uniforms and Snort's wife Trollypot had given them a hand, sewing traditional elven garments. Sidonia and Svanhild smiled at the strange assortments of colours and materials that they were wearing.

'How much better than the black you set out in,' laughed Sidonia. 'Once home, our seamstresses will quickly see you in the finest elven wear.'

Laughter and cheer resounded around the fire, until Starlight suggested they catch some sleep and rise early to prepare for the journey home.

Next morning, Sidonia and Svanhild discovered that their elven friends had left the lodge and moved outside. They found them seated on logs around a campfire sipping a drink of roasted dandelion roots. Svanhild sat down by Starlight's side. Remorse dwelt in those black elven eyes. She sensed the torment in his mind and took his hand.

'Fear not elven friend. All who walk this earth slip and stumble. I nearly fell into greater peril. The magic and the power of the great enchantress drew me in her wake and I barely escaped its fatal pull. The currents of the mind run deep. The chaff rises to the surface and blinds our vision and we fail to see the beacons that mark a safe journey for the voyage of the soul.'

Starlight cast Svanhild an astonished glance. The Swannemaiden, this loveliness sitting on the log by his side, had strayed and erred and had nearly been seduced by the power of the great witch. It dawned suddenly on the elven youth that others too, had faced agonizing choices.

'The Elven Queen surely will rejoice at your return Starlight,' continued Svanhild. 'Archers from your native land will travel to Esteria to oppose the evil that looms beyond yonder mountains. Some of your friends may wish to join.'

All the Elves rejoiced at the prospect of serving their Queen and proving their loyalty.

Time flew by as they chatted around the fire and it was nearly noon when they rose to leave.

Svanhild had talked to Starlight about the trail ahead. The Elves had come from a different direction but Starlight knew that the trail dropped down again and that once more they would have to make their way through three or four miles of dense and damp forest.

Sidonia embraced each one of the seventeen Elves. Svanhild followed behind shaking hands. When she came to Timmy Tightstring the small Elf stood tiptoe and whispered into her ear.

'I have wandered far and wide around the camp because I am restless, that's why they call me Tightstring. Perhaps I suffer from hypertension. I pick up things others cannot hear. Strange high pitched voices I heard in yonder hills. A scratching sound that grates the marrow in your spine.'

'Thank you, Tightstring Timmy. If shrill and strident voices are carried on the wind, we will give them a wide berth.'

They shouldered their packs and walked through the sun-filled glade. Elven voices echoed across the landscape. 'Fare thee well Swannemaiden. Godspeed elven sister.'

33

Scornbirds

$\mathcal{T}$he giant spruce rising on both sides of the trail dwindled the slight travelers and a dreadful smell of mould suffused the air as they trudged on through the dank forest. Their feet sank deep into the soggy moss and when they pulled them up, they could hear the water sloshing in their boots. Crossing a swamp, black insects descended biting their necks and faces. On reaching firmer ground they came across a beck and washed in the cold clean water. It soothed the itching bites.

No ray of sunshine reached down to the forest floor. Exotic mushrooms, the size of dinner plates appeared in the moss, some a deep red with white dots, others with big white stems and shining canopies, their silver surfaces emitting a strange light. Svanhild was fascinated by the mysterious colours glowing amidst the luminescent green of mosses. She reached out to pick a brilliant red canopy, but Sidonia stopped her.

'Svanhild, even touching can be fatal, so poisonous are they!'

Svanhild recalled old Fiddlehead's warning and wondered what magic had bewitched this trail. They trudged on in sheer desperation wondering if the trail had an end at all. Suddenly Sidonia sang out.

'On yonder hill rays of moonlight penetrate the canopy, the spruce are thinning, we are nearing the end of this dark passage.'

The path began to rise and the ground became firmer. The spruce were not so dense and birches appeared amidst the evergreens.

Sidonia took some cakes from her pack and they nibbled as they climbed uphill. Revived by elven cakes, they moved at a fair clip. The air improved as they left the damp forest behind and the going became easier. They came to a clearing filled with moonlight. There was no hope of reaching the Lake of the Coloured Fishes before nightfall.

'If overnight we must Sidonia, why not set up camp in this meadow? The light of the moon will cheer us and a fire will keep the flies away.'

Sidonia began to gather twigs. Svanhild took a wooden container out of her pack and headed toward the sound of a babbling brook. Skipping down to the water's edge she leaned over and filled her bowl. When she returned, flames were leaping into the night sky. For a moment she stood still taking in the image. Slim would have painted it, but she etched it in her mind. A scratching noise startled her from her reverie. It was a raspy sound, like broken voices, shrill and strident. Suddenly it stopped and all she could hear was the faint babbling of the brook. Seated by the fire she told Sidonia.

'The scratching noise Timmy Tightstring mentioned, I think I heard it down below.'

'All I can hear Svanhild, is the crackling of the flames, yet I take Timmy's warning seriously.' The little creature is hypersensitive and I doubt not that he has the second sight.'

They roasted the chestnuts that Hester had put into their packs and Svanhild made tea. Blissfully, the faint rasping voices were not heard again and they were able to enjoy a few moments of quiet. Just when they were taking out their sleeping bags, crude laughter echoed off the rock face at the end of the clearing. This time they were alarmed.

'Timmy Tightstring's caution was no idle fancy. Away at once!' urged Sidonia.

They were just rolling up their sleeping bags when bats dropped from a tree, sheering overhead. Svanhild took a burning branch and threw it, but it was of no use. The bats kept coming. Desperately flailing at the swarming pests, they managed to stuff most of their belongings into their packs and hurried away. Precious time had been lost.

High pitched noises drifted across the moon shadows of the forest. Sidonia and Svanhild looked at each other and wondered if they should turn back. Silently they strode forwards, hoping that they would pass unseen by the source of the sickening noise. For awhile it seemed that they were out of danger. Then, without warning, a shriek rang from behind. They turned and beheld the creatures that had made the racket.

Facing them were three tall birds. They resembled giant flickers with dark red bands encircling their necks. The feathers, dirty brown in colour and in an awful state of disarray gave the impression that the birds were in a perpetual state of moulting. Fierce green eyes burned in their sockets and the large black beaks opened and shut with a clapping sound.

When they saw Svanhild and Sidonia's astonished faces, the birds let out a snide laugh. The tallest, in the centre, who stood as high as Svanhild, screeched in a raspy voice.

'Travelling to the Lake of the Coloured Fishes, Svanhild, you and your pretty companion from elvenland? Going to visit the ore thief and his roly poly wife?'

A cascading laugh made his beak clatter like a pair of castanets and the flunkies by his sides joined in. The sound was jarring and cold shivers travelled down Svanhild's spine. Sidonia tried to compose herself and practice creative visualization but any positive images were scattered by the dreadful vibes coming from the birds.

Svanhild caught her breath and undertook to stand up for her friends, Oarflake and Ambrosia. 'Don't call Oarflake a thief. He is a healing master and saved the lives of many a wounded creature in the forest.' Her words were wasted. The foul-feathered creature rattled with laughter.

'The Gnome Oarflake, a healing master? Oh, yes, and I am a dancing swan.' This last line seemed to amuse his fellow birds and there was a lot of beak clacking and frightful laughter.

Svanhild realized that the creatures knew about Slim and the dancing swans and wondered who they worked for.

She mastered her anger and turned her back on the repulsive creatures.

Sidonia took her hand. Slowly they started walking up the incline with the birds following close behind, pecking at their shoulders. Then some yards ahead, four other birds stepped into the trail in front of them, blocking their passage.

In anger Svanhild turned around and faced the spokesbird.

'Shame on you! Who are you and your feathered companions, that you dare touch us with your filthy beaks? What business do you have foul-mouthing the noble Gnome and his generous wife. Beware of Ambrosia's psychic powers.'

For a moment Svanhild's warning had a sobering effect.

'Psychic powers, my tail feathers,' scoffed one of the other birds. 'Don't bluster us hussie.'

Svanhild's face flushed red and Sidonia touched her arm for fear she would raise it in anger and hit the scamp.

'Take it easy, Swannemaid,' rasped the tall fowl facing her.

'Swannemaid?' screeched one of his flunkies. 'Maid no more. Spent the year travelling in the woods with the Marquis deCygne.'

'Travelled with His Excellency in the bush or should we say, His Corpulency,' quipped Whopper, a brawny character standing behind her. The birds' randy chuckling echoed through the forest. The mortification and humiliation of their captives only encouraged the hooligans who decided to punctuate their witty remarks by sinking their beaks into the girls' shoulders.

Sidonia had to restrain Svanhild from reaching for her slingshot. Resting her hand on Svanhild's right arm, she looked up and faced Scruffers, the lead bird.

'Elven lore speaks of the feathered outcasts from the garden of bliss, Scornbirds. You are the Scornbirds!'

It was the words about the garden of bliss that silenced the rowdy lot. The fire of derision burning in their eyes dimmed, but not for long.

Soon the jeering and screeching resumed full force and they crowded close around Svanhild and Sidonia. The mass of scuzzy feathers began to move and the girls were dragged along through a small clearing and onto a side trail. When they tried to run away, the birds started pecking their arms and shoulders. Resistance was useless. Caught in the centre of a tight circle of Scornbirds, they were pushed forward until they came to a garden overgrown with weeds and vines. Svanhild and Sidonia were startled to see, standing in the centre, a spacious cedar lodge. Large windows showing pots of dried up flowers flanked its heavy oaken door, the thatched roof was overgrown with green moss.

The door opened revealing a hunched greybeard standing on the threshold. When he saw Sidonia and Svanhild ringed by his frazzled flock, an evil grin spread over the dotard's face.

'See what my precious birds brought home,' mused the old hunchback. 'A fine catch my feathered friends. Svanhild in the company of an elven maiden. Welcome to Scornlodge, my daughters, welcome!' croaked the old rascal.

Svanhild looked at the face in the doorway. She had seen it before, but could not recall where. Sidonia recognized it instantly. She turned to Svanhild.

'It is Banewort, once councillor to King Arcturus, and banished from the court for slander and impertinence.'

'Come in my children, come in. My faithful birds have escorted you here safely. Yes, I have trained them well.'

They had no choice. The birds were crowding behind them, pushing and shoving until they found themselves inside. The birds too, entered the lodge perching on chairs and the beams above. The interior was in a state of disarray. Feathers covered the floors and kitchen counters and the smell was foul.

Sidonia and Svanhild sat down on a low bench by the grate. Here at least they were free from the smothering feathers and the sharp beaks. A small fire was burning in the grate and they were relieved to be able to warm themselves and dry their damp clothing. They were dazed and puzzled by the events of the day. Had the wily master of the Scornbirds brought them here to vent his anger or did he know about their mission?

The Scornmaster was delighted. He did a kind of two-step around the lodge, his disfigured body hopping about with amazing agility. At the sight of their master's antics the birds began clapping their beaks. Banewort danced in step with the chorus of clattering bills. He seemed immensely pleased about the day's events. When he finished prancing around, he raised his hands and the birds stopped their clattering.

Svandhild and Sidonia were bewildered by the mad scene. Banewort, out of breath, slumped down onto a raggedy old sofa. When he came to, he looked at the girls sitting on the other side of the grate.

'Great honour to have visitors from the Kingdom, my doves. You will be my guests for one or two, or perhaps many days.'

'Master Banewort, said Sidonia who had managed to keep calm, 'Our time is precious. We must leave tonight.'

'My dear elven child you don't mean it. It would be hasty and quite impolite,' rasped the old toad. 'I cherish pretty companions in this lonely outpost, a feminine touch to make this pigsty into a cosy place. I am used to elegance. Once I lived in the Royal Palace.'

'And were banished by King Arcturus,' added Svanhild. Hatred sprang into his eyes.

'The King was a doddering old fool. I tried to counsel him, Lord Imbrun tried, but to no avail. In the end he paid with his life.'

The air of gaiety had vanished from the face of the Scornmaster. A caustic light dwelt in his eyes.

'The dreams of the King were the dreams of a child, the simpering simpleton. To enhance his power, Elves, Swannepeople, Dwarves, Outlanders, Mountain Fairies and Gnomes were forced into one nation.' Svanhild was about to burst out in anger but just in time Sidonia took her hand and spoke up.

'It is not true, Master Banewort. A conference was called at Mount Oneisis and the people gathered there voted for unification.'

'And where did it get them?' chuckled their host. 'When King Arcturus united the Kingdom, he raised the ire of the Dark Lords. He lost his life and his daughter. The Kingdom is in shambles. Some dream that the Princess will be freed. Idle dreams, the stuck up wench is imprisoned in the old Alcazar, soon to be moved to the palace of my Masters'

Horror and disbelief struck Sidonia and Svanhild.

'Ah, I see you are shocked, my pretties. Appearances can be deceptive. The angel faced Princess that you remember, that symbol of purity, has allied herself with Salan, the lustful leader of the Seven, in the Land of Darkness.' The Scornmaster's face screwed up and his disdainful chortle filled the room.

'A priceless match. The wedding will be soon and I shall attend it.'

Shock and indignation showed in Sidonia and Svanhild's faces. It only fuelled their host's glee.

'The union of the faithless Princess and the lusty Lord, a delicious arrangement. I shall be there and you shall be there. Hi ho, hi ho, to the palace we go, and we will feast together. Oh yes, my ladies the friendly Grolls will be your guard of honour and travel with you to the palace. There, we shall meet and make merry. The prospect brought tears of laughter to the Scornmaster's eyes. Svanhild and Sidonia were horrified. What fiendish plot was hatching in the rapscallion's tarnished mind?

A glint of cunning appeared in the Banewort's eyes. Evil to the core, he had shrewd intuition.

'A visit to the palace will be more exhilarating than spending time with the dull witted ore thief. Yes, it is true that the exiles on the shore of the Lake of the Coloured Fishes have a sixth sense for gold. Is it a golden tablet you are looking for?' In a vague and undefined way the Scornmaster seemed to sense the purpose of their journey.

'No golden tablets will be found, my pretties. Golden tablets are but an idle dream. The golden rim to which the hopeless cling. Wake up my deluded maidens, waste no time chasing specious visions. Hi ho, hi ho, to the palace we go and there we shall make merry.'

Marching around the table, his evil laughter filled the lodge and the scornbirds joined in a raspy chuckle. The sound of the birds grated on the girls. All that they held dear and holy had been soiled and sullied. Their beloved Princess had been maligned and derided.

'Go and rest your weary bones my dears,' said Master Banewort,' pointing to a corner in the lodge.

Svanhild and Sidonia moved to the empty space, unpacked their sleeping bags and spread them on the wooden floor. Dead tired they were, yet the cackling of the birds kept them from dozing off.

'The King, a simpering simpleton, the Princess leaves her crumbling Kingdom, Oarflake the ore thief, wears a mask of saintliness. Vanity, all is vanity!' cried the feathered choristers. For a few moments the din subsided and then Banewort piped up.

'When the proud Elven Queen joined the Kingdom, half her people rebelled and fled from her tyranny.'

Sidonia ignored the taunt. Sleep was not possible. They sat up leaning against the wall and Master Banewort walked over with two mugs of hot huckleberry wine. He placed the drinks on a small table and seated himself on a stool. Svanhild cast him a withering glance. 'Is nothing sacred to you Master Banewort?'

'I have learned that lesson in the long weary years that I served the King in the palace in Lambarina, tinsel on the outside and rot within. A fool was King Arcturus, deceived by his underlings. He would not listen to Master Banewort.' scoffed the misshapen figure leaning on one elbow.

'Princess Yaconda, all loveliness and purity in the eyes of the innocent. It was the Princess who seduced Lord Imbrun. They sailed off on his yacht to conclude the affair,' laughed the old scoundrel. 'Charades, palace charades and no one looked behind the masks. Wake up my innocent children, wake up. The Kingdom is lost. They would not listen to old Banewort and cast him out for cheek and slander. My day will come when sense and sensibility return. When the Seven rule the Kingdom, this shadow play will end.'

At last the ranting and raving came to an end and Banewort wandered off. Svanhild and Sidonia sank down to the floor, pained, exhausted and their souls in agony. Their vision of the world had been twisted. Sidonia sat up again and began creative visualization. Svanhild, feeling the healing power that emanated from her elven friend, fell asleep.

Sunlight filled the lodge when they woke next morning. They stuffed their blankets into their packs and looked around. Feathers floated in the bright beams of light. The scruffy birds were perched everywhere and clutter covered the floor. It was hard to get around and they began to clean up best they could. If they were to spend some time here as the involuntary guests of the mad Scornmaster, they had to make the place habitable.

After sweeping up the muck and piles of feathers they scrubbed the floor. Svanhild found some oats and cooked porridge. Sidonia's hand touched Svanhild's shoulder.

'I trust there is no truth in the words of the Scornmaster. Princess Yaconda seducing Lord Imbrun.'

Svanhild looked at Sidonia. They both knew the slander of the wicked Banewort, was rooted in bitterness and malice, pure fantasy. Yet it had left an impression, no matter how faint. It was fortunate that Svanhild knew how Lord Imbrun had kidnapped the beautiful, Princess Yaconda, and cruelly imprisoned her.

'My dear Sidonia, it was Lord Imbrun who delivered her to the Seven. The Mountain Fairies Edel and Weiss discovered the Princess imprisoned in the tower of the old Alcazar, in the western desert. There she languishes under the watchful eyes of the cruel Grolls.'

Sidonia sighed with relief and chided herself for the shadow that had crossed her mind.

'Svanhild we must escape from this dreadful lodge before we become mired in this morass of spite. Disdain dwells in Banewort's soul, disdain for all that is fine and noble and all he says is echoed by the tattered feathers, Scornbirds!'

They sat down to breakfast and enjoyed a few minutes of repose before Banewort began scurrying around the lodge. He pushed open the front door and fresh air filled the large open space, then the birds came down from their perches and marched outside.

The Scornmaster closed the door behind the birds, joined the girls at the table and helped himself to the leftover porridge.

'A lovely morning my dainties. How pleasant to have one's breakfast cooked by such lovely creatures. I cannot let you go. It would break my heart.'

Svanhild and Sidonia kept silent. After he had finished breakfast, he limped over to the window and looked outside. Rubbing his crooked hands he whispered to himself.

'The snow is gone and soon the Rover and his Grolls will arrive. They'll pay a pretty penny for those two. The Seven Lords will be delighted to have Svanhild and an elvenmaiden among the wedding guests.'

The thought of the girls in the midst of a troop of grizzly Grolls tickled him and he burst into a devilish laugh. They feel hard done by now. Wait until they arrive at the palace of the Seven. One had to keep in the good graces of the Seven Masters. It would be a worthy gift.

'Make yourselves at home my pretties. Go for a walk and enjoy yourselves. You are safe at Scornlodge.'

Banewort, waddled off to a corner of the lodge, sat down at a small desk and opened a ledger. Yes, his wealth had been increasing and the prospect of a hefty reward was enticing. The rays of the morning sun caught the rapscallion resting his head in his hands and he sailed off into a light slumber.

A grating sound came from the corner of the lodge. Svanhild looked around and saw the Scornmaster's head sinking on his desk. He was now in a deep sleep. Svanhild sprang up, quietly, catlike, she slid over to the woodstove and picked up the cast iron frying pan. Tiptoeing carefully over to his corner, she raised her arm. But before she could bring the mass of iron down on the scoundrel's head Sidonia caught her arm.

'For mercy's sake my love. Do not kill him. It is not ours to judge.'

Svanhild went limp and Sidonia guided her back to the dining table. Banewort woke for a moment, muttered some incoherent sentences, and went back to sleep. Sidonia, sitting across from Svanhild, took her hand.

'My beloved friend, do not be cross with me. We must not kill. It is too heavy a burden to bear.' Svanhild calmed down and the fire in her eyes dimmed.

'Thanks Sidonia. It is better this way. Much good would it have done. The birds would have turned on us.'

They walked out of the lodge and into the sunshine. Some of the birds were leaning against the wall of the lodge enjoying the spring sun. Slowly Svanhild and Sidonia sauntered to the foot of a hill at the end of the garden. The birds seemed to take little notice, but out of the corner of one eye, Scruffers had been watching them. When they reached the top of the hillock, he flapped his wings and made after them. Others followed and Svanhild knew that there was little chance of breaking away. They turned around and calmly walked back to the lodge.

Each day, they followed the same routine. They cooked and cleaned, went for walks and coped best they could with their pettifogging host and the chorus of Scornbirds echoing his endless slander.

One night, after a trying day Svanhild's patience was wearing thin. While on their daily walk she suggested to Sidonia, that they try and outrun the Scornbirds.

'It would not work Svanhild. They would overtake us and everything would be the worse for it. Patience my love, our chance will come. In two days time it will be full moon. Already the birds are becoming restless, we must wait until then.'

The full moon rose in all its splendour, its rays softened by spruce branches, shed a soft light on the garden and the lodge. Svanhild and Sidonia with their packs ready sat quietly by the stove. Banewort, a glazed look in his eyes wandered restlessly around the lodge. He appeared to get more agitated by the minute and began reciting the injustices that he had suffered at the Royal Palace. He vilified the Elven Queen, the Sisters of the Secret Crossing, and the great Wizard Isumatak.

Moonbeams fell through the large front windows and the Scornmaster began hippety hopping around the lodge. The birds paraded behind him skipping and flapping their wings.

'Moonstruck, flipped!' whispered Svanhild, 'Now is our chance.'

They moved quietly along the wall to the front door and slipped out. Only when they reached the end of the garden, did they start to run.

The frenzied scene at the Scornlodge went on until Banewort exhausted, slumped into his old rocker. Wiping perspiration from his forehead he looked around the lodge. The girls had disappeared. They had used the party atmosphere to make a getaway. But not for long. The moon was full and his precious Scornbirds would track them down. The birds would make pincushions of the two fugitives. His feathered thralls sensed that something was amiss and turned towards their master. An evil fire gleaming in his eyes, he seized a poker from the woodstove and yelled.

'Sharpen your beaks, my warriors. The treacherous maidens made a getaway. After them!'

Scruffers pushed open the heavy door and looked over the moonlit clearing. There was no sign of Svanhild and Sidonia. He rushed out followed by his flock of scruffy feathers. Scornbirds are incapable of true flight, yet hopping, skipping and flapping their wings, they moved swiftly. Once the path took a down turn, they began gliding short distances.

Adrian and Anneke, a newlywed beaver couple, were sitting at the edge of their pond, enjoying one of those rare moments of repose in beaver life. The water levels were just right and the moon was bright.

They were flummoxed when Svanhild holding Sidonia by the hand rushed by. But once the Scornbirds came into sight, Adrian figured it out. The feathered mischief makers were up to no good. Baring his huge cutters Adrian looked at his mate and in record time the two hauled a freshly cut spruce across the path. It caught Scruffers by the talons. The huge bird went catballing down the slope and landed in a puddle. Mud dripping from his wings, he cast a vile look at the beavers.

After a few minutes of delay, the birds resumed the chase. It was not long before they caught sight of Svanhild and Sidonia running uphill. Making a mad dash through an open field, they surrounded the pair.

Scruffers knew that the Scornmaster would catch up with them in a short time and decided to wait for instructions, before needling their captives. The birds spent the time sharpening their beaks on the large rocks that lay scattered about.

Svanhild and Sidonia stood hand in hand, fighting off an overwhelming sense of despair. An eerie silence prevailed, only broken by the sound of the long black bills grinding against the surface of the rocks.

In Miranda the seven swans moved silently on the moonlit lake. Folks in Miranda were astonished and delighted to have the swans stay in town. Many couples were seated on the benches lining the shore, enjoying the panorama. It added a touch of loveliness to the little lumber town.

One night after the swans performed a ballet, many of the onlookers remained to watch the light of the full moon playing on the water and the swans floating by. Great was their surprise when on the far shore appeared a long line of elves, gaily skipping along in the moonlight, and heading for their town.

Cornelius, the Mayor and his wife Annabelle rubbed their eyes and looked again.

'Elves, hubby, a troop of elves dancing along the far side of the lake with swans floating in the foreground. A double blessing for Miranda. Romance and art have come to hick town.' Annabelle had been raised in the capital and after twenty years of isolation, a touch of beauty and enchantment was heaven sent.

At the Golden Goose, Hester Hollyhock and daughters, Fragrance and Fairlight, were cleaning the dining hall when Starlight and his companions bounded into the old inn. Hester couldn't believe her eyes. Visits by elves were rare. Sidonia had been the first elf to visit in years, and now, there stood seventeen of them. Starlight introduced himself and told Hester of their meeting with Svanhild and Sidonia and of the Elves' decision to return to the realm of Queen Orchidae.

Fairlight and Fragrance were thrilled to have Elves visit the inn. Fairlight went upstairs to prepare beds for the seventeen elf visitors and Fragrance added extra tables in the dining room.

On seeing the Elves enter the Golden Goose, Cornelius and Annabelle walked to the inn to join the Elves at dinner. Other folks, anxious for news in these uncertain times, dropped in for coffee and dessert.

Starlight told Cornelius and Annabelle of his meeting with Svanhild and Sidonia and reassured their friends that he expected that they had arrived safely at the Lake of the Coloured Fishes.

Timmy Tightstring did not share Starlight's optimism. A feeling of unease had plagued him during the day and he was strung tighter than ever. Starlight had noticed it and blamed the full moon for Timmy's fidgety state of mind. The Elves were enthralled to be back in the Kingdom, talking to Swannefolk and enjoying the jolly atmosphere of an old inn. Some asked Hester if they could play the instruments hanging on the wall and before long song and dance filled the hall.

The mirth and jollity tapered off by midnight. Timmy Tightstring, playing the utelli, had sung an ancient elven chant. When he climbed onto a chair to hang the utelli back in place, his eye caught sight of a silver ring. He picked it up and returned to his table. Raising the ring, to a candle flame, he saw mounted on it, an oval stone. A rose ringed by flames had been engraved in the centre. He surmised that the ring belonged to Svanhild. Holding it in the palm of his hand, he felt a flow of energy. His eyes moved to the candle and focussing on the flame, an image appeared. He saw Svanhild and Sidonia standing in a forest, countless spears flying towards them. A conviction seized the tiny elf that the swannemaid and his elven sister were in peril. He rushed out of the inn and to the water's edge.

Pavlova, too, had had a foreboding that Svanhild and Sidonia were in danger. When she saw Timmy Tightstring running out of the inn, she lifted her wings and flew to shore. Timmy kneeling by the water's edge, told Pavlova of his vision. Limonides and the others formed a half circle around the Elf.

Ancient memories passed on from generation to generation rose in Limonides and Pavlova's minds and a vision of Scornbirds, in a dark forest, appeared to them. Within seconds Limonides became airborne and the others rose in swift pursuit. At lightning speed, flying in formation, they skimmed the treetops. An inner compass guided the swans in a straight line to their goal.

The Scornmaster was slow in catching up with the birds. When he reached the clearing where the prisoners stood surrounded by his plumed servants, his evil face lit with glee. They had almost flown the coop, but they would not try it again. He would see to that.

'Go to it fellows. Drive them home and don't spare your bills.' The Scornbirds huddled around their prey and sank their dark bills through the tough canvas jackets into Svanhild and Sidonia's shoulders.

Svanhild was overcome with fear and pain, but Sidonia remained conscious of all that happened around her and it was she who descried the moon shadows of many wings move across the clearing. Scruffers looked up and shrieked with fright. Limonides hovered over him and with a stroke of his powerful wings, knocked him to the ground. The other Scornbirds had cowered at the sight of the swans. They lay cringing in the meadow, the swans hovering over them.

Sidonia and Svanhild were mesmerized by what they saw. The Scornbirds seemed to be shrivelling up and their feathers began to fall off.

'They are paralyzed with fear Sidonia, they think the swans will kill them.'

'It is not fear, my love, that brings their agony. They see, floating over them, the grace and the beauty of the swans.

'Now they have seen what might have been. In the mists of time they had a close affinity to the swans. The swans too, were not the same then that they are now. Their feathers had been frazzled and grey, their necks short and stubby. One day a small swan, the youngest among them, had a vision of another world, far from sodden moss and glowering spruce. A world of streams and lakes and sunlit meadows. Restlessly they searched the forest for a way out of darkness. When they chanced upon a path that would lead to liberty and light they invited the scornbirds to follow but they sneered and rejected the path that would have led to grace and beauty. Secure in their damp and dark surroundings, they remained in the forest.'

Svanhild was horrified when she caught sight of the Scornbirds. They dragged their shrivelled naked bodies through the long wet grass and from sight vanished for ever.

The Swans formed a circle around the maidens. Svanhild knelt in front of Limonides and Pavlova and let her hands glide down their long necks.

'In your souls, you knew the peril that surrounded us and you were still in Miranda when the call came.'

Sidonia whispered a prayer of thanks and looked at the swans around them. Then she thought of the Scornmaster. What had happened to Banewort? Had he rushed back to the Scornlodge?

She wandered downhill and discovered the prone figure of the Scornmaster. Two beavers, shaking their heads, stood by his feet. It seemed that the Scornmaster on his flight downhill had been hit by a falling log.

Sidonia looked at the tall beaver standing at the other side of the Scornmaster. A wide grin spread over his face revealing magnificent ivories gleaming in the moonlight. She spoke gently to the beaver and his wife.

'It is better this way, his time had come. We thank you for your aid for it was you who cut the log that tripped the scornbirds and hastened the end of their Master. I marvel at your skill in felling trees. What a sense of timing.'

The compliment was well received. The beavers made a polite bow, flapped a cheery ra-ta-ta with their tails and walked away. As they splashed into the pond, Sidonia could see their brown pelts glisten in a ray of light.

Like most elves, Sidonia was endowed with psychic powers. She beheld two transparent figures hovering over Master Banewort, as he breathed his last. The spirits were busy wrapping the Scornmaster in a black shroud. When he moved his lips, Sidonia could not hear his words but one of the spirits answered him in a bell-toned voice.

'Evil is in the eye of the beholder.'

Svanhild was still kneeling within a circle of swans when Sidonia joined her. She understood now that Limonides' decision to delay his departure for Cascade had sprung from an inner urge. The noble swan explained how Timmy Tightstring had seen in the candle flame, a vision of the danger threatening and had rushed to the water's edge to share his vision with the swans.

'Wonderful synchronicity.' exclaimed Sidonia. 'The seven swans were there when Timmy Tightstring found the ring and saw the terrible fate hanging over us. Heaven be praised. We are not alone. Praise and thanksgiving to the cosmic forces that surround us.'

Limonides and the swans had a sense of fulfillment. This last meeting with the shadows of their past had been part of their destiny. They experienced a spirit of freedom which seemed to lighten their being and with joyous wings they took flight. Svanhild and Sidonia waved farewell as the seven swans circled the meadow. They rose swiftly and Svanhild lost sight of them. Sidonia watched them soaring high above the forest, the rims of their wings silhouetted against the full moon.

Svanhild took Sidonia's hand and they walked down into the next valley. Neither had any thought of sleep. They wanted, before anything else happened, to reach the quiet haven at the shore of the Lake of the Coloured Fishes.

The spruce gave way to larches, birches and a sprinkling of maples. Clearings became more common and when the first light of dawn cast a rose tint over the land, they found themselves close to the homestead of the Gnomes. Exhausted, their clothes tattered by the bitter beaks of the Scornbirds, they trudged on by a sheer effort of will.

By sunup they reached the height of land and could see light glistening upon the water. The trail came to an end at the far side of the Lake of the Coloured Fishes. When they reached the shore, they slumped onto the fine sand and quenched their thirst. Across the lake they could see the homestead of the Gnomes and Sidonia espied Oarflake working in the garden. Still, it was nearly an hour's walk to reach their friends' home.

Sidonia gathered birch bark and moss and Svanhild struck a spark. When the silver bark burst into flame, a column of dark smoke rose into the air.

Ambrosia walking on the porch with a basket of laundry saw the signal.

Oarflake was raking the garden when Ambrosia called out. 'Into your boat old Gnome. Smoke is rising on the far shore, I am sure it is Svanhild returning.'

Oarflake straightened up, dropped his rake and ran down to the rowboat moored at the end of the jetty. When Oarflake's boat slid onto a sandbank at the end of the lake, Svandhild was waiting for him.

Clinging to him with a sense of despair and gratitude, she planted a kiss on the wrinkled cheek. Oarflake looked at the waif in her tattered rags. He didn't bother to ask questions. He simply picked her up and placed her gently into the back of the boat.

Sidonia climbed aboard and on their way across the lake she related to Oarflake their adventures and expressed the hope that Oarflake would be able to take them to the land of the Sea Gnomes.

'It is well you came, my dear. The Sea Gnomes are more likely to trust an elven maid than fellow Gnomes. They are suspicious of any one who might covet their treasures on the ocean floor. It will take time to gain their trust.

Ambrosia was waiting on the dock when the little vessel glided alongside. Svanhild, somewhat revived, climbed onto the wharf to fall into Ambrosia's generous arms.

34

Matista Learns of a Wedding

Soft sunlight filtered through the lace curtains of Matista's boudoir. The sorceress, seated on a satin covered sofa, reached for a hand mirror on the dresser. In daylight the sight of her face always unnerved her. It was Isumatak's curse that had robbed her of her daylight beauty. Night was her domain. Deep in thought she paced back and forth. Much was left to be done. The Seven in the Land of Darkness must be cautioned. Salan had become cocky. Power had gone to his head. Would he let his guard down? Well he might, for centuries had passed and dulled the edge of his prudence. The Seven Lords had enjoyed youth and immortality and never had their power been challenged.

The United Kingdom on their northern border was a cause of vexation to the Seven. Resistance was stiffening and the fear lingered that a tablet would be found that could undo the incantation which had secured their power and their youth. Infiltration had not worked and their armies stood poised to storm the mountain passes and rush on to occupy the Kingdom. Matista, at times, questioned the wisdom of the enterprise. Would it be wiser to leave the Kingdom in peace? It posed no threat, but anger and the urge to control silenced the voice of caution.

Old scores must be settled. This time Isumatak would not escape her wrath. The wizard's tricks would be of no avail when overwhelming force surged down the mountainside. These cheerful thoughts calmed Matista.

Princess Yaconda was safely tucked away at the old Alcazar guarded by Grolls and soon to marry Salan, the leader of the Seven. Once the people of the Kingdom learned that Salan had married their beloved Princess, their will to resist would dwindle. Salan has reason to be pleased. It was a shrewd move by the steamy old fox. Got himself a pretty maiden and removed the heir to the throne in the bargain.

Yes, the Seven should be pleased, their reign secure and their lifestyle enhanced by all the little perks that power brings. Matista knew about the new villas, the sparkling waters of their private pools and the pretty hostesses. Absorbed by power, and joys of the flesh, their vigilance might falter.

A voice within urged her to travel to the palace and tell the Lords to move with caution. Their sense of invincibility must not go to their heads. Yes, she would hasten thither and arrive in time for the wedding. Salan and Yaconda at the altar together. How droll!

Yaconda had been taken care of. Matista remembered how the people of the Kingdom adored her. The thought overwhelmed her with jealousy. Long ago she too had been adored as the future bride of Prince Norvalt, son of the great King Stanislav. Well wishers and admirers had lined the streets and cheered their future Queen. Power and fame had been within her grasp when outrageous fortune struck. The Prince married Princess Netilda, a nobody amongst princesses, and yet she captured his heart. Matista shook with anger. She had been jilted. Her beauty and brilliance cast aside. The memory, centuries later, still grated. She sat down by the magic mirror holding her face in her hands. Yes, there had been pain, but sweet the revenge. Her incantation had sent King Norvalt, Queen Netilda and all their subjects into a deep sleep. It was then she had handed the reign of power to Salan and his Lords. It had been a great victory.

She must pack her bags and travel to the palace. She imagined the agony of Princess Yaconda being dragged to the altar into the welcoming arms of the lusty lord. A shrill laugh filled the room. The whole thing would be quite exquisite. It was pleasant to visualize the scene and it lifted the sense of depression that had settled upon her during the winter.

She went downstairs and walked outside. The soft westering sun highlighted the white roses blooming in the garden and in the distance she caught sight of the lake ringed by stands of spring flowers. She walked around the garden delighted by signs of life returning. Meadow, looking down from the chateau, hadn't seen her happy since Svanhild's escape. Life had been dreadful at the Chateau for many months.

Matista passed through the orchard touching some of the buds on the fruit trees. It was going to be a lovely spring and there was much to look forward to. To make sure all was well, before retiring, she would have a peek at the magic mirror.

Back in her boudoir, she sat in front of the Mirror of a Thousand Fragments.

The first image was one of armies marching on the shore of the Wasa River. The time of reckoning was nigh. She moved her fingers over the glass and could feel the fine fissures that divided the mirror in a thousand pieces. As her fingertips continued to explore the mirror, images of people and places around the world flashed in front of her. Suddenly a sharp pain shot through the middle finger of her left hand. It travelled up her arm and she cried out in anguish. A feeling of dread beset her, unusual for an enchantress of the highest spheres. What was the power of this mirror that a small cut on the edge of the glass caused such pain?

She looked closer and saw that a fragment of the mirror was missing, leaving a razor sharp edge. Who had dared to steal a fragment from her beloved glass? Who else, but her onetime apprentice, the bedevilled maid from Swanneland. The cheek of the girl to filch a sliver from the mirror.

Her mind spun with fury. Once Svanhild was captured by the armies of the Seven, it would fare ill with her. She looked through the window at canopies of cedar and spruce bending with the west wind and rested her eyes on the sea of green caught in the last flash of sunlight.

Her left arm and hand still ached but her mind was calm. It was dusk, the hour of transformation. She raised her small hand mirror and felt a sense of triumph as her shrivelled countenance metamorphosed into a bewitching comeliness. Her beauty at that nocturnal hour never ceased to amaze her. The pain in her arm vanished, the bleeding stopped and she sighed with relief. If only the night could last forever. How she despised the light of day. It was then she heard a voice speak her very thoughts,

'Oh enchantress, take heed when thou speakest in that vein. Do not despise the light, lest thou be cast in outer darkness. Hearken to a voice from ages past. It was I who received the priceless mirror crafted by the Dwarves and it was I, the Elven Queen who yielded to its magic whisper,

A beauty that transcends,
all who dwell in Elvenlands,
it shines beyond compare,
ah, such radiance is rare.

'The mirror that enchanted me spun a net of vanity. It cast a shadow on my soul. At the hour of death I prayed that the mirror never again would reflect the beauty of one face but mirror forth the glory of the human race. The mirror did much good enchantress, until it fell into thine hands and became a servant of the dark power. Oh, ye who pray for darkness take heed ere thou art cast into a darkness, whence there is no escape.'

The enchantress burst into derisive laughter that echoed through the house. Marie and Gertrude, working in the kitchen, could hear the dishes rattling and shivers travelled down their spines.

'Oh, Elven Queen, from realms yet unseen,' exclaimed Matista drawing herself up, 'do not waste your warnings. Darkness is my realm, there I thrive and work. Who are you to judge whether the mirror that was once yours, is used for good or ill? Now the mirror is mine and I will use it as I see fit!'

There was no response from the apparition standing by the side of the mirror. Matista looked up and caught a glimpse of her supernatural visitor's turquoise eyes. Never did she see the tears of light on that face, shining with an unearthly beauty.

When Matista looked again the vision had vanished. The incident had been disturbing. Now whenever she looked at The Mirror of a Thousand Fragments, a faint image of the Elven Queen rose in the background.

A frightening thought occurred to the enchantress. If the prayer of the Elven Queen, carried on her dying breath, had bestowed the miracle of world vision onto the glass, would her spirit living in the realms above, have the power to undo the miracle?

She focussed on the mirror. The images were still there. Her eyes moved over the surface and found the spot where she had cut herself. To the right Gnomes appeared standing on the beaches of the Eastern Ocean. Silver and gold lying on the sand glistened in the setting sun. Matista frowned. Gnomes had never before been seen near the sea. Anxious to know more, she scanned to the right of the missing fragment. Behold, a galley flying the banner of the Seven Lords rowed across her field of vision. The slaves strained at the oars for the galley had a barge in tow. Richly ornamented was the floating platform and in the centre stood a large canopy.

Matista shrieked with laughter. Seated under the canvas were the Crown Princess Yaconda and her maiden Dominique. The whole thing was delightful. It was the Princess on her way to the palace to celebrate her nuptial feast. An evil chuckle escaped her lips. The sight wiped from her mind the Elven Queen's disturbing visit. It was time to start packing

She got up from her chair and was about to cover the mirror when she decided to have one last look at the Gnomes on the beach. Sea Gnomes living on the isolated shore of the Eastern Ocean. It would be wise for the Seven Lords to have a Rover check it out. She looked again at the glass but suddenly the image darkened, only the silver frame glittered in the candle light. She brought her face close to the mirror. It was of no avail, the image went black. She shifted her eyes back and forth. It was useless! A black vapour had enveloped her secret window on the world. The ghastly truth dawned, the Elven Queen on her return to the spirit world had undone the power of the Mirror of a Thousand Fragments. The carrier wave that had energized the image had disintegrated.

The Enchantress flushed with anger. She stood up and in a fit of fury seized the wondrous silver frame and tossed it through the open window. It sailed through the night air and landed upon the stone patio. This time the silver frame crumbled and glass covered the paving stones. The merewings startled from their perch and flapped their oversize wings in fright.

Distraught, Matista walked down to the studio and slumped down into her chair by the open fire. Looking into the flames she consoled herself with the thought that the mirror had served its end. The final battle was near and about the outcome there could be no doubt. The image of Princess Yaconda clinging to her handmaiden flashed into her mind.

'Ah yes, I will be at the palace in time to attend the wedding.' giggled the evil witch. She felt a surge of energy and began collecting her finest dresses and ornaments for the festivities.

35

At The Alcazar

A violent rainstorm swept over the dunes and the remains of the old Alcazar presented a dismal sight. A lone tower rose from the ruins and pelting rain entered the top chamber through slits in the wall.

It was now almost two years since the Princess Yaconda and her handmaiden Dominique had been imprisoned in the crumbling tower.

Throughout the day they would huddle by a small coal fire. On the Princess' loom stretched a half finished blanket. Weaving had kept her mind from dwelling on her fate. The blankets were traded with the guards for food and coal.

When the Groll Captain Homerus disappeared, a small detachment of Grolls, under the command of the giant Groll, Puff, had replaced him. The grim scaly appearance of the creature was deceiving. Puff was a softy at heart. Grolls were generally cruel, callous, creatures. But a beam of light from his Troll forefathers had found its way into Puff's heart.

Dominique had been grateful for Puff's many acts of kindness. The supply of food and coal for the little stove had much improved. Nonetheless, the winter had been trying. Storm after storm had battered the tower and the cold and dampness had been intense. Dominique's companionship and her merry spirit had kept the Princess from wilting in her stone bower.

One morning Dominique looked at the design taking shape on Yaconda's loom. The sun highlighted seagulls soaring over a cerulean sea. It bode well for the future. Dominique smiled. Many of the throws and blankets that had come off her loom throughout the winter had reflected dark and sombre themes. A shoot of hope must have sprung up in her mistress' psyche. It would be her task to foster it until help came in sight.

The Princess was in deep slumber on the straw mattress that covered the stone bench along the wall. Dominique looked at Yaconda's pale and wan face. She had never doubted that deliverance would come, but when? Did she have the strength to last?

She walked to the narrow window and looked at the desert landscape and the sea beyond. In the wake of the storm, long swells broke upon the shore. Sunlight glistened on the wet sand and gave lustre to the cacti blooming in the sandy soil. When Dominique turned away from the window Princess Yaconda was sitting up on her mattress.

'Oh Dominique!' cried the Princess, 'When will all this end? The isolation, the not knowing. It is hard to bear. They murdered my father to break the unity of the Kingdom. Why am I still alive, a prisoner in this forlorn ruin?'

'Take heart Yaconda, for all things there is a reason oft hidden from mortal eyes. Despair not my love. In the end all will be well.'

Yaconda rose and kissed Dominique on both cheeks.

'Thank heaven that you followed me into exile Dominique.' Dominique pressed her hand before walking downstairs to fetch the breakfast makings. She approached the heavy oaken door and knocked three times. The iron bar outside squealed on its hinges and Captain Puff swung the door outward. A smile played on the scaly Groll face.

'A lovely morning, the sun ablaze and I am greeted by a pretty pair of eyes. It is a pleasure to serve your Highness.'

'Silly Captain Puff, you know I am not your Highness.'

'No difference my pretty, when I look at you, I see a princess.'

Dominique looked at the huge creature, his dew covered scales glistening in the sunlight. They were flatterers, the gnarly creatures, but the memory of Captain Homerus, who had almost done her in, was fresh in her mind. She must not take any chances.

'I must make haste Captain Puff to cook breakfast for the Princess. Could you let me have some eggs and a loaf of bread?'

'Indeed I can my idol.' Puff turned around and shouted an order to one of his underlings.

'Any news from the palace? Dominique asked quietly, lest any of the other Grolls should overhear.

A sombre look appeared on the scaly giant's face. He had developed a protective feeling towards his captives. Dominique suspected that he was hiding something from her and looked him straight in the eye. Puff surrendered and decided to tell the truth.

'It was yesterday that a merewing flew into our camp.'

'It carried a message from the Seven Lords?'

'It did so Dominique. Our stay here is to come to an end.'

'To an end Captain Puff,' cried out Dominique.

'We have been recalled to the palace.'

'We will be abandoned to our fate in this wretched ruin?'

'Were it only so,' lamented the goodhearted Captain .

'Talk straight,' demanded Dominique, 'So, we will not imagine the worst.'

'I fear it is the worst. You and the Princess are to join us on our return voyage to the palace. Dominique stared at Puff, a look of horror on her face. She saw his scales scintillating in the sunlight and noticed they became smaller as they reached his neck. She knew there was no malice in his heart. He resembled a good natured dragon and tears actually sparkled in his eyes.

'Heaven be praised,' she whispered, 'Puff is a rare find amongst Grolls.'

The large green eyes in the massive head were veiled in mist and whatever fear she might have had of Puff vanished. She stepped outside, seating herself on a rock in the warm sunlight. Puff sat on a small dune, his head resting on his hands.

'Is there more Puff?' asked Dominique.

'Your Princess, my dear.'

'What about my Princess, Puff?'

'Only hearsay ma'am, whispers on the wind.' Puff looked uncomfortable.

'Tell me Puff, I must know!'

'There is talk of a wedding, the Lord Salan is to wed the Princess. Heart-rending are the tidings I bring,' blubbered Puff, who had grown fond of the Princess and her maid.

'Marry the Princess,' Dominique exclaimed.

'Alas, my dear, nothing can prevent it.'

'When will we travel to the Land where the Seven rule?'

'The galley with the barge in tow will arrive today, Dominique lady.'

'Ye Gods above.' burst out Dominique, afraid to go inside and tell the Princess. There was no need. Her mistress was standing in the doorway when Dominique turned towards the tower.

'What is afoot Dominique,' sternly asked Princess Yaconda. 'Tell me now. Death, I do not dread my faithful maid.'

'Not death, Princess, hearsay of a crime worse than death. We must travel to the palace of the Dark Lords. You are to be Salan's bride.'

It was as if a veil fell from the Princess' eyes. In a flash she could see the fiendish plot. The throne of the Kingdom would never be occupied. In despair her people would yield to the pressure of the Seven and would fall under the sceptre of darkness, without an arrow loosed or a spear flung.

'There is time Princess,' soothed Dominique, 'Much can happen to foil Salan's plans.' Princess Yaconda took Dominique's hand and they walked inside the tower.

'We must prepare for the journey,' said Yaconda in a tone of resignation.

When they had finished packing their few belongings, Dominique walked up to the window and looked out to sea. On the gentle ocean swells sailed a handsome galley, towing in its wake a festive looking barge. Before reaching the dock, the many oars propelling the craft came to rest and a Rover at the helm skilfully brought the vessels alongside the quay.

The Rover, dressed in the uniform of Salan's bodyguard, jumped ashore and walked up to the tower. Dominique and Yaconda had walked down the stairway and were standing in front of the Alcazar. The Rover greeted them, pulled an epistle out of his vest pocket and without further ado began reading a proclamation.

'From the seat of power, in the Land of the Seven, flow greetings and salutations to the Princess Yaconda. Lord Salan invites the Princess and her maid to board the royal transport to attend a reception at the palace. Princess Yaconda will be treated as a guest of honour and accorded all the privileges of her station as the future bride of the great Lord.'

Dominique was struck by the envoy's cold mechanical voice.

She cast a glance of contempt at the Rover, flawlessly attired in an elaborate uniform.

'And what if we refuse the invitation, my puppet?'

For a moment the scar on his left cheek flushed red, but the Rover had been trained since childhood to suppress emotion. He answered in a flat voice.

'Consequences very unpleasant, dungeons under palace damp and cold. Pools of cold water, dangerous reptiles!'

'Some invitation.' scoffed Dominique.

Princess Yaconda had been watching Puff standing a few paces behind the Rover. The Groll's desperate mimicking told her that Dominique should hold her tongue.

Dominique was still seething and muttering something about foul reptiles on the upper levels of the palace when Princess Yaconda took her by the hand and walking past the envoy headed towards the harbour.

Puff picked up the baggage and carried it to the barge. Then, hurrying back to the tower, he returned triumphantly, carrying the loom above his head. Yaconda silently blessed the gentle soul who lived in that fearful body. When Puff had placed the loom on the deck of the barge, he ran back to the tower and picked up the many bags of wool and yarn that had been left behind. He caught up with Yaconda and Dominique on the jetty.

The barge was an extraordinary sight. Colourful and attractive decorations along the sides swayed in the gentle breeze and in the centre stood a pavilion made of mauve coloured canvas. Two pretty hostesses from the palace had been sent along on the expedition. They stepped onto the dock, curtsying before Yaconda.

'Princess Most High, welcome to the royal transport. We will see to your comfort and obey your commands.'

The Princess made a slight bow and walked up the gangplank followed by Dominique and the hostesses. Exotic birds were perched on gaily decorated posts and the Princess and her maid were utterly amazed by the luxury and festive arrangements that met their eyes. Walking through a passage flanked by potted azaleas, Yaconda and Dominique entered the stately tent.

Not in her wildest nightmares had she walked through portals of doom, so splendid and festive in their array. The whole thing seemed preposterous, unthinkable.

'Dominique, Salan is up to some terrible mischief.'

'We must pray for time Princess, there is much that can happen to forestall his evil designs.'

Once they were seated on the comfortable pillows, the hostesses came in with food and refreshments. They could not resist the delicacies spread before them. Nothing like it had been served since they landed on these forlorn shores.

It was not long until they could hear the Rover shouting orders at the sailors. Dominique walked onto the deck and watched the men coiling the mooring cables. The galley was already moving seaward. The towrope tightened and following the lead of the galley, the barge began a slow turn.

On the rear deck of the galley, Grolls were celebrating their return to the homeland with bottles of beer.

They knew they would be joining the troops for the final push into the Kingdom and looked forward to the looting which would follow in the wake of the conquest. A good distance away from the frolicking Grolls, stood the lonely figure of Puff, gazing at the vanishing shoreline.

Dominique returned to the tent and joined her mistress seated on the sofa. The Princess leaned her head on Dominique's shoulder. All that could be heard now was the splashing of the oars and the gentle lapping of the ocean around the bow. Dominique watched the Princess close her eyes but just before she floated off into a light sleep she heard her whisper, 'No one knows of our fate or comes to our aid.'

On a small dune top near the shore stood a tall pelican watching the vessels sail past. He had seen the Princess and her maid embarking on the colourfully decorated barge. His keen eyes had not failed to notice the veil of tears on the lovely face. Fragments of conversation and some lewd remarks by the Grolls had led him to draw his own conclusions about the procession. The cruise presented a merry image to unsuspecting eyes, but Peli 1 had been in intelligence long enough to know that an evil plot was in the making.

'Dreadful, dreadful,' muttered Peli to himself, 'an innocent maiden on her way to the altar of sacrifice.'

It was against his better judgement but he wanted to speak a word of hope and encouragement before taking wing. In the twilight he espied tropical birds perched on the roof of the barge's pavilion. He soared over to greet his feathered brethren, striking up a conversation with a parrot. The moment he saw that the entrance to the tent was no longer under surveillance, he bid his friend good night and sailed undetected into the canvas enclosure.

Dominique was astonished to see a pelican glide into their sanctuary. She knew that pelicans were bold, but this was unheard of. There was something in the way that he stood and gazed at her, that made her realize that this was no ordinary bird. Princess Yaconda awoke from her slumber and looked at Peli 1. She had visited the home of the Mountain Fairies and was well acquainted with Queen Tuluga and her Secret Flyers. Their courier services had been much prized by King Arcturus and she sensed that the pelican facing her was no wild bird but rather a highly trained member of the elite group.

Standing ramrod straight, he saluted the Princess and introduced himself.

'Peli 1 your Highness, from the court of Queen Tuluga. For several days I have had the convoy under observation and have a pretty good idea of your predicament. With your permission, I will report to the Queen. The Queen will bring Salan's plans to the Council at the Manor deCygne. No doubt, they will act to forestall the diabolical scheme of the shameless Lord.

'The Council at the Manor deCygne?' asked the Princess in an astonished tone of voice.

'Begging your pardon your Highness but after the death of the King, your father, there was no one to lead the nation. Lady Erica called a Council representing Mountain Fairies, Elves, Gnomes, Outlanders and Swannefolk. Lambarina was too dangerous so the Council moved to the Manor in Cascade.

'You didn't mention the Dwarves Peli 1.'

'The Marquis deCygne led a mission to the Dwarves. They support the Council and will defend the passes. The Dwarf Scimitar has been captured by the Rovers, but I hear that an attempt at rescue is afoot.'

'Heaven be praised,' exclaimed Princess Yaconda, 'I feared after the death of my father that long buried hatreds amongst the people in our Kingdom would rise again. You bring good tidings, my clever bird.'

Although a cool customer, Peli's light pink feathers flushed to red and he made a slight bow. The stress the Princess had put on 'my clever bird' was gratifying. He looked again at the Princess' noble features and understood why she was so beloved by her people.

'Could one look at those eyes and not weep for the Princess whose fate had taken such a tragic turn?' For once Peli 1 admitted to himself that it was hard to maintain professional detachment. A voice within told him that not a moment was to be lost. With a polite bow he turned, shot out of the tent and into the dark night.

'Oh Dominique, there is much to be grateful for. The Dwarves are fierce fighters and let us pray that Scimitar is freed. The Council will assure the unity of our people. Removed from the intrigues and dangers of Lambarina, they are safe at the Manor deCygne, the home of the Lady Erica, an erudite woman gifted with the second sight. Perhaps help will come our way.'

'I trust it will. Now rest, my Princess, and gather your strength for the days ahead.'

36

Under the Shadow of the Black Peak

Stripped to the waist, lifting blocks of marble on a handcart, Scimitar glistened with perspiration. The heat was stifling and dust from the quarries under the Black Peak made breathing difficult. Not far off, iron was mined and smoke from the smelters darkened the horizon.

Lashes from Groll overseers had left a kind of cross-hatching of welts on his back. The prisoners toiled in the marble quarry from sunup to sundown. When the sun vanished behind the mountains and darkness descended, Scimitar and the other prisoners on his team would drag their weary bones to a cave in the mountainside. There, over a small fire they would warm up the mush that was brought around by the Grolls, provided they had met their daily quota.

Scimitar did his share of the work, but at night when his fellow prisoners sat around the fire talking or playing cards, he would retire to a tunnel at the end of the grotto.

How often he chided himself for getting caught. Why had he paddled his canoe to an island in the Sanctus? After Helga's father had been bitten by the black hound, he should have stayed at the Wendell Farm and consoled the mother and the lovely Helga. What had blinded him to their grief and driven him on? It was in this year of toil and suffering that he had come to realize that he loved the Swannemaid. Why had he denied it for so long? He had always thought Dwarves were above that kind of nonsense. Then it came to him in a flash of insight. As a youth he had lost his heart to a young maiden and his peers had teased him mercilessly. Then he had been sent to work in one of the remote tunnels in the Finnian Range. When he became a warrior, his skill and ambition propelled him to leadership. Amongst dwarf warriors, love for a maiden was a sign of weakness, to be shunned and banished from the mind.

He thought of his brother Smithereen the poet, misunderstood by his fellow Dwarves and suffering from the moping illness. Only the cheer and patience of Sunflower had kept him going. It was in this lonely prison camp surrounded by misery that Scimitar experienced new feelings and energies rising up from the depth of his being. They were bursting through the crust of culture that for so long had contained his life.

Wives had always been carefully selected for Dwarves. Marrying an outsider was unthinkable. A year earlier he had tried, by fasting for seven days, to flush the image of the Swannemaiden from his mind. It had worked after a fashion but as a prisoner in this hellish place he spent much time in thought. Pain and suffering had lowered the threshold of his unconscious. A surging sea had swept away the dykes of years. Amongst thoughts and images drifting into daylight was the image of the lovely Helga. In true dwarf fashion, he was spending his time thinking and agonizing. The map of his world was changing and he had to come to terms with it.

He had dismissed all thought of escape. The stone wall surrounding the complex, topped with broken glass, stood twelve feet tall. Guard towers manned by archers were strategically placed. Even if he were to make it over the wall, he had no way of defending himself against the patrolling Grolls and the fearsome dogs. Toil and suffering were his daily fare and in a strange way he felt he deserved no better.

At midnight when all were asleep, Scimitar wandered out of the cave and into the moonlit quarry. He sat down on a slab of marble and rested his head in his hands. A feeling of hopelessness overcame the Dwarf and his mind drifted to the days before his capture. The mad rush on the river to reach the capital. The horrible attack on Helga's father, Helga kneeling by his side, tears glistening in her eyes. The enchantress Amaranth had appeared before him on the night that he had been captured. He recalled the enchantress' parting words.

'When in peril call on me my stalwart Dwarf. Let not pride bar thee from invoking my aid. Call on me. Speak my name.'

For the first time in his life despair overwhelmed Scimitar. Despair of life, despair of the mission that he had failed to accomplish, despair over the fate of Helga. He found himself sinking on his knees, calling aloud.

'Amaranth, Amaranth.'

When he rose a soft light appeared in a niche in the rock face and as Scimitar moved closer, he beheld the enchantress. Her golden tresses and turqoise dress reflected the scant moonlight and her finely shaped hands shone with a white radiance.

'It took this much pain Scimitar, to bring you to your knees and to call my name. Your friends have not forgotten you, Scimitar. Even now they are on their way to help you escape from this horrible quarry.' Amaranth opened her hand, revealing a crystal vessel. 'For seven days at the break of dawn you must drink of this elixir. It will restore your strength and enable you to scale the wall at full moon. You are needed Scimitar to lead the struggle that looms ahead. The enemy will storm the passes. Let not pride blind you to the strength of others. All must play a part in the storm that threatens the Kingdom. Fare thee well my Dwarf.'

The image of the enchantress was fading quickly. Scimitar stood gazing into the darkness of the alcove. It was as if she had never been, yet he was holding a small vessel in his hand. Moonlight sparkled in the crystal and Scimitar felt a sense of hope and wonder and perhaps for the first time in his life, humility. Once more Amaranth had come into his life when all seemed lost.

He tucked the bottle into his pocket and walked slowly back to his cave. There was no hope of escape unless he regained his health. Amaranth had said his friends would be in touch with him. How were they to scale the barrier or to evade the Grolls guarding it?

Once inside, Scimitar, spread his bed roll and lay down near the opening. Millions of stars twinkled far above. His mind travelled through the firmament and pondered the mysteries of the heavens. What secrets did these countless bodies of light contain?

Like most Dwarves, Scimitar believed in the power of heavenly bodies to move events on earth. For seven days he was to take a drink from the crystal flask at the break of day and in seven days the moon would be in full radiance.

Would he have the strength to scale that formidable wall and would friends be waiting on the other side?

The eerie silence under a canopy of dark spruce was lightened by the gay crackle of a campfire. Seated around the blaze was a company of seven. Duckie, Slim and Moose were warming their hands with mugs of hot coffee while Bullneck and Rick the Reamer were enjoying the traditional dwarf drink of hot spruce beer. The Mountain Fairies, Edel and Weiss, who abhorred alcohol and seldom drank coffee, had boiled up a pot of mint tea. Below their campsite stretched a panorama of meadows and parkland. Beyond, in the distance, rose the Black Peak.

Travelling all night they had taken advantage of the thin crust of snow on the alpine meadows. Edel and Weiss leaping, sliding and slithering. The others had skied down. The Dwarves had taught Moose Martin and Slim the art of skiing during the long winter that they had spent in the village of Turania.

For more than five nights they had travelled and were too weary to go any farther. Tomorrow they would scout around and find the right place to set up base camp for the rescue of Scimitar.

The next day, after breakfast, Moose and Slim walked towards an escarpment on the horizon. An hour's walk brought them to a steep rock face and scouting carefully along the cliff side, they discovered a crack in the mass of solid rock. A short passage led to a large cave. It would protect them from the weather and it was far enough from the prison camp to avoid detection.

Moose stayed behind to explore the cave while Slim returned to the campsite to lead the remainder of the party to the grotto. Moose discovered that at the far end of the large rock chamber was a short tunnel leading to a natural chimney, where could be seen, a shaft of daylight. The chimney would permit them to have a fire. In the distance the smelters below the black peak were spewing clouds of black smoke. The likelihood of a thin column of smoke being spotted would be slight.

By sundown they were settled in and resting comfortably around a small fire. The faint howling of black dogs in the distance was disquieting but the prevailing wind was from the south and their scent was unlikely to carry. Nonetheless it was a reminder of the peril that surrounded them. Bullneck and Rick the Reamer took turns patrolling the camp through the night.

In the morning Moose gathered firewood while Slim built a fireplace out of rocks and lit a pile of kindling. He knew he could never fight so he tried to make himself useful in other ways. When there were no chores he would sketch scenes from their travels, filling several books with sketches and watercolours.

Slim was also a sharp observer. At night he listened to the barking of the dogs. Guessing at the direction, he tried to figure out the pattern of the Groll patrols around the vast prison complex.

When the others rose they were pleasantly surprised by the sizzling of pancakes and the smell of coffee. They had a strenuous journey behind them and now they took their time relaxing over the first hot meal in five days.

Leaving his comrades around the fire, Slim set out to scout the area. He crossed the meadows in front of the escarpment and wandered into the woodlands. Poplar, birch and maple were just coming into leaf. Rambling through the undergrowth, he was startled by an unexpected movement in the shrubbery. Taking cover behind a spreading honeysuckle, he carefully peeked between the branches. A figure was kneeling on the forest floor. He moved forward to get a better look and to his surprise he descried an old woman on her knees picking herbs. Startled by branches cracking behind him, he turned and saw Bullneck crouching in the bushes. Concerned for Slim's safety the Dwarf had followed him.

When they moved forward, the woman raised her head and seeing the bulky figure of the Dwarf staring down at her, she mumbled in a frightened voice.

'Pardon me sir,' I work in the kitchen that cooks for the brass. I only slipped out to gather herbs for dinner. Mint and marjoram sir, for your dinner.' Bullneck couldn't help smiling when he looked at the wizened face, half hidden in a bower of snow white tresses. It dawned on him that the woman kneeling in the patch of mint took him for one of the overlords in the prison complex.

Slim knew that Bullneck as leader of the expedition faced a dilemma. If the woman returned to the prison camp, she might talk and describe the meeting with the Dwarf. The results could be disastrous.

'We must talk to her,' volunteered Slim. Bullneck nodded. 'You tell her Slim.'

The woman rose holding a basket of herbs in her right hand. She brushed back her white hair and the artist in Slim saw the beauty that once must have graced her face, now edged with grief. She stood the height of Slim and looked at his deep black eyes and comely face. A tear swam into her eyes and she burst out, 'You are not one of them!'

'We are not, lady,' smiled Slim. 'I come from the Land of the Swans and my friend Bullneck is a Dwarf.'

'Then the Dwarves are still a free people, not enslaved by our Masters?'

'We are a free people my good woman, and are now part of the federation, The United Kingdom of the Seven Mountains.' Astonishment shone in her eyes. Slim took her hand and said gently, 'Come and meet our companions.'

'I have but an hour before I will be missed in the kitchens, sir.'

'Call me Slim and tell us your name.'

'Call me Arabella. Arabella.' She whispered the name over and over again as if it had vanished and reappeared from the mist of time.

The companions around the campfire were surprised to see Slim and Bullneck appear in the company of an unexpected visitor. They stood up and bowed to the stranger in their midst. Arabella sat down on a log and Slim explained to the friends the strange encounter.

Edel brought her a cup of the rosehip tea and sat down beside her. Then Weiss leaped over the fire to bid her welcome. She looked at the shining faces of the light-footed creatures and it came to her from memories long forgotten, that these were fairies, fairies who lived far away from the land of the Seven Masters, fairies that her mother had sung about in her childhood, fairies who lived in a world of song and dance and happiness.

Edel and Weiss looked at the white hair moving in the morning breeze, and the blue eyes staring at them.

'Edel,' whispered Weiss, touching his hand. 'She is a noble soul shrouded in a tale of sadness, a romantic tragedy no doubt. Perhaps she will tell us her story.'

The glazed look in the woman's eyes cleared. It dawned on her that she was among friends and could speak freely.

'Arabella is my name. How sweet its sound when my mother whispered it and my husband returning from the forest sang out, "Arabella". How it broke my heart, when his last breath whispered, "Arabella all is well, God bless thee Arabella."

'We lived in the land of the Seven Lords and village life was fair. Then one evening my boys were captured by a press gang. The Rovers take the youngsters and train them in their regiments. My husband, working in the garden heard my cries for help. He seized an axe and killed two of the

Rovers. A groll archer hidden behind a hedge loosed the arrow that slew him. All I had, all that was dear to me, gone in a single day. My golden hair turned white, like that of many women in the village. Few families were left untouched.'

Tears welled in the eyes around the fire. Bullneck nodded. He knew all about the cruel practice of seizing children and raising them in the discipline of the Rovers.

'The women supported one another and helped hide the few children still left in the village. Smuggled across the border, the children found refuge in Esteria. Our troubles were just beginning. Four years later the women were recruited for slave labour on the farms along the shores of the Wasa, and a few of us were sent to work in the mines by the Black Peak. For fourteen years I have worked in this wretched place.'

Edel and Weiss were overcome by the tale of woe.

'This goes beyond romantic tragedy, Weiss, I wonder if there is word for that kind of tale?' Whispered Edel.

'I think not Edel, it takes us to the heart of darkness, to a world beyond words.'

The company knew Arabella could be trusted. Slim spoke first.

'We feel your grief and we are grateful that you shared with us, your story.'

Arabella looked at the faces seated around her. Sensing the men were on a secret mission, she said softly, 'I can guess why you are here and you can count on me.'

Bullneck spoke sternly, 'A brave offer Arabella. One of us must enter the camp undetected. Our leader, Scimitar is a prisoner in the quarries and you can help us plan his escape. You know the risks?' She stood up before speaking.

'Death I welcome. I will do anything I can to oppose the evil that has fallen upon us.'

Slim knew that Arabella must return to the kitchens in time and offered to walk her back through the woods. When they came to a small lily pond Arabella whispered, 'No farther Slim. The pond marks the southern point of the Groll Patrol. Return to your camp and meet me at ten tomorrow.'

Slim watched her vanish into the rhododendron bushes at the far side of the pond. For a moment his eyes rested on the water lilies blooming. He wondered how such beauty could flourish in the shadow of the Black Peak?

Next morning early he left for the Lily Pond and found Arabella gathering herbs at the water's edge. Slim carried her basket filled with herbs as they walked to the Cave. He spoke of Swanneland and told her of his dancing Swans. Arabella was enchanted with tales of swan ballet and of gondolas sailing on the moonlit Sanctus.

When they reached the grotto, the men were seated around the fire and Edel and Weiss had perched on a ledge above. Bullneck bade Arabella welcome and reminded her that they needed to smuggle one or two of their men into the camp.

'Arabella, is there a way to get through the barrier?'

'No sir. You can neither pass through the wall nor scale it. The few prisoners that made it to the top were slain by arrows from the watch towers.'

'How do you pass back and forth, Arabella?' asked Slim.

'There is a small wicket guarded by two Grolls. They open it for me when I go gathering herbs. The officers like their dinners well enough.'

'And they open it again when you return with your bundle of herbs?'

'They do Slim. We cook for hundreds of men and some days I take two trips.'

'Could anyone follow you, hiding under the bundles of herbs that you carry on your arms? Slim glanced up at Edel and Weiss.

'They would have to be awfully small Slim!' laughed Arabella.

The Mountain Fairies jumped down from their lofty perch and knelt before Arabella.

'We will follow you,' said Weiss, 'Edel on one side and I on the other.'

Bullneck nodded. He had hoped to get into the compound himself, but his massive frame was an obstacle. The Mountain Fairies were the only ones who could hope to succeed.

Before taking leave, Arabella asked the company to gather herbs, flowers and a few water lilies for the dining table. Her time outside the wall was limited. Slim, Edel and Weiss spent the rest of the day picking flowers and herbs.

When Arabella arrived next morning, she burst out laughing at the sight in front of the cave. Edel and Weiss, wearing crowns of daisies were standing by a mountain of herbs and flowers. She seized in each arm a huge bundle of herbs and flowers. Edel and Weiss lined up by her side and poked their heads into the lush greenery. The dress rehearsal was a success. It was the kind of fantastical performance that one might have seen at a Mountain Fairy masquerade.

Slim made a quick sketch before Edel and Weiss reappeared from under the camouflaging greens. There was no time to be lost. The company shook hands and wished them well.

After they vanished from sight, Bullneck wondered how the tiny creatures could aid Scimitar's escape. Yet there seemed to be no other way. The wall and the defences were formidable. He felt frustrated. His hands itched to swing his ball and chain and to cut a swath through the ranks of his enemies. The kind of action that soothes a Dwarf's nervous system.

Alas, this assignment required the kind of artfulness and jugglery that few Dwarves possess and Bullneck thanked his lucky stars for Slim and the Mountain Fairies. Duckie was a kind of wild card. Of Moose Martin he didn't know what to think. 'An odd chap,' he mumbled, 'his maps are useful, but he wouldn't hurt a fly, I fear.'

Bullneck stood up and went about the cave checking out his weapons. Moose returned to mapmaking, drawing escape routes and Duckie joined Rick the Reamer, who had been teaching him spear throwing. During the next few days they managed to keep busy. Every morning, hoping for news, Slim went down to the lily pond.

When Arabella and the Mountain Fairies, came close to the compound, Arabella stopped and Edel and Weiss took up their places by her side. They ducked their heads under the fragrant heaps of greenery.

'We must be quite a sight Weiss.' laughed the irrepressible Edel.

'Quiet, silly goose. Greens don't talk.' The warning came in the nick of time. A passing Groll seeing the huge bundles of greens and flowers commented.

'A savoury meal tonight for the big wheels.' Grolls were crude creatures but they did take pleasure in fine dining. Their table manners were another matter. They were close to the wall now and the guard at the narrow gate saw Arabella approaching.

'Good morning cook,' shouted the Groll, 'quite a mountain of herbs you gathered. Must be a special occasion, let me give you a hand.' The Groll bowed down ready to seize the bundle that was Edel.

'Off with your lobster paws,' screamed Arabella, 'you would crush the life out these delicate greens.'

'Begging your pardon ma'am,' stammered the rebuffed Groll, 'just trying to give you a hand.'

'All right Scaly,' Arabella relented, 'you are a good natured fellow, now open the gate for me.'

Arabella and her bundles of greens squeezed through the narrow opening. Scaly seeing her walk away with a kind of strange wobble, figured she was suffering from the joint-ill. At the next checkpoint a Rover Captain waved her on. Food was important to them at this isolated post and they were lenient with the kitchen staff. The pleasing fragrance of the herbs sailing by augured well for the evening meal.

Arabella crossed the courtyard and walked into the cookhouse. The other women were relieved to see her. She had been away longer than usual and they had been worried.

'Are you going into business Arabella?' asked one of the women looking at the huge heaps of herbs.

'Not so, my sisters. We'll dry them for the long winter ahead. Arabella trusted the women in the cookhouse, most of them had come from her own village. Yet one never knew and the Rovers had ways of making them talk.

Carefully walking behind counters which kept the suspicious bundles out of sight, she reached a row of storage cupboards at the back of the kitchen. Opening one of the doors, she shoved the Fairies inside.

Edel and Weiss found themselves in a large cupboard and once their eyes became used to the dim light, they looked at one another in their outlandish outfits and burst into soft laughter. Stripping off their floral array, they reclined on a couple of flour bags.

It is difficult for Mountain Fairies to sit still for long periods of time, yet they would have to wait till dark before they could hope to begin a survey of the camp and find Scimitar's whereabouts. Undeterred by the small space, they managed to perform a number of acrobatic tricks. A wooden dowel at the top of their cubicle allowed them to hang upside down by their feet for a change of posture.

At dusk, when most of the women had retired, Arabella appeared in the doorway. At the sight of Edel and Weiss hanging by their toes from the bar above, she burst out laughing. There was something so quaint, so droll, about her tiny guests. It gave her hope and faith for another world beyond the confines of the dark camp.

Arabella placed on the floor a tray with their evening meal and a pot of mint tea.

'Any time you want to get in touch with me, Edel and Weiss, shove three mint leaves in the crack under the door. You can explore the camp during the night but you must return before sunrise. Take heed my buttercups. Spies abound in the camp. Most of the women in the cookhouse can be trusted, if the need arises, otherwise talk to no one.'

Edel and Weiss, now in an upright position thanked her and seated themselves on the bulgy flour bags to enjoy their meal. Arabella waved the two a kiss and closed the door.

Near midnight when all was silent, Edel and Weiss, decided to leave their hiding place and begin their trip through the camp.

The door of the cookhouse was locked, but they slipped out through a window. Once in the courtyard they could, in the distance, see a tall chimney spewing smoke and sparks into the sky. A fiery glow shone through the windows of a building at the foot of the chimney. Weiss guessed that it was the place where the ore was melted.

'We better check it out Edel in case Scimitar works there.' A fine rain had begun to fall and there was little chance that they would be spotted. Once close to the building, they saw a door standing ajar and slipped inside. Three furnaces burned brightly, and men stripped to their waist, tipped buckets of molten metal into moulds. Then came a frightening hissing sound as some of the prisoners doused the red hot metal with cold water. A Groll wielding a whip spurred them on. The men worked like fiends. The fires and the glow of molten ore cast a red sheen over their drenched bodies.

Their hearts ached for the prisoners toiling in this inferno. They knew that no one could survive long in this hellish place. Weiss pressed Edel's hand and whispered, 'No sign of Scimitar, let us move on.' They slithered along the wall until they reached the door.

'The fires of hell Weiss, why this terrible suffering?' They walked silently in the rain.

'In our country, Edel such horrors are unknown. We sing and dance and felicity dwells amongst us. The Lords of Darkness are obsessed with power and ambition.' Edel looked puzzled. The only ambition he understood was the quest for glory and romance. They could see in the distance the lights of the armouries. Weiss put his hand on Edel's shoulder.

'Let us thither and see the weapons being crafted for the coming war.'

The rain had stopped and a shaft of moonlight darted among the fleeting clouds. In the distance they could hear the din of hammers hitting anvils.

When a dark cloud veiled the moon Weiss took Edel's hand and they ran across the yard. Once they had reached a clump of bushes they relaxed and surveyed the scene. They could see sparks flying in the windows of the armoury. Slinking carefully up to a window and standing on tiptoe they peered inside. Grolls were pushing bellows, firing a huge forge and smiths were hammering steel into swords, spears, and arrowheads.

No trace of Scimitar. He must be in another part of the camp. They were just about to turn around and retrace their steps when Edel espied, in the distance, a building surrounded by trees and bushes.

'It could be the living quarters of the Camp Commandant, Weiss,' suggested Edel.'

'I think not Edel, Arabella said that the Chief lived in a two storey house between the kitchens and the quarries.'

Curiosity got the better of them. Carefully they wound their way through the trees and bushes. Once they had come close they saw that the building was a sizable log structure. Light shone through an open window and the sound of voices carried on the wind. They slithered up to the window and listened to the conversation inside.

'Fine weapons have been coming out of the armouries, Professor, but we will need something that will scare the Dwarves out of the mountain passes. We would lose many troopers if the Dwarves were to hold the passes for any length of time.

'I know General. We are perfecting a secret weapon.'

'That isn't good enough Professor. The time is now.'

The General rose from his seat, walked to the open window and leaned out. Edel and Weiss sank to ground level and looking up, they beheld the barrel chest and puffed cheeks of the General, commanding the prison complex.

When the General returned to his seat, Edel and Weiss popped up and looked inside. Opposite the General, behind the table, stood a lanky figure with long dark hair and black eyes. The withering look of the General had turned the Professor pale but he hadn't lost his cool.

'Tell me, Professor, about this secret weapon that will send the Dwarves stampeding down the Mountain. Another brain wave to make us the laughing stock of the camp? The Seven Lords have been patient, Professor, very patient. What have they seen for their money? Drums and trumpets that were to scare the Dwarves. Forget about all those harebrained ideas. The sound of your giant drums scare the Dwarves? They wouldn't scare a rabbit. I smell trouble, Professor. They will recall you to the palace and drill some sense into you. Remember the crocodiles in the dungeon. That was your idea. It may come to haunt you.'

Edel and Weiss, tired of standing tiptoe and anxious not to miss anything, dragged an old crate under the window. Throwing caution aside, they poked their heads into the window casing.

The Professor was pleading with the Camp Commander.

'My assistant assures me, General, another day or so and we can stage a demonstration.'

'Very true, your Highness,' piped up a shrill voice. 'The effect of our new invention will devastate the Dwarves.' When Edel heard the new voice, he squeezed Weiss' arm.

'By the dragon's tail Weiss, I swear I know that voice, an elven voice.'

'It can't be Edel,' whispered Weiss, 'There are no Elves here.'

They did not have to wait long for an answer. A tall Elf attired in a black cape and cap climbed onto a stool and was clearly visible in the lamplight.

'Cobalt!' exclaimed Edel in a muffled voice. 'The devilish imp that plucked me from the river Mork and presented me to the Grolls as an appetizer.' Weiss, who knew the story well, put a hand on his shoulder.

'Calm down, Edel and listen.'

'Meet my research assistant, General,' said the Professor who had recovered his balance. 'Cobalt, Captain of the Black Elves.'

The General chortled at the sight of the dapper figure behind the table.

'You are welcome Captain Cobalt, I hope that you will help the professor make good on his promise.' Cobalt made a polite bow.

'We are close to a breakthrough, General. Our new invention will blast the Dwarves out of the mountain passes. Once ignited, the magic powder that we have concocted will produce an awesome explosion.' The professor cast his assistant a scathing look.

'I have made an important discovery and it is true, the little Elf made a small contribution to the project.'

The General knew the Elves were bright and this fellow Cobalt could have come up with an important idea. He decided to give the Professor and his assistant another chance.

'I want to see results now. No further delays.' Cobalt looked a bit peeved. He didn't like having to play second fiddle to the Professor. He bit his lips and decided to bide his time.

Cobalt had been a precocious youth. While the other Elves played and sang, Cobalt had dabbled in the art of alchemy. Once he had combined green, black and silvery powders and when a spark touched the mixture, a frightful blast had destroyed his equipment. It was after that disaster that Cobalt became interested in politics. He suffered from delusions of grandeur and politics was a perfect outlet. It was then that he founded the independence movement, led his followers out of the Kingdom and in the end, fell under the shadow of the Seven Lords. When assigned as research assistant to the Professor, he recalled the green and silvery powders and mixed them with charcoal. He had not forgotten the spark, and some early trials had been promising.

The Professor motioned the General to follow him. The three vanished out the back door.

Edel and Weiss looked at each other and stepped down from their crate. Moving carefully around the side of the building, they hid amidst a clump of cedars. They could see the Professor and Cobalt pouring powders into a pot. Holding on to a large pine tree, the General watched the experiment. Patches of moonlight sailed over the blue-tinted lawn. Edel and Weiss had a clear view of all that was happening.

The Professor, stroking his goatee, peered intently at Cobalt. The ingenious little Elf was making a fuse out of dry moss. Lighting the moss with a flint he ran back to a clump of trees. The flame travelled swiftly along the fuse to the pot of powder which had been sunk into the earth.

The blast knocked Edel and Weiss over. The General's massive frame didn't budge and provided support for the professor. Cobalt, who knew what was coming, held on to one of the branches of a birch. A dark cloud of smoke rose up and a broad smile appeared on the General's face.

'The Dwarves will be running. The foul fiend himself couldn't have done better. How much of the precious powder have you stored?'

'The small log hut in the back is filled with the mixture, ready for use.' piped up Cobalt.

'Ample,' shouted the Professor, 'to scatter all the rogues in the alpine meadows.'

Edel and Weiss had seen enough. Swiftly and silently they slipped back to the cookhouse and retired into their temporary cupboard home. Once inside they lit a candle and to their delight they saw standing on the floor, a pot of cold mint tea and a dish of wild strawberries. They looked at each other and burst out laughing. Their faces were dotted with black smoke and bits of earth.

'By gosh Weiss, it is an awesome weapon, the Professor has invented.'

'Not the Professor, Edel. It is the devilish mind of the Black Elf that conjured it up.'

'We must warn the Dwarves, Weiss.'

'We can do better than that Edel. We will light a fire against the back wall of the log hut. I say, it will be the end of their stock of powder.'

'Dear friend and companion of my youth, it will blow us to kingdom come.'

'Not so, dear Edel. We will make a fuse, like the one we saw Cobalt use. Once we light it, we run like the wind. When Arabella goes agathering herbs to morrow we will ask her to bring dry reed and we will braid a fuse.'

'Brilliant Weiss,' shouted Edel, now quite on fire with the idea, 'the explosion will be monstrous.'

'More important, chaos will reign in the camp and that may give Scimitar a chance to scale the wall.'

'We must find him first, Weiss.'

'If he is in the camp at all, he will be in the quarries, Edel. The day after tomorrow is full moon. We must send a message to Bullneck, to be at the lower end of the wall near the quarries, two days hence at midnight.'

'Tomorrow we must find Scimitar. The prisoners who work in the quarries retire after sundown to their caves. It will have to be in daylight, Weiss. It will be our only chance to find the Dwarf.'

Edel and Weiss looked puzzled. They knew that it would be folly to reconnoitre during the daylight hours. They would be arrested on sight. Weiss pulled his hands through his golden locks and pondered the problem. For awhile they sat silently on their flour sack. The candle was burning down and they were terribly weary.

'Let us sleep now Weiss,' said Edel, snuffing the wavering flame between his fingers.'

'Sleep sweetly, companion of my youth,' whispered Weiss. 'In sleep the flutter of our thoughts is stilled and the secret voices in the depth of our being may speak to us.'

It was near dawn when Edel woke with a start, reaching for Weiss' hand. 'Weiss, I have the answer!'

'Well then Edel, tell me now. How can we stalk around in broad daylight and not end up in a cabbage roll at a Groll dinner?'

'It is simple. We dress up.'

'Dress up like Grolls or Rovers. You silly duck, we are less than half their size.'

'Weiss, if Cobalt is here, his troupe of black Elves must be in the camp. We dress up as Black Elves. We are slighter but near the same height.'

A sunbeam travelling through a crack in the door lit Weiss' face.

Edel could see that the idea of resembling a Black Elf presented a problem to Weiss.

Just then they heard on the plank floor, the soft tread of Arabella's slippers. She opened the door and breathed a sigh of relief to see her fairy friends safe and sound. Hardly had she put down the breakfast tray, when Edel spoke up.

'Arabella, dear, we saw Cobalt last night, the Captain of the Black Elves. Are the other members of his troupe in the camp?'

'Yes they are so my love. The black pests arrived in winter and have been working for the Rovers. They strut about in their black capes and spiky helmets as if they owned the place. They spy on the workers in the camps and run messages for the Rover Captains. When they have nothing on hand, they come and torment the women in the cookhouse. Wags and whippersnappers they are, the black scamps.'

'Arabella,' Edel exclaimed in a subdued voice, 'they are the same height as Mountain Fairies. Could you and your friends make us Black Elf outfits?' Then we would be able to walk around the camp in daylight and look for Scimitar.'

A twinkle danced in Arabella's eyes. 'I will have to tell some of the women from my village that you are here. Fear not. They can be trusted. They will do anything to help you on your quest. Tomorrow morning I will bring the costumes.'

Weiss had been horrified at first, yet the idea appealed to his sense of drama. Before Arabella left, they asked her to fetch some dry reeds on her herb gathering trip.

Once the door closed, they knew that they would have to stick it out in their dark cupboard for four and twenty hours. It was a challenge. After breakfast, to stretch the time, they lingered over a pot of mint tea. Then several hours of handstands on the flour sacks and some acrobatics from the overhead bar. They had a sleep in the afternoon to catch up with last night's adventures and on waking, one of Arabella's friends appeared with a splendid supper. She had a young face yet her hair was streaked with white. Speak she did not but the sad black eyes cast a smile so sweet that it sent Edel and Weiss spinning a tragic tale of romance. Long after she left they were still working on her life story until emotionally exhausted, they fell asleep.

Dawn was breaking when Arabella knocked on the door and opened it. Weiss and Edel rubbed their eyes and looked up into the early light.

'Good morning, Arabella. You came early this morning!' said Weiss, between yawns.

'All night we worked on your costumes my fairies fair.' Arabella raised her arms and Edel and Weiss stared at two floppy black elves dangling from her hands.

'It is perfect,' shouted Edel who could hardly wait to put on his costume.

'We are grateful to you and the other women,' said Weiss clasping her fingers between his tiny hands. 'One more thing Arabella, could you leave a message for Bullneck? Tell him that the rescue party should be at the far end of the wall, near the quarries, by midnight.'

'Tell him, added Edel with a glint of glee in his eyes, 'we will stage a fireworks to distract the guards!'

Arabella had tears in her eyes when she left. At last they were able to do something, something that might crack the millstones that had ground their lives to bits. Well she knew the risks, but it didn't matter. The Mountain Fairies had left her with a sense of joy. They made her think of fountains, sunlit waters and rustling leaves. She sang as she set the tables in the cookhouse that morning.

Edel and Weiss wasted little time getting into their new costumes. It was only after Arabella left that they noticed the two pair of black boots standing by the side of the cupboard. They quickly put them on. Thank goodness, Arabella had thought of the boots.

Edel had spent enough time in captivity to watch Black Elves closely and he put on for Weiss, a demonstration of their deportment. Born actors, they soon perfected the walk and the stances of the Black Elves. When they sat down to breakfast all they could talk about was their new adventure and the stories that they would tell if and when they returned to their homeland.

After breakfast they fastened the last buttons and placed the spiked black caps on their heads. When Arabella opened the door she couldn't believe the likeness.

'It is perfect,' she exclaimed, 'even the arrogance is there.' Edel and Weiss thanked her again and told her that they would be back by dark. There were no guests as yet in the dining room and they walked confidently through the large space and left by the main entrance.

'We must try to avoid meeting the real Black Elves face to face Edel. Their uncanny sight might do us in.'

They drew their black helmets deeper over their foreheads and tried the kind of forbidding Black Elf look. They did quite well until they looked at one another and broke up laughing.

They marched across the open space between the dining halls and the quarries. As they passed the residence of the Camp Commander, they saw the General standing on the porch, talking with the Professor and Cobalt. They saluted smartly but kept their distance. All went well.

At the edge of the quarries they halted and looked at the hundreds of prisoners cutting marble and granite blocks, stacking them on carts and hauling them away. They realized that they would never have been able to find the Dwarf at night. Even now in daylight it would not be an easy task.

The ground near the great wall had not been excavated and a path ran along the wall to the end of the quarries. They marched along carefully, scanning the workers in the pits below. Whenever they met a Groll or Rover they saluted. Like the Black Elves in the messenger corps, they had black canvas bags strapped over their shoulders. Nobody seemed to give them a second thought. Black Elves reported directly to the Camp Commander's office and Grolls went out of their way to please them.

At times they could hear the cracking of whips and the Fairies cringed at the lot of the prisoners toiling below. When they came to the last section of the quarries where the marble was cut, they sighted among the prisoners, a Dwarf.

'It must be Scimitar,' said Edel. 'No other Dwarves have fallen into the hands of the Seven.'

A short distance from Scimitar, for indeed it was that ill-fated Dwarf, stood a Groll. He had spotted the Black Elves on the ledge and wondered what was up. Weiss ran down a ramp leading to the bottom of the quarry and stopping short of the Groll, saluted in the Black Elf fashion, casting him a sharp look. The Groll was taken aback at the appearance of the Black

Elf. Rumour had it that they could get you into hot water in a jiffy and he decided to cooperate.

'Your name please,' demanded Weiss.

'My name?' stammered the scaly giant.

'Your name,' shouted Weiss, poking his swagger stick between the Groll's scales.

'Fonz is my name your Blackness, commanding the guards in the section reserved for dangerous criminals.'

'It is well Fonzie. Stand at ease. I have been ordered to make a list of all the prisoners in your section and to make notes on their performance. First I will speak to the Dwarf loading the cart at the end of the quarry. Your cooperation is appreciated and will be mentioned in my report.

'I am grateful your Blackness,' said the Guard Captain playing it safe. 'If there is any trouble, you call Fonzie.'

Edel had been watching the scene some twenty feet away and was overcome by the sheer gall of his bosom friend.

'You take the notes mate,' said Weiss, nodding to Edel.

Scimitar had just finished loading a huge block of marble and was wiping his forehead when he saw the black creatures. Black Elves often had raised his ire and he looked annoyed when he saw the two strutting across the yard, heading straight for him. He knew that tonight was full moon and Amaranth had warned him to be prepared. He couldn't risk a dose of solitary. He would try to keep his cool with the pesky Elves. Scorn dwelt in his eyes when he spoke.

'What brings the traitors back to this end of the quarry?' Undeterred by the ease with which Scimitar tossed a colossal slab of marble onto the cart, Edel and Weiss stood in front of him. Scimitar rubbed the perspiration out of his eyes and looked at the two. These black Elves were different from the usual bunch who would have trembled in their boots when he lifted the marble.

He retreated a few steps into the shadow of his loaded wagon. The Fairies followed him. Scimitar peered at his visitors. A light danced in their eyes unlike those of other Black Elves.

'Scimitar,' whispered Weiss.

'By the Great Spirit,' exclaimed the Dwarf. 'You are Mountain Fairies.'

'It is true,' said Weiss. We needed the disguise to find you. We come from the Kingdom. We spent the winter in the alpine meadows at the home of Smithereen and Sunflower.'

Scimitar's eyes filled with wonder. The words of the enchantress had come true. But how unlike his wildest expectations, yet messengers from home had come.

'There is little time Scimitar. Tonight, at midnight, there will be fireworks to distract the guards and Bullneck and his party will be on the other side of the barrier.' Scimitar cast a look at the high wall.

'Pile some blocks of marble at the bottom of the wall, Scimitar,' suggested Weiss, 'It will shorten the climb.'

Edel and Weiss knew that they had to be brief. They might be watched.

With remarkable ease they slipped back into their official role and before turning on their heels, smartly saluted Scimitar in Black Elf fashion.

At sundown Scimitar returned to his cave and thought about the day's events. He couldn't believe that those will-o-the-wisp creatures had undertaken the dangerous task of getting in touch with him. He stroked his beard mumbling, 'Mountain Fairies, strange indeed, I have done them an injustice. It calls for a paradigm shift.'

His mind travelled back to times long ago when he had visited the land of Queen Tuluga. All he could remember was nights of music, dance and play. Never a serious conversation, just light-hearted banter, the kind that Dwarves consider to be an utter waste of time. In his solitude, he meditated upon the paradoxes of life. Mountain Fairies, of all creatures risking their necks to save his life and gain his freedom.

He opened the small bottle that the enchantress Amaranth had given him and drank a few sips. Strength had flooded his being since Amaranth's gift seven days ago. A week earlier he could barely move the marble slabs, now he lifted them with ease. He planned to leave some slabs of stone at the bottom of the wall and felt confident that he would be able to climb to the top. The guard towers presented a much more serious threat. Weiss had talked of fireworks, and Scimitar could only hope that they would distract the archers posted in the towers.

Edel and Weiss marched jauntily across the camp. They had packed fuse, flint and provisions in their backpacks. It would be best to wait until after sundown before approaching the research laboratory and the log hut where the magic powder was stored.

At dusk, prisoners began returning to the dormitories. Without raising an eyebrow, Edel and Weiss mixed in with the flow of workers.

Edel, elated by his new role as a Black Elf, played it to the hilt. He pulled his helmet at a rakish angle and assumed a manner of conceit that a real Black Elf would find difficult to match. He dreamed already of what it would be like in the telling. Weiss kept an eye on Edel. He well knew the ups and downs of his bosom friend and Edel was now having a high. He strutted around with sublime arrogance, poking Grolls with his swagger stick.

When they passed the officers' mess, Edel took an unexpected turn and walked up the steps leading to the entrance. Weiss was horrified but before he could reach him, Edel had slipped into the building.

Weiss walked on until he came to a quiet area and then he vanished into a stand of alder bushes. Once out of sight he worked his way through the shrubbery to the back of the mess. There were two small windows high up and beyond Weiss' reach. He looked around for something to stand on, but no barrels or crates were in sight.

Rays from the sinking sun caught the top of a tall stand of aspen. Weiss noticed, in the vanishing light, a streak of gleaming yellow. Was it an eagle from the Celestial Covey? Suddenly it flashed through his mind that he better not be taken for a Black Elf and hastily he removed his spiked helmet.

Fortunately for Weiss, eagles have remarkable eyesight and the moment he removed the helmet, Nightglider recognized the laughing eyes of the Mountain Fairy. Weiss heard the swish of wings and the great bird touched down on a rock by his side. He rejoiced to see it was his old friend from the Covey.

'Nightglider, what a relief to see you here.' In a few words Weiss explained their disguise and Edel's folly. Nightglider nodded gravely. Master Grimmbeak had suspected the mischievous imps would end up in trouble and had dispatched him to check on the pair.

Weiss took a rope from his backpack and Nightglider fastened it to a beam jutting out from under the roof of the building. He climbed up in a flash and found that the small window afforded a good view of the mess hall.

Edel was seated at a round table amidst a group of Rover Officers who took a great deal of delight in the lively Black Elf. He had them all enchanted with his fantastic tales and the young ladies serving the officers at the table were thrilled by his performance. Edel helped himself generously to the food and wine, for two days in the cupboard had whetted his appetite.

Nightglider perched on a small aspen tree and his grave eyes beamed in on Edel. He held his breath as he watched the Fairy, who had to the delight of the Rovers and hostesses crowded around him, begun yodelling a Mountain Fairy song.

'Thank heaven, Nightglider, there are no real Black Elves in the canteen,' he may yet get away with it.' whispered Weiss.

Nightglider just shook his head. Such foolishness was hard to fathom.

The Rovers kept filling Edel's glass. Edel appeared elated with the part that he was playing. He had the Rovers in stitches and their applause and laughter resounded throughout the mess.

Only when Edel had finished his dinner and emptied a bottle of wine did he bid farewell to his enthusiastic audience. Weiss, too, relaxed. He saw Edel dancing nimbly through the crowd, waving to his new found friends, until he reached the door.

Nightglider, satisfied that the prankster had made his way safely to the door rose up from his perch, dipped his wings as he passed Weiss and headed back to the Celestial Covey.

Weiss was just about to lower himself in order to meet Edel at the front of the building when he took a last peek through the window. To his horror, he saw the Captain of the Black Elves walking through the main entrance, a groll servant at his side. Edel deftly stepped aside to let the pair pass, but it was too late. When his hand reached the door handle, it was seized by the Groll's claw. Scorn dwelt in Cobalt's eyes as he knocked off Edel's helmet. Had Cobalt had his way, it would have fared ill with Edel. As luck would have it, just then the bulky frame of the Camp Commander walked through the door. The General picked up Edel and when he saw that the fairy like creature had been dressed up in a Black Elves' uniform, he roared with laughter. Walking through the mess, he held him up to the light and examined him as if he were a large unusual insect.

'A kind of butterfly without wings. Charming, I will keep it in my office for observation.' The General, a devoted naturalist, treasured his collection of insects and reptiles. He was delighted with the new find.

The Rovers seated around by the table where Edel had entertained them, were relieved to see Edel in the hands of their Commander. The wisp of a fellow had impersonated the pesky Black Elves. Weiss could hear them shouting.

'The fingerling put the black imps in their place. Well done butterfly. He is a jolly good fellow. Don't pin up the poor mite, General.'

Weiss slid down the rope and sat down in the alder bushes. He thanked his lucky stars that Edel's knapsack had the provisions and that it was his own that had the flint and the fuse. For a few moments he sat still and tried to meditate. Mountain Fairies are not deep meditators but he was at his wit's end. He focussed on his breathing and repeated softly the words that the old elven Sage Seraphim had taught him: leoth stroem, the light streameth forth.

He retained the lotus position for more than five minutes and felt a renewed sense of purpose and peace. Edel was in the hands of the enemy, but at least General Veldbloom had taken a personal interest in him.

He had to get on with his task, too much depended on it. He checked the contents of his back pack. Thank heaven the flint and the fuse were still there. There was no time to lose and he must avoid any further risk of meeting Black Elves. He crossed through the alder bushes until he came to the rear of the building where the ore was melted and he could see the red glow in the small windows. He kept his distance and when he reached the research station he sought shelter in a clump of cedars. Bright moonlight filled the square in front of the station. He could hear the cloppety clop of boots on the stones and peeking from his hideout saw Captain Cobalt striding to the laboratory.

'Feathers and folderol,' muttered the Black Elf, 'Fairies here, Fairies there, Fairies everywhere. There must be others in the camp. Tomorrow we will comb the place.'

Weiss stayed in the stand of aspen until the raving Captain had vanished into the building. Fortunately, the log hut where the magic powder was stored, was well behind the laboratory and Weiss quietly made his way through the bushes until he reached the rear of the hut.

It would take awhile for a fire to burn through the logs and it wouldn't be necessary to use a fuse. He gathered dry moss and birch bark, tossed the coiled fuse of dry reeds on top and fired the moss. He added windfall from the trees nearby and soon a healthy blaze sprang up. The hut looked rather small and he wondered if the blast would be loud enough to create havoc amongst the guards.

A macabre feeling stole over him. What terrible force was about to be unleashed? He was mesmerized by the dancing flames, when suddenly he realized that the dry logs of the hut were burning fiercely. Time had run out. He grasped his backpack and throwing caution to the wind, leaped into the open. Moving like a whirlwind, he reached a small pavilion near the research station.

Crouching behind a bench, he saw flames reaching the top of the hut. Just in the nick of time he covered his ears and lay down flat. The earth trembled under him, shockwaves uprooted trees, and half the research station tumbled down. When the din subsided Weiss stood up and saw a black mushroom cloud rimmed with golden moonlight.

He could hear shouts coming from different parts of the prison camp, and Grolls were running in all directions.

Before leaving, he took a look at the research station. He could see Cobalt and the Professor silhouetted in the window in a section of the building that had not been destroyed. Curiosity got the better of him and he moved closer. He could hear now the agitated voice of the Professor.

'We lost our entire store of the magic mixture. You must tell us Cobalt where the silvery powder can be found. We have the charcoal and the green stuff, but only you know where the silvery powder is mined.'

Weiss listened carefully but Cobalt didn't speak. His eyes looked faraway and the Professor was getting desperate. A silver haired figure in a white coat joined the two. 'You are wasting your time Professor. The Black Elf suffers from amnesia. He was in the path of the blast and has lost his memory.'

'Lost his memory,' shouted the Professor, 'Impossible, he has no business losing his memory.'

Weiss had heard enough. The Professor would never be able to make good on his promise of a lethal weapon. Leaping, ten feet at a time, he flew across the open space until he reached the quarry.

By now pandemonium reigned in the camp. Rovers were running towards the clouds of black smoke near the research station, and guards abandoned their watchtowers and rushed towards the centre of the melee. Commander Veldbloom stood on the porch of his house yelling for somebody to tell him what was happening.

When Weiss reached the end of the quarry, he could see Scimitar standing before his cave. The other prisoners had rushed over to the site of the explosion.

There were no guards left on the tower nearest Scimitar's cave. Weiss motioned Scimitar to follow and swiftly crossing the quarry, they arrived at the place where Scimitar had piled the marble slabs. Weiss took a rope from his backpack and clenched one end between his teeth. With amazing agility, the blithe Fairy shot up the wall. His tiny feet found a footing in the pitted cement where no other creatures would have found a hold. Once atop, he tied the rope to a sturdy branch of a neighbouring tree.

Scimitar marvelled at the performance of his pint-sized friend. He seized the rope and wetted his lips with the last drops of Amaranth's elixir. Strength flowed through him and with ease he pulled up his heavy frame. Weiss was already standing in a patch of fern when Scimitar came sliding down. There was really no time for ceremony, but the Dwarf wanted to express his admiration for the featherweight by his side. He rested his heavy hand on Weiss' shoulder and pulled the empty crystal vessel from his pocket.

'Pure crystal from the hands of the great enchantress, it is yours noble spirit. My life is forfeit. It is best you take it as a token of my gratitude.'[9]

Tears welled in Weiss' eyes and carefully he placed the sparkling crystal in his pack. Scimitar looked at the trees around him, breathed deeply and softly muttered, 'Free, free at last.' He had been spared the disgrace of death in a prison camp. He might die in battle, but was not that the dream of every Dwarf?

He looked again at the figure by his side. Then it dawned on him that Edel was not there. 'But there were two of you. Edel and Weiss, named after my favourite flower. Where is Edel?'

'Alas, Scimitar, now it is only Weiss, Edel was captured by Cobalt, Captain of the Black Elves. Angels in heaven be praised. He wasn't left in the hands of the Black Elves. Commander Veldbloom took an interest in him and keeps him in his office as a pet.'

There was no more time to talk, the cry of a whip-poor-will could clearly be heard. It was Rick the Reamer's signal call. Only seconds later Bullneck and Rick appeared among the trees and greetings were of the no nonsense kind. But shake hands they did. Weiss showed no surprise at the cool reunion. He had lived with the Dwarves long enough to know that there would be no hugging. Emotional restraint was hard to fathom for Mountain Fairies who danced with joy when meeting long lost friends.

But a smile appeared on Scimitar's face when Bullneck handed him a sword. The sword was Scimitar's own. Sergeant Crusher, after his trip to the Convent of the Sisters of the Secret Crossing, had returned it to Smithereen for safekeeping. Scimitar seized the haft and the blade emitted a blue light. The magic edge bestowed on the blade had been Amaranth's gift.

---

9   *The crystal vessel has survived through the ages and is now on display in the Museum of Fine Art and Folklore in Lambarina .*

Slim, standing in the background amongst the trees, now walked up to Scimitar and took his hand. Scimitar was astonished. Not only were there Mountain Fairies in the rescue party, but Swannefolk as well.

'Perhaps,' he mused, 'my talk to the men in the coffee room at the Graceful Neck had its use, Swannefolk have come to our aid.'

Bullneck stepped onto the path anxious to push forward, but Slim raised his hand.

'Not yet Bullneck, I have worked out the pattern of Groll patrols and in a minute or two, they will come by. We must wait.' Scimitar cast the Swanneyouth an admiring glance. Yes, there were other ways to serve than by the sword.

Slim had calculated that there was a small window of opportunity for their getaway and he signalled to the party to draw farther back into the bushes.

Moments later they heard the faint slapping sound of Groll feet on the forest floor and a fierce looking guard with two black hounds passed in the distance. Since they were upwind the party went unobserved. Now Slim took the lead and moved forward on a narrow trail, the others followed single file.

Back at base camp, Moose and Duckie sat in the shelter of the grotto, warming their hands by a small fire. They had a clear view of the moonlit meadows stretching to the edge of the forest.

The sound of the explosion had reverberated through the caves and they hoped that it had given Scimitar a chance to scale the wall. Moose trained his eyes on the edge of the forest where soon the rescue party should emerge into the open.

They had roasted venison for supper and now were quietly sipping coffee from wooden mugs. Moose put down his mug and walked closer to the opening to get a better view. Duckie saw an ominous expression on the face of the old ferry Captain. Something unexpected was afoot.

'Quick Duckie, to the tunnel at the back of the cave.' Moose threw a bucket of sand on the fire and followed Duckie. At the end of the tunnel they came to a space where a shaft of moonlight shone down between two rock formations.

'What did you see in the meadow, Moose?' queried Duckie.

'A Groll with a black hound heading towards us. The cursed hound may pick up the scent of the venison. If he raises the alarm we are gonners.'

'I think the Groll would search for loot, before calling his fellow guards Moose.'

'Perhaps that is all he is interested in,' sighed Moose. 'Try and climb the chimney Duckie and once the Groll enters the cave, run down the rocky slope and head for the forest to forewarn Bullneck and his party.'

Duckie pressed his back against the shady part of the chimney, placed his feet against the moonlit face and began to wiggle up. The Dwarves had taught him rock climbing and he moved quickly up the narrow passage.

Once Duckie had vanished from sight, Moose breathed a sigh of relief. From the top Duckie slithered down the rocky slope, keeping out of the Groll's sight. Hiding behind a rock he could see the dog galloping towards the cave with the Groll running behind. The moment that they entered the cave, Duckie raced down to the meadows and onto the forest hoping to intercept the rescue party.

Moose stood frozen at the bottom of the chimney. He hoped the Groll would be content merely to ransack their belongings. He heard the dog pawing the buried deer bones and his huge jaws began cracking them. Then all fell silent. Only a sniffing sound travelled down the cave. The black brute was closing in on his scent. The Marquis's agony flashed through Moose's mind and he prayed silently that he might be spared that fate.

The dark shape drew closer. Moose could now see the black fur glistening in the moonlight. It couldn't be true. It must be a horrible nightmare.

'Sit Cruncher!' shouted the Groll and the hound sank on his haunches.

The Groll leaned forward, supporting himself on his sword and eyed his victim.

Moose emerging from his cocoon of fear looked at the grim pair facing him. He was a strong man and during his years as a ferry captain he had knocked the heads of a few rowdy sailors together, but he was not a fighter. His only hope was that Duckie would reach the Dwarves in time.

The Groll gazed at the innocent eyes in front of him. To kill the Captain would be too easy. He would make a useful shield when the remainder of the party returned and judging by their packs there were at least five of them.

'Out, step outside, redhead,' shouted the Groll. Moose got up and walked toward the cave opening.

'Faster redhead,' hissed the Groll, who for some unknown reason seemed irritated by the Captain's red mop of hair. Once outside, Moose looked over the meadows. There was no sign of Duckie or the Dwarves. The Groll pointed at the cliff rising behind them.

'Climb up, on the double.' yelled his captor poking him with his sword. Moose hurried up the narrow trail that led to the top of the escarpment. When they emerged on top, the Groll goaded him towards the very edge of the abyss. Looking down, Moose felt dizzy and raised his eyes towards the wall of green at the end of the meadows. There was movement amidst the moonlit trees and a ray of hope entered his heart. He saw three Dwarves slashing the undergrowth and storming into the meadows. Duckie had found the party.

Despite his poor night vision, the gruesome creature sensed something was afoot and rested his sword on Moose's right shoulder. Before long the Groll descried the warriors, swords raised high, dashing across the meadows. They were short in stature but the Groll knew the Dwarves to be formidable warriors.

Scimitar, leading the charge was the first to hear the Groll's warning shout. He stopped in his tracks and saw, silhouetted against the moonlight, the strange threesome standing on the edge of the cliff.

The Dwarves grasped the situation instantly. The black dog was seated a few steps back from the ledge beside his master, whose sword was now poised between the Captain's shoulder blades. Unless they laid down their weapons and walked back to the forest, their friend and companion would be pushed over the edge into the abyss. It would give the Groll time to attract the attention of other patrols and they would all end up prisoners in the quarries or worse.

Slim and Weiss stood farther back in a patch of wild raspberry bushes, mortified at the drama unfolding on the cliff's edge.

True to the dwarf warrior code, they would readily give their lives to save their friend. Bullneck and Scimitar threw down their swords and the Groll looked pleased as he heard the metal clatter on the rocks. Rick the Reamer was just about to toss his bow away when a piercing cry from Slim and Weiss startled him. He looked up in time to see Moose Martin step forth into the abyss. Instantly, before Moose's body touched the earth below, Rick sent an arrow soaring, striking the Groll in the chest. He too, toppled over the edge. The next arrow caught the dog racing down the trail. It spun him around and he vanished into a crevasse.

Slim's eyes moved from the drama on the height of the cliff to the entrance of the Grotto, where the lifeless form of his close friend had come to rest. Moose had often told him that he couldn't bear the thought of fighting or killing anyone. Yet, it was Moose who won this battle. High up on the cliff he had stood and in a flash of intuition it came to him, just one step would save the lives of his friends. The step that took him over the edge had purchased both their freedom and their lives.

The Dwarves knew that they must move quickly. They built a cairn of rock and lifted the remains of Moose Martin inside. Bullneck said that memorial services would be celebrated on their return to Turania. The gentle Captain from Swanneland who had dwelt among them would forever dwell in the hearts of the Dwarves. His would be the first name of an outsider, to be carved on the face of the Sacred Mountain. The first of the Swannefolk to be on the lips of their troubadours, chanting the praise of the immortals.

Slim cast a last glance at his friend and companion. He knew that life itself was a walk on the edge of an abyss, but to save their brethren, few would take that fatal step.

They packed their belongings and lost no time in getting ready for the long trip home. Dawn was breaking when the small party began the long climb to the alpine meadows.

Weiss lingered behind. He was the only one not carrying a heavy load. Fleet of foot, he would catch up. His finely tuned spirit sensed the soul of Moose Martin leaving this earthly plane and seated by the rough cairn, his sweet voice intoned words of parting,

> *my captain leaves the shell*
> *he loved so well,*
> *to thee a fond farewell*
> *for I hear voices welcome thee,*
> *praise the deed that set thee free*

When Weiss had finished the chant, he could feel the spirit of the ferry boat captain sailing rivers and seas he had never dreamed of. He knew in his heart of hearts that Moose Martin would find his way on those uncharted waters.

He cast a last look at the dismal scene and defying gravity, jumped lightly from rock to rock until he caught up with the solemn column marching towards the alpine village of the Dwarves.

It was Slim who guided the party through the spruce forests on the lower slopes of the Finnian Range. Making use of the maps that Moose had drawn, he led them safely back to the mountain meadows.

Walking alone ahead of his companions, his thoughts wandered through the terrible and wonderful things that had happened. He had loved Moose Martin, and his death was a terrible shock. Slim's mind travelled to the village of Cascade, the quiet joyful pace of life, his dancing swans, the cottage by the river, his mother singing by the hearth and Svanhild seated by her loom. He heard the shuttle flying and saw the wondrous golden flowers she was weaving on a purple field.

Sergeant Crusher, at his guard post by the south gate, was the first to spot the party climbing up the snow covered meadows. He counted the tiny figures in the distance. Six there appeared to be. But seven had set out. Sergeant Crusher looked dismayed. Scimitar not rescued and one of the party lost. Before running off to tell Sunflower and Smithereen, he looked again. A tiny sprite was flying across the white slopes. One of the Mountain Fairies? No other creature could leap from rock to rock like that, especially if they were ten feet apart. Out of breath and wiping perspiration from his forehead Weiss, leapt onto the wall opposite the Sergeant.

'Welcome back my fairy. Glad to see you. You may as well give it to me straight my tiny friend, I am an old warrior.'

'Scimitar is with us Sergeant Crusher, but two are lost. Moose Martin saved the party but paid with his life.' Sergeant Crusher was shocked. 'And your tiny friend, where is he?'

'Captured by the Black Elves and handed over to General Veldbloom.'

The light hearted imp that had brought cheer to all through the long dark winter, now betrayed by the Black Elves and in the hands of the Camp Commander. Sergeant Crusher wrung his hands in a motion that suggested a Black Elf might be wriggling between his fingers.

By now the remainder of the party had reached the gate. Dwarves from the village gathered about and there was rejoicing at the sight of Scimitar. But soon the story of Moose Martin made the rounds and there was genuine grief. The gentle Captain, always ready with a helping hand, the Captain who couldn't hurt a fly had given his life to save his fellow travellers. It was the kind of action that is close to a Dwarf's heart and the news travelled like wildfire. The loss of Edel was another blow, but at least there was a chance that the corky little creature might be able to wiggle out of his captivity.

Sunflower and Smithereen were shocked at the sight of Scimitar. The once barrel-chested Dwarf was a shadow of his former self. Smithereen hugged his brother and Scimitar kissed Sunflower on both cheeks. Sunflower was truly astonished. Her brother-in-law had actually shown a sign of affection. When she looked at him, there was a new light in his eyes. She kept staring at those green lakes in their bony sockets. The once turbid waters were clear and she could see great depth. The suffering had changed Scimitar and had touched the hidden layers of his psyche. What a joy to have him back.

Scimitar and Smithereen walked home together. Sunflower waited for Slim and Weiss, put an arm around each shoulder and walked with them to the cottage.

A few days later a memorial service was held for Moose Martin. Smithereen unveiled the tribute to the Captain, carved in the face of the Sacred Mountain. He, an outsider, had joined the ranks of Dwarf heroes. The men, women and children gathered by the site, raised their right hand in a last farewell. Smithereen's deep voice praised the stranger that had lived amongst them.

'From the land of swans he came, a stranger, he did not share our past. Yet, our future he does share, which is greater than the past. With the one step he took on that forlorn cliff side he stepped into our lives. My Captain, you are one of us.'

In his deep voice Smithereen quoted a few lines he had penned that morning.

one step and
down sailed the captain
one step, and a leap into eternity
to you who dwell
in heights ethereal
we bid farewell

Master Grimmbeak and young Theodorus perched on the cliff side, watched the ceremony. Master Grimmbeak had been trying to harden the oversensitive bird to the facts of life, but with little success. Tears flowed from the young eagle's eyes. To tell the truth, Master Grimmbeak himself had been moved by the tribute. The mention of ethereal heights was dear to the eagle's heart. The Grandmaster decided that Smithereen was a poet of note.

A few days after the memorial service Weiss offered to travel to Cascade and to bring news of Scimitar's rescue to the Council gathered at the Manor deCygne. The Dwarves were dismayed to see him leave but it was urgent that the Council receive news of all that happened. Weiss would travel more swiftly than any of them and was less likely to be detected.

37

To The Eastern Shore

The Scornmaster and his fierce birds had brought pain and humiliation to Svanhild and Sidonia. Although safe at last at the cottage of the Gnomes, they felt spent and worn out. The home of Oarflake and Ambrosia was a haven of rest.

Beside the log house stood a small building used by Ambrosia to nurse back to health, ill and injured animals. When Oarflake and Ambrosia first arrived at the Lake of the Coloured Fishes, the forest dwellers had resented the intrusion by the banished Gnomes. Over the years mistrust had vanished. Ambrosia's healing powers became widely known and many animals and birds sought her aid.

Ever since Ensten had asked Leonardo to keep an eye on the Gnomes, the grey wolves had always been there in time of need and in return many a sick wolf had come to the Gnomes to have bones set or to recover from illness.

Sidonia and Svanhild basked in the warmth of Ambrosia's hospitality. Between meals they would sit on the porch and enjoy the autumn sunshine. Oarflake was harvesting root crops for the winter and they could hear him singing as he worked in the garden.

In the evenings they would linger around the supper table and tell Ambrosia and Oarflake about the Council at the Manor deCygne in Cascade and their adventures on the journey to the Lake of the Coloured

Fishes. Of their captivity at the home of the Scornmaster, Ambrosia couldn't hear enough. She was thrilled to hear how Timmy Tightstring had sensed their desperate plight and sent the swans to their succour. Oh, how she would love to meet the tiny Elf. Sidonia assured her that one day she would come to the court of Queen Orchidae and meet many Elves.

Oarflake knew that the mission to find the Sea Gnomes was urgent but after the traumatic encounter with the scorn birds, Sidonia and Svanhild must first regain their health. The journey to the Eastern Shore would be long and arduous. They would cross the Finnian Range at one of the southern passes and trek through enemy territory to reach the shore. Luckily the region was uninhabited and there was little risk of meeting enemy scouts. Once on the other side of the mountain range they would follow the headwaters of the Little Wasa. Oarflake hoped they would be able to set up camp by the riverside and build a raft to float down the river to the settlement of the Sea Gnomes. Ambrosia would stay behind, finish the harvest, and nurse the animals in her care. Oarflake saw the look of concern in Svanhild's eyes. He reassured her that Leonardo and his girl friend Andante would call and check on Ambrosia. In case of need they would carry a message to Esteria.

On a brilliant fall morning they set out on the path along the lake. Svanhild and Sidonia were enchanted by the bright coloured fishes flitting about. The waters beneath the surface resembled a spectrum of startling colours constantly changing and moving about.

Several times they turned and waved farewell to Ambrosia. At the end of the lake Oarflake and Svanhild lost sight of her, but Sidonia could still see her wandering about the vegetable garden.

The first few days they made good headway. Oarflake knew every nook and cranny in this part of the forest and there were plenty of fine campsites. Only when they came close to the top of the mountain range did the nights become uncomfortably cold. In the morning they would scrape the hoarfrost off their camping gear and swing their arms and stamp their feet until Oarflake got a blaze going. Sidonia always ate lightly but Oarflake and Svanhild took time to eat a solid breakfast.

Two more days were spent climbing the bare slopes of the Finnian Range. The sunny weather was a blessing and by late morning the air warmed up. Only the tall grasses on the alpine meadows stayed wet, soaking their footwear through and through.

Near the summit they found a narrow pass flanked by high cliffs. Throughout the pass, a crust of ice supported them and they were able to make good headway. By afternoon the weather turned. Purple clouds scudded across the summit and an eerie light filled the gorge. Anxious to find shelter they quickened their pace. Snow began to fall and without warning violent shifting winds sculpted the snow into strange and eerie drifts. In the lee of a large rock, Sidonia and Svanhild clung to each other, while Oarflake wandered about seeking a refuge for the night. Gnomes, like Dwarves, have a sixth sense when it comes to finding caves and cracks in seemingly solid walls of rock.

Wading through the heavy snow, Oarflake made slow progress until he stumbled upon fresh tracks. He trudged along for a while and suddenly the footprints stopped. He espied a narrow entrance in the face of the cliff. It would be the only chance of finding shelter for the night and he backtracked to find his companions.

Svanhild laughed when she saw the snow covered face of their faithful guide. Snow had frozen into his beard and eyelashes and the howling wind made it difficult to hear a word he said. He beckoned them to follow. Holding hands, Oarflake leading, they fought their way through the blizzard. Svanhild, walking behind Oarflake, was startled to see him melt into the rock face. The wind ceased to whip their faces and the blinding white gave way to utter darkness.

'Ah ha, ah ho,' echoed Oarflake's voice, 'if there is an opening in the mountain, a Gnome will find it.'

Oarflake knew that other creatures had found their way into the cave. He asked Sidonia and Svanhild to stay near the entrance and carefully he slunk deeper into the tunnel. Once his eyes adjusted to the faint light, he made better progress. The light grew brighter and now he could hear voices. At first he was baffled. Soon however a light began to dance in his eyes and he called out in the ancient Gnome tongue, 'Hail to thee, cousins from the sea.'

Svanhild and Sidonia knew from the tone of Oarflake's voice that all was well and they caught up with him. Turning a corner, they could see the light of many candles reflected in crystal and stalactite.

Oarflake, entering a domelike chamber, saw three gnome youths standing behind a small wooden table, their faces showed a mixture of both fear and astonishment.

Listening to their voices, he realized that they still conversed in the old gnome tongue and familiar with ancient texts, he spoke to them as best he could. The warmth of his approach, the sparkle of laughter in his eyes and his kindly tongue dispelled any misgivings that the youths might have had. They bade him be seated.

They had been astonished at the appearance of a strange Gnome but when Svanhild and Sidonia entered the grotto they couldn't believe their eyes. Their legends spoke of Elves and Swannefolk but never had they imagined meeting them. Oarflake introduced himself and his travel companions.

The youngsters seemed delighted and did everything they could to make their guests comfortable. One of the young men lit a fire. At first smoke filled the grotto, but soon it vanished in the large cracks between the rocks. The damp cold retreated before the flames and Svanhild and Sidonia stopped shivering. The smallest of the three boiled a pot of water and served tea.

The youths were friendly and thrilled to have visitors from lands long since shrouded in mystery. Yet, Oarflake felt they were ill at ease. He asked them about their village by the sea. It soon came out that they had left the settlement without their parent's permission. When they first heard Oarflake's footsteps they feared that men from the village had come to take them home.

For centuries the cave had been used as a shelter by the Sea Gnomes. Every spring and fall they would travel up into the mountains to drive timber and firewood down the Little Wasa.

'But when you spoke,' laughed Folderol, the eldest, 'we guessed right away that you must be a Mountain Gnome, a member of the tribe that our people had left long ago.'

'You guessed well, Folderol. I am delighted to meet our distant cousins. Our sagas tell of your forefathers' departure from the mountains in search of distant shores. I have often dreamt of discovering our long lost cousins by the sea.'

'Why did you leave your village and your family Folderol?' asked Svanhild.

'It was the way of life, Swannelady,' said Folderol in a solemn tone. 'All our people were concerned with was the search for treasures, the riches that rest on the bottom of the ocean.'

'Piling up wealth and more wealth to no purpose,' added Flink, who was seated next to Folderol.

'We wish - wish - wished for another kind of life.' stammered Trickle, the smallest of the three. 'We had heard about King Arc - arc- turus and the Sacred Book of Common Lore. We are sear - searching for another kind of life.

We hoped the Sacred Book might tell us about the meaning of life. We are searching for the Kingdom. We dream of mee - meeting the King.'

Oarflake nodded, well he knew the pressures in the traditional gnome communities to pile up riches.

Svanhild cast a loving look at the small Gnome who blushed a deep red.

'Don't be upset Trickle,' soothed Svanhild, I admire what you said.

'I am not upset!' burst out the tiny fellow. 'You are so very beau -beau – tiful, Lady of the Swans, and nobody has understood us before.' Oarflake put his arm around Trickle, who had put his head on Oarflake's shoulder.

Sidonia and Svanhild took off their wet boots and set them by the fire to dry. Folderol served more mugs of steaming tea and passed around a plate filled with thick slices of the homemade bread that his mother had baked.

Then Oarflake stood up. Looking at Folderol, Flink and Trickle, he said in a solemn voice, 'I will tell you the story of a Gnome obsessed, not with the meaning of life, but with the search for gold.'

The three youngsters were mesmerized when they learned how Oarflake had been banished for the theft of gold, of the decades Oarflake and Ambrosia had spent in the remote forests and of their spiritual journey. Tears ran down Trickle's face and hope sprang into his eyes.

'One day all of you will come to the Kingdom and learn about the Common Book of Sacred Lore. The Mountain Gnomes gave up their independence many years ago. We joined Elves, Mountain Fairies, Outlanders, Swannefolk and Dwarves to form the United Kingdom. At present the Kingdom is threatened by the Seven Masters in the Land of Darkness. Your lives would be in peril if you were to travel to the Kingdom at this time.'

Once this darkness passes,' added Sidonia, 'a new life will dawn and barriers between people will be no more. You will come to the Kingdom, visit the land of the Elves and meet our Queen Orchidae.' At the thought of travelling to the land of the Elves, a light sparkled in the eyes of Folderol, Flink and Trickle.

'Your families must be terribly worried. It is best you return home,' counselled Oarflake who guessed that they were afraid to face their parents and the Elders of the village.

'We will travel with you and speak to the Elders.'

'We would be grateful if you could sir!' exclaimed Folderol. 'And we will build a raft and travel with you down river. We have made the trip many times.'

'I think,' piped up Trickle, 'we were meant to come up here and meet you.'

Sidonia laughed. 'I believe that too, Trickle. It is one of those strange coincidences that pop up in life to remind us that we are not alone. The Elves call it synchronicity.' The three youngsters had never before heard the word and they were astonished at all the new ideas they learned about that evening. They had set out to find new horizons but never made it beyond the borders of their homeland. Yet new worlds were opening before them.

More tea was poured. Svanhild unpacked Ambrosia's sausages and Trickle deftly arranged them on a grill over the fire pit.

Talk went on deep into the night. The three youths had an unquenchable curiosity and only when Oarflake dozed off, did the party come to an end. Svanhild and Sidonia unrolled their sleeping bags on the rough bunks at the end of the grotto. Folderol, Flink and Trickle settled down around the glowing embers in the fire pit. After all, their search for the outside world had been a success. Although different from what they had imagined, a success just the same.

A ray of sunshine entered the cave through a crack in the rocks and caught Folderol holding a coffee pot. Trickle was beating batter for hot cakes. A few moments later, Flink walked in with a pile of firewood and reported that the wind had packed the snow tight and that the crust would easily support them.

By the time Oarflake and the girls joined in, the pancakes were sizzling in a cast iron pot and coffee was on the boil. Thoughtfully, Trickle had made tea for Sidonia.

'Wonderful to see the sun again,' said Svanhild, 'I hope that we will be able to travel today.'

'I have been outside. The snow is hard and we can descend quickly. By evening we can reach the headwaters of the Little Wasa. By the water's edge stands a large stockpile of logs and a fine raft will carry us to the sea. My father is a river driver and many a raft he and I have built.'

'That is wonderful news Flink,' said Oarflake, 'How long will it be to raft down the river to the sea?'

'A good day's travel will take us to the shore.'

'How blessed we are to have found you on this forlorn mountain top in the midst of a storm.' exclaimed Sidonia, 'Our mission is urgent and no time must be lost in reaching your village.'

Oarflake thought it best to explain to the boys the reason for their journey. He spoke about the power of the Seven, the threat that they posed to the Kingdom and the legend of the golden tablet with the mystic writ.

'But the tablet could be anywhere,' wondered Flink.

'The village of your people is our last hope Flink. Agents of the Seven have combed the land in vain in search of the golden plate.'

'There is no knowledge of your settlement on the Eastern Ocean. The sagas of the Gnomes only speak of the departure of your forefathers, there is no word of their arrival,' said Svanhild. 'Only when I stole a glimpse at the Mirror of a Thousand Fragments at the Chateau of the sorceress Matista, did I see the Sea Gnomes standing on the beach, surrounded by a wealth of jewels, gold and finely crafted silver. I removed the tiny piece of glass from the mirror. Let us hope and pray that Mastista did not see the settlement in the abutting fragment. The treasures of the Sea Gnomes is our only hope of finding the legendary plate.'

Folderol, Flink and Trickle thrilled to hear of the extraordinary events happening far away from their tiny isolated settlement. Yet, it was clear that sooner or later, the Sea Gnomes too would be drawn into the chain of events unfolding in the outside world. The three boys realized the importance of finding the golden tablet. It was Trickle who spoke first.

'The sea is full of treasures. Many a ship has floundered on the reefs near our shore. Our divers bring up more gold in a day than Mountain Gnomes mine in a year.'

Oarflake felt goosebumps spread all over his skin. He quickly whispered a silent prayer that never, never, never, would gold fever seize him again.

Flink, who came from a family of deep sea-divers, couldn't recall seeing any golden plates.

'Golden vases, and marvellous ornaments, jewels and bracelets are brought up every day from the deep, yet many wrecks remain untouched. Those by the outer banks cannot be reached, the water is too deep.'

'Alas,' sighed Oarflake, 'the chances of finding the tablet in time are scant.'

'But we must pursue every lead,' exclaimed Svanhild, 'too much is at stake.'

Packing took no time at all and with Folderol leading they entered the tunnel and walked out of the cave. Emerging from the semi-darkness of the grotto, the sunshine and glistening snow took them by surprise and it took several minutes before their eyes adjusted to the light. Folderol, whistling a gay tune, led them down the snowy slopes. Walking, gliding and tumbling they made speedy headway and by late afternoon crossed the tree line. The dark green needles were a balm to their eyes.

Farther down the mountainside the weather became milder and they began peeling off layers of clothing. Emerging from the spruce forest, they found themselves walking through glades ablaze with the deep red of blueberry bushes and clumps of golden poplar. The ground became soggy and small rivulets appeared. Rills flowed together and formed streams; the headwaters of the Little Wasa. They followed the river and soon the sound of rushing water made it hard to hear one another talk. Sidonia was the first to spot the mountain of logs in the distance.

'The logs, I can see them stacked by the shore.' Folderol, knowing that they were still several miles away from the log pile, was amazed that Sidonia could see them in the fast dwindling light. Before reaching the logs, they came to a cabin. It had been built by the river drivers as a temporary lodge.

The cabin was comfortable. A stove stood at one end and kindling had been stacked against the wall. In a few minutes a fire was started and warmth spread throughout the cabin. Bunks had been built along the walls and a trestle table stood in the centre.

They combined their provisions for a potluck supper and when the sun dropped below the horizon, lit candles and cooked a fine dinner.

Folderol, Flink and Trickle knew their parents would be relieved to know that they were safe and sound. Just the same there would be punishment in store.

Sidonia smiled. 'Your presence here was heaven sent. I will speak to your parents. They will understand and appreciate what you have done for us. We must anticipate the best. Our Queen, Orchidae, taught us creative visualisation. In your mind's eye you must see your fathers and mothers as loving understanding beings. It takes practice and attention but it works, I assure you.' The youth were amazed at all the new ideas the strangers brought.

On waking in the morning, Sidonia and Svanhild saw no sign of the Sea Gnomes. As they rolled up their sleeping bags they heard a series of loud splashes coming from the river and rushed outside.

'Look Sidonia,' shouted Svanhild, 'They are launching the logs and building a raft.' Folderol and Flink, standing atop a pile of logs wielding their pewees, rolled the logs over the edge sending them down into the river.

On the river, jumping from log to log was Trickle. He looped a long rope around the logs tying them together. At the next bend in the river he managed to jump ashore and anchor his catch to a tree stump. As soon as there was a goodly number of logs in the water, Folderol and Flink joined Trickle and they lashed the logs tightly.

Svanhild and Sidonia returned to the cabin to boil some coffee. There were blueberry cakes left and they carried the coffee and cakes out to the three river drivers who took time out to enjoy breakfast. Oarflake cleaned the cabin and brought the luggage out to the landing.

After breakfast the young Sea Gnomes loaded the raft. Folderol fetched the pike-poles lying by the side of the cabin and they took their place on each side of the raft.

Sidonia, Svanhild and Oarflake were standing in the centre of the slippery platform when Trickle loosened the rope holding the raft to shore and clambered aboard. Skilfully, Folderol and Flink maneuvered the unwieldy craft among boulders and rocks.

Flink and Folderol knew all the bends and sandbanks in the river and the raft, carried by the current, floated swiftly through the changing landscape of woodlands and green fields.

Only one incident marred the joyful spell of sun and water. Sidonia had spotted, miles away and high above the horizon, the black shape of a merewing speeding to his homeland. Why had the black bird, with the purple beak, strayed into this unknown region of the world? When she told Svanhild a shadow crossed her face. Was it possible that Matista had caught a glimpse of the Sea Gnomes in an adjacent fragment of the mirror? Svanhild's mind travelled back to the Chateau. She had heard the sorceress' footsteps on the stairs when she removed the first fragment. There had been no time to do more.

They neared the coast and the river widened. Marshlands appeared on both sides and Oarflake watched with wonder as the river began to split into many channels. Flink and Folderol never faltered. They knew from childhood all the twists and turns and skilfully guided the rough craft through the delta.

Oarflake offered a silent prayer of thanks. Had it not been for their meeting with the young Sea Gnomes at the summit of the mountain, how could they have found their way through the myriad channels?

It was now late in the day. The sky still a deep blue, Sidonia, seated at the front of the craft, looked over the marshlands stretching to the horizon. Although they were still miles from the coast, she could see thin lines of dark grey streaking into the sky. Perhaps charcoal pits in the village were burning hardwood. She beckoned Trickle to join her.

'Can you see the dark streaks yonder, Trickle? The men are burning charcoal perhaps?' Trickle had good eyesight but he couldn't see smoke that was more than fifteen miles away.

'No smoke in sight Elven lady. The charcoal pits are not near the village, it could be the forge working.

'There are many tiny puffs on the horizon Trickle,' said Sidonia, a slight tremor in her voice. They floated deeper into the delta. Oarflake and Svanhild joined Sidonia at the front of the raft.

'What is it Sidonia?' asked Svanhild, sensing a note of alarm in Sidonia's voice.

'The smoke Svanhild, it is turning black and shooting straight up.'

Svanhild knew that elven eyes seldom err and she wondered what could have happened on the coast. Half an hour later, all could see the smoke darkening the horizon. Folderol stopped singing and looked at the strange sight.

'A fire in the village!' shouted Flink.

'The whole village must be burning!' cried out Folderol.

'I fear,' whispered Svanhild to Sidonia, 'that the sorceress caught a glimpse of the Sea Gnomes in the Mirror of a Thousand Fragments. I suspected trouble when you saw the merewing.'

Oarflake had the same thought. 'A raid by a Rover and his troop of Grolls?' The young Sea Gnomes had gathered enough from Oarflake's tales to know what was up. Fear of wrath on their homecoming turned into concern for the well being of family and friends.

Working their pike-poles hard they moved the raft swiftly through the delta and within an hour reached a dock several miles distant from the village. The sun was sinking over the sea and an amber glow stood out against the darkening sky. Folderol and Flink were about to run off to their homes when Oarflake called them back.

'We must approach with caution, boys. Some of the raiders may be left behind. Is there a path that provides cover when approaching the village?'

Flink pointed to a shallow valley of shrubs and berry bushes.

'Yonder trail will take us to a ridge above the village.' The moment that Folderol docked the raft, Trickle jumped on land and tied it to a mooring. Following Folderol, they hurried down the jetty and came onto a trail flanked by wild roses and alder shrubs.

Once in the valley, particles of soot floated in the air. An acrid smell made breathing difficult and climbing up the ridge they felt a faint sense of nausea. Sidonia offered to go ahead and take a look from the top of the ridge. Oarflake nodded. Lightly tripping up the sandy slope, hiding behind juniper bushes, she scanned the horizon. In the distance huge waves were crashing on shore, but down below there was utter devastation. Most of the houses were burnt to the ground. Only at the south end of the settlement, a dozen or so remained standing.

Her eyes searched the dark expanse of ocean. Miles north of the ruined settlement, she spotted the silhouette of a galley. A sail and many oars were propelling the vessel back to the palace of the Seven. The rays of the setting sun glistened on gold and silver ornaments piled on the rear deck.

'Heavens above,' whispered the elven maid, 'All the treasures the Gnomes raised from the bottom of the sea sailing to Salan's Palace. But praise be, the raiders have left.'

Turning around, she beckoned her companions. They were horrified by the sight of the burning town. A stream of men, women and children could be seen moving towards a part of the village where a small number of homes were still standing. There, atop a shallow dune, stood a tall Gnome, white locks and beard flowing in the wind. The villagers formed a semi circle at the foot of the dune.

'It is the Elder, Findhorn, speaking to the meeting,' burst out Folderol, 'We must fly thither!' The three youth ran towards the crowd below.

Oarflake, Sidonia and Svanhild saw them storming into the circle and their parents running up to embrace the three runaways. Findhorn came down the dune to shake their hands and Folderol talked to him at length. Oarflake looked reassured.

'I think they have told the Elder and their parents about our presence here.'

'It is true,' said Sidonia, 'The Elder they call, Findhorn, is turning our way, a smile in his blue eyes. Now he beckons us.'

Oarflake, taking Svanhild and Sidonia by the hand, walked down the sandy slope towards the dune. Any fears that Oarflake still harboured about his meeting with the Sea Gnomes vanished when he saw the venerable elder, with outstretched arms, striding towards him. Oarflake found himself in a warm embrace.

'Welcome, Oarflake, welcome. The returned prodigals told me your name and spoke of your mission. The flight of the three boys up the mountain has caused anxiety and anger, but after the devastating raid on the village, all that was forgotten. Our treasures are gone, but heaven be praised, no lives were lost.'

'Long have I waited for this moment!' exclaimed Oarflake. 'As children, how often did we hear the saga of your forefathers' trek towards unknown shores.'

Oarflake resting his hand on Findhorn's shoulder, introduced Svanhild and Sidonia.

'Welcome my children,' beamed the Elder, 'welcome to our home and hearth. What is left of them we will share with you.'

'Did you have warning of the raid?' asked Oarflake.

'One of our divers spotted the galley and raised the alarm. We hid in the deep tunnels that we excavated years ago.'

'Alas, the silver ornaments, the jewels and gold that our divers brought up from the deep are gone. They raided our homes and cellars before firing them.'

Oarflake smiled and took Findhorn's hand. 'Find not your joy in treasures. If that is all that is lost, you are blessed indeed.'

'Yet my people are disconsolate and heartbroken. The fruit of years of dangerous and arduous deep sea diving gone and many homes in ruins.'

Findhorn led his guests down to the circle of villagers. The sight of the strange Gnome, an Elf and a Swannemaiden startled the men and women at the foot of the dune and for a moment they forgot their loss and distress. Findhorn introduced them and then led Oarflake to the top of the dune and asked him to speak. All eyes were on the ancient Mountain Gnome.

'Friends, fellow Gnomes,' sounded Oarflake's deep baritone. 'What a joy to be here amongst my own people. Your forefathers left their mountain home centuries ago to settle these remote shores. Providence led us to you at a time when the Seven Lords threaten our Kingdom. It is their troops that have assaulted your homesteads and robbed you of your riches, the fruit of many years of labour. Grieve not my brethren. No lives were lost and homes can be rebuilt. I too lost all the gold that once I mined.'

All eyes were riveted on the stranger on the dune top. Oarflake told of his greed, banishment and of the mine of spiritual riches which had become his true coinage.

When Oarflake finished, tears sparkled in Findhorn's eyes. He embraced Oarflake and introduced him to the men and women who wanted to shake his hands and thank him for sharing his story. Folderol, Flink, and Trickle brought their parents to meet him. The events of the day and Oarflake's talk had changed much and the youthful rebellion of the three met with new understanding.

The moon shed an eerie light over the ruins of the village. Many of the men and women were busy either setting up tents or building temporary shelters in the dunes. Findhorn's home had been spared and he invited Oarflake to stay with him and his wife. Before leaving, Findhorn turned to Sidonia and Svanhild.

'I have asked Alexa to take you in.' Findhorn could hear a couple of women mumbling.

'They are going to stay with old toddy head. She is daft. Old Alexa talks to spirits at full moon.'

Findhorn turned, an enigmatic smile on his face. 'I have a feeling that they will enjoy their visit with Alexa. Her house is still standing, too!'

Trickle walked Svanhild and Sidonia to the home of Alexa. She had never married and at one hundred and forty-four, was the second oldest resident in the settlement. So pleased was she to have strangers stay with her, she hustled and bustled around her small log home and cooked the company a late evening meal. While stirring the stew on the hob she sang merrily an old ditty.

Alexa had always been young at heart and even now in her hundred and forties she was a child's spirit in a bent and wizened body. The presence of an Elf and a Swannemaid in her house simply entranced her. Sidonia looked into the innocent blue eyes, an innocence that she had only seen in elven eyes.

'A woman without guile,' she mused.

Svanhild and Sidonia spoke of their home and family, dancing swans and elven lore. Like a child enchanted by a fairy tale, Alexa was mesmerized by the strange and wonderful tales. The spell was only broken when Svanhild and Sidonia fell asleep in their chairs. With a deep sigh Alexa got up and made their beds.

After her guests were bedded down, sitting by the dying fire, Alexa dreamed of swans floating on the Sanctus, by the light of the harvest moon. This visit meant so much to her. It seemed that all these years she had been waiting for it.

The morning sun caught Svanhild at the breakfast table. She was slowly coming to with a cup of coffee. Alexa had brewed rosehip tea for Sidonia. She felt a great love for the elven maid and tears welled in her eyes when Sidonia asked her to come, when peace returned to the Kingdom, and stay in elvenland.

Svanhild was fascinated by the aged woman so keen to please them. Yet when she closed her eyes, it was as if a child were scurrying around the kitchen instead of an old biddy.

'How old are you Alexa?' Asked Svanhild overcome by curiosity.

'Ah, my dears, does it matter? Over a hundred years or more I have walked these shores. Never did I marry, the young divers didn't even look at me, too busy they were chasing gold and silver. Yet for all the treasures gathered at the bottom of the sea, happiness eluded them.' A smile played upon her face. Yesterday had seen the labour of years vanish in the twinkling of an eye.

Svanhild and Sidonia looked with wonder at their hostess.

'Ah, my children, for years I nursed my ailing father. He was one of the village's divers. Now to supply my daily needs, I knit sweaters'

Alexa walked over to the living area beckoning them to follow. On the round table were displayed dozens of sweaters in many colours and designs. Dolphins danced, gulls soared and one sweater in midnight blue showed seven swans rising. Alexa, seeing the astonished look on Svanhild's face, told her that the image had come to her in a dream.

'The sweaters are a great joy to me.' said Alexa, taking Svanhild by the hand to show off her wool collection in the alcove. Svanhild smiled when she saw the amazing variety of colours and the delight that Alexa took in her designs.

Sidonia had gone back to the kitchen table. Sitting by the stove, she looked around the tidy space. Above the woodstove ran a ledge, the length of the wall. On it were crowded pretty plates made of stoneware and silver. The dinner plates depicted men and women dancing, laughing faces and festive dress.

'Thank Heaven,' mused the elven maid, 'Gnomes make merry betimes. Not like the priggish Dwarves.' The silver plates had engravings celebrating births, marriages and anniversaries.

When Svanhild and Alexa returned, they went out to have a look at the rebuilding of the town. It was fortunate that the men had organized a log drive in late summer and many logs had been floated down the Little Wasa. Men and women were working together clearing debris and placing new logs on the old foundations. Gnomes have enormous strength and easily can lift three or four times their body-weight.

Findhorn and two other Elders had taken Oarflake under their wing. They walked out of town into the dunes until they came to the entrance of a tunnel, well concealed by an abundance of wild rose bushes. The raiders had never spotted the entrance.

When Oarflake mentioned the legend of the golden tablet, they could only tell him that there were but few gold plates among the treasures stored in the underground cave.

Two Elders, carrying torches, went ahead, Findhorn and Oarflake following close behind. When they came to a large vault, the Elders raised their torches and Oarflake stared at a mound of treasures. Never in his life had he seen such riches. He waited until the goose bumps subsided and then calmly walked towards the heap of gold and silver.

Findhorn held up some exquisite silver work and explained that many of the ornaments had been crafted in a remote Elven Kingdom across the Eastern Ocean and salvaged from shipwrecks. They were held in trust by the Elders.

Feverishly, they worked through the mound. Wondrous stones and ornaments glittered in the torch light. By day's end, Oarflake's hopes had begun to fade. They came across a complete set of golden plates but no engraved characters anywhere. When the last necklace and silver ornaments were set aside, Oarflake knew that no golden plates containing the secret were to be found in the vault. Could it be that the raiders had found the golden plate in one of the homes they ransacked?

Findhorn reading his thoughts put his arm around Oarflake's shoulder.

'It is not likely, Oarflake. I have seen all the treasures in the settlement, never did I see a golden plate with writings etched on its rim. Perhaps it only lives in legend. Had it been crafted in the mists of time we must believe it lost forever.'

Shaking his head, Oarflake followed the Elders back into the tunnel. When they emerged into the dune landscape the setting sun cast a red sheen on the long ocean swells. Findhorn took Oarflake's hand and walked him to Alexa's home. The Gnome was heavy at heart, he had so wished to bring a glimmer of hope to Svanhild and Sidonia after all their efforts and sacrifice.

Findhorn too was saddened. Their settlement, at long last, had been discovered by the Seven. Well he knew that after the Kingdom had been conquered, the Lords' dark gaze would turn towards the forlorn settlement on the coast. If not enslaved on the galleys, their men would be made to dive for their new masters.

Slowly they wound their way to Alexa's cottage, passing through stands of poplars and evergreens. They could see candles flickering gaily in the cottage windows. Oarflake felt a tingling in his fingers and when they drew closer his face began to burn. Goosebumps spread over his skin.

'Gold,' he burst out, swinging open the door. Startled by Oarflake's outcry, Findhorn followed him inside. Sidonia and Svanhild cast an anxious glance at Oarflake, but he didn't see them. Rushing into the kitchen his eyes fastened on the ledge above the stove. Climbing on a chair, he pushed his right hand between two plates of stoneware decorated with pretty flowers. He could feel the touch of solid metal and a current of excitement ran through his fingers. Handing the pottery to Svanhild, he lifted the plate out of its hiding place. The gold reflecting the light of the candles filled the room with a bright sheen. Carefully, he passed it to Alexa who placed it on the table. After he stepped down from the chair he raised the plate.

'Solid gold, of the highest grade!'

Alexa standing by his side couldn't help laughing at the enchanted look in the strange Gnome's eyes. She put her hand on Oarflake's arm.

'An heirloom, my dear,' soothed their hostess' youthful voice. 'I love the flowers on the pottery and the plate got pushed behind. The golden tablet hails from distant shores, the gift of an Elven King. Caught in a savage storm his ship was wrecked on the outer banks. It was my Grandfather who waded, shoulder deep into the towering waves and pulled him to shore. At the foot of the dunes, dying in Grandpa's arms, he spoke his last.

"The tablet is yours, a source of light, the key to justice, and a balm for healing."

'Say no more!' exclaimed Oarflake bustling with excitement. 'Sidonia look! Elven characters, engraved on the rim of the noble gold.' Sidonia had already recognized the fine lettering that adorned the round edge of the plate. Legends in her home land, had spoken of elven Kingdoms beyond the seven seas. She had often looked at ancient manuscripts and had no difficulty deciphering the characters, edged finely, in the outer rim of the plate. Eyes sparkling, she recited the first verse,

child of innocence
step into the halls of night
sing out my elven daughter
sing out with laughter
let waves of light
lift the curse of night
joy for ever after

All eyes were on Sidonia who was trying to make out the last lines at the bottom.

when darkness falls
a child will raise the call
her voice will speak
words in golden deep

They looked at one another other in utter amazement. There was little doubt that this was the golden plate of which Isumatak had spoken. The tablet Matista had feared might yet be found. But the text appeared incomplete. Svanhild was the first to speak.

'Is it possible that there is a second plate, a mate to this one, hidden in the golden deep?'

More gold is scattered on the ocean floor,' reflected Findhorn. 'In fine weather the gold can be seen in the deep waters beyond the outer banks.'

'Perhaps that is what is meant by golden deep.' Oarflake reflected aloud.

'The second plate could be on the ocean floor.' Faces around the table fell. Only Alexa smiled.

'Could the golden deep allude to the centre of the golden plate?All looked at Sidonia reaching for the plate. It took both hands to raise the heavy golden disk to the candle flames. She peered intently at the centre and burst out in laughter.

'The answer to the riddle!' she sang out in her soft lilting voice. 'It is hidden. Deep at the core of the golden disc, where only elven eyes would spy it.'

'Praise be.' Oarflake and Findhorn exclaimed in unison.

It took Sidonia some time to decipher the minute characters engraved in the centre of the plate and she was almost afraid to whisper the incantation.

selveeos altara
zervos nimos
liahath ovara

'Strange and powerful words,' sighed Alexa. 'I am all shivery.'

Everyone sensed the power of the incantation, and silence prevailed around the kitchen table until Oarflake raised his deep voice.

'Providence has led us to the tablet. It was Alexa who solved the riddle and showed us the incantation that can break the shackles of oppression.'

Svanhild spoke a word of caution.

'We still face many dangers and uncertainties but the tablet brings hope of victory. We must find the way to the Federation of the Moles where the elven children found refuge.'

'That we will do,' smiled Oarflake. 'Before the first snows we will return to the Lake of the Coloured Fishes, whence by wolf sled to the Kingdom of the Moles.'

Svanhild saw the look of wonder in Alexa and Findhorn's eyes.

She took Alexa's hand and told of the old prophecy.

'An elven child, innocent and radiant of heart, must speak the hidden verse. The Mountain Fairy, Edel, met the elven children in the tunnels of the Moles. Elmira, the youngest, has the gift of spirit travel and appeared in a vision to Ensten, the sculptor. In wood he carved her likeness. A face wreathed in smiles, eyes like mountain dew and a laugh like falling water.' Alexa was enchanted.

'Did you see the carving my dear?'

'I did Alexa and I know that it is Elmira, the elven child, who will carry the golden plate into the halls of darkness.'

Alexa and Findhorn had tears in their eyes. For centuries, the Sea Gnomes had lived in isolation in this remote settlement, now a new world was unfolding and they wanted to be part of it.

'Oarflake,' suggested Findhorn, 'Let me travel with you as far as the summit. The trek up the Finnian range is treacherous. Following the shore of the Little Wasa is difficult and slow. Having travelled the trails throughout a lifetime, I know many a shortcut.' Oarflake put his arms around Findhorn's shoulder.

'Distant cousin and fellow traveller, we are delighted.' Sidonia and Svanhild looked relieved. To have a friend and guide along who knew the terrain intimately would ease the trip to the summit.

Alexa put a pot of juniper wine on the hob and from the oven she took a tray of steaming scones. Sidonia and Svanhild looked at each other, and broke into laughter. The solemn atmosphere dissolved into celebration. Oarflake's talents were not limited to hymns and he burst into merry song. Svanhild and Sidonia danced around the parlour and Findhorn beat time with a set of wooden spoons. Alexa forgot her age and waltzed around the kitchen table.

When the din subsided all collapsed on the chairs around the kitchen table. The juniper wine flowed freely and the scones and goat cheese vanished quickly. The toasts honoured Alexa who had solved the riddle of the golden deep. Spirits rose. Sidonia shared elven lore. Svanhild told of the great swan festivals in Cascade, of teams of swans with silver crowns sailing on the moonlit waters of the Sanctus. Alexa's blue eyes shone. Svanhild saw the longing in her face and whispered, 'You too will come to Cascade Alexa, and sail in our gondola.'

'At full moon, my angel?'

'At harvest moon, Alexa.'

It was past midnight when Oarflake and Findhorn walked through the dunes to Findhorn's home. Svanhild and Sidonia were already fast asleep in Alexa's attic.

Next day, under a clear blue sky, the people of the village gathered in the dunes to hear Findhorn speak.

'My friend, Oarflake, has shed new light on the terrible attack we suffered two days ago. The Lords of Darkness have discovered our refuge on this forlorn coast. We have lived here for hundreds of years and amassed riches untold. Our wealth has been seized and our homes destroyed. Still we are a free people. Alas, it cannot last. We must join our distant brethren and throw in our lot with the Kingdom. Oarflake has spoken to me of the Sacred Book of Common Lore, writings collected by King Arcturus from the sacred traditions of the people in the Kingdom. The book has been accepted by Gnomes, Dwarves, Elves, Outlanders, Swannefolk and Mountain Fairies alike. The lore of all enriches its pages, which speak of the world of the spirit, of treasures that cannot be seized, of love enduring. With your consent I will ask Svanhild and Sidonia to tell the Council in Cascade that it is our wish to join the Kingdom in opposing the evil that threatens us.'

The Sea Gnomes, chastened by the calamity that had befallen them, eagerly raised their voices in support. When Findhorn finished speaking many of the men came up to talk to Oarflake. Women, fascinated by elven lore, crowded around Sidonia. Many were the questions Sidonia and Svanhild answered, but of the discovery of the golden tablet, they did not speak. The company that had witnessed the disclosure of the magic words knew that it was best to keep silent.

It was near noon when Findhorn tapped Svanhild on the shoulder. It was time to bid farewell. Findhorn and Oarflake shouldered their packs and Svanhild and Sidonia, accompanied by a handful of men and women, returned to Alexa's to fetch their gear. All watched when Svanhild wrapped the golden plate in a length of purple silk. Carefully she placed it inside her pack. They embraced their youthful hostess and reluctantly left the cosy cottage to face fresh perils.

When they reached the fields sloping up towards the summit, most of their entourage left, except for Folderol, Flink and Trickle. The boys hiked along with them for several hours insisting upon carrying Sidonia and Svanhild's packs. When the trail narrowed, Findhorn hinted tactfully that it would be wise to find their way home before dark. Oarflake thanked them again for all their help. The boys got a kiss from Svanhild and Sidonia, which they cherished in the secret chamber of their hearts. Few mortals have been kissed by an Elf and a Swannemaiden.

The trail quickly steepened and the going became arduous. It was fortunate that Findhorn led the way. Often he would lead them away from the river's edge and follow shortcuts through the meadows and woodlands.

They spent the night in a blueberry patch. A sheltered campsite and a bonfire kept them warm through the night. They started again at dawn and hoped to reach the cabin by the river that night.

At twilight they passed the launching site of the logs and shortly after they stepped into the cabin. Flink had replenished the supply of firewood before they started their trip down river. Within minutes they had a hearty supper on the hob and rested their weary limbs by the warm stove.

After the evening meal Sidonia and Svanhild dozed off. Oarflake and Findhorn pulled up a couple of chairs to the stove, lit their pipes and talked gnome lore deep into the night.

When Oarflake opened the door next morning, wet snow covered the land. The going would not be easy. They had a quick breakfast and made an early start. Most of the morning they trudged through mud and snow but their spirits never faltered. They could hardly believe that they had found the plate, the golden plate of lore and legend. Now, in the eleventh hour, would it still be possible to turn the tide? Svanhild reached behind and felt the solid round shape in her pack, Praise be, it was not a dream the plate was there.

As they gained height, the temperature dropped and the snow hardened. It was late afternoon when they reached the summit. The weather had cleared and Oarflake suggested that they carry on. It was here they had to bid Findhorn farewell. They embraced the venerable Sea Gnome Elder. His blue eyes sparkled and as he spoke a gust of wind lifted his long white beard.

'The time for parting has come. Fare thee well my friends and tell the Council that the Sea Gnomes will play their part.'

A few minutes later Findhorn was only a speck on the white hillside, descending towards the tree line. A tear rolled down Oarflake's cheek.

'Many pass through the chambers of our hearts,' he mused,' but few linger to become part of our lives.'

They crossed the summit of the Finnian Range and began their descent towards the Lake of the Coloured Fishes. The snow was firm and by dusk they could see the dark edge of the spruce forest down below.

Every time that they stopped for a break Svanhild felt the bottom of her pack and made sure the plate was there!

'How do we find the tunnels of the Moles, Svanhild?'

'I have no idea Sidonia. Only Edel or Weiss would be able to tell us that.'

They skipped easily over the frozen snow, humming a melody or singing a song for they were light of heart. Tomorrow they would be back in the homestead at the shore of the Lake of the Coloured Fishes. The jagged wall of spruce looming ahead was draped in an eerie light and black clouds chased overhead. At first Svanhild and Sidonia were enchanted by the dramatic sky. Oarflake looked worried and quickened his pace. When the girls caught up with him, snowflakes, whipped up by a rising wind, were flying.

They were walking amongst dwarf birch and small spruce, forerunners of the forest ahead. The snow was coming down in sheets and soon reached to their knees. Sidonia looked at Oarflake carrying a heavy pack and breaking trail. She knew that he was near exhaustion and whispered a prayer for relief.

They could hardly see four or five feet ahead and slowed almost to a halt. Svanhild checked with her right hand for the golden plate. It was safely stowed away but what good would it do if they didn't reach their goal?

'Don't think of it Svanhild, we will get there.' came an elven voice out of the swirling snow. So often had Sidonia read her thoughts that Svanhild wasn't surprised anymore.

They came to a halt and held hands. Between two gusts of wind, Sidonia caught a faint knocking sound. It seemed to come from a fair sized tree close by. She moved forward and could now hear a loud hammering. When the snow eased a red blotch became visible. Wiping snow from her face, she saw a woodpecker perched on a branch level with her eyes.

'Roland Hammerfast at your service elven child. If I am not mistaken the Swannemaiden is standing by your side.' Svanhild recognized his staccato speech pattern, the result of years of hammering. It was the very bird that had warned them before they fell into Matista's trap at the retreat of the Sisters of the Third Woe and who had acted as her guide in the spring.

Svanhild couldn't raise her voice above the storm, but she touched Roland's rich feathery coat with her right hand, by dint of recognition. The jaunty woodpecker knew this was not the time to waste words. He fired a salvo of loud knocks which seemed to signify, 'Follow me.'

Struggling through the deep snow, they trudged behind the red beacon until suddenly Oarflake lost his footing and sank down below the snow. Their feathered guide who had perched on a fallen tree, hammered out in measured language. 'Excellent, he fell precisely into the right place. The cavern under the hollow tree is warm and safe.'

They could hear Oarflake shout from below. 'Step down the hollow. It will give us shelter.'

Sidonia bent over the hole where Oarflake had vanished, when suddenly the snow gave way and she too slid down onto the soft peat floor of the hollow.

Svanhild broke some spruce branches from a nearby tree and laid them over the hole. Shouting a warm thanks to their guide, she slid between the branches. Roland Hammerfast tapped out his signature tattoo by way of farewell. Svanhild remembered the syncopated beat from their earlier meetings.

Seated by Sidonia's side at one end of the hollow, Svanhild lit a candle. The faint light revealed a space about eight feet long. They could see Oarflake, collapsed from exhaustion leaning against the far wall of the shelter.

Roots of trees ran along the walls and the peat floor was damp and soft to the touch. Svanhild picked a piece of root and poked a breathing hole through the snow cover, she could tell the drifts were gaining height and couldn't help wondering if their refuge might turn into a tomb.

'No Svanhild. It is your thoughts that will entomb you, not the snowdrifts. Somebody will hear our call.'

Svanhild could see the faint gleam in the elven eyes. She huddled by her friend's side and fell into a deep sleep.

38

Queen Tuluga At The Manor

A westering sun had turned the land of the Mountain Fairies into brilliant reds and gold. Forests of birch, maple and evergreens surrounded the village of Windekind at the bottom of the valley. Queen Tuluga, standing on the terrace of the Royal Residence, let her eyes travel over the panorama of bright hues interspersed with green meadows.

She had been pondering the encircling dangers. Armies of the Dark Lords were gathering behind the Finnian Range and no news of Princess Yaconda's fate as yet. Her mind went back to the reign of King Arcturus when the Mountain Fairies had yielded their independence to join the United Kingdom of the Seven Mountains. Queen Tuluga could not help thinking how remarkable a union the good King Arcturus had brought about.

Yet, the people in the Kingdom were so unlike each other. Well she knew that in the eyes of the stern Dwarves, Mountain Fairies were lighthearted dreamers who danced their way through life. Those deep souled Dwarves spent their lives tunnelling in the Finnian Range and their leisure hours boring into the caverns of their psyche. Carrying a yoke of guilt on their shoulders, they were a sombre lot, concluded Tuluga. Yet in this time of turmoil and peril, all played a part. Where would they have been without the dwarf warriors? She wondered what had happened to Scimitar. Had a rescue been attempted? Yes, she must travel back to the Manor and see if there were news of Scimitar. The Dwarves were formidable warriors and without them the legions of the Seven could easily break through the mountain passes and freedom of all would be at peril.

Alas, her own people were not warriors. Dreams of glory might have led a few of them on strange and hair-raising adventures, but fighters they were not.

The Mountain Fairies were musicians and dancers who spread mirth and merriment throughout the land. Queen Tuluga knew very well that her people didn't ponder the roots of life. They were butterflies sipping nectar from the bloom. Never mind the roots, they would leave those for the Dwarves. Her people were not thinkers. They were lovers. In a strange way they had enriched and brought joy into the lives of all the people in the Kingdom, lightening their burdens. Dwarves had little use for Mountain Fairies, yet always when her people danced and sang, they crowded the seats on the lawn of the Graceful Neck. She had heard them grumbling and mumbling, foam and fiddle-faddle. But when the Fairies celebrated the miracle of life in song and dance, the dour Dwarves were always there.

Queen Tuluga strolled back and forth on the terrace. Strains of music from the village carried on the wind and looking down at the square below, she could see groups of maidens and young men dancing around the fountain.

Life in Windekind was festive to a fault. String quartets were popular and wonderful violins were crafted by local artisans. The instruments were carved from almond wood and the strings came from the web of the giant forest spider.

Everyday of the week was devoted to the arts, except for Sunday night, when her people gathered at court to hear their Queen read from the Sacred Book of Common Lore.

Queen Tuluga laughed at the merry scene below. When she raised her eyes she caught the gold and red on the mountain side. Only moments later the sun sank behind the summit but high up in the sky the vanishing rays caught Peli I in a shower of light. Moments later the pelican banked into a steep dive soaring straight towards the palace.

When Peli touched down at the far end of the terrace, Queen Tuluga, anxious for news, rushed to meet him. She perceived a touch of sadness in the bird's eyes and feared the worst. The poor pelican was exhausted and she ordered her maid servants to bring water and fresh fish. After Peli drank and ate some trout, he summoned enough courage to tell the story of Princess Yaconda's voyage to the palace of the Dark Lords and the unholy union planned between the Princess and Salan. It was appalling news and Queen Tuluga knew she must travel to the Manor in Cascade. She stood the same height as Peli 1. Stroking his wings, she spoke words of encouragement to the bedraggled bird, and praised his talent for intelligence gathering.

Many merewings had been recalled by the Dark Lords to prepare for the final assault and the sky was safe. Queen Tuluga decided to travel the next day to the Manor deCygne and report to the Council. Peli 1 needed the rest and tonight her presence was required in Windekind for the beginning of the autumn festival.

When she walked out into the rose gardens, she could hear the singing of nightingales blending with the music from the town below. Night descended and she gazed at lines of fire winding through hill and valley. Carrying flaming torches Mountain Fairies from outlying hamlets were travelling towards Windekind to participate in the festivities.

The fate of Yaconda and the forces of doom gathering at the borders of the Kingdom pressed heavily upon the Queen, yet her heart responded with joy at the sight of the merrymaking. For the remainder of the evening the tiny Monarch was transported into a world of cheer. Orchestras played and dancers from many villages performed. The slender beauty of a fairy maiden floated on stage to sing the song cycle of the Enchanted Forest and dancers of the Royal Ballet brought the evening to an end with a dazzling performance of 'Flight of the Hummingbirds.'

At dawn Queen Tuluga awoke refreshed and gladdened. In her heart she knew the joy and beauty expressed by her people to be an affirmation of life and that could not be quenched by the doom that threatened.

When the morning sun kissed the hills around Windekind, the Queen was airborne. Five pelicans carried her in a net of finely woven silk. Peli 1 spearheaded the formation.

The Gnomes Gritt and Gneiss, patrolling the grounds around the Manor, were the first to notice the party soaring overhead and they rushed up to the Manor to announce their arrival. Lady Erica and the Elf Silfida entered the garden just in time to see Queen Tuluga emerge from a path between two beds of roses. Lady Erica clasped the tiny Queen in her arms and looked at her jet black eyes. She knew that ill tidings had brought her hither but she refrained from asking questions.

The Gnomes bowed before the Queen of the Mountain Fairies. Volker, the quaint Outlander and secretary of the Council, stood in the background whistling a merry jingle by way of welcome.

Svanhild's mother Annabelle and Martha, were busy setting the table in the sunroom, when Lady Erica and her guest walked in. Annabelle put an extra pillow on the chair for the slight guest of honour.

Queen Tuluga smiled. She was not embarrassed. Her height had never bothered her, and neither did it diminish her authority. Her slight body bespoke an iron will and her coal black eyes caught friend and foe in a magic noose. When all were seated she shared the news about Princess Yaconda.

It came as a terrible shock and all knew in their hearts that the diabolical union conceived by the depraved minds of the Seven must be forestalled at any cost. After lunch they moved upstairs and took their seats around the table. Silfida read a prayer and then there was a moment of silence.

'A terrible fate threatens the Princess,' said Silfida, 'but let us project in our minds, a positive image. Every time we think of the Princess in this time of trial we must see Yaconda triumphant and restored to the throne.'

'Our elven friend speaks in truth,' affirmed Martha. 'Help will come my dear friends.' Volker whistled a doleful tune and Martha's face broke into a smile.

'You must believe, Mr. Volker, I can feel the fermentation in the unseen world. Seeds are germinating, seeds of hope.'

'Salan will announce the coming wedding. The Princess is beloved throughout the land and this act of treachery will strengthen the people's will to resist,' reflected Lady Erica.

'Peli 1, brought more news,' exclaimed Queen Tuluga. 'I should have mentioned it earlier. The Eagles have declared for the Kingdom. Master Grimmbeak has abandoned the long standing tradition of neutrality.'

Clapping and cheering dispelled the sombre mood. Volker wrote it all down. Silfida looked over his shoulder to learn his method of note taking. She had offered to take over the secretarial work when Volker left for Esteria.

Queen Tuluga offered to stay at the Manor and keep the Pelicans nearby to carry messages. Lady Erica thanked her and suggested that Peli 1 should attempt to enter the palace of the Dark Lords and gather intelligence.

Queen Tuluga walked to the window, raised a small silver whistle suspended from a finely crafted pearl necklace and blew three ascending notes. In less than a minute Peli 1 appeared in the window.

Lady Erica stood up and addressed the Queen's feathered agent.

'Our gratitude Peli 1. You have carried out many a daring and perilous mission.' Peli 1 knew the words of Lady Erica to be well deserved praise. But he had to watch that it didn't go to his head. Early in his career, bitter experience had taught him that lesson. Once this wretched business was over, he would let his feathers down and indulge in a bit of glory.

'There is one more mission that we would like you to undertake, Peli. Fly into the heart of darkness, the palace of Salan in the Land of the Red Earth.'

Peli bowed politely. His eyes had the hard glint befitting a secret agent. The mask of indifference the noble bird presented to the world was indeed deceptive. His heartstrings had been plucked by the grieving Princess and the cruel fate awaiting her. In a gesture of respect, he lowered his great beak towards the Council Members, cast a look of gratitude towards Lady Erica and took wing without further ceremony.

At the North Pond, Peli 1 stopped long enough to bid adieu to his four feathered comrades floating leisurely on the silent waters. For meal breaks during the long and dangerous flight ahead he stuffed some fresh trout into his beak.

Lady Erica watched the shadow of the pelican streaking across the sunlit lawn. When she turned around she was astonished to see the secretary of the Outlander's Council, busy packing. Lady Erica watched the lanky secretary stuffing camping gear into his rucksack. She smiled.

'Volker are you joining the last group of volunteers to travel to Esteria?'

The enigmatic Outlander whistled a few melancholy notes.

'Lady Erica, great upheavals are afoot, events of historic significance will unfold in the land of Esteria. Who will record it all for generations to come? It is my duty to travel thither and to write down all that happens.'[10]

---

10   *In the latter days the name Volker is still remembered in the annals of journalism as one of the first war correpondents in ancient history. A statue in front of the Writers Guild building shows the secretary in a musical attitude whistling a tune.*

'A perilous mission Volker,' sighed Lady Erica.

'Perilous times must still be witnessed and recorded Lady Erica. History sheds light on the past and the future. Perilous but wondrous times. Its tales will touch lives in millenia to come. No trace of these happenings may remain, but perchance manuscripts will be found and read in the latter days.

'Volker,' laughed Lady Erica, 'if no traces be found, these tales may be regarded mere fantasies and myths.'

Volker was not at all perturbed. He seemed quite sure that one day remnants of the Land of Darkness and the United Kingdom would be found, and that he was destined to record these momentous happenings for the children of the future.

The next morning the Council bid Volker Godspeed. The lanky Outlander strapped a heavy pack on his back and appeared somewhat top heavy as he swayed down the path to the river.

Lady Erica was standing at the wharf when Volker joined the last group of volunteers to board the vessel that would take them on the first lap of their journey to Esteria. As they pulled from shore, she could hear the secretary whistling a soulful tune.

Most of the people in Swanneland had seen through the treachery of the Rovers. Some had paid with their lives when they refused to carry out Rovers' orders. There were a few collaborators left who stubbornly believed they would be better off under the rule of the Seven Lords.

During the Council's morning session Lady Erica suggested that Silfida talk to the collaborators. All felt that Silfida's non-threatening personality would be able to reach them. Silfida gladly undertook the mission. The Gnomes Gneiss and Grit would follow her, accompanied by the bear Grumpuss, in case of trouble.

The two tough Gnomes with their axes stuck in their belt, walked often through the village where they had begun to organize a resistance movement. If Silfida's gentle soul failed to change the mind of the few turncoats left, Gneiss and Gritt had other ways of persuading them. The collaborators had been intimidated by the Rovers and their black hounds, but the sight of those blue elven eyes had an amazing effect on them. Many had a change of heart. The sight of the Gnomes and Grumpuss hovering in the background were an additional incentive for some diehards.

After sunset the remaining Council Members gathered around the open fire in the great hall. During the long fall evenings they shared legends and lore from their different traditions

It was a moonlit night and Gritt had joined the company by the hearth. The wine goblet had made the rounds and the grim Gnome had loosened up. Accompanying himself on a one-stringed instrument, he began to recite an ancient gnome ballad. His stern face became animated and celebrating victories of his forefathers in song he danced merrily around the room.

Norma and some of the other kitchen servants sneaked into the hall and stood by the back wall. All were enthralled as the Gnome took them to battles at mountain tops, to the deliverance of maidens incarcerated in impenetrable castles and to the discovery of a mother lode, yielding vast amounts of gold.

Gneiss stood watch that night in the rose garden, Grumpuss pacing back and forth behind him. The bear was restless. Had he picked up a strange scent?

Gneiss climbed up the trellis on the side of the small pavilion and once atop the roof he scanned the pine forest rising to the north and the moonlit path leading to the Convent of the Sisters. A fleck of grey moved along the path and he suspected someone was approaching the Manor. He rushed over to the house and quietly slipped into the hall where Gritt was performing. He knew better than to butt in. Gently tapping Silfida on the shoulder he beckoned her. Silfida crossed the rose gardens and effortlessly climbed atop the pavilion. Her sharp eyes, scanning the moonlit scene, picked up the grey shape bounding down the ridge.

'It is a wolf galloping down the trail from the Convent, Gneiss.' She looked again, 'I see a rider on its back and they are advancing swiftly. I suspect it is the Mountain Fairy Weiss with news from the land of the Dwarves. I must return to the hall and tell the news.'

Silfida clambered down and skittered back to the Manor. Gneiss had a serious talk with Grumpuss. He explained to the restless bear that there were wolves and then there were wolves and that the Great Grey approaching the garden was a noble member of the species. It was confusing for the great bear, but he had spent enough time with Gneiss that he could sense the gist of the Gnome's talk.

When Silfida breathed into the hall, Gritt was still holding forth. He was narrating a daring raid by Gnome warriors into the land of the Fire Eaters. Storming up the slopes of a volcano, leaping over streams of glowing lava, they arrived in time to forestall an act of human sacrifice. A maiden kidnapped from the valley below was about to be tossed into the crater when the Gnomes snatched her from the high priests' hands. The company in the hall were enchanted and Gritt got a warm hand for his performance. Only when the applause died down, did they see Silfida standing in the doorway.

'It is Leonardo coming from the Convent of the Sisters, a Mountain Fairy riding on his back, I cannot tell whether it is Edel or Weiss.'

Fifteen minutes later, Gneiss accompanied Weiss into the front hall. He walked straight up to Queen Tuluga and bowed the knee before her. She motioned him to be seated by her side.

'We bid you a warm welcome, Weiss, news of your adventures reached the palace. You and Edel have done us proud. I trust that Edel is well and thriving in the land of the Dwarves?' As an afterthought she asked, 'He is keeping out of mischief, is he not?'

Weiss, taking a sip of tea from the cup that Norma had passed him, looked at the circle around him.

'Alas, my Queen and members of the Council, it breaks my heart to be the harbinger of ill tidings. Edel is in the hands of the enemy. Moose Martin, gave his life to save his friends. His name stands now amongst the great and is carved on the face of the Sacred Mountain. But Scimitar, Scimitar is free.' Weiss had observed Annabelle's anxious face.

'Fear not mother. Your son returned from the rescue mission. Slim is safe and sound in the home of Sunflower and Smithereen.' As Weiss' tale unfolded both joy and grief swept the faces around the hall.

Before going back to guard duty in the gardens, Gneiss made a quick detour into the kitchen and picked up a dish of roasted meat for Leonardo. Walking into the clear night air, he saw Grumpuss leaning against the pavilion in the rose garden. At the entrance, caught in a beam of moonlight, Leonardo's long snout rested on the threshold. The two seemed to be on the best of terms. Leonardo was resting comfortably after the long run from the Convent and he got up just long enough to swallow his dinner. After licking his chops he slumped down again and fell asleep.

Inside the Manor, Weiss finished telling the amazing story of Scimitar's deliverance and Silfida read a prayer for the soul of Moose Martin who had given his life to make it all possible. Lady Erica stood up.

'Friends, Edel and Weiss have rendered wonderful service. Our thoughts go out to Edel and we pray for his safe return from the Land of Darkness. Tell us Weiss, how did you find your way down to Cascade?'

'After the rescue expedition I returned to the village of the Dwarves. There I rested for a week and then joined a group of woodcutters travelling down the mountain to a camp close to the Lake of the Coloured Fishes, whence I made my way to the home of Oarflake and Ambrosia. Only Ambrosia was home. Oarflake had left with Svanhild and Sidonia for the land of the Sea Gnomes. After a few days rest, I told Ambrosia that it was urgent that I move on and travel to the Manor deCygne to bring news to the Council.

That evening Ambrosia sounded the Unicorn horn and Leonardo appeared at the door. The noble wolf offered to carry me hither and travelling fast we made it in two days. Last night we enjoyed the hospitality of the Sisters of the Secret Crossing. We had a splendid time.'

Lady Erica laughed. She quite understood that the Sisters must have been delighted to have Weiss and Leonardo stay at the Convent.

'Weiss, did Ambrosia have a hunch when Oarflake, Sidonia and Svanhild might return?'

'She did not, Lady Erica. I know that Ambrosia has the second sight but she could not tell.'

Martha, who had been nodding silently throughout Weiss' story, raised her voice in soft, lilting, tones,

> *Snow swirling in the tree*
> *weary the travellers three*
> *feet founder in the snow*
> *round and round they go,*
> *the darkness in these eyes of mine*
> *is brightened by a golden shine.*

Lady Erica looked upset. 'Does it mean that Oarflake and the girls are lost?'

'Lost they may be, Lady Erica, but these eyes of mine are brightened by a golden shine.'

'You think Martha,' sang out Lady Erica, 'they found the golden tablet with the magic incantation?' A smile played on the wrinkled face.

'I see a golden shine, my love. Of writing, I cannot see a trace.'

A tremor of excitement fluttered around the hall and they talked late into the night about Martha's vision. It was after midnight when Queen Tuluga rose.

'My friends and fellow counsellors gathered at the Manor, the tablet is our only hope. We must believe Martha's glimpse behind the veil revealed the truth. I think Oarflake, Svanhild and Sidonia are lost and we must do everything possible to reach them.'

'The Wood Owls,' Weiss piped up, 'Half a day's journey on wolfback will take me to the hereditary woodlands of the owls. Solomon and Kasper have mastered the art of celestial navigation. Surely they will find them and guide them to the Lake of the Coloured Fishes.' Queen Tuluga put her left hand on Weiss' shoulder.

'Then you had better go to bed and get some rest my faithful Fairy. Tomorrow I will rise at dawn to bid you Godspeed.' A lot of sleepy heads nodded their consent and Lady Erica ended the meeting with a short reading from the Sacred Book of Common Lore.

Everyone left the room to catch some sleep except for Silfida who was trying to fill in for Volker. She was still busy writing down everything that had been said, at least as well as she could remember it.

At dawn the next day Queen Tuluga and Lady Erica walked with Weiss to the rose garden. Leonardo was doing his morning stretches and was ready for a good run. Queen Tuluga stroked his heavy pelt and spoke words of encouragement and praise. Although his verbal skills were very limited Leonardo had an uncanny genius for grasping the crux of the matter. The noble beast felt loved and appreciated.

Weiss explained to him that they were headed for the land of Solomon and Kasper. Leonardo knew the owls and remembered the time that they had guided him to the palace of the Queen of the Marshes.

Weiss shouldered his pack, which the thoughtful Norma had filled with provisions and then sprang on the wolf's back.

Grumpuss gave Leonardo a friendly slap on his flank and the great wolf leaped forward. Weiss, holding on for dear life, could only dimly hear a few of the good wishes that Lady Erica and Queen Tuluga sent after him.

39

A Magic Signal

$\mathcal{A}$ veil of blue light enveloped a stand of pines and the full moon revealed the silhouettes of many forest owls perched on branches of the tall trees. Every full moon a meeting was called, but the great birds were fiercely independent and often didn't bother showing up. Wars and the rumours of wars had led to speculation that the Kingdom might fall and with it their hereditary rights. Attendance had shot up.

Solomon, perched a couple of feet above the rank and file, had explained the situation. One of the old boilers hooted out,

'It is not the end of the world if the Kingdom falls, we can negotiate with the new regime!' Solomon cast him a stern look.

'One problem, Profundo, the new regime does not negotiate.'

'Hoity toity, you don't say,' muttered the old timer who had his own opinion in the matter. Kasper, perched just one branch below his Chief, raised his voice to the right pitch for speaking in his capacity as Deputy.

'Feathered comrades, thank your lucky stars that King Arcturus bestowed, in perpetuity, our rights to the forest. If the armies of the Seven overrun our forest, we'll be in the soup in perpetuity, owl soup.' These were strong words and they took the wind out of the old birds.

'Well put, Deputy,' hooted his Chief.

A rush of air and the flapping of wings broke the silence. A young owl touched down on the pine next to Solomon and cast a questioning glance at his Chief.

'Any news Gregory?'

'A grey wolf is leaping through our hereditary woodlands.' Here Gregory was interrupted by angry grunts and shouts.

'Carry on,' hooted Solomon with an encouraging nod.

'A strange creature, Chief, was riding on the wolf's back, slight as a reed, and long golden hair streaming in the wind.'

Solomon consulted Kasper before he held forth.

'It is Leonardo the grey wolf and one of the Mountain Fairies riding on his back. I fear the good wolf is lost again. We helped him out last year and I think it would be best to check on the pair. Terrestrials have a poor sense of direction.'

Satisfied that they had dispelled any illusion of treating with the Seven, Solomon adjourned the meeting with a scale of ascending hoots. He had picked up a lot of information during his visit to the Manor deCygne and he knew that the Great Grey and the Mountain Fairies had played their part in opposing the forces that threatened their independence.

The Chief and his Deputy took to the air and within a few minutes sighted the great wolf passing through a stand of birch. His long red tongue was hanging out and it was clear that he had been trotting at a good clip. Soaring overhead, the owls gave a couple of deep hoots and Leonardo, coming to a sudden stop, sent Weiss sailing through the air until he came to rest in a patch of fern. Leonardo was resting on his haunches catching his breath and Weiss, regaining his footing, spotted the owls perched on a rock.

'Solomon, Kasper, we have found you at last.'

'Perhaps it was we who found you and your noble charger my fairy fair.' Solomon's large saucer eyes were almost laughing and Leonardo wagged his long bushy tail.

'We carry greetings from Queen Tuluga, wise birds. Svanhild, Sidonia and Oarflake are feared lost in a snow storm on the Finnian Range.' When Weiss mentioned Svanhild a light began to gleam in the owls' eyes.

'They must be high up the mountain,' suggested Solomon, 'only little snow fell here near the Sanctus.'

'Martha the blind prophetess saw them lost in the swirling snow. She has the second sight,' explained Weiss. Solomon and Kasper had studied psychic phenomena and they knew that second sight was not to be trifled with. Both had met Martha at the Manor and they took the message seriously.

'We will fly up the mountain and attempt to find the lost travellers. You and your wolf friend are exhausted. Travel on to the homestead at the Lake of the Coloured Fishes and rest. The owls will take charge.' Solomon hooted decisively.

'A massive search will be launched!' beamed Kasper. Leonardo got ready to carry Weiss to the homestead of the Gnomes.

The shadow of many wings passing over the forest floor caused considerable commotion amongst the forest dwellers. A number of weasel families watched the large flock of owls winging their way towards the Finnian Range. The weasels hoped the owls were leaving the forests for good. There had been some nasty incidents involving the owls and life would be a whole lot more predictable without those great birds around. There was much clapping and cheering and before long an all night party was in the works. Weasels live very much in the present and the thought that the owls might return did not occur to them.

Squirrels, beavers, badgers and other animals given to long range planning, took a more sinister view of the event and thought that the mass exodus might signal an approaching catastrophe. They took no chances. Some disappeared into deep tunnels, others fortified their homes and checked their stockrooms.

Soaring over the tree tops the owls flew soon into sheets of snow and the forest below was veiled in white. When they reached the steep slopes of the mountain range, Solomon asked the owls to fan out and attempt to find traces of the lost travellers. It was a hopeless task. The snow had wiped out all tracks and signs of life. The storm blew unabated. It was only their remarkable inner navigation system that enabled the owls to return to the spruce tree where Solomon had perched. Solomon counted his flock, forty owls huddled on the branches of the great spruce. Their wings had iced up and some had barely succeeded in making it back. Solomon scratched his head with his wingtip.

'Forty owls,' he mused, 'but there should be forty two. Of course he had forgotten to count himself that made forty one. Solomon's great strength was wisdom, not arithmetic and he felt a little puzzled. He counted again and came to the conclusion that one of the birds hadn't made it back.

He hooted a deep note and others joined in unison. They hooted an entire octave up and down again. Seconds later young Gregory appeared from a cloud of snow.

'Chief Solomon,' shouted the youngster, 'my apologies, I heard a faint knocking and flew on to find its source. It was Roland Hammerfast banging out a tattoo. He told me that the travellers found shelter in a deep hollow and will guide us thither.'

Solomon rubbed the snow out of his eyes and then beheld the bright red figure of the woodpecker. He had met the dapper bird before at a meet of Feathers for Freedom and knew him to be a trustworthy fellow.

Solomon thanked all the members of his flock, especially Gregory and suggested that they return to the hereditary forest.

'Kasper and I will follow Roland and look for help to uncover the travellers in the snow covered hollow.'

The owls lifted off and soared down the mountain, anxious to return to their private sanctuary and milder weather. Solomon and Kasper found themselves alone with the brave woodpecker.

'There is no point, wise birds, in following me to the snowdrift over the hollow. We must find terrestrials who can dig them out, it is one of the things birds cannot attempt.' Solomon and Kasper nodded. Woodpeckers were known for their common sense.

'Splendid, young Hammerfast. If you stay here we will find help at the cottage of the Gnomes, Ambrosia will be home.'

'It is done Chief Solomon. I shall be here rapping out my tattoo.'

The Chief and his Deputy shook the snow off their wings and rose above the white wilderness. The snow had eased and they had no difficulty finding a heading for the Lake of the Coloured Fishes.

Flames blazed cheerily in the open hearth at the Gnome home, yet Ambrosia, knitting in her rocking chair, could find no peace. She got up and took her deerskin parka from a wooden peg and slipped it on. Outside only a few flakes floated in the air and swift moving clouds occasionally allowed a moonbeam to highlight the landscape. She sighted the owls soaring over the lake. Their wide wings were perfectly still, as they sailed towards the cottage, touching down on the porch railing. She was pleased to see Solomon and Kasper and bade them welcome.

'Ambrosia, the travellers are lost, believed to be buried in a drift below the tree line, we must find help. Young bird Hammerfast is at the scene.'

Ambrosia gave the birds a grateful look. For a few moments she remained silent watching the play of light and shadow on the lake, a plan of action shaping in her mind. She rushed back into the cottage and seized a horn from the wall. It was the horn taken from the dying unicorn. The Gnomes had been deeply touched by the gift of the beautiful whorly ivory. Whenever they sounded the horn a deep melancholy sound echoed over hill and dale, only recently did they discover that the oscillations were carried through the ether, hundreds of miles distant. Since then, when travelling, Oarflake always carried a crystal on a silver chain around his neck. Wherever he might be, when Ambrosia set the horn to her lips the crystal was energized and sparkled brightly.[11]

Silently praying that her hubby was still conscious and would be able to pick up the signal, Ambrosia put the horn to her lips. Nine times she sounded the horn and the deep tones resonated through the wilderness. Many forest animals heard her call and wondered what was up. For the Great Grey it was a signal to rush over to the homestead of the Gnomes. With Leonardo away at the Manor, Andante led the team and loping through the deep snow it was only a short time before they appeared in front of the cottage. Ambrosia already had brought out the sled and quickly explained to the wolves the fate that had overtaken Oarflake and the girls. The wolves lined up single file with Andante in the lead and in a jiffy Ambrosia hitched them up.

Solomon and Kasper became airborne and led the way. The Great Grey shot forward with Ambrosia holding on for dear life as the sled swept over the frozen lake.

The badgers Ludwig and Berend now lived near the shore of the Lake of the Coloured Fishes. They had been forced to relocate. Matista had got wind of their complicity in Svanhild's flight and the peace and serenity so much prized by the two badgers had been shattered. Whenever they stuck their heads outside, branches from a huge oak tree would come crashing down and for no good reason paintings on the wall suddenly would drop. Seated by the fire at night drinking hot chocolate and eating bran muffins, they could feel the sorceress' dark eyes staring at them. Ludwig had been close to a nervous breakdown. Berend had taken the matter in hand and

---

11 *The horn believed to be the only genuine Unicorn horn on the planet, can be seen in the Museum of FineArt and Folklore in Lambarina. Next to the horn suspended from a silver stand is the silver chain with the crystal that Oarflake wore throughout his life! In the latter days it was this horn that inspired inventors and led to the discovery of wireless telegraphy!*

decided that they should move to the Lake of the Coloured Fishes. It was a safe distance from the sorceress and close to Ambrosia's house of healing. Old age was creeping up and altogether it seemed to be a good move.

When the moon appeared that night, the two friends, stepped outside and beheld the wolf team flying across the lake.

'By Jove Ludwig, what a splendid way to travel.' Ever since he had taken up skating, Berend had been enthralled by speed. To his fertile mind, the wolf team was an inspiration.

'Berend, don't even think about it,' sighed Ludwig. 'Wolf travel is more dangerous than skating on thin ice.' Berend took a longing look at the vanishing sled before stepping inside. Ludwig had the hot chocolate and the bran muffins ready and seated by the fire, once more they enjoyed their evening snack in peace and serenity.

Buried beneath a huge snowdrift, Svanhild and Sidonia had been nursing Oarflake back to health. The Gnome had been exhausted and with this new trial seemed to have lost heart. Their shelter was cool and damp and after four days they had run out of candles. Oarflake sat propped up against the roots of the spruce that hovered above their shelter and Sidonia and Svanhild huddled together at the other end of the hollow. The loss of light had a terrible effect on them. Svanhild had to struggle to keep alive any hope of rescue. In this hour of darkness she fell into a dream state. She saw Ensten seated by his work bench, his long slender fingers holding the woodcarving of the laughing elven child. Then she saw herself standing in front of him, holding a silver tray with a red rose. Their eyes met and Ensten took the rose and raised it to his lips. She woke with a start and pressed Sidonia's hand.

'I dreamed that I offered Ensten a red rose, and he pressed it to his lips.'

'Perhaps it took this time of darkness to hear your higher self tell you that you are in love.'

'Sidonia, all my maidenhood I dreamed of youths, valiant and gallant, famous and flamboyant, to match my longing for drama and adventure. And now I am in love with a shy woodcarver from a small frontier town. But in his eyes Sidonia, there dwells all the adventure and drama that I shall wish for.' Sidonia prayed that the dream might come true, even on this earthly plane.

Svanhild dozed off again but Sidonia remained alert. The darkness was so intense, even her phenomenal sight could not penetrate it. Suddenly she saw a sparkle of light at the far end of the hollow. She thought for a moment she was seeing things but then it happened again. The crystal pendant on Oarflake's chest sparkled brightly.

'Svanhild look!' she burst out, squeezing Svanhild's hand. Svanhild opened her eyes and saw the crystal on Oarflake's silver chain light up.

They both shouted. 'Oarflake wake up! The crystal, the crystal on your silver chain is energized.' Oarflake, startled by Sidonia's voice, raised the crystal. It glowed and sparkled.

'Heaven be praised!' called out the Gnome, 'It is Ambrosia's signal. They are searching for us. She is sounding the unicorn horn. The crystal receives the energy waves and succour is on its way.' The light from the crystal brought new hope to the three.

Sidonia visualized a safe return to the homestead of the Gnomes. Svanhild sang softly of shining waters and white wings, of swains and maidens in the spring. The light from the crystal and Svanhild's singing dispelled the deep torpor that had crept over them and now they listened intently for any sound from the outside world. Sidonia was the first to hear the pit pat of wolf paws on the hard snow. Then came the swoosh of the sled sliding sideways when the team came to a sudden halt. Ambrosia's voice called through the breathing hole, 'We are here my love, hold on!'

Solomon, Kasper and Roland looked on as Ambrosia unhitched the wolves and took a shovel from the sled. Roland's hammering had enabled the owls to hone in on the exact location and no time had been lost in flying around.

Ambrosia took the shovel and removed the crust of ice from the snow drift. No sooner was the ice gone then the wolves took over. Their great front paws sent snow flying in all directions and the huge drift quickly dwindled.

It was fortunate that Oarflake sat at one end of the hollow and the girls at the other end, for suddenly the centre caved in and two wolves came crashing down. Oarflake managed to stand up and Ambrosia helped to pull him out.

Stiff as a board, he could hardly move. To loosen him up she took him by the arm and made him walk. The fresh air and the moonlight revived Oarflake and he burst out.

'My love, we have found the plate, the golden plate!' Ambrosia's eyes filled with hope and joy.

Andante now could see Sidonia and Svanhild emerging from the snow. Gently she grabbed Svanhild by the collar of her jacket and hauled her up. Sidonia clambered out by herself and embraced each of the gallant wolves.

Suddenly panic swept over Svanhild's face.

'Oh my stars, where is my pack with the golden plate?' All eyes turned to her but Andante saved the day. She dived into the snowy hollow and after some frantic digging surfaced with the precious bundle.

Once Svanhild gained her footing, she tightly clutched her pack, running one hand along the bottom. Thank Heaven the round shape was still there. When her eyes adjusted to the moonlight she saw the three birds perched on a low branch. She went up to Roland and thanked him for finding shelter in the midst of the storm. The young woodpecker didn't want Svanhild to make a fuss. He bowed politely, said he was entirely at her service, tapped his signature tattoo and took off.

Svanhild, stepping between Solomon and Kasper, put her arms around the owls. The large eyes lit up and the stern look mollified.

'My faithful friends, thank you, thank you!' whispered Svanhild before taking her leave and joining the others on the sled.

The Chief and his Deputy felt rejuvenated. 'All in the line of duty, Chief,' hooted Kasper, 'owls are wise as well as service oriented!' Solomon gave his Deputy an admiring glance.

'Well spoken, Deputy. Wise and service oriented. I like the sound of that and it will raise us in the public eye. A feather in our cap!'

As the sled began to slide forward, Svanhild and Sidonia waved a last kiss. Oarflake and Ambrosia called out to Solomon and Kasper, urging them to come and visit soon.

The sky was clear and the upper layer of snow frozen solid. The wolf team galloped over the icy surface and at dawn they arrived at the homestead of the Gnomes. To their surprise, Leonardo was dozing on the porch. When the team came to a halt in front of the house, Leonardo woke, did a couple of stretches, jumped down the steps and gave Andante a friendly lick on the snout. Ambrosia gave the wolves a hug and removed their harnesses.

When the party went inside they found Weiss sleeping on the bench. At the sound of their footsteps, he woke with a start. Jumping from the bench, he ran up to Svanhild and Sidonia. Both embraced the Fairy at the same time and Weiss found himself in a tight squeeze.

Ambrosia was relieved to have Oarflake back safe and sound. She forgot her fatigue and started cooking breakfast. Svanhild brought out a pot of stew to the wolf team. It was all gone by the time Weiss appeared to bid farewell, but Leonardo was still there and Weiss stroked his deep fur. Leonardo understood the gesture and before taking off gave a friendly howl.

After breakfast Svanhild took out the golden plate and placed it in front of Ambrosia.

'Oh my stars, goose bumps all over!' she cried, 'and this time it is not for the gold my dear, it is the hope that springs in my heart that our people will live in peace and that the shadows over the Kingdom will clear in the light of a new dawn.'

40

At The Palace

On the red sandstone plateau surrounding Salan's palace seven lovely villas had sprung up. Salan himself had designed the project. He despised traditional building styles and his eye for architecture had served him well. The villas were striking in design. Six were modest in size, but the seventh, an imposing structure, was to be his own. All of them had a splendid view of the River Wasa and the Fire Mountain rising up from the desert. Towards the east stretched the red sands and a small rise on the horizon marked the descent into a canyon.

Colourful gardens and pools surrounded each dwelling. Trained overseers and slave labour had completed the work in record time. Now after long meetings at the Palace, the Seven could return to their own villas. The tension had subsided, no longer did they grate upon one another in the evening hours. At night they enjoyed privacy by the poolside. Pretty maidens would massage their tense bodies and sooth frayed nerves.

Salan was pleased with himself. The plan had worked. Splendid design, calming colours and charming hostesses had taken the grit out of his opinionated fellow Counsellors.

The atmosphere at the Council meetings relaxed and the six were falling into line. The conquest of the United Kingdom was at hand and the raid on the village of the Sea Gnomes had been a complete success. Once more the intelligence Matista had gathered from the Mirror of a Thousand

Fragments had served them well. The last place in the world where the fabled golden tablet might have turned up had been searched. No tablet had been found but to the delight of the ladies in the palace, wonderful treasures had been brought back by the raiding party. Salan had liberally bestowed jewels, bracelets, diamond broaches and golden headbands upon all the serving staff. The beautifully crafted silver work, bowls, vases, candelabras, plates and cutlery he had kept for the palace dining tables.

His fellow Counsellors were contented. The last place where the golden plate might have turned up had been thoroughly searched and the myth had been laid to rest. The old prophecies had been the fantasies of an oppressed and enslaved people. It was no wonder their misery caused them to indulge in such thoughts.

Dawn was breaking over the land of the red earth. The sun's rays intensified the red pigment in the soil and to Salan, standing by the window in the palace, it appeared as if the plains below had caught fire. The drama of the scene delighted him. The river Wasa looked like a black ribbon winding its way through crimson sands to reach the ocean.

The scene below began to show signs of life. Army units were exercising and slave ships glided gracefully on the shimmering river. Beyond the river a small column of smoke could be seen rising from the Fire Mountain, the volcano which, in ages past, had poured streams of lava over the land.

The stark landscape, in a dark romantic way pleased Salan. Soon the Counsellors would arrive for their daily work. Salan prized the privacy of the early hours.

The tiptoe of dainty feet broke his reverie. Precilla, his favourite handmaiden, entered with a silver tray bearing coffee and an apple fritter.

Cheered by recent events, the stern Lord cast a smile at the pretty maiden. She blushed and quickly turned around. The sight of her lovely shape moving away turned his mind to that other lady, soon to enter his life.

'The maiden Princess would have scruples about their union but it was so logical, so delightful. A thrill went through his being. How could she resist him. He took a mirror from his drawer and raised it up. Stern, yet youthful and handsome! His jet black locks and goatee gleamed in the sunlight. Chiselled features gave him a noble air. 'Hard to resist,' he whispered softly as he put the glass away.

The tinkling of silver bells ended his reverie. He straightened and turned towards the heavy oaken door at the end of the hall. The door swung open and Lord Imbrun walked in. Salan had been pleased with his services. Years ago he had planted the handsome young man as a spy in the royal household of King Arcturus. After masterminding the demise of the King he had kidnapped the heir to the throne. But whispers had reached Salan's ears that at one time the Princess Yaconda had taken a shine to the nobleman. It would benefit the delicate hands of the handsome Lord to do some honest work.

'My dear Imbrun, I have a message on my desk. The Princess Yaconda arrives within two days. It might upset her to see the man who dispatched her dear father to the great beyond. A change of place, a new challenge?'

Lord Imbrun turned white. Others, before they vanished without a trace, had been addressed in those very words.

'No Imbrun, fear not, a simple transfer. The dungeons have been in a state of chaos, guards have walked off in the middle of their shifts. A strong hand is needed down there. The crocs have been neglected.' Lord Imbrun was dismissed. Salan felt relieved, it was an elegant way of solving a painful problem and of saving the Princess heartache. He did not expect to see Lord Imbrun in the near future. After he finished his coffee, a messenger rushed in and knelt before him.

'Your Highness, two parties have arrived at the palace, the great sorceress Matista and her servant Finch. The enchantress will wait upon you after sunset.' Salan smiled, for he well knew the sorceress aversion to daylight meetings. Secretly he was relieved that the powers of his protectress had been clipped by the old wizard Isumatak. The enchantress could be meddlesome and to have her around twenty four hours a day would have been trying.

'Very well Victor,' said Salan, 'What is the other party?

'Commander Veldbloom, in charge of the quarries and armouries under the Black Peak.'

'Bring him in, my boy.'

It was fortunate indeed for the Commander that Salan was in merry spirits and willing to listen to an explanation of Scimitar's escape. Otherwise the Camp Commandant might have been consigned directly to the dungeons. When Victor told him that Salan would see him, he breathed a sigh of relief. At least this little detour upstairs implied a window of hope.

With him, on a long leash, was the latest acquisition to his butterfly collection. Before entering the great hall, he tied the unhappy Mountain Fairy to a column.

Salan listened carefully to the Commandant, who stressed the fact that carelessness of the Professor and Cobalt, Captain of the Black Elves, had lead to the massive explosion in the weapons research laboratory and how the ensuing chaos had made it possible for the Dwarf Scimitar to scale the barrier and make a successful get away. For a moment Salan looked annoyed and the image of the reptiles in the dungeons danced before the Commandant's eyes.

Scimitar had been a thorn in Salan's side. Many an ambush had the Dwarf sprung on unsuspecting Rovers and Grolls, but now the time of the Dwarves was up. His armies, standing in readiness, soon would overwhelm the passes, Scimitar or no Scimitar, that would be the end of it.

The Commandant saw the black cloud lift from his Lord's countenance and thought the time opportune to mention his gift.

'Allow me Your Highness, to present a small gift, a token of my loyalty.'

'More stuffed animals, Veldbloom, or pinned up butterflies from your collection?'

'No my Lord, this time it is a live specimen for your amusement, a Mountain Fairy.' Salan burst out laughing.

'A Mountain Fairy, Commandant, I thought you collected butterflies.'

'It is like a butterfly, Master, although larger and without wings. It resembles an Elf, yet slighter.'

Salan was intrigued. He reached for an ancient volume on his desk, a Guide to Nature's Wonders. He leafed through it until he came to Mountain Fairy. A chuckle could be heard and the Commandant felt that once again he had cheated the crocs in the dungeons.

'Mountain Fairies,' Salan uttered a chortle and read aloud, 'Mountain Fairies, the slightest of intelligent beings, harmless imps and tricksters. Fleet of foot and wonderful performers. Shine in dance and song. Procreation unlike other intelligent beings, Mountain Fairies are conceived in the large white flowers of the Night Lily. Details thus far have escaped naturalists. See also Dreamchild and Windflower.' Salan closed the book and laughed aloud.

'You did well Bloomveld. Fetch me this slightest of intelligent beings.'

Edel had overheard some of Salan's words and knew that if he was going to be of any use at all he would have to play the part for which he had been cast.

The Commandant, who had become quite fond of Edel, regretted having to part with his tiny friend. The camp tailor had sewn for his pet a white costume with golden wings jutting out at the shoulders. He took the leash and walked Edel into the great hall.

Edel curtsied before Salan. Salan couldn't help smiling at the whimsical appearance by his desk.

'On a leash, Commandant,' thundered the great Lord. You got the Dreamchild on a leash? What in heaven's name are you afraid of Veldbloom? Did you not hear what it says in the book? Harmless, known for their lightness of being and you, a warrior, tie him up. Those years of isolation have gone to your head, my friend. Take some time off and chase butterflies on the plains. Now free the innocent waif and let him roam the palace. He will delight the ladies and bring mirth into these sombre halls.'

After setting Edel free, the Commandant attempted a word of caution and mentioned that Edel had been caught in the disguise of a Black Elf.

'That is just what I read,' said Salan good naturedly, 'they are light-hearted pranksters.'

The Commandant held his tongue and counted his blessings before retiring.

Salan cast a pensive look at the will-o-the wisp standing by his side as if awaiting orders.

'It is well my imp,' Salan spoke softly as if afraid to shake the fragile creature. You have the freedom of the palace. Report back to me at this hour tomorrow. Entertain the guests and charm the ladies.'

Edel danced a kind of a jig before making an obeisance and gracefully waltzed out of the hall.

Salan rubbed his hands. This Windflower served his purpose well. It would add a merry note to the wedding feast. The blithe Fairy would be a kind of court jester. Royalty and high placed nobles always had retained such creatures to lighten the burden of office. It could not have come at a better time.

Edel, once more free as a bird, sailed through the palace halls. What a relief to be without that wretched collar around his neck. At first the thought of escape occurred to him, but even if he were able to leave the palace, whereto then? The grounds around the palace were filled with soldiers.

Being cast as a court jester was a new experience. There would be ample scope for his talents and it would give him access to places and people in the palace. Had providence turned the foolishness that led to his captivity into an opportunity? If that were the case, there was still hope for creatures like himself.

He roamed the corridors, hippety hopped through the kitchens, alarming, surprising and delighting the kitchen staff. He climbed the spiral stairway to one of the observation towers, saluted the Rover on duty and told him that he was a page to the great Lord himself. The Captain lifted him up onto the parapet and pointed out the interesting features of the surrounding landscape. Before jumping down Edel scanned the winding waters of the Wasa River, far in the distance he caught sight of a brightly coloured barge being towed upstream.

'Tell me Captain, the festive vessel miles down the river. Whence does it hail?'

'Ah, my little Lord, it hails from the Alcazar, where the two oceans meet.'

Edel wondered if the Princess Yaconda would be on the barge?

He thanked the Rover, saluted smartly and pranced down the spiral steps.

Back on the main floor, the sound of music drew him to a set of double doors at the end of the hall. One of the doors was ajar and he peeked inside. It was the women's pavilion where the pretty hostesses spent their time between tours of duty in the palace and the villas. Edel was astonished at the sight of girls playing the lute and utelli. Above the music he could hear shuttles flying. He tiptoed into the hall and turning left he saw three large looms. Marvellous fabrics were being woven, deep reds with golden dragons spitting fire, blue waves with fishes flying and on the last loom, sheets of silk, white as virgin snow.

Seamstresses were sewing festive dresses, reflecting all the colours of the rainbow. At the very end, seated by large windows, two girls worked on a long white dress. The pure white silk, embroidered with myriad precious stones, gleamed and glittered in the sunlight.

Edel, fascinated by the scene approached the pretty weaver seated at the first loom. The moment she saw him, she dropped her shuttle, sprang on her bench and shrieked.

'The creature, look at the creature! The music stopped and a dozen pair of lovely eyes looked at Edel. Undaunted he danced around the circle of artisans and quick as lightning made up a little ditty to set their hearts at rest.

be not frightened pretty ladies
no mouse is in the house
I am no salamander or armadillo
not a snake under the pillow
nor a beast rough and hairy
I am Edel, the Mountain Fairy

Edel's lilting soprano voice disarmed the maidens and laughter and cries of delight echoed through the room. And once more Edel was the darling of the company. He made the maidens laugh, admired their beauty and was in great form.

When a light lunch was served, they shared their food with him. Edel had to answer endless questions about Mountain Fairies. All wanted to touch him and to make sure that he was real.

The girls at the end of the hall asked if they could comb his hair. Gaily whistling, he danced through the long space and kneeled before the lovely pair. His eyes were level with the silk dress covered with countless jewels. When the girls on his left began to brush his golden locks he asked about the dress.

'A wedding dress my pixie. In three weeks time wedding bells will ring across the land. Did not you know my pretty pixie that a Princess from across the ocean will wed our Lord, the great Salan?'

Edel was surprised for a moment and then it came to him the prospective bride was none other than their beloved Princess Yaconda. It was the Princess travelling on the gaily decorated barge that he had seen from the observation tower.

Edel knew in a flash that if this blasphemous union were to take place, it would dash the hopes of the people of the Kingdom, crush their will to resist. It was an act of infamy to be forestalled at all costs.

Under the gentle hands of the seamstresses plaiting his locks into a single braid, Edel fell into a daydream. Of course he would perform some heroic act that would foil Salan's devilish plot and earn the eternal gratitude of the lovely Princess. When he came back to earth he knew that whatever he did, he must play his part as the court jester and not betray his feelings. He thanked the girls, bowed to the company and walked out of the pavilion.

Wandering through the halls, he landed in a luxurious wing of the palace where the guests of the Seven resided. One of the doors stood open and seated on a red sofa, he spied a sweet old lady. Time's unforgiving needle point had etched its lines and furrows on the face of the ancient one. Yet, a surprisingly youthful voice called out.

'Come in my innocent waif, and cheer one weighed down by the sorrows of years.' Edel's gallantry got the better of him and he walked into the room. She motioned him to a small stool by her side.

'You must wonder who I am my dear child?' He thought for a minute and said.

'You are the mother of the Lord Salan, my lady.

'Not the mother, butterfly.'

'The grandmother?' Edel ventured.

'That was naughty my insect,' she laughed pulling one of his golden wings.

'Adviser to the great Lord, I am. Friendly counsel I give, ah it isn't always taken. The Seven forget sometimes what I have done for them. It causes me grief my child.'

Again Edel was astonished by the voice. When he closed his eyes he saw a bewitching beauty.

'I think you are a Mountain Fairy. How did a little windflower end up in the palace, my dear?' She asked, taking his hand.

It was the touch of the shrivelled hand that sent a tremor up his arm and put him on his guard. He withdrew his hand, laughed heartily and without blushing lied through his teeth.

'Oh Ancient one, I was a rebel in my own country and joined up with The Black Elves. At the prison camp I worked for Commander Veldbloom and it was he who brought me here. I too serve Lord Salan, not with wisdom but with foolishness'

Standing up he sang:

on the stage of life
I play the clown
and turn upside down
the trouble and the strife
that blinds us seeing
the foolishness of our being

'The new court jester that I have been told about.' She giggled and patted him on the back.

'At your service milady,' said Edel backing out of the room and with a quick bow slipping into the hall.

He ran all the way to the other side of the palace and spotting a bench under the archway leading to the kitchens, he sat down and wiped his face. He felt he had slipped out of a spider's web. That voice of youth and beauty still rang in his mind. Of course! Now he remembered! Slim and Moose Martin had spoken of the betrayal in the retreat of the Holy Sisters. An old biddy had enticed them in. Her voice, too, had belied her age!

'By the teeth of the great dragon,' he whispered to himself. 'It was she, the great enchantress, Matista. Only few mortals have met her, perhaps I am the only Mountain Fairy. What a tale to tell.' He forgot that in the end, even fewer escaped her clutches.

When he looked up he beheld a kindly looking woman standing under the archway. She handed him a cup of tea.

'Here drink this, my pet and when you come to a little, join us at the supper table. Edel thanked her and took a few sips of tea. When he felt better he walked over to the long wooden table and sat down to have supper with the kitchen staff.Once more he found himself the centre of attention at a jovial supper party. At the end of the meal, a tall lanky figure wearing a chef's hat, sauntered towards them.

'The chief cook is coming to check you out,' smiled the lady next to him.

Edel looked up into a friendly pair of eyes. The chef put some dainties on the table.

'To honour our tiny visitor,' he laughed. Edel stood up and made a polite bow.

News had travelled fast through the palace and the Chef knew that the Mountain Fairy was court jester to the great Lord himself. Before walking back he took a good look at the tiny figure with the golden wings sticking out from his shoulders and a sparkle danced in his eyes. He turned and walked away but one of the girls at the far end of the table could hear him mutter.

'The arrival of the foreign Princess must have changed the dark Lord's ways. Once gloomy as the night, now he wants delight and surprise. And by golly he shall have it. I will perch the butterfly on the seventh storey of the wedding cake, iced and all!

As commanded by Lord Salan, next morning, Edel presented himself in the great hall. To his surprise all seven Counsellors were there. Three were seated on each side of the long table and Salan was at the head. Edel jumped onto the end of the table, ran across its full length and kneeled before Salan, all to the annoyance of the Counsellors and to the amusement of their leader.

'Sit by my side my butterfly,' laughed Salan. 'You shall be my adviser on poppycock and merry making.' The other six were not amused and Torzak cast a suspicious look at Salan's new court jester.

'Today, my friends, is a day of celebration. Our armies marched at dawn, and at noon they will reach the passes. The Dwarves will be crushed and the Kingdom overrun. Today is a day of double celebration. Princess Yaconda will arrive at the palace this morning, and three weeks from today wedding bells will toll.'

You will wed the pretty lady,' butted in Edel.

'I will Butterwings! She will be mine, mine, mine!' cried out the great Salan, in an outburst of emotion.

'Now run along Dreamchild and when the royal party sets foot in the palace, be there to cheer them, and bid them welcome to the land of promise.'

Edel lost no time leaving the hall. The cold stares from some of the Counsellors had made him shiver. The moment he had slipped out, Counsellor Torzak piped up.

'And who is the insect you call Butterwings, my Lord?'

'Suspicious you are, Torzak, and true to form. He is a gift my dear fellow, a Mountain Fairy, a Dreamchild or Windflower. Harmless, the book tells us. Times of fear and worry are gone Torzak.'

'And the golden tablet Lord Salan?'

'No trace of it amongst the Sea Gnomes' treasures. The golden tablet, Torzak is a figment of the imagination. Wipe that frown off your forehead. Levity and glee must fill the palace.'

Torzak made an honest effort, but the frown was etched deep into his forehead and refused to disappear.

Edel, by now, knew his way around the palace and walked to the guest wing. Carefully he tiptoed past the sorceress' suite until he reached the end of the hall.

A stairway joined the hall at this point and he could hear heavy footsteps climbing up. A huge Groll appeared carrying a set of wooden frames on his shoulders. He entered the suite at the end of the hall. Edel peeked in and saw boxes and luggage spread around. At the very end of the room stood Dominique. When she heard the pitter patter of feet she looked up.

'It can't be,' she whispered, 'A Mountain Fairy dressed up as a butterfly.'

She blinked her eyes as if to dispel any illusion and called out.

'You are the Mountain Fairy who saved my life at the Alcazar. Which part of the alpine flower are you my love, Edel or Weiss?'

'Edel at your service,' he laughed. Walking up to Dominique, he cast a look at the Groll, who was now putting together Yaconda's loom.

'Don't mind him, Edel,' Dominique said quickly, 'Puff is good hearted and can be trusted.' Dominique gave Edel a hug and standing back, took a good look at him.

'Edel you have sprouted wings!' Edel laughed and explained how the Camp Commandant, to please his fancy, had dressed him up.

'No one must know that we met before, Dominique,' said Edel casting a glance at Puff. Puff smiled and raised a finger to his lips. It was the first time in his life that Edel had seen a Groll smile. He walked up to the giant and standing on his toes reached for the claw-like hand. Puff was touched by this show of trust and affection and Edel knew that if the need arose, he had an ally in the palace.

Dominique had rushed out of the suite to warn Princess Yaconda of Edel's presence. When the Princess, accompanied by two hostesses, walked through the double doors, she bit her lips at the sight of the golden wings and managed a serious look.

When the hostesses left, the Princess hugged Edel and kissed him on both cheeks. Edel knew there was little time and as best he could, he filled the Princess and her handmaiden in on events. To his credit, he included the bit of foolish bravado that led to his capture and in the end brought him to Salan's palace.

'We are grateful that you are here Edel,' sighed Yaconda.

They could hear footsteps coming down the hall and waving to Yaconda and Dominique, Edel made a quick getaway.

Dominique saw the gleam of light in her mistress's eyes and knew that the Mountain Fairy had sparked a ray of hope in the Princess' heart.

41

The Assault

The short burst of colour in the alpine meadows was nearing its end. At night temperatures fell below freezing and smoke spiralled up from the log cabins' chimneys in the village of Turania. Usually at this time of year the Dwarves would be cutting timber in the valley below but Scimitar had asked them to prepare for war.

It was Sunflower's care and cooking that had restored Scimitar's health. Within in a few weeks his emaciated figure had regained the typical barrel-chested look of dwarf warriors. Yet, Sunflower sensed that Scimitar had changed. At night, lost in thought, he would sit by the fire. One night the flames in the hearth cast a dreamy glow on Scimitar's face. Sunflower, stirring a pot of beans, cast a concerned look at the brooding warrior. Her uncanny intuition told her that, this time, Scimitar's mind was not on the approaching battle. He seemed far away. Then it dawned on her. Scimitar was in love and this time he knew that he was in love!

'It is the Wendell girl, Skimmy, I can read your thoughts.' She said laughingly.

'You always could, Sunny.'

Sunflower marvelled at the change in the fierce warrior since his imprisonment and escape. He seemed now to be in touch with the deeper currents of his psyche. Scimitar sent a ring of smoke up to the ceiling and looked at his sister-in-law.

'I fear for Helga and the Wendell family. If the enemy overruns the Kingdom, the suffering will be terrible.'

'I thought that Helga was working at the Convent of the Sisters of the Secret Crossing,' reflected Sunflower.

'The Convent would not be spared Sunny.'

Scimitar got up quietly, gave Sunflower a hug and walked out of the kitchen.

Sunflower, wonderstruck, watched him leave. He had actually hugged her. A male warrior had shown his feelings. Changes were afoot in dwarf culture. Sunflower laughed as she ambled over to the wood box. Scimitar in love with the Wendell girl. For her grim brother-in-law to fall in love was a singular event, but with a Swannegirl!

'The maiden must have a special gift.' she mused, 'what made her volunteer in the Convent of the Sisters?' For Scimitar's sake she hoped that Helga Wendell hadn't joined the novitiate of the Sisters of the Secret Crossing. How dearly she would love to meet the girl whom Scimitar, for years, had banished from his mind. Suddenly she felt a tingling in her spine and a vision came to her of a maiden with golden tresses tiptoeing towards her. A sense of foreboding came upon her. Before long she would meet the enigmatic Helga.

Master Grimmbeak had supplied important information about the enemy's movements and Scimitar and Bullneck anticipated an attack at the Crystal Gate, the deep gorge affording a narrow passage across the summit of the Finnian Range. Men, women and children worked day in and day out building ramparts and fortifications. To block the pass, a large number of logs had been brought up from the forests. They would be unable to stop the overwhelming number of Groll regiments preparing for the assault on the other side of the range but Scimitar hoped to delay the armies of the Seven reaching the Kingdom.

An observation tower was erected on the heights bordering the pass. Once completed it was manned day and night. Nightglider or Master Grimmbeak brought daily reports on enemy moves and Scimitar knew there were but few weeks left before they could expect an attack. At a frantic pace the Dwarves carried on their preparations.

When Slim was leaving for Esteria, Scimitar had asked him to send news about the volunteer forces gathered under the command of the Marquis deCygne. Scimitar had doubts about the Marquis' military skills.

Esteria was the second line of defence and vital to the protection of the Kingdom.

One morning Master Grimmbeak arrived at the cottage of Smithereen and Sunflower. Sunflower had a pot of scrambled eggs and bacon on the hob and she invited the great bird in. The Grandmaster, peckish after a long flight from Esteria, joined them for a hearty breakfast.

The bacon was not entirely kosher, for the Eagles of the Covey had forsworn the consumption of higher life forms, and stuck to a diet of fish and eggs. But the smell of bacon was overpowering and unwilling to offend his hostess, the Grandmaster acted on the principle that top birds can make an exception to the rules, if wisdom demanded it.

When they had finished breakfast, Grimmbeak asked Sunflower to take a message out of the leather vessel fastened around his neck. Sunflower took the note out of the container.

'A note for you Scimitar from Slim.'

'Please read it Sunflower,' said Scimitar reaching for his coffee mug. Sunflower unfolded the paper and held it to the light.

'Dear Scimitar, arrived in Esteria a week ago. Marquis deCygne organizes splendid parades, entertains dignitaries, many parties, much song and dance, morale excellent. No preparations for defence, no fortifications, no military exercises. Yours Slim.'

Master Grimmbeak nodded solemnly. Reprimand shone in his eyes.

'Alas, overflights by Nightglider and Servatius confirm Slim's report. The command has gone to the nobleman's head, I fear. It was only a year ago,' reflected Master Grimmbeak, 'his body torn by the tainted fangs of the black hounds that the Marquis stood at the edge of the great beyond. Yes, in that hour of agony, the Marquis had manifested remarkable humility and meekness. Quite commendable. The birds of the Celestial Covey were touched. Alas, friends, the glitter of the world is hard to resist. I fear he is quite his old self again.' Sunflower wiped a tear from her eye.

'Master Grimmbeak, the loss of Dorothea must have changed his heart.'

'Aye, for awhile it did so but the light of vanity is blinding.' lamented the Grandmaster of the Covey with a sad shake of his yellow beak.'

Before speaking, Scimitar filled his pipe and sent a circlet of smoke into the air. 'I must travel to Esteria without fail. It is in Esteria that we must stop the enemy. There are too few of us to defend the pass at the Crystal Gate. We may be able to hold out for a few days, a week perhaps, no more.

In Esteria we stand a chance to stem the tide. The volunteers gathered there must be whipped into shape.'

'Leave today Scimitar,' urged Smithereen. 'Bullneck will command the defence of the Crystal Gate and I shall stand by him. In Esteria you must take charge of the troops, let the Marquis look after the ceremonies.'

Scimitar got up and started packing. Grimmbeak wished him well before taking his leave. Urgent business required his presence in the Celestial Covey.

Later in the day, walking into a snow flurry, Scimitar, Anvil and Sergeant Tuffkote began their long trek down the mountain to Esteria.

Bullneck, who had now been left in command, was busy showing the warriors where to pile rocks above the narrow passage of the Crystal Gate. Once the rocks were set in motion, an avalanche of stone would pelt the enemy troops.

A group of women placed sharp pointed posts in the ground. Others were dragging branches into the narrow pass and pouring pitch on them. These were to be fired when the enemy advanced.

High up in the observation tower Sergeant Crusher scanned enemy territory. He could see the line of dwarf archers hidden behind rocks covering the slopes leading to the Land of Darkness. Bullneck had instructed the archers to save their arrows for the legions of black dogs, likely to be in the vanguard.

Angelica, the goat lady, had gathered a store of healing herbs and friends in the Mole Confederacy had supplied her with a shipment of roots.

She had dried the roots and ground them to make special ointments for the healing of wounds. One of the compounds, made from the roots of beech trees, stopped bleeding.

Anvil's brother Sledge, the local blacksmith, had invented a steel trap that, on impact, would break the legs of black hounds. Hundreds of the devices had been concealed on the bare mountain side in front of the Crystal Gate.

Day and night the village buzzed with activities. Men, women and children worked on defences and escape routes. Several miles from the village there was a hidden entrance into the side of the Sacred Mountain and a tunnel leading to a series of grottos. Torches and provisions had been stacked inside the Mountain, in case the entire village had to go into hiding. Bullneck knew they could only hope to hold out for a week, at the most. The Grolls would surely destroy the village and any Dwarves that they could find.

Once the end was near, they would fire the pitch-covered branches at the end of the pass and under cover of smoke and fire, the women and children would hide inside the grottos.

The herbal remedies of the goat lady, the rescue of Scimitar and the company of the Mountain Fairies, had brought a healing to Smithereen. The moping illness had left him. He began to write poetry again and no longer tried to hide it. Although the Dwarves were still mystified by his verses, they had ceased to snicker. Some actually had begun to read his poems in secret.

Edel's captivity was a cause of grief to Smithereen. How often had the tiny Fairy's mirth lifted him out of the cavern of depression. If ever the Black Elves came within arm's reach, he would do justice to his name.

To let off steam Smithereen would practise his ball and chain technique, bringing the heavy steel ball up to phenomenal speed. One night after a strenuous workout, Smithereen was standing on the porch studying the spectral shapes of snowdrifts veiled in a bluish light when wing shadows moved over the snow.

'The great bird himself,' mused Smithereen, 'no doubt there is important news.'

A minute later the Grandmaster of the Covey touched down on the porch railing. A stern look gleamed in the yellow eyes.

'Time is up Smithereen, Servatius and Nightglider flew over the Wasa River, troops are moving up the mountain and assembling at a base camp, close to the Finnian Range. The assault likely will be launched at full moon, seven days from now.'

Smithereen nodded. 'We are ready Grimmbeak. We shall not be able to hold the pass for long, but once they enter the Crystal Gate they will pay a price.'

'I doubt it not,' said the Grandmaster with an expression that came as close to a smile as eagles are capable of. 'From the air I see a black circle when you swing that ball, poetry in motion. The Celestial Covey approves of poetry, that is to say the right kind of poetry of course. Would you honour the Covey with a poem next year at our twenty-fifth anniversary? We would be pleased to have a few verses.'

Smithereen was delighted that the Grandmaster appreciated his poetry in the martial as well as the literary field and he graciously accepted the commission. Grimmbeak, anxious to return to the Covey, turned to Sunflower standing in the door way and made a polite bow.

'We too shall play our part sunny lady. On the flight back I shall stop off at the birch wood where the Dauntless Divers perch. I will tell them to get ready.' Smithereen and Sunflower welcomed the news. They had never seen the heavy black birds with their fierce red combs in action. But they knew their steel like neck muscles enabled them to dive bomb anything that moved below without dislocating vital parts.

Grimmbeak didn't waste any time, taking wing for the birch wood to confer with Red Flash, Chief of the Dauntless Divers.

When first they set out for Esteria, Scimitar, Anvil and Tuffkote were overtaken by snow squalls. It was all down hill but snow and later freezing rain made the footing treacherous. By the time they reached the tree line, they were sore, wet and tired. A lean-to in a stand of spruce was quickly built and a hot blaze lifted spirits and dried their garments.

When sunlight peeked over the ridge, they jumped out of their sleeping bags and cooked a hearty breakfast, they packed quickly and dashed off. On the morning of the third day large stands of silver birches appeared and by afternoon they entered the gentle parkland surrounding the city of Esteria.

Sunlight captured the distant spires of the Monastery of the Luminous Horizon. Under the guidance of the great sage and wizard Isumatak, the monastery had flourished. It had been a source of comfort to the men and women in the town below, for the monks gave advice, settled family quarrels, healed the sick and taught the children to read and write. Neither the monks nor the people in town knew how long Isumatak had been there. In time not remembered, he had travelled hither from the arctic wastes. Legend told of a great sorceress who had taught him the secrets of the cosmos. With her, there had been a falling out and he had entered the Monastery.

Esteria was a town of loggers and woodworkers. In their isolated enclave they had, for centuries, enjoyed a peaceful life. The influx of volunteers had overwhelmed the quiet town folks. Any spare rooms in town had been taken up by Outlanders and Swannefolk who were the first to arrive. When the Gnomes came with their axes and shovels they dug tunnels into the hills and built comfortable quarters inside. Swannefolk were horrified to see them in their underground dwellings without windows but the Gnomes felt perfectly at home. The elf archers, the last to appear on the scene, had found space in the Monastery of the Luminous Horizon which was situated in the hills behind the town.

The Esterians spared no effort to make their guests comfortable. Esteria was an independent enclave, yet its survival was closely linked to the fate of the Kingdom.

The blending of Esterians, Outlanders, Gnomes, Swannefolk and Elves had led to a great deal of excitement. All were loyal to the throne and committed to the values they shared in the Sacred Book of Common Lore. Quarrels and old prejudices popped up at times, but generally they were amicably resolved.

A small group of Mountain Fairies marching into town carrying violins and other string instruments, had caused quite a stir but none of the onlookers thought for one moment that the will o' the wisp company of musicians had come to fight. Instead they turned out to be splendid entertainers. Every night parties and feasts were organized to celebrate an expected victory. Lore and songs from different traditions resounded around campfires well into the early morning.

The Marquis, acting in his capacity as Commander in Chief, had donned a magnificent uniform with many gold stripes and often was seen visiting the camps or attending festivities in his official capacity.

Ferdinand deCygne, after much soul searching, had at last decided that his true genius was in the military field. For years he had wavered between the path of the warrior and that of a holy life in one of the great monasteries, perhaps reaching the station of sainthood. Fame came to him when in a fit of rage, he had slain half a dozen Grolls. Legend already had multiplied that figure many times. The local tailor had produced a dazzling uniform and wearing it confirmed him in plans for a military career. Only when he visited the Monastery on the hill did he feel a pang of nostalgia for the path of the pilgrim that once he had contemplated.

The Marquis had established excellent relations with the leading burghers of the town. He had staged a number of colourful parades which had been enjoyed by all and often he was invited to official and unofficial dinner parties. Ensten, the woodcarver and a handful of Esterians, wondered about military preparedness and fortifications but most of the town enjoyed the unusual activities. The colourful spectacles gave everyone the feeling that all would be well.

A comfortable mansion in the centre of town served as the Marquis' residence and headquarters. The Marquis was delighted when Duckie arrived on his doorstep. He had him fitted out in a uniform and reinstated the dapper youngster as his page. Duckie had wanted to join the warriors in the frontline, but his protests were to no avail. The Marquis had an uncanny sense of self preservation and he remembered occasions when the quick witted Duckie had pulled him out of the soup.

When Volker reached Esteria, the Marquis had invited him to stay at his official residence. Town people took Volker to be the Marquis' private secretary and the Marquis did little to discourage the notion. Volker was content with the arrangement, it gave him a role people understood and left him free to record the historic events that were unfolding.

An amazing sight greeted Scimitar, Anvil and Tuffkote when they reached the meadows outside the city wall. Gnomes were seated on the wall smoking their long meerschaum pipes, Swannemen played ballgames in the meadows and Elves were stringing up decorations for an evening of festivities.

When the three fierce looking Dwarves approached, the merry hubbub faded to a mere whisper and rumours spread like wildfire that the good times were over.

The Dwarves marched straight through the merry scene, passed under the arch of the city gate and only came to a halt when they reached the town square. The Marquis was standing on the front steps of his Mansion. He warmly welcomed the three warriors, but Scimitar's piercing eyes gave him a feeling of unease. Scimitar had learned many lessons during his imprisonment and displayed unusual tact. He praised the Marquis for the arrangements that he had made for housing and provisioning the volunteers and for maintaining excellent relations with the town people. Pleased and flattered the Marquis invited the Dwarves in for refreshments. They were comfortably seated by the open hearth, enjoying hot coffee and buns, while Scimitar filled them in on all that had happened. Volker scribbled as quickly as he could, trying to catch every detail of Scimitar's adventures. Once Scimitar finished, the Marquis turned to him.

'I trust that the Dwarves will hold the passes Scimitar, wonderful warriors they are.'

Then it dawned on Scimitar and his companions that neither the Marquis nor any of the volunteers had ever seriously entertained the idea that the enemy would force the passes and descend upon Esteria. Scimitar smiled.

'I am afraid not, Ferdinand deCygne. Dwarves are savage fighters and they will inflict heavy losses upon the enemy. Hold the passes? Perhaps for a day, a week at the most. The armies of the Dark Lords, will in the end, overwhelm us. Rover officers, Grolls and black hounds will storm through the Crystal Gate and head for Esteria.'

The Marquis' hand fumbled for his pipe and drops of perspiration danced on his noble brow. The mere mention of the black dogs revived the trauma of his earlier experience. The idea that they might have to fight was dreadfully upsetting.

At this point Scimitar suggested that he would be willing to take over military operations if the Marquis could shoulder the overall command and manage supervision of the fortifications and relations with the town's dignitaries. Considering the unsettling news Scimitar had brought, the Marquis was relieved and then and there promoted Scimitar to Commander in Chief. Before leaving, Scimitar caught a glimpse of Duckie working at a table in the room next door and the young Swannelad got a hug that he never forgot.

A song and dance fest had been planned for the evening and wisely Scimitar did not interfere. It turned out to be a jolly night and even the Dwarves enjoyed themselves. But one of the locals had heard Scimitar whispering to his companions, 'The party is over.'

Next morning, while Scimitar, the Marquis and Volker were sitting at breakfast, Slim walked in. The great warrior welcomed him with open arms. He had grown fond of the quiet self-effacing swanneyouth who had played such a vital part in his rescue.

Since his arrival in Esteria, Slim had been staying at the home of Ensten and Ulrik. The brothers had helped him to complete surveys of the surrounding country and he handed Scimitar a folder with maps and sketches. Scimitar lost no time poring over Slim's work and realized quickly that his mapping skills were important for planning the defence. Walking home in the evening, Slim heard the town crier announcing a midday meeting for the volunteers with Commander Scimitar.

Next day at noon, Scimitar, flanked by Anvil and Tuffkote, walked into the meadow on the south side of the town. Leaving his comrades, Scimitar climbed a slight rise. A ripple of anxiety travelled through the crowd and the volunteers gathered at the foot of the hillock had a feeling that life as they knew it was about to take a major turn.

The Marquis and Volker stood off to the side. Scimitar knew the volunteers had enjoyed months of leisure in Esteria, confident the Dwarves would carry the burden of battle.

'Outlanders, Gnomes, Elves, Swannefolk, Fairies and Esterians.' called out Scimitar, 'Marquis deCygne has asked me to prepare you for the battle ahead.'

Eyes, filled with disbelief, stared at the lone warrior facing them.

'Battle ahead,' the words echoed through the throng and for a few moments hopes rose that the new Commander was talking about some other battle, a safe distance away.

'In a few days time the enemy will launch a full-scale attack on the pass at the Crystal Gate. The Dwarves are prepared and will defend the pass. They will stop the enemy for a day, two days, perchance a week. Then the troops will take the pass and rush onward towards Esteria. They could be here in a fortnight.'

A wave of fear moved through the meadow. That they might actually have to fight came as a terrible shock. They had heard about the Grolls and the black dogs, but had no idea how to stop them. All eyes were on Scimitar, anxious to know what they could do to forestall the calamity looming on the horizon.

'Friends, while there is yet time, we will build a line of defence and learn the art of warfare. Night and day will we toil to build barriers and booby traps. We will steel ourselves for the suffering that must be endured.' Scimitar's deep voice carried an ominous note, and a hush fell over the crowd.

'Those of you willing to fight raise your right hand,' thundered the Dwarf.

To a man Outlanders, Gnomes and Elves raised their hands, but none of the Swannefolk responded to the challenge. The Swannemen grouped together at the edge of the meadow looked embarrassed. A tiny chap stepped out and hesitantly walked forward to face the Dwarf on the hillock.

'Commander Scimitar, we may as well be honest about it, we who come from the Land of the Swans, are no fighters. Generations back, our ancestors mastered the art of warfare, but long since we have abandoned physical conflict, our nervous systems have evolved and are too finely attuned. The very idea of bashing somebody over the head or worse being bashed on the head ourselves, gives us the shivers.'

Scimitar's gaze froze their spokesman into uneasy silence. But the wisp of a chap wriggled out of the spell, and piped up.

'We will build the fortifications and look after the wounded, Sir Dwarf.'

Scimitar broke into a smile, he had expected as much. Swannefolk were great showmen, but they abhorred fighting. Scimitar remembered the tiny spokesman from earlier meetings at the Graceful Neck in Cascade.

'It is well Elzevier, I trust the volunteers from Swanneland will turn these charming meadows into a formidable line of defence.'

Later that afternoon Scimitar worked with Slim, designing different types of obstacles that would slow the enemy's advance. Slim did a series of sketches and took them to the Swannemen who had gathered outside the town wall.

The next day, the Marquis ventured into the meadows to see his fellow Swannemen erecting barriers and driving stakes into the ground. Under the guidance of the Dwarf Anvil, they turned into skilful sappers.

The Marquis was amazed at the speed at which the men worked and the ingenuity of the devices that they put together. Sharp pointed poles that would puncture Grolls' large floppy feet were driven into the ground. Deep trenches were dug and covered with branches to scatter the enemy's ranks and fray their nerves. Scimitar hoped the booby traps would cause the enemy column to split and to move to the forested areas on both sides of the meadow, where elf archers would be hiding in the trees.

Scimitar and Tuffkote worked with the Elves, Gnomes and Outlanders.

Gnomes were wonderfully skilful with their axes and the Elves excelled in archery. The tall Outlanders had few martial skills but Scimitar taught them to throw heavy spears that could pierce Groll scales and stationed them at the main approaches to the town. The elf archers found hiding places behind bushes and some climbed trees, whence they would loose their arrows upon the enemy.

The Gnomes practised hiding behind bushes and rocks in the outer perimeter. When Scimitar blew a whistle, like quicksilver, they would fly at an imaginary enemy. With their axes they could slash the Grolls below the knees where there were no protective scales. If not slain, at least the Grolls would be disabled and useless for further action.

Scimitar's strategy aimed at diverting a direct attack. Fierce resistance in front might tempt the enemy to encircle the town and to venture into the soggy marshlands. Ponds and puddles covered with a thin layer of ice, offered a deceptive footing. The heavy Grolls, would sink into the muck.

A deep moat filled with water ringed the town itself. The moat had been dug to drain the swamps, but now it became part of the defence system. Fall rains and early snow showers had raised the water level and even Grolls were likely to lose their footing. If they made it across, they would have to scale a dyke of stone and gravel that had been built up over centuries. Many houses stood against the dyke and if Grolls climbed atop, missives from the upper storeys would be raining down.

Scimitar, knowing that he needed all available hands, asked the men and women of Esteria to volunteer for the defence of the town itself. The peaceful lifestyle of this enclave of woodcarvers and lumbermen had not been jarred by violence for generations. Scimitar discovered to his delight that archery had always been an honoured pastime amongst the Esterians. Many of the men could send an arrow true and at a hundred feet, split a post. To pick off troopers that made it across the moat, archers were stationed at the upper windows in the log houses. Women worked night and day piling missiles on the second and third storeys of other buildings on the outer ring. On woodstoves, large pots of boiling oil and molten lead were bubbling for a warm reception, in case Grolls or Rovers appeared on the dyke.

During the day Slim drew maps and diagrams of the fortifications but at night he retired to Ensten and Ulrik's cottage to share an evening meal and relax playing a game of cards or shuffleboard with Ulrik. Ensten would sit by the open hearth, lost in thought or working on a carving.

One night when Ulrik had retired, Slim joined Ensten by the fire. Ensten asked about Svanhild. Slim sensed that the friendship between Ensten and Svanhild ran in deeper channels and he knew that Ensten was worried about her. Slim's thoughts often went out to Svanhild. They had been close yet so unlike each other. Like other Swannemen the idea of hand to hand combat or killing another living creature was unthinkable to Slim. But Svanhild had a fiery temper and would not hesitate to send an arrow at a foe or to loose a stone from her slingshot with deadly aim.

One night, after a day of mapmaking in the pouring rain, Slim arrived home soaking wet. It had been a hard day for everybody, Scimitar had driven the volunteers to the point of exhaustion and Slim felt despondent but a blazing fire in the hearth and Ensten's smiling face cheered him. What was the woodcarver up to? Ensten reached behind his back and brought forth a large carving of a swan in flight.

'It is yours Slim.' It was a woodcarving of Slim's lead swan, Limonides.

Slim couldn't help but marvel at Ensten's memory. Only once had the woodcarver seen Limonides perform aerial ballet. It had been more than a year ago in the town of Miranda, yet the gift was a perfect likeness and Slim was delighted.

Scimitar spent the evenings studying the drawings and sketches that Slim brought to him and he worked on planning earthworks for the defence. During the day he was in the field with the troops, directing mock attacks and manoeuvres. The volunteers were eager to learn and under the command of the Dwarves, developed into an effective fighting force.

At a recent meeting, Scimitar, the Marquis and Volker speculated how long the town could stand a siege. If the winter snows came early, the enemy would have difficulty in supplying the troops and the Grolls were not used to winter warfare. Yet all knew that the long range prospects were dim.

One morning a glimmer of hope flew in. Slim saw the dark raised wings of the owls, reducing speed for a landing on the front steps of the Mansion. Slim greeted Solomon and Kasper and invited them in. Scimitar bade them welcome and for a perch, pointed to the backs of two finely carved chairs. Solomon looked at the sombre faces around the table. He was pleased to be the harbinger of good news.

'Svanhild, Sidonia and Oarflake are back home at the Lake of the Coloured Fishes,' began the Chief of the owls. Everyone around the table was full of apprehension. A ripple of amusement swept the yellow eyes of the deep bird and to heighten the drama of the scene, he paused for a moment.

'They searched the settlement of the Sea Gnomes and almost had given up hope, when Oarflake's sixth sense for the presence of gold impelled him to reach behind a set of pretty dinner plates to find a tablet cast in solid gold.'

'The golden tablet with the secret incantation found!' Exclamations and shouts sounded around the table. Enjoying the commotion that they had wrought, Solomon winked at Kasper. It was Scimitar, of course, who brought the company back to earth. '

'It is true friends. The news brings a glimmer of hope but the chances of the tablet reaching the palace before the armies of the Seven destroy the Kingdom are scant.'

Solomon took the floor again, 'The pixie Weiss.'

'Mountain Fairy, Chief.' corrected Scimitar who had a new respect for the light hearted creatures.

'Weiss, the Fairy from Windekind, will accompany Svanhild and Sidonia to the Federation of the Moles where they hope to find Elmira, the youngest of the elven sisters. Elmira, whose radiant laughter Ensten captured in his carving, who received the gift of spirit travel, the elven child of ancient prophecy, harbinger of light and bearer of the golden tablet.'

'A noble tribute Chief,' muttered Kasper.

Scimitar cautioned the others that the barriers around the Palace of the Seven were formidable and even if a way were found to penetrate the stronghold, it might be too late.

Solomon and Kasper promised that they would keep an eye on Svanhild and her fellow travellers. Any flimsy reason would send them off to check on the Swannemaiden.

Scimitar walked the owls to the front porch and thanked them for their concern and support. Grave was the expression in the eyes of the great birds as they winged their way over the once peaceful town that now resembled an armed camp.

'The end of the world could be at hand Chief,' groaned Kasper, 'our hereditary rights to the woodlands, conferred by the King in perpetuity, could be at risk.'

Solomon let out an impatient grunt. 'Rights in perpetuity. Poppycock, horse feathers, Deputy. Rest in perpetuity! We'll be lucky if we don't end up in a Groll's stew pot, owl feathers filling expensive cushions in the Lords' palace. They might embroider an owl on the covers.'

When the Chief's sense of humour turned sour, things were serious. For a while the birds flew on quietly until Solomon broke the silence.

'I apologize Deputy, I lost my temper. Svanhild is on her way to the Land of Darkness. She has not lost heart and neither will we.'

'We will stand by her until our last feathers are scattered over the winter snows Chief.'

'Poetry Deputy, sheer poetry!

The arrival of the Dwarves had put an end to parades and pomp and the Marquis' prominence in town diminished. A frown had settled on the nobleman's brow and he began to slide into a deep depression. At night he would sit by the open hearth and stare at the flames. The image of Dorothea sprang back into his consciousness. He was horrified to think that during his short meteoric military career, his mind had repressed the image of his beloved Dorothea. His splendid uniform had attracted admiring looks from the local ladies.

'By the Great spirit,' he mused, 'am I so inconstant? Has my heart turned to stone?'

As the days slipped by, the Marquis resorted to meditation. He remembered the words of the elven sage, Seraphim, at the Graceful Neck.

'If all else fails, meditate.' At times, a vision of Dorothea would come to him. Once he actually felt her hand upon his forehead. It was she alone who had truly loved him. It was her love that had saved him and his companions from Queen Marsha's evil clutches. The Queen whose curse, in a fit of anger had petrified his beloved Dorothea. So, Ferdinand deCygne, spent his evenings looking into the fire, whispering Dorothea, Dorothea, as if the flames could turn the cold marble into flesh and blood.

In the alpine meadows on the Finnian Range, the Dwarf Village had been in a state of constant motion. Tension had been unbearable, but now that the hour of trial was at hand, a strange quiet settled over the dwarf stronghold. It was Master Grimmbeak, who brought the news that the enemy was on the march and had set up base camp on the other side of the range, well above the tree line. They would attack at dawn.

The men and women of Turania were ready. Smithereen had joined the warriors at the Crystal Gate and Sunflower led the women of the village to a high plateau above the pass where thousands of rocks were piled high. Once the enemy drew close, an avalanche would greet them.

Dawn found Sergeant Crusher and Bullneck standing side by side on the watchtower peering down the range. Ground fog covered the slopes and there was no sign of troop movement. Suddenly rising from the mist, a huge Groll appeared. Sergeant Crusher was horrified to see him advance towards the watchtower. Twice the size of the usual sort, he seemed totally unconcerned about being detected. When he caught sight of the Dwarves on the tower, he burst into raw laughter and quickening his pace, headed straight for Sergeant Crusher and Bullneck. The Dwarves rung the great bell and raised the alarm. When the monster reached the tower, Bullneck saw that his head came within five or six feet from their platform. Huge claws seized the corner post and began shaking the wooden structure. The tower swayed perilously. The Groll, enjoying himself immensely never saw the Dwarf approaching from behind. Unfortunately for the brute it was Smithereen whirling his giant ball at lightning speed. With great precision it hit the ruffian at the knees and with a yell of anger the Groll hit the snow covered rocks. When the dazed figure rose to a sitting position, Smithereen brought the ball up to speed again and this time the steel globe silenced the Groll for good.

The tower veered back to its original position and Bullneck and Sergeant Crusher could see the regular troops marching towards the pass. Sunflower and the other women, alerted by the ringing of the bell, already were halfway up the mountain and on a signal from Sergeant Crusher, would be in place to start a rock slide.

Upon their first attempt to storm the Crystal Gate, the enemy suffered heavy losses. When they thronged into the narrow pass Sunflower and the other women sent the rocks crashing down. The Rovers leading the Grolls ordered an immediate retreat but for many it was too late.

Bullneck and Sergeant Crusher expected another attack but an eerie silence prevailed. The next day the enemy changed tactics, they marched single file into the pass presenting less of a target for the falling rocks. Many Grolls were wounded or killed, but they kept coming. Those that made it through the pass were met by warriors whirling ball and chain.

Most of the archers in front of the pass had loosed their last arrows. Their hiding places had been detected by enemy scouts and they were forced to retreat. Running trails high up in the mountains, most of them were able to make it back to the village. To cover Sunflower and her women, Bullneck sent some of the archers up the high cliffs.

Sergeant Crusher, on top of the observation tower, felt sick at heart. As far as the eye could see columns of troops covered the wintry slopes. The enemy kept coming. It mattered not how many were felled or wounded, others would take their place

The women ran out of rocks and now lit pitch covered branches, stockpiled by the edge of the cliff. On a signal from Sunflower they seized long poles and began pushing the burning pyres off the edge turning the entire passage below into an inferno. The Grolls, who abhorred fire, were frightened out of their wits. Many panicked and tried to turn back but the Rovers with their long whips drove them on. They managed to hold the pass that day but the Dwarves feared for the morrow. Seven Dwarves had fallen in battle and twice that number had been wounded.

At dawn Sergeant Crusher espied a long column moving forward in light snow. The snow slowed them down on the steep slopes but they kept coming.

From her high mountain post, Sunflower saw the line split into two. The main force headed for the pass but the second group seemed to be heading for the very summit on which she was standing. It was clear the women had done an excellent job raining rock and burning timber on the troops and the enemy had determined to put an end to it.

The Grolls' large duck feet didn't handle the icy surface very well and they kept sliding back on the steep slopes. They were still hundreds of yards away and making little progress.

Before retreating the women cast a look at the Grolls, slithering and sliding on the mountainside. They couldn't help laughing at the spectacle and for a few moments they stayed to watch. It was Pristina, standing next to Sunflower who shouted a warning. She had spotted a dark patch moving at great speed across the snow.

'Stars above, Sunflower, a black horde moving across the snow. Black hounds in full gallop.' In the distance they could hear clicking sounds, like popping corn, as many of the dogs were caught in Sledge's traps. Those caught, went mad with rage and attacked their masters. The Grolls had few scales below the knees and the huge jaws clasped their lower legs. A few dogs managed to avoid the traps and one of the Rovers directed them up the mountain plateau, where Sunflower and her women were sending down the ravine, their last reserves of blazing logs. A few of the black hounds were halfway up the slope. Their huge paws dug into the snow, overtaking the stumbling Grolls, they loped swiftly to the top. Sunflower could see white foam bubbling on their black jaws.

Pristina grasped her hand and for a moment they stood motionless as the drama unfolded before their eyes. When the first hounds reached the steep incline near the summit, she gave the signal to retreat.

One of the archers who had joined them, picked off two of the seven dogs climbing up the slope but the others kept coming. Sunflower and Pristina were running towards the village when Sunflower's right foot caught on a burning branch. When she picked herself up a large black shape sprang towards her. She seized the blazing twig and threw it. Then suddenly her right hand grew cold and stiff and time seemed to stand still. She looked at her hand as if in a dream and then saw the foaming jaws slowly release her arm and drop down to the ground. The feathers at the end of the arrow that pierced the black hound, fluttered in the wind.

Dazed with pain, Sunflower began to slide down the mountainside. Pristina guided her as best she could and at a clump of small birches they came to a halt.

'Leave me here Pristina and lead the women and children to the Sacred Mountain and hide in the tunnels. My end is near, I will die. The illness of the tainted fang leaves no hope.'

'The men will carry you to the Convent of the Sisters of the Secret Crossing. The Marquis recovered.'

'Not at this time of year my love. The snow is deep and the Sanctus barely frozen. None can save me.'

'There is hope,' pressed Pristina sternly. 'We will find a way.'

Two archers who had seen Pristina bending over Sunflower's snow white face, rushed up. They joined hands, seating Sunflower between them and carried her down to the village.

Over thirteen of the Dwarves had fallen in battle. By late morning a heavy snow squall had forced the enemy to retreat. Smithereen, ball and chain slung over his shoulder, saw the crowd gathered in front of his cottage.

'It is Sunflower,' he murmured, 'Angels Above! Sunflower has been hurt.' The men and women parted when Smithereen approached. Walking through the door he saw, Angelica, the goat lady, kneeling by Sunflower's side pouring a dark coloured liquid into her mouth. A wave of horror engulfed Smithereen. No words were needed. He had seen the black horde flying up the mountain. The liquid was the mixture of Devil's Claw and Deadly Shade of Night, the potion that had given the Marquis a window on life. The bleeding hand and the fang marks told all. He kneeled, his lips touching her forehead and took her hand.

'We will find a way, Sunny.'

'It matters not my dearest,' whispered Sunflower. 'I am ready to leave this plane.'

Pristina, standing by Smithereen's side, cast a loving look at her friend.

'Leave us and delight the Angels with your laugh? Certainly not my love, we will not let you go, not yet.'

'The men must not risk their lives in vain, Pristina.'

'There is another way. Bullneck raise the Black Dragon.'

The huge Dwarf looked astonished but he knew better after all these years than to question Pristina. He rushed out to fetch the standard and raise it on the flagpole in the village square. Within minutes it fluttered at the top of the pole, a black dragon on blood red, the symbol of mortal peril.

Nightglider and Servatius had just completed a surveillance flight over the Finnian Range. They circled the Dwarf village but snow squalls had reduced visibility. They were about to fly home when there was a break in the weather and Nightglider, catching a distant glimpse of the village, descried a fleck of red. It was enough to raise the eagles' interest and they went into a steep bank. When the snow abated, they could see the Black Dragon on the red field.

'The sceptre of death, Servatius. Mortal peril threatens. Follow me.'

Nightglider nosedived and only pulled up when they saw the crowd gathered by the home of Sunflower and Smithereen. Bullneck, standing, on the porch had seen them streaking down. The moment that they perched on the railing, he called out.

'It is Sunflower, one of the black hounds caught her in the hand.'

Nightglider was shaken but kept his cool. He knew that the tainted fang illness must be treated within ten days. The snow was too deep for terrestrials to transport Sunflower to the Convent. The Covey must rise to the occasion. He turned and faced Bullneck.

'We will fetch the eagle team. Have Sunflower wrapped in furs. We shall return.'

With those words Nightglider and Servatius rose in a steep climb. Flying at lightning speed, high above the Finnian Range, they reached home base in record time. The sky had cleared and they could see the entire Covey perched in a great circle. In this time of crisis all the birds attended the sessions. When Grimmbeak saw them shooting down, he suspected something was up. They pulled out of a steep dive seconds before perching in the centre of the circle. One of the old boilers shaking his head, muttered.

'Cutting a dash again.' A flash from Grimmbeak's burning eyes silenced him.

'Chief,' stammered Nightglider. 'It is Sunflower, her right hand torn to shreds by a black brute. The goat lady's medicine will give her ten days. The snow is too deep for the dwarf runners and the Sanctus cannot be crossed at freeze up.'

Instantly Grimmbeak grasped the situation. The great bird had deep feelings for Sunflower whose laugh had a strange way of cheering his spirit and a film of moisture gleamed in the deep yellow eyes.

'Brethren in the flight of the spirit,' thundered the Master's voice echoing against the cliff side, 'The Celestial Covey will meet the calamity that has befallen the sunny lady and will rise to this mission of mercy. It will take seven birds to carry Sunflower to the Convent of the Sisters. Wingspan and stamina are what it takes. Which of you twelve-footers volunteer?'

To a bird, the eagles raised their right wing. Master Grimmbeak picked six large birds and decided to lead the formation himself.

'Theodorus,' barked the Master, 'Fetch the net from storage.' The young bird hastened to the cliffs below and pulled a large piece of triangular webbing from the crevasse. The nets were woven with thread from the webs of giant forest spiders. Many a squirrel stuck in the fierce spiders' webs had been rescued by the eagles.

Theodorus handed the webbing to Master Grimmbeak. Knowing that he didn't have the wingspan for the mission, he was content to stay behind and assist Nightglider and Servatius in their surveillance flights.

Master Grimmbeak, followed by his covey brethren, soared up in a steep climb. As the formation sped to the village of the Dwarves, moonlight rimmed the great wings with a band of light.

The snow squalls over Turania had vanished and Sergeant Crusher, on his tower, looked up at a million sparkling stars. Only the distant fires in the enemy camp were a reminder that the peaceful village stood in peril. Staring over the magic winter snows, he spotted the seven eagles. They approached at great speed and he called down to one of the sentries to run with the news to Sunflower and Smithereen's home. As soon as they got word they wrapped Sunflower in furs. The moment the eagles touched down, Sunflower was carried out and placed in the middle of the net. No time was to be lost. Smithereen kissed her forehead and the large birds hooked their talons through the strands. Master Grimmbeak, standing at the apex of the webbing, gave the signal. Instantly seven pair of wings moved in unison. Their pinions beat with such force that a powerful gust of cold air enveloped the men and women standing on the porch.

It seemed to Smithereen as if the seven eagles and Sunflower were gliding up on moonbeams. Only when they turned south towards the Convent of the Sisters of the Secret Crossing, did Smithereen lose sight of his beloved Sunflower.

He went inside the cottage and knelt by Sunflower's loom. For the first time in his life he prayed, prayed to that unknown force that his artist friends in Lambarina had told him about. It was in Lambarina he had once asked his friend Maedi to teach him about prayer, the white haired poet had quoted from his own work.

> *How mere words on ether floating*
> *bring light and seeing*
> *guide the course of our being*
> *no words of mine can tell*
>
> *forged in the furnace of despair*
> *words soar in the air*
> *enter secret portals*
> *to change the fate of mortals*
>
> *that mere words softly whispered*
> *succour do bring, I know full well*
> *what labyrinthine path they travel*
> *I cannot tell.*

How true those words rang now. He prayed to that great unknown presence that surrounds and suffuses all creation and from the depth of his heart, he asked for Sunflower's healing.

When he looked up at Sunflower's loom, on a golden field appeared the weft of alpine flowers, bursts of white, purple, blue and red. A joyous image. New faith sprang into his heart and admiration for Sunflower's art. Had all the verses he had written over the years brought such joy? There on the ancient loom sang Sunflower's poetry.

He stood up and walked to the window. Bullneck was directing the women and children towards the hidden tunnels. Tonight the warriors must leave the village. Smithereen donned his leather jacket and slung ball and chain over his shoulder. Bullneck met him outside and told Smithereen that he had asked some of the warriors to stay with the women and children in the grottos in the Sacred Mountain. The remainder of the men would travel to Esteria and join the last line of defence.

Smithereen and other warriors went up to the pass and set fire to the pile of logs at the entrance. It would provide a smoke screen and slow the enemy down for a few hours.

The Dwarves shouldered their packs, picked up their weapons and made their way down the mountainside towards Esteria. It was still dark and when Smithereen looked back he could see the great fires burning at the foot of the pass. A few more hours and the Grolls would pillage the village. Nothing would remain.

42

The Siege of Esteria

*T*he elf archers were the first to see the dwarf warriors emerging from the forest. The news travelled fast and shockwaves moved through the ranks of the volunteers. It could mean but one thing, the Crystal Gate had fallen. Within days violent Grolls and savage dogs would be upon them.

Two quick-thinking Elves jumped out of the trees and ran up the hill reaching the Dwarves before they would walk into the line of booby traps set for the enemy. Carefully zigzagging through the defences, the Elves guided the warriors safely to the Town Gate. Scimitar hugged Smithereen and breathed a sigh of relief when he saw how many warriors had survived the battle at the Crystal Gate. They were badly needed to strengthen his army of novices. The news of Sunflower's fate came as a terrible shock.

That evening at the Mansion, delegates from the volunteers and the Esterians joined the company to hear Bullneck and Smithereen tell of the battle at the Crystal Gate. Large numbers of Grolls and Rovers had been slain, but it was clear that the enemy had vast reserves. They were glad to learn that many black dogs had been caught in traps. The hounds were dangerous but worse still, the sight of them terrified and demoralized the troops.

A happy note was carried to the meeting by the arrival of young Theodorus. Theodorus had flown to the Convent of the Sisters a day after Sunflower's arrival. Sister Esmeralda had taken Theodorus to the room where Sunflower, wrapped in her nettle suit, was resting. A young Swannemaiden with blue eyes and long golden tresses, had been holding her hand, singing a lullaby. When Theodorus left, Sunflower had fallen into a deep sleep.

Gratitude showed in Smithereen's eyes and Scimitar had a feeling that it was his Helga who had sung Sunflower to sleep. A nagging doubt sprang in Scimitar's mind and gently he touched the young eagle's wing.

'Theodorus, the name of the young woman who sang to Sunflower, do you recall?'

'Sister Helga, a gentle soul from Swanneland.' Theodorus saw a ripple of unease cross Scimitar's features. 'Sister Helga is one of the nine lay sisters that came to the convent to help with victims of the tainted fang illness.' Scimitar tugged again at Theodorus' wing.

'Did you say lay sister noble bird?'

'It is true Sir Dwarf. Lay sisters they are. They will stay at the Convent until peace returns to the land. A heavy weight fell from Scimitar's shoulders He actually smiled and thanked Theodorus for the welcome tidings.

At daybreak, rays of the morning sun, caught Scimitar standing by the town gate. Hoarfrost covered the clumps of birches in the meadows.

He marvelled at the sight. What irony that this sparkling canopy of beauty within hours would turn into a bloody battle field.

Peering into the morning haze, he could see the black silhouette of a single bird, its large wings sailing majestically towards him. Scimitar welcomed Nightglider as he perched on the town gate. Nightglider confirmed that the vanguard of the enemy would reach Esteria by noon.

Scimitar had expected as much, but he was relieved to learn from Nightglider that the Rovers had driven their troops on to Esteria and that there had been no time for looting and pillaging. The women, the children and the wounded, were safe in the grottos of the Sacred Mountain.

'Look up Scimitar,' said Nightglider.

'Scimitar raised his eyes and saw, above the sparkling haze, a number of black dots on the horizon. They moved swiftly and he recognized the outlines of eagles, but not the familiar shapes of the birds of the Covey. The bodies were heavier and with a shorter wingspan. Within a few hundred yards they banked into a steep dive and perched on the gate. The Dauntless Divers had arrived.

Red Flash, head bird for the Divers, made a polite bow and Nightglider introduced him to Scimitar. The fierce eyes, the ruffled feathers and the mangy appearance crowned with a blood red comb, made an impression. The scruffy appearance and the lack of finesse didn't fool Scimitar. These birds were tough customers. Master Grimmbeak had told him that they were diamonds in the rough. Scimitar, knowing that he was going to need all the help that he could get, heartily welcomed the leader of the Dauntless Divers. Expecting a number of black hounds in the vanguard, Scimitar asked Red Flash to have his divers airborne at the first sign of enemy troops approaching and to maintain altitude. As soon as the black dogs appeared the Dauntless Divers were to put them out of action. It was the kind of assignment that Red Flash and his fiery birds cherished.

It was now but a matter of hours. All the volunteers had moved into position. Bullneck and Smithereen had placed the seasoned dwarf warriors amongst them. The elf archers were waiting for the hoarfrost to melt before climbing the tall spruce trees. Their bows were cleverly constructed from different layers of wood strapped together. The night before, quivers filled with arrows had been placed in the trees. It was mid-afternoon when elf scouts came running down from the high forest to raise the alarm. The enemy was approaching.

Commander Zervos and his brother Zenon, next in the line of command, walked at the head of the column of Grolls marching down the mountain towards Esteria. They had paid a heavy price at the Crystal Gate, but a few weeks earlier spies had brought reassuring news. Esteria would be a piece of cake. Merewings had reported parades and ceremonies with that useless figurehead, the Marquis deCygne, prancing around in a glittering uniform. No signs anywhere of military activity.

Zervos and Zenon were shrewd and ruthless men, they trusted no one and least of all each other. They wanted to finish the business quickly and to march on to Lambarina, where Zervos was to be installed as Governor. To speed things up they had called for a pack of black hounds to spearhead the troops. It would frighten any volunteers who actually were prepared to fight.

The time had come to send the dogs flying down to Esteria, and Zervos called out to the master of the hounds to give the command.

At the sound of three short whistle blasts, the black horde rushed from the forest into the parkland surrounding the town. An awesome spectacle unfolded. The Dauntless Divers, circling high above banked into steep dives. Wings folded back and slowly rotating on their bodies' axis, they bore down on the black shapes moving across the meadows. With amazing precision they honed in on their targets, stunning the foaming brutes. Quick as lightning the Gnomes moved in with their axes and finished them off. Within a short period more than thirty four had been slain.

There was no sign of the Grolls yet and all those who had watched the extraordinary performance cheered and clapped. Red Flash stepped forward and bowed to the cheering crowd as if the whole thing had been performed in a circus.

When Zervos emerged from the forest and raised his sight to survey the terrain he found that the ground was littered with black hounds. He hissed between his missing front teeth. No doubt Master Grimmbeak of the Celestial Covey had a hand in this. He would deal with the eagles in days to come. No time was to be wasted now and he ordered the troops to take the town before sunset.

The wave of Grolls rushing towards the town wall, were met by hundreds of poisoned arrows fired by Elves hidden in the trees. If not slain by arrows the Grolls often were disabled. Gnomes carrying their axes and Dwarves whirling ball and chain darted across the battlefield and made sure that they didn't get up again.

The booby traps that the Swannemen had constructed spread dismay among the enemy. Grolls suddenly would lose their footing and fall into deep pits, others had their large floppy feet pierced by stakes. Scimitar's strategy worked well, and that night, Commander Zervos cancelled plans for a frontal attack. At dusk, Scimitar supervised an orderly withdrawal to within the town walls.

On the morrow the enemy pressed closer to town. Booby traps and a group of esterian archers stationed on the dykes quickly thinned their ranks. The Esterians who thus far had only shot arrows in friendly archery matches, struck Grolls and Rovers at more than a hundred yards. Few arrows missed their aim.

A small number of enemy troops making it through the hail of arrows waded across the moat and up the high dyke on the other side. The women of Esteria were ready. Large rocks, boiling oil and lead, had a powerful effect on the brutes.

Zervos changed his plans and diverted troops to surround the town. Numerous Grolls got stuck in the frozen marshes and others sank through the thin ice on the ponds. The enemy had large reserves of manpower but only a handful of black hounds were left. It took Zervos' troops two days to find safe passage through the marshes and invest the town.

Scimitar knew merewings flew messages back and forth between the realm of darkness and the Commanders in the fields. The merewings with their huge wingspan could fly at high altitudes and in vain the eagles had tried to bring one down.

That night, certain of a quick victory, Zervos sent news to his masters.

A merewing carrying the small wooden vessel had been spotted by Red Flash of the Dauntless Divers. A haze hung over the forest and the faint moon, ringed by fog, was hardly visible and the black bird with the purple beak was forced to fly at a low altitude. Red Flash, under cover of a fogbank, soared high above the merewing and in a lightning dive, knocked the bird cold. Unfortunately, he tumbled down among the campfires of a Groll regiment. Red Flash could see the outline of the stricken merewing. Soaring at ground level, he touched down by the lifeless bird and managed to sever the leather band with the container attached. He seized it in his beak and before Grolls had a chance to pull their bow strings, he was airborne.

Directly, Red Flash presented Scimitar with the container, he opened it and read the contents aloud to the company.

'Esteria invested. Victory within reach. Within a few days the Kingdom will be yours. Your humble servant Zervos.'

'Alas,' murmured Scimitar, 'It is the truth.'

Bullneck, standing by the window, beckoned Smithereen to join him. Looking out, they saw trees waving in the wind and sheets of snow sweeping down upon the town. The warriors looked at each other and faint hope rose in their hearts. They knew that Rovers and Grolls were not prepared for winter warfare. The climate in the Realm of Darkness was tempered by the Eastern Ocean and snow or ice seldom were seen. The blizzard would confound the enemy and give their own men a chance to regroup and to strengthen fortifications but for how long?

The rattling of the shutters drew Scimitar to the window. The storm had intensified and huge snow drifts were forming. The enemy would be forced to stay in the trenches and their simple shelters. Pacing back and forth Scimitar addressed them.

'We have been granted a brief reprieve friends. The winter snows will delay the enemy for weeks. Resupply will be difficult and they will run short of food and clothing. This will give us time to dig in and prepare for a lengthy siege. We are the last line of defence and none of us know the outcome of the battle. How often in the past has aid come from strange and unexpected sources. We must hope and pray.

All the volunteers were now within the city walls. The Elves had not been able to return to their quarters in the Monastery, located on the high ridge, miles behind the town. When the enemy encircled Esteria communication with the Monastery had been cut off. Families in Esteria, vied to have Elves stay with them, and very quickly they were absorbed. The Gnomes, too, had found shelter within the walls.

There was no let up in the weather. Snow kept falling and by the end of December it had reached the second storey of most homes.

The Grolls suffered terribly. Many had frozen feet and there were severe food shortages. At night, parties of Dwarves on skis would race across the frozen wastes setting fire to their camps and many were left without either shelter or food.

Zervos had a log cabin built for himself and like a caged bear, spent days pacing his small office. Menacing messages from the Palace arrived with clockwork regularity. Zervos knew that his masters simply didn't believe his reports of terrible winter conditions and placed the blame squarely upon his shoulders. Many of his men had died or been disabled and he knew that his hands were tied until the weather improved and new troops and supplies could travel across the Finnian Range.

Scimitar had stocked enough supplies to feed the people of the besieged city and the volunteers had managed amazingly well. Crowded together, often in uncomfortable quarters, they kept up their good cheer. A number of festive gatherings had helped to shorten the winter evenings and Mountain Fairies danced and sang their way through the dark season bringing merriment where ever they performed. Everybody kept in shape shovelling mountains of snow.

Smithereen had met old friends amongst the volunteers from Lambarina.

Many were poets and artists and evenings were spent reciting poetry, song cycles and displaying works of art. Smithereen, at last, surrounded by kindred spirits, felt he had come home.

In daylight hours Scimitar worked with the volunteers, spent time on the ramparts scanning the enemy camp or talking to the sappers who were always busy thinking up new devices to surprise the enemy. They had just built a huge catapult that would throw a bucket of rocks a hundred yards or more.

Slim did sketches of scenes around town and had begun painting portraits. He mastered the play of light and shadow in a wonderful manner, giving life and depth to his work. Encouraged by fellow painters from Lambarina he completed a number of canvases.

At night, Scimitar studied the plans and drawings of the defense perimeter. When Slim visited the Mansion, he was fascinated to watch the Dwarf at work. Intensity dwelt in that face and a strange light shone in those steel-grey eyes, the light of courage and devotion. After watching the Dwarf for several evenings, he worked up the courage to ask permission to paint his portrait. It took persuasion but Scimitar, knowing that he owed Slim a debt that could never be repaid, consented. Every night Slim would come to the Mansion and while Scimitar worked out new strategies, Slim was absorbed in his artistry. Fellow artists, who viewed the canvas, knew a work of art had come into being. In time the painting became known as Light of the Brave.[12]

At the Convent of the Sisters of the Secret Crossing, Helga had spent the night by Sunflower's bedside. The sun's early rays kissed the pretty face wreathed in nettle leaves.

'You know Scimitar?' queried Helga.'

Sunflower couldn't help laughing even though the slightest movement intensified the burning on her skin.

'You look surprised, Helga, but in a strange way our lives are interwoven. Scimitar is my brother in law. Come closer my love.' Sunflower's voice fell to a whisper, 'In ordinary times I would not have spoken of his love for you, but peril is upon us all. Nobody knows whether the Kingdom will survive.'

Helga blushed, for Scimitar always had a place in her heart, ever since the day that they had met at the Wendell farm. Helga had never spoken to anyone about her secret, but she felt a bond with Sunflower and told her

---

12   *The painting survived throughout the ages and hangs in a small chapel in the Lambarina Museum of Fine Art and Folklore. An illuminated manuscript below the painting gives details of the life of Scimitar. In the lower right corner is the emblem of a Swan and a faint outline of the artist's name, but only elven eyes can see them. The painting has faded except for the eyes, where dwells a radiance that inspires visitors to face the battles in their own lives.*

how she had met Scimitar in the cherry orchard. Together they had ambled to the shore of the Sanctus. There seated by the swiftly flowing waters, they talked until sundown. Then without another word and without bidding her farewell, Scimitar suddenly had boarded his canoe and paddled away. Sunflower took Helga's hand.

'The warrior that faced a thousands foes flees at the sight of a maiden, a Swannemaiden in a cherry orchard!' She burst out laughing.

'Dwarf males are puritans my dear, they simply don't permit themselves the little pleasures of life. The notion that he had fallen in love was absurd to Scimitar. Dwarves don't fall in love, they take a wife from their own. To banish your image from his mind, he fasted for seven days. It was the suffering and imprisonment that unlocked the secret chamber in his heart, to which the maiden in the cherry orchard, had been exiled. Praise be, my dear that in these times of turmoil, dwarf culture is changing. The people of the Kingdom have been thrown together in strange and unexpected ways and when this evil passes, life will be different for all of us. Soon the young eagle, Theodorus, will return to the Convent and I will pen a note to Smithereen for him to carry back. Would you care to send a card to Scimitar?'

'It would be forward of me, Sunflower.'

'No, my love, not in time of peril. Scimitar lives on the edge of the abyss. It is better that he knows he is loved, before storming into battle.'

When Theodorus hopped into the room and perched at the end of Sunflower's bed, a small vessel containing two messages was sealed. While the young eagle related to Sunflower the happenings in Esteria, Helga tied carefully the leather strap with the messages attached around the eagle's neck.

Scimitar had been always a mystery to Slim. He had a deep affection for the Dwarf. One night, Slim noticed that Scimitar's eyes had wandered away from the maps and drawings on his desk and he was gazing at the fire. He wondered where his secret thoughts took him.

The silence in the room was broken by a peck on the window. Smithereen opened the door and saw Theodorus perched on the railing of the front steps. He beckoned to the young eagle and Theodorus perched on his broad shoulder. When they walked into the front room, all eyes were on the bird. Theodorus hopped on the back of an armchair and Smithereen undid the leather strap that held the small container. He took the note out, recognized the handwriting and a smile spread over his face.

'All angels be praised, friends, Sunflower is well.' Smithereen held the note closer to the chandelier and in a deep sing song voice read, 'A few more weeks my love, and I will shed these nettle leaves. Thanks be to God. An angel has hovered over me and nursed me through this dark night. I can see light again. Helga has embroidered red roses on a white dress, and I dream of the day when I shall shed these burning leaves and slip into the dress she is sewing for me.'

Laughter and relief spread around the table but Scimitar looked far away. Only when Smithereen put his arm around his brother's shoulder did Scimitar look up. 'A note for you, Skimmy, from the Convent.' Scimitar walked to the mantelpiece and opened the neatly folded card. Slim thought he saw on the unflappable Dwarf's face a slight blush, or was it a glow from embers in the fireplace? Scimitar carefully folded the card and retired to his room.

The Marquis had not been well and he spent much time in his room. When Duckie came in he would find his master seated by the window, looking out over the snow covered town. Seldom would the Marquis don his splendid uniform or his white feathered hat and he had refused all invitations to dine at the homes of leading burghers in town.

The nobleman sank into a deep depression. He reflected that all he had done was merely to parade around town in his dazzling outfit. Admiring looks from the pretty girls had made his head spin and his love for Dorothea had slipped into the recesses of his mind. He felt burdened with guilt. It was she who had saved him from a fate worse than death and he should have been searching for a way to undo the terrible curse that had petrified his Dorothea.

What could be done? He was confined in this town and come spring, violent Grolls would overrun Esteria. He felt caught between two millstones. Sitting by his desk, his head resting in his hands, the image of Seraphim came to him. One evening at the Graceful Neck, the white haired sage had spoken on the Dark Night of the Soul.

'Great God,' he had cried out, 'that is where I am, in the very middle of that dreadful night. Vanity has been my downfall.'

After days of agonized soul searching, Dorothea's image began appearing in his dreams. She rose up from the deeper layers of his psyche and entered his consciousness. He felt her slender hands touch his face. The faint light of dawn rose and broke the spell of his soul's dark night.

At the end of February the appalling weather took a turn for the better. Snow began to melt and as suddenly as the winter had come upon them, it vanished. Milder weather lifted the gloom.

The Grolls had suffered terribly from cold and hunger, but now a few transports with food and clothing had reached Zervos' army and with the return of the spring sun they recovered their usual insolence. Already they were talking about the loot to be had in Esteria and Lambarina. Some cast covetous eyes upon the Monastery on the hill behind the town, but strict orders had come down the lines to leave the monks in peace. Zervos knew that the Monastery would not be in their line of march and taking it would mean a loss of men and resources. The commander was superstitious and deep in his heart he feared supernatural retribution.

The next day a merewing brought news about more recruits and supplies crossing the Finnian Range. Zervos smiled, soon he would smash the wretched Dwarves and their volunteers.

The return of sunshine mesmerized the people of Esteria. For a few days they just sat in snow banks soaking up the sun. Scimitar and the Dwarves knew they had several weeks grace before the enemy would be able to move and before starting drills, they let the volunteers enjoy a few days of spring weather.

At the beginning of the week preparations were once again in full swing.

For ten days they worked from dawn to dusk. One morning at sunup, Scimitar saw Nightglider circling high above. Minutes later he perched on a wooden shield that the sappers had built to protect the archers. Nightglider read the question in Scimitar's eyes.

'Time is up, Scimitar. Reinforcements have crossed the summit.'

'How long Nightglider?'

'Three days Scimitar.'

He thanked Nightglider and rushed over to the Mansion to report the news. On the third day they saw the new troops trudging through the mud, drawing a tight circle around the town.

Scimitar had expected a large scale attack from all sides but the first enemy columns broke through the wild southern marshes. A sudden and violent assault at a single point took the town by surprise and nearly broke their line of defence. A half dozen Grolls penetrated into the town, but quickly were slain. Many of the retreating Grolls were struck by the deadly aim of the Esterian archers.

The attack had been a shock and several Dwarves had fallen in battle. The mood was sombre and the exhausted Dwarves and volunteers retired to catch some sleep. Their respite was not to be long lived. Elves, standing on the tower of the town hall, scanning the moonlit marshes, spotted Grolls emerging from stands of cedar. No night attack had been expected. The elven guards seized their trumpets and blew the warning signal. The trumpet blast caught Scimitar resting by the hearth. Seizing his sword, he rushed outside and ran towards the south gate. The renewed assault, hours after the retreat, had been totally unexpected. He realized that it would take the warriors a few moments to dress and to rush to the wall. It might be too late.

By the light of the full moon the Grolls were moving quickly. A troop of Grolls, carrying a ramp, was going to span the moat and force the gate. Scimitar could see their scales glistening in the moonlight. When he unsheathed his sword, the edge glowed a deep blue. The moment that the ramp touched the gate, he jumped down and rushed across. The glowing blue steel unnerved the first row of Grolls and they fell back.

Slim, who had been working late, had heard Scimitar leave. He dressed quickly and only minutes later hurried after him. Climbing atop the town wall, he froze at the scene before him. At the far end of the ramp stood the solitary Dwarf, wielding his magic sword and scattered by the moat lay a number of Grolls. Precious time had been gained. More Dwarves and volunteers were now arriving at the wall. The Esterian archers began sending their deadly arrows creating havoc amongst enemy troops.

Slim shouted to Scimitar to retreat but his words were drowned by the din of battle. To his horror he saw a Rover sidle along the edge of the moat. The Rover waited until Scimitar turned aside and then let fly the heavy steel shaft. The razor edged point pierced Scimitar's chest and felled the valiant Dwarf. Smithereen, who had just arrived at the gate, jumped down, swirling ball and chain. The formidable weapon scythed down the Grolls advancing on Scimitar and gave him a few precious moments to pick up his brother and carry him to safety. Ready hands reached out to help him up the wall. The surprise attack had failed and a Rover Captain blew the retreat.

Scimitar, resting in Smithereen's arms, smiled at the circle gathered around. 'Friends I have failed you. Forgive me.'

'It is not so Scimitar.' Smithereen said gently. 'You have always led the way and ventured where others dared not go.' Scimitar's head sank on Smithereen shoulder and his hand rested on his arm.

'Hark, my brother, the sound of trumpets calling in the distant mist.' These were the last words spoken by the dwarf warrior and Volker was there to record them for posterity.

Scimitar lay perfectly still, the thin spirals of breath, condensing in the cold air, becoming fainter and fainter. When Slim raised his eyes he beheld the figure of a lady rimmed in light.

'Amaranth,' he whispered, 'the enchantress has come for Scimitar.' Now Slim could see Scimitar rise and take the outstretched hand of his spirit guide. Swiftly they ascended and vanished in a haze of light.

43

Journey To The Moles

Gingerly, Svanhild placed the golden plate on the oak shelf above the open hearth. Catching the rays of the rising sun, it filled the room with a golden sheen.

After their ordeal in the snowy hollow, Svanhild, Sidonia and Oarflake had spent several weeks recovering from lack of food and exhaustion. The strain of the last year had taken its toll and it took an effort of will to even think about leaving again and finding their way to the Kingdom of the Moles. Only Weiss was full of bounce. Edel had talked often about the time he had spent in the tunnels of the Moles and Weiss was keen to see them.

Ambrosia was cooking breakfast for her guests. How she had enjoyed their company! Every night they had gathered around the glowing embers in the hearth. Oarflake would light his meerschaum and Ambrosia, taking up her knitting, would look at Sidonia, pleading silently for another tale of Elven Lore.

Their departure had been delayed by winter storms and deep in her heart Ambrosia had been grateful. She had dreaded the idea of another winter in isolation. Many a lonely winter they had spent in exile. The isolation became more forbidding as the years went by. Ambrosia knew that Svanhild and Sidonia had no choice but to set out again. She would miss them terribly.

It was the beginning of February and soon the sun would brighten their days. Thank heavens, Oarflake would stay home this time, his girth was too substantial to crawl into mole tunnels.

Svanhild, Sidonia and Weiss would travel together. Leonardo had promised to take them to the Lake of Shadows, close to the realm of the Seven. Hot springs fed the Lake of Shadows and the warm waters of the long lake affected the climate. Once they reached the lake, there would not be enough snow left to travel by wolf sled and they would make their way on foot through enemy territory, travelling through the marshes and the great pine forest until they reached the sands of the red desert.

Weiss had never travelled in the land of the moles but Edel had often spoken of his experiences. Weiss knew that the moles had splendid underground tunnels and that mole guards were posted at each entrance, in the red desert, to their underground complex. By daylight, merewings patrolled the desert and it was dangerous to travel. They would have to be careful and try to attract the attention of moles on guard duty. Weiss had a fair idea where they were likely to find an entrance to the tunnels.

When Svanhild saw the sun rising above the lake, she wanted to leave that morning but Oarflake suggested they depart the next day. The wolf team had to be assembled and provisions prepared. No sooner had they finished breakfast, when Oarflake walked across the room and seized the magic horn. He stepped outside and raised the spiral ivory to his lips. Three times the sound of the horn resonated over hill and dale, the deep tones awakening all the creatures that breathed the air of spring. Bear and squirrel turned over in their winter sleep. The badgers, Ludwig and Berend, sprang out of bed and peeked out their front door, but by now the badgers were used to the sound and decided to go back to sleep.

Leonardo and Andante, enjoying the early sunshine in front of their lair, were galvanized by the sound and in an instant the wolf pair was speeding through the snow towards the Lake of the Coloured Fishes. Only when they arrived in front of the cottage did they come to a full stop. Resting on their haunches, they let out a joyous yelp.

Oarflake rushed out to greet them. With long red tongues hanging out and thick winter fur glistening in the sun, they stared at him. He saw the twinkle in their eyes and heartily congratulated them. Already he knew their secret; over the holiday season they had become life partners. The badgers, Ludwig and Berend, had spilled the beans. Ludwig had complained a good deal about wild partying by the wolf pack but Berend had done the sensible thing and joined the Great Gray in the merry making and a jolly good time he had of it.

Oarflake explained the mission to the wolves. Always anxious for adventure, they promised to round up the team and return on the morrow.

Oarflake spent the day preparing the sled, harnesses and provisions. He strung a new bow for Svanhild and made sure that her quiver was filled with arrows. Ambrosia cooked a splendid farewell dinner and that night, seated around the table, they drank a toast of blueberry wine to the success of the journey. During the evening they recalled the many strange and wonderful adventures that they had shared. A feeling of finality about the upcoming trip bound them close together. It was the last chance to turn the tide.

When they arose next dawn, Ambrosia was stirring porridge on the stove. Already Oarflake had carried out their packs and tied them down on the sled. They were seated at the breakfast table when the wolf team galloped across the frozen lake, clouds of fine snow glittering in their wake.

Oarflake and Weiss hitched the wolves. Svanhild double-checked the round shape at the bottom of her pack before putting it on the sled. The three made but a light load and the wolves shot forward speeding across the lake and vanishing quickly into the trees on the far shore. Ambrosia and Oarflake waved from the porch but even Sidonia could not see them for the cloud of flying snow behind.

By late afternoon the distance between the evergreens flashing by had increased. Birch and aspen appeared and soon they found themselves on the edge of the marshes. Through most of the day, the wolves had been galloping at top speed, now they began to slow down.

When Svanhild saw a stand of cedars, she called out to Leonardo. The team came to halt on a gentle rise covered with trees that promised to make a fair campsite.

Svanhild untied the large burlap bag of wolf food and fed the team. The Great Grey were speedy eaters. When they had finished licking their chops, they formed a ring around their charges and sank into a deep slumber.

Weiss who had gone off in search of firewood returned with birch bark and dead branches. They quickly got a blaze going and stew on the boil. Seated by the bright flames and ringed by a team of sleeping wolves they felt perfectly safe.

Next morning they started out in a fine drizzle and by noon were splashing through puddles. They were nearing the Lake of Shadows, a large expanse of water fed by hot springs and surrounded by lush vegetation.

At lunch they peeled off their winter jackets. Most of the snow had disappeared and by early afternoon Svanhild saw that the wolves were straining hard to move the sled through the slush. From here on they would have to travel on foot. She threw her arms around Leonardo and Andante and thanked the great beasts. The long red tongues gave her an affectionate lick.

Shouldering their packs, they began a long trek through the marshes. For some time they could still hear the wolves howling a sad farewell. Although Svanhild knew that gladly they would have risked their hides, nothing could be gained by travelling farther south with the Great Grey. The snow was gone and the team would likely be detected by enemy patrols.

Svanhild had attached the quiver of arrows to her belt and carried her bow in her right hand. Sidonia was close behind but Weiss skipped ahead reconnoitring the terrain. Dusk had fallen over the marshes, but they plodded on. At a small cedar grove they rested for a couple of hours and nibbled on the snacks that Ambrosia had provided. By midnight the rain stopped and moonlight shimmered on puddles covering a peat bog. Chances of detection would be slight at night and they decided to keep moving. Weiss was always sprinting ahead to the next clump of bushes and signalled when all seemed clear. They knew they were in no man's land, close to the border of the Land of Darkness. Enemy patrols could appear at anytime.

They joined Weiss in a stand of stunted cedars and stopped to catch their breath when Sidonia espied silhouettes moving in the distance. Weiss was about to take off again for a copse of willow bushes on the horizon but Sidonia put her hand on his shoulder.

'Wait Weiss, until that patch of moonlight travelling across the marshes reaches the willows.' Moments later her sharp eyes descried three figures against the rays of the moon. Shrouded in haze rising from the marshes, they prowled through alder bushes. Sidonia knew by their size that two were Groll warriors but a tiny figure in front, partly hidden in the fog, appeared be an Elf.

Svanhild held her breath as she looked at her elven friend's startled expression. Sidonia taking her hand, whispered a warning.

'A Black Elf is leading the patrol. They are using the Black Elves because of their extraordinary vision.' A bright patch of moonlight revealed the Black Elf speeding ahead of the Grolls, leaping across the marshes and swiftly approaching their hideout.

'He must have seen us, quick, duck behind the shrubs.'

It was too late. The black shape was flying towards them, bounding from knoll to knoll. Now all could see him, his black cape fluttering behind and skilfully navigating between ponds and puddles.

Svanhild gazed at the dark Elf darting over the marshes. Through the last year they had faced peril and privation, their goal was within reach and now the black imp was threatening to put an end to it all.

A wave of anger seized her and she reached for her bow. Never before had she drawn in anger. Sidonia whispered softly.

'It is Lightfoot, Captain Cobalt's right hand and second in command of the Black Elves.'

Svanhild placed an arrow on the string and using every ounce of strength, pulled it back. Her right eye was fixed on the tiny figure dancing through the reeds. At the edge of a small pond he hesitated for a second before leaping across. His black shape was silhouetted against the moonlight when the arrow caught him in midair, Svanhild whimpered as the traitor tumbled, headfirst, into the water.

Sidonia saw that the Grolls were still waiting for a signal from their elf scout. With their poor night vision they had probably failed to see Lightfoot's demise. Svanhild was stunned by her deadly aim. The gentle Sidonia, who never in her life had contemplated violence, put an arm around her shoulder.

'It had to be, Svanhild. Don't give it a second thought.' It was Weiss who broke the spell. He took them by the hand and pulled them out of the grove.

'Quick my friends,' he urged, 'Quick. We must run for the pine forest. A bank of fog shielded them from the Grolls still looking for Lightfoot. He appeared to have vanished without a trace.

They ran swiftly, sometimes up to their knees in water or thrashing through willows and alder copses. As they gained height the going became easier.

Stopping to catch their breath Sidonia could see on, the hills ahead, a broad band of green. It was the pine forest they would have to cross before reaching the red desert sands in the land of the Seven Lords.

Moonlight flooded the marshes that they had just left behind. Looking back it was only Sidonia who could see the outline of two Grolls bending over a pond. They had found their elven scout with a telling arrow in his breast.

As they gained the higher ground the going became lighter. Soon they reached the first stands of pine. The moon's rays filtered through the canopies of the pines and illumined the carpet of needles down below. From time to time they walked through a valley where pines mingled with stands of birch and oak in bud. Holding hands, with Weiss leading, they covered many miles before the first signs of dawn forced them to seek a hiding place in which to pass the daylight hours.

Weiss spotted a clump of rhododendron bushes. He knew that often they grew around water. They penetrated deep into the mass of rhododendrons, brushing away the green shiny leaves. Stands of stinging nettles were everywhere but desperate to find a safe haven, they paid no heed to the itching and burning. On reaching a small pond, they quenched their thirst and soothed their nettle burns in the cold water. Svanhild slumped against an ancient tree trunk. She was shaking and kneeling in front of her, Sidonia took her trembling hands.

'Sidonia, Sidonia,' sobbed Svanhild, 'I have killed a living being, I have taken an elven life.' Sidonia's voice sounded unusually stern.

'You have served the cause of justice, Svanhild. Your arrow pierced an evil heart.' Svanhild cast a grateful glance at the loving eyes hovering over her and she pressed Sidonia's hand before sliding down on a bed of leaves.

Weiss awoke in bright daylight. Gingerly he crept through the bushes until he could see sunbeams shining on the forest floor. Judging by the light it was late afternoon and perhaps they should have an early start. He bounced back through the bushes to wake Svanhild and Sidonia. They washed in the pond and ate the dried meat that Ambrosia had put in their packs. It was still bright out and Sidonia suggested they wait until dusk. Patrols might have been alerted after Lightfoot's death. They would have to be doubly careful.

Weiss tiptoed to the outer ring of rhododendrons and scanned the pine forest. All seemed clear. He lay down resting his head on a needle covered knoll. The lattice of light and the singing of the pines soothed him and a feeling of peace stole over his soul.

Then unexpectedly Weiss was startled out of his reverie. Above the singing of the pines, high above the range of mortal ear, soared a voice. It was a frequency only Fairies could hope to catch. He raised himself and looked up. A golden sheen veiled the top of the great pine. The singing became louder and slowly the golden haze descended. Then a single fleck of gold emerged from the cloud and glided towards him on a ray of sunlight. Only when it came close could Weiss see it clearly. His astonishment knew no bounds when a minute Fairy hovered before his eyes.

The golden wings moved like a hummingbird's and the tiny translucent body was exquisitely shaped. Weiss, well versed in fairy lore, knew that the creature was a Golden Fairy, the minute species from which his own race had sprung. Barely had he regained his composure when jubilant laughter greeted him.

'Greetings to you, my Mountain Fairy. We feared we had lost touch with our offspring. And here you are in a strange and dangerous forest far from your beloved lake and mountains. How fares the noble Queen Tuluga?' Weiss was both pleased and astonished by how much the Golden Fairy knew of his people. He told her of their dangerous plight. When he had finished talking, the Golden Fairy's laugh cascaded up and down an entire octave.

'Mountain Fairies always were adventurers, Weiss. And that romantic streak in your soul has once more landed you in a fine pickle. Will you slay dragons and snatch the Princess from the altar? We shall do what we can to assist. We have no love for Grolls and Black Elves. They destroy our forests and steal our honey.' Weiss looked astounded.

'You make honey?'

'We keep bees and high up in the canopy of the great pines we tend our hives. Pine honey heals the ill and energizes the body. Our Fairies will bring refreshments to the rhododendron bushes where you and your friends are hiding.'

Weiss was fascinated by the tiny shape hovering before him, its wings oscillating at phenomenal speed. He felt a sense of kinship with the creatures who were the ancestors of his own people. Their extraordinary hearing in the upper registers had been transmitted to the Mountain Fairies. Yes, it was true long ago, fairies had been airborne creatures. Never in his life had he imagined that the mythical beings still lived on earth.

'Wait until Edel hears this,' he mused. The musical voice of his airborne friend broke his trend of thought.

'And who might Edel be?' sang the golden voice.. Tears welled in his eyes. 'My name is Weiss. Edel, companion of my youth and bosom friend, is a captive of the Seven Lords. A Black Elf betrayed him.'

Edel and Weiss, how charming! I pray you will be reunited,' sang out his visitor. 'My name is Bloom and I am the speaker for our people. We will try to guide you safely through the forest. The Black Elf scouts and the Grolls patrol the area but we will raise the alarm when they pass this way'

'How will you warn us, Bloom?'

'How did you hear us in the first place Weiss?'

'I heard a second harmonic of voices rising high above the singing of the pines.'

'Weiss, hearken carefully for only you can hear the range of our singing. We will sing our favourite hymn praising the miracle of life, the miracle of life which encompasses all being.'

'Encompasses all being,' pondered Weiss aloud.

'Yes, Weiss, all being. Even Matista and the Seven Lords play a part on the stage of life.'

'Now listen well, my Fairy fair. When we are singing, all is well and you can travel safely, the moment we stop, danger threatens and you must hide.' Bloom laughed at Weiss' puzzled expression.

'Fear not, my friend, you will hear the silence and if you fail to listen I will buzz you. Now hasten back Weiss. At dusk my Fairies will come to the rhododendron dell with refreshments.

Weiss thanked the Golden Fairy. The tiny creature had a compelling presence and inspired a sense of reverence even in a Mountain Fairy. He bowed the knee before her and ran all the way back to the pond to share news of his amazing encounter with Svanhild and Sidonia. They were astonished and could hardly wait for the Golden Fairies to descend.

Weiss dipped his tired feet in the pond and leaned back against a rhododendron shrub. Soon he dozed off but at sundown he woke with a start and looked up. Above the rustling of leaves rose the enchanting melody of the hymn, celebrating the miracle of life. This time many voices were singing.

'Hark Sidonia, Hark Svanhild, the Golden Fairies are singing.' They gave him a puzzled look, for the singing soared above their range of hearing. Gazing upwards they perceived the golden haze descending and then they heard tiny feet landing on the rhodo leaves. The Fairies now sang in a lower key and Sidonia and Svanhild could clearly hear their voices, such voices they had never heard before.

myriad the miracles around us
wonders that astound us
fairies see the mystery
in the lily and the rose
and read the secret code
of the force that made her
the signature of the creator

The golden voices lifted their hearts and they felt transported to a new dimension. In the semi darkness, the Fairies emitted a soft golden light.

Bloom flew forward landing on the tip of a large leaf, Svanhild and Sidonia stared in wonder at the translucent body of the minute Fairy now so close to them. The singing stopped and another Fairy joined Bloom at the tip of the leaf. She presented to Svanhild a crystal vessel and then gazed deep into her eyes as if reading a secret that dwelt there.

'Beloved Swannemaiden, keep this crystal vessel filled with magic nectar, until you reach the desert in the land of the Seven. Even a drop will quench your thirst and render strength. I trust it will last until you gain entrance into the tunnels of the Mole Confederacy.'

Before Svanhild and the others had a chance to thank them, Bloom and her companion had disappeared. Now other Fairies descended carrying silver trays. Some were laden with wafers and honey, others came with bottles of fermented nectar and transparent candies.

Seated by the waters of the small pond they enjoyed the delicate dishes. Directly they finished eating, drowsiness stole over them and they were lulled into a deep sleep by the voices singing in the pine canopies high above.

When they woke at dawn, they felt refreshed and rested. Looking around they discovered that while they slept, the Golden Fairies had paid a visit. By the edge of the pond was spread a splendid array of dishes. They took their time nibbling at the dainty food. There was no reason to hurry until Weiss could hear the singing, giving the all clear signal. It was nearly noon when Weiss's face lit up.

'Above the whispering of the pines I hear voices singing. Sidonia, Svanhild we must hurry and travel while we can.'

They shouldered their packs and walked out of the rhododendron dell. Needles and leaves covered the forest floor and the going was smooth.

Marching swiftly for several hours, they reached the southern end of the forest. Already the pines began to thin and by late afternoon the vegetation had changed. The singing continued and Weiss was so used to it by now that he startled when suddenly it ceased. Svanhild and Sidonia were not aware of any change but Weiss sounded the alarm.

'Quick,' he whispered, 'The Golden Fairies have finished singing.'

Svanhild spotted a pile of rocks and the trio ran towards it. They slipped through an opening between two huge boulders. Near their shelter, strange contorted trees and shrubs with fierce thorns and flaming red flowers, provided some protection from the afternoon sun.

Sidonia, peeking between the rocks, reeled in horror at the sight of two Black Elves followed by a Groll and a black hound. The huge jaws were covered with foam. She shuddered and turned away.

Though they were well hidden from sight, the black dog likely would pick up their scent. Sidonia looked again and saw the hound sniffing restlessly. Black Elves were looking behind trees and shrubs. In their eyes she could see the anger at the recent loss of one of their own.

The dog came within thirty yards of their hideout, when suddenly he became disoriented. The reason soon became apparent. A horrid smell carried by a light breeze wafted into their shelter. It was dust from the giant Purple Cloud mushroom. When touched, the mushrooms emit a profusion of dark purple dust, which makes breathing difficult. They had to fight the urge to sneeze lest the sound betray them. After a few minutes the air cleared and Sidonia took another peek. The black hound, confused by the overwhelming scent, aimlessly wandered around. Suddenly Weiss smiled and Sidonia and Svanhild looked at him in wonder.

'Laughter,' he whispered, 'I hear peals of laughter high above. When Sidonia looked again the patrol had vanished among the trees. Soon a golden cloud drifted towards them and Bloom landed on a stunted olive tree in the centre of their shelter. She lowered her voice so all could hear.

'Our lookouts saw them coming. When the hound caught your scent, we dropped down and danced on the violet canopy of a huge mushroom until clouds of purple dust blocked the light of the sun.'

Before they had a chance to thank them again, Bloom and her Golden Fairies were floating high above and only Weiss could hear the sound of their laughter. When the mirth died down and the singing began, Weiss knew that the coast was clear. They set out once more.

Leaving the last trees behind, the heat grew intense. They entered the land of the red earth where a few withering shrubs survived amidst a myriad of blooming cacti. A shallow ridge provided shelter from the sun and here they rested until dusk. In the daytime it was perilous to traverse the expanse of desert, the heat was sweltering and merewings easily could spot them. It was safer at night and the desert would be cool. They drank the nectar from the crystal vessel Bloom had given to Svanhild and a surge of well being enveloped them. Just before midnight they set out again. The moon cast enough light to travel by, and they moved swiftly over the desert sands. Weiss knew that they would soon reach the Confederacy of the Moles and they began looking for signs of an entrance to the underground tunnels.

It was close to dawn and they had not yet found a trace of the Moles. They made for a distant cliff and just before sunrise reached a steep rock face. Weiss scouted around the cliffs and found a small cave. It was large enough to give shelter from the sun and they decided to rest until dusk. Comfortably bedded down on the warm sand Sidonia looked through a crack at the desert landscape. The first rays of the rising sun turned the sand bright red and the desert stretched as far as the eye could see. How would they ever find an entrance to the tunnels of the Moles, in this unending sea of sand?

High above the Lake of the Coloured Fishes soared the Wood Owls, Solomon and Kasper. Svanhild had been much on their mind. They had been worried about the fair Swannemaiden and the slight Elf. That Weiss made up one of the party was another cause of concern. The owls didn't think much of the light hearted Mountain Fairies. A romantic impulse or a chance for glory would send them dashing off where even angels fear to tread.

They swooped into a steep dive levelling off near the cottage of the Gnomes. Ambrosia, who had seen the dark shadows moving over the ice, stood in the doorway and invited them in for a snack of smoked meat.

'Culture has its advantages, Deputy. Smoking meat enhances its flavour.'

'Very true Chief, terrestrials have made many useful inventions. Ingenious when it comes to the how of things. Owls focus on the why. Wisdom is our domain and that's where we have made our reputation.'

'Well put, Deputy, precise wording. Your literary talents please me.'

Oarflake explained to the owls that the party had left several days ago and by now should have reached the pine forest.

'I fear that they may be hard put, Chief Solomon, to find a tunnel entrance in that desert of red sand.'

'It will be our pleasure to lend a helping hand,' the owls hooted in unison.

Oarflake and Ambrosia cast them a grateful glance. It was dusk when the owls lifted off but a gibbous moon supplied enough light to survey the terrain below.

Solomon's night vision was phenomenal, even for an owl. Flying over the marshes, he spotted activity below. Black shapes were moving around a stand of weeping willows. The owls went into a steep dive and landed in a stand of cedars. To their astonishment they beheld, laid out on a bier of woven willow branches, a body wrapped in a black cape, a peaked cap rested on its chest. Numerous Black Elves had gathered around their fallen comrade.

'Deputy, it is the scoundrel Lightfoot, second in command of the black pests. Dead as a doornail. It was he and Captain Cobalt who led the separatists out of the Kingdom.'

'Justice triumphs in the end, Chief. Perfidious knave, he had it coming!'

'Perfidious knave, I like it Deputy, a sensitive way of putting it but I am afraid a battle may have taken place. We must make sure that Svanhild and her friends have not been taken prisoner by the black imps.'

'Follow me, Deputy,' said Solomon rising from the cedar tree and flying across the marshes. They scanned a large area, but there was no sign of the three travellers. They decided to fly over the forest and search the desert on the other side. Slight were the chances of finding the lost travellers amongst the trees. When they reached the other side of the great forest they perched in a tall pine and there rested for the remainder of the day. There was a real danger of encountering merewings over the red sands. The black birds would be able to spot them miles away. In the dark they would be no match for the owls.

At dusk they set forth flying over the rapidly thinning trees. Once in the desert they enjoyed sailing on the updrafts rising from the hot desert sands. The darkness deepened and beams from a rising moon illumined the cacti, many of which only bloomed at night. The Chief and his Deputy were fascinated by the yellow, white, gold and purple splashes against the desert sand.

'Remarkable, Chief, a very different world from the hereditary forest.'

'Beautiful, Deputy, but no trees to perch in. Those huge cacti sprout fearful spikes, the only place to land is sand or rocks.'

They were rather enjoying the splendid nightscape until columns of black smoke rising from one of the armouries reminded them that they had penetrated into the heart of enemy territory.

Minutes later they spotted the brightly lit palace of the Seven. They banked sharply west and began flying a grid pattern over the desert.

Down in a hollow, sheltered by a large rock stood two mole guards.

'Lovely night, Alfredo,' piped the tallest of the pair.

'Tolerably so, Horatio. The moonlight is hard on the eyes, but the air is cool and pleasant. One gets a different perspective of the earth, by standing on top of it.'

'Very true, my friend. Point of view is everything.' A high pitched whistling sound put an end to the conversation.

'Owls diving!' yelled Horatio, scurrying towards the tunnel. As he disappeared underground, Alfredo was right at his heels.

When Solomon and Kasper touched down on the rock they were disappointed. The moles had vanished and they might have had news about Svanhild and her friends. At the tunnel opening, they could hear a faint yelling.

'Owl warning, red alert!' Fortunately Ben the Mole, Chief Justice of the Confederacy was standing nearby as the terrified guards rushed down the tunnel. When they saw the figure of the imperturbable Judge they stopped in their tracks.

'Owls, Chief, owls at the door.' The judge folded his hands in a gesture of peace.

'Fear not, my friends. It is more than a generation ago that one of our brethren was taken by the wide eyed birds. The owls have had a change of heart when they learned about our evolved way of life. I received assurances from Chief Solomon that Moles have now been added to the list of protected species.'

Leaving Alfredo and Horatio standing with their mouths wide open, Ben the Mole strode forward and stuck his head through the tunnel opening.

The owls loomed awfully large and the moonlight, reflecting in the yellow eyes, took his breath away. Some quick breathing exercises helped to regain his balance. An inner voice told him all was well, the owls had come for a reason. He made a slight bow and said politely, 'Welcome great birds, we trust your mission is one of peace. Ben the Mole, Chief Justice of the Confederacy, at your service.'

'Greetings, Chief Justice. We have come to enlist your help. We fear for Svanhild and the elven maiden, Sidonia, travelling towards your realm.'

Ben the Mole looked perplexed and his glasses almost slid off his long nose as he rested his head on his right paw and thought deeply.

'Chief Justice,' said Kasper, 'does the name Weiss tell you something. Weiss is their travel companion.' In the tiny mole eyes a light went on.

'Ah so, my winged friends, Weiss, the Mountain Fairy, Edel's Weiss, his bosom friend. For some time Edel was an honoured guest at my home. Now it all comes back to me. I hope and pray Edel made it safely back to the land of the Dwarves. He was a volatile chap, but a charmer of the first water. We enjoyed having him.'

'Edel returned safely to the land of the Dwarves, my dear Judge, but he got himself into a pickle not long afterwards.'

'Ah so, I thought as much,' sighed Ben, 'he was a bit of a dreamer, I wonder where he ended up.'

'That is another story, Ben the Mole,' said Solomon, 'no doubt Weiss will fill you in, that is if the party isn't lost in the desert or worse.'

'We will do all that we can to find Svanhild, Sidonia and Weiss. Our wards, the elven children would be delighted to have a visitor from the land of the Elves. Mole guards will scout the desert, my dear owls. If they made it safely out of the forest we will find them. There are many of us you know!'

The owls smiled and flapped their wings signifying their farewell. Solomon nodded to Kasper and lifted off. They felt that they had done all that could be done and knew the noble moles would leave no stone unturned.

Ben the Mole waved farewell and hastened back into the tunnel to confer with the other Judges. It was not long before a decision was reached and a battalion of warrior Moles scurried into the desert in search of the lost party. For protection from the cold night air they wore down filled jackets and stuck in their belts were huge knives. In their pockets they carried wooden goggles with tiny slits, in case they failed to return before sunrise.

All night long a legion of moles crisscrossed the desert sands. Close to dawn, just when the search was to be called off, a young mole warrior spotted a merewing circling high above a distant rock formation. Summoning the other moles in his unit, he rushed toward the spot where moon shadows of wings moved over the sand, in front of a cliff face. They spotted another merewing sitting by a cave entrance. There were fifteen Moles and when they drew their fearsome knives the bird thought the better of it and took off. The Moles entered the rock enclave and found Svanhild, Sidonia and Weiss wrapped in a deep slumber. Some recognized Weiss and woke him first.

Weiss was astonished to see a mole guard standing by his side.

'Hurry up mate,' shouted the mole, 'merewings know your hideout.'

Weiss, instantly awake, sprang into action.

'Delighted to see a mole, at last!' he shouted and heartily shook his paw. The mole guard knew he had found the right party, for Weiss looked the spitting image of Edel, at least in the mole's foggy eyesight. Sidonia and Svanhild were sitting upright by this time and the guard explained the need for haste.

Already the desert was bathed in red light. The Moles donned their wooden goggles and although small in stature, they looked quite fierce. Flanked by the Mole warriors, the trio walked several hundred yards until they came to a dense stand of cacti. The yellow cactus flowers which had bloomed all night now were closing their petals to keep out the rays of the desert sun, yet they still looked beautiful and Sidonia halted for a moment to admire them. The patrol leader walked through a thicket of shrubbery and beckoned them to follow. The tunnel entrance was well concealed by several rocks.

'Heavens above,' exclaimed Svanhild, 'I can never squeeze through there.' But before she knew it, the mole warriors, small as they were, had moved one of the rocks aside. Svanhild crawled in, followed by Sidonia and Weiss.

Once their eyes had adjusted they could see that the tunnel gradually increased in size. Soon they were walking upright. Sconces on the wall supported tall flickering candles casting a soft light throughout the tunnel. The underground pathways did not seem as forbidding as they had imagined and they breathed a sigh of relief.

After a short walk they turned into a wider tunnel illuminated by torches. Doors opened on both sides of the tunnel and heads popped out to stare in astonishment at the strange procession.

Coming to a large circular space they could see tunnels running in all directions and following their guides they passed through an archway into a wide corridor ending in an antechamber. At the far end was a set of solid oak doors. Their guide let fall a heavy brass knocker. The door opened revealing the imposing figure of Ben the Mole and two other Judges, seated behind the bench.

'It is Benjamin, Chief Justice of the High Court,' one of the guards whispered into Svanhild's ear.

'Chief Justice,' Svanhild burst out, 'we have come on an urgent mission and entreat your aid.'

'Of course your mission is urgent, why would children of the light come to the tunnels of the moles, if it weren't urgent? Ah, I see the fire in your eyes. You have a temper but haste does not work here, dear lady of the swans. Think of our tunnels, what would happen if they had been built in haste? They would crumble and the old tunnels reaching to the Palace of the Seven would be beyond repair.'

Svanhild realized the old mole knew a good deal more than she had guessed and kept her silence.

'Come closer dear friends, and let us have a look at you. Even under the best of conditions, our eyesight is marginal.' The three of them walked up to the bench, bowing politely before the three judges and Ben the Mole addressed them in his formal capacity.

'Welcome to the Confederacy, I apologize to you, my weary travellers, for this formality. Alas, it is the law. All who enter our realm must be cleared by the court. All are considered dangerous, unless proven otherwise. It stands to reason does it not?' The other judges, all clad in black robes, nodded solemnly.

'A spotless character profile is required to enter into these sacred halls. That at least is the theory,' he concluded with a smile.

'Now let me introduce my colleagues, Orpheus on my left and Nimbus on my right.'

Orpheus adjusted his glasses which continually were sliding down his wet snout and took a good look at the trio facing him.

'Ah so,' he muttered, 'strange creatures indeed, yet the vibrations seem to be positive. If I am not mistaken we have here with us a maiden from the Land of the Swans, an elven lady and another Mountain Fairy. Yes I remember that fellow Edel, who seemed to be in perpetual motion.'

'It makes the matter quite simple,' chuckled Ben the Mole, 'Weiss the Mountain Fairy is the latter half of Edelweiss. Since Edel passed our inquest with flying colours, I vouch for Weiss.'

The logic seemed irrefutable and the other judges nodded vigorously.

'Svanhild's fame already has reached our ears and Sidonia is an elven maid from the land of Queen Orchidae. That says it all.'

'Not so quick, Ben the Mole,' objected a severe looking Orpheus, 'remember that there have been Black Elves.'

'But they were not elven maidens, Orpheus. Look at her lovely features, my dear mole.' Orpheus once more adjusted his glasses and took a good look.

'Quite right, Ben the Mole. The countenance inspires trust. The aura around her head shines brightly and I vote in favour.' Nimbus too raised his paw in support and recorded the approval of the court in a black ledger.

Ben the Mole stepped from behind his bench and shook their hands, officially welcoming them to the Confederacy.

Afterwards Benjamin took the three of them aside and asked about the golden tablet. Svanhild was again astonished by how much he knew and told him that they had recovered the golden plate and were trying to find a way into the palace.

'My dear friends,' explained Ben, 'you know that the elven sisters are our wards and Elmira, the youngest, has the gift of spirit travel, she has told us of your mission and already we have sent out our champion diggers, to explore a network of abandoned tunnels that lead all the way to the palace. They will report back within two or three days.

'There is nothing that we can do until the team reports back, so for the next few days you must rest and gather your strength for the days ahead.'

Ben's wife, Rochelle, had been very fond of Edel and Ben knew that she would insist on having Weiss stay with them. Nimbus invited Sidonia and Svanhild to be guests at his own home.

Nimbus and Consolata had been married for many years, all their children had left home and there was plenty of space for guests. Weary though the guests were, Consolata's warm welcome lifted their spirits and touched their hearts. When the silver-furred mole lady took their hands between her paws, it felt like an electric current passing through their arms and they felt energized and reassured. The small creature seemed to be a channel for celestial energy.

They had long talks with Consolata who was eager to learn of their adventures. At night she played her miniature violin lulling Sidonia and Svanhild into a peaceful sleep.

After a hearty breakfast of roots and a cup of dandelion coffee Consolata suggested that they meet the elven children. They followed their hostess through the front door and into a labyrinth of well-lit tunnels many of them decorated with murals.

A short walk took them to the central plaza. Orchestras played at outdoor cafes. Shops and sidewalk stands displayed a variety of goods. Svanhild and Sidonia were amazed at the wide selection of roots and spices. Some of the shops carried silverwork made in the dwarf smithies and traded for roots and rare minerals.

In the centre of the plaza sparkled a fountain lit by torches. Svanhild and Sidonia were fascinated by the fine mist of water rising.

'The fountain is fed by underground springs,' Consolata explained, 'one of our engineers came up with the idea.' They walked around the fountain and on the other side of the water curtain, seated on the low wall they beheld the three elven sisters. The moment that they caught sight of Sidonia, they sprang up and rushed towards her.

'Elven sister,' called out Elmira the youngest of the three, 'you have come at last.' Sidonia embraced the three.

'My dear Elmira, how did you know that we had travelled hither?'

Consolata, standing on the fountain wall, whispered into her ear.

'Did not you know Sidonia, Elmira has the gift of spirit travel? When the three sisters found refuge amongst us the enchantress bestowed a special gift on each. Annabelle received the gift of music, Galatea, beauty and Elmira, spirit travel.' The three sisters were delighted to meet Svanhild and lightly they kissed her cheeks.

Sidonia, looking down one of the tunnels leading to the plaza, saw Orpheus and Weiss sauntering towards them. As soon as Weiss saw them, he leapt forward and bowed before the elven sisters. All three had met Edel and they realized that it must be Weiss who was standing before them. Elmira's laughter welcomed him. Never before had he heard laughter like that. It reminded him of sparkling water and tinkling bells. He understood why Ensten had carved Elmira's face, wreathed in laughter.

Sidonia, sensing that Elmira was anxious to talk, took her hand. They sat down at a small table at a nearby café. Sidonia explained to Elmira about the golden tablet and the ancient prophecy. Elmira only smiled and she asked no questions, it was as if she had known all along. When Sidonia had finished, she asked her about elven land and Queen Orchidae, and spoke of her longing to return to the land of her foremothers, once peace had returned to the Kingdom.

Svanhild and Consolata joined them and Svanhild asked how they might find a way to the Palace of the Seven.

'You must ask the Judges,' suggested Consolata, 'Come to our home tonight for supper. Orpheus and Benjamin are coming too and we shall find a way to reach the palace.'

That night the fur of many moles glistened in the candlelight at Nimbus and Consolata's home. The mole ladies' coats turned deep silver in later life and Svanhild thought them very beautiful. Consolata opened a set of sliding doors, doubling the size of the dining room.

Ben the Mole and Rochelle arrived with Weiss and the elven sisters. While they were waiting for Orpheus to appear, Weiss told stories of his homeland and the love for music that his people shared with the moles. There were many questions about Edel who was fondly remembered. Tears glistened in many eyes when they heard of Edel's capture by the Black Elves.

At first, Svanhild and Sidonia had felt awkward being so much taller than the moles, but now they were quite used to it. Sometimes when the moles wanted to make sure that they could hear their voices, they would jump onto a stool to be face to face.

When Consolata and Rochelle appeared in black gowns offset with gold ornaments, Svanhild and Sidonia held their breath. The mole ladies looked glamorous. Orpheus, who arrived late, was wearing a black suit.

When all were seated, Consolata, assisted by two small girls, served dinner. There were dishes of roasted root, prepared with a variety of spices. Although the food was unfamiliar, Sidonia, Svanhild and Weiss found it surprisingly tasty. While they were enjoying dandelion coffee and sweets for desert, the elven sisters performed. Annabelle's angelic voice, the bewitching beauty of Galatea's face and Elmira's bell-like laughter brought enchantment to the underground dwelling. They were transported to another world, where beauty blossomed and no tears did flow.

'Only the enchantress Amaranth could have bestowed these gifts,' reflected Sidonia. Nimbus stood up and with a silver spoon touched his glass.

'We know why these visitors have come to our subterranean world. They have a sacred mission. If they reach the palace and our elven daughter intones the incantation of the ancient elven Kings, the spell will be shattered, the spell that for centuries has cast its shadow. How will they reach the palace?' For a few moments there was silence. Then Orpheus rose.

'My friends, all my life, I have lived in these dark tunnels. Generations of moles have dug deep under the desert floor. Hundreds of miles of tunnel have fallen into disuse. I can recall one tunnel that reached all the way under the palace of the Seven. Tomorrow the survey party will return with a report and we shall see what we shall see. Gather here tomorrow night and I will share with you their findings.'

Later in the evening they enjoyed some spruce wine. The year before the Dwarves had traded the wine for healing roots. Ben the Mole asked Weiss to share some of his adventures. He leaped at the opportunity and kept the company entertained till midnight.

When the guests were about to leave, Svanhild asked them to gather around her at the end of the table. She reached under the table and raised a package wrapped in silk. She folded back the cover and all beheld the golden plate.

The guests stared in wonder at the mystic writ. It was as if the power and majesty of the ancient elven King, who had carried the tablet to the eastern shores, were pulsating in the room. Recognition sprang in Elmira's eyes. Sidonia now understood that the elven child's gift of spirit travel was not limited to space. She travelled in time and had met the King who dwelt in the distant past.

At breakfast next morning, Consolata and Svanhild detected a trace of sadness in Sidonia's face.

``I heard you speaking to Elmira in the ancient elven tongue, did something upset you Sidonia?'

'My beloved friends, Elmira and I did indeed speak in the ancient tongue. We did not want to dampen the high spirits at the party, but Elmira's spirit has visited Esteria. Scimitar himself and many other Dwarves have fallen, famine has ravished the city. It is a matter of days, a week at most, before all will perish.'

Svanhild sank her head onto her knees. Consolata walked up to her and with her slender paws touched her forehead.

'Fear not maiden of the swans, moles are lowly subterranean creatures, but once challenged they can perform wonders. A special Digger Corps will open the tunnels that have caved in over the years.'

That evening they learned that the survey party had been able to penetrate close to the palace, and two days later a troop of mole sappers had finished repairing the passages.

The very next day Svanhild and Sidonia shouldered their packs and followed Consolata to the plaza where Weiss and Elmira awaited them. They embraced Consolata and followed a party of mole guards to the south end of the town. Here they left the gaily-lit tunnels behind and entered into dark passages. The only light visible was cast by the torches carried by the mole guards. The moles removed obstacles and rocks in their path and their cheerful marching songs kept up their spirits. The tunnels widened at times into large caverns, where crystal formations and colourful minerals flickered in the torchlight.

As they drew closer to the palace, a sense of foreboding settled over the company. Svanhild felt a sense of despair. How could they ever succeed against such overwhelming odds? Folly, it is all folly, kept running through her head.

Sidonia understood Svanhild's mood swings and pressed her hand.

'We are playing our part, my love. It is all that matters. Trust in the world of the spirit. We are not alone, Svanhild.' Svanhild held her hand tighter.

'Had it not been for you, Sidonia, I would have given up long ago.'

They trod on, often damp and always dead tired. Sometimes the tunnels were shallow and often it was necessary to crouch for hours on end. On the third day, they came to a series of connected grottos. The guards knew that they were exhausted and suggested a rest. Placing torches in clefts in the walls, two guards left to explore the underground passages ahead. They returned hours later with a broad grin on their faces.

'We are close to the dungeons of the palace,' announced the Captain of the guards. Stay behind and rest. We will scout for access to the palace vaults.'

There was a sigh of relief. The tramping and crouching through the damp tunnels had come to an end. For better or for worse, they had reached the end of their journey.

The guards, who had stayed behind, shared their provisions with Svanhild, Sidonia, Elmira and Weiss. One of the moles took a small camp stove from his rucksack and boiled coffee.

Hot drinks, the camp stove and light from the torches brought some solace and warmth into the dark damp space. They began to unwind, while awaiting the return of the Captain. They didn't have to wait long. The Captain walked back into the Grotto, a grim look on his face.

'Alas, the only entrance is barred by a heavy grate, behind the grate crocodiles splash in pools and puddles.'

Once more the way was barred. They had come so close. All huddled around the oil stove and Sidonia prayed that a way might be found.

44

Heart of Darkness

The once gloomy palace of the Seven now exuded a veneer of cheerfulness and the High Lord Salan appeared in a merry mood. That very morning a merewing had landed on the terrace with a message from Commander Zenon, the siege of Esteria was in its last phase. In a matter of days the armies would be moving into town. Most of the nasty Dwarves had fallen and among them, that crafty military genius, Scimitar. And then there was the forthcoming wedding. The lovely Princess would be his. Yes, he would carry off the delicious damsel and the Kingdom with her!

Precilla, favoured handmaiden to the High Lord, still danced to his wishes but deep inside that fair lady burnt the fire of jealousy. How pleasant it would have been to be consort to the great Lord. How well she would have played the part. All her dreams, shattered by a foreign Princess!

Bright murals adorned the once sombre halls. Silver candelabras, stolen from the Sea Gnomes, shed a soft light and pots of lovely flowers appeared throughout the palace.

Edel had done his share to amuse the Seven. The light-hearted Mountain Fairy had turned out to be a born court jester and Lord Salan allowed him a good deal of freedom. He managed to produce smiles on the Lords' grave countenances and at times laughter echoed around the conference table. Only grim faced Torzak never succumbed to Edel's clowning. He was suspicious of the little tramp.

Princess Yaconda had been confined to an ornate apartment. Pretty hostesses served the finest delicacies and attended to her every need. Yet, she was in a state of despair. It was Edel's visits that always kindled a ray of hope and kept her from jumping off the balcony onto the red rocks, seven stories below.

Dominique, faithful handmaiden, could sense the Princess' moods and when despair gleamed in the royal eyes, she stayed close by her side.

'Two days, Dominique, before Salan will force me to the altar and seal my doom. The end of the royal line, the end of the Kingdom. Death alone can bring solace.' Dominique took her hand.

'Beloved Princess, two days is an eternity. Every minute of every day can bring tidings of events not foreseen or expected. Every ripple in the stream of time can bring surprise and redemption. If you choose death, don't jump from the balcony. On my walks through the gardens, I have collected sap secreted by the thorns of Purple Wraith.'

Yaconda knew the shrub well. It grew in abundance along the edge of a small stream in the palace garden. Only at full moon did it bloom, its deep purple flowers radiating a mystical and deadly glow.

'On the morning of the wedding, the phial will be yours, my Princess. Swear, you will not touch it until the ceremony is over.'

Yaconda gave her word and Dominique relaxed. Her mistress had given her word and she no longer needed to keep her eyes fixed on the glass door opening onto the balcony.

One of the servants came in with a tray of refreshments and Dominique accompanied her mistress to the dining table. For a short time they sat together in silence, sipping tea from golden beakers.

After tea Yaconda went back to her loom, sending the shuttle flying. It had a calming effect and kept her mind from spinning frightful scenarios.

She was grateful to Puff, the kind-hearted Groll, who had dismantled the loom and transported it to their new suite. Almost everyday he dropped in to check if they were comfortable or stood in need of any supplies. Nothing was too much for Puff, unlike most Grolls, a fluke of nature had transmitted to him the kindness of his forefathers, the ancient Forest Trolls. His devotion to Yaconda knew no bounds.

For two days now there had been no sign of Puff, and Dominique was wondering what could have happened. Just then Edel, in a flurry of excitement, flew in to the apartment.

'Puff, poor Puff, he has fallen into disfavour with the Captain of the

Guard, and has been sent to work in the dungeons.'

'It is all my fault,' lamented Yaconda, 'he has helped us out so often. No doubt he raised the Captain's suspicion. Our only friend among the palace staff has been taken from us. Good Puff now is in that horrible dungeon with the crocodiles.'

'Perhaps there is a wisdom in this too,' whispered Dominique. Yaconda sighed and squeezed her hand.

Edel knew the Princess was sinking into a slough of despair. Frantically he started thinking about some heroic deed that would change the tide. So overwhelming were the odds that even a Mountain Fairy's fertile imagination couldn't come up with a wild scheme to whisk off the Princess. He decided to cruise the palace and look for clues. Gaily flapping the wings of his butterfly suit he skipped down the long palace halls. It had occurred to him to find his way down to the dungeon and talk to Puff about some desperate plan to snatch Yaconda from Salan's clutches.

Wandering down the stairs, he passed the entrance to the palace kitchens. He had forgotten the Chef's jest about putting him on top of the wedding cake but when he passed the archway leading to the kitchens, a long arm caught him around the middle and drew him inside.

'Ah, my butterfly, just in time,' chuckled the Chef. 'We are putting the icing on the seventh story. I better hang on to you and make sure that you are here when we put the finishing touches on the wedding cake.' The Chef rubbed his hands. To have an iced butterfly on top of his masterpiece would create a sensation.

It dawned on Edel that the Chief Cook had not spoken in jest. He tried to get away but the Chef's long arm scooped him up again. The kitchen staff was delighted to have Edel flutter around but they kept a close eye on him.

Puff, who adored the Princess and her handmaiden, had done everything he could to make life more comfortable for them. He had brought flowers from the garden and attended to all their needs.

When some ruffians in the guard regiment cornered him, sharing a few ribald jokes about the Princess and her maid, mild mannered Puff seethed with anger. A coil of wrath unleashed in the huge frame of the peace-loving Groll, and the sound of Groll skulls knocking together, echoed through the halls. Many of his colleagues were out of commission for weeks. 'Pussyfoot', his nickname through the years, fell into disuse.

Shortly after this incident, he learned of his new assignment, permanent guard duty in the dungeons. There, on a low stool, sat poor Puff watching the crocodiles swarming in the pond. The fierce reptiles were feared by slaves and soldiers alike, for anyone who thought of mutiny or incurred the displeasure of the Seven had met a bitter end in the dungeon reservoirs. During periods of inactivity the crocs became bored and amused themselves by harrying the guards. One croc crawled ashore and snapped at Puff's feet. Puff quickly discouraged him. Jumping into the water, he seized the monster's tail and spinning the reptile round and round, sent it flying. At the place of impact an indelible impression was etched upon the dungeon wall. The image subdued the unruly reptiles and Puff was left in peace.

He had spent the night on a bench in front of the guard post wondering what he could do for the Princess, when a grating sound woke him from his reverie. It appeared to come from one of the underground passages.

He walked to the entrance and looked in. It was dark and there appeared no sign of any movement. After a short silence the scraping began again and now he could hear the snapping of crocodile jaws. He lit an oil lamp and walked into the tunnel until he came to the iron grate, barring strangers from entering the dungeons. Raising the lamp he saw a Fairy stuck in the ironwork and on the ground two crocs snapping at the unfortunate captive. In an effort to free himself, the buttons of the creature's jacket had popped off and lay scattered on the ground. At the sight of the new guard the crocs fled.

When Puff looked closer he saw that the creature caught in the grate looked like a Mountain Fairy. At first it occurred to him that it was Edel playing a prank. He expected Edel to burst out laughing, but this Mountain Fairy seemed terrified by the sight of him.

Puff scratched his head. He was bright enough, but his thought processes moved slowly. Suddenly, a light went on inside that huge head.

'Weiss, Weiss,' he shouted, 'you are Weiss, Edel's bosom friend.' Puff's laughter echoed through the caverns throwing the crocs into a panic.

Weiss stopped squirming and looked up in astonishment. He suddenly realized that life was not going to be squeezed out of him by the huge hands in front of his eyes. He let out a sigh of relief, the tension in his body vanished and he slipped through the bars landing at Puff's feet. Puff raised him in one hand and whispered over and over again.

'Weiss, my tiny pal's bosom friend. Fear not little one, you are in good hands.' Weiss didn't doubt it judging by the huge palm supporting him.

'Puff is a friend of the Princess, Weiss, and we must find a way to forestall the wedding of the Princess and the Lord Salan.'

'That is what we have come for Puff,' exclaimed Weiss. 'Tell me about Edel, is he safe and sound?'

'Edel is safe enough,' chuckled Puff.' He is the darling of the palace.'

'That is what I'm afraid of,' said Weiss bursting into laughter. 'Edel plunges into a role with heart and soul and when the play is over, he doesn't know how to move off stage. This was too deep for Puff. All that mattered was that Weiss had come to save the Princess.

'The wedding is at noon today , Weiss. What shall we do?'

'My friends, Svanhild and Sidonia, are waiting in the grottos beyond the gate but we have to find a way to bring them through the iron grate. I was the only one who could squeeze through the narrow opening.

Puff put Weiss down and looked at the grate. He put one foot against the wall and with both hands seized the iron bars. He took a deep breath and with one sudden effort tore the gate from the rock face, hinges and all.

Weiss couldn't believe his eyes and thanked heaven that those hands belonged to a good-hearted creature. He quickly stepped through the opening where the gate had been and whistled three times. First the mole guards came out to make sure that it was not a trap. Weiss assured them that Puff could be trusted and that they were free to return home. The moles tripped back to the Grotto and told Svanhild, Sidonia and Elmira that Weiss had entered the dungeon and was waiting for them. Thanking the moles for their help, they rushed ahead to find Weiss.

The three girls stopped in their tracks when they caught sight of the giant Groll, but Weiss quickly put their fears to rest. Seeing, Sidonia and Elmira, Puff's heart melted. As a child he had often dreamed of Elves and now here, they were standing before him. He went down on his knees to greet Svanhild and the Elves and offered his services. Weiss told them that Puff was as good as his word but that wasn't necessary, Sidonia could gauge a person's level of trustworthiness at a glance.

When Puff kept staring at her, she smiled, 'You are not dreaming Puff, Elves do exist, Elmira and I are very much alive.' Puff was delighted.

Weiss explained that the wedding was planned for that very day.

'Is there a way of entering the palace without being detected Puff?' asked Sidonia.

'No my lady, there is a guard with a black dog at the head of the next flight of stairs. I think I could climb up and knock him over the head,' volunteered Puff. He was still down on his knees to make communication easier and Sidonia put her hand on one of his fingers.'

'Thank you Puff, but it would make a racket, I fear.'

Puff admitted the dog's barking would be plenty loud and echo throughout the palace halls. They were lost in thought, there didn't seem to be an easy answer. Once again, Sidonia surprised them. 'Violence will not work. In elven lore there are other ways to face an enemy. I will walk up the spiral stairway and confront the guard and his dog.'

Svanhild didn't protest, by now she knew that Sidonia had special powers. Yet, all held their breath and prayed silently as Sidonia quietly stole away to begin the long climb up the rough stone steps. Reaching the column at the head of the stairs, she caught sight of the Guard and the dog standing beside him. Softly she intoned an ancient elven chant.

Only when she came closer did the guard see the ephemeral elven maid. For a moment he thought that he had taken leave of his senses. To make sure he was not dreaming he rubbed his eyes. No, the wisp of a creature before him was not a phantom and the hideous face broke into a grin.

Even the dog by his side failed to growl. Sidonia walked on until she reached the huge jaws. Slowly raising her hands, palms facing outward her hazel eyes beamed at the fearsome creature. The dog rolled on his back and sank into a coma, paws falling slowly to one side. The crystalline sounds of the elven maiden's singing echoed around the walls and mesmerized the guard. His limbs began to relax and slowly he slid from his chair coming to rest on the floor.

Sidonia beckoned Weiss who was standing at the foot of the stairway. The Mountain Fairy was wonderstruck when he saw the formidable Groll and his hound in a deep sleep. He beckoned the others to come. Puff climbed the stairs as quietly as Grolls can climb, Svanhild and Elmira, following upon his heels, were astonished to see both guard and dog sprawled on the stone floor. Puff, who knew every nook and cranny in the palace, now took the lead, guiding them through the empty halls.

In the morning Two Rover Captains came to the Princess' quarters, to accompany Princess Yaconda and Dominique to the palace chapel.

Dominique had helped her don the splendid wedding gown sewn by the palace seamstresses and Yaconda had not objected. The wedding dress was truly beautiful and the white silk had been embroidered with myriad small pearls. A coronet of jewels, heisted from the Sea Gnomes, adorned her head. When Yaconda stepped forth into the sunlight, Dominique clapped her hands. Her mistress' radiant beauty captivated all around her.

What astonished Dominique was that the Princess had consented to wear the wedding gown. Princess Yaconda, sensing her wonderment put a hand on her shoulder and whispered. 'My beloved handmaiden, I will walk down an aisle that leads to a higher temple to celebrate a union in the celestial realm. Adorned in this raiment will I enter the portals of eternity.'

Dominique was horrified. Seized with grief and anguish she spoke in stern tones.

'Princess, Princess, do not rush your dream to enter heaven's halls, a tragic queen. Leave not the world's stage before the curtain falls.'

The Princess was staring in the distance. Dominique feared that she had slipped into another reality and was relieved to hear her voice again.

'I have given you my word, Dominique, only after the high priest solemnizes this unholy union, will I drain the deadly draught, and walk down that nobler aisle that leads to a realm beyond tears and sorrow.'

Thus it was that when the Captains of the Guard came to lead her to the chapel, she did not remonstrate and willingly followed them. Dominique prayed silently that Yaconda would return to the here and now and cling to a ray of hope for deliverance.

In the chapel, the six Lords were seated in the front row. Strains from stringed instruments filled the great vaulted space. Salan and one of the few remaining old priests stood behind the altar. The order of priests had been eliminated by the Seven but a few of the old men had been retained to perform traditional functions. The ancient one entrusted with the ceremony had for years been Salan's soothsayer and the great Lord trusted him to read the words that would sanctify the union.

Guard Captains and hostesses were seated in the middle rows. Behind them were the palace servants, many of whom had been recruited as children and forced to work in the palace for most of their lives.

The musicians on the balcony were the first to behold the Princess, framed by the graceful arch at the back of the chapel. When Princess Yaconda, full of grace and majesty, walked up the aisle, their fingers froze on the strings and a profound silence fell over the multitude. Sunlight shining through the stained glass windows cast her in a veil of many colours. Never before had they seen such a sight. It was as if the Princess belonged to another world, a world they had heard about in fairy tales, long before they had been seized from their parents arms' and raised to serve the cruel Lords.

Salan feared that the festive spirit had vanished. To his relief, nine cooks dressed in white, carried in the seven story wedding cake and standing atop was a butterfly in pink icing. Cheers and laughter greeted the sight and the musicians struck up a wedding march.

Dominique had found a seat close to the front. Her eyes never left the Princess. She had sewn a pocket in the folds of Princess Yaconda's gown to hide the tiny phial. If the their union were sealed it would deliver her from her agony. An extra stitch at the top of the pocket ensured that the Princess would not be able to seize it on impulse. Dominique was ready at the sight of any untoward movement, to rush up to her mistress and intervene.

Looking around the chapel, she espied, seated on the sill of one of the windows, a tall pelican. His plumage was wonderfully coloured by sunlight filtering through the stained glass. Only a handful of people had observed the silent figure, high above the crowd. Peli 1 gravely observed the proceedings.

The old priest, facing the Princess and the High Lord, stood behind the altar, waiting quietly for the music to end and for the excitement of the crowd to ebb. Salan was impatient and he wanted the ceremony over with. A sense of foreboding had come to him. All had gone well. Yaconda had willingly come to the altar. Force would have been used, had it proved necessary.

'Yet there is many a slip between the cup and the lip,' he mused and with a gentle kick prodded the Priest. The old man hastily intoned the first words of the ancient wedding chant, but a hysterical cry interrupted him. It was Precilla, the Lord's handmaiden, overcome with jealousy, yet bewitched by Yaconda's beauty, she burst out in anger.

'False-hearted man, this act of treachery will cost you dearly.' Turning to the crowd she called out in despair, 'Stop this act of sacrilege. Save the Princess from this evil fate.' The last few words were garbled, for the guards had already seized her and were carrying her out the chapel.

Salan shot the priest a fiery look and this time the old man raised high his voice, so as to block out any competing sounds. He was only halfway through the wedding chant when all eyes turned to the wedding cake itself and a thunderous wave of laughter drowned his voice.

The pink butterfly on the seventh story of the cake had stirred. The icing cracked and out walked Edel in his butterfly suit. Flapping his wings he hopped down one level. Salan was very fond of his court jester but this time he had gone too far. He would pin him up in his collection with the other insects. Seething with anger, he waited for the laughter to die down. His eyes flashed fury at the guests who were now standing up, cheering and clapping as Edel, with icing sugar falling from his flapping wings, pretended to fly down the wedding cake.

Counsellor Torzak, who had never trusted the Mountain Fairy, didn't laugh. He turned to the enchantress seated on his right and touched her shrivelled hand.

'Matista, I fear that the Fairy is up to no good. There is gypsy doodle in the works and the little imp will pay for this. Matista needed no warning for the strings of her soul were vibrating to strange and dangerous chords. The enchantress had a finely honed inner warning system. Many a time it had saved her from disaster. Mysterious forces were moving through the palace but she could not identify them.

Salan too felt a strange sense of urgency to complete the ceremony, he seized the Princess' right wrist in an iron hold and with the other hand he gripped the arm of the soothsayer as if to squeeze the words out of him. The old man in a panic, groped for words that would not come. At last he raised his scroll and haltingly began to read the fatal words that would bind the pair.

Edel, after his performance, quietly had moved to a seat next to Dominique. Dominique knew that there were but minutes left, yet her mind was clear. She raised her eyes as if beseeching aid from some higher power. It was then that she caught sight of three shadows on the balcony wall moving swiftly forward. An inner voice told her deliverance was near. She stared at Yaconda and to her horror saw her hand moving closer to the pocket in her gown. Horrified she turned to Edel.

'Edel do something, anything to gain time!' Edel flapping his wings and literally flying up to the stage landed between Salan and Yaconda and burst into a wedding song. The old priest, at the sight of the sugar coated butterfly, stopped in mid-sentence and broke into a fit of laughter. Salan was not amused. He took Edel by the end of one of his wings and sent him whirling through the air.

Dominique breathed easier. In the commotion, Princess Yaconda had moved her hand away from that fatal pocket with the phial of Purple Wraith.

Matista was on guard, her restless eyes searching the hall and the balconies that ringed the upper half of the building. She too saw the shadows of three small figures against the upper section of the wall. Her dark eyes flashed a warning to Salan.

High above, Weiss, Svanhild and Elmira moved silently and swiftly. Reaching the balcony above the altar, they came to a halt. By now many of the guests had noticed the mysterious figures. Svanhild looked down at the appalling crime being perpetrated, and for a moment a wave of anxiety swept over her. What if the incantation didn't work? No such doubt beset Elmira. With a remarkable concentration of energy, her slender arms raised the tablet and her laughter echoed through the chapel sending a ripple of dismay among the guests below.

The tablet catching the sunlight filtering through the stained glass burned with a deep golden light. The eyes of the multitude were mesmerized by the slight white figure holding the golden plate, shimmering with a brilliance that blinded eyes.

The priest, too, turned around and the sight of the elven child holding the tablet in a golden haze was more than he could take. He dropped the scroll and fell to the ground. The moment that Matista saw the light shining on the Golden Plate, she knew that the one thing she had feared had come upon her. The old witch's eyes were stabbed by the elven child's radiant beauty.

At the sight of Svanhild standing by her side, her fury knew no bounds. The maiden she had chosen to be her apprentice had become the instrument of her doom. In a last desperate effort she tried to utter a curse, but the syllables froze in her throat.

It was then the elven child sang out the words that the ancient elven Kings, had endowed with mystic power.

> *selveeos altara*
> *zervos nimos*
> *liahath ovara*

The incantation resounded from the chapel's vaulted ceilings and cries of anguish could be heard from the six Lords seated in the front row. Only Salan remained silent, a stoic expression on his face. He had released Yaconda and the priest from his grip and Matista had joined him on the stage before the altar.

Commotion was rampant among the guests and many stood up to get a better view of the drama unfolding before them.

Yaconda rushed over to Dominique, who was seated in the second row, and they watched the six Lords as their hair turned white and their youthful faces withered. They writhed in agony and despair. Their bodies shrank and their skin shrivelled. The Mystic Writ of the ancient elven Kings enshrined in the Golden Plate had broken the cycle of lasting youth and power that had been theirs. Reduced to a pitiful condition, they stumbled to the back of the chapel and out the palace doors. Their cries of despair and regret carried a note of repentance.

Not so, for Matista and Salan. Defiance shone in their eyes. Everyone stared at Salan expecting him to lose his youth and vigour like the other six, but nothing happened. Matista was seen whispering. Would her magic protect the High Lord? A wave of apprehension moved through the ranks of the servants. They had seen the humiliation and agony of the six Lords and a glimmer of hope had entered their hearts. They had spent their lives in forced labour but now, for a moment, they caught a glimpse of freedom.

The enchantress' hand rested on Salan's shoulder. A veil of dark purple light enveloped them and then almost imperceptibly their bodies diminished. Within minutes nothing but a black purple haze remained at the place where they had stood.

The Grolls and Rover Captains in the audience had been terrified by what they had witnessed and fearing that a similar lot might befall them, rushed out the palace. Only the servants and the hostesses remained in their seats. Sidonia understood what was happening and reassured the remaining guests that there was no cause for fear. When her voice sang out all eyes looked up at the elven maid on the balcony.

'The power of the Seven has been broken. The six Lords have fled into the desert, dragging their shrunken bodies to the eastern shore. The span of their ignoble lives has run its course. The High Lord Salan and the evil enchantress have dematerialized. Never again will you see them in their earthly form. Yet take heed! Their spirits dwelling in the realms of darkness can enter into the psyche of unsuspecting men and women and lead them astray.'

Weiss, standing on the balcony, looked down upon the pink butterfly flapping its wings. He knew in a flash that the creature was none other than his bosom friend. He jumped from the balcony, lightly landing on the stage and embraced the butterfly. Edel and Weiss, reunited, danced around the stage in a frenzy of joy.

Streams of people emptied out of the great hall. Many Rovers had fled the palace, hoping to reach the villages from which they had been recruited. Most of them perished in the desert. The Grolls who had escaped army duty and served in the palace had nowhere to go, but they lost no time in helping themselves to the many treasurers in the palace and sacking the seven villas of their overlords. Confusion and chaos reigned everywhere.

Puff, who had been watching from the back of the chapel, rushed to the front and took charge. He told Princess Yaconda and her friends to stay close behind him. Swinging his huge arms, he cleared a path through the chaotic crowd and safely shepherded the Princess, her handmaiden and friends away from the palace and into the desert.

But how were they to find their way across the Finnian Range?

They were standing at the edge of a sea of red sand that reached to the horizon. Puff looked lost. In the distance they could hear Grolls sacking and looting the palace and the villas. As they stood huddled together, a shadow of outspread wings passed over the brightly lit desert sand. Then they saw perching on a rock nearby, Peli 1.

'Not a moment is to be lost my friends,' sounded the grave voice of Queen Tuluga's secret agent. 'Follow me!'

Peli 1, hopping from rock to rock, led them on through the desert. For hours they walked with only one thought in their mind, to leave far behind the horror that they had lived through.

'Thank heaven for the faithful pelican,' whispered Svanhild to Sidonia, 'without Peli 1, we would have been lost.'

Trudging on, hand in hand, they still could not quite believe the nightmare was over. What had happened and what would the future hold? Had the armies of the Seven destroyed Esteria and overrun the Kingdom?

Only Edel and Weiss bubbled with good cheer. They were convinced that all would turn out well and rejoiced at the thought of the hair-raising stories which they would bring to the merry gatherings in their homeland. They would be in the limelight for years to come.

45

Esteria Relieved

General Zervos whistled softly as he looked down upon the ruins and rubble of Esteria, highlighted now by the fiery red of the sinking sun. The back of the town's defences had been broken. Were it not for the wretched Dwarves the town would have fallen months ago. The snotty Commander Scimitar, had perished, but his brother Smithereen had wreaked havoc amongst his Groll regiments. Swirling, at lightning speed, his cursed ball and chain, he had cut a terrible swath through the troops.

At last Zervos could rejoice. The fortifications had been weakened and Rover and Groll regiments soon would break through the barriers and trample the remnant of defenders.

Alas, it had taken months, not days, to capture the town, but the day of reckoning had come at last. The foolish Dwarves and the volunteers had delayed the victory. Now one push and the town would topple. Yes, they would pay a terrible price for their foolhardiness. The arrows of Elves and Esterians had picked off his best men. As for the women, ah the women, they had signed their own death warrant. Their generous libations of boiling oil and molten lead had tormented his men and he was content that the revenge would be sweet.

Lighting a pipe, the General scanned the sky over the Finnian Range. The last rays of the setting sun caught the mountain peaks in a flash of light and the shadows of night were veiling the range in darkness, but high above the mountains a last ray of sunlight revealed dark shapes soaring towards the camp. Zervos knew them to be merewings, their huge wings permitted them to fly at altitudes which no other birds could reach. No doubt a message from the Seven to seize the town or else! The merewings came down in a long glide, perching near the communication hut. A Captain of the guard rushed up and unfastened the leather container, carried by one of the birds. Zervos standing in the doorway, snatched the vessel from his hands, tore off the cap and walked over to the oil lamp. The Captain, standing nearby, saw a frown form on the cruel forehead. As he read on however, Zervos' eyes brightened.

'The Seven are no more. The golden tablet was found and the mystic writ etched in the plate by the elven Kings has burnt the magic shield forged by Matista's spell. Six Lords shrunk and diminished, Salan and Matista vanished. Do not expect they will ever reappear. Chaos at the palace. Hasten back. Restore order. The power will be yours.'

Zervos rubbed his hands in a gesture of pleasure. The note had come from a trusted informer whom he had planted in the palace. This was the chance he had waited for. Never mind Esteria, a small sacrifice for the power and the glory that would be his. He would rule with an iron hand.

He blurted out orders for the army to head back to the realm of the late Seven Lords, not a moment was to be lost. Zenon might get wind of it. Zenon had his own spies in the palace and would lose no time in challenging him. At that moment the Captain standing by his side pulled his sleeve and pointed upwards.

High above, a single moonbeam caught a merewing descending over the city in the direction of the second army headquarters. Within minutes his brother Zenon would receive the news! They must leave this instant. Orders flew through the camp and everywhere Rovers and Grolls ran around rousing the troops and preparing for the long trek up the mountain. Burning fires, half cooked meals and supplies were left behind, as the pressure to march grew.

Zervos drove his troops mercilessly, through the foothills and up the slopes of the range. Once above the tree line he halted and looked back. His haste had been well advised. In a patch of moonlight, marching in narrow columns Zenon's second army wound its way through the marshes east of the town. Once Zenon reached the mountain slopes, he would challenge his supremacy. Shouting to his captains, he drove the troops on towards the ridge. There he would set an ambush for Zenon. Many a time had he been outwitted by his halfbrother. Now, once and for all, he would settle the score and make sure he did in the slippery eel.

Slim walked silently along the stone wall in the town park. The wooden plaques, edged with flowers, were the work of Ensten. Engraved in the centre of each was the name of a Dwarf fallen in battle. Dawn was breaking and light danced on the blossoms of the shrubs surrounding the graves. A deep melancholy settled on his soul as he counted the graves. There were too many. He walked on, climbing the dykes behind the cemetery and surveyed the surrounding hills draped in sunlight. It might be the last time that he would see a sunrise over Esteria. The town had reached its breaking point. Many were the breaches in the dykes and fortifications and at strategic points the deep moat had been filled with rocks.

Before returning to Ensten's and Ulrik's cottage, Slim decided to walk along the defence perimeter to check for signs of movement in the enemy lines. Upon reaching the north gate he halted and scanned their encampments. A strange silence prevailed and no clattering of arms could be heard, no bugle calls to rally the troops. Even stranger was the fact that no smoke was rising from the many huts and camps. Slim thought at first it to be a clever trap to entice the remnant of the warriors outside the walls.

He plucked up his courage, slid down the dyke and walked towards the enemy positions. No sign of life, a few fires smouldered here and there, but it was clear that they had been lit the night before and supplies were scattered over the grounds. Everything pointed towards a sudden departure.

Ulrik and Volker, walking on the dyke, had seen Slim going through the enemy camp and they watched anxiously. Fitting an arrow to his long bow, Ulrik climbed down and headed toward Slim. Volker trailed behind.

Unexpectedly a Rover Captain came out of one of the tents. Ulrik raised his bow to cover his friend. It wasn't necessary. The moment that he saw them, the Captain raised his hands. Once within earshot he called out, declaring himself a deserter.

Quickly he explained that the power of the Seven had been shattered and that the news had reached first Zervos and then Zenon, causing both to rush back to the palace to seize power. Volker wrote it all down in his zeal to record these wondrous happenings for the benefit of generations to come.

Their first reaction to the disappearance of the armies was one of immense relief and gratitude. They had been spared a terrible fate, but what if the armies returned? How could they be sure?

When the news spread among the people within the town walls, there was joy and bewilderment. They had seen death approaching and had taken leave of their loved ones. Many had raised their hands skyward as if to touch the hand of their maker, a common practice among Esterians at the hour of death. Had there been a miraculous reversal of fortune? The siege had been lifted but for how long?

Smithereen, now in charge of military operations, took a cautious view of the situation. Working together with the Marquis, he organized parties to bring supplies and arms left by the troops into the town. All enemy encampments were destroyed, just in case and the volunteers from Swanneland were busy repairing fortifications.

Slim drew sketches of the enemy camp for his diary. Working close to the hills, he was the first to hear the distant pitter patter of paws and hoofs. Jumping onto a knoll, he scanned the rising hill country. A throng of creatures came galloping down the hills, kicking up a cloud of dust. Passing through the enemy camp, they slowed down and seeing Slim and Volker, came to a stop. Slim knew by the sorry sight of the furry crowd that the animals had been terrified. He overheard a group of badgers mumbling, 'The end is near. The great catastrophe is upon us, at last!' A small fox worked his way to the front and made a polite bow.

'Noble Sirs,' he began in a shaky voice, 'never before have we seen or heard the like of it. A terrible battle raged near the ridge of the Finnian Range and the clanging of arms echoed through the mountains. Deep in our holes the ground shook, waking us from our winter sleep. The din terrified us.'

Smithereen and several Dwarves had joined Slim and Volker. It did not take them long to figure out that the armies of Zervos and Zenon had clashed in moonlight on the alpine meadows.

Slim assured the animals, that the battle was over and it would be quite safe to return to their winter holes. There was a good deal of discussion and milling around, but it was only when Solomon and Kasper arrived and reported that not a single survivor could be found on the mountain slopes that the animals decided to return to the forest in the foothills and try falling asleep again.

Smithereen bid the owls a warm welcome and invited them to the gatehouse. Perched on a bench by the long wooden table, Solomon cast a stern glance at his audience.

'Flying over the Finnian Range at midnight, thousands of swords flashed in the light of the moon. We perched in a nearby tree and felt the earth tremble as the armies of Zervos and Zenon rushed upon each other. The sound of steel on steel reverberated through the mountains. The violent vibrations awoke the spirits in the Firemountain and black smoke rising veiled the moon's rays. The din of battle reached a frightful pitch. The sound of thousands of hammers pounding anvils shook my tail feathers. Such violence never before has been witnessed by mortal bird.'

At this point the Chief of the Owls fell silent, overcome by the awesome sight that he had witnessed.

'Frightful indeed,' butted in Kasper, 'brother rose against brother and after a savage battle they slew one another. Arms locked together they fell into the blood red waters of a small pond, never to rise again.'

'How can this be?' exclaimed Slim.

'My dear ballet master from the Land of the Swans,' hooted Chief Solomon solemnly. 'It is written in the Owl's Book of Wisdom, that deep within the psyche dwells a judge. He weighs our deeds and pronounces sentence. Secretly, we set the stage for our own fate.'

Kasper cast an admiring glance at his Chief. This was deep stuff. Then and there he resolved to take up, once more, his studies of the Book of Wisdom. Three volumes! The prospect was daunting, but then he did want to be Chief one day.

Sergeant Crusher, the Marquis deCygne and Ensten entered the gatehouse and greeted the owls. Kasper and Solomon again had to describe the scene that they had witnessed.

At last it dawned on Slim that the power of the Seven had been crushed. Svanhild, Sidonia and the elven child had reached their impossible goal. The mystic words engraved by the ancient kings had shattered the evil spell that had empowered the Seven. Elmira had intoned the incantation on the golden plate.

The Marquis knew that the situation called for an official address and town criers went around summoning everyone to the square in front of the town hall.

The news of the mysterious departure of the enemy troops had spread like wildfire. The men and women of Esteria who had been preparing to face their maker that very day were overwhelmed with joy and jubilation.

They hastened to the square and joined the many volunteers and the surviving Dwarves.

The Marquis, aided by Duckie, had managed to don his gala uniform and quite splendid he looked standing on the steps of the town hall, medals and gold braid glittering in the sun. A wave of inspiration moved the Marquis to raise his voice.

'Citizens of Esteria men and women alike, volunteers, noble Dwarves, to you who will be honoured by future generations and remembered in the annals of history, to you, I pay my tribute.

> *you who endured when hope had fled,*
> *raised arms when strength had ebbed*
> *and clung to life when none was left*
> *you stemmed the tide that swept*
> *the land of hopes and dreams*
> *and might–have–beens*
> *a new day dawns*
> *of hope and peace*
> *but for the dead we weep*

There was laughter and weeping and some voices enquired whether the armies might return. The Marquis told them of the undoing of the Dark Lords and of the thundering clash which had destroyed the armies of Zervos and Zenon.

Only now did it dawn on the multitude that the war was over. The evil Lords were no more, their frightful armies lay in tatters in the shadows of the mountain peaks, where ice and snow and avalanches would wipe out the last traces of that terrible battle. The darkness had lifted and they stood at the threshold of a new age of light and peace. There was gladness and rejoicing, dampened only by the terrible losses that all had suffered.

The Marquis asked Smithereen to come forward and then he paid homage to the great warrior and his brother, Scimitar, who had fallen in battle. He praised the monks of the Monastery of the Luminous Horizon south of the town. How often had soldiers on the dykes seen a haze of light rising from the Monastery at dawn, when the monks prayed for the relief of the town. They could not raise a hand in anger, but the men and women of Esteria knew that their prayers had sustained them in hours of trial.

Later that day the Marquis led to the cemetery, a procession to sprinkle over the graves of the fallen, the petals of thousands of spring flowers.

As Master of Ceremonies, the Marquis was in his element. His melancholy vanished and he experienced a thrill of excitement.

The crowd filed slowly through the cemetery's iron gate and after a while began drifting back to town but Ferdinand deCygne stayed behind. Standing amongst the graves, his thoughts travelled back to Dorothea. An incantation had reduced the Seven to mortals and had crushed their power. Was it not possible that in the secret well of cosmic knowledge, there dwelt a magic spell that would undo the cruel curse Queen Marsha had uttered, petrifying his beloved Dorothea.

He looked out upon the southern hills. The massive Monastery of the Luminous Horizon caught the last rays of the setting sun. As he stood meditating upon the merits of a monastic life, a vision appeared before him. The great Wizard, Isumatak, beckoned him to come to the Monastery. Was it an answer to his silent prayers? He donned a warm cape and walking through the town gate, headed for the Monastery.

His mind went back to Dorothea. Moments ago he had been caught up in the excitement of victory now he plunged into the depth of despair. His mind should have focused on his love, entombed in marble. He should be grieving for his Dorothea, striving to find a way to undo the curse. The image of Isumatak reappeared and he saw the spires of the abbey looming in the distance. A voice inside urged him to seek the help of the sage. Before dusk he entered through the archway leading into the gardens. Seated in a pavilion he descried Isumatak.

'Isumatak,' called out the stricken nobleman, kneeling in front of the wizard, 'I beg you to undo the evil that has befallen Dorothea.'

The wizard rested a hand on Ferdinand's shoulder. 'My beloved friend, not I, it is you alone who can perform the miracle that will set Dorothea free. Once you find the love that burns within your heart, cleansed from worldly desire, the intensity of its light will guide you to Dorothea.'

The words raised the curtain of melancholy, yet, Ferdinand was shaken, before there had always been someone else to help him out. Then he remembered the hero within and the time he slew a dozen Grolls. He had paid a price for that. Yes, he must look within.

'You must be our guest in this house of contemplation and stay until you find the light within. My days on earth are drawing to a close. Once I depart for other spheres my powers will be enhanced and I will be with you on your quest.'

Isumatak embraced the dazed nobleman and departed.

A monk approached him and led him to a cell. Seated on a cot, he regained his composure and began to meditate. His thoughts flashed back to events of the past, to his parents, to Dorothea, and his striving for a station in life, be it warrior or saint. He thought of Moose Martin who gave his life for his companions. Would he have stepped over the cliff's edge to save his friends? He struggled with his demons. Of the food the monks brought to his cell, he ate but little.

A burning sensation suffused his body. It grew in intensity. He closed his eyes and fell into a trance. Flames leapt up around him, after a period of time the pain became excruciating. He was walking through an inferno, creatures emerged from the flames reaching out to him and hampering his progress. It seemed an eternity before the flames subsided. He came to an iron gate. Desperate, he fell upon his knees and knocked. When the door opened he beheld a maiden surrounded by light. She greeted him and reached for his hand. From her flowed a sense of peace, a peace he had never known before. It dawned on him that the presence facing him was his own soul, his secret companion on the journey through life.

When he woke from his trance the sun's first rays caught him in a flash of light. The burning pain was gone. He felt reborn, a love for all creatures great and small dwelt in his consciousness. The image of Dorothea was etched in his mind. He would free her from the marble prison in which she had been entombed. He felt Isumatak's love surround him and urge him on to the deeper layers of his psyche. There he would find a source of strength that would never fail.

The Marquis felt electrified. He had no idea how things would unfold, but he left his cell, bade farewell to the monks, and walked out the gate. For two days he followed a trail through the forest until the trees dwindled in size and marshes appeared. He knew he was drawing close to Queen Marsha's palace. Of Isumatak there was no sign, yet he felt his presence.

When the mudsprites caught sight of the Marquis entering the water gardens surrounding the palace, they perceived a change in his bearing and a light shining in his eyes.

'Gracious God,' exclaimed the Marquis, 'my friends, Greenpiece and Theophilus. The power of the Lords is broken, the end of your suffering is nigh. I must see the Queen, kindly help me enter the palace.'

The sprites could tell that momentous changes were afoot and hastened to take the Marquis to the secret entrance leading to the palace dungeons.

Greenpiece knocked the secret code and the heavy door opened. Ferdinand deCygne strode forwards, through the dungeons, up the spiral stairway and into the great hall.

At first the Queen's handmaidens seemed pleased to see their former playmate. His vanity and innocence had been amusing. Yet there was something about his stride and the light burning in his eyes that frightened them.

When Queen Marsha appeared, for a moment, the Marquis wavered but a new power surged within.

Queen Marsha too could see the transformation that had taken place. She could sense that the power of her seven masters had ebbed. Once she had manipulated her visitor like a marionette. No more. His love for her former handmaiden had been purified, and an aura of light surrounded Ferdinand de Cygne. The brightness of which frightened her.

At that instant a loud clap echoed through the palace halls. The statues of the evil Lords standing in the centre of the seven fountains cracked and toppled over. The sight so terrified a few remaining Grolls that they fled the palace and rushed into the marshes, where they perished in patches of quicksand.

Queen Marsha had fallen to her knees. She looked at the Marquis and read the question in his eyes. At first she remained silent but the light around him rose to such intensity that she yielded to its unspoken command and intoned an incantation.

No sooner had she uttered the last syllable, than Ferdinand heard the cooing of a dove. For a moment he was mystified, but then recalled the dove, petrified on Dorothea's shoulder. He sprang up and rushed to the small bower by the waterfall. Standing amongst the rhododendron flowers was his beloved Dorothea, exactly as he had left the marble maiden and the dove, more than a year ago. But now the little bird was singing and life suffused through the cold marble. Then, flapping its wings, the dove flew up and perched on a branch. Dorothea raised her right hand and the Marquis kneeling, at her feet, spoke words of gratitude and praise for Isumatak's guidance, a parting gift to an undeserving lover.

'Rise my love,' sang the lilting voice of his beloved Dorothea, 'I too thank the spirit of Isumatak for this gift of life. But before we leave this dreadful place, a debt must be redeemed. The green moaners must be transformed to their former state.'

Hand in hand, they walked back to the dining hall and beheld the

Queen standing alone. When she looked up Queen Marsha was moving towards the far end of the hall. Swiftly Dorothea overtook the Queen and placed a hand on her shoulder.

'There is one act you will perform, before you slink away, to join your masters wandering in a desert of desolation and oblivion, for the few days that are still theirs. I pray, it will lighten the burden that you will carry on your journey.'

The Queen trembled when she looked at the once meek handmaiden, for in her eyes shone a greatness that had eluded her in all her own strivings for control and power. Well she knew what was being asked of her and she spoke the magic words that would lift the curse that had changed the travellers from Lambarina into toads and mudsprites. Now unable to bear the light any longer she rushed out the hall, followed by a few faithful handmaidens.

The Marquis looked at his love and took her hands in his. Dorothea burst out laughing and they danced around and around in a circle of joy.

Only the sound of many feet on the stone stairways leading up from the dungeon caused them to pause and listen. Joyful voices greeted them and a group of young men knelt before the Marquis and Dorothea. She gently touched their foreheads.

'My dear brethren Jeremiah, Fynn, Theophilus, Greenpiece, and others whose names I have forgotten, heaven be praised for your transformation. Thus it is true; frogs can be turned in princes.' A handsome young man with a warm smile bowed before her.

'No words can describe our gratitude for overturning the terrible judgement that the Queen had laid upon us. For years we lived as frogs and mudsprites building dykes and tending the Queen's water gardens. We were in the depths of despair when the Mountain Fairy, Weiss, came to us last year with a ray of hope. Glory be, no longer are we mudsprites and green moaners. We are the free men from Lambarina.'

'We all learned a lesson from the terrible night that we lived through, my dear Theophilus. Soon you will be back with your families in Lambarina. The Marquis and I will travel with you to the Kingdom for there is comfort and safety in numbers.'

The next morning a warm spring sun highlighted the flowers in the water gardens. As the travelers stepped onto the terrace they were greeted by loud cheers. Neatly lined up in two rows stood Master Ratticus' troopers, their splendid ivories glittering in the sun. Master Ratticus lifted his red hat and bade them safe voyage.

They all thanked the great rat heartily. The Marquis remembered how the Master and his fierce troopers had saved his party from capture by the Grolls. The loud farewell shouts of the rats could still be heard as they left the gardens and began the long trek to the river Sanctus.

In Esteria life was returning to normal. Everyone had pitched in repairing the worst damage and now the Dwarves and volunteers were getting ready to go home.

Slim and Ensten were worried about Princess Yaconda, Svanhild and the Elves. Yet there was little that they could do. They decided to travel back to the Kingdom with the other volunteers. Slim and Ensten had considered travelling to the Palace of the Seven, for fear that turmoil and chaos might have prevented Svanhild and her companions from leaving the Land of Darkness but Smithereen had advised against it. It was likely that they had managed to slip away, nonetheless, he sent Sergeants Crusher and Tuffkote to the Palace of the Seven to look for them.

When the volunteers from the Land of the Swans began the long trek home, Ensten and Slim joined them. Moose Martin was not among them, yet his spirit lived in their hearts.

Thanks to Puff and Peli 1, Princess Yaconda, Dominique, Svanhild, Sidonia, Elmira, Edel and Weiss were all safe. They had found their way to the edge of the desert and already were within sight of the Finnian Range.

At last they were leaving that dreadful red sand and their eyes feasted on the green leaves of the aspen and poplar stands on both sides of the path.

Edel and Weiss had recovered from the frightful drama before anyone else and contemplated their triumphal return. Rushing ahead they nearly bumped into two moles guarding the entrance to one of their tunnels. The moles knew them, of course, and asked if they could help. Weiss explained that they were looking for shelter. The moles, who knew all the nooks and crannies in the area took them to a comfortable cave. While Weiss held the moles enthralled with Queen's Yaconda's miraculous deliverance from the edge of the abyss, Edel raced back to the party with the news that a safe cave had been found. Heartened by the prospect of shelter and rest, they trudged the last weary mile to the cave entrance.

When Peli 1 saw that they were in good hands, he dipped his wings and flew on. He would alert Master Grimmbeak to their plight. The eagles might be able to fly them over the range.

When the mole guards saw the Princess walk through the entrance to the cave, they bowed and bid her Royal Highness welcome. Puff had to take his heavy pack off before he could squeeze through the narrow entrance. Edel had started a small fire and Puff had enough provisions for a meagre supper. After a skimpy meal and hot drinks, all fell into a deep slumber. The moles scurried back to the Confederacy to inform the Judges about the momentous happenings.

In the morning, gazing at the sunlit mountains, Sidonia saw two eagles soaring towards them. She rushed up a knoll waving an aspen branch. The moment that the eagles saw her signalling they dropped down, levelling off at a hundred yards. Edel and Weiss recognized them and sang out in chorus. 'Master Grimmbeak and young Theodorus.'

The eagles landed on a boulder and Master Grimmbeak saluted the party. When the noble birds saw, in the entrance of the cave, a lovely maiden with a wedding dress showing under a fur jacket, they bowed. It dawned on Master Grimmbeak that he stood in the presence of the Princess, heir to the throne. Princess Yaconda expressed her pleasure at meeting the Grandmaster. She told him that she was well acquainted with the high ideals of the Celestial Covey. This pleased the great bird and he tried to think of ways he could be of service to the Princess.

He called Sidonia aside and offered to airlift the members of the party to a safe haven, of course, with the exception of Puff who was simply too heavy.

Svanhild and Sidonia suggested that the Princess and Dominique travel to the Convent of the Sisters of the Secret Crossing. There they could recover before returning to Lambarina, once order was restored in the Capital.

Master Grimmbeak ordered Theodorus to fly to the Covey and return with four eagle teams and the necessary webbing. An hour later, a formation of twenty-eight birds touched down on the red sand.

No sooner had they landed, than four triangles of webbing were spread and Yaconda and Dominique took their place in the centre of two nets. At a sign from the Grandmaster, the teams rose in unison and headed towards the Convent. Minutes later the last two teams took off, one carrying Svanhild and the other Sidonia and Elmira.

As the teams gained altitude, Weiss and Edel looked at each other and wondered when their turn would come. The next day Servatius and Nightglider soared over the horizon and touched down by the cave. They told Edel and Weiss to climb on board. The Mountain Fairies were thrilled to soar once more on eagle-back over the mountain peaks. What joy, what a fitting end to their great adventure.

Poor Puff was left behind. His weight was well beyond the capacity of the Covey to airlift. Yaconda had promised him a job at the palace, so he got up and started the long trek to Lambarina.

46

New Age Dawning

Nettle leaves covered the floor in the Convent's tower. It had now been weeks since the last victims of the tainted fang illness had shed their nettle suits. As Helga swept up the leaves, she prayed that the suffering that had touched so many lives would come soon to an end.

Looking out the tower window, Helga espied four V-shaped formations flying towards the Convent.

'Eagle teams, bringing more victims of tainted fang?' she wondered.

She seized the bell rope. The heavy bronze bell tolled, alerting the Sisters to an unexpected party approaching the Convent. The sound resonated through the halls.

The Sisters rushed into the courtyard and great was their joy when the first team touched down and Svanhild stood up and walked out of the webbing.

'Welcome Svanhild,' sang out many voices. Svanhild embraced Sister Esmeralda and Helga.

'Two other teams will arrive within a few minutes, carrying Princess Yaconda and her handmaiden Dominique,' called out Svanhild.

The Sisters looked wonderstruck.

'Svanhild,' burst out Sister Esmeralda, 'the Princess has been delivered from her tragic fate?'

'It is true Sisters, Elmira raised the golden plate and sang out the mystic words of the elven Kings. At the eleventh hour, Salan's devilish plot came to naught and the Princess and her friends in the chapel escaped into the desert. The power of the Seven is ended, the Kingdom is safe.'

Shouts of jubilation subsided only when the second team of eagles soared overhead. Descending in a graceful spiral, they touched down in the circle of Sisters and lay workers.

When Princess Yaconda stood up, the Sisters cheered and applauded. Mother Hyacinth embraced her and taking the Princess by the hand, accompanied her into the Convent. Moments later, Dominique arrived to a warm welcome.

Most of the Sisters remained in the garden awaiting the arrival of the last team carrying the Elves. Elven visits were rare and the spectators rejoiced when Elmira and Sidonia glided down into the garden. The elves had been wrapped in blankets and it took them a few minutes to clamber out of the webbing. They enjoyed a royal reception and surrounded by the Sisters and lay workers, entered the Convent.

Inside the Convent, Svanhild had sought out Helga and led her to a small alcove lit by candles. She had to tell Helga of Scimitar's death, but she didn't know how to begin. The flames of the candles danced in Helga's deep blue eyes and taking Svanhild's hand she whispered, 'I will relieve you of your burden my dear friend, I know that Scimitar fell in battle. The Sisters on the other side have seen him on the shore of the opal sea.'

'You loved him, Helga?'

'I love him still Svanhild. And now that he has left this plane, I will join the Sisterhood. Come with me, my dear Svanhild. There is someone here who is keen to see you. Helga led her to a room at the back of the Convent and opened the door. Svanhild didn't know whether to cry or to laugh. Standing by the bed was Sunflower. She had long since shed her nettle suit and wore a lovely white dress, edged with roses. She approached Svanhild and embraced her. It was the first time that Svanhild and Sunflower had met and yet they felt an instant bond. Holding hands they sat down on the bed. The Dwarf's wife and the Swannemaiden, the two heroines who had changed the traditional role of women in the Kingdom, talked deep into the night.

Spring flowers were blooming around the Convent. The morning sun had warmed the stone wall that encircled the Convent and a few cumulus clouds stood out against an azure blue sky. Seated on a low wooden bench and leaning against the warm brick were Sister Esmeralda and Helga. Sister Esmeralda's arm rested on her shoulder and her free hand wiped the tears from Helga's cheeks.

Svanhild had confirmed Scimitar's death and Helga suffered a deep sense of loss. Love for the noble Dwarf had always dwelt in her heart and perhaps this was the reason that she had not joined the novitiate before.

After a sleepless night, they rested in the spring sun. A whirlwind of emotions spun in Esmeralda's heart. She grieved with her friend and spiritual sister, and yet deep within she rejoiced. The moment that she learned of Scimitar's death, she knew that Helga would join the order of the Sisters. No words were spoken that morning, both knew!

The hares, Philip and Alexander, had a healthy respect for Sister Esmeralda swinging her garden rake. This morning, however, the hares could tell that she was out of it. The coast looked clear. Philip and Alexander, working swiftly and silently, completed a successful raid on the root cellar, transferring a bushel of carrots to their own storage facility.

It was dusk when Servatius and Nightglider arrived, carrying Edel and Weiss. Kyria was the first to see the eagles fly over the north tower and she couldn't believe her eyes when she saw two tiny creatures clinging to the eagles' necks. Svanhild had told the Sisters that the Mountain Fairies would arrive and when the bell tolled they rushed out into the courtyard in a flurry of excitement.

The eagles touched down in the middle of a bed of daffodils. The dark feathered birds ringed by yellow flowers made a striking image. Sister Ursula, the Convent gardener, felt they could have been more discreet in their choice of a landing site, but the wise old woman knew that this was not a time for reproof.

The Sisters, looking at the tiny figures seated on the backs of the great birds, thought that they were statuettes. Their arms seemed to be frozen around the eagles' necks, in fact they could hardly move; flying at high altitude the cold had been intense.

The Sisters gently loosened their arms and legs and helped the poor creatures to dismount. They wrapped them in blankets, carried them into the convent, and placed them near the hearth. Mountain Fairies bounce back very quickly and after a few minutes near the glowing embers there were definite signs of life. When they became conscious of the Sisters standing around in a semicircle, anxiously watching, their speech returned.

A number of hot drinks and the stimulus of an eager audience brought them back to their old bubbly selves. Edel and Weiss, recounting their flight on eagle back over the Finnian Range, became the centre of a circle of adoring eyes.

A festive spread graced the table for the evening meal and for so rare an occasion the Sisters opened a bottle of wine.

Mother Hyacinth began the banquet with a prayer of thanks and a toast to the Princess. The guests were still terribly weary and to their relief, Edel and Weiss took responsibility for entertainment. Spurred on by food and wine, their hair-raising tales mesmerized the Sisters. Svanhild and Princess Yaconda hardly recognized their adventures and were amazed how truth can be embroidered in the art of telling. For seven days the friends stayed at the Convent. Every night the Sisters travelled with Edel and Weiss to the Confederacy of the Moles, the Palace of the Seven, Esteria, the Alpine meadows of the Dwarves and the banished Gnomes at the Lake of the Coloured Fishes.

One night Sidonia spoke of the discovery of the Golden Plate. The Sisters could hardly contain their excitement when Svanhild took the plate out of her pack and let the Sisters pass it around. When touching the shimmering gold engraved with mystic writ, they sensed a current of energy.

Svanhild wondered what to do with the golden plate when she returned home. She did not want to keep it, for the gold might be a temptation to thieves. She asked Sidonia and Elmira and the solution came to the three of them at the same time. They offered the golden plate to the Sisters, to be kept in the Convent's archives. Mother Hyacinth graciously accepted it. And in the Convent the golden plate remained.

The next day a messenger on horseback arrived from Lambarina. The volunteers had returned to the Capital and order had been restored. The men and women of Lambarina had learned of the Princess' rescue and were overjoyed. The palace was ready for her return and planning for the coronation was in full swing.

A carriage drawn by two horses arrived at the end of the week to take the Princess, Dominique and their companions to the Sanctus. From there they would continue their journey on the river. They bid the Sisters a fond farewell and promised to return once a year for a reunion.

The barge that awaited them was decorated splendidly and the journey was made in comfort. When they docked at Cascade, Princess Yaconda embraced Svanhild, Sidonina, Elmira, Edel and Weiss and promised to return to Cascade for the Spring Festival.

When the spires and rooftops of Lambarina appeared on the horizon, Princess Yaconda burst into tears. The Princess and her handmaiden could see men, women and children lining the shore. Music drifting across the water from a floating orchestra, blended with the jubilation and the cheering from the crowd. The news of the fall of the Seven had reached the town earlier, and the palace had been decorated for Princess Yaconda's coronation.

That very evening the Princess was crowned Queen and took her rightful place as Sovereign of the United Kingdom of the Seven Mountains. Standing on the palace balcony addressing the multitude, Yaconda asked that the celebrations be moved to Cascade to coincide with the great Swan Festival to honour the Swannefolk whose courage and sacrifice had saved the Kingdom. Svanhild, the nation's heroine would attend the festival. Many of the Outlanders were unaware of the part that Svanhild and her friends had played, but when Volker arrived back in his native town, he spoke in halls and coffee houses of the part Swannefolk had played in saving the Kingdom. The Outlanders spared no efforts to prepare for the festival in Cascade.

Cascade rejoiced at the return of Svanhild and her friends. Annabelle, in tears when Svanhild stepped ashore, insisted she come home to rest for a few days in the cottage by the river. Lady Erica deCoscoroba invited the Elves and the Mountain Fairies to stay at the Manor.

Sidonia, saw the twinkle in Lady's Erica's eyes and wondered what secret joy dwelt there. When she spoke to the Elves, there was a tremor in Lady Erica's voice.

'In early morning I gazed in the black pool and beheld Gustav amongst his fellow prisoners, they were crossing the Finnian Range and should reach the Sanctus within two days. Uncle Svend and two men are sailing upstream to meet the men returning from slavery. My dear elven child, Gustav will come back to me. Never did we know the tender green of love in spring, yet in the golden bower of autumn love, we shall dwell.'

After two days of rest, standing in the sunroom of the Manor, Sidonia sighted a vessel on the Sanctus. Seven great swans, their wings spread to catch the wind sailed in its wake. Running down the hill, she saw Svanhild standing near the water, calling out. 'Sidonia, Sidonia, it is Slim standing on the stern talking to the swans.' Sidonia looked at the frail vessel, and saw Slim and many of the other men returning from Esteria. Then she caught sight of Ensten and she squeezed Svanhild's hand

'And there near the prow, stands Ensten!'

Now Svanhild could see him too and rushed to the dock. The very moment Ensten saw her waving he jumped into the water, waded ashore and scooped her into his arms.

As the boat docked, Sidonia saw, to her surprise, a young maiden standing amongst the men. Snow white was the lovely face and she knew it to be Dorothea. The only trace remaining from the ordeal in marble was the colour of her face. White as the newly driven snow it would ever remain.

The moment that Lady Erica beheld the comely girl and the Marquis walking hand in hand to the Manor, she realized that Dorothea had been brought back to life. Someone had found the antidote for petrification. She herself had spent days looking in the waters of the black pool, for the command to undo the curse. Heaven be praised, a great wizard or enchantress had succeeded where she had failed. When the Marquis told her later that it had been Isumatak's last act of charity, before ascending, tears of gratitude welled in her eyes.

After greeting his friends, Slim slipped quietly away to spend some days with Svanhild and Annabelle in the little cottage by the river. Just to be able to walk down to the water and listen to the rustling of the poplars was such joy. Slim had learned from volunteers in Esteria that his old flame Rosemary, the pretty waitress at the Graceful Neck, had married a wealthy businessman. Sitting by the river's edge, the thought came to him that in summer he would celebrate his thirty sixth-birthday, the age at which Swannemen could marry. Now after that long wait Rosemary had walked out of his life. Perhaps he would never marry.

When he walked back to the Cottage he saw old Martha's bear, Grumpuss, sitting by the apple tree cleaning up the windfall. Walking through the doorway he beheld the blind prophetess seated by the hearth, enjoying a cup of tea and a raspberry square. Old Martha put down her teacup and took Slim's hand in hers.

'Grieve not for Rosemary, my love. There are a dozen Rosemarys in every town, but only one Fragrance.'

Slim laughed, he recalled a day in the Golden Goose and the magic in the emerald eyes of the landlady's daughter. He would lose no time in travelling to Miranda and inviting Fragrance to be his guest at the Spring Festival. Then it would be only a short hop to the Convent of the Sisters, for Slim had decided to attend the wedding of the Marquis and Dorothea.

Marquis deCygne had arranged with Mother Hyacinth to have the wedding at the Convent and the Sisters rejoiced for they had grown fond of the Marquis. When tainted fang disease had brought him to the edge of the grave, they had spent months nursing him back to health. The prospect of meeting Dorothea threw them into a flurry of excitement. Dorothea, who had lived through the trauma of petrification and had gone through a near death experience of the nearest kind, might be able to share some of her visions from the other side.

Slim's mission to Miranda had been crowned with success and a smile played on his face when he arrived at the Convent for the ceremony.

Amidst flowers and song, Sister Esmeralda joined the Marquis and Dorothea in a union that would bind them on their journey through this world and beyond.

At night there was a splendid banquet. After the meal and several goblets of excellent wine, the Marquis settled down by the open hearth and gazing into the glowing embers, pondered the mysteries of life. There, seated by Esmeralda's side, sat his lovely Dorothea. She had slipped her earthly moorings but a kind providence had returned her to him, to bring him joy and the assurance that the spirit lives, no matter what happens to our mortal coil.

Sister Esmeralda asked Dorothea to speak of her out of body experiences. She gladly told the sisters of the time she spent in the worlds beyond, while her body of cold marble rested down below. But only the sisters shared her tale, to no others did she ever speak of it.

Slim had made some rough sketches of the wedding party and the next morning he filled in the details. Later in the day, in a brief ceremony, Helga was received into the Convent and entered the novitiate of the Order of the Sisters of the Secret Crossing.

Walking at night through the long corridors, Slim found Helga seated in an alcove, a single candle cast her face in a warm glow, a book of prayer rested on her knees. Slim sat down, a sketchbook on his knees. Once home in Cascade he finished the painting and sent it to the Convent as a gift.

The day before the Spring Festival, Queen Yaconda and Dominique arrived in Cascade on the Royal Barge. A carriage drove them to the Manor where they would be the guests of the Marquis, Dorothea and Lady Erica.

When Queen Yaconda and Dominique walked through the rose garden, a slender figure, white locks and beard reaching to his shoulders, stood by Lady Erica's side. The Queen knew in her heart the gaunt appearance to be Gustav, returned after years in the galleys of the Dark Lords. She looked at the dark eyes sunk deep in their sockets, her heart bled and she threw her arms around him.

From everywhere guests began arriving, some travelled on land, some on water and others in the air. Queen Tuluga of the Mountain Fairies, had been carried hither by her pelicans, with Peli 1 leading the team.

Solomon, Chief of the Wood Owls and Deputy Kasper flew in at night perching on the hen house behind Annabelle's cottage. Their arrival raised serious concerns among the barnyard fowl. They need not have worried, the owls ignored them. The Chief and his Deputy dozed, anxiously waiting for the dark eyed Swannemaiden to appear.

At sun up, Svanhild welcomed Kasper and Solomon and invited them to be her guests for the festival. She served breakfast and brushed their feathers. When she went back into the cottage, the owls had a twinkle in their eyes.

'A striking appearance, Deputy. Those eyes bore deep into one's subconscious, stirring the archetypes.

'Quite so, Chief, She is a gem amongst terrestrials, I daresay.'

'An elegant way of putting it Deputy!'

Slim had gone out that morning to enjoy a cup of coffee and a croissant at one of the outdoors cafes on the Beechway, the main street through the town of Cascade. To his amazement nearly all the tables were occupied. Gnomes, Mountain Fairies, Elves and Outlanders seemed to have taken over the entire town. After wandering a while he found an empty table. Savouring his morning coffee and croissant he watched strangers pouring into town.

He was delighted to see the Dwarves marching under the arches formed by the great beech trees. The sturdy warriors were led by Smithereen, but lo and behold, by his side walked Sunflower. Right behind came Bullneck and Pristina. To Slim's astonishment a number of Dwarves had brought their wives. It was simply unheard of!

The years of darkness and suffering had brought the people of the Kingdom closer together and dwarf culture had begun to change. Once prudish, priggish and sour-faced, the warriors now smiled occasionally. They became jollier as time went by and no longer felt that they carried the world on their backs. Now they actually took an interest in the appearance of their wives and didn't grumble when money was spent on a pretty dress. They even accompanied their families on picnics. One of them invented the game of soccer and now dwarves channel their martial energy into chasing a ball around the alpine meadows.

The Mountain Fairies, too, had been affected by all the events they had lived through. Now they spent two evenings a week reading from the Common Book of Sacred Lore and hymn singing, of course, the other five nights they still party.

Lady Erica de Coscoroba, standing by her bedroom window, looked over the silent waters of the great River Sanctus. Sweet providence had brought back the love of her youth.

She turned around and beheld standing on her dresser the portrait of Gustav as a young border scout. What time and suffering had wrought! She had hardly recognized him when he limped up the lane towards the Manor, snow white locks and beard ringing the sunburnt, shrivelled face. But when he spoke in that singsong lilt she knew so well, she opened her arms to the stranger. Now for the remainder of this mortal journey she would care for him and share his joys and sorrows.

When she walked back to the window, she could see Slim's team of swans performing water ballet on the Sanctus. A large number of visitors sauntered along the shore. She hastened to get dressed, for soon the Marquis would be opening the Festival.

Thousands had gathered on the lawns that ran from the Graceful Neck down to the shore of the Sanctus. Dwarves, Gnomes, Mountain Fairies, Outlanders, Elves and Swannefolk intermingled freely. Some sat on small stools, others remained standing, depending on their height.

Master Grimmbeak, Servatius and Nightglider had perched in a stand of poplars with a clear view of the stage in front of the Inn.

The Graceful Neck was packed with visitors and the top floor had been reserved for guests of honour. For the overflow, several outbuildings had been pressed into use.

Slim, Ensten, Svanhild and Sidonia moved amongst the crowd greeting friends from distant lands. They were delighted to meet again Findhorn, Alexa and the three youths, Folderol, Flink, and Trickle. It had taken seven days to travel from the village of the Sea Gnomes to Cascade. Alexa's eyes sparkled with excitement, as she embraced Svanhild and Sidonia. She was still the child in an old body.

For Sidonia there were tearful reunions with the many Elves who had journeyed to the festival. She was delighted to see among them, Timmy Tightstring and Starlight. The elven community had rejoiced at the return of the seventeen, who had broken with Cobalt and the Black Elves. Queen Orchidae had granted a full pardon and no lingering prejudice remained.

At ten o'clock, a flourish of trumpets announced the opening of the Festival and the hubbub subsided. All eyes turned to the Marquis standing on stage in front of the Graceful Neck. Resplendent in his gala uniform and bolstered by admiring looks from the citizens of Cascade, he exuded a new confidence. He had good reason. The story of the twelve Grolls that he had slain in a fit of rage now topped one hundred and forty four.

The Marquis welcomed Queen Yaconda, Queen Tuluga of the Mountain Fairies, the elven Queen Orchidae, the Chief elder of the Gnome's Sacred Chamber, Smithereen, Volker of the Outlander Council, and honoured guests. Eloquently, he described the horrendous events of the past year and the humble part that he had played in the great drama. He was holding forth with marvellous zeal when Dorothea, sitting behind, pulled his coattail and whispered. 'Don't forget the Queen's speech.'

Taking the hint, the Marquis deftly concluded his narrative, welcomed all the visitors, and thanked providence for the Queen's safe return to the Kingdom.

Queen Yaconda's golden tresses had been braided, a delicate silver crown adorned her head and her long gown of dark blue silk embroidered with golden stars swept the stage. She raised her hands in greeting to the thousands standing before her and when the applause diminished, spoke in a soft singing voice, 'Standing before me I behold a mosaic of beauty, a mosaic of Dwarves, Mountain Fairies, Gnomes, Elves, Swannefolk and Outlanders. Beloved friends, it is to you that I owe my life and my Kingdom. You have paid dearly to bring about victory and this Festival celebrates the end of that long night and the dawn of a new day.'

Yaconda watched the waves of cheering men, women and children on the lawn and her eyes filled with tears.

'When I said beloved people, I include all the creatures who have laboured and risked their lives to banish the evil that had fallen upon us, be they terrestrial or celestial.'

Master Grimmbeak and the other eagles of the Celestial Covey could be seen nodding their great beaks and flapping their wings in appreciation of the Queen's thoughtfulness.

Yaconda knew that the ordeal her people had lived through had brought them closer together and had diminished cultural barriers. She ended her speech by expressing the wish that the great festival would mark the beginning of a new age of light, prosperity and unity.

The clapping and jubilation left her with a sense of immense joy, nonetheless, she felt enervated by the events and asked the Marquis to take over the duty of conferring the medals. Before stepping down there was one honour that she had to bestow herself.

She beckoned Svanhild to step forward. The Queen took the wreath of golden roses which Dominique was holding and gently placed the wreath on the heroine's silver tresses.

'My Sisters and brethren, mark well this moment. A maiden amongst us wears the golden wreath for bravery, the highest honour in my power to bestow.'

For a few minutes silence reigned. It was as if the audience needed a few moments to realize fully the portent of the event.

The women were the first to burst into applause. Then Smithereen's deep voice boomed a hearty cheer. The Dwarf warriors looked bewildered but after a couple of minutes they stomped and chanted lustily. This was the signal for the Gnomes and others to follow their example. If those stout warriors recognized a maiden heroine, times must be changing and they might as well join in. The result was that a tumultuous ovation echoed through the entire valley.

Lady Erica and Gustav threw flowers onto the stage.

When the clapping and cheering subsided, Queen Yaconda and Svanhild, holding hands, walked towards the Inn, leaving the Marquis in charge of the official award ceremonies.

The first tribute was to Moose Martin and Scimitar. Gold medals, in their memory were to be placed in the Museum of Fine Arts and Folklore in Lambarina. Smithereen, too, received a gold medal for bravery.

The massive warrior standing on stage wiped the perspiration from his face. The medal roused mixed emotions in Smithereen. He detested fighting and had his hopes set on receiving an award for literary achievement. Alas, only his bravery was rewarded. Like many poets, his artistry was recognized only in the latter days and today his poems can still be found in texts of ancient literature.

Solomon and Kasper were called to the stage and each received a beautiful wreath woven with silver cords. The wreath's golden tassels flickered in the sunlight. Being wise, the owls hid successfully their pride and feigned to be reluctant to accept the award.

When they returned to their perch on the boat house Kasper could no longer contain himself. 'A marvellous distinction, Chief, we are the first owls to receive the Wreath with Golden Tassels. We shall wear the Wreaths at the next meeting in the hereditary forest. Solomon cast a benign look.

'It is true, Deputy. Status symbols have their place, but humility is a great virtue.'

'Quite so, Chief, one that we owls can take pride in.'

Solomon blinked and advised Kasper to spend more time studying the Owl's Book of Wisdom. 'All three volumes Deputy.'

Next the Grandmaster of the Celestial Covey was summoned. The Marquis thanked him for sacrificing his traditional neutrality and for coming to the aid of the Kingdom. He placed a small silver helmet on the eagle's head. 'Congratulations Master Grimmbeak. To you and the Celestial Covey, a distinguished award for vigilance and outstanding service to Queen and country.'

Red Flash of the Dauntless Divers received a gold ribbon for his remarkable service in the defence of Esteria.

Peli 1 had been standing quietly apart from the crowd. Used to keeping a low profile, he was surprised when his name was called. The Marquis praised him for his services and proclaimed his appointment as Royal Messenger to the court of Queen Yaconda.

There were more speeches and medals, but the crowd breathed a sigh of relief when a blast by the trumpeters announced a break for the midday meal.

Splendid tables laden with delicacies had been prepared and there were beer gardens brimming with sparkling brew welcoming the eager guests.

The organizers of the festival had allowed several hours for lunch, which proved a wise arrangement. Sidonia took a plate of elven wafers and a cup of mint tea to the water's edge. Nibbling on the wafers and scanning the vast expanse of water, her attention was drawn by water splashing near the far shore. She put down her plate and cup and raised her hand to shield her eyes from the sun. She could see near the opposite shore, two furry creatures on a raft trying to paddle across the river, but the current was swiftly carrying the fragile craft downstream.

She called out to Slim pointing to the river. Slim could hardly discern the fleck in the distance, but taking Sidonia's word for it he jumped into a small skiff and rowed toward the distant shore. Some Swannemen who had heard Sidonia shouting for help, manned a larger boat and followed in Slim's wake.

When the boats reached the raft, Slim couldn't believe his eyes. Two moles had been swept into the water and were holding onto a raft for dear life. With the help of the men in the other boat, Slim pulled the moles from the water and headed back.

Sidonia was relieved to see two moles wrapped in blankets, seated in the bow of Slim's skiff. She recognized Ben, Chief Judge for the Mole Confederacy and his wife, Rochelle. The bedraggled couple, none the worse for wear, hopped onto land. Holding hands, they climbed up the embankment amidst the cheering of the crowd. Sidonia rushed up to them.

'Ben and Rochelle, welcome to the festival.'

'My dear elven lady,' said the dripping mole, 'We apologize for our late arrival, but our legs are short and our boating skills elementary.'

Sidonia rubbed their wet fur with her scarf and with the help of the spring sun, it was soon restored to its deep grey lustre.

Edel and Weiss came up to greet their old friends and to accompany them to the Manor where Lady Erica welcomed them. Although there were many guests at the Manor, finding a tiny space for the Moles was easy. Slim had taken their soaking backpacks to the kitchen and Norma washed and ironed their clothes.

After a prolonged luncheon banquet, Mountain Fairies opened the afternoon entertainment by playing their violins. Elven choirs sang and Gnomes did their hammer dance. To everyone's surprise, the Dwarves performed acrobatics, forming a human pyramid nine stories high. The Esterians, whose extraordinary marksmanship had sealed the doom of untold enemy soldiers, gave an archery demonstration.

Then a spectacular performance by Slim's swans drew the guests to the shore. Limonides and Pavlova danced a Pas de Deux . Oarflake and Ambrosia, practically standing in the water, were spellbound and joined in the enthusiastic applause.

In late afternoon a light meal was served in the gardens of the Graceful Neck. The moles, recovered from their eventful journey, walked down the lawn. It was the first official visit by moles from the Confederacy and many heads turned as they passed. Rochelle wore a dark purple gown over her silver fur and a dainty hat and high heels added to her stature. Ben wore a black suit with a black beret. Everybody was kind and attentive to the small visitors, who had done so much for the cause of freedom.

When the full moon rose over the Sanctus, two ceremonies took place at the Manor. The first one united in marriage, Svanhild and Ensten. Annabelle who had worried for years that Svanhild would never find a husband, glowed with pride.

A light sparkled in the eyes of Slim and Fragrance as they acted as witnesses in the simple ceremony. In four weeks time Slim would turn thirty-six and be eligible to marry.

'And not a day later!' whispered the happy ballet master. Fragrance squeezed his hand.

Then Queen Yaconda stepped forward, she took Lady Erica and Gustav by the hand and spoke the simple words that sealed their union.

'A bond forged in the fire of suffering and sacrifice can never be severed. Then walk hand in hand on this journey without end. My blessings and my love go with you.'

The Queen's eyes filled with tears as she embraced Lady Erica and Gustav, and then accompanied them to the terrace to drink a toast.

Slim and Fragrance had rushed off to the river to decorate the Gondola that would carry the newlyweds on the moonlit waters. The carving of the laughing elven child was placed on the bow. Spring flowers were woven through the arches that spanned the gondola. The scent of hyacinths and hundreds of spring flowers filled the air as Ensten carried his bride to the Gondola and placed her under the canopy of flowers. Limonides and his team would propel the bridal vessel.

They were still moored by the shore when Svanhild was startled by a strange moaning sound. She looked up and found herself staring at Leonardo's wet snout. The long red tongue touched her cheek. She leaned over, nearly tipping the gondola, and threw her arms around the noble wolf's head. Andante, too, gave her a quick kiss but then the Gondola moved forward and Svanhild threw a parting kiss to the wolf pair.

Adorned with small silver crowns, the seven swans glided over the moonlit waters. In Ensten and Svanhild's wake sailed another vessel filled with Mountain Fairies playing their tiny violins. Then in a long slender Gondola pulled by twelve swans, came the guests of honour, Queen Yaconda, Dominique, Lady Erica and Gustav, the Marquis and Dorothea, the Mayor of Miranda and his charming Annabelle, Smithereen and Sunflower, Sidonia and the Elven Sisters.

Gondola after gondola drawn by teams of swans floated past the Graceful Neck. On a small hillock overlooking the procession, stood Slim, Fragrance and Volker. Never before had such a long train of gaily bedecked vessels plied the sparkling waters of the great river. Volker was still taking notes for the great historical work he was contemplating. Slim had planned to sketch but the event was simply too exciting, he etched it in his mind instead.

When Oarflake and Ambrosia floated by, they were delighted to see Slim with a lovely maiden by his side. Ambrosia waved a kiss. In the same gondola, seated behind the Gnomes, was Alexa. She was enchanted by the graceful swans silently moving on the moon-filled waters. The sound of violins and of elven voices singing brought a magic to a scene that would live in time.

When the last gondola floated by, people began flooding the lawn by the old Inn. The Dwarves had a surprise in store. They had carried a supply of fireworks down from the mountains and now began firing small missiles above the waters of the Sanctus. Brightly sparkling designs ornamented the heavens. Bouquets of flowers in brilliant colours burst into the night sky, dolphins somersaulted in a sea of light, and golden spirals skipped over the surface of the Sanctus until they vanished into the deep waters. The fireworks signalled the end of the official festivities, but dancing and music went on until the hours of dawn.

At midnight, the small circle of friends who had shared in the great adventure, gathered for an intimate dinner on the Manor terrace. This, their last meal together before returning to far flung parts of the Kingdom, was a celebration of the bonds that had been forged between them.

Martha, the blind prophetess, had left her bear Grumpuss at the entrance to the laneway leading to the manor. Grumpuss would ensure some privacy for the event. He wouldn't hurt a soul, unless the vibes were bad, of course. Then the noble bear would turn into a ball of fury. Just seeing him leaning against the oak tree near the entrance was enough for people to change their mind about walking up the lane.

The light of many candelabras sparkled on the crystal plates. Seated at the head of the table were Queen Yaconda, The Marquis and Dorothea. The Marquis' countenance, flushed with pride, contrasted starkly with the snow white face of his love. The marble whiteness would always remind people of the near death experience through which she had lived and the sacrifice that she had made in the pathway of love. Her eyes shining with happiness, she beamed at all the loving faces that surrounded her.

Slim and Fragrance were there as well as Martha, Annabelle, Dominique, Svanhild and Ensten, Lady Erica and Gustav, Smithereen and Sunflower, Sidonia, the three elven sisters and, of course, Oarflake and Ambrosia. On a large cushion at the other end sat Ben the Mole and Rochelle.

Although the moles had not been on the guest list for this event when the Queen heard of the long trek that the small creatures had made and their harrowing mishap on the river, she requested that they be included.

Duckie had been invited but he backed out preferring to be with Norma in the kitchen. When reports reached Norma that Duckie had been impervious to the charms of the maidens in Queen Marsha's palace, she had begun to worry. But Duckie had grown in the last two years and doubts about his hormones were quickly laid to rest.

Queen Yaconda lifted her glass and the tinkling of crystal resounded in the still of the night. Suffering still from the trials through which she had lived in the year past, her speech was brief.

'Beloved friends, who traversed the flames of suffering that purifies the soul, let us join hands and pray that my father's vision will come true. May Elves, Gnomes, Mountain Fairies, Outlanders, Swannefolk and Dwarves, work hand in hand to build the great nation of King Arcturus' dream, a nation where all creatures great and small shall find refuge and live in peace and joy.'

After a short silence the company turned to share in the splendid spread on the table. Little was said and little needed to be said, for no sword could sever or fire consume the golden thread that bound them.

The seven swans had danced several times during the day and there had not been time to honour Limonides and his team. Svanhild and Slim had asked the swans to come to the banquet after midnight. Svanhild had just finished the story of how the seven swans had saved Sidonia and herself from the fierce Scornbirds, when the moon shadow of many wings moved across the table. The swans touched down on the low stone wall at the end of the terrace.

Queen Yaconda rose and placed a golden bracelet around each of the graceful necks. Once the bracelets had snapped into place they would never unlock again. It was a clever device crafted in the smithies of the Gnomes.

The swans made a deep bow. Then upon a nod from Svanhild, Limonides moved his powerful pinions and rose swiftly in the night sky. Pavlova and the other swans rose up behind him.

Queen Yaconda remained standing at the end of the table. There was one last distinction to be conferred. She asked Edel and Weiss to stand up.

'Edel and Weiss, no earthly reward can reflect the noble deeds and the joy that you have brought your Queen.'

'Your Majesty,' Edel and Weiss sang in unison, 'no earthly reward do we desire. To serve but in the shadow of your glory is our hearts' desire.'

'Then your desire is fulfilled, my dear Fairies. Hereby, I appoint you Companions of the Throne, an office which will require you to spend much of your time at my palace in Lambarina.'

Edel and Weiss looked at each other, their eyes sparkling with joy. They jumped onto the table, grasped each other's hands and spun around in a whirl of excitement. A number of glasses were shattered and several candelabras ended up on the terrace floor. Seeing her Companions of the Throne pirouetting on the table, Queen Yaconda had a fleeting doubt about the arrangement that she had made, but the Mountain's Fairies' unbounded joy quickly dissolved any momentary reservations that passed through her mind. The Queen's laughter resounded around the table, infecting all.

When Edel and Weiss returned to their seats, Svanhild raised her glass and shared a message that had lifted her heart. Gertrude and Marie who had helped her escape from Matista's chateau had found refuge at the Convent of the Sisters of the Secret Crossing.

Silence descended upon the circle of friends. They stood together at the threshold of a new dawn, this unique privilege they shared and it would bind them throughout time.

So began an era of lasting peace. There were trials and tribulations, earthquakes, floods and other calamities, but never again did men raise a hand in anger.

Millennia passed and only in the latter days has evidence been found of the great struggle that inaugurated a cycle of peace and enlightenment.

A peasant staking peat in the great bogs north of the Frivoli, found Volker's manuscript sealed in a clay pot. Modern readers became fascinated with the great work. At first it was considered a remarkable book of classic fiction.

An aged archaeologist had second thoughts and suggested that the book could have been based on historical events. His ideas were dismissed by the professional community, but he persisted and started doing field work on his own. He trekked across the Finnian Range and after several years of digging and suffering great hardships, discovered the remains of the Palace of the Seven. His find caused a furor among his professional colleagues and some unkind remarks were flung at the old professor.

Later, young admirers of the scientist unearthed the Convent of the Sisters of the Secret Crossing. A cedar chest was found containing Helga's diaries and the oil painting of Helga meditating, which Slim had donated to the Sisters.

When towards the end of their dig they found the golden plate, it put to rest all lingering doubts. Volker was acclaimed as one of the great writers of ancient history. A team of foremost linguists deciphered the text engraved by the ancient Elven Kings. The golden tablet, on display in an armour plated glass case, is the pride of the Museum of Fine Art and Folklore.

One young student combing carefully through the ruins of the Convent discovered, wrapt in silk, a small piece of glass. It was the sliver that Svanhild had taken from the Mirror of a Thousand Fragments.

The curator of the Museum was delighted with the piece of glass and had it mounted on a slab of black alabaster. The curator's delight might well have been tempered had he known the consequences of this precious addition to his collection.

Sophia, the curator's only daughter, a girl of grace and beauty, had entered a national beauty contest. The night before the event she couldn't fall asleep. She got out of bed and wandered through the moonlit halls of the museum. Upon entering the wing that contained finds from the Convent of the Sisters, she descried, glistening in the moonlight, the fragment of glass.

After reading the text below, she raised her eyes and gazed at the magic fragment. Suddenly she startled, for there appeared before her, veiled in light, a radiant beauty.

'The elven Queen, you are the elven Queen, whose prayers transformed the Mirror of a Thousand Fragments!' exclaimed Sophia.

What passed between the spirit of the elven Queen and the comely maiden and the words that she whispered to Sophia, remain to this day a mystery.

The next morning much to the consternation of her family, Sophia cancelled her entry in the Beauty Contest and signed on with a foreign aid mission. Within weeks she had travelled overseas to a remote part of the globe and for years laboured in relative obscurity, bringing relief and solace to the poor and downtrodden.

Close to the display of the piece of glass that Svanhild had lifted from the Mirror is an alcove containing the oil painting of Scimitar. Placed alongside is the recently discovered canvas of Sister Helga meditating.

The paintings have become known as Light of the Brave and Light of the Heart, and the story of Helga and Scimitar's love has inspired great works of art throughout time.

ISBN 141207962-4